WIRRAL'S WAR WITH THE FRENCH

MARTIN ROBERTS

All photographs and maps by the author, except 'Historic Warships in the East Float Dock' by Frank Smith, and 'HMS Bronington' by Ted Rodden, both copyright The Warships Preservation Trust. As the Warships Preservation Trust no longer exists, the author has been unable to obtain permission for the use of the pictures in this book, but he hopes that their inclusion serves as an appreciative acknowledgement of the work of the Trust in trying to perserve our naval heritage.

For the purposes of this book, 'Wirral Council' is an entirely fictitious organisation, and any similarity to real local authorities is unintentional and coincidental.

First Published 2009 by Countyvise Limited,
14 Appin Road, Birkenhead, Wirral CH41 9HH.

British Library Cataloguing in Publication Data.
A catalogue record for this book is available from the British Library.

ISBN 978 1 906823 12 2

Dedicated to my wife and children for their support, patience and understanding, and to the part-time soldiers of the Territorial Army, who were the inspiration for this book.

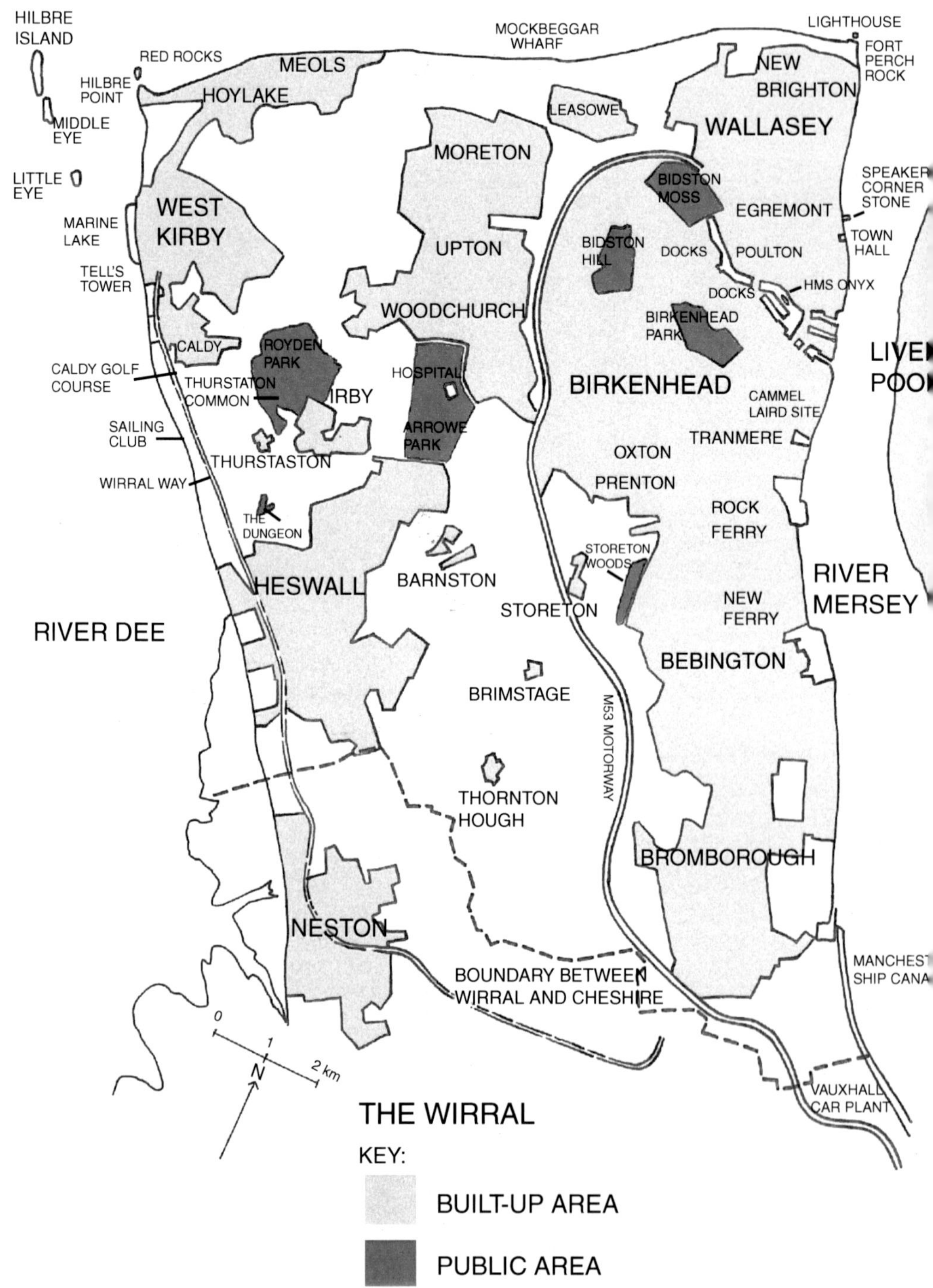
LIVERPOOL BAY
HILBRE ISLAND
RED ROCKS
HILBRE POINT
MIDDLE EYE
LITTLE EYE
MEOLS
HOYLAKE
MOCKBEGGAR WHARF
LEASOWE
LIGHTHOUSE
FORT PERCH ROCK
NEW BRIGHTON
WALLASEY
MORETON
WEST KIRBY
MARINE LAKE
TELL'S TOWER
CALDY
CALDY GOLF COURSE
ROYDEN PARK
THURSTATON COMMON
IRBY
SAILING CLUB
THURSTASTON
WIRRAL WAY
THE DUNGEON
UPTON
WOODCHURCH
HOSPITAL
ARROWE PARK
BIDSTON MOSS
BIDSTON HILL
DOCKS
BIRKENHEAD PARK
SPEAKER CORNER STONE
EGREMONT
TOWN HALL
POULTON
HMS ONYX
BIRKENHEAD
CAMMEL LAIRD SITE
TRANMERE
OXTON
PRENTON
ROCK FERRY
STORETON WOODS
HESWALL
BARNSTON
STORETON
RIVER DEE
NEW FERRY
RIVER MERSEY
BEBINGTON
BRIMSTAGE
M53 MOTORWAY
THORNTON HOUGH
BROMBOROUGH
NESTON
BOUNDARY BETWEEN WIRRAL AND CHESHIRE
0
1
2 km
N
VAUXHALL CAR PLANT
THE WIRRAL
KEY:
BUILT-UP AREA
PUBLIC AREA

GLOSSARY

APWT	Annual Personal Weapons Test (army marksmanship test)
BATCO	Battle Code (for sending secure radio messages)
Bergen	Rucksack
'Binlid'	Helmet
Bivvi-bag	Waterproof sleeping bag cover
Bunker	Underground shelt or firing position
Callsign	Reference code to identify individual radio user
CAP	Company Aid Post (location where casualities are treated initially)
Casevac	Casualty evacuation
CEFO	Combat Equipment, Fighting Order (webbing, daysacks, helmet, weapon)
CEMO	Combat Equipment, Marching Order (CEFO plus bergen)
CO	Commanding Officer (the colonel commanding a battalion)
Comms	Communications
CQMS	Company Quartermaster-Sergeant
CP	Command Post
CSM	Company Sergeant-major
CWS	Common Weapon Sight (image-intensifying night sight)
Daysacks	Small rucksacks, which can be attached to main bergen to form side pouches
DPM	Disruptive Pattern Material (camouflage clothing)
ERV	Emergency Rendezvous
Fireteam	Half of a section (ie. four soldiers)
FRV	Final Rendezvous
FUP	Forming Up Point (where troops move into attack formation)
GPMP	General Purpose Machine Gun (belt-fed 7.62mm medium machine gun)
H-Hour	Time at which first troops cross the LOD
ICFT	Infantry Combat Fitness Test (timed speech march in full kit)
LAW94	Light Anti-Tank Weapon 94mm
LOD	Line of Departure (start line from which units advance)
LSW	Light Support Weapon (magazine-fed 5.56mm light machine gun)
LUP	Lying Up Position
M16	American 5.56mm assault rifle
Minimi	Belt or magazine-fed light machine gun
NBC	Nuclear, Biological or Chemical (warfare)
NCO	Non-commissioned officer

OC	Officer Commanding (the major commanding a company)
OP	Observation Post
PAWPERSO	Battle preparation mnemonic (Protection, Ammunition, Weapons, Personal camouflage, Equipment, Radios, Specialist equipment, Orders)
PSI	Permanent Staff Instructor (regular NCO attached to a TA unit)
PUP	Pick Up Point
RV	Rendezvous
RLC	Royal Logistics Corps (sometimes nicknamed 'The Really Large Corps')
RSM	Regimental Sergeant-major
Sangar	Fortified structure, often made of sandbags
Section	Eight-man sub-unit commanded by a corporal, compromising two fireteams
SA80	Standard British Army 5.56mm assault rifle
SOP	Standard Operating Procedure
'Stag'	Sentry Duty
'Tab'	Movement on foot, usually in full kit

STRUCTURE OF THE WIRRAL REGIMENT

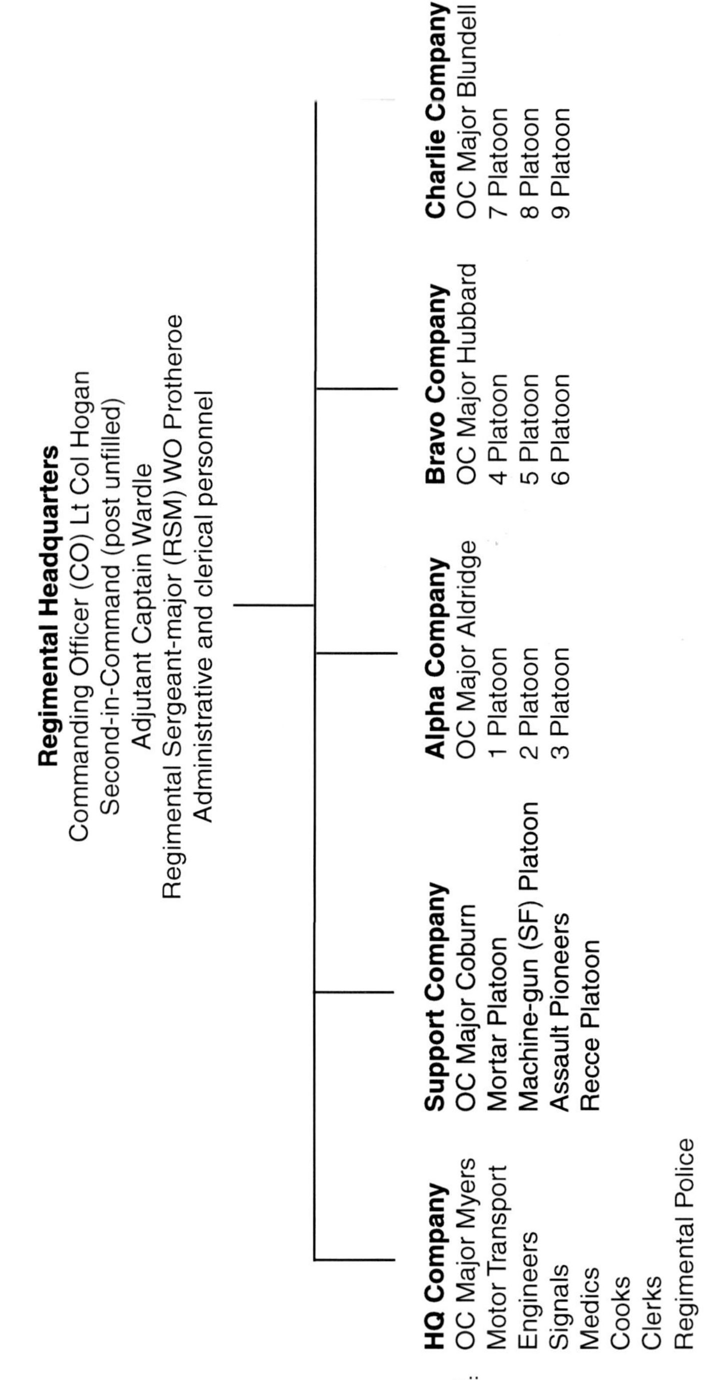

CHARLIE COMPANY STRUCTURE

Officer Commanding (OC) - Major Blundell
Second-in-Command (post unfilled)
Company Sergeant-major (CSM) - Warrant Officer 'Taff' Jones
Company Quartermaster-sergeant (CQMS) - Colour-sergeant Morris

Company HQ	**Seven Platoon**	**Eight Platoon**	**Nine Platoon**
Motor transport	Lt Saunders	Lt Grudge	Lt Evans
Signals	Sgt Carter	Sgt Murphy	Sgt Collins
Stores	1 Section	1 Section	1 Section
Medical	2 Section	2 Section	2 Section
Armourer	3 Section	3 Section	3 Section
Clerical			
Catering			
Snipers			

EIGHT PLATOON STRUCTURE

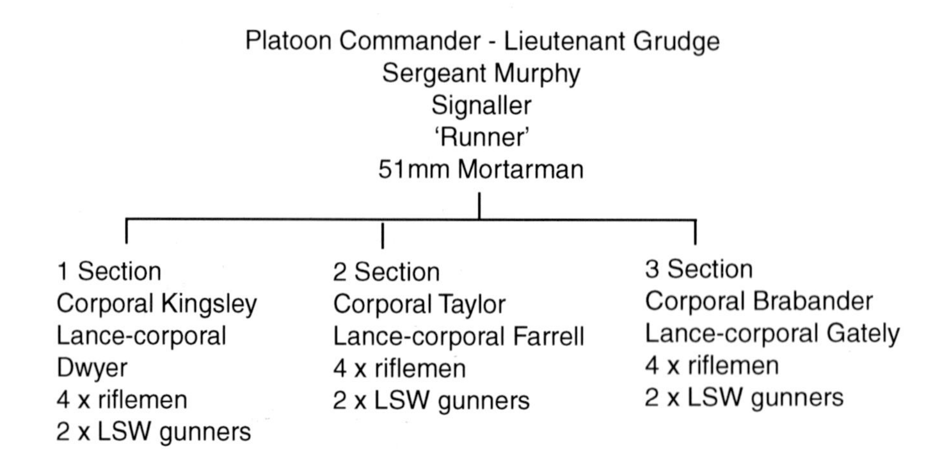

CHAPTER 1

All at Sea

I don't like this book. I don't know why, I just don't like it. It failed to grab me at the start, the ending failed to satisfy, and the intervening pages were similarly uninspiring. They say everyone has one book inside them; I wish Mr Roberts's one had stayed there, but now it's out I hope he's satisfied and goes back to the day job.

Ivor Stammer
Literary Planet

Mr Roberts replies:
I frankly don't give a damn what you think. I've had a book published, you haven't, end of story.

Council Leader Gerald Radley cleared his throat but paused before speaking. This was the moment towards which his entire life had gravitated, and he wanted to savour it.

"Fighting men of the Wirral," he began, "you are about to make history. Tonight, or rather, this morning, you will follow in the footsteps of your forefathers in the great tradition of D-Day, to attack and defeat an aggressor who has wronged our dear homeland so deplorably. How appropriate that you are to land in the area once known as Gold Beach, where British soldiers landed in Nineteen Forty-Four. How appropriate that I speak to you now in this historic wardroom, where the surrender of South Georgia was signed by the Argentinians during the Falklands War. And how appropriate that your enemy is the French, against whom we Englishmen have a long and noble history of conflict. Yours is an honourable fight, and in undertaking this adventure you will forge a legend which will surely stand alongside those of Wellington, Nelson and Henry the Fifth."

He paused for dramatic effect and glanced around at his audience of officers and NCOs. Their faces were streaked with green and brown camouflage cream, which made their eyes appear strangely white and staring, so it was difficult to judge their response to his oration. He fancied, however, that it was going well.

"You Happy Band of Brothers carry the pride of Wirral and of England with you. If you fail, we all fail. But if you succeed, as I know you shall, this will be your finest hour. Yours will be the glory. Never will so much have been owed by so many to so few.... You alone will be able to hold your head up high and say '*I was there. I dared, and I won.*' Consider yourselves privileged, in a way, for many will envy you and regret not being part of this noble undertaking. To quote Henry the Fifth, '*Men now abed in England will hold their manhood cheap*'."

Radley looked regally at the video camera which was recording his performance for posterity, or rather for his own future self-analysis and self-gratification. He glanced at his watch - a purely theatrical gesture, as he knew precisely what the time was - and pretended to draw his speech to a premature close.

"Gentlemen, I wish you luck. You have preparations to complete so I shall detain you no longer. Listening to Major Aldridge's orders just now, I'm certain that you'll be ashore and have secured your first objectives by midday. It shouldn't be long then before we can force the French into a satisfactory settlement and get you back home to your loved ones. I wish I were going with you. For my part, I hope I can do better than Churchill, by offering more than blood, sweat, toil and tears....Instead I offer you as much assistance as the Council can possibly provide. I promise that no expense shall be spared to keep you supplied and supported during this campaign. Children in Wirral will go without before you do. I have complete faith in your ability to succeed, and in your professionalism and determination. May God be with you. Wirral expects that every man will do his duty..."

Going into battle without first emptying his bowels was not Corporal Robert Taylor's idea of fun. In fact, as he had come to realise, going into battle was not his idea of fun at all. And having treacherously palpitating bowels - which threatened to unleash a fear-induced flood of diarrhoea at any moment - simply added a final touch of abject misery to his already wretched situation.

Robert was standing in a sickeningly swaying corridor aboard *HMS Plymouth*, a decrepit frigate brought out of retirement to become the flagship of Gerald Radley's task force. In her wardroom an hour previously the Council Leader had delivered his eve of battle speech, which had been received with silent contempt by most of the soldiers present, including Robert. It had been during the monologue that he had felt pressure welling up inside his intestines. Since then he had made several attempts to use one of the ship's toilets, but had encountered queues of soldiers in a similar predicament to his own, all the victims of nervousness and the Territorial Army's predilection for changing deadlines at short notice. H-hour – the time at which the troops would leave *Plymouth* in small boats to invade Normandy – had originally been set for 5.00am, which allowed plenty of time for bowel-emptying and other essential preparations. Suddenly, for undisclosed reasons, it had been brought forward to 3.00am, and everyone was panicking. Panicking and cursing the senior staff, or 'Head Shed', as incompetent or indifferent or just 'a bunch of tossers'.

The ship rolled and swayed and he steadied himself against a bulkhead, trying to move obligingly out of the way as several soldiers in full kit pushed past in the crowded confines of the red-illuminated corridor. Steaming in the darkness, close to the French coast, *Plymouth* was at battle stations and all white light was forbidden, in case any escaped and penetrated the night to warn the French of their presence.

Frantic activity was evident all around – men scurrying to and fro on errands, NCOs shouting instructions, bulky equipment being hauled clumsily through narrow spaces with no regard for bystanders like Robert. He felt strangely detached from events, and slightly guilty that he was not making a greater contribution; he was essentially an outsider amongst these men, who mostly belonged to Alpha Company, The Wirral Regiment. Robert's own unit, Charlie Company, was back in Wirral, engaged in cushy training exercises and Homeland Security operations. A few of Robert's friends from C Company were elsewhere on the ship, but for the moment he was alone among indifferent strangers. Deprived of the *esprit de corps* engendered by the familiar comrades of his own unit, he felt isolated and dejected.

He used the momentary lull in the proceedings to conduct a quick check of his personal state of readiness, making sure that his webbing pouches were securely fastened, all of his pockets were done up, and items such as field dressings, camouflage cream, torch, cigarette lighter, penknife and notebook were all where they should be. Then he checked that his rifle's safety catch was on, the change lever was set to semi-automatic, and the protective plastic muzzle cover was fixed securely over the end of the barrel with black electrical tape. Electrical tape was an essential item in the TA infantry. It was used everywhere – to prevent torches turning on accidentally, to customise webbing, secure helmet covers, repair radio handsets....sometimes it seemed as if the entire Territorial Army was held together by nothing more than black electrical tape and its stronger counterpart, gaffer tape.

"Hurry up and let's get this over with," muttered the corporal next to him, who happened to be the company signaller. Robert certainly did not envy him, going into action encumbered by heavy radio kit, with its frustration of snagging wires. "I hate all this hanging around," the corporal grumbled. "If we're gonna go, let's go."

Robert nodded. "Or better still, let's turn around and go home. I don't care what that prick said just now about our finest hour and all that – this whole thing is a load of bollocks."

Suddenly the queue of men waiting in the passageway began to shuffle forward in response to some inaudible instruction further down the line. Robert heaved his heavy bergen onto one shoulder and followed the signaller until he emerged into the gloomy but relatively cavernous space of the ship's helicopter hanger, where some semblance of order was in the process of being established. As he crossed the metal threshold a red torch beam was shone into his face.

"Who've we got here?" demanded a voice, which Robert recognised as belonging to the Company Sergeant-major.

"Corporal Taylor from Charlie Company – I've been attached to Company HQ."

"Right, I need you and the rest of HQ along this wall here." The

CSM pointed with his torch, and Robert moved obediently into position, together with the signaller and several other soldiers. He disliked this phase of any large operation, when individuals lost their personalities and became insignificant drones, to be herded like wretched cattle. H-hour would restore his individual status when the troops were unleashed from the ship, but right now he felt small, insignificant, uncared for and afraid. Thoughts of his girlfriend repeatedly flooded into his mind and had to be suppressed. He knew that, if he allowed them to take hold of his consciousness, he would be unable to function as required by the machine of which he was a small but significant part.

In the red dimness it was possible to distinguish the silhouettes of men being lined up into formations. Each eight-man section had 'fallen in' and was being inspected by its corporal, who moved along the row of soldiers, checking equipment by torchlight and asking random questions such as, "Is your water bottle full?" or, "Have you oiled that weapon?" or, "What's the password?"

Robert overheard the voice of an officer nearby and recognised it as that of Lieutenant Whitham, who commanded One Platoon. That meant that his friend Mark Conrad should be somewhere nearby.

Robert took a chance. "How goes it, M.C.?" he called out into the darkness. If no-one had answered he would have appeared a fool, but after a few seconds a familiar voice gave the hoped for response:

"Not good, not good, R.T.," Conrad shouted from somewhere across the hanger. He pushed his way through to where Robert was standing. "Where are you, Rob? Ah – there you are…So - ready to give Harry Hun a damned good licking?"

Robert smiled in the darkness and replied as the routine demanded, quoting from the television comedy *Blackadder Goes Forth*. "Er, I think you'll find it's the Frenchies we should be licking."

Conrad feigned outrage. "Don't be disgusting, darling - I wouldn't lick a Frenchie if he was glazed in honey!"

Robert became serious. "All I want to do is get ashore," he confessed quietly. "Actually, Mark, all I want to do is go home. This whole operation is frankly ridiculous and I think we're going to get our arses kicked."

"I think you may be right. Just keep your head down, mate. This isn't our fight – it's A Company's, the bunch of Muppets. Our job is to stay out of it and get back to Charlie Company in time for tea and medals. Look on the bright side - at least you're with the Head Shed – you'll be alright with Aldridge. God knows where I'll end up with Wally Whitham."

Robert could sympathise. His own attachment, to Company Headquarters under Major Aldridge, was likely to be less risky than Mark's posting, which would involve being on the front line under the command of an officer who did not inspire complete confidence. Every TA battalion, it seemed, had one or two officers who were surplus to requirements, without an obvious role in the grand scheme of things.

Whitham had been such an officer in Charlie Company - Robert had always referred to him as '*Officer Without Portfolio*'. When A Company had been formed three months previously, Whitham had been transferred across to the new unit and put in charge of One Platoon, and no one in C Company missed him.

"There's always the old underpants on the head and pencils up your nose trick, if all else fails," Robert joked. "Let them think you've gone mad."

"Can't you see? I've already got my underpants on my head, and these pencils are killing me! But seriously, Rob, one thing really bothers me..."

"Do tell."

"Well, it's just occurred to me - this is supposed to be our Grand Invasion, the big, no-expense-spared offensive against the French, right?"

"Supposedly..."

"Then why is Aldridge in command? I mean, no offence to the guy - he's a good enough officer - but only a few months ago he was our second-in-command in C Company, a mere captain. If this invasion is so crucial, why isn't the CO leading us in, or at least Major Blundell? And why send A Company, when everyone knows that Charlie Company is by far the most experienced unit in the regiment? To me, that suggests something..."

Robert felt uneasy. "You're right. We're expendable."

"Corporal Conrad!" an agitated voice called out from the gloomy ranks of One Platoon. "Corporal Conrad! Where the hell are you?"

"Better go. Take care, mate."

"You too. And remember: Adventure...excitement...a Jedi craves not these things!"

Mark disappeared back into the ranks, just as the voice of the CSM shouted above the background noise of the ship's engines: "Right, Mr Whitham, I need you to move One Platoon over by the doors so we can get Company HQ sorted out..."

More soldiers entered the hanger, which was becoming increasingly crowded. It had been designed back in the 1960s to accommodate one small helicopter, not sixty soldiers with weapons and equipment, who were struggling to keep their balance and suppress nausea as the ship rocked and swayed and rose and fell. Troops who had been absorbed throughout the ship during the voyage from Wirral were now being funnelled into an inadequate space and tempers began to fray as the new arrivals, directed by seemingly oblivious senior ranks, pushed and jostled and kicked and elbowed their way into the crowd. Someone stumbled dizzily and almost started a domino effect. Fear and excitement were building to a critical mass. The Company Sergeant-major took control, moving the men of One Platoon, who were ready to go, over to one side of the hanger to create more space.

At that moment Major Aldridge arrived to take charge of the Company HQ contingent of which Robert was reluctantly a part. As a corporal who usually commanded a rifle section, he felt a certain arrogant superiority over the motley assemblage of signallers, cooks, clerks and storemen with whom he would be going into action. Robert knew that some of these men fired their rifles as little as once a year, to qualify for their TA bounty, and he sincerely hoped that they would not be involved in any serious fighting.

"Where's Corporal Taylor?" the major asked, unable to identify Robert due to the darkness and the camouflage cream.

"Here, sir."

"Aha! Good - glad to have you with us, Corporal T. I need you with me at all times until further notice, okay?'

"Right, sir." Robert was fairly content to be serving with Aldridge, whom he regarded as a competent yet approachable officer. The major peered at the luminous dial on his watch and sighed, as if resigning himself to the inevitable.

"Okay Sergeant-major. We need all lights off now. Let's get everyone outside and into the boats."

A few moments later the metal shutter of the main door slid up with a loud metallic clatter, and a cold, salty wind blew away the stuffy air from inside the hanger. It sounded wild outside. One Platoon shuffled out into the forbidding night and moved unsteadily past the tethered Agusta helicopter in single file, before descending the starboard flight of steps which led down to the quarter deck at *Plymouth*'s stern. Company HQ followed shortly afterwards, using the steps on the port side of the vessel and congregating on the opposite side of the quarter deck, clutching the handrails for support. Members of the ship's crew were busy loading the huge three-barrelled mortar – a relic of the frigate's original anti-submarine role – which would shortly be used to fire improvised smoke bombs at the French coastline. Bumping impatiently in the surf at the *Plymouth*'s stern was a flotilla of small craft, including fishing boats, cabin cruisers and yachts. These would carry the soldiers ashore.

In the darkness, a wake of white foam caught Robert's attention. Peering into the night, he could just make out the ghostly silhouette of the Mersey ferry *Royal Daffodil*, steaming parallel to the *Plymouth* about a hundred metres away. The *Royal Daffodil* was carrying the men of Two and Three Platoons, who would no doubt be in the process of boarding their own fleet of small boats. It was like Dunkirk in reverse, Robert thought to himself.

"Good luck to you all!" shouted a voice from the helicopter deck above. Robert glanced up to see Gerald Radley standing at the handrail, flanked by two sinister Special Council Workers armed with sub-machine guns. The Council Leader was watching proceedings with great interest.

Not for the first time, Robert contemplated his bizarre situation, and tried to make sense of how he had arrived at it. It was less than a year since he had led a completely unremarkable life as a Wirral schoolteacher and part-time TA soldier. Now, incredibly, he was part of an invasion force which was poised to land on French soil, with a very real possibility of being killed, injured or captured in the near future.

The fear, excitement and anticipation which had been steadily building-up in his body now reached a climax, and his strength seemed to drain away. His bones felt icy-cold, his skin tingled, his bowels palpitated and his stomach was hollow and nauseous. He steadied himself against the handrail, breathed deeply and opened his eyes wide into the damp, salty wind to clear his head, while trying to convince himself that his queasiness was due to sea-sickness rather than fear. Major Aldridge had already begun to climb down into the yacht below, and now it was Robert's turn to descend the boarding ladder. He dropped his bergen down to a crewman in the yacht's cockpit, pulled his rifle strap tight, checked his lifejacket, and swung his legs over the handrail. As he climbed unsteadily down the swaying ladder, he glanced resentfully up at the silhouette of Council Leader Radley, and fancied that their eyes met for a fleeting moment. '*One thing's for sure*,' Robert thought bitterly to himself, '*if anyone's responsible for this mess, it's that bastard*.'

CHAPTER 2

Origins of a Mad Scheme

I must confess to having been somewhat confused whilst reading Chapter Two, until I realised that it's actually the real start of the story, the chronological beginning. Chapter One turns out to have been merely an attention-grabbing appetiser, a tantalising flash-forward presumably intended to lure us into the novel and engage our interest. Well, it certainly didn't succeed in my case...

Carruthers Hinterglow
Retired Reader magazine

Mr Roberts replies:
Bah humbug!

Some men are born great, others acquire greatness, and some have greatness thrust upon them. Most men, of course, never achieve greatness, but some pursue it with such obsessive recklessness that they cause a lot of damage.

Gerald Radley was one such man. Essentially a small-hearted and egocentric individual, he had risen to the lofty heights of leader of Wirral council through a combination of ambition, luck, and sheer bloody-mindedness. Blissfully oblivious to his own shortcomings, he had pursued every promotional opportunity that had come his way, regardless of how well suited he was to the position in question. In the race to reach the top, many of his more talented competitors had fallen by the wayside, either languishing too long in jobs for which they had a particular aptitude, or devoting too much time to families or leisure pursuits, or being deterred from applying for certain promotions by an awareness of their own limitations. Gerald Radley possessed no such awareness, and had attained several prime positions by default, simply because no other suitable candidates had applied for them. He was also not encumbered by distractions outside the workplace, with no serious recreational interests and only a limited commitment to his wife and two daughters. To him, a family was largely an accessory - a mandatory commodity to be possessed because it was expected of someone in his position, and bestowed an air of respectability which helped mask some unsavoury aspects of his character.

Radley began his career as a lawyer, working first in private practice before moving to the Corporate Services department of Wirral council. Within the legal profession, local authority jobs were generally regarded as a safe haven for the lame and undynamic, and Radley found himself a shark amongst cod, his obsessive ambition giving him a competitive advantage over his more pedestrian colleagues.

So he had risen steadily and inexorably toward the top of the hierarchical pyramid, gradually surrounding himself with reliable allies or obsequious fools who could be easily manipulated. He found that his career progression became easier the higher he climbed, thanks to a tradition of mutual back-scratching amongst senior officials. Within the safety of such a coterie it was relatively easy to avoid the repercussions of any serious professional blunders, as highly-paid colleagues would always be willing to engineer cover-ups for each other to protect their salaries, perks and pensions. Wherever possible, Radley assisted the promotion of those he liked and hindered the progress of those he disliked or regarded as potential threats. People who fell foul of him, for whatever reason, soon found themselves isolated and vulnerable, their conduct scrutinised continuously and mercilessly under the guise of routine performance management reviews until, inevitably, they slipped up and were forced to resign or take early retirement. Basically, Gerald Radley was an unscrupulous bastard.

Then, after almost twenty years as a council employee, he made a bold and potentially risky career move. He resigned his senior position in the local authority and accepted a partnership in a private law firm based in elegant Hamilton Square. The move cost him a drop in salary, but enabled him to stand for election as a councillor two years later. His local authority background – and in particular his well-established relationships with many senior council officials – equipped him with experience and inside knowledge which so impressed his fellow party members that they decided to make him their leader. And so, after a resounding victory in the local elections, Gerald Radley became arguably the most powerful figure in the borough.

As leader of Wirral Council, Radley set about cultivating connections across the peninsular. By the time he embarked upon his second term in office at the age of forty-seven, he had contacts in the police and judiciary, the health service, local schools and sports associations, the Rotary Club, Chamber of Commerce, various pressure groups and a multitude of private companies ranging from ship repair to legal and financial services. For the first time ever, his party held a huge majority in the council, emasculating effective opposition, and Radley's position seemed unassailable. Ensconced securely within a bureaucratic kingdom populated by loyal friends, acquiescent puppets and easily intimidated minions, he exercised his powers in an increasingly Draconian way, and few dared challenge him.

But there was a problem. Despite his undeniable success within the realms of local government, he remained fundamentally dissatisfied. For Gerald Radley yearned desperately to be a *great* man, and deliberating over planning applications, discussing waste recycling policy or visiting schools neither inspired him nor satisfied his need for *greatness*.

His long-suffering wife frequently tried to reassure him: "But what you do *is* important. It's great in its own way..."

He remained unconvinced. "It's trivial and humdrum. In ten years' time nothing I've done will be remembered and no-one will remember me. I want to make *history*."

Unfortunately, Gerald Radley did not want to be a great council leader. He wanted to be great in the tradition of Winston Churchill or Genghis Khan. From an early age he had considered himself unfortunate to have been born too late, forced to exist resentfully in the mediocre doldrums which had superseded what he referred to romantically as 'The Age of Greatness'. This noble era had, in his opinion, drawn to a regrettable close shortly after the end of the Second World War. Since then, he believed, the country had been in decline, and potentially great leaders had become so disempowered by the curse of collective decision-making that it was no longer possible for a visionary, like himself, to achieve anything of consequence. He was adamant that, had he been born a hundred years earlier, his legendary deeds would have made him a household name and his statue, in marble, would grace a prominent position in Westminster Abbey.

"Britain today has gone to the dogs," he declared one day, pausing to hit a ball on the seventh tee of the links course at Caldy. "And the sad thing is, no-one seems able to do anything about it. That was an awful shot....bugger – in the rough. I mean, anyone who wants to do *anything* has to go through so much *damned* consultation with so many other *damned* people, all giving their own *damned* opinions, that by the end of it all the original idea is so watered down it's not worth doing."

His friend and colleague Terence McCarthy positioned his own ball and took a practice swing. McCarthy, the council's chief executive, was a large, bulky man in his fifties with a ruddy face and an impressive thatch of white hair. "You're head of the council, Gerald," he said devilishly, "why don't *you* do something about it?"

"Why don't we all do something about it?" interjected Duncan Silverlock, a small, weasel-like man with thinning hair and glasses, who was the director of the council's Finance Department. "If there're enough of us who feel the same way, surely together we can make some changes..." He watched McCarthy take his shot – a good one, then fastidiously balanced his own ball on a tee and selected a number three wood.

"And what exactly are we going to do something about?" McCarthy asked innocently. He actually knew perfectly well, as they had held this conversation many times before, but he enjoyed playing Devil's advocate.

"Everything," Radley said simply. "Everything that's gone wrong with society and the country as a whole. Yob culture. Anti-social behaviour....Low quality people leading low quality lives at the expense of decent hard-working people." For a moment he floundered, struggling to find the words to express himself. "The lack of values, the rudeness, the absence of ideals or noble struggle or *greatness*. We need some *greatness*. It used to be Great Britain. It certainly isn't now."

"Too true," McCarthy agreed with passionate cynisism. "We need a return to British values – the things that made Britain *great*. Cricket. Work in the mine or mill all week, football on Saturday, church on Sunday…roast beef and Yorkshire pudding…and war with the French. We were always great when we were fighting the Frogs!"

"I sometimes think we could do with a war," Radley said quietly. "It'd shake away some of the complacency and kick society back on track. People need something to *strive* against, to unite them in a common purpose - otherwise the rot sets in like it has since the Fifties."

"Hitler regarded war as a great purifier," contributed Silverlock, absent-mindedly.

McCarthy was enjoying the conversation immensely. "Why don't we declare war on France, dig some trenches in Normandy or somewhere, and send all of our low quality people to go and fight in them? Wouldn't that be splendid?"

Radley looked at him thoughtfully. "It wouldn't be easy. The government would never let a part of the UK go to war on its own. We could only do it if we had autonomy. And it would cost a lot to fight even a small war…"

"Gerald you arse!" laughed McCarthy. "I was joking!"

Radley stared out across the River Dee without expression. "I wasn't…"

Later, in the club house, they joined a group of four other council officials who had just returned from their own round of golf and were standing at the bar sipping drinks.

"Gerald wants to declare war on the French," McCarthy announced joyously, "and he's serious!"

"And the first thing I'll do when we're at war is have you shot!" Radley responded. He found the chief executive frankly irritating when he was in such a mood. Although the two men were friends and had worked together for years, they were very disparate personalities. McCarthy, although committed to his job, was essentially a relaxed, jovial character whose priorities were home, family and recreational pastimes - especially sailing and golf. Radley, by contrast, was obsessed with a nebulous concept he called '*The Strategic Vision*', which involved relentless change in pursuit of an administratively perfect society. Such a bureaucratic Holy Grail was, of course, unattainable, but Gerald Radley was driven by the quest, not the ultimate outcome. He was the sort of man who, upon finding himself in Utopia, would immediately make a list of unsatisfactory issues, and start formulating policies to rectify them.

"It's an interesting idea, a war with the French," remarked a rather dashing, well-groomed man in his mid-thirties, thoughtfully scratching his neatly clipped moustache. He was Alastair Blundell, Assistant Director of Housing. Radley was particularly keen to have his participation in the conversation because, as a part-time major in the Territorial Army, Blundell commanded Wirral's only Infantry company.

"Would your boys fancy a bit of a scrap with the French, if I can arrange it?" Radley asked him casually, as if he were proposing another round of golf. "I don't mean the whole of France, I'm thinking smaller scale, say Wirral versus Normandy, or something like that..."

Blundell laughed, then shrugged. "I'm sure the lads'd be up for it, if you pay them enough. How would we go about it?"

Radley looked thoughtful. "Well, we'd need the cooperation of the French, of course. That's why I suggested Normandy – Birkenhead is twinned with Caen, as you know, and I was talking to their mayor and some of their councillors a few months ago, during the Cultural Friendship Exchange."

"A crafty title which I dreamt up", interjected McCarthy proudly. "The real name should be '*Excuse for a piss-up at the council-tax payer's expense*.' We had a great time..."

Radley ignored him. "As I was saying, Monsieur Lebovic expressed similar views to my own – he believes that there's social and moral decay in his country, and it seems that many French people feel the same way. In fact, there have been several public protests in Normandy against decisions made by the French government and the EU...The Frogs are far less apathetic than us Brits."

"And what does he think about going to war with us?" Blundell asked, curiously.

"I don't know, I didn't ask him. But I got the impression he might be receptive to the idea."

The whole group was listening now, unsure as to whether to take the conversation seriously or not, but intrigued nonetheless, and greatly entertained.

"The government will never allow a part of the UK to do anything like that on its own, it simply won't happen," declared Simon Beatty, director of the council's 'Adult Health and Social Care' department.

Radley shrugged. "So we detach ourselves from the UK, like Cornwall did last year. Provided Europe upholds our application for limited autonomy we'll be free to do as we please, without interference from Westminster. It's one of the big things in Europe at the moment – '*The right of geographically or ethnically distinct peoples to determine their own identity*'. I was reading about it the other day. We're a peninsular surrounded on three sides by water. Surely that makes us geographically distinct."

"Wouldn't Europe stop us having a war, the spoilsports?" asked McCarthy.

Duncan Siverlock shook his head confidently. "No, Europe will stop us exporting bread or milk or subsidising our farmers. As long as we don't contravene any trade agreements, and pay our annual contributions, and hang an EU flag on the town hall, we'll be okay. The European Parliament is too obsessed with trivial matters like making sure all council documentation is printed in sixteen languages, just in case someone from Romania turns up at the town hall and wants to read our parking policy...."

McCarthy downed his pint and put the glass down hard on the bar. "What about the cost? Wars cost money, Gerald, and you can't very well fund it from the council tax. How would we pay for it?"

"Through the sale of surplus council-owned assets, and the granting of licences. There are still some school playing fields and large public parks left, with developers queuing up for the right to build. And there are plenty of roads where we could introduce parking charges. Then there are all the savings we'll make if we're independent and I can actually run the place the way I'd like to..."

Simon Beatty looked unconvinced. "So what's the point? In fighting the French, I mean?"

"Society gets a focus," Radley replied. "And with focus comes unity. And if we're at war we can use it as the justification for the sort of policies and laws which are needed to sort this country out once and for all. Some people need to be forced to behave in a certain way – the *right* way. They won't do it of their own accord. Under wartime conditions we can force the population to do the right thing. We don't actually need much of a war – in fact, if there were too many casualties it would be counter-productive. It's the *idea* of war I'm interested in. I think it could be the only way back to *greatness* in this country."

Beatty was clearly uncomfortable. "Gerald," he said awkwardly, "I hope you won't take this the wrong way, but...Are you really, seriously, considering breaking away from the rest of the country and declaring war on the French?"

Radley smiled like a viper. "I'm not sure. Let's see what the good people of Wirral decide."

Radley had chosen his moment perfectly. He knew that there was a growing resentment amongst local people towards central government in London and the European Parliament in Brussels, due to a number of recent policy decisions which were perceived as treating the region unfairly. Liverpool had received a massive injection of funding associated with its status as *European Capital of Culture*, but little of this development money had benefited Wirral, leaving the peninsular's population feeling like the poor relations of Merseyside. This discontentment had increased after Downing Street outraged local residents by approving the creation of a huge centre for asylum seekers in downtown Birkenhead, and when Prime Minister Adare also gave permission for French nuclear waste to be stored on the peninsular prior to being shipped to Sellafield for reprocessing, Wirral's population became convinced that Westminster held some sort of grudge against them. Other controversial proposals which were creating disaffection included the use of the Cammel Laird shipyard to break-up vessels contaminated with toxic waste, and the construction of a potentially polluting refuse incinerator at Eastham. To make matters worse, Adare was suspected of complicity in allowing the Vauxhall factory at Ellesmere Port to be taken over by a rival French car manufacturer, and rumours were circulating that the new owners intended to close the plant after stripping its assets. Although Vauxhall's was located in neighbouring Cheshire, many of its workers lived on the Wirral and depended on the factory for their livelihood.

All of these factors meant that, when the council-produced leaflet entitled '*Time for a Change?*' was posted through the letterboxes of the peninsula, it was not treated with the indifference or even ridicule which it would undoubtedly have received a decade earlier.

CHAPTER 3

Wirral Decides

This is one of those books where the reader repeatedly feels like shouting 'Get on with it!' Obviously a plot has to be allowed to develop, but the author can only expect so much loyalty from his readership before they simply lose interest or start skipping pages to get to the 'good stuff'. Chapter Three is particularly frustrating – a collection of mini-chapters jumbled together in a disjointed hotchpotch. Surely we should be entitled to expect greater skill from our author in crafting his storyline?

Edmund Smedley
Basingstoke Evening Gazette

Mr Roberts replies:
Every letter, word, sentence and paragraph of my work has been carefully chosen and exquisitely crafted into my masterpiece. I'm an artist!

In the living room of their rented terraced house in Tranmere, Mark Conrad and Ben Spencer were watching television. It was an old set, donated by Spencer's mother on a generous 'Either you have it or it's going in the skip' basis, and the poor-quality picture was tinged with green. On the screen, a fat man with tattoos and a vest was painting the walls of a house while making supposedly humorous remarks to the camera. He did not flinch when an empty beer can bounced off him.

"You'll break the TV, you Muppet!" scolded Spencer, before downing the contents of his own can and throwing it at the television.

"It's sucking my will to live!" Conrad exclaimed. "Why are we watching this shite? Why are we watching some fat cockney bastard paint his house? If I paint this house will they send the cameras round?"

"It's reality TV..."

"It's reality shite!" Conrad leapt angrily from his festering armchair and rummaged through the pile of video cassettes at the base of the television. The video player was only slightly newer than the TV, another hand-me-down from a relative. He found a tape and sighed with satisfaction: "Ah – *Wayne's World*. Party time, excellent."

Spencer disappeared briefly to his room and returned with his Webley Tempest air pistol. By the time Robert Taylor arrived back from work, looking rather incongruous in his shirt and tie, his two housemates were taking it in turns to shoot beer cans off the top of the television. Fortunately there was a wall rather than a window behind, but Robert wondered who would repair the damaged wallpaper before the landlord saw it and deducted the cost from their deposit. He stared at Mark and Ben and shook his head despairingly.

"My God, and this is the intellectual future of the nation! Don't you bloody students ever do any work?"

Conrad pulled the trigger and sent a beer can somersaulting into the air. "Save it for the judge!" That was one of his favourite phrases.

"I'm not a student anyway," declared Spencer defiantly.

"Oh, I forgot, you dropped out. So you're Unemployed Man. Or is it Unemployable Man?" Robert and Mark laughed, but Spencer looked hurt and defensive.

"Actually I've got a job at Aldi, starting on Monday."

Robert sat down cautiously on the sofa, which was damaged and could swallow an unsuspecting man whole. "Good. Then you can pay me back that hundred quid you owe me."

"And that hundred and twenty quid you owe me," added Mark.

Spencer looked sheepish. "Give me a break guys. I'll pay you back, it's just not easy at the moment. No one does me any favours..."

Robert feigned sympathy. "My heart bleeds for you, Ben. But if you can't afford to live here you shouldn't have moved out of your parents' house." Spencer had borrowed the money for his deposit and first months' rent from his TA friends.

Robert turned to Mark Conrad. "Don't you find it rather unreasonable, my dear Conrad, that this guy here claims he's so poor, yet in his room there's a brand spanking new TV and DVD player, yet we're here watching this ancient relic which makes everything look green? There's something wrong somewhere."

Conrad nodded. "I reckon his TV and DVD should become house property until he pays us back. He owes Simon and the Mullah money as well, did you know that?" Simon and 'The Mullah' were the two other tenants who shared the house.

Robert shook his head in disbelief. "Where does all this money go, Ben? Are you a drug addict or something? Actually, if you are you'd better watch out." He picked up a tatty copy of *'Time for a Change?'* which was lying on the sofa beside him. The picture of Gerald Radley on the cover had several pellet holes through its head. "If this thing about Wirral governing itself goes ahead, then bag heads like you are going to find themselves in the shit. It says here that Council Leader Radley's going to take a hard line against you."

"I'm not a bag head!" Spencer protested.

"Save it for the judge!" Conrad growled, before lifting his buttocks from the sofa and braking wind noisily in Robert's direction. "It's away!" he exclaimed, in the voice of an X-wing pilot from the film *Star Wars*.

"Is it a hit?" Robert asked, hopefully.

Conrad shook his head with disappointment. "Negative. It just impacted on the surface." This exchange of dialogue took place whenever anyone farted in the living room.

"Changing the subject," Robert said, "have you voted yet, Mark?"

"Nope. You?"

Robert shook his head. "No."

"May I be so bold as to ask how you intend to vote?"

"You may. I'm not sure, but I think I'll probably be voting yes. I don't like the way the country's being run at the moment, so I reckon I've got nothing to lose."

"Any idea what happens to Charlie Company?" Conrad was army-barmy, the keenest part-time soldier Robert knew, and as an impoverished student he relied heavily on his TA income, so the future of their unit was of great importance to him.

"If the overall vote is no then nothing changes. From what Major Blundell was saying the other day, if the vote is yes, then Wirral gets whatever TA assets are within its boundaries at the moment. That basically means us, the Engineers and the Really Large Corps. Oh, and the cadets. Then we'll all get organised into some kind of mini-army, I think. That's the idea anyway."

Conrad was sceptical. "Doesn't sound that great to me. What about training days – how will they be affected?"

"Well, from what I gather, they'll increase for the first few years. Apparently Council Leader Radley's eager for the new force to be highly regarded, and he's prepared to spend money on equipment and training. Who knows, he might even buy us a decent rifle."

"Then I think I'll vote *yes* as well," Conrad declared.

"And so shall I", added Spencer. "If I can find the form…"

Conrad stood up decisively. "Right," he announced proudly, "I feel beaucoup movement down below, so I'm going upstairs to the toilet, where I shall produce something which, when it reaches the Irish Sea, will be a danger to shipping…"

A week before the final deadline for the submission of voting forms, Radley, McCarthy, Silverlock and Blundell went sailing on McCarthy's 30ft yacht *Alacrity*. They set out from a mooring on the River Dee at high tide, and sailed down the estuary towards the wind turbines out at sea. The trip had the air of a conspiracy about it – indeed, Radley had specifically chosen the boat as the venue for the gathering as it guaranteed privacy, with no danger of conversations being interrupted or overheard. As they approached the mouth of the river, with the Hoyle sandbank to port and Hilbre Island to starboard, the wind picked up, filling the sails and sending the boat surging forward in a most satisfying way.

"So, Gerald, are you nervous?" McCarthy asked.

"About what?"

"You know! About the vote."

Radley leaned back in the cockpit, enjoying his gin and tonic. "No, I'm not nervous, Terence. I'm confident that it'll go in our favour and in a week's time we'll actually have the power to do something meaningful in the borough."

"Can we cheat? I mean, print twenty-five thousand extra voting forms and fill them in ourselves, or something like that?" There was a mischievous gleam in the chief executive's eye.

"Not possible, I'm afraid," Silverlock told him. "The EU is sending a team of inspectors over to make sure it's all done by the book. They'll check voting forms against the electoral roll, so we can't make up imaginary voters."

McCarthy puffed his pipe thoughtfully. "But not everyone in the Wirral will vote. Can't we get our ICT department to come up with a computer programme that'll tell us who hasn't voted, then produce fake forms for those people?"

Silverlock shook his head patronisingly. "The inspectors are going to pick names at random and visit them to make sure that they not only exist but also that they actually voted, and that their vote was correctly recorded by us. If they turn up at someone's house and the person says they didn't vote, then the whole thing will be declared null and void and we'll have enough egg on our faces to make the world's biggest omelette."

Radley appeared irritated. "We don't need to cheat. We're going to win."

"We've certainly produced enough propaganda and made enough promises," mused McCarthy wryly. He was referring to the persuasive literature – mostly leaflets and adverts in local newspapers – which had been produced by the council's public relations department in recent weeks and delivered to households, at considerable expense. The literature had extolled the merits of partial autonomy while vilifying the arguments against it, as well as making promises aimed at swaying those who might be on the borderline between voting *yes* or *no*. Included in these promises was a pledge to clamp down on immigration, and create hundreds of new jobs within the council which would be reserved exclusively for local workers.

Blundell had remained quiet during the proceedings, but now he spoke with a thoughtful and slightly distant expression. "Gerald?"

"Yes."

"Have you spoken to Monsieur Lebovic recently?"

"I have."

"What did he say? I mean, did you mention You Know What?"

Radley smiled proudly and pompously. "I did. And he's thinking about it. Actually, he thinks it's a good idea, but he needs to sound out some of his colleagues before he can give a definite thumbs-up. Obviously it depends on our vote next Friday..."

"So we may actually be going to war at some point in the future?"

"That's the plan."

"The reason I ask is that if – when – we're a self-governing region, the British government won't supply us anymore. From a military point of view that means no more ammunition, fuel, spare parts, boots or anything else we need."

"I realise that. So what's your point, Alistair?"

"My point is that, if we're going to fight the French, we need stuff to do it with. Now, as far as I'm aware, the rules state that any region applying for partial autonomy gets whatever military assets it possesses at the time the result of the vote is declared."

"That's correct. And?"

"Well, the Battalion has a big field firing exercise next weekend, which means Charlie Company will get a lot of things it doesn't normally have: shed loads of ammo, grenades, mortar bombs, anti-tank missiles – the lot. If you could somehow delay the result of the vote until Saturday morning we might get to keep it all."

Radley was impressed. "An excellent suggestion. I'll see what I can do."

Robert Taylor was having a bad day at school. He had taught five one-hour lessons, with each class presenting its share of irksome challenges, and now his stress levels were being swollen to bursting point by a twelve-year-old boy. The child was running around the science lab, making strange shrieking noises and terrorising other pupils, many of whom were looking understandably uneasy. Robert's teaching objectives for this, his final lesson of the day, had been projected onto the whiteboard for the past ten minutes, but so far no progress had been made due to the disruptive antics of the boy, whose name was Simon Smythe. Smythe was a skinny runt of a child with shaved ginger hair and freckles – a classic Merseyside 'scally'. He was notorious throughout the school for his atrocious behaviour, and today's exploits were nothing unusual.

"Simon, I asked you to sit down," Robert said firmly.

Smythe stopped and looked at him with a defiant smirk. He tilted his head to one side and let out a strange squawking sound, then climbed onto a stool and started leaping from bench to bench, laughing and kicking pupils' books onto the floor.

Robert tried to stay calm, but could feel his blood pressure rising. The arteries in his neck started to pulsate, an indicator of the anger and frustration which were welling up inside him. Smythe's performance was beginning to incite several other pupils to misbehave, and the situation threatened to escalate out of control.

"Simon, get down off the table – *now*!" he shouted. Smythe ignored him and jumped onto a bench located by an open window. His trainers slipped on the shiny laminate surface and for a moment Robert's heart missed a beat: if the boy fell out of the third storey window then he, the teacher, would be held accountable and possibly prosecuted. Fortunately Smythe regained his balance, and laughed at his lucky escape.

"Simon Smythe, get down now!" Robert screamed in his best infantry corporal's voice. The boy looked momentarily startled, then leapt from the table and ran across the room. Robert strode after him, resisting the temptation to run, which would have seemed undignified; earlier in the term, he had chased a pupil along a crowded corridor, only to make a fool of himself by almost knocking over an innocent child and then dropping his wallet in front of dozens of amused schoolchildren.

"Simon, if you can't sit down and settle down I'll keep you behind at the end of the lesson,' Robert warned, aware that his threat sounded pathetically feeble.

"Easy, tiger," Smythe goaded. Some members of the class laughed, others grinned with amusement but were secretly appalled.

Robert lost his temper. "Get out! Stop wasting my time and get out!" He had almost cornered Smythe but the boy dodged past him and escaped from the room like a slippery delinquent rat. For a moment, the room fell silent and Robert breathed a sigh of relief. Then, suddenly, Smythe stuck his head back in through the doorway and announced, in a Bugs Bunny voice: "The-the-the-the-that's all f-f-f-f-f-folks!"

"Get out, fool!" Robert shouted, pushing the door shut and holding it closed. Sometimes he really hated his job. It would have been possible to tolerate pupils like Smythe, and even find them amusing, were it not for the fact that the rest of the class would be expected to achieve a certain standard in the forthcoming exams, and disruptive pupils jeopardised their chances. And if the class under-achieved, it would be Robert, not Simon Smythe, who would be held accountable. He sighed, turned towards the rows of expectant faces and resorted to some of his standard teacher clichés.

"That clown is stopping you from learning and he's messing up your education. I don't think he has the right to do that...It's not funny, Ryan. Don't encourage him. Just because he's going nowhere in life doesn't mean you have to follow him..."

Several pupils started sniggering and Robert turned to see Smythe making faces through the glass panel of the door before running away. Robert cursed whichever government minister had decided to save money by closing special schools and forcing pupils like Smythe into mainstream education, where he did not belong.

Resuming the lesson was not easy, as the pupils had lost their concentration and Robert had to inform the school office that Smythe had left the room without permission and was probably wandering the corridors causing mayhem. Hopefully a senior member of staff would catch the boy and discipline him appropriately, although this was unlikely: those in authority at Robert's school were increasingly reluctant to leave the comfort of their offices to do battle with the unruly hordes.

Finally, the lesson ended and Robert dismissed the class. He stood by the doorway and watched scores of pupils streaming past in a jostling juvenile torrent which flowed turbulently along the corridor towards the stairs. Suddenly he noticed Simon Smythe amongst the crowd, grinning defiantly, safe within an impenetrable phalanx of bodies.

"I hope you enjoy your detention tomorrow, Simon," Robert called after him, knowing full well that Smythe would simply defy him once again by not turning up. It all seemed hopelessly futile. The balance of power had shifted so far from teacher to pupil that only the well-behaved children respected the school rules, while the miscreants largely did as they pleased. Robert sighed and wondered how he could possibly do this job for another thirty years. He felt exhausted, and his throat hurt from all of the shouting he had been forced to do that day. Ironically, he often shouted more during a day's work as a teacher than he did as a TA corporal.

The flow of pupils along the corridor subsided to a trickle and he noticed his colleague Martin Higgins, who was standing in the doorway opposite.

"Another day, another dollar," Robert said wearily. "Thank God it's Friday tomorrow."

"What was the delightful Simon Smythe up to?" Martin enquired.

"What he does best: wrecking my lessons."

"They need to increase his Ritalin."

"They need to shove a great big Ritalin suppository right up his arse!"

Higgins shook his head. "No, that'd cost too much – they'd have to pay his parents even more benefits then. You know what'd really do the trick with little bastards like that?"

"What?"

"A good old-fashioned beating," Higgins declared. "And I'm hoping he might be getting one in future, if the council gets its way and we become independent. I'm dropping my voting slip into the polling station tonight and it'll definitely have a cross in the 'yes' box."

Later, sitting in the Green Bar in central Birkenhead with his friends from the TA, Robert ranted about the increasingly poor behaviour of pupils at his school and the stress it was causing him. The others listened with limited sympathy. They enjoyed hearing about the outrageous antics of certain unruly youths, but were of the opinion that teachers had a relatively easy life, with good pay and excessively long holidays, and should consider themselves fortunate.

"You know what you should have done?" said Mark Conrad, when Robert had finished describing the afternoon's incident involving Simon Smythe. "You should have pulled out your sword and given him the good news!" This was a phrase he had picked up from a member of the Royal Green Jackets: 'sword' was the term for a bayonet in that regiment.

Robert sighed. "I sometimes wish I could. But half the time it's not the kid's fault. If they were brought up properly by parents who cared about them they'd probably be alright…"

They were joined by Karl Brabander, the slightly oriental-looking call centre manager who was also a TA corporal in the same platoon as Robert. Returning from the bar with a round of drinks and a packet of crisps, he sat down opposite Robert and scowled. “Oh you’re not still whinging about how hard it is being a teacher, are you Tayl? All that holiday and home by four o’clock! It must be hell for you!”

Robert refused to rise to the bait. Brabander had a reputation for being highly antagonistic, in a good-natured sort of way. He was also an extremely competent section commander, someone from whom Robert and Mark had learned a lot over the years. His seven years in the TA had included a tour of duty in Iraq with the regular First Battalion.

Robert grinned. “No, I was just saying how civilised it was to have an intelligent conversation without you.” He leant across the table and snatched Brabander’s crisps, then nonchalantly opened the packet and offered it to Conrad. “Crisp, good sir?”

“Don’t mind if I do.” Conrad reached over and pulled out a crisp of such gargantuan proportions that it seemed to take forever to emerge from the packet. “Oh-oh!” he exclaimed with delight, “it’s a whopper – must be my lucky day!”

Deprived of the item which had constituted the bulk of its contents, the crisp packet seemed to collapse in on itself, an empty husk devoid of nourishment. Brabander stared at it in a combination of amusement and silent rage.

“It’s alright, Brab,” Robert reassured him with a snigger. ‘There’re still a few bits in the bottom....hmm, tasty.” He plucked out the last remaining crisp fragments and stuffed them into his mouth, then handed the empty packet back to its rightful owner.

Brabander slowly turned the packet upside-down, and looked distinctly unimpressed as a few pitiful shreds fell out onto the table. He focused his ‘Vietcong sniper stare’ on Mark Conrad. “Well, Con, you’d better hope you stay in Taylor’s section because if you ever end up in mine you’re gonna be doing a hell of a lot of stagging”. He turned to Robert. “And when I’m platoon sergeant, Taylor, your section’s gonna be doing all the shitty stuff – you’ll be out doing patrols and ambushes and anything else that’s going. You’ll be sitting all night in some Sennybridge forestry block in the rain while everyone else is snug in their gonk bags. Don’t you worry, boys, I’ll make sure you’ll both be sorry that you nicked my crisps. Won’t they, Murph?”

Paul Murphy smiled and nodded obligingly. He had been sitting contentedly in quiet detachment, semi-listening to the conversation while sipping his beer and slowly drifting into sleep. Brabander’s question had caught him off guard and, like a daydreaming schoolboy, he was unsure as to what answer was expected of him. Murphy was the third section commander in Eight Platoon, along with Robert and Karl Brabander. At thirty five, he was the oldest by seven years - highly experienced but, by his own admission, “Getting a bit long in the tooth.”

Robert noticed an untouched beer on the table and remembered that one member of their party was missing.

"Anyone seen how Spencer's getting on?" He stood up and peered through the crowd towards the bar, where Ben had last been sighted, trying to chat-up a girl who worked in Tesco. Suddenly there was a commotion over on the other side of the room. Robert noticed violent movement out of the corner of his eye, and turned to see the bouncers carrying a rabid, screaming youth towards the exit. The boy squirmed and writhed like an eel, and Robert recognised him as Ryan Smythe, older brother of Simon, who had left school the previous year without taking any exams. As a pupil, Ryan's behaviour had been arguably worse than Simon's, and he had evidently not improved in the intervening period. Robert was impressed by the business-like manner in which the bouncers dealt with the troublemaker, carrying him roughly but without inflicting any real injury. Smythe spat and cursed and threatened, then cried out as he was bundled through the glass doors and knocked his head on one of the chrome handles. Outside, the 'head bouncer' leant close to Smythe's face and spoke to him with quiet malice. No sound penetrated the thick plate glass windows, but Robert could guess that the youth was being warned in no uncertain terms of the consequences of returning to the establishment to cause trouble. Seconds later, Smythe was dumped unceremoniously onto the pavement. He lay there for a moment in tears of rage, then picked himself up sulkily and limped out of view.

"That'll learn 'im!" remarked Conrad with satisfaction.

"He used to go to my school," Robert said. "He's the brother of that little scroat I was telling you about just now. Small world, isn't it? I never taught him, but I know he was a real pain in the arse. Pity we couldn't deal with him like that when he used to mess around in lessons...." He looked perplexed. "What I can't understand is, how is it that a bar is allowed to have a more effective discipline system than a school? How can that be right? Schools are supposed to benefit society, whereas this place only exists to make a profit and get people pissed. Yet here they can pick you up and throw you out if you cause trouble."

"Write to the Government and ask them," Brabander suggested with an indifferent shrug. He downed his beer, slammed the glass on the table and stood up. "Right, I'm off!"

Robert nodded. "Yep, time to go. Are you playing soldiers this weekend, Brab?"

Brabander shook his head. "Nah, Liverpool are playing." He was a fanatical 'Reds' supporter.

Mark Conrad put his jacket on. "Big day tomorrow. We should find out whether we're a '*Semi-Autonomous Self-Governing Region*' or not."

Brabander burped as loudly and grossly as possible. "I can't wait."

The following evening, Robert was sitting on the hard slatted bench seat in the back of a Bedford four-tonne truck, trying to keep warm as the vehicle sped south through Wales towards the Sennybridge Training Area in the foothills of the Brecon Beacons. A cold draught penetrated the lorry's canvas cover, and the noise and fumes from the engine combined with the cigarette smoke and farts from his fellow passengers to create a distinctly unpleasant environment in which to spend four hours. He began to wonder whether, after six years, it was time to leave the TA. Most people, he reminded himself, did not spend their Friday evenings wedged into a rickety truck with a bunch of rough-and-ready men wearing camouflaged '*disruptive pattern material*', or 'DPM' as it was referred to in the Army. Most people did not voluntarily spend their precious leisure time being cold, wet, filthy, deprived of sleep, physically exhausted and put under pressure. Most people relaxed at home or socialised with friends in clean, civilised surroundings. It occurred to him - not for the first time - that perhaps his part-time TA life was a substitute for a fulfilling normal life, a sanctuary he had taken refuge in because he was too socially inadequate to be a successful full-time civilian. He decided, on reflection, that this did not really bother him; the TA only occupied one or two weekends a month and, regardless of whether it was indicative of personal deficiencies, the simple fact was that he really enjoyed soldiering.

From the seat behind, Mark Conrad leant over and shouted in his ear. "Linda phoned last night. There's a message on the answerphone. Sorry, I forgot to tell you earlier."

"What did she say?"

"She wants you to phone her."

"Right. Thanks."

Linda was Robert's girlfriend of eight years. They had met at university and been happy together as students, but after graduation the search for suitable jobs had resulted in geographical separation, forcing them into a long-distance relationship which had dragged on far too long. As time passed, the passion and romance and, he had to confess, the love, had dwindled to the point where there was little point in their being together. Robert was aware that the decent thing to do would be to end the relationship without further procrastination, putting it out of its misery with an honourable *coup de grace*. But he was too loyal, both to Linda and to the memory of their past happiness, and too scared of being single after eight years. He often wondered why she had not finished with him. The most likely explanation was that she was waiting to meet someone better, but her 'knight in shining armour' had not yet materialised.

"Have they announced the result of the vote yet?" asked Conrad, shouting over the whir of the vehicle's transmission and the flapping of the rear canvas panel.

"Say again?"

"The vote – the autonomy thing. Have you heard the result?"

“No. Last I heard they were still counting.”

“Oh.”

It was too noisy in the back of the truck to hold a proper conversation, so they sat in silence, keeping their thoughts to themselves. Gradually, the wind blowing through gaps in the canvas began to make Robert feel progressively colder. He pulled up the hood of his combat smock, put his gloves on and pushed his hands deep into his pockets. For a while he felt warmer, but the effect was short-lived and once again the chill crept back into his body. It was like sitting in a wind tunnel. Years before, as a recruit, he had believed that discomfort had to be endured – almost enjoyed – with some sort of masochistic pleasure if one was to be considered a good soldier. Then, one night, he was sitting under the dripping conifers of a rain-drenched Welsh forestry block, wearing his normal combat clothing and deliberately not donning his waterproofs because he thought it would be a concession to weakness, when the corporal in charge – who was snug in his Gore-Tex suit – asked him why he was allowing himself to get so wet.

“I don’t mind, Corporal”, the naive recruit Taylor had replied with a casual shrug. “Getting wet’s what it’s all about, isn’t it?”

“Put your Gary Gore-Tex on,” the corporal told him sternly. “Any fool can be uncomfortable.”

Since then, the phrase ‘*Any fool can be uncomfortable’* had become one of his TA maxims. It echoed through his brain now, as he sat hunched in the breezy truck, and galvanised him into action. Fumbling in the gloom, he pulled his sleeping bag out of his bergen and spent the next ten minutes struggling to pull it up around himself. With boots on this was no easy task, because the bag kept snagging on his heels as he squirmed and wriggled and tried to force his way in. Sometimes it seemed that sleeping bags deliberately resisted entry by soldiers desperate for warmth and sleep, clamming-up uncooperatively to deny access. Eventually, amidst protests of annoyance from Murphy and Spencer on either side of him, he succeeded in pulling the quilted cocoon up under his arms and was soon feeling deliciously warm. He slumped down happily on the seat, closed his eyes, and wondered what to do about Linda.

By nine o’clock the next morning, Charlie Company had been split into groups and dispersed over the various firing ranges of the Sennybridge training area. Mark Conrad had gone to practice fire and movement drills using live ammunition, Murphy was on the 51mm mortar range, and Spencer was throwing grenades. Robert found himself in a group which included his platoon commander, Lieutenant Andrew Grudge, waiting in a bunker behind the LAW94 firing range. The LAW94, or ‘Light Anti-tank Weapon, 94mm,’ was a throw-away rocket launcher designed to give front-line infantry soldiers a realistic chance of destroying modern tanks on the battlefield.

"Have you heard anything about the independence vote yet, sir?" Robert asked, partly to make conversation but also because, if anyone was likely to know the result, it would be Grudge.

The officer shook his head. "No. I was speaking to the OC earlier – he works for the council, as you may know – and he said the computer system counting all the votes crashed yesterday afternoon and they've been working all night trying to sort it out. I bet that'll really impress the EU inspectors!"

"Are you for or against it, sir?"

Grudge thought for a moment. "I don't know. From the point of view of a Wirral resident I'm in favour of it. From the point of view of a TA soldier I'm against it. I want to stay part of the British Army, not some half-baked Wirral Muppet Home Defence Force. I tell you one thing, Corporal T, if we become independent you can kiss goodbye to the sort of training we're doing this weekend. We'll be lucky to fire enough rounds each year to pass an Annual Personal Weapons Test."

Robert respected Grudge. He was a competent and enthusiastic platoon commander with a passion for soldiering, but was unpopular in the officer's mess because he did not always conduct himself in the manner expected of a subaltern. Grudge was relatively old at thirty-two, slightly overweight and with dark brown hair going grey at the temples. His background was working class and he was not afraid to voice opinions which might differ from those of the Colonel or Regimental Sergeant-major. This had given him a reputation as something of a maverick, a loose canon with ideas above his station. What really antagonised senior officers, though, was his relationship with his platoon. An ex-NCO himself, Grudge seemed to prefer socialising with the men he commanded than spending time in the officer's mess, which was disapproved of by his commissioned colleagues. Only his undeniable achievements as an officer, which included commanding the sole platoon in the Battalion at full strength, prevented him from being told politely but firmly to take his talents elsewhere.

"What are we waiting for?" Robert asked, peering outside to where the platoon sergeant, Pete Collins, was standing impatiently beside a stack of boxes containing the anti-tank weapons. Collins was wearing a fluorescent yellow vest over his combats, identifying him as one of the range officers who would be supervising the firing. Captain Aldridge, the company second-in-command, was in overall charge of proceedings but was nowhere to be seen.

"What's going on, Sergeant Collins?" Grudge called out.

Collins walked over to the bunker. "As you know, sir, we were supposed to start firing at nine o'clock. It's now quarter past but the OC has told us to wait until he arrives before we start firing. Captain Aldridge is on the radio trying to find out where he is. Hang on a minute...Oh dear, this isn't good..."

An altercation could be heard outside, with one angry voice and one defensive one.

"Shit, it's the RSM," Collins said. "I should stay in here if I were you, sir..."

The Regimental Sergeant-major was the most senior NCO in the Battalion, a figure to be feared, even by officers. He was speaking to Captain Aldridge, and was most displeased. His angry tones could be heard even from within the bunker.

"You were supposed to start firing at nine o'clock, Captain. I don't care what Major Blundell said, this is a Battalion exercise, and if Charlie Company don't stay on schedule they screw it up for everyone else. Now, either start firing now, sir, or your boys will be doing Infantry Combat Fitness Tests all day while everyone else uses their allocation of ordnance."

The RSM stormed off in his Land Rover, leaving Aldridge looking deflated and indignant. He was annoyed at having been reprimanded for something which was not his fault, but there was no point arguing with the RSM, who was always right.

"Okay, gents," he said decisively, "let's get started. Lieutenant Grudge, you're first. Make sure you've got your respirator and ear protection."

Grudge left the bunker and headed for the firing point. Robert and the rest of the group waited. After a short while there were two loud *thuds* in quick succession. Then the lieutenant returned, scowling. "A sodding mobility kill. I hit the track."

It was Robert's turn next. He followed Collins to the firing point, which consisted of a wall of sandbags with an opening in it. Beyond the sandbags the ground dropped away into a large hollow, at the bottom of which lay the blackened hulk of a Russian T62 tank. Due to the powerful blast from the missile launcher, he had to wear the correct protective equipment – a respirator, ear plugs and ear defenders, as well as his helmet. All of this made him feel cumbersome and slightly detached from reality, like an astronaut or a deep sea diver. Sergeant Collins handed him a LAW94 and he began to prepare the weapon for firing. Removing the polystyrene end caps was easy enough, but he struggled to extend the firing tube.

"Come on, Tayl," the sergeant goaded with delight. "There's a main battle tank roaring towards you and if you don't get that thing open you're going to be history..."

Sweating inside the rubber respirator, Robert was not amused. Despite his best efforts, he could not extend the rear half of the launcher. He was used to training with inert drill launchers which were loose from repeated opening and closing, but a new, live weapon was far stiffer. Desperation turned to focused anger and with a violent tug he finally managed to pull the rear tube out until it clicked into place. With relief he cocked the weapon, flipped up the sight unit and aimed over the top of the sandbags at the tank hulk in the hollow below.

"Fire all five spotting rounds, then the main armament," Collins instructed. "And remember – as soon as you've fired the HEAT round, get down behind the sandbags." Robert was disappointed – he had hoped to be able to watch the missile hit the tank.

"Okay, if you're ready, Corporal T," the sergeant said, "*tank action!*"

Aiming the weapon while inhibited by the restricted visibility of the respirator was no easy task, as the sighting system featured a holographic aiming grid which could only be seen from certain angles. Getting the respirator, sight and missile launcher all correctly aligned was a real challenge. Eventually, Robert succeeded in bringing the weapon on target, estimating the range to be about one hundred metres, and fired the first of his spotting rounds. These were tracer bullets designed to help a soldier correct his aim and find the correct aiming mark before unleashing the expensive armour-piercing warhead. The spotting round made a white flash as it hit the top of the tank's turret – too high. Robert adjusted his point of aim and fired again. This time his shot was low, striking the caterpillar tracks. Such a hit was classed as a 'mobility kill', or 'M' kill, as it would immobilise the tank but not put it out of action completely. His third shot was right on target, hitting the base of the turret: a 'K' kill, which should, in theory, destroy the tank. After repeating the feat with his fourth and fifth spotting rounds he knew precisely where to aim. Each LAW94 cost one-and-a-half thousand pounds, which increased the pressure to score a direct hit with the armour-piercing warhead.

Sergeant Collins crouched down beside him. "Right, Tayl, that's your lot – HEAT round now. Remember to check the back-blast area."

Robert turned around awkwardly to make sure there was no-one behind him who might be injured by the exhaust gases which would blast from the rear of the tube. Satisfied that the back-blast area was clear, he slid the selector lever to main armament, took aim, gripped the weapon tightly and pressed the trigger. The missile fired with a terrific bang and a blast of smoke. Robert ducked down behind the sandbags as the armour-piercing warhead hit the tank with a *thud!*

Collins patted him on the back. "It's a good one, Rob. 'K' kill, well done. Right, go back to the troop shelter and send along the next firer."

Robert glanced quickly over the sandbags. There was a lot of smoke swirling around the tank, but no obvious damage was apparent. Almost swaggering with pride, he hurried back to the bunker, but when he reached it no-one was interested in his tank-killing achievements. They were too busy loading the crates of missiles onto one of the company 4-tonne trucks. Lieutenant Grudge saw Robert approaching and called out to him.

"Corporal T, go and tell Sergeant Collins to close down the firing point and get back here asap. The vote's just come through – Wirral's got partial autonomy so we're no longer part of the Mercian Regiment - or even the British Army. As soon as we're loaded up, we're off."

CHAPTER 4

'Enough's Enough'

It would appear that Mr Roberts has a grudge against Local Authorities. He certainly paints us in a very bad light, depicting council officials as power-crazy vultures seeking only to serve their own interests at the public's expense. This amounts to slander- we're not like that! We work hard for the benefit of the community, we have the community's interests at heart, and we certainly do not possess as much power as Mr Roberts suggests.

Anthony Farquar
Senior Local Authority Executive

Mr Roberts replies:
You have plenty of power! You take five percent of my annual income, you decide which schools will close, where and when and how new building will take place, where I can and cannot go, and what I can and cannot do when I go there. You set the budget for the emergency services, dictate whether I can recycle plastic bottles, and determine the type of surfacing on the pavement outside my house. The decisions you make frequently affect my life to a greater extent than those of central government. Of course you have power! And you sometimes abuse it...

The result of the vote was a huge relief to Gerald Radley, although he conveyed the impression to the contrary, shrugging-off his victory as if it had been a foregone conclusion. He had taken an enormous gamble with the whole affair and his arrogant hubris had paid off. In his grand scheme of things, the independence referendum had been the one element over which he had no control, and had the result been a 'no' vote, his career might have collapsed in tatters. But the people of Wirral had risen to the occasion, supporting him in his hour of need, and from now on everything else would be relatively straightforward.

Radley was aware that it would be unwise to make too many radical changes too quickly. It was tempting to allow his newly acquired power to go to his head - it was indeed an intoxicating sensation - but he had learned long ago that all major administrative decisions had to appear to be the result of some form of consultation process; consultation - even sham consultation - was the best way of ensuring that blame for poor decisions was not shouldered by an individual like himself, but rather was shared and dissipated amongst groups or departments, or even the community as a whole.

So he bided his time, concentrating his efforts on internal changes within the council which had little immediate impact on the public. Initially, the most pressing task was to complete Wirral's bureaucratic transition from an ordinary part of the United Kingdom to a 'Semi-Autonomous Self-Governing Region'. In-house staff and teams of highly paid accountants, lawyers and other consultants from the private sector worked ceaselessly to produce a new financial and legal framework which would enable the peninsular to function under its new designation. Wirral had not severed itself completely from the Motherland - it was neither practical nor desirable to do so - but being semi-autonomous opened up a plethora of administrative minefields in areas such as taxation, law and order, land ownership and the benefits system. Issues too detailed and specific to have been given any serious consideration before the vote suddenly surfaced and demanded immediate attention...One such matter related to whether convicted criminals from Wirral who were currently held in prisons elsewhere in the UK should be sent back to the peninsular. It transpired that Wirral would either have to pay an exorbitant fee to keep its miscreants incarcerated at their present locations, or they would be repatriated at the end of the month. As Wirral possessed no suitable facility in which to accommodate them, Radley reluctantly agreed to pay the fees for the time being, but he immediately issued instructions for the fort at Perch Rock in New Brighton to be converted from a museum into a high-security prison for serious offenders.

Hesitantly, the council began to adjust to the new system, albeit at the expense of some of its usual, more prosaic services. Radley's main concern was that Wirral should not suffer economically as a result of its newly acquired autonomy, and to this end his priority was to make sure the region's finances were secure. He and Duncan Silverlock spent many hours with a team of advisers, working out the revised figures for the council's budget now that central government was largely out of the equation. Under the model established by Cornwall the previous year, some tax revenue would still be paid to the British Treasury, and Wirral would receive certain limited entitlements in return, but essentially the peninsular was now self-governing and would have to generate its own income.

Fortunately, the area had been a net contributor rather than beneficiary under the old system, which meant that, if the population simply paid to the council what it had formerly paid to the British Treasury, it should be possible to not only balance the books but also accumulate some surplus funds which could be discretely paid into Radley's secret war coffers.

After several days of deliberation and some very fine working lunches, the senior executives decided that, with immediate effect, the word 'council' should always be spelt with a capital 'C'. They also decreed that the term 'council tax' should be replaced by the more locally appropriate designation 'Wirral tax'. Radley and his cronies were careful to ensure that, when residents received their first Wirral tax bill, it amounted to slightly less than the sum total of their pre-autonomy council tax, income tax and National Insurance contributions collectively, thereby convincing people that they were now better off. The Public Relations department produced a glossy pamphlet which emphasised this fact, and extolled the virtues of various other independence-related benefits.

Now that he possessed the power he had always craved, Gerald Radley was itching to introduce some radical reforms and drastic new social policies, but Terence McCarthy urged restraint.

"Don't do too much too quickly, Gerald," he warned. "You don't want people to think you're some kind of power-crazed dictator who did this autonomy thing so he could become a modern-day Hitler. Take your time, sort out all the boring, mundane stuff, and wait for people to start complaining that you haven't delivered what you promised on some of the more controversial issues. It's always better to introduce measures by popular demand rather than doing them off your own back. Makes you appear democratic. And it covers your arse if something goes wrong..."

Eventually the tedious transition process was complete and Radley was able to turn his attention to matters of greater interest. He drew up a plan for restructuring the Council, creating, merging or abolishing divisions and sections. Ostensibly this was to make the organisation more 'streamlined and locally sensitive', but its real purpose was to disempower his opponents while simultaneously creating an administration better suited to fighting a war. Radley would ideally have liked to create a nucleus of power based entirely around himself, McCarthy and Silverlock, but at this stage he could not risk scandalous accusations of cronyism, so was forced to operate within the constraints of the existing council system. This meant that, in theory at least, all the elected representatives - including those from other political parties – had to be involved in the decision-making process. Radley's friends and allies dominated the cabinet, so this was unlikely to cause any serious problems, but it posed the potential threat of a minority of dissenters being able to obstruct new policies or leak controversial information to the media. McCarthy came up with an ingenious way of circumventing this potential problem through a new system which he called 'administrative devolution.' In future, rather than the entire cabinet convening to discuss a particular issue, it would be considered by a system of select committees, working parties and steering groups made up only of 'relevant representatives'. And, as Radley himself determined the composition of these groups, the new system enabled him to marginalise those whose loyalty could not be guaranteed. One by one, his opponents found themselves bypassed, left sitting in their offices while matters of great import were discussed in meetings to which they had not been invited. They were aware that they were being sidelined, but could do little about it, because 'administrative devolution' had supposedly been introduced by popular consent. The real brilliance of McCarthy's brainchild was that it could be justified as an efficiency measure, as it reduced the number of senior officials involved in meetings, and therefore was guaranteed to win favour with the electorate.

"Why do we need a gathering of the whole Council to discuss, for example, a highly technical legal issue which few if any of the members will understand?" Radley had argued, while proposing the new system to sceptical colleagues. 'Surely a smaller group of suitably qualified experts would be more appropriate, reporting directly to myself..."

At the same time as he was overseeing the restructuring of the Council, Radley also gave approval for the amalgamation of Wirral's army assets into a single composite regiment comprising infantry, engineers and logistics corps units, plus a cadet force. The Wirral Regiment, as it was known, officially came into existence during an impressive ceremony in Birkenhead Park. All personnel wore the same cap badge featuring the legendary Wirral hunting horn, but riflemen, sappers and drivers were distinguished from each other by a special emblem worn on their shoulders. The three TA centres continued operating as usual under their existing commanders, although they were now administered and funded by the Council rather than the Ministry of Defence in Whitehall, and had a new Commanding Officer, or 'CO'. Radley had considered putting Blundell in overall command, but the major had asked to remain with C Company, and in any case was probably too young and too biased towards the Infantry to be a suitable candidate. Fortunately, a golfing acquaintance of Radley's was a retired Royal Artillery colonel, who agreed to take command of the new regiment, unaware that the appointment - which he accepted as something of a retirement hobby - would involve bloodier conflict than he had experienced as a regular soldier. His name was Alan Hogan.

The new regiment required administrative support, so an office was established within the town hall to deal with issues such as pay and the provision of supplies and equipment. A young executive from Corporate Services, Steven Saunders, was put in charge of a small 'Defence Procurement Team' which began negotiating contracts with suppliers worldwide for items as diverse as socks and hand grenades. The creation of this team was kept secret from the public.

In the immediate post-autonomy period, the peninsula's soldiers were unable to train outside the barbed wire compounds of their TA centres, due to the fact that no other military land existed on the Wirral and the new regiment was not entitled to use MoD facilities elsewhere in the UK. At Blundell's request, several areas of Council-owned land were made available to the TA for training, and a new law was passed giving the military the right to conduct exercises over the entirety of the region's countryside; for the purpose of this law, 'countryside' was defined as farmland, forestry, common land, seashore, and all public open space – basically everywhere except the built-up areas. To appease the part-time soldiers, who had become increasingly frustrated by inactivity, large sums of money were made available for training. The infantry conducted a series of weekend exercises involving reconnaissance patrols, ambushes and observation posts, with cadets acting as enemy, while the engineers and logistics corps men worked at building facilities on the newly acquired Council sites to turn them into useful military training areas.

None of this greatly impressed the public and, as McCarthy had predicted, complaints began to trickle in from people dissatisfied by the apparent lack of significant change. Radley knew that he had to respond to these grumbles with tangible action, ideally involving a high-profile crusade against an issue of concern to the general population. He struggled to select a suitable focus, until he received a copy of a free local newspaper which carried the headline: *'Vandals Target Cemetery Again'.* After reading the article, he turned to his wife with an expression of incredulous rage.

"What sort of feral vermin are we breeding here - who don't even respect their own dead? We seem to be encouraging the proliferation of hordes of low quality people who are spiritually, morally and culturally bankrupt!"

Radley had finally found his crusade. His top priority, he decided, would be to tackle the anti-social behaviour which had become the scourge of Wirral, while a secondary initiative would involve the creation of a large number of new non-administrative jobs within the Council. Ironically, both issues turned out to be connected, with the latter emerging as the solution to the former.

Radley was eager to be regarded as a man of the people, and to this end he went out into the community on 'walkabouts' to talk to the masses and hear their grievances. His critics cringed at what they regarded as a tacky charade, but the tactic boosted his popularity considerably and achieved its aim: after two weeks of knocking on doors and visiting numerous community centres, pubs, working men's clubs, sports centres and supermarkets, Gerald Radley had won approval from many hitherto hostile members of the public and acquired a much greater understanding of what concerned them. He was reassured to learn that anti-social behaviour was high on most people's list of concerns, especially where it involved gangs of marauding youths who seemed able to terrorise neighbourhoods with virtual impunity. The problem had reached such endemic proportions in some areas that the police had admitted to being unable to respond effectively due to 'lack of resources', resulting in a feeling amongst law-abiding citizens that they had been abandoned to mob-rule. This was precisely the issue which Gerald Radley wanted to address, and he threw himself into the task with ruthless enthusiasm.

"Tackling this menace will not be possible without changes to the law," he told resident after resident. "Society and the State have become so disempowered that the thugs have taken control of the streets. We need to reverse this situation and give some power back to the communities. We need an effective way of identifying these people, catching them and making sure they change their ways. Do I have your support?" Invariably he did.

As part of the Council restructuring programme, a new section had been created with the specific purpose of formulating a revised legal framework for the region. Radley now turned to this team of lawyers, solicitors and magistrates – many of whom he knew personally – and instructed them to produce legislation which would reflect the public opinion expressed during his walkabout tours.

"The existing definition of what constitutes anti-social behaviour can remain unchanged," he told them. "What I want is greater powers to deal with these troublemakers. I want anonymity for witnesses so they can give evidence without fear of reprisals. I want to reinforce the public's rights of citizen's arrest so they can catch these damned yobs themselves and hold them until the police arrive. I want that stupid duty of care clause abolished – if a burglar falls through someone's roof, they can damn well pay for the roof, as well as being prosecuted - there'll be none of this suing the owner nonsense. I'd like to see anyone convicted of more than two anti-social offences lose their right to the protection of the law. Put them outside society. They can't have it both ways – showing contempt for the law one moment then expecting it to protect them the next… Let them become the victims of revenge attacks from the community – see how they like it! And finally, what I'd really like - and the public really want - is an immediate and effective punishment system, based on a combination of corporal punishment, meaningful fines and community service. For example, if some little bastard vandalises a library or something and is caught in the act, there'll be none of this drawn-out prosecution process: he'll get an immediate on-the-spot beating to teach him a lesson, then his family will be fined for the cost of repairs plus administrative fees. If they say they can't afford the fine, we confiscate property to the appropriate value, forcibly if necessary. If they're on benefits, the benefits stop. And when we've recovered the money, we make the little bastard pick up litter or dog shit for a month to atone for his sins….Can you express all that in legalspeak?"

At that point, several members of the team made their excuses and left. The remainder, untroubled by moral scruples, simply replied. "You're the boss, Council Leader," and obligingly got on with the task.

Radley left them to work with words and hurried back to his office to arrange a meeting that afternoon with McCarthy and Silverlock. It was inconvenient that their offices were nowhere near his own – indeed, McCarthy had to travel from a completely different building – so to remedy this unsatisfactory situation a contractor had been commissioned to convert some redundant rooms on the top floor of the town hall into a purpose-built executive suite. When complete it would feature a conference room, luxurious lounge, several studies with attached bedrooms, a kitchen and a bathroom. There would also be a communications cubicle equipped with broadband computer links, secure phone and fax connections and video conferencing facilities. The idea was to create a self-contained control centre from which senior Council officials could run the borough, in comfort and safety, without having to ever leave the building. How much the suite cost to build was never revealed.

The meeting that afternoon was an informal one and no minutes were taken. Had there been an agenda, the main item on it would have been the identification of the priority issues to be addressed now that the Council possessed the power to do so.

"Let's consider for a moment where we're at," Radley began. "We've successfully completed the administrative and financial transition, and although it's still early days, I must say I think it's gone better than I dared hope. Society hasn't collapsed like some people said it would, we've got more money than we used to have and the property market has moved back up to where it was before the vote. In fact, it seems that more people are trying to move into the area than ever before, presumably because they like the sound of what we're doing. We've restructured the Council so that it better suits our needs, and the military are happy for the time being at least. So far we've done nothing controversial, but people are beginning to complain that controversial policies were what they wanted when they voted for us."

"So let's do something controversial," Silverlock suggested eagerly.

Radley smiled. "We're going to. As you know, I've instructed the legal team to draw up some draft legislation covering anti-social behaviour, which seemed to be the number one priority for people on the street. When they've done that we'll get Paul Ryder in Public Relations to produce another leaflet outlining the proposals and asking for comments. We'll do some newspaper stuff as well."

"What if the plebs don't go for it?" McCarthy asked.

"Oh, they will. I'm sure they will. Besides, no-one's monitoring us now – we can do what we like. We can make up figures to suit our needs if we have to...For example, pick a number between five and twenty."

"Thirteen."

"Okay. So, we only had thirteen people oppose the proposals.'" Radley grinned deviously. "Great, eh? Like I said, we can do what we want."

"What about Internal Audit?" asked McCarthy dubiously.

"Internal Audit were a victim of the restructuring programme," Silverlock reminded him. "Our fundamental integrity puts us beyond question, which made their job unnecessary."

"Anyway, back to controversial policies," Radley continued. "Obviously there's a time delay in getting new policies implemented, so we need to start thinking about what we want to do in advance. We need to have our next batch of ideas ready in a few days to give to the legal team, so that they can turn them into laws and we can implement them as soon as possible. Now that we've started the ball rolling, let's keep up the momentum. So, fire away."

"Youth crime," said McCarthy, without hesitation.

"Under-age pregnancy," was Silverlock's contribution.

"Discipline in schools."

"Drugs."

"Benefits culture."

"Immigration."

"The justice system..."

Radley held up his hands. "That'll do for now. Right, so we need to decide what we don't like about the way these issues are handled at the moment, and how we'll improve things in future. Oh – and I'd also appreciate suggestions from either of you on how we can convincingly start our war with the French..."

Two weeks later, Robert Taylor picked up a new Council-produced leaflet, entitled *'Enough's Enough',* from the doormat, just as he was about to leave the house. He glanced through it quickly with an expression of bemusement, then wandered back to the lounge, where Mark Conrad was watching the film *Zulu* on video.

"Can you believe this?" Robert asked incredulously. "It says here that people caught doing anti-social things can be given on-the-spot beatings by the authorities."

Conrad did not avert his eyes from the screen, on which Michael Caine was patronising Stanley Baker by offering to 'get my man to clean your kit.' *Zulu* was one of Conrad's favourite films. He took the pamphlet from Robert's outstretched hand and perused it briefly. "Good. Hang 'em high and hang 'em long and hang 'em till you can't hang 'em no more, that's what I say! It's about time someone had the balls to challenge these bastards instead of appeasing them all the time."

"Yeah, but who will they get to do the beating? It'd better not be teachers!"

Conrad shrugged. "I'll do it, if they pay me enough."

"Ever the mercenary. '*Mark Conrad - will beat his own grandmother if the price is right!*'"

"Save it for the judge!"

"I will. See you later."

Robert went out to his car, an elderly Vauxhall Vectra, and was dismayed to find that the wing mirror had been smashed yet again – the third time in four months. Other cars in the road had been similarly vandalised. "Bastards!" he spat. What was really frustrating was that he had a fairly good idea of who was responsible for the damage – a gang of local youths who congregated around Birkenhead Central Library and roamed the surrounding streets in hooded tops – but he was powerless to do anything about it. Suddenly his attitude towards

Enough's Enough changed. Conrad was right – it was time to stand-up against society's anti-social elements, and deny them the impunity they had enjoyed for too long.

Robert drove through the Birkenhead Tunnel under the River Mersey to meet Linda when her train arrived at Liverpool's Lime Street station. He saw her approaching through the crowd on the platform, and felt confused and empty. Their eyes met and they smiled weakly. Once, they would have run to each other like characters in some clichéd romantic movie, and embraced passionately. Now, their reunion was celebrated with a token lifeless kiss.

Driving back to the Wirral, their conversation was awkward and perfunctory. He talked about work and the proposed measures outlined in the Council's leaflet; she told him about a party she had attended the previous weekend, and repeatedly mentioned the name of a male colleague who had evidently made quite an impression. Robert wondered if she was doing it deliberately to try to make him jealous...If so, the tactic failed to achieve the desired result.

"Why don't we just call it a day, Linda?" he was tempted to say, but lacked the temerity. Beyond the fragile shell of their relationship loomed a gaping void of loneliness and isolation which he was not eager to enter. At least Linda offered some feminine softness and intimacy in a world which would otherwise consist mainly of his stressful teaching job throughout the week and TA training at weekends. But staying with her presented him with a moral dilemma, as he had always prided himself on being an honourable man who would not maintain a relationship with a girl unless he loved her. And he was pretty sure that his love for Linda had died.

"We're having another get-together next weekend," she told him. "You could come along if you wanted to - meet some of my friends..."

"I'd sooner socialise with lepers" he almost replied, but thought better of it. Instead he said, "I can't, I'm afraid, I've got TA. There's a big exercise on and I've already said I'll go. Sorry..."

"Never mind, then." A few years ago she would have been disappointed, and a few years before that, heartbroken. She would have wondered why he chose to spend his time in the rough company of men, training to kill imaginary enemies, when he could have been with her, doing 'nice' things. But now, she did not really mind – in fact, it suited her that he was not intruding into her successful new life which was blossoming down in Peterborough. People appreciated her there. Men appreciated her there...

That night they shared a bed but there was no passion. Robert lay on his back in the darkness, staring at the ceiling, not daring to touch his corpse-like partner for fear that she might flinch and recoil, like a frigid anemone.

Needless to say, the measures proposed in *Enough's Enough* entered Wirral's fledgling statute books with, according to the Council, 'negligible' opposition. However, it was soon to become apparent that simply creating new laws would achieve little without an effective means of enforcing them. This became painfully evident when Gerald Radley decided to involve himself personally in implementing the new legislation for the first time.

Radley was well acquainted with Wirral's chief of police and was generally regarded favourably by officers on the beat, who appreciated his tough stance on crime and criminals. Here at last, they believed, was someone who had *their* interests at heart – a man who would not be intimidated by society's undesirables and would give the police the power they needed to gain the upper hand. So, when a youth was caught in the act of smashing the glass of a bus shelter, the constables who dealt with the incident were only too happy to inform the Council Leader, as he had requested. Upon receiving the telephone call, Radley leapt to his feet in excitement.

"I'm off to Bebington," he told his secretary, grinning manically. "It's time to kick some arse!" It occurred to him then that someone in his position ought really to have a personal aide whose duties would include acting as his bodyguard and chauffeur. He resolved to ask Alistair Blundell if he knew of a suitable individual – ideally a competent young up-and-coming Council employee with past or present military experience. Whatever their background, the chosen person would have to be completely trustworthy and reliable, as they would have access to the very heart of Radley's administration. For the time being, however, the Council Leader had no such aide, and would have to drive himself.

When he arrived at the scene of the crime he found two policemen in high-visibility jackets restraining a scrawny youth who was perhaps fifteen years old. The boy had a shaved head and was wearing the standard uniform of a typical Birkenhead 'scally' – tracksuit with hooded top, cap and trainers; essentially an outfit chosen to enable the wearer to become unidentifiable in seconds and make a quick getaway. A Council worker in green overalls was sweeping up the fragments of broken glass from the vandalised bus shelter, and a small crowd of onlookers had gathered to watch proceedings.

Radley parked his BMW behind the police van and introduced himself to the constables. "So, gentlemen," he said pompously, "can you tell me what's happened here?"

Before the policemen had a chance to reply, the boy they were restraining blurted out, "They're accusing me of smashing this glass but they're lying, cos that's what the Busies always do, and I'm gonna sue that gimp over there for grabbing me arm."

"Be quiet," Radley snapped. "I'll speak to you in a minute." He turned to one of the policemen. "So, what actually happened, officer?"

"Well sir, according to witnesses, this boy threw a brick at the glass and then ran away, but the gentleman over there managed to grab hold of him and restrain him until we arrived."

Radley looked approvingly at a man in his late fifties who was standing at the front of the crowd, clutching a red-stained handkerchief to his nose.

"Officer, why is his nose bleeding?"

"Er, it seems the boy hit him several times to try to make him let go, sir."

Radley's eyes narrowed to furious slits and he clenched his fists in rage. For a moment it seemed as if he might be about to strike the boy. Then he regained his composure. "You piece of filth," he said slowly. "Do you know what happens now?"

"You can't call me that," the boy said defiantly. "I know my rights. Don't you go speaking to me like that, you fuckin' gimp, or I'll find where you live and break yer windows."

Radley was outraged, but managed to preserve a calm exterior. He was new to situations like this, and realised that a truly great leader would not be antagonised by someone so insignificant. So he smiled serenely: this was a moment to savour.

"Listen, my lad, you are going to pay for the damage you've done."

"Oh yeah? I 'aven't got any money."

"Then we'll take it from your parents. And then you're going to be sweeping this road for two weeks."

"Oh yeah? Try and make me, ya fuckin' gimp!"

"We will." Radley turned to the policemen. "We're wasting our time being reasonable with this boy, officers....Beat him."

"I'm sorry, sir?"

"Beat him. I think it's the only thing he'll respect – a damned good beating. Maybe then he'll take us seriously."

It was hard to tell who looked more shocked, the boy or the constables. For a moment there was silence. Then one of the policemen said awkwardly, "Council Leader Radley, we don't do that sort of thing. It's not our job. We're police officers, not thugs...."

"So you're refusing to beat him? Aren't you aware the law's changed? It *is* your job now!"

"I'm sorry, sir..." The two officers shuffled uncomfortably and looked at the ground.

The Council Leader felt betrayed. His new-found power was slipping away before he had even had the chance to exercise it. And now he was in danger of being made to look an emasculated fool in public. There was no alternative – he would simply have to beat the boy himself, or lose all credibility. But he had not engaged in physical violence for years, and it was completely inappropriate for the most influential man in the entire borough to be resorting personally to fisticuffs in order to enforce his own laws. Radley's mind raced, frantically searching for a way out of the situation. Then he noticed the Council worker who was still sweeping up the broken glass. The man was large and powerful, with tanned skin, a shaved head and tattoos on his strong forearms. Radley walked swiftly over to him and spoke furtively.

"Good afternoon. I'm Council Leader Radley. I suppose that makes me your boss."

The man was unimpressed. "Hello." He continued sweeping.

"Erm, what's your name?"

The man stopped sweeping and looked straight at Radley with an expression of mild irritation. "Daniel Price."

"Listen, Mr Price. I need someone to do a job for me. It'll only take you a minute or two and I'll pay you a grand - cash, in half an hour..."

Two minutes later the bus-stop vandal was lying on the ground in tears of rage with two black eyes, a bleeding nose and numerous bruises. Of the group of onlookers, several had walked away in horror but the majority stayed to watch and cheer. Radley looked down at the boy with smug satisfaction then turned to the man who had caught him.

"Would you like to put a few kicks in, sir?" the Council Leader asked. "To pay him back for your nose?"

The man shook his head. "I think he's had enough, the little bastard."

"Fair enough. Right, officers, take him away to a police station and lock him up. Find out where he lives - we need to start getting the money for the glass from his parents, if he's got any. Mr Price, come with me please."

Driving back to the town hall, Radley took a long circuitous route which enabled him to visit a bank and speak to his saviour in the privacy of his car.

"Mr Price, I'm very grateful to you for what you did just now. If you hadn't come to my rescue then everything I've tried to do to make Wirral a better place would be for nothing. I'd like to make you a proposal..."

"I'm already married."

The comment bounced off Radley's humourless exterior without effect. "No, you misunderstand me. What I'd like to ask you is: how would you like to work for me, doing things like you've just done? The pay would be twice what you're on now."

"I could be persuaded, I suppose..."

"Excellent. And do you have any friends within the Council who might also be interested...?"

Thus was born the organisation which came to be known - and feared and loathed - as 'The Special Council Workers.'

CHAPTER 5

Gerald's Private Army

I'm still not sure whether this is supposed to be a serious novel or a tongue-in-cheek one. While many of the later chapters are gritty and grim, the earlier ones chronicling the rise of Gerald Radley to a position of supreme power are satirical to the point of being ridiculous. Even the author must admit that the idea of a local authority councillor acquiring that sort of omnipotence is frankly absurd.

Arthur Aldenham
Aspiring Critic magazine

Mr Roberts replies:
Of course it's tongue-in-cheek. But it's serious as well. And consider this: if you wrote a fictitious story about a failed artist who ruthlessly exterminated millions of people because of the shape of their noses, everyone would say it was preposterous. Yet it happened. Never underestimate the ability of lunatics to get into power.

The incident at the bus shelter had shaken Gerald Radley's confidence, and he subsequently directed all of his energies into ensuring that such a situation would not arise again. He had originally assumed that the police would enforce his new regime, but it had become glaringly apparent that they could not be relied upon. In disgust, he telephoned Chief Inspector Joseph Richards, the man in charge of the borough's police force, and demanded assurances that his officers would uphold the recently introduced laws.

"My people will do whatever the law requires of them," Richards promised, although his voice lacked conviction. "They're professionals. And they *do* appreciate the new powers you've given them in the fight against crime."

"Then why didn't the two constables at the scene punish the boy as the law required? I made a note of their numbers, by the way, and I expect them to be disciplined for dereliction of duty."

At the other end of the telephone line, Richards hesitated. When he finally spoke, he sounded defensive and uneasy. "I think it's this idea of on-the-spot punishment – corporal punishment – which my officers are uncomfortable with. In the past their job was to catch criminals, and they're happy to continue doing that job under the new legislation. But when they caught them, they used to hand them over to the courts for trial and sentencing – they weren't expected to beat people in the street, and I don't think you'll find many of them who'll be happy to do that now. You'll find a few, but not many…"

"I see. Well, thank you. At least we know where we stand." Radley put the phone down. He was disappointed yet not entirely surprised, and resolved to penalise the police by reducing their budget next year. But that would not solve the pressing problem of how to enforce his new social policies. Who else could he use? He considered asking Blundell for military support, but suspected that TA soldiers might harbour the same reservations as police officers, and in any case all army personnel would be needed in their units if and when his planned war ever came to fruition. Daniel Price and his friends seemed the most promising option.

The phone rang and his secretary informed him that a certain Mrs Gardner was demanding to speak to him. He looked perplexed.

"Mrs Who?"

"Mrs Gardner, Council Leader. Apparently you met her son yesterday, something to do with a bus shelter...?"

Radley stiffened with anxiety. The boy was clearly a juvenile psychopath, and as such was likely to have fully-fledged psychopathic parents, friends and relatives. People like that had no respect for the law or civilised standards of behaviour, and when they considered themselves to have been wronged, they expressed their anger with fists and feet, with bricks and bottles, with abusive phone calls and petrol and matches, with baseball bats and knives...Suddenly, Radley felt very vulnerable - afraid, even. All the trappings of his authority within the Council - all the computers and plush furniture, the headed paper, the eloquent letters and polite e-mails, the *Investors In People* certificates on the walls, the protocols and directives – none of it would protect him from the simple physical aggression and violence of the gutter. He needed to buy some time.

"Maurine, tell her I'm out. Take her details and say I'll call her back. As soon as you've done that, call Mr McCarthy, Mr Silverlock and Mr Blundell and tell them to drop whatever they're doing and come over here for an emergency meeting now!"

"What I realised yesterday," Radley declared solemnly, "is that there's absolutely no point in continuing with any of our reforms unless we have the physical muscle to actually enforce them. It seems the police won't do it, so we need to recruit people who will – and recruit them quickly."

"How many do you think you'll need, Gerald?" asked Alistair Blundell.

"I don't know exactly, but I'd've thought at least a hundred. That way we can have twenty or thirty on duty at any one time, on a shift system."

McCarthy gave an appreciative whistle. "And how do you propose to recruit people like that – an advert in the local newspaper?"

Radley smiled. "Why not? What I mean is, the guy who came to my rescue yesterday works for the Council. Okay, I had to go to the bank and pay him a grand of my own money, but the point is he had no moral scruples about beating the shit out of that little scally bastard.

And he's got friends he works with who'll be prepared to do the same thing. I reckon I've found our own private army, and the best thing is they already work for us."

Silverlock was impressed. "And we're in the process of advertising for three hundred more!"

Radley looked positively animated. He was really proud of himself. "Exactly. These manual workers - labourers, repairmen, hedge cutters and the like - are ideal. They're fit and strong, and they'll happily put the boot in without asking questions, if you pay them enough. All we have to do is select the hundred most suitable ones - and by that I mean the most reliable, aggressive, disciplined, etcetera - pay them some extra money and give them some training, and we'll be sorted."

"What sort of training?" Blundell asked.

"Oh, I don't know, we'll have to devise a programme...It shouldn't involve too much – loyalty tests and basic thuggery, that sort of thing..."

"Basic buggery?" Silverlock said mischievously. Radley had always had doubts about the sexual orientation of his unmarried colleague.

"Who'll be in charge of them?" McCarthy asked, a little nervously. "You'd better be careful, Gerald – recruiting people like that could easily backfire on you..."

"Well, we'd be in overall control, but on a day-to-day basis it'd be the same person who's in charge of them now: George Lawton. I'm going to speak to him as soon as we finish this meeting."

George Lawton was a fearsome fifty-two year old Yorkshireman who presided over what remained of the old Council Department of Works – the section of the local authority which actually 'got its hands dirty' as opposed to doing office-based administrative work involving phones and computers. Over the years, Lawton had watched bitterly as his empire shrank around him and the number of Council-employed tradesmen and labourers dwindled, to be replaced by private contractors brought in on a job-to-job, hire-and-fire basis. His loyalty to Gerald Radley had been assured by the Council Leader's promise to discontinue the practice of using external agencies, and expand the ranks of the Council workforce once again. Lawton would be a powerful ally. He was a staunch traditionalist, a self-confessed 'belt'n'braces' man (whatever that meant), a man who spoke his mind, called a spade a spade and did not suffer fools at all, let alone gladly. His workers respected him because he had worked his way up from the bottom, was harsh but fair, and because, despite his age, he remained a force to be reckoned with. An ex-boxer, Lawton had been known to take disgruntled apprentices outside and offer them the chance to take their grievances out on him with their fists. Those that took up the challenge usually ended up getting hurt. He was the ideal person to lead a bunch of Council-employed ruffians.

Together, Radley, Silverlock and McCarthy finalised arrangements for the creation of the new organisation. Some of the personnel would be new employees, while others would be recruited from the existing Council ranks. Silverlock would be in charge of the recruitment and selection process, while Radley, McCarthy and Blundell would devise a training programme and arrange for the purchase of the necessary equipment and clothing from a secret fund. Radley was eager that the new unit became operational as soon as possible, so proposed they recruit Daniel Price and several of his friends immediately as a nucleus around which to build. Once the Special Council Workers were properly established as a fully functioning entity, the number of police in Wirral would be reduced, and their role largely limited to detective work. In future, duties such as patrolling the streets, guarding suspects in custody and dealing with civil unrest would largely be handled by the Special Council Workers.

There remained one more issue to resolve.

"What do I do about this wretched mother harassing me about her wretched son, no doubt to threaten me or sue me or something?" Radley asked in desperation.

"That's easy," McCarthy told him. "In a way you've only got yourself to blame for that one, Gerald. It's all very well telling the public they can contact you because you're a Man of the People, but can anyone phone the Queen or Prime Minister whenever they're unhappy about something? Of course not."

"Your point, Terence?"

"Make yourself uncontactable. That's what I've done. Anyone who tries phoning my office gets a recorded message saying I'll be happy to speak to them but they're number eighteen in a queue. The message changes every ten minutes but the caller is never nearer than number eleven in the queue, so they eventually give up."

"I've done even better," said Silverlock proudly. "People who try to get a contact number for me are referred politely to the website. Now, a lot of them are elderly folk who don't have access to a computer, so that cuts down the number of potential callers. Once on the website, it's very tricky to find the phone number. And if anyone does find the number, I've got Terence's queuing system. So basically I don't get any unwanted phone calls."

Radley looked at the pair of them and shook his head. "You're totally unscrupulous! I'm not sure I feel comfortable working with people as unethical as you two!"

Later, after his colleagues had returned to their offices, the Council Leader received another phone call from his secretary, informing him that Mrs Gardner was in reception. She was screaming abuse and making threats about what she was going to do to "That Radley bloke". The police were called and removed the woman quickly and efficiently, but the incident increased Radley's sense of vulnerability and outrage. How dare a proletariat minion challenge his authority with her mob-rule tactics! It would take several days for even a small unit of SCW heavies to be recruited and briefed, so Radley immediately contacted Alistair Blundell and requested temporary military assistance. Fortunately, it was C Company's drill night that evening, so the major was able to arrange for two members of what Sergeant Collins called 'The Dole Patrol' – men without regular employment who were able and eager to do extra duties – to go to the Council Leader's house and act as his personal bodyguard. The men – a lance-corporal and a private – wore civilian clothes and each was issued with an SA80 rifle, a bayonet and a pick-axe handle, concealed in a sports bag. They spent the night in Radley's living room and accompanied him to work the next morning. During their five day attachment, which passed without incident, their main challenge was combating boredom. This they achieved admirably with the help of a portable TV, some paperback novels and a stack of pornographic magazines. Easy money.

Within a month, Gerald Radley's private army of Special Council Workers was up and running under the leadership of George Lawton, who entered into his new role with sinister zeal and determination. In an extravagant gesture of appreciation, Radley furnished him with an ideal headquarters location: the old brick pump-house at the far end of the East Float dock, in the area known as 'The Four Bridges'. The disused building was notable for its blackened clock tower, which resembled a crenulated castle turret and dominated the surrounding landscape like a decayed fang. Public funds were used to completely refurbish the interior and build cells and interrogation chambers, but the exterior was left untouched: both Radley and Lawton agreed that the soot-blackened bricks created a malevolent impression which was entirely appropriate to the building's new function.

To avoid possible scandal, SCW personnel were ostensibly employed in ordinary capacities as grass cutters, street cleaners, maintenance workers and such like, but were paid a secret bonus in recognition of their elite status, and received a lucrative hourly rate for any time spent performing 'special Council duties', which basically meant doing Gerald Radley's dirty work. He put them to good use immediately: within two days of the first five Special Council Workers swearing their oath of allegiance, someone poured petrol through Mrs Gardner's letterbox in the middle of the night and burned down her house, with her in it.

CHAPTER 6

If It Ain't Raining It Ain't Training

Despite all of the usual assurances that this book is entirely fictitious and any similarity to persons living etcetera is entirely coincidental, I recognise the Corporal Gorpe character in Chapter 6 as myself, and I should just like to inform readers that, having served alongside the author in the TA for over five years, he wasn't such a great NCO himself.

Dwayne Shagwich
The real Corporal Gorpe

Mr Roberts replies:
I never said I was...

On a cool, blustery Saturday morning in April, Corporal Robert Taylor led his eight-man section on a patrol. His platoon – Eight Platoon - had spent the night bivouacked in a 'tactical harbour' in a small conifer wood somewhere between Bebington and the village of Brimstage in rural mid-Wirral. With a multitude of duties to perform during the hours of darkness, including digging shell scrapes, preparing equipment, doing guard duty and receiving orders for the following day's mission, there had been little opportunity for sleep, and the men were already tired when they lined up for inspection and kit check the next morning after a hurried breakfast. Eight Platoon was deploying three patrols that weekend, to separate locations across Wirral. Each was to conduct a training exercise throughout the day, followed by a 'real' operation during the night. Robert's section was to be taken by four-tonne truck to a drop-off point near West Kirby in the north-west corner of the peninsular. From there, the men would patrol between various checkpoints until they reached an as yet undisclosed location, where they would try to capture an enemy agent. The 'real' phase of the operation would take place that night in Arrowe Park, where the patrol would carry out a special mission at the request of Council Leader Radley himself. All movement during both phases was to be 'tactical', which meant operating as if a real enemy was in the area.

To keep them on their toes, Major Blundell had arranged for some cadets, under the command of Corporal Gorpe from Nine Platoon, to act as hostile forces in the patrol area. Gorpe was one of those annoying part-time soldiers who gave the TA a bad name. He tried to be more army-barmy than the keenest regular soldier, and his excessive use of jargon could be especially irritating. Gorpe did not walk, he 'bimbled' or 'tabbed'. His rifle was a 'gat', his food 'scoff' and instead of sleeping he got 'shut- eye', 'kip', or 'kopped zeds'. A four-tonne truck was a 'wagon' or 'bus', and helicopters were 'wocker-wockers'. Sometimes it was as if he were speaking a different language, to the point where Robert once remarked to Mark Conrad:

"It's like the *Monty Python* sketch '*RAF Banter*', except with him it's 'TA Banter'...I can't understand a word he's saying, can you, chaps?"

Whereas most TA soldiers bought the cheapest tubes of greasy green and brown camouflage cream, Gorpe had a hinged metal compact case - like a ladies make-up set - featuring a mirror and four different colours, which he applied painstakingly until he resembled a character from a Vietnam War movie. What made the whole situation even more ridiculous was that Gorpe's level of fitness and general competence left a lot to be desired. He almost defined the acronym 'STAB', as used by the regular army, which stood for 'Sad TA Bastard'. Blinkered by an unjustified self-confidence, and hopelessly in love with the sound of his own voice, he was notorious for subjecting anyone unfortunate to find themselves trapped in his company to tedious anecdotes, from which they could only escape by concocting plausible spur-of-the-moment excuses, such as needing the toilet urgently. For this reason, Gorpe was referred to by many of his more cynical fellow soldiers as *Corporal I'm Off For a Shit*. He relished being put in charge of the cadets, who were generally too young and impressionable to recognise bullshit, and therefore revered him as an army deity, fuelling his ego like petrol on a fire.

Robert was determined not to be caught or even seen by Gorpe and his troupe of camouflaged adolescents, so he carefully planned his patrol route to make maximum use of all available cover – hedgerows, sunken tracks, scrubland, woods and so forth. He knew that Gorpe only had about twenty cadets at his disposal, and these would be dispersed over a wide area looking not only for his own patrol but also those led by corporals Brabander and Murphy. In theory that should mean that the 'enemy' would be spread very thinly and should therefore be easy to evade. Only incompetence or sheer bad luck would result in Robert's patrol being compromised.

Sitting in the back of the Leyland DAF four-tonne truck on the way to the drop-off point, Robert heard rain pattering on the canvas roof overhead. It quickly became heavier and from the back of the vehicle he could see veils of falling water drifting in squalls across the landscape. This was advantageous from a tactical point of view, as poor weather was likely to demoralise the cadets and reduce their effectiveness as enemy. He could picture Gorpe now, moving gleefully amongst his disciples and responding to their grumbles with Army clichés such as, "Come on boys – it's mind over matter: I don't mind and you don't matter!" or, "Don't worry lads – if it aint raining it aint training!"

As the lorry neared West Kirby, Robert made some final checks to make sure his section was ready to deploy as soon as they reached the drop-off point. Everyone was seated in the correct 'order of march' for the patrol, their camouflage cream was good and they had all fitted yellow blank firing attachments to the muzzles of their weapons, as they were not using live ammunition during the initial phase of the exercise. They had also donned their waterproofs. The truck slowed and shuddered to a halt, the tailgate swung down with a crash, and on Robert's command the men jumped out and took up positions in 'all round defence', covering overlapping arcs in a circle around the vehicle. The drop-off point was in a cul-de-sac near the coast on the southern edge of the town, with a row of bungalows on one side and a litter-strewn grass strip leading to the beach on the other. It seemed farcical to be deploying tactically in such a location. As the lorry rumbled away and the men crouched in the rain, Robert noticed an elderly lady watching them from her front room window. She waved at him. He waved back.

The patrol moved off in the direction of the first checkpoint, with Private Stevenson acting as scout in the lead. Robert usually put Stevenson on point because he was young and keen and 'switched on'. There were many TA soldiers who slipped into a sort of daze while patrolling – what was referred to as 'switching off', or, to use Gorpespeak, 'bimbling along in mong mode alpha'. Of all the members of a patrol, the scout had to be especially alert at all times, maintaining communication with the NCO behind him while simultaneously looking ahead for enemy, booby traps, or more mundane hazards such as ditches or barbed wire.

The weather deteriorated still further as a strong wind developed and blew the rain almost horizontally at the soldiers. Sometimes, Robert fancied, it seemed as if the forces of nature did not approve of a particular operation and would do their utmost to thwart it. This appeared to be the case today – the wind kept changing direction capriciously so that it blasted the rain into the men's faces, regardless of their direction of movement. It was the sort of unrelenting, merciless rain which drenched everything and eventually penetrated even the best waterproof clothing, finding vulnerable entry points through the Gore-Tex defences.

Under Robert's direction the section advanced in staggered file along the Wirral Way, a popular footpath and bridleway running north to south across the peninsular along the line of a disused railway. Tactically it was an unsound route, but with a residential area on one side and the exposed beach on the other there was no real alternative. The men proceeded swiftly but nervously, half expecting to be ambushed at any moment. Stevenson had set his rifle to fully automatic and Robert made sure he had a smoke grenade at hand, in case they came under attack and had to break contact and withdraw in a hurry. The most potentially dangerous location was at Caldy, where a secluded car park next to the footpath offered an ideal site for Gorpe to mount an ambush. Robert split the patrol into two four-man 'fireteams' so that each could cover the other as they crossed the danger zone. No threat materialised, and with considerable relief the section proceeded south, to where the Wirral Way cut across Caldy golf course. Eager to regain some freedom of movement, the sodden soldiers pushed and kicked their way through the dripping bracken and bramble at the edge of the footpath, climbed precariously over a post and rail fence and jumped down onto the grass of one of the fairways. They relaxed a little: Gorpe and his cadets could only hope to cover the obvious routes through the area, and crossing the golf links was an unpredictable move which should ensure the patrol was not ambushed. Robert squinted against the squalls of rain blowing in across the River Dee and peered through his rifle's SUSAT sight at the landscape ahead, but the lenses were spattered with droplets of water, and wiping the eyepiece with his finger only served to produce a smeary blur. He hoped that the weather was impairing the enemy's ability to see as much as it was his own.

Several stoic golfers regarded the soldiers with disdain as they trudged grimly across the precious, sodden turf. The rain seemed to be getting steadily heavier, and it poured off their helmets and pooled in the hoods of their waterproof jackets before trickling down their necks. Then a message came in over the radio from Lieutenant Grudge, instructing the patrol to proceed to a certain grid reference where enemy activity had been sighted. The grid reference was sent in Battle Code, or BATCO, so Robert brought everyone into the shelter of a small copse while the radio operator, Private Finnegan, decoded it.

Robert deliberately opened his map so that the blank side was uppermost, then stared at the white paper and shook his head despairingly. "By God it's a bland, featureless desert out there!" he exclaimed to Mark Conrad with a grin, before turning the map over.

"Where have we got to go?" Conrad asked, after Finnegan had converted the BATCO message into a normal six-figure grid reference.

Robert used the romer on his Silva compass to pinpoint the location on the map. "Looks like the Dungeon."

The 'Dungeon' was a small wooded valley, situated in farmland on the gentle hillside which sloped up from the River Dee towards a ridge of high ground overlooking the estuary. On the map the feature resembled an isolated green wishbone in an expanse of white. Robert had walked there with Linda on several occasions and remembered it as a dank and gloomy place, with a small stream cascading through a muddy ravine, and abundant ferns which created an almost primordial landscape.

He glanced at the members of his section, who stood dejectedly under the trees. They should really have been crouching in all-round defence, watching alertly for any signs of the enemy. Instead, several individuals were beginning to 'switch off' as their morale was sapped by the incessant rain. Robert was particularly concerned by skinny Private Harding, who had his hands in his pockets and was staring sulkily at the ground. Karl Brabander always referred to Harding as 'The World's Only Human Invertebrate', the joke being that he was 'completely spineless'.

"You alright, Harding?" Robert asked, in as caring a voice as he could muster under the circumstances. In reality he had little sympathy – the patrol had only been going for an hour, and if Harding could not hack it then frankly he should find some other way of occupying his weekends. Brabander's attitude towards the sickly soldier would simply have been: "*If you don't like it, Harding, hand your kit in and join the Brownies.*"

Harding nodded weakly. "I just don't see why we're doing this when they want us to do a proper OP tonight. Why couldn't we just be dropped off at Arrowe Park tonight so we'd be fresh?"

"I don't know," Robert replied. "Ours is not to reason why, ours is just to do or die…It's what we've been told to do, so it's what we're going to do. That's how it is…"

"It's mushroom management, Harding," commented Private Hughes 42 in a fatherly voice. "You know – kept in the dark and fed on shit..." He chuckled. Hughes - whose surname had to be accompanied by the last two digits of his army number because there were so many other Hughes's in the regiment - was an 'old sweat', an ex-regular who had served in the TA for over ten years and had become something of a Charlie Company institution. He seemed to spend most of his life propping up the bar at the TA Centre, sharing his inexhaustible supply of jokes and consuming vast quantities of alcohol. Now he looked imploringly at Robert. "Can we have a quick smoke, Corporal Taylor?"

Robert glanced around. The weather was so foul that there was no chance of cigarette smoke betraying their position to anyone.

"If you're quick," he said. "Two minutes, then we're off. Stevenson – I need you to go over there as sentry to make sure no-one's coming after us."

While the private soldiers enjoyed a quick cigarette, chocolate bar or mouthful of tea from a thermos flask, Robert and Mark Conrad moved a short distance away and talked quietly.

"I hate to say it," Conrad said, "but I agree with the Invertebrate. We've done this sort of thing loads of times before. All this is achieving is making the boys cold, wet and pissed-off before we even start our proper mission tonight."

"I agree. But that's Major Blundell for you. We both know he derives a perverse sense of satisfaction from running us ragged. And I bet he's warm and dry at the moment."

Blundell had a reputation as a slave driver with a penchant for inflicting unreasonable hardships upon his men, often from the relative comfort of a camp bed in the company command post, or 'CP'.

The section continued patrolling in a general south-easterly direction, leaving the golf course and entering farmland. Here the soldiers moved in single file, hugging the vegetation of the field boundaries in case Gorpe had an OP positioned somewhere on the ridge above. Where possible they avoided gateways, forcing their way directly through the hedgerows which divided the fields, although the brambles and briars snagged and tore their Gore-Tex suits like nature's barbed wire. After a while they reached a road which cut directly across their route and was completely straight for half a kilometre in either direction. This presented a real problem, as it was an ideal feature for Gorpe to use as a surveillance aid; all he had to do was sit in his Land Rover at one end of the straight section of road, and he would be able to see anyone who tried to cross. The patrol had no alternative but to trudge uphill, staying close to the hedgerow, to where a bend in the road provided a more secluded crossing point. From there it was only about a kilometre to the Dungeon, so they pressed on through the rain.

The patrol reached the edge of the woodland surrounding the Dungeon valley and Robert decided to reconnoitre the objective area. He selected a suitable drop short point, or DSP, positioned the section in all round defence, and left Conrad in charge while he and Stevenson went ahead to investigate the specified grid reference. The pair crept forward through the trees, thankful for the pattering of the rain which drowned out the rubbing sound of their Gore-Tex clothing. Robert's heart was beating rapidly - even during a mere training exercise, it was surprising how the combination of nerves and excitement caused the adrenalin to flow.

Nature clearly still disapproved of the soldiers' activities, as the rain continued unabated and gusts of wind swept the area like malevolent spirits. At the drop short point, Lance-corporal Conrad crouched by a hawthorn bush and scanned the trees, watching for Robert's return – or for the approach of enemy personnel. The other men were concealed in the long grass at the woodland edge, leaning on their soggy bergens and staring over their weapons as rain dripped from their helmets. Thankfully it was not long before Robert emerged from the undergrowth with his arms outstretched to show that he and Stevenson were 'friendly forces'. He crouched next to Conrad.

"Right mate, the objective area is a small re-entrant, about two hundred metres in that direction." He pointed. "There's a clearing about thirty metres back from the edge of the valley – that can be the Final Rendezvous and rear protection party location. We need to put some more foliage on our helmets and shoulders, so we're not sky-lined when we look down into the re-entrant."

"Sure. Then what's the plan, Stan?"

"Well, the tricky part is that we're supposed to try to capture the agents or insurgents or whatever they are, and you know what'll happen – as soon as we move in they'll just leg it, no matter how many blanks we fire. So, Mark, I want you and Farrell to go round to the opposite side of the re-entrant so you can grab anyone who tries to run and physically drag them back up to us. The cadets never play dead so we won't either."

Robert drew a quick sketch of the re-entrant in his waterproof notebook and used it to brief the rest of the patrol. Their current location, the drop short point, would now act as the emergency rendezvous, or ERV, to which everyone would return if things went wrong and the patrol became fragmented. The soldiers hid their bergens in the long grass beneath some bushes and then, working in pairs so that half of the section remained covering the arcs of fire at all times, supplemented their personal camouflage with extra vegetation. When Robert was satisfied with the results, he gave the signal to advance in single file to the final rendezvous, or FRV, which he had selected a short distance from the small valley in which the enemy were expected to appear. At the FRV the men once again went into all round defence, but this time they lay in a very tight circle with their legs overlapping and their weapons pointing out in every direction while they waited, watched and listened. After several minutes, Robert decided it was safe to proceed, and sent Conrad and Private Farrell off to occupy a position on the opposite side of the re-entrant.

Leaving privates Finnegan and Harding at the FRV to provide rear protection, Robert, Stevenson, Spencer and Hughes 42 crawled forward through the mud and leaf litter to a position from which they could peer down into the little valley. Robert cursed the blank firing attachments on the end of their weapons: it was forbidden to camouflage these in any way, yet their bright yellow paint could easily give away the position of an otherwise well camouflaged soldier. Meanwhile, Mark Conrad and Private Farrell skirted around the re-entrant, giving it a wide berth before working their way back up on the other side to reach a concealed position directly opposite Robert's team.

The rain deluged down and the inactive soldiers began to shiver. Robert yawned and rested his chin on his rifle to relieve the strain on his neck. Once again, he wondered why he chose to do this at weekends, for half the daily salary he received as a teacher – in fact, it was nearer a quarter, if calculated on an hourly basis, as a day's work in the TA often involved a full twenty-four hours of hard graft. Yet, despite the discomfort and the tiredness, he felt strangely and intensely alive... *That*, of course, was why he did it.

In the dell below, the stream that was usually a feeble trickle was today a muddy torrent, but there were no signs of human activity. Robert wondered how long they were supposed to wait here for. Lieutenant Grudge had instructed the patrol to be in position by two o'clock, but had neglected to give any further timings. That was probably a deliberate oversight – the 'fuck about factor,' or FAF, as it was known to Robert and his friends.... the TA thrived on abbreviations and acronyms. 'FAF' was often incorporated into training exercises to test morale and push soldiers to their limits, in keeping with the principle '*Train hard, fight easy*.'

In his radio headset, Robert heard the three short bursts of static which was Conrad's signal that he was in position. He scanned the vegetation on the other side of the re-entrant and eventually spotted his second-in-command, lying at the base of a tree. They gave each other the thumbs-up.

At that moment, Ben Spencer sneezed loudly, then began fumbling noisily with the water bottle pouch on his webbing. Robert kicked him and subjected him to a harsh stare of disapproval. Spencer stared back with a questioning expression of innocent surprise. Robert mouthed the words 'Shut up,' and Spencer looked away. Although he was a friend, who was good company in social situations, Spencer could be a complete liability as a soldier.

After an hour, the men began fidgeting restlessly as the parts of their bodies in contact with the ground slowly went numb. Spencer's eyes kept closing and he had to be kicked awake. Then, just as Robert was considering sending two men back to swap with the FRV party, there was movement in the re-entrant below.

A man came into view, wearing an old army greatcoat and a woolly hat, his hands nonchalantly in his pockets as he walked slowly up the footpath from the direction of the estuary. When he drew nearer, Robert recognised him as Lance-corporal Dudley from the C Company stores. Dudley - or 'Duffer Dudley' as he was affectionately known, was an affable but undynamic TA soldier in his thirties who had jumped at the opportunity to get out of the rifle sections and into the stores, where he could relish the power of controlling the issue of kit, make endless mugs of tea, and furtively smoke cigarettes outside the back door. Robert watched as Dudley loitered by the stream about thirty metres away, lighting a cigarette in a theatrical gesture reminiscent of a character in a cold war spy film.

A few moments later, two figures in camouflage clothing and berets appeared from the trees and ferns to the left of Robert's field of view, moving down-slope towards Dudley. Their outdated 58-pattern webbing and manually-operated rifles identified them as cadets. Upon reaching Dudley, one of them handed over a small rucksack. Aware that the three men might suddenly disperse, Robert decided to act - it was now or never.

"Army! Halt or I fire!" he shouted.

In a real-life situation with live ammunition, the men in the hollow would almost certainly have surrendered immediately for fear of sudden death, but now, in a training scenario, they were prepared to take their chances. The two cadets turned and started running back the way they had come. Dudley stood still for a moment, glancing around frantically as he tried to work out where Robert's shout had come from. Suddenly, Mark Conrad and Private Farrell burst from cover and sprinted down the muddy slope to intercept the fleeing cadets. Seeing them, Dudley decided to make his escape, but went in the wrong direction - running up the slope directly towards where Robert and his men lay concealed in the ferns.

Mark Conrad slipped in the mud and slid halfway down the slope, but he regained his balance and dived onto one the cadets, pulling him to the ground. The other lad was too far away to catch, so Farrell fired a burst of blanks at him as he fled. As expected, the cadet was evidently bullet-proof and carried on running. More cadets appeared further up the re-entrant and, ignoring the fact that one of their number was in the way, began firing at Conrad and Farrell.

Slipping and sliding in the mud and leaf litter, Dudley struggled up the slope, glancing frantically behind him. He was startled when Robert suddenly stood up out of the vegetation in front of him and fired a warning shot into the air. Dudley skidded to a halt and raised his hands in surprise.

"Search him," Robert shouted to Hughes 42, and the hapless storeman was pushed roughly to the ground. Stevenson aimed his rifle at Dudley's head while Hughes searched him for weapons or important documents.

In the muddy re-entrant below, Conrad was dragging the captured cadet by his webbing while Farrell was providing covering fire. To aid their escape, Robert threw a smoke grenade down into the hollow, with the intention of creating a smoke screen between his men and the group of cadets. However, the canister hit the branch of a tree and fell short, narrowly missing Conrad and isolating Farrell on the wrong side of the developing curtain of smoke. Fortunately, the private realised what was going on and acted quickly, kicking the grenade in the direction of the cadets before catching up with Conrad and helping him with his prisoner.

When Conrad and Farrell reached him, Robert immediately gave the order to withdraw. As they departed, he tossed a thunderflash – a sort of enormous firecracker – down into the smoke-filled hollow to simulate a claymore mine. It fizzed and sparked for a few seconds before detonating with a terrific *bang!* which made the ground shake.

The patrol regrouped at the FRV, where Robert made sure that everyone was accounted for before giving the command to withdraw back to the emergency rendezvous. Dragging their two captives, they ran through the trees to the edge of the wood, where they retrieved their bergens and lay in all round defence to catch their breath and make sure they were not being followed. It was still raining heavily. After several minutes, with no sign of pursuing enemy, they moved on, heading uphill towards the top of the ridge. Robert tried contacting Grudge on his radio but could not obtain a decent signal, so he dropped back and walked alongside Finnegan to use the more powerful set in the private's bergen.

"Hello Two-Zero, this is Two-Two Charlie, message, over."

There was a short delay followed by a burst of static, then the lieutenant's modulated voice came back through the handset. "*Two-Zero, send, over.*"

Robert wanted to know what he and his men were supposed to do now, but the requirement to use correct voice procedure over the radio net made him struggle to express himself. After some hesitation he said: "Two-Two Charlie, mission accomplished, be advised we have two Papa Oscar Whiskies, no casualties...Er, where to now, over?"

Twenty minutes later, the weather-beaten patrol were waiting beside the main road which ran along the top of the ridge, watching a Land Rover approach through the torrential rain. Robert had expected to rendezvous with Lieutenant Grudge, but when the vehicle pulled up alongside him and stopped, it was Colour-sergeant Protheroe, the company Permanent Staff Instructor, who leaned out of the window to greet him. Every TA infantry company had a PSI, who was a senior NCO seconded from the regular battalion to give advice and ensure that the part-time soldiers received proper training. Permanent Staff Instructors were usually sergeants who were promoted to Colour-sergeant for the secondment, and most of them initially resented being posted to the TA but ended up enjoying the assignment. Protheroe was no exception. His early grumbles about 'STABs' had not lasted long, as he began to appreciate the efforts of the part-time soldiers and enjoy the relative freedom of his new life away from the regimentation of the regular battalion. A highly experienced and professional soldier, Protheroe was destined to become the Regimental Sergeant-major when the Wirral Regiment expanded to wartime strength.

"Good effort, lads," the PSI said, climbing out of the Land Rover to take custody of the two captives. "Your next RV is at grid 246858."

Robert worked out where the grid reference was on the map and his face fell.

"That's Royden Park."

"That's correct, Corporal."

"But I thought our OP mission tonight was in Arrowe Park..."

"You thought right, Corporal Taylor."

Robert was distinctly unimpressed by this latest development. His clothes were wet from sweat and rain, his shoulders ached from the weight of his heavy bergen, and the excitement of events in the Dungeon during the afternoon had sapped his energy.

"But Royden Park is north of here, almost back the way we've come! It's right out of the way for Arrowe Park..." he protested sulkily.

"That's how it is, I'm afraid," Protheroe said, with some sympathy. "The OC wants you to RV at Royden Park at nineteen hundred hours so he can give you a final briefing before you proceed with the next phase of the operation."

"Ah, the OC....I should have known." Robert sighed. "Right, I suppose there's no point whinging about it – we'll see you there. Ours is not to reason why...and all that."

Protheroe nodded approvingly, revved the engine and engaged first gear. "Well done, Corporal T. Good effort, lads - keep it up!"

The PSI drove away in a northerly direction, his Land Rover emitting a distinctive whining sound which remained audible long after the vehicle had disappeared from view. Robert sighed and briefed his men on the latest requirements of the mission, trying his best to placate their grumbles with a reassuring, “It’s only about 3K away, we’ll be there in just over an hour...” A sudden gust of wind blasted him with yet more rain, as he set a new compass bearing and led his patrol in the direction of Royden Park.

In order to reach the specified rendezvous location, the patrol had to cross Thurstaston Common, an expanse of woodland, heath and sandstone outcrops which were a navigator’s nightmare. A maze of minor paths criss-crossed the area, but there were few landmarks or distinguishing features which were visible from a distance greater than fifty metres or so, due to the dense vegetation. In such terrain a map was virtually useless. Robert had done some orienteering there in the past, and on numerous occasions had walked with Linda up to the trig point on the sandstone ridge, which offered views of Liverpool to the east and Wales to the west. He was aware of how easy it was to get disorientated and then thoroughly lost on the common, so today he led his patrol directly to the trig point, from where he knew the route through the birch trees, bracken and heather to Royden Park. His intention was to arrive at the RV early to give his men time to sort themselves out and have some food before the evening’s operation commenced. If they reached the RV on schedule at seven o’clock, Blundell would almost certainly be waiting for them and would no doubt send them off again as soon as he had given his briefing. And if that happened, it was probable that at least one member of the patrol would ‘go down’ that night...

‘Going down’ was a generic army phrase which basically meant that a soldier could no longer function effectively. Usually, men ‘went down’ as a result of being cold, wet and exhausted. Sometimes the affected individual was actually suffering from hypothermia, heat stroke or some other medical condition, but more often the incapacity was attributable to mental capitulation and collapsed morale. As a general rule, the most competent and experienced soldiers, who kept themselves warm and fed and alert, never ‘went down’. Certain members of Eight Platoon – the ones whose hearts were not really in soldiering – were notorious for ‘going down’ when the going got tough. Robert’s money tonight was on Harding or Spencer, or both.

On numerous occasions in the past, Robert had discussed with Conrad and Brabander the qualities which made a good soldier. Having never experienced actual combat, he could hardly claim to be an expert on the subject, but he considered that his six years of TA experience entitled him to at least express an opinion. It was his belief that the most essential attribute of any infantry soldier was not physical fitness, aggression, intelligence or marksmanship skills, although these were undeniably important. No, the most essential quality was the ability to endure extreme discomfort and prolonged tiredness. For discomfort and tiredness featured heavily in an infantry soldier’s life. A man who could run a four-minute mile or kill someone without remorse was of little use if he simply 'threw in the towel' when he became tired, cold, wet, filthy, hungry or degraded.

The patrol skirted around the trig point, avoiding the top of the ridge so as not to be silhouetted against the brighter patches of sky to the west, where the sun was setting behind the clouds. On days like this it was hard to imagine that the sun still existed. In the fading light, Robert caught sight of his boots. The abrasion of coarse grass and heather had scuffed off the polish, exposing the bare leather and allowing water to soak through.

His feet had been wet for several hours now and he could feel tender hotspots on his heels and one ankle, which would develop into blisters if given the chance. He regretted not following Brabander's example of wearing waterproof socks, and resolved to buy a pair at the earliest opportunity. Urging Stevenson at the front to quicken the pace, Robert guided the patrol across the common and into Royden Park, heading for the car park near the entrance, where they were to rendezvous with Major Blundell. Gusts of wind spat squalls of rain at the eight soldiers as the weather made one last-ditch, all-out attempt to stop them reaching shelter, but they trudged on indifferently.

It was five-thirty when they arrived at the parking area beneath tall trees, which swayed frantically in the gale. Only a few cars belonging to diehard dog walkers remained parked in the gloom, and the warden was locking up the toilets. He looked a little startled as the grim-faced soldiers emerged from the woods and Robert Taylor hurried over to speak to him.

"Can you leave these open for a bit longer?" Robert asked, pointing at the gents toilet. "We could really do with getting out of this rain for a while."

The warden shrugged. "I suppose so. How long for?"

"About an hour, if that's okay. We won't make a mess, I promise you."

"Alright. I've still got some things to do before I leave tonight – I'll come back in an hour. No mess, mind."

The bedraggled soldiers filed gratefully into the toilet and dumped their squelching webbing and bergens onto the floor. It was a standard old-fashioned public toilet, with plenty of spiders, reeking urinals full of yellow disinfectant blocks, and a permanently running cold tap. But it was shelter, and after the ravages of the day's foul weather it was nirvana to the weary men. All they wanted was to be out of the wind and the rain. Had they been given a suite at the Savoy, with complimentary champagne and call-girls 'on the house,' they could not have been happier. Their contentment was consummated by the discovery that the hot-air hand drier actually worked, and for the next hour it was in continual operation, providing hot air bliss to the cold and dejected.

Within minutes the soldiers had their hexamine stoves out and were brewing tea and heating-up their boil-in-the bag meals. The hexamine tablets were not supposed to be used in confined spaces because they produced toxic fumes which could make a man sterile, but no-one cared: at that moment, future fertility was a lower priority than tea and hot food. The soldiers shook the water out of their Gore-Tex jackets and trousers, put on warm clothes, and took it in turns to stand in front of the hand drier. Gradually their reserves of morale were replenished, and when Major Blundell and Lieutenant Grudge arrived on schedule at seven o'clock, they found the patrol in surprisingly good spirits.

CHAPTER 7

The Boys in the Car

Mr Roberts is evidently not aware of current trends in Army parlance. 'Muppet' and 'mong mode alpha' went out of fashion years ago.

A serving soldier
'Gung Ho' magazine

Mr Roberts replies:
Who cares, you Muppet!

Standing in the doorway of the toilet, Robert heard vehicles approaching and stepped out into the gloom as a Land Rover and four-tonne truck pulled up outside, their headlight beams illuminating the drops of rain which still refused to abate. Blundell, in beret and waterproof jacket, climbed down from the passenger side of the lorry and hurried over to where Robert waited.

"Good work this afternoon, Corporal Taylor," the major said, ducking into the toilet doorway, "although, obviously, the important stuff will be tonight - hopefully. Now, this will be the first time you've done an operation like this – in fact, it'll be the first time any of us have been involved in this sort of thing. How you perform tonight will pretty much decide how Council Leader Radley regards the whole company. What I'm trying to say is, don't mess up. Confident?"

"I'd be a lot more confident if we weren't all knackered from your pointless fuckabout-factor exercise this afternoon," Robert was tempted to reply, but instead he nodded and said: "We'll do our best, sir."

"Good, I have great faith in you, as you know."

Blundell held Robert in perhaps unreasonably high regard, partly due to his track record of competence as an NCO, but also because he was educated, well spoken and of good character. On several occasions in the past, the major had urged Robert to apply for officer selection, but he had politely declined. Robert was content to remain a corporal, or 'full screw', as the rank was known in Army slang. 'Best rank in the Army,' someone had once told him. 'Higher pay than a lieutenant - and no mess bills!' Not only did Robert prefer the more informal, down-to-earth social life enjoyed by NCOs, he had also realised long ago that the Army – or at least the Infantry – was basically run by corporals. *Remain a corporal*, he told himself, *and you'll remain indispensable*.

The section's mission that night was classified as being 'in support of the civil power,' and officially did not exist. The men were to set up an observation post, or OP, in Arrowe Park to watch for joyriding youths who had demonstrated a predilection on Saturday nights for dumping stolen cars near the children's play area and setting them ablaze. If they repeated the practice tonight, the soldiers were to apprehend them before they had a chance to burn the vehicle and then hold them until such time as they could be passed to the police. It sounded simple, yet the operation would be the culmination of two weekends and four evenings of meticulous planning and rehearsals. In many respects it was a similar exercise to that carried out at the Dungeon during the afternoon, except that the 'enemy' tonight would not be playing by any rules. In recognition of this, the patrol would be issued with live ammunition.

The soldiers lined up outside in the rain to unload their weapons, remove the blank firing attachments and empty their magazines of blank rounds, which Lance-corporal Conrad collected in a sandbag. After Lieutenant Grudge had inspected every man's rifle, magazines and webbing pouches by torchlight to make sure that no-one still possessed any blanks, the section went back inside to 'battle clean' their weapons. This involved pulling flannelette patches through the bore, reaming carbon deposits out of the gas system and squeezing copious quantities of oil into and around the breech block. Then Robert summarised the detailed set of orders which he had delivered to his men the previous night. He paid particular attention to the purpose of the mission, how it was to be executed, and each man's role in the operation. Blundell and Grudge listened with approval. Finally, after watches had been synchronised, passwords and callsigns memorised, radio and night-sight batteries checked and camouflage cream reapplied, the weary soldiers lined up outside again and were each issued with a single magazine containing ten live rounds.

"Keep your safety catches on and do not make ready until Corporal Taylor tells you to," Grudge instructed. "We don't want someone having an ND between here and the objective." ND stood for 'Negligent Discharge' – when a soldier allowed his weapon to fire unintentionally. Even when using blank rounds, a ND was a regarded as a serious military offence, but an incident involving live ammunition in a public place would be considered an act of unforgivable incompetence.

The lieutenant turned to Blundell and said: "Can I have a word, sir?"

"What is it, Lieutenant Grudge?"

The two officers walked a short distance away from the men but Robert could just make out their conversation over the background hiss of the rain.

"I was just thinking, sir," Grudge said, "it might make sense to drop them off a bit closer to the objective, save them having to tab the whole way on foot. They've worked hard today and if they're too chin-strapped they won't be able to function well tonight."

Blundell rubbed his wet moustache and considered the suggestion before declaring dismissively, "Oh, it's only about 3K.

Come on, Lieutenant, they're soldiers…if they ever find themselves in a real war they'll have to contend with a lot worse than this, I'm sure… Let them go on foot – it'll do them good."

Two hours later, the section was concealed in its OP location and it was still raining. Arrowe Park, which surrounded Wirral's main hospital on three sides, was a varied landscape combining natural forest with recreational facilities such as playing fields, a golf course, tennis courts and children's play areas. Robert sat in the mud and leaf litter in the impenetrable darkness at the edge of some woodland, and peered out through the foliage of a bush. The murky panorama to his front comprised an expanse of grass, a tarmac service road, and a small playground featuring a swing, a slide and a boarded-up ice ream kiosk.

Hidden in the musty vegetation alongside Robert were Privates Farrell, Harding and Spencer. The remainder of the patrol had been carefully positioned in concealed locations around the area to form a trap. Lance-corporal Conrad and Private Stevenson were concealed beneath the branches of a large cedar tree a short distance away, while privates Hughes and Finnegan were hiding in the shadows behind the ice-cream kiosk. The grass clearing in the centre of the soldiers was a favourite spot for joyriders to dump their stolen cars; the turf was scarred by tyre tracks and burned patches, and littered with broken glass.

Robert had fitted a CWS night vision sight to his rifle and he used it now to scan the area for signs of activity. The sight magnified what little ambient light there was, making everything appear as varying shades of green or black through the eyepiece. CWS images were grainy and two-dimensional, which made it very hard to judge distances with any degree of accuracy, so Robert tended to alternate between using the sight and his 'mark one eyeball'. The problem with this technique was that squinting into the illuminated eyepiece caused the pupil to constrict, resulting in temporary loss of vision in that eye. Robert remembered the first time he experienced this phenomenon and had panicked, fearing that the Army had blinded him.

After staring at the gloomy patchwork of shadows for a while, the darkness began to play tricks on him. Black patches of shadow metamorphosed into ghostly figures, grey shapes in his peripheral vision seemed to move but were motionless when looked at directly, and it was almost impossible to decide whether certain dark blobs were large objects in the distance or small ones close by. Concentrating on such a confusing panorama was a real challenge and gradually his mind wandered. He began wondering what Linda was doing now, and how she would feel if she knew that her boyfriend was currently sitting in a public park holding a loaded rifle with bayonet attached, waiting to ambush joyriders. It occurred to him – surprisingly for the first time – that he or one of his comrades might injure or even kill someone tonight. His part-time soldiering had undergone a transition to an altogether more serious level, which pleased him: it was about time that C Company put some of its endless training into practice.

By midnight the novelty of sitting in the mud on a 'real' mission had worn off. Robert was cold, damp, uncomfortable, tired, and bored. He struggled desperately to keep his eyes open, but his eyelids became progressively heavier and he started dreaming fleetingly during his increasingly prolonged blinks. What concerned him most was the realisation that, if he was finding it so difficult to stay awake, it was likely that less disciplined members of the section such as Harding or Spencer were already asleep. The patrol had been in position since nine o'clock and had orders to remain there until five in the morning. Robert was just wondering how he could possibly remain alert – or even awake – for another five hours, when the screeching of tyres and the growling of loud engine exhausts roused him to a state of full consciousness.

Two cars approached at speed along the service road which bordered the pitch-and-putt course. In the lead was a Vauxhall Corsa, closely followed by a heavily modified Fiat Punto sporting full body kit of add-on bumpers, sills and spoilers. The two vehicles appeared to be racing each other.

The Corsa swerved onto the grass and performed a handbrake turn only metres from Robert's position, churning up the turf as its wheels spun in the soggy ground. It lurched forward suddenly and stopped. The Fiat pulled up alongside, spluttering from its oversized exhaust pipe. The drivers exchanged a few words which Robert did not catch – he was too busy writing the registration numbers onto his hand with permanent marker pen – then the Punto roared around in a wide arc and screamed away. The Corsa's engine died and three youths climbed out, looking around furtively. One of them took a container from the boot and began pouring liquid – presumably petrol – into the interior, sloshing it over the seats with howls of delight. Robert squeezed the prestle switch on his radio three times to alert Conrad and Hughes, then moved slowly and stiffly into a crouching position. The excitement and nervousness were almost paralysing, but he knew that at any moment the youths might disperse into the night. Trembling, he stood up in the shadows, took a deep breath, and screamed, "Army! Halt or I fire!"

He burst from cover with Farrell, Spencer and Harding following close behind, setting-off one of several trip flares which they had placed around the area. The flare ignited with a hiss, bathing the scene in a fiery orange-white light.

Moments later, Conrad and Stevenson, and Hughes and Finnegan, erupted from their respective hiding places, setting-off additional trip-flares and screaming "Army! Halt or I fire!" as they converged on the car. It all happened so quickly that the joyriders froze in terror as eight sinister silhouettes, brandishing what appeared to be spears, materialised out of the darkness and charged towards them like demons against a flickering backdrop of satanic fire.

"Don't move!" Robert yelled. "Don't fucking move or you're all dead!"

The boys were wearing tracksuits and trainers, and had they simply run away into the night they would almost certainly have escaped. But the soldiers' sudden appearance paralysed them momentarily, like startled rabbits in car headlights, and they found themselves surrounded by a ring of bayonets.

Robert aimed his rifle at the three boys and told them "Lie down! Lie down now! On the ground - *now! Move it!"*

Mark Conrad darted forward, snatched the petrol can from one of the youths and threw it away, then pulled the boy backwards and tripped him over onto his back in the muddy grass.

"Don't do anything stupid, now, mate," the lance-corporal warned, touching the trembling boy's throat with the tip of his bayonet.

When all three captives were lying face down on the ground with their legs apart, Hughes 42 secured their hands behind their backs with cable ties supplied by Finnegan, who was an electrician in civilian life. Conrad searched the boys' pockets and confiscated matches, cigarette lighters, mobile phones and a Stanley knife. Robert despatched Farrell and Harding to block the service road in case the other car returned, then used Finnegan's radio to report to Lieutenant Grudge, who instructed the patrol to wait by the car until further notice.

As the adrenalin wore off and his body relaxed, Robert suddenly felt very cold, very hungry and very tired. Events around him seemed distant and surreal. He knew that he was starting to 'switch off'...

"Better get these boys away from the car, Corporal," suggested Hughes. The smell of petrol was very strong, despite the dampening effect of the rain.

Robert blinked several times and became alert again. "Good idea. And take these bayonets off, before someone hurts themselves." The bayonets had provided excellent intimidation value but now they were frankly liabilities, serving only to cause accidental injury. It had been his idea to fit them to the rifles, and he would consequently carry the blame for any wounds resulting from their unorthodox use in this operation.

"What're you gonna do with us?" whimpered one of the boys, who could only have been about fourteen.

"Quiet, lads," Robert said sternly. He bent down and grabbed the youth's ankles, intending to drag him face-down away from the petrol-drenched car. But when he felt the boy's legs shaking violently with fear, and smelt the excrement in his urine-soaked tracksuit, he changed his mind.

"Spencer, come here and give me a hand with him."

Together, they carried the trembling, wretched boy away from the car and put him down in the shadows under the trees. Conrad, Stevenson, Hughes and Finnegan moved the other two youths, keeping watch on them with torches taped under their rifle fore-ends with the ubiquitous black electrical tape.

"Make sure you don't leave anything which shows we've been here," Robert instructed. Blundell and Grudge had been very specific on that point – nothing was to be left which might betray the fact that this had been a military operation. Spencer and Finnegan were sent to collect the spent trip-flares and associated wires and pickets; they poured water onto the still smouldering flare-pots before putting them into a sandbag. One of the boys began to cry and tell everyone how his mum and dad were going to kill him.

They waited in the rain, expecting the police to arrive, but after ten minutes two unmarked white vans approached along the service road before being stopped by Farrell and Harding. Robert hurried over. A stocky, brutal-looking man wearing a black bomber jacket sat chewing gum in the passenger seat of the lead vehicle.

"Er, who are you?" asked Robert hesitantly. He took an instant dislike to the man, and sensed that the animosity was mutual.

"Special Council Workers, mate. We deal with this sort of thing now. I hear you've caught three of the little bastards. Pass them over to us and we'll take it from here."

"Follow me."

The vans dimmed their headlights and drove slowly behind the soldiers to where the three boys lay. Several black-clothed SCW men climbed out of each vehicle. The one who had spoken to Robert, and appeared to be in charge, said: "We'll deal with these lads now. You've done your job, corporal."

At that moment, one of the boys must have realised that he was being passed into the custody of the Special Council Workers. He started writhing around frantically, struggling desperately to break free, to no avail.

"I don't want to go with them!" he shouted in panic. The SCW had only been in existence for a few weeks but had evidently carved a reputation for itself amongst the peninsular's law-breaking youth. "Get the police!" the boy demanded. "Get the 'busies'. I want to go to the 'busies'…"

"Shut up or I'll knock your teeth out!" the senior SCW man snarled with contempt, unclipping a telescopic baton from his belt. "Don't worry, we'll get the police for you, son…all in good time." He turned to his crew. "Right, fellas, get 'em into the vans."

Robert felt suddenly surplus to requirements, and a little cheated after all of the patrol's hard work during the preceding hours. He had expected to hand the boys over to appreciative police officers, but now it felt as though the section's glory was being stolen by this ungrateful bunch of unsavoury characters. However, he reminded himself, his men had done their job and done it well, and now it was time to get some well-earned rest.

"Okay, Two Section, let's go. Good effort tonight. Make sure you've got all your kit and follow me."

Without looking back at the Special Council Workers, he led his fatigued patrol back into the darkness of the trees and onto one of the woodland paths, pulling the radio handset out of Finnegan's bergen and speaking into it as he walked.

"Hello Two-Zero this is Two-Two Charlie, message, over."

There was a pause, then Grudge's voice crackled back to him over the radio net.

"*Two-Zero, send, over.*"

"Two-Two Charlie, message is 'Zebedee'. Moving to Papa Uniform Papa now, Echo Tango Alpha figures fifteen minutes, I say again, fifteen minutes, over." Zebedee was the pre-arranged codeword for 'mission accomplished.'

"*Two-Zero, roger your last, well done, out.*"

Leaving the scene of the night's operation, Robert felt troubled. There was something not quite right about how the mission had ended...He was not happy about handing the joyriders over to the Special Council Workers.

"Mark," he said to Conrad, "take the section a hundred metres down the path and wait for me there. Remember we're still tactical. I want to check something..."

The patrol proceeded onwards, while Robert dumped his bergen by a prominent tree and crept back towards the clearing. He approached stealthily, carefully planting each foot to avoid snapping twigs. The white vans were still there, with two Special Council Workers standing outside, smoking cigarettes and chatting quietly. But the vehicles were rocking on their suspensions, and muffled shouts and screams could be heard coming from within. Then everything went quiet. As Robert watched through his night-sight, the rear doors opened and the boys were brought out. Their hands had been untied but their bodies were limp and lifeless, sagging like dummies. The SCW men carried them over to the Corsa and placed them inside – one on the back seat, the other two in the front. Robert felt intrigued yet uneasy, and his growing sense of foreboding turned instantly to horror as the Special Council Worker leader nonchalantly flicked his glowing cigarette at the petrol-soaked car. It hit the side of the vehicle and fell onto the wet grass, glowing faintly.

The man laughed. "I was trying to get it in the sun roof..."

A competition ensued, with all of the men throwing their cigarette ends at the petrol-soaked car, which refused to catch fire.

"Come on, we're wasting time," the leader declared. He found an empty beer bottle beneath on of the van's seats and used it to prepare a Molotov cocktail. Then he casually lit the cloth and threw it at the car, which burst into flames. Within seconds the vehicle was a raging inferno. Robert looked away in revulsion, but his eyes were drawn back to the spectacle – to the dark shapes just visible through the roaring flames and billowing smoke inside the car. The glare from the conflagration penetrated the woodland and illuminated him, but the

Special Council Workers' attention was focused on their handiwork, and they did not notice as he crept silently away.

"What the hell was that?" asked Conrad when Robert rejoined the section. The flickering glare was visible through the trees.

"The car's on fire."

"How?"

"I don't know. I couldn't see..."

A short while later the patrol left the woodland and emerged onto the mown grass of some playing fields. Robert checked his map and compass for the last time.

"The pick-up point is in the car park on the other side of these football pitches," he told his men. "It can't be more than three hundred metres. Lead on, Stevenson."

With the promise of rest and hot tea only a short distance away, the soldiers' moods lightened. Private Farrell – the platoon joker – began to sing the 'Elephant's Marching Song' from the film *The Jungle Book*:

"Hup two, three, four – keep it up, two, three, four,
Oh the aim of our patrol
Is a question rather droll,
But to march and drill over field and hill –" (he trumpeted like an elephant)
"Is a military goal,
Is a military goal...
What - whuhohohoho...a man cub!"

Robert grinned with amusement, but he wanted his men to create a good impression when they arrived at the pick-up point. "Come on Farrell" he urged good-naturedly, "save it for the four-tonner ride back to TAC."

"Let's hope we are going back to the TAC," said Hughes sceptically. "That bastard Blundell might have something else lined up for us tonight."

When they arrived at the PUP they found the Company Sergeant-major, Dai 'Taff' Jones, waiting for them by the dark bulk of a Bedford truck. It was still raining, albeit less heavily.

"Well done, boys," Jones said as they sloughed off their bergens and stretched their aching, compressed spines.

"Tell us that's it for tonight, sir," pleaded Hughes.

"Private Hughes, it's not even two o'clock in the morning, and you're getting paid for a whole weekend. The major wants you to tab back to the TA Centre."

Everyone's heart sank.

"Then he can kiss my great big hairy arse!" Hughes declared defiantly. "I'm having an official sense of humour failure. Give me my teddy so I can throw it in a corner..."

The CSM grinned in the darkness.

"Only joking, boys. Get your kit on the wagon and let's get back to the TAC. You've worked hard tonight."

"There is a God!" exclaimed Private Farrell joyously. "And He is a kind and merciful God!"

When the men of Two Section arrived back at the TA Centre they were greeted by a jubilant Major Blundell.

"Well done, lads," he said, as they climbed stiffly down from the Bedford and shouldered their kit once more to take it inside. "Really well done. Council Leader Radley's delighted with you."

"Then maybe he'd like to sit in the rain next time, sir," muttered Hughes, who had a naturally hostile disposition towards anyone above the rank of lieutenant.

"Perhaps you'd like to tell him that yourself, Private Hughes. He's here now."

They went inside, squinting in the bright light, and dumped their webbing and bergens onto the woodblock floor of the drill hall. Robert staked his claim on a prime spot by a radiator and, feeling tired and drained of energy, quickly put on a dry T-shirt and jumper. Lance-corporal Dudley had made tea and soup, which were available on a side table, kept hot inside large thermos urns known as 'Norwegians'. Robert was in the process of pouring himself a cup of tea when Lieutenant Grudge appeared, accompanied by a smartly-dressed man of well-fed appearance.

"Council Leader Radley," Grudge said, "May I introduce Corporal Taylor, one of my section commanders."

Radley extended a soft, chubby hand. Robert's own hands were damp and filthy, and he wondered momentarily whether he should wipe them before shaking hands with the Council Leader, but decided against it. In contrast with the tall, impeccably dressed Gerald Radley, whose neck bulged slightly over the top of his shirt collar, Robert felt like a wretched, scrawny street-urchin.

"So, Corporal," Radley said, "it sounds like you've had a successful mission. You and your men should be proud of what you've achieved tonight."

"Thank you."

"I'd like you to do more of these operations in future," Radley continued. "They really put you guys to good use. And everyone's a winner. I mean, you're getting good training, and the borough is getting the benefit of your services in the fight against crime…"

"I suppose so."

There was an awkward silence. Then Lieutenant Grudge, whose responsibility it was to prevent awkward silences in this situation, said: "Corporal Taylor's a teacher, Council Leader Radley."

"Oh really? Which school?"

"Ridgefield."

"Good, good…that's quite a 'challenging' one, isn't it?"

"It is."

"And have the recent Council policies made things any easier for you as a teacher?"

Robert was determined to be honest. "Er, not really...It's all very well saying that teachers can physically punish children, but it's been so long since it was last allowed that it's no longer part of the school culture, or even society's culture. Teachers don't feel comfortable with it and the kids and their parents won't accept it. I mean, with some of our pupils, if you went to slap them or cane them for something they'd done, they'd probably hit you back, and later you'd have their psycho parents or friends or relatives waiting for you when you went home. You can't introduce a policy like that overnight."

"I see. So what's the solution, in your opinion, Corporal Taylor?"

Robert thought for a moment. "Well, I've never understood why we don't have some sort of school 'bouncer' to deal with the disruptive and aggressive pupils. That would allow the teachers to teach, which is our job, rather than doing crowd control all the time."

"That's a very interesting point. I'll make a note of it." From his expensive suit, Radley produced a small electronic notepad and pulled out its tiny stylus. He fiddled with it for a while, trying to get it to work and taking several times longer than he would have done with a conventional pen and paper. Eventually he succeeded in writing 'school bouncers?' on the screen, before putting the device away.

Major Blundell hurried over to them. "Corporal Taylor, I need you and your section in classroom one now for your debrief. Might as well get it out the way now, before the other patrols come in - then you can get your heads down. We've just heard from Corporal Murphy – One Section's caught some fly-tippers in Bebington...Right, just bring your weapons, leave the rest of your kit here...Council Leader Radley, perhaps you'd like to join us?"

"I'd love to."

As they walked along a corridor towards the classroom, Robert sidled up beside the Council Leader and said: "Councillor Radley, can I ask what's going to happen to those boys we caught earlier?"

Radley hesitated for a moment. His natural instinct was to tell the corporal to mind his own business, but, caught off guard, he was unable to think of a way of doing so tactfully. After a momentary pause he said: "Oh, they'll be taken into custody and made aware of the errors of their ways, probably given a good clip round the ear, so to speak, you know, that sort of thing..."

"So they won't be joyriding again?"

"Good God no. We'll make sure of that."

Robert caught the Council Leader's eye for a fleeting moment then looked away. In that brief glance he became suddenly aware that, regardless of whatever other qualities Gerald Radley might possess, he was definitely not a man to be trusted.

CHAPTER 8

A Gathering Storm

Mr Roberts' story is about as far from original as it's possible to be without incurring lawsuits for blatant plagiarism. The idea of parts of the United Kingdom declaring themselves independent has been explored on numerous occasions in the past - 'Passport to Pimlico' springs to mind. And more recently, Wirral writers used the theme as the basis for a play about their own peninsular...This tu'ppenny ha'penny author really should be ashamed of himself...

Diedre Manrancour
Northwest Gazette

Mr Roberts replies:
You're right of course, Diedre, although you must admit that your own novel, 'A Passion for Fashion,' which follows the fortunes of a working-class girl who finds success and romance in the glamorous world of the designer clothing industry, was hardly original either.

In the days immediately following the Arrowe Park mission, Robert Taylor suffered attacks of conscience which made him tense and self-absorbed. His intestines churned uncomfortably and he lost his appetite. At work he found it hard to concentrate or summon any enthusiasm for his job, and when a pupil in his tutor group asked, "Sir, did you hear about them boys who got burned?" he almost confessed to involvement in their murder, so desperate was he to shed the burden of his guilty secret. It subsequently emerged that one of the boys had been the brother of a pupil at the school, and rumours began to circulate that the burned bodies had not been removed from the car. This was confirmed by an article in the local free newspaper, the *Wirral Herald*, which was delivered to Robert's house four days after the mission.

Under the headline '*Burned Alive*', the article revealed that a wire mesh fence had been erected around the Vauxhall Corsa and the bodies left inside while forensic tests were carried out. As a result, the site had become something of a macabre visitor attraction, especially amongst local youths, who asked the Special Council Worker security guards for permission to peer through the fence at the charred corpses. Some took photos with their mobile phones, and the images inevitably ended up on sick websites with titles such as '*Just Desserts*' or '*That'll Learn 'Em*'. The distraught parents of the three joyriders were understandably outraged, and tried repeatedly to contact the Council to demand that their sons be laid to rest with dignity. But their protests fell on the deaf and compassionless ears of answer-phones, recorded voice messages and an indifferent secretary who promised to return their calls but never did. The parents, along with a small army of friends and relatives, marched on the town hall to demand an audience with Council Leader Radley; they arrived to find the doors locked and a sign in the window stating that the building was closed for 'essential maintenance'. So the burned boys remained in the blackened shell of the car, staring out of the windows with fixed grins and grotesquely protruding teeth.

During that same week, it was announced that Special Council Workers would be posted to certain 'challenging' schools in the borough to enforce discipline. "They'll act a bit like bouncers," Gerald Radley was quoted as saying. Within days they arrived at Robert's school – two stocky brutes with no necks, who patrolled the corridors like Rottweilers. Pupils swiftly learned to fear them, for unlike the ineffectual teachers, they had no qualms about using force against those who defied authority. Disruptive children were given one chance to change their ways and co-operate before they were taken – by force if necessary – to the foyer to await collection by their parents, who were subsequently fined a thousand pounds. One boy decided to call the system's bluff and put up a fight. His punches served only to enrage the Special Council Worker, who retaliated with huge tattooed fists and left the boy sobbing on the floor in front of his classmates. He was subsequently expelled.

The teachers in general had an ambivalent attitude towards the new security staff. Most felt uncomfortable about the use of physical force in school and found the two men intimidating and unsavoury, but they were aware that they risked appearing ungrateful or hypocritical: for years, teachers had been demanding that tougher measures be taken against severely disruptive or aggressive pupils, so they could not very well complain about the heavy-handed tactics of the Special Council Workers. And it was undeniable that there had been a massive improvement in discipline since the men had arrived...

One day, Robert was teaching a lesson about digestion to a class which included the bane of his life, Simon Smythe. Smythe had already been disciplined twice by the SCW 'bouncers' and was trying hard to control his behaviour, but the innate desire to be disruptive and seek attention and was hard to suppress. Also, he was struggling to adapt to the absence of the drug Ritalin, which had been banned by Gerald Radley because the Council Leader refused to acknowledge the existence of Attention Deficit Hyper-activity Disorder, or ADHD, which Smythe supposedly suffered from. "It's just making excuses for naughty children and poor parenting," the Council Leader opined dismissively. "I find the idea of rewarding people for producing anti-social brats frankly obscene. From now on there'll be no more money for the drug itself, or for all of the benefits paid to the parents of these fruitcakes."

Smythe waited until Robert's attention was focused on another pupil, then surreptitiously threw a pen across the room. But just as the biro left his fingers, Robert turned around at the crucial moment and caught him red-handed.

"Simon Smythe! I saw that! Throw anything else and you're out! Now, pick up the pen and get on with your work."

Smythe grinned defiantly. "I didn't throw anything."

"Yes you did, I saw you."

Suddenly the door opened and one of the Special Council Workers stuck his scarred, skull-like head into the room.

"Everything alright, sir?"

Robert glanced at Smythe and saw the colour drain from his face. There was a pleading expression in the boy's eyes.

"Is he giving you trouble, sir?" the Council Worker persisted, staring malevolently at Smythe. "I've come across that lad before. He's on his last warning."

"It's okay, thanks," Robert replied. "He just dropped his pen and had asked permission to pick it up. Go and get it, Simon."

Smythe walked silently across the room, a paragon of obedience, and retrieved the pen. The Special Council Worker glared at him disapprovingly.

"Let me know if he causes any problems, sir, and I'll deal with him. Okay?"

"Okay, thank you."

The door closed and the bouncer disappeared. Robert looked at Smythe and said: "That's one you owe me, Simon."

The month of May saw the TA conducting three more weekend operations 'in support of the civil power', and Robert entered a state of perpetual fatigue. His entire life seemed to have been consumed by his two jobs; when he was not teaching or preparing to teach, he was soldiering or preparing to soldier.

Then, during one operation against vandals who had repeatedly attacked the Hoylake lifeboat station, a youth pulled out a knife and was shot in the leg by Farrell. In the ensuing confusion, two vandals escaped, and Army involvement could no longer be kept secret.

"We'd better move house," Robert said to Mark Conrad when they returned home after the mission and were cooking their respective evening meals in the squalid kitchen. Robert was amused to notice that the impoverished Conrad's dinner that night consisted of a single boil-in-the-bag meal from an Army ration pack.

"Hmm, that looks good..." he joked, peering into Mark's saucepan with mock envy. "Is there enough for me, too? Seriously, though, once Wirral's low-life realise that we're helping to catch them, the TA will be as unpopular as the police or Special Council Workers. And people round here probably already know we're in the TA because they'll've seen us in uniform, or packing our kit into the car."

"You're right," Conrad replied. "And when we move we'd better make sure no-one knows what we get up to at weekends. No more leaving the house in uniform - it'll have to be civvies only. Any suggestions where we should go?"

"Wherever we can afford, and at least a couple of miles from here. New Ferry? Rock Ferry? What do you think?"

"I don't mind. But we'll lose our deposit on this place for leaving before our six months contract is up. I don't think I've got the cash for another deposit, and I bet Spencer hasn't either."

"Well, let's just pay the man, and damn his impudence! Don't worry, I'll pay. I never get the chance to spend any of the money I earn these days. I'll even pay for The Wastrel..."

At around the same time as Robert, Mark and Ben Spencer were making arrangements to move their meagre lives from one rented house to another, Gerald Radley and his cronies were making arrangements for war. By now the triumvirate of Radley, McCarthy and Silverlock were firmly established in the new executive suite in the town hall. In addition to the Council Leader and his two deputies, the rooms housed three secretaries, a pair of SCW guards, and two members of Blundell's 'Dole Patrol'; as Radley's programme of social reform gathered pace, he realised that he was making himself unpopular with some potentially dangerous people – people who might possess greater firepower than the fists, steel toecaps and batons which were all he could legally arm his Special Council Workers with. So once again he requested military support. It really frustrated him that he could not legitimately arm his SCW units with guns, but he had to acknowledge that McCarthy was right when he said that such a move would not be acceptable to the public at this stage.

The inner circle of Radley, McCarthy and Silverlock, which collectively liked to be known as the 'Senior Executive Committee,' or SEC, held a meeting in the conference suite which was also attended by a trusted clique of loyal councillors and officials including the likes of Alistair Blundell and George Lawton. Colonel Hogan, the head of the Army, had not been invited because he was still something of an unknown quantity, and Radley did not want him to know that the war, when it came, was a deliberately engineered artificial event. No formal minutes were taken: the meeting was one of a growing number of informal gatherings which officially did not exist. Conspicuous by their absence were several elected councillors and four out of the total of six departmental directors, whom the Council Leader regarded as potential threats to his authority. Gerald Radley may have been head of the Council, but for the time being he was by no means an omnipotent dictator wielding absolute power. The executives in charge of the six principal local authority departments, and the elected members of the cabinet, varied in their allegiance to Radley. There were no unequivocal enemies as such, but only Jonathan Powell in Technical Services and Tony Williams in Finance were guaranteed allies. The directors of the other four departments were generally supportive, but could not definitely be relied upon to support Radley, as their views on many issues tended to be rather more liberal than his own.

Of greatest concern to the Council Leader were Brian Salter from the Regeneration Department, and the elected councillor with whom he worked closely, Sylvia Fadden. Both were competent and professional - respected figures of integrity who commanded considerable loyalty within the Council, and as such had to be treated carefully. Radley had known them both for a long time, and in the past had always regarded them in the way that a lion might regard an elephant – as prey probably too large and dignified to tackle, and which presented no real threat anyway, so was probably best left well alone. But now that he possessed far greater power, the presence of two influential people who were not necessarily on his side made him distinctly uneasy. Fadden and Salter had never been openly hostile towards him, but they were certainly not acquiescent puppets and might oppose him on certain key issues if given the chance.

So he decided not to give them the chance. By simply not inviting the pair to meetings on the grounds that the matters to be discussed were outside their area of responsibility, he effectively excluded them from the decision-making process and removed a potential source of opposition to some of his more controversial schemes.

A minion brought in a tray of coffee and biscuits and Radley waited until she had served the drinks and departed before commencing the meeting.

"Right, okay...Firstly I'd like to thank you all for being here and for your efforts over the past few months. What I'd like to do today is review where we're at now and discuss where we go from here. I think we can all agree that so far things have gone remarkably well. In particular our campaign against anti-social behaviour has been a real success story, and for that I'd like to thank George for managing his SCW units so effectively, Duncan for masterminding their recruitment and training, and Alistair for providing military support."

The three men nodded in acknowledgement. Radley took a sip of coffee and continued.

"What I'd like to do now is take the whole process further. A few months ago, Terence, Duncan and myself drew up a list of the main target issues which concerned us, and we've been formulating some policies to try to address them. But many of the remedies will require some fairly hard-hitting measures, and I honestly don't think they'll be palatable to the public in the current cosseted peace-time environment...So I'd really like us to be at war as soon as possible.

"I've spoken to Monsieur Lebovic and he feels the same – if we're going to do this, we should do it sooner rather than later. The tricky thing is, how do we start our war without it being blatantly obvious to the public that the whole thing's artificial? I've been putting a lot of thought into this, but I'm still not convinced I've found the answer. I believe that our first priority must be to cultivate as much anti-French feeling as possible, and there are several issues we can exploit to achieve this. As you know, it seems that we are going to have to pay over three million pounds for breach of contract because we're now refusing to take the nuclear waste which Whitehall volunteered us for before we became autonomous...the French government has got its lawyers onto us like piranhas. The public won't be happy about that, or about what's going on at the Vauxhall site – I reckon most Wirral people will blame the French for the latest redundancies."

He turned to Paul Ryder, the head of the Public Relations division. Ryder was a tall, gaunt man of fifty-one, fastidious and professional and totally humourless.

"Paul I want you to work in conjunction with the local media to get as much propaganda value out of these things as you possibly can."

Ryder gave an expressionless nod. "Will do, Gerald."

"At the same time, I'm proposing we organise some form of cultural exchange visit again, like we did last year, to promote closer links with Caen and Normandy...I'm sure if we put our minds to it we can find a way of ensuring that the visits achieve the exact opposite of their supposed purpose of fostering good relations..."

"We need the French representatives to run over a local child or something when they come over here," mused McCarthy. "Couldn't we arrange for a Birkenhead scally to run out in front of Lebovic's car or something? If that happened I reckon the North End would declare war on France without any encouragement from us!"

"That would be good,' Radley agreed. "Something like that would be ideal - we need something to outrage our people so much that they actually want to go to war. We need our own Pearl Harbour, or sinking of the Lusitania...Anyway, have a think about it, and let me have any ideas as soon as possible."

The Council Leader paused momentarily, checking his handwritten agenda for the next item.

"Now, funding. Fighting the French will cost money, and my main concern is that, once we're at war, investors will pull out of Wirral and the economy will suffer. So, we need to raise as much capital now, while things are going well. I've asked Duncan to come up with some fund-raising ideas..."

On cue, Silverlock ceremoniously produced a piece of paper from his combination-locked briefcase and held it up proudly.

"Thank you, Gerald. I've put together a list of suggestions, in no particular order, for generating income for the War Fund. Firstly, before war is declared, we make a concerted effort to sell all remaining school playing fields and areas of public open space which we've identified as surplus to requirements. This might include parts of Birkenhead Park, Royden Park and Arrowe Park. All remaining Council housing will be sold off to housing associations or private-sector landlords, which will bring in substantial sums. I also think we should start charging a greatly increased fee for the grant of all planning permission, whether it's for an estate of houses or a single conservatory. I suggest an arbitrary figure of, say, ten percent of the project's value."

Radley nodded approvingly. "Sounds perfectly reasonable. And we can always increase it in future if we need to. What else?"

"Well, as you may be aware, we've made some money for the Fund already by overpricing major projects and splitting the extra profit between ourselves and the contractors. For example, converting the New Brighton fort into a prison was officially budgeted at 4.6 million but it actually only cost about 3.4, so we pocketed a straight million and the contractor got two hundred grand for keeping quiet. I suggest we continue this practice wherever possible – it should be easier now that Internal Audit is no longer with us.

"There are also various other schemes in the pipeline which we've devised to generate smaller sums on an on-going basis, such as putting pay-and-display machines in all Council car parks including schools, libraries, sports centres, the benefits office, police stations, parks, etcetera…Resident's parking permits will no longer be free and we'll make every road within five miles of Birkenhead town centre a resident's parking zone. Anyone not paying £10 for a permit will have their car clamped, with a £200 removal fee. We'll continue to raise money through the current system of SCW-enforced fines for anyone breaking the law – this has already netted us considerable sums. Oh – and there's a possible way of making money from wheelie bins… George, I'd like to speak to you about that after the meeting, if I may." Lawton nodded.

"Just out of curiosity, Duncan," asked Alistair Blundell, "how much is in the fund at the moment?"

"Just over five million."

There were appreciative whistles from several of those present, but Radley was more down-to-earth: "Five million doesn't buy a lot nowadays, I'm afraid, gentlemen. However, that money is only to make the preparations necessary to start the war. Once the fighting begins, we can justify tax increases to fund it. And we can start being ruthless with spending cuts. I reckon at least a quarter of our existing Council staff may have to go, which will save us a fortune. The way I see it, every administrative post we cut means an extra soldier in the field. Anything else on funding, Duncan?"

"Er, That's pretty much it for the time being, although I've asked Finance to set up a programme to put pressure on employees to increase their pension contributions, so we should be able to use those funds in future. I'm also looking into the possibility of setting up a system of war bonds, where Council staff would receive part of their salary as bonds rather than cash."

"Sounds promising…Right, thank you. Good work there. Start implementing your measures as soon as possible. In the meantime, we continue our current programme of stamping-out anti-social behaviour. Judging by the letters in the local papers, most people seem to approve of what we're doing, although there's a minority who are vehemently opposed."

"Most of them are the anti-social ones who can't get up to their old tricks anymore," interjected George Lawton, clenching and unclenching his scarred fists on the table.

"Or the do-gooder libertarians who live in cloud-cuckoo land," added Duncan Silverlock with contempt.

Radley steered the conversation back on track. "What I wanted to say was, we need to make sure we still have popular support. I'd like you all to try to gauge the mood of the public. Ask your friends what they think of what we're doing, and get them to ask their friends as well. Remember, I want to keep the *majority of* people happy the *majority* of the time. I'm not particularly concerned if we offend a few minorities along the way. We'll meet again next week and I'd like some feedback then. Right: Any Other Business..."

The meeting closed and people started drifting towards the lounge for drinks and casual conversation. Radley called out to Blundell before he reached the door.

"Alistair, can I have a quick word?"

The 'quick word' was to become a hallmark of Gerald Radley's management style, enabling him to discuss issues in private, on a one-to-one basis, under the guise of a friendly chat. It was an excellent way of ensuring that only he was truly aware of what was going on, so that no-one – not even McCarthy or Silverlock – ever knew the full extent of his machinations.

Radley closed the door discretely and the two men sat down.

"Alistair, we need to talk about how we're going to run this war, and the resources we'll need to do it. As you know, I don't want to involve Colonel Hogan at this stage, so you're still my main military adviser at the moment...Now, you're aware of what I'd like to achieve. I want enough real fighting to make the people of Wirral appreciate that we're actually at war, so we can then benefit from the social policies made possible by a state of emergency. But I certainly don't want mass carnage, and neither do the French. In fact, Monsieur Lebovic and I have already agreed that all fighting should be confined to rural areas – under no circumstances do we want street battles in our towns. At some point in the future I'd like to mount a limited invasion to establish a front on the French mainland, and I'd expect them to do the same to us. So, how many men will we need, and what kit will they require?"

Blundell thought for a few moments, although he had already given the matter considerable attention in the preceding months.

"I reckon we'll need at least three infantry companies, plus support. You can't really do much with anything less than a company..."

"And how many men are there in a company?"

"About a hundred. Now, from what you've been saying, we might expect to have a company in France, a company holding the front line against French forces on our soil, and a company in reserve, training or resting. We'll also need some of the transport and engineering assets we've already got, plus admin personnel. And unless you want your war to be some kind of glorified paintball game, we'll need a support company."

"What does that do?"

"Supports the rifle companies. It usually has machine guns, mortars and maybe assault pioneers or a recce platoon."

"So how many men in total?"

"I reckon about six hundred, minimum. And we'll have to allow for attrition – wars produce casualties, and they'll need replacing."

"And how many troops do we have in Wirral at the moment?"

"On paper, about two hundred and fifty. In reality, less than two hundred."

"Hmm. So we need to draw up a plan for recruiting, training and equipping another four hundred men...That's going to be a big job. And expensive."

At that moment there was a knock on the door and George Lawton leaned into the room, smiling triumphantly.

"Council Leader Radley," he declared proudly, "I've thought of a way to start your war: *football!*"

CHAPTER 9

The War Kicks Off

Presumably we're all supposed to regard the character of Gerald Radley as some sort of tyrannical fascist bogey-man intended to make us appreciate how mild and moderate and liberal our real leaders are. Well, from my point of view, I'm sick to death of the whole ineffectual bunch of political fops who currently run our country, and if someone like Radley came along he'd get my vote any day!

Gunter Gauleiter
Campaign for the Preservation of Traditional England

Mr Roberts replies:
I'd keep quiet about that if I were you, Gunter.

As spring became summer, the Council did its utmost to subversively incite anti-French feeling amongst the general population. The Public Relations department produced a Council newsletter, delivered free to all households, which was laced with subtle anti- French propaganda. At the same time, a website was set up to enable people to express their views about the general state of affairs in the borough; much to Gerald Radley's satisfaction, the majority of responses were either supportive of his social policies or acrimonious towards the French - or both. In fact, unknown to Radley, some of the respondents were actually Council staff working for Duncan Silverlock, who wanted to ensure that his leader's zeal was fuelled rather than dampened.

Wirral had two local newspapers – the *Gazette* and the *Herald* - which were published each week and delivered to every household free of charge. The *Gazette* was undeniably independent - and frequently criticized the new regime and its leader - but Radley was personally acquainted with the editor of the *Herald*, and usually enjoyed favourable reporting within its pages. One way in which the paper served him especially well was by selectively publishing letters from its readership. At the Council Leader's insistence, the considerable quantity of correspondence which criticised his leadership and dismissed Wirral's burgeoning anti-French sentiment as prejudiced bigotry was discarded, and the journal concentrated instead on publishing letters such as this:

Dear Editor,

It should come as no surprise to your readers that we in Wirral are experiencing difficulties with the French. They have been our historic enemy for hundreds of years, and even as our ally have proved untrustworthy and unreliable, always putting their own interests first. Due to the politically-correct attitude towards history which has regrettably prevailed in Britain for several decades now, many readers will be unaware of this one-sided relationship, but I shall attempt to enlighten them with a few pertinent details. During the First World War, even though Britain had millions of troops fighting and dying to stop the Germans reaching Paris, the French charged us £200 to allow each of our casualty evacuation trains to use their track. In the Second World War, British soldiers were killed by Vichy Frenchmen manning coastal defences in North Africa. DeGaulle fled to London after his nation capitulated, but after the war he actively opposed Britain's entry to the Common Market – gratitude indeed! In the Falklands War it was French Exocet missiles which sank our ships, and in the second Gulf War they turned their backs on their old allies, without whom they would now be speaking German and eating bratwurst. The French wasted no time in banning our beef during the BSE scare, and they regard our cooking as inferior, yet this is a nation which gorges itself on horses, frogs and snails. In the past we have pandered to them, but it's about time we told them une grande 'Non non NON!'

Wilfred Underlever
Irby

This was exactly the sort of poisonous, xenophobic vitriol that Gerald Radley desired, but publicly he conveyed the impression of being appalled by it. In the press and on local radio he appealed for calm and a spirit of trust and friendship. He invited dignitaries from Birkenhead's twin town of Caen to visit Wirral to help rebuild some cultural bridges, and subsequently led a reciprocal trip to Normandy. These 'Friendship Exchanges' featured various forms of entertainment, ranging from dances by schoolchildren to theatre performances, restaurant meals, industrial visits, military inspections, and tours of local sites of interest – all justified on the grounds of hatchet-burying and enabling the leaders of the two regions to forge closer ties. Unknown to everyone except the three members of the Senior Executive Committee, the exchanges also involved several private meetings between Radley and Monsieur Lebovic, in which arrangements for war were discussed and finalised. Then, a week after the French contingent had returned home, a leaked memo informed the media of the exorbitant cost of entertaining the visiting dignitaries, and the *Gazette* published the information. People were outraged, but fortunately for Radley, few citizens seemed to blame the Council for the profligacy, and most of the public's anger was directed towards the Normans - who were regarded as having cynically squandered tax payers' money in an orgy of wanton extravagance.

Finally, in a desperate bid to restore good relations, the two leaders arranged a football match between Wirral's *Tranmere Rovers* and Caen's team, *Normandie Dynamique*. "Where politicians and politics have failed, ordinary people and football may succeed," Radley was quoted as saying. The match would be held at Tranmere's ground at Prenton Park.

Two days before the date of the game, Radley left the town hall by a side exit at six o'clock in the evening and walked to his car, accompanied as always by his usual entourage: a pair of Special Council Worker 'heavies', two soldiers from the 'Dole Patrol' and his recently appointed personal aide, Sean Simms. Formerly a clerical officer in the Technical Services department, Simms had served for just under a year with Charlie Company and had come to the attention of Alistair Blundell, who had recommended him to Radley. The ambitious twenty-three year old had been a reasonable part-time soldier, but had quickly realised that the TA would never make him rich and interfered with both his social life and his full-time career. He had leapt at the chance of being Radley's aide, recognising the role as a possible springboard to greater things. After being selected for the post, Simms was sent on numerous courses including driving proficiency, basic administrative skills, martial arts and bodyguard training. Blundell had even agreed to sign-out one of C Company's Browning pistols to him, on condition that he passed a handgun skill-at-arms course at the newly completed firing ranges at Mockbeggar Wharf on the peninsula's north coast. The major was reluctant to lose control of any of his unit's weapons, but arming Simms would obviate the need for the 'Dole Patrol' to protect Radley and so, the loss of one pistol, Blundell would regain two soldiers and their rifles. As each new string was added to Simms's bow he became increasingly arrogant and self-assured, which was exactly the sort of personality the Council Leader desired.

Radley had almost reached his BMW when an unknown voice shouted his name, and he turned to see a man running across the car park towards him. The two SCW bodyguards blocked the stranger's path and Simms moved close to protect his boss, while the 'Dole Patrol' soldiers reached into their sports bags for the rifles hidden inside.

"Stop right there, mate," one of the Special Council Workers barked, raising his hand.

The man slowed to a halt. "Council Leader Radley?" he said, with a strong scouse accent and the hint of a sneer in his voice. He was aged around forty, and looked quite respectable.

Simms stepped around the neckless bulk of the SCW bodyguard and confronted the man. "If you want to speak to the Council Leader you'll have to do it through the correct channels, sir, you can't – "

"Don't try to fob me off with that crap!" the man spat. "You know as well as I do that you can't get through to anyone in the Council these days. I want to speak to him now, or is he too scared to talk to the ordinary people who pay his wages?"

He circled round to try to out-manoeuvre the bodyguards, but at that moment Radley stepped out from behind his human shield, smiling pleasantly.

"What's the problem, sir? You seem agitated by something..."

“Too fucking right I am!” The man’s eyes narrowed. “I want to speak to you about my son.”

“Your son?” Radley was genuinely bemused.

“Yeah, my son. My son, who was burned to death in Arrowe Park and left sitting in a wrecked car for three days, while people gawped at him and took photos. My dear son, Tyler McMinn…” His voice faltered, and there were tears in his eyes.

“I see…” Radley said awkwardly. “I was very sorry to hear about that tragedy, Mr er…?”

“McMinn.”

“…Mr McMinn, and you have my deepest sympathy, but with all due respect, what has it got to do with me?”

McMinn regained his composure and gave Radley a fearsome look of utter malice. “I want to know who was responsible for him being left in that car, and all the signs point to you…”

For a moment there was an awkward silence, then Radley said: “I see. Then in that case I think we’d better discuss this inside…”

The group returned to the building and entered via a side door which Simms opened using a combination of security code and electronic key. Once in the foyer, Radley ushered the group towards the lift and pressed the button for the basement.

“We’ll go down to my office, Mr McMinn,” he said.

‘*We’ll go down to my office*’ was a pre-arranged signal to trigger a procedure which had been rehearsed in advance for just this sort of eventuality. The lift arrived and the two Special Council Workers entered first and stood against the back wall.

“After you, Mr McMinn,” Radley said politely, extending an open palm towards the lift cubicle. They entered and the doors closed. It was crowded in the confined space – certainly too crowded to swing a fist. Radley glanced at one of the SCW heavies and raised his eyebrows. Without warning, the bodyguard immediately reached forward and clamped an enormous arm around McMinn’s throat. At the same time, the other Special Council Worker embraced both men in a smothering bear hug, pinning McMinn against his colleague and effectively preventing him from using his arms or legs to defend himself.

“Get off me, you fucking apes!” McMinn screamed, writhing frantically but to no avail.

The lift reached the deserted basement, which housed the boilers and was only used for storage, and the doors slid open. McMinn’s shouts and screams echoed around the damp corridors and reverberated amongst the dusty pipes and ducting, but were heard by no-one.

“What do you want us to do with him, sir?” asked one of the SCW bodyguards, struggling to restrain the enraged father.

Radley replied as if he were speaking to a child or a simpleton. “Why, beat him, of course. Beat him to within an inch of his life. And then beat him some more…”

The two SCW men went to work on Mr McMinn with their batons and boots while the others watched. Simms pulled a lock-knife from his pocket and stood at the ready, in case McMinn broke free and tried to attack the Council Leader. The two soldiers, secretly appalled, watched uncomfortably with expressions of disdain. After a while, McMinn stopped screaming or trying to protect himself. In fact, he stopped doing anything at all. He lay still on the hard floor, his body responding to the telescopic truncheon blows and kicks from steel toecaps in the way that a sack of sand might. Eventually the Special Council Workers stepped away from the motionless figure and looked enquiringly at Radley.

"That enough, sir?"

The Council Leader nodded. He looked pale and his forehead was damp with sweat, but his eyes burned with a malicious fire. "Is he dead?"

Simms crouched hesitantly beside McMinn and pressed two fingers into the recess next to his Adam's apple. "He's alive, sir," he declared. "I mean, he's got a pulse. I think..."

Radley, Simms and the two soldiers departed, leaving the Special Council Workers to deal with the tricky problem of a nearly dead man. Several hours later, when it was dark, Mr McMinn was pushed unceremoniously out of the back of a white van as it sped along a stretch of country road known as Barnston Dip. Left lying in the road on a blind bend, he was hit by several cars before the emergency services arrived, and was pronounced dead on arrival at Arrowe Park hospital. The coroner – a personal friend of Radley's - would later declare that the cause of death was injuries sustained from vehicle impacts. Radley congratulated himself on dealing with such a potentially difficult problem with ruthless efficiency, but the McMinn family was to prove a thorn in his side once again...

"It's bloody typical, isn't it?" Robert Taylor exclaimed indignantly. "The day we move house is the day of this sodding football match."

He and Mark Conrad were loading up the Vauxhall Vectra with all of their possessions as they prepared to move to new digs in Rock Ferry. The match was not due to start for several hours, but already the spare parking spaces in the road were beginning to fill-up with cars belonging to fans who arrived early in order to patronise the local pubs before kick-off.

"I reckon we'll need at least two trips," Robert remarked, as they carried the cumbersome television and video to the car through a fine, dismal drizzle. "The problem is, when we come back for the second lot, I bet we won't be able to park anywhere near the house...Hold it a second – whoahoa! Towards you a bit...sorted." With the huge TV in place on the back seat, he looked up resentfully at the miserable sky and asked, "Why does it always rain whenever I move house and have to pack and unpack all my worldly goods?"

"Life's a shit sandwich and you've just taken a bite," Conrad replied philosophically.

Ben Spencer appeared in the doorway. "Any room for my stuff, guys?" he asked sheepishly.

"No!" they replied in unison. Then, seeing Spencer's panicked expression, Robert had an idea. "I'll only take your gear if you agree to put your TV and DVD player in the lounge for us all to use. Otherwise you'll have to get a taxi."

Spencer looked dejected. He was by nature an inveterate sponger, and having to make concessions to get his way went against his personal code of scrounger ethics. But he was broke, as usual, and could not afford a taxi, so he reluctantly agreed to Robert's terms.

Sure enough, when they returned to the road after depositing the first load of possessions at their new address, there were no parking spaces anywhere near their house. Robert left the car in the middle of the road while they hurried in and out of the house, transferring all of their remaining possessions to the back of the Vectra. It was only possible to fit everything in if all of the rear seats were utilised, which left no room for Ben Spencer.

"Start walking," Robert told him. "As soon as we've dumped all this stuff off I'll come back and pick you up."

A steady trickle of fans was walking along the pavements, moving good-naturedly in the direction of the imposing blue-grey corrugated bulk of Tranmere Rover's football ground, Prenton Park, which towered above the surrounding houses. Robert had to drive slowly and carefully to avoid supporters who spilled off the pavement and into the road.

"So," he asked as they crawled slowly past the ground, "do you think a bunch of men in shorts kicking around the modern day equivalent of a pig's bladder will heal a rift which dates back a thousand years or more?"

Conrad peered through the misty windscreen at the crowds of French fans disembarking from a line of coaches, separated from the home supporters by a police cordon. Already some hostile jeering could be heard.

"I wouldn't bet on it..."

A concerted advertising campaign and subsidised tickets meant that Prenton Park was full to capacity for the 'friendly' football match between Tranmere Rovers and Normandie Dynamique. Ten minutes before kick-off, Gerald Radley and Claude Lebovic walked out onto the pitch together and addressed the crowd. Using a megaphone, they thanked those present for supporting the event, pledged their commitment to a Wirral-Normandy alliance, and expressed the hope that the match would not only entertain but also help usher in a new era of friendship and cooperation between the two semi-autonomous regions. White doves were released, together with a thousand 'friendship' balloons in two contrasting colours. The players came onto the pitch, the crowds roared, and after the respective national anthems had been sung, the Welsh referee blew the whistle and the game commenced.

Despite the players' best efforts to please and entertain, the match was a disappointment. An early one-nil lead by Tranmere was equalised by a French goal just before half-time, and there was tangible frustration amongst the home supporters during the interval. The standard of play in the second half was distinctly lacklustre, with increasing friction between the two teams resulting in several fouls. One of these by a Tranmere player left a Frenchman with a badly injured knee and gave the visiting team a free kick, which flew into the back of the net. Many of the home supporters booed and jeered, while others prayed desperately for an equaliser as they watched the minutes tick painfully away. Then, two minutes before the final whistle, with the score at two-one in Normandy's favour, someone hurled a bottle and triggered an outbreak of missile throwing. Objects which should not even have been in the ground, including bottles, stones and batteries, went flying through the air between the two rival groups of fans, and shortly afterwards complete pandemonium broke out.

The players sprinted for the tunnel and cowering families hurried towards the exits as fighting erupted between opposing groups of male fans, many of which were actually Special Council Workers in disguise. It was a very ugly scene. Police flooded into the ground and began prising apart the combatants and dragging them away. Suddenly there was the sound of gunfire.

It was impossible to say exactly how many shots were fired, or from where they originated. But the loud succession of reports echoed around the ground and acted like a collective slap in the face for those fighting on the pitch and terraces. For a moment they restrained their feet and fists and looked around in alarm. Many people were screaming, but several voices were amplified by genuine anguish and rose above the others, shaming them with grief.

"My boy's been shot!" one man exclaimed in disbelief. "Jesus Christ – he's been shot!"

"Oh my God!" a woman screamed. "Someone help my husband, please help him!"

The agony was not one-sided. From the opposite side of the ground could be heard the plaintive cry, "Ma fille! Ma fille!"

When the police, stewards and uniformed Special Council Workers finally got the situation under control it became apparent from the distribution of casualties that shots must have been fired from at least two locations within the ground, although this fact was suppressed in the subsequent press releases. On one side of the pitch a local man was dead and three other people, including a boy, had been injured; on the other side, French casualties were two dead and four wounded.

The fighting had spilled out of the football ground onto the surrounding streets, and although most of the French fans made it back to the relative safety of their guarded coaches, some were cut off by the numerically superior home supporters and were chased through the surrounding streets. The penalty for not running fast enough was a severe beating. A few foreigners managed to escape by jumping over fences and hedges into private gardens. Sirens wailed as ambulances and police vehicles nudged their way through the melee, carrying the dead and wounded to Arrowe Park hospital. The drivers of the French coaches closed their doors with a hiss and steered their vehicles urgently south in convoy, leaving behind a number of their countrymen who would be repatriated later by plane. Radley's and Lebovic's attempt to foster good relations between their people had ended, as intended, in disaster.

That evening, Gerald Radley announced on local radio that he would be making a speech the following morning in Birkenhead Park to address to population and inform them of 'grave news'. He urged everyone to attend the event in person to demonstrate solidarity.

One man listened to the radio announcement with particular interest. He was Jeffrey McMinn, older brother of the man whose body had been dumped at Barnston Dip, and uncle of one of the joyriders who had burned to death in Arrowe Park. An electrician by trade, he was a fairly timid man of fifty-two whose world had just collapsed. Being unmarried and without children, his close relatives were of paramount importance to him, and in the space of three cruel weeks both his beloved brother Phillip and wonderful nephew Tyler had died in suspicious circumstances.

"This Councillor Radley bloke and his regime are corrupt and evil, I'm tellin' ya, Jeff," Phillip had declared furtively in the Halfway House pub only a week before. "They left Tyler in that car deliberately, to make an example of him. And I reckon this is just the start of it. You wait and see, Jeff..." He downed his pint and slammed the empty glass down on the table. "I'm gonna find this Radley bloke and have it out with him. If people like us don't stand up to him now, he'll walk all over everyone."

Now Phillip was dead, and there was little doubt in Jeffrey's mind that Radley was responsible. A sense of outrage and offended family honour compelled him to act. His timid nature would have rendered him powerless had it not been for his hobby - smallbore rifle shooting. Every Thursday evening he took his Anschutz .22 target rifle to a club near West Kirby and focused all of his energies upon shooting small holes through the centre of ten black circles on a piece of paper positioned twenty-five metres away.

"I don't know why you don't just use a hole punch," Phillip used to tease. "You'd save a fortune on all your gear and bullets, and you' be sure to get it in the middle. *And* the hole would be neater! I think you just like all those kinky straps and clips and stuff."

Only a month before, Jeffrey had been ecstatic to achieve his first ever 'possible' score, with every shot a top-scoring 'bull'. Such was his elation that he had taken Phil to the pub for a celebratory drink. Now, the achievement seemed pathetically meaningless and futile, and his one burning obsession was to exact vengeance upon the man he regarded as responsible for the deaths of his brother and nephew.

On the morning of Radley's speech, Jeffrey McMinn got up early and put his bolt-action rifle in the boot of his Peugeot estate car, hiding it under a dog blanket. His pet springer spaniel darted around with excitement, spinning like a dervish and jumping up at him with imploring whimpers, begging to be allowed to come on the trip. Jeffrey thought for a moment, and decided to take the dog.

Wirral was too small and densely populated to have any truly remote areas, but there were some country lanes which would be relatively quiet at this time in the morning. McMinn headed for the village of Brimstage and drove along a secluded road with farmland on either side, until he found a spot which suited his purpose. The lane bisected an avenue of trees which had once connected wealthy Lord Leverhulme's grand house in Thornton Hough with his soap factory in Port Sunlight. Jeffrey McMinn parked his car by an old bricked-up pillbox and let the dog run around to legitimise his presence; a dog seemed to automatically bestow respectability upon people who would otherwise have appeared suspicious. For a few minutes he stood by the car, watching his lively spaniel and listening forlornly to the sound of birds and distant traffic noise from the motorway.

Seeing or hearing no evidence of human activity in the area, he inflated three party balloons and weighted them by pushing the rubber knots under the ring pulls of unopened cans of beer. Then, ignoring a sign saying 'Private', he climbed over a gate and walked up the middle of the avenue of trees, counting his paces to estimate the distance from the car. He placed one of the weighted balloons at 100 metres, one at 150 metres and one at 200 metres – the maximum range at which he could realistically expect to hit anything with a .22 rimfire bullet.

Returning to his car, Jeffrey was startled by a cyclist who flew past silently in full racing gear. McMinn waited for several minutes, in case the man was part of a cycling team or even a race, but no-one else appeared. Then he discretely removed his rifle from its case and slid the weapon through to the front passenger seat before lowering the nearside window. By moving the seat forward and removing its headrest he was able to create a stable support, from which the rifle could be fired out of the window without any of the barrel protruding from the vehicle.

He loaded a single tiny cartridge and took one final furtive look around. There was a row of cottages about fifty metres away, but they were largely hidden from view by vegetation and it was unlikely that, when he fired, enough sound would escape from the car to cause any alarm. Nevertheless, when he took aim at the nearest balloon and pulled the trigger, the shot sounded like a thunderclap to his guilty ears. The balloon burst instantly, but that did not surprise him because he had shot competitions at that range before and knew the correct sight adjustment. Hitting the one at 150 metres was more challenging, requiring two shots and a point of aim considerably higher than expected. He took four shots to burst the most distant balloon, aiming so far above it that he estimated that, if he sighted on Gerald Radley's head at that range, the bullet should hit him somewhere in the chest or abdomen.

A large crowd had gathered in Birkenhead Park to hear Gerald Radley deliver his speech, although there were fewer people than the Council Leader had expected. Wirral's population was well in excess of three hundred thousand, but there could not have been more than one percent of that figure surrounding the makeshift platform which had been hurriedly erected to elevate the Council Leader above his subjects. Radley wondered what everyone else was doing that afternoon. Probably shopping, he decided bitterly. The Age of Greatness was truly gone, but today's announcement would herald its return.

"People of Wirral," he began grandly, speaking slowly into the microphone, "this is a time of crisis. As you are probably aware, relations between us and the French province of Normandy have been increasingly strained recently, and attempts by myself and others in the Council to calm the waters have failed. Yesterday, matters came to a head during the football match which we had intended to be a celebration of cooperation and reconciliation. As you may have heard, French infiltrators fired indiscriminately into the crowd, killing one local person and injuring three others, one of whom I understand has since died in hospital. The French authorities under Monsieur Lebovic have refused to accept responsibility for this outrage, or apologise, or even allow our police to make enquiries pursuant to catching the perpetrators. As you can appreciate, this is a very serious situation indeed, so an emergency meeting of the Council cabinet was held last night to discuss our response to the atrocity. It was decided that the magnitude of the outrage puts it above resolution by diplomatic means and that only one course of action remains open to us. It is therefore with great sadness and a heavy heart that I must inform you that, as of midnight tonight, a state of War will exist between Wirral and the French province of Normandy…"

Jeffrey McMinn arrived at the park just as the Council Leader was starting his speech. The entrance nearest to Radley's podium was blocked by Special Council Workers and police, so McMinn drove around to the other side of the park and, much to his surprise, found an alternative gateway guarded by a single SCW man.

"Can I come through to walk my dog?" McMinn asked nervously. "I bring him here every day…"

The man scrutinised him for a moment, as if assessing his potential as a threat, then nodded and stepped aside. Scarcely able to believe his luck, McMinn drove around the ring road which encircled the park, heading for where he could see a large crowd of people. He was astonished by the lax security at the event, and became suddenly hopeful that his assassination attempt might actually succeed.

In fact, the ease with which Jeffrey McMinn gained access to the park was largely the fault of Gerald Radley himself, as he had made the mistake of giving George Lawton complete control of all police and SCW units at the event. Lawton may have been good at managing gangs of tradesmen and labourers, or directing the activities of his SCW thugs, but he was no security expert. Wrongly perceiving the main threat to the Council Leader's safety as coming from hooligans or disgruntled citizens armed with bricks, bottles or knives, Lawton had positioned most of his personnel in a human shield around the platform, with the remainder distributed throughout the crowd in the immediate vicinity. The possibility that someone might try to take a long-range pot-shot at Radley was not something he had considered, and as a result McMinn managed to get to within two hundred metres of his target.

"The road ahead will not be easy," Radley warned the assembled masses, "and sacrifices will have to be made by all of us. But if we stand together as One People, unified in our struggle and our determination to succeed, and emulating the stoic fortitude of our forefathers, I know that we *will* win, and good *will* prevail over evil. Quite how the situation will develop from now on is –"

There was a muted *crack*! and the Council Leader flinched and swayed slightly, reaching for his shoulder with a confused expression. After a moment he sat down heavily as attendants rushed to his aid, while somewhere beyond the crowd a Peugeot estate car accelerated away, with a dog barking furiously in the back.

CHAPTER 10

Phoney War

I am the sort of person who is abusive and violent towards hospital staff and I personally object to being referred to as 'a disease which must be eradicated.' If I find out where this Martin Roberts lives, he's going to get well and truly leathered...

Kyle Heath
Letter to *Wirral Herald*

Mr Roberts replies:
You cannot hold me responsible, good sir, for the words or actions of my characters who are, after all, works of fiction.

Gerald Radley had achieved his aim of initiating an artificial war with the French, but being shot by a rogue sniper had never been part of his game plan. He had intended to savour the period following the declaration of hostilities, revelling in the sense of excitement and apprehension, shouldering the heavy weight of responsibility with noble fortitude, and generally appreciating the increased potential for *greatness*. Instead, he spent the time in Arrowe Park hospital, being operated on for a gunshot wound to his left shoulder. The tiny bullet had shattered his collar bone and been deflected upwards before it tumbled out of his body.

"You've actually been very lucky, Mr Radley," declared the surgeon who operated on him. "When the bullet hit your clavicle it could have gone up or down. Fortunately it went up. Had it gone down we probably wouldn't be having this conversation now."

"Would it have killed me?" Radley asked curiously. He was lying in bed, his dutiful wife sitting patiently by his side. Simms sat by the door, reading a magazine, and two Special Council Workers were standing guard in the corridor outside.

"Probably not, unless you didn't receive any medical treatment. But you would have lost a lot more blood and suffered a lot more tissue damage."

The surgeon's name was Angus Henderson. Formerly an army doctor with the rank of major, he had joined the National Health Service five years previously and exploited his military experience to become Arrowe Park's leading expert on gunshot wounds and other injuries more usually encountered on the battlefield. Although outwardly cordial towards Radley, the surgeon in fact considered his patient an unsavoury character and found a degree of poetic justice in his injury.

"It's a pity it wasn't something bigger, like a 7.62..." he joked confidentially to one of his colleagues at the sterilising basins. "Then all that would need to be done would be to bury him and reverse this ludicrous autonomy thing. Wirral's not a country in its own right, any fool can see that, surely..."

That afternoon, the Council Leader was visited by Terence McCarthy, leaving Duncan Silverlock to hold fort in the town hall.

"How are you, Gerald?" the chief executive enquired.

"Well, I've got a smashed collar bone, but apparently I'm very lucky, according to the doctor."

"I've got to say that you look a hell of a lot better than the guy who shot you," McCarthy remarked. "Jesus – you should see what Lawton's boys have done to him..."

In his panic to escape, Jeffrey McMinn had driven the wrong way, towards the park exit which was blocked by Special Council Workers and police. Upon realising his mistake he had slammed on the brakes and tried to reverse, but his car was rammed by one of the ubiquitous white vans which shunted it into a tree. Within seconds McMinn had been dragged from the vehicle, bundled into the back of the van, and driven away. During the short trip to the New Brighton prison fort he was severely beaten.

"Have you found out his name?" Radley asked curiously.

"We have, although I can't remember it off the top of my head. As far as we can tell he's just an ordinary person, a nobody."

"Why did he shoot me?"

"I don't know, but I'm sure Lawton will find out for us in due course... Oh – I took the liberty of leaking a memo to the press saying that you were shot by a French infiltrator. I thought that might suit our needs better than having to admit it was a member of the public who did it."

"What a brilliant idea," Radley said approvingly. "That should stir things up a bit...Any news from Lebovic?"

"A message came through this morning, in gobbledegook. I hope you can decipher it because no other bugger can." McCarthy dug into his pockets and pulled out a piece of paper upon which was written a seemingly meaningless jumble of letters and numbers.

Radley waved it away. "It's no good showing it to me now. I can't decode it without my cipher notes, which are in my office. I really need to be out of this bed and getting back there..." Becoming suddenly animated, he leant forward and tried to sit up, but his wife and McCarthy pushed him gently back down against the pillow.

"Easy, tiger," McCarthy urged, "you've just been shot."

"But we're at war! The French might attack at any moment!"

"What are they going to do – bombard us with frog's legs?" McCarthy scoffed. "You need to rest. Believe it or not, Gerald, things can get done without you."

"But I don't want them done without me!" Radley protested like a spoilt child. "I'll have to start holding meetings here, it's the only solution. Right - tomorrow I want to see Alistair and Colonel Hogan. We've got to start getting ourselves prepared in case the French attack."

"Okay, if that's what you want," McCarthy said sceptically. "But I still think you need to rest..."

Radley looked agitated. "Oh, Terence – can you do something for me, as a matter of urgency?"

"I'll try."

"Get in touch with Richards at police HQ. Apologise on my behalf for the recent breakdown in relations and tell him that we are eager to work more closely with the police from now on - and we'll be reviewing their budget very soon. Oh, and mention to him that I need a personal security adviser on a part-time basis and he'd be an ideal candidate for the job, if he's interested."

McCarthy smiled cynically. "Okay, I can do that, Gerald...And what do you want from him in return?"

"Ask him to provide a list of names and addresses of everyone on the Wirral who holds a gun licence. We need to start confiscating these weapons immediately. I mean, it's outrageous – members of the public being allowed to have guns, but my Special Council Workers not..."

The following day, Major Alistair Blundell and Lieutenant-colonel Alan Hogan visited Radley in hospital to discuss the Army's requirements for fighting the French. Now that hostilities had been declared, both officers were in uniform and had a bodyguard in the form of Hughes 42 from Robert's section, armed with a rifle. Duncan Silverlock also attended the meeting.

Radley greeted them warmly. "Good morning, gentlemen. Sorry to drag you over here, but I needed to see you urgently...I want you to tell me what you think we're going to need to get this war off the ground. I can't promise to be able to get you everything you ask for, but I promise I'll try...Obviously money will come into it, which is why Duncan's here. So, gentlemen, fire away..."

"The main issue we need to start addressing right away is manpower," Blundell declared without hesitation. "The Colonel and I both agree that we need to recruit a minimum of around four hundred extra personnel, which will be a tall order, considering we could never recruit enough to be at full strength with one company in peacetime, let alone three or four companies during an actual war..."

"Although," interjected Hogan, "more lads tend to want to join up in wartime. It's surprising but true – recruitment offices get the most enquiries when there's a real war on."

Blundell looked sceptical. "Even so, I doubt we'll get four hundred suitable candidates queuing up to join the infantry..."

Hogan shrugged. "Okay, so we look at other options. When the regular army is short of men it calls on the TA and the Reserves – "

"I thought the TA was the reserves," said Radley, with a confused expression.

"The TA is part of the reserve forces," the Colonel explained. 'There are also reservists who are ex-soldiers - men who've left the

Regulars but can be called-up again in times of need. Perhaps we can put out an appeal asking for anyone who's left the Regulars or TA in the past two years to report for duty. Perhaps we could offer them a higher rate of pay or accelerated promotion in recognition of their experience - give them an incentive to get back in uniform..."

"Sounds like a good idea," said Duncan Silverlock. "What age range would you specify?"

The two officers looked enquiringly at each other.

"I'd go for seventeen to thirty-two," said Blundell. "That's the range we've traditionally recruited from in the TA..."

"It might be an idea to raise the older limit," Hogan advised. "Otherwise we may find we're still short of men after having turned away people who would have made perfectly good soldiers but were too old. I'd consider going up to thirty-eight, or even forty. The priority is to get up to strength. We can always boot people out later on, or put them into reserve units. The selection process and basic training will sort out the wheat from the chaff, regardless of age...Anyway, I'd rather have a fit, switched-on thirty-five year old in my regiment than a nineteen year old couch potato who doesn't know his arse from his elbow."

"What about 'lumpy jumpers'?" Blundell asked the Colonel.

Radley looked bewildered. "Lumpy jumpers?"

"Females," Hogan explained. "I hadn't really given the matter any thought, to be honest.

"Then don't," Radley declared with an expression of disdain. "I'm not keen on the idea of women on the front line. Wirral's maidens should be at home, looking after the children and supporting their menfolk at the front...Anyway, where were we? We were discussing recruitment. So, we run an advertising campaign to encourage people to join up, especially those with previous military experience. Let's assume we end up with enough suitable applicants. What then?"

"They'll have to be trained," the Colonel replied. "We should be able to come up with a suitable selection and training programme using our existing resources. Might take a while to get everyone through the training mill, though..."

"How long – roughly? Give me a ball park figure."

"Difficult to say. But each man will need at least three weeks' basic training, then some time to be assimilated into his platoon so he can actually make a useful contribution. Oh – and they'll need to be clothed and equipped, of course."

"Of course. Draw up a list of essential items and I'll get Steven Saunders in Procurement to start ordering. Anything else?"

"They'll need arming as well, Gerald," remarked Blundell quietly.

"Naturally, if they're to beat the French. So we buy some guns."

"The question is," said Hogan, "what guns do we buy?"

"Surely the same ones they've already got," Radley replied indignantly.

"I'm not sure we can," said Hogan. "I don't think the SA80 is in production any more. And they're not great rifles anyway. Perhaps this could be the ideal opportunity to equip our men with something better."

"How about M16s?" Blundell asked hopefully.

The Colonel nodded. "That'd be the obvious option, but presumably it'll depend on what's available, how much it costs and who will supply us now we're at war. I doubt the British Government will. We might end up having to buy Kalashnikovs from Russia or something like that..."

The Council Leader fidgeted impatiently, allergic to any conversation in which he did not have a pivotal role. "Er, gentlemen, let's not get too bogged down with technical details at this stage.... You're the experts, I'll leave it in your capable hands to come up with your preferred choice of rifle and a couple of reserve options, then we can pass the matter over to Saunders for him to make detailed enquires and get some quotes for the cost. So, what else do we need?"

"GPMGs," Blundell said and then, seeing Radley's confused expression, added: "General Purpose Machine Guns. As many as we can get."

Hogan nodded. "I agree with Alistair. The GPMG is probably about the most versatile weapon we can buy...But what about artillery, have we thought about that?"

The Council Leader squirmed uncomfortably in his hospital bed. He did not like the sound of artillery. Both he and Lebovic had tacitly agreed that the destructive power of any weaponry used in their war should be limited; under no circumstances did Radley want his beloved Heswall reduced to rubble. But he could not tell Hogan that, having decided that the Colonel should not, at any point in the future, learn that the war was artificial. So after a pause he said:

"Sounds expensive. I don't think we'll be able to afford heavy weapons..."

"How about mortars, then?" suggested Blundell. "They're basically the portable artillery of the Infantry. They'll give us an indirect fire capability at a fraction of the cost of artillery."

Radley looked more enthusiastic. "What can they do?"

"Deliver high explosive, smoke or illumination bombs to a range of over four kilometres. They can be carried on men's backs and there's practically nothing to go wrong with them."

The Council Leader was impressed. "And how many would we need?"

"I think there's normally at least three barrels in a mortar line, isn't there, Colonel?"

"I think so. I'm not an infantryman, remember."

"So we buy three mortars," Radley declared, then changed his mind. 'Actually, we'll buy four..."

They continued discussing the requirements of the enlarged army until their conversation was interrupted by the sound of shouting outside. It was a man's voice, very loud and very aggressive, the slurred speech liberally adorned with profanities and threats. Fearing another attack on the Council Leader, Simms and the two officers drew their pistols while Hughes 42 cocked his rifle. Then Blundell stayed in the room to protect Radley while the others hurried out to investigate.

In the main ward outside, a violently struggling man was being restrained by Radley's two SCW bodyguards. A nurse sat on the floor, clutching her face and being tended to by colleagues as blood dripped between her fingers. Other medical staff - nurses, doctors and porters - formed a nervous semi-circular cordon around the man, who was unshaven and had vomit down the front of his jacket.

"Let go of me, you bastards!" he screamed at the SCW men, spitting on the floor. "Fucking bitches – give me some fucking morphine!"

At the sight of the armed posse emerging from Radley's private room, the man's eyes suddenly widened. He looked genuinely confused. "What the fuck's going on? What the fuck is this?"

"Be quiet or I'll have you shot!" declared a contemptuous voice. Gerald Radley appeared in the doorway of his room, dressed in his pyjamas and with a morphine drip in his arm. He regarded the man with an expression of extreme disdain, then turned to Angus Henderson. "Doctor, what's going on here?"

"Er, this patient is being abusive, sir," the surgeon replied, without averting his gaze from the rabid man. "He's demanding drugs which he can't have."

"Let me go!" gasped the man, pulling in vain at the tattooed forearm which one of the Special Council Workers had clamped around his throat.

Radley turned to the group of medical staff. "You carry on with your important duties, please. We'll deal with this gentleman. He won't cause any more trouble, I promise you. Right, let's get him into my room for a chat..."

The writhing man was bundled through the doorway into Radley's private room.

"What do you want us to do with him, sir?" asked one of the SWC bodyguards, who was struggling to restrain the man's legs.

Radley shrugged. "Why, beat him of course. Take him outside the building to somewhere quiet and beat him to within an inch of his life. Then beat him some more. I want it so he'll never walk or speak again, and will spend the rest of his miserable life eating and pissing through a tube. Mr Simms, go with them and make sure they do a thorough job. Any problems, kill him."

At this, the drug addict found new, almost superhuman strength induced by fear, anger and desperation.

"Shit, I don't think I can hold him!" shouted the bodyguard responsible for restraining the man's legs and lower body.

Simms reacted quickly. He slid his pistol back into its shoulder holster, unfolded his lock-knife and rushed towards the man's flailing feet. A moment later the drug addict was screaming in pain and resisting noticeably less. There was blood on the floor and on the blade of Simms's knife.

"Come on lads, let's get him downstairs," Simms told the Special Council Workers, and they hurried into the corridor towards the lift, dragging the hysterical man, whose legs now dangled limply and left a red trail behind them.

Radley was intrigued. "Did anyone see what he did? I couldn't see..."

"It looked like he cut his Achilles tendons," said Alan Hogan, appalled.

Radley was delighted. "Then it certainly looks like you chose the right man to be my aide, Alistair. He's utterly ruthless. That's a quality I admire." He walked unsteadily out into the corridor and waved to attract the attention of Dr Henderson. "Can you find me a wheelchair, please Doctor?"

"I really don't think you should be going anywhere yet, sir..."

"It's not for me. It's for that piece of filth. When my men have finished with him I want him patched up and put in a wheelchair with a sign round his neck warning people like him that that's what happens to abusive patients. Have a porter wheel him around the wards...make an example of him to deter others. Scum like that are a disease which must be eradicated. I simply will not tolerate aggressive behaviour towards medical staff...Oh – and we'll send a monthly bill to his next of kin in respect of 'ongoing treatment'..."

In the weeks following the declaration of hostilities, Wirral slowly but surely readied itself for a possible attack by the French. No-one, not even Radley himself, knew in what form this might come, so preparations were made to cover all eventualities. A high barbed-wire fence was constructed along the southern boundary with Cheshire, closing all roads into and out of Wirral except for the M53 motorway and the A540. Checkpoints were constructed where these two highways crossed the border, so that the SCW could search cars and check the identity documents of anyone entering or leaving the peninsular.

Building a fence was relatively easy, but when it came to formulating a credible defence plan to protect against French attack, the inescapable problem remained the conspicuous shortage of manpower. Being a peninsular, Wirral had a large coastline relative to its total area, and there were simply insufficient troops to man an effective number of defensive positions around the clock. This problem was exacerbated by the part-time status of the TA soldiers. Radley knew that he was at liberty to mobilise all troops to full-time service if he so desired, but Silverlock advised against this on grounds of cost, as it would swallow funds which were urgently needed for the recruitment of extra men and the purchase of equipment. In any case, it was unlikely that the enemy would be able to mount a significant offensive for at least a few months, in which case fully mobilised troops might be standing idle on full pay – an abhorrent notion to someone of Radley's character. At present, the majority of TA soldiers paid more to the Council in tax contributions from their civilian jobs than they received as pay for their military service, so Radley effectively got troops for free - a felicitous situation he was naturally eager to prolong. There would inevitably come a time when it would be necessary to mobilise all soldiers to full-time status, but for now Radley decided that they should remain part-timers for as long as possible.

Radley and Blundell had discussed the theoretical defence of the peninsular on numerous occasions in the past, but now that Hogan was involved and Wirral was officially at war it was time to draw-up a proper plan. This was achieved during a meeting attended by Radley, Hogan, McCarthy and the three majors who commanded the existing TA units: Blundell from the Infantry, Hubbard from the Engineers and Myers from the Logistics Corps. By this time the Council Leader was out of hospital, although his arm remained immobilised in a sling to protect his shoulder while it healed.

After much deliberation, a flexible defensive strategy was devised which would be refined and strengthened as more money and troops became available and the likelihood of a French attack increased. Initially, every member of the current TA force of around two hundred soldiers would report for duty two days each week, although the days would not necessarily be consecutive nor confined to weekends as had always been the case previously. Attendance would be compulsory, with unauthorised absence being treated as desertion, a very serious offence in wartime.

By staggering the days on which men reported for duty, the stop-gap system would ensure that at least seventy troops were available at any one time. Some of these would be based at the TA centres to guard the armouries, while others would be stationed at key defensive locations such as Hilbre Island or Perch Rock lighthouse. The remainder would conduct training exercises or work on building coastal defences - digging trenches, laying barbed wire, constructing pillboxes and so on. As a precautionary measure, the work parties would be organised into Quick Reaction Forces, or QRFs, which would be ready to deploy by vehicle to any part of the peninsular in an emergency. All other TA personnel - those who were not on duty - would continue working in their tax-paying civilian jobs as usual, but would be required to do so wearing army uniform and have all of their equipment, minus rifle, packed and close at hand. They would also need to have a switched-on mobile phone on their person and be contactable at all times, rather like lifeboat crew or retained fire-fighters. In the event of an attack, each part-time soldier would be sent a coded text message informing him of a secret location to which he was to report for duty and collect his weapon. The idea was that the QRFs would keep the enemy at bay long enough for the rest of the Army to get itself mobilised and effectively deployed.

"The key to successfully repelling a French attack at the moment, with our limited resources, will be early warning," Hogan declared. "The more notice we get that they're coming, the better able we'll be to defend ourselves. Now, we don't necessarily need soldiers as lookouts. There must be civilians we can use – existing Council staff, or even volunteers..."

"How about the bird-watchers?" suggested Major Myers. "They sit for hours along the coast, looking out to sea with powerful telescopes. I'd say they'd be ideal lookouts."

Runnaud nodded enthusiastically. "And if we're making the entire coastline a restricted area, like we discussed, we could give them a special pass or something as an incentive – you know, a favour for a favour...they can keep watching their curlews and godwits so long as they agree to keep us informed of anything unusual they see around our coastline."

"Good idea," McCarthy agreed. "I know for a fact that there are lots of old codgers who'd love to feel that they're making a contribution to the War Effort. In fact they'd probably pay for the priviledge..."

"That's assuming their eyesight's good enough to see anything," commented Hogan with a wry grin. "We don't want to put everyone on alert every time a fishing boat or Irish ferry sails by. Actually, do we have any boats available? We could do with some stationed offshore to act as early warning sentinels."

McCarthy chuckled. "I belong to a sailing club, and there are plenty of members who'd be only to happy to help. I'll ask the commodore to provide a list of people willing to take their boats out on a shift system to watch out for the French."

"What about the lifeboats?" asked Major Hubbard of the Engineers. "They'd make good fast patrol boats, wouldn't they?"

"They would," Blundell agreed. "With some troops on board armed with a GPMG and an anti-tank weapon they'd be a useful first line of defence. I'll speak to the lifeboat people and arrange for some of our lads to start training with them."

Radley nodded approvingly, enjoying the creative flow of the meeting, but Colonel Hogan looked troubled. "Unfortunately," he said solemnly, 'if we're actually going to take this war to the French, we're going to need much bigger boats – ships, in fact – and the men to crew them. As a soldier I hate to admit it, but it was the Navy that really made Britain great, and we haven't got one."

"Yes we have!" declared Major Hubbard excitedly. "Right here, under our noses – floating in a dock less than a mile from where we're sitting now! We've got something the French haven't got..."

Radley and the others stared at him blankly, until McCarthy finally realised what Hubbard was referring to.

"Of course!" the chief executive exclaimed. "The Historic Warships!"

Radley beamed with delight. "My God! The Historic Warships! Our very own private navy!"

"Actually, Gerald, if you want to use those ships you'd better be quick," McCarthy said soberly. "I seem to remember you authorised the conversion of the dockside warehouses into luxury flats about a month ago. The ships are due to be scrapped..."

The Historic Warships were a local tourist attraction, a museum comprising a shore-based German U-boat which had been raised from the ocean bed, and three floating British naval vessels: *HMS Plymouth*, a Type 12 frigate aboard which the Argentine surrender of South Georgia had been signed during the Falklands War; *HMS Onyx*, a diesel-powered submarine distinguished for its role in landing special forces on the islands during the same conflict; and *HMS Bronington*, a wooden-hulled minesweeper notable for being Prince Charles's first and only naval command back in the 1970s. The vessels had been moored by a disused warehouse in the East Float dock for years, immobile but maintained in reasonable condition by a team of dedicated volunteers whose tireless efforts with paintbrushes kept the insidious corrosion at bay. Restoring the ships to seaworthy condition would not be easy, but Radley was determined that Wirral's history of shipbuilding, refitting and repair would ensure that they would, in due course, be added to his inventory of military assets.

While Steven Saunders and his Procurement Executive team made urgent enquiries pursuant to getting the ships operational again, the Personnel department placed advertisements in the local press to recruit sailors and ex-sailors from the Royal and merchant navies. Anyone who had ever served on a Type 12 frigate or Ton class minesweeper was particularly in demand. These adverts supplemented those already published each week seeking ex-regular or TA soldiers, with the emphasis on infantrymen and especially those with specialist mortar or machine-gun training.

Standing on the edge of the cliffs by the bird-watching hide on Hilbre Island, Robert Taylor stared out to sea and savoured a pleasant moment. It was a beautiful summer's evening, warm and still and tranquil. To the west, the sun was setting behind the Welsh hills, bathing Wirral in a soft orange light. The tide was high, so the island was completely surrounded by water and cut off from the mainland, and small waves lapped gently against the sandstone below. Every so often the dog-like head of a seal would surface out of the brown, turbid water and stare at him curiously, making him smile. On evenings like this, even a hardened cynic would struggle to deny that the world was a wonderful place.

There was no doubt in Robert's mind that, of all the duties he could potentially have been allocated this weekend, the Hilbre observation post was definitely the most agreeable. During the day, a work party of Engineers had begun constructing a small pillbox on the rocky platform upon which he was currently standing, but they had run out of concrete and departed before the tide came in. That left Robert and his three C Company comrades as the island's only occupants, hopefully until about noon the following day, when water levels would recede sufficiently for men and vehicles to cross the sand flats from West Kirby. Unless anyone came out by boat, or during the night-time low tide, the four soldiers would have the island to themselves, and Robert would be ruler of his own mini-kingdom. It felt wonderful to be left alone, free from the contradictory instructions, frantic duties and general fuck-about-factor which usually dominated army life.

With no-one barking orders at him and no urgent tasks to perform, Robert made the most of the opportunity to relax and reflect upon his current situation and his life in general. Ironically, the war had given his existence a new sense of direction and purpose which had previously been lacking. Ten years ago, aged eighteen, Robert had nurtured dreams of achieving great things, of really *being someone*. He had positively throbbed with ambitious vitality, intellectual promise and creative energy, but his youthful optimism and exuberance had steadily waned as each successive year passed and he remained an insignificant nobody. Now, at twenty-eight, he was reluctantly resigning himself to the disappointing realisation that he would never be a movie idol, rock star or tennis champion. A life of anonymous, unfulfilled mediocrity had loomed depressingly ahead...Until, that was, war had been declared and he was transformed from Sad TA Bastard to one of 'The Few', the elite band of noble defenders upon whom the safety of the entire peninsular depended. Perhaps here, at last, was the yearned-for opportunity to achieve something honourable and memorable, a chance to elevate his existence above the mediocre and mundane, to undergo a rites-of-passage experience upon which he could look back in later years and be proud. In many respects, Robert Taylor suffered from the same cravings for greatness that afflicted Gerald Radley, although his altruistic nature set him apart from the Council Leader by dictating that his own achievements should not be at the expense of anyone else.

Over on the mainland there was a distant rumble as one of the Engineers' bulldozers pushed hardcore into a large hole excavated as the foundation for an octagonal pillbox, sited to command the sand flats between West Kirby and the three islands of Little Eye, Middle Eye and Hilbre. The sound shook Robert out of his introspective state and back to the job in hand. He reminded himself of his duties as guard commander on the island: to observe and monitor all shipping which approached nearer than the wind turbines, reporting to HQ any vessel which seemed to be acting suspiciously; to ensure the island was patrolled at least once every three hours; to maintain communications with the mainland through hourly radio checks; to supervise the digging of two shell scrapes at strategic locations, using sandbags if the soil proved too thin to achieve the correct depth; to provide anti-aircraft fire against enemy aircraft which came in range; and, lastly and most importantly, to defend the island in the unlikely event of a French invasion. Quite what sort of attack his four-man fireteam was supposed to repulse with a general purpose machine gun and two LAW94 missiles had not been explained. There was an additional, sixth, duty, given to him personally by Major Blundell, who was aware of Robert's talent for drawing and had asked him to produce a sketch map of the island showing as much detail as possible, and especially those features of military significance such as 'dead ground,' arcs of fire and potential amphibious landing sites.

Robert climbed the ladder which led up into the bird-watching hide, perched atop the sandstone walls of the derelict lifeboat station. Inside, the hide had been reinforced with sandbags, and a certain Private Wharton was sitting on a stool, peering out through the observation shutters past the heavy barrel of the GPMG. Unlike the flimsy and generally unsatisfactory Light Support Weapon (LSW) which had been in service with the TA infantry since the early Nineteen Nineties, the General Purpose Machine Gun (or 'Jimpy' as it was affectionately known to squaddies) was a real soldiers' weapon capable of delivering much greater firepower. Corporal Karl Brabander had once described it thus: "It's the Isembard Kingdom Brunel weapon – lots of big steel parts and some great big fuck-off rivets along the side for good measure!"

"How's it going?" Robert asked Wharton.

"Alright, Corporal."

Robert did not know Wharton well, as he was usually in Murphy's section, but he seemed a reasonable soldier, if a little inexperienced. Due to the overlapping shift system which had recently been introduced, in which each soldier served two days per week as dictated by a complex schedule, the usual composition of each section (known as the 'ORBAT') had been completely disrupted and Robert rarely found himself working with his familiar team. At present only he and Wharton were on duty on the island; the other two men were relaxing or sleeping in one of the bird-watchers' bunkhouses about a hundred metres away.

"Seen anything worth reporting?"

"No, Corporal. I was watching that ship there but it looks like it's heading into Liverpool. It's an Irish ferry isn't it?"

Robert squinted through his binoculars. "Looks like it. I'll report it anyway, just to let them know we're awake. Then I want you to keep watch here while I go for a wander around the island."

He contacted HQ on the radio to inform them of the vessel, then left the hide and walked around the perimeter of the island, enjoying the last vestiges of daylight and the sense of space, freshness and freedom. He tried using his mobile phone to call Linda, but got through to her answerphone and could not think of anything to say, so sent a text message instead. Shortly afterwards he was surprised when she phoned him back. Even more surprising was her tone of voice – she did not seem completely bored and uninspired when talking to him. They shared a reasonable conversation which, while not in the same league as the passionate exchanges of their early years together, was pleasant enough. She even expressed interest in what he had to say, and wanted to see him in the near future. When they had finished talking, Robert resumed his patrol and wondered what had caused the sudden transformation in Linda's attitude. Perhaps a potential suitor had turned out to be married, or gay, or psychotic, he thought cynically.

He made his way carefully along the sandstone cliff top on the west side of the island, peering over the edge as if expecting to see French commandos scaling the rock faces with daggers in their teeth. Despite having a magazine of live rounds loaded into his rifle, with another five in his webbing along with two hand-grenades, he had still not adjusted to the fact that there might be a genuine, hostile enemy out there who would try to kill him if given the chance. He wondered about the form in which an attack might come. Would it be a stealthy assault by special forces, who would slip unseen onto the island like seals and slaughter the defenders mercilessly with silenced guns and combat knives? Or an all-out invasion, employing shock tactics and maximum firepower to obliterate any token British resistance? He shuddered. If the French did mount an attack, the island was likely to be one of their initial key objectives. Suddenly, Robert felt very isolated and vulnerable, and the Hilbre observation post duty no longer seemed such a cushy number after all.

It was around this time that all civilian gun owners in the borough received a letter from the Council informing them that their weapons were required as part of the War Effort, and anyone failing to hand them in to the police, SCW or army immediately would be guilty of treason and sentenced to ten years' hard labour. With such draconian consequences for non-compliance, it was perhaps not surprising that the confiscation process was completed in two days. To soften the blow, each gun owner was given an official receipt and a form with which to apply for compensation in respect of firearms or shotguns which they had 'donated' to the cause of winning the war, although not a penny was ever paid nor a single gun returned to its rightful owner.

When the deadline for surrender of all legally owned guns had past, Gerald Radley visited C Company to examine the assorted weapons. There was an impressive array of longarms of different makes, models and calibres. After some discussion with Blundell and Hogan, it was decided that the .22 bolt-actions would go to the cadets for teaching basic marksmanship skills, while the centrefire rifles in calibres ranging from .222 to .375 would be given to the infantry for possible sniping use. That left the .22 semi-automatics, fullbore lever-action carbines and manifold shotguns, all of which would be issued to the Special Council Workers for their 'personal protection'.

"I'll need the Army to run some sort of weapons handling course for my Council Workers," Radley told Colonel Hogan. "Many of them will not have used guns before and I don't want any accidents...Oh, and I'll need something for myself of course..."

The guns had been laid out on the drill hall floor and Radley walked up and down the rows, looking at each weapon in turn with an expression of almost perverse excitement. It was not long before he selected an exquisite double-barrelled twelve-bore shotgun.

"This is the one for me," he declared, admiring the beautiful engraving and the hand-cut chequering of the polished walnut stock. "Of course, I'll need the butt cut down and the barrels sawn off..."

CHAPTER 11

Hesitant Combat

In these modern times of increasing European unity and cooperation, it is both disappointing and disturbing to see the publication in England of such a blatant anti-French book. What is it with the English and us French? Why do they hate us so?

Sophie Carsoux
La Citizen magazine

Mr Roberts replies:
I do not hate the French at all! The French are great. In contrast to us British – who try to please everyone but end up pleasing no-one, least of all ourselves – the French always do what is best for themselves. And I respect and admire them for it.

Despite the seemingly purposeful military activity which was evident across Wirral, it was the French who took the first meaningful action in the early stages of the artificial war. The British had made the mistake of delaying serious preparations until after war had been declared, whereas shrewd Monsieur Lebovic had initiated some long-term measures as soon as the idea of possible conflict had first been mooted by Gerald Radley. While Wirral's dithering Council were indulging in endless meetings, the French authorities had been discretely training four reserve soldiers as parachutists, and funding a local pilot to hone his night flying skills. Ironically, the money for this training was siphoned from an EU 'cultural enrichment' grant to which Britain had been the main contributor, a fact which Lebovic found highly amusing.

On a dark, cloudy night in July, a twin-engined aircraft with specially modified long-range fuel tanks took off from Normandy on a pre-arranged flight to Preston. During the trip, the plane deviated slightly from its authorised flight path, ostensibly due to navigational error caused by the co-pilot mistaking the River Dee for the Mersey. The detour took the aircraft over south Wirral and, as it flew low over the peninsular, four parachutists jumped out and floated silently down into a farmer's field, while the few British soldiers awake at the time stared obliviously out to sea.

The French infiltrators gathered in their parachutes, shouldered their heavy packs and hurriedly vacated the landing site, heading north-west in single file at a rapid pace to make the most of the few remaining hours of darkness. By the time the sun came up they had gone to ground amongst the birch trees and bracken of Thurstaston Common, and in the days that followed they laid low and furtively dug a pair of foxholes in a dense area of vegetation well away from any path. Each grave-like space was just large enough to accommodate two men lying side by side with their equipment at their feet, and was roofed over with branches overlaid with green plastic sheet and covered with soil, turf and live vegetation. Only a narrow entrance hole remained visible from outside, which could be concealed with tree bark and ferns. These claustrophobic cells became the soldiers' home during the weeks that followed. They spent the daylight hours resting in claustrophobic discomfort, and emerged at night like nocturnal wraiths to conduct ghostly reconnaissance patrols of the surrounding countryside and the British positions along the Dee estuary.

When Gerald Radley's shoulder had healed sufficiently for the sling and most of the dressings to be removed, he decided to visit the prison in the converted fort at New Brighton, in which thirty-four men convicted of serious crimes were incarcerated. During the fort's conversion to a jail, Radley had insisted that no money or effort be spent on providing comfort or luxury in any form. There were to be no televisions or pool tables, or even an exercise yard; this was to be an austere, dismal place in which the guilty suffered remorse, atoning for their sins in abject misery and squalid degradation. The design had been based on American prisons, with small cage-like cells arranged along both sides of a central corridor. To add a final touch of superfluous cruelty, the Council Leader had instructed that a stone trough be placed in the centre of the corridor, into which a droplet of water would fall every few seconds from a pipe in the ceiling. The sound echoed ceaselessly around the cold, bare walls day and night, relentlessly eroding the inmates' sanity as the water itself would slowly and imperceptibly erode the stone of the trough.

Word of Radley's visit must somehow have reached the prisoners because, as soon as he and his entourage stepped into the main corridor, the men leapt like rabid animals to the front of their cells and began to rattle the bars while repeating a chant which had obviously been pre-rehearsed:

'*Coun-ci-llor Ra-der-ley*

What a big fat prick is he!'

Radley flinched a little as he passed through the gauntlet of abuse, flanked by Simms, two Special Council Workers and a prison guard. Then he smiled, as if amused by a personal joke, and glanced briefly and defiantly at the prisoners.

"You won't be smiling if we get hold of you!" someone shouted.

The Council Leader ignored the remark and walked on, until he reached the last cell in the row. Its occupant was not standing at the bars, chanting. He was lying on the floor, his body partly covered by a blanket. The guard unlocked the heavy barred door and slid it open just far enough for Gerald Radley to step into the dank, gloomy cell. The man on the floor tilted his head slowly and peered up through eyelids so swollen from bruising that he could barely see. Outside, the chanting continued.

"Mr McMinn," Radley said impassively, "you have been a very bad man, shooting me like that..." He hesitated. For once, the Council Leader seemed lost for words. Then he turned to his two SCW henchmen. "Pick him up and take him outside."

The bodyguards heaved Jeffrey McMinn to his feet and draped his arms over their shoulders. He dangled like a rag doll between them, his legs trailing limply as he was dragged out into the corridor, in full view of the other prisoners. Radley looked around slowly, meeting the stares of the men behind the bars and smiling at them wickedly. The chanting died away until there was silence in the corridor, punctuated only by the infernal sound of dripping water.

"Thank you, ladies," the Council Leader said, as if addressing an audience from the Women's Institute. He pointed to Jeffrey McMinn. "This man tried to kill me, so I don't like him. Let me show you what I do to people I don't like."

He reached inside his leather trench coat, pulled out the sawn-off shotgun and pointed it at a patch of dried blood on McMinn's chest. It had been Radley's intention to subject his victim to a few final moments of terror, but McMinn's head lolled forward to such an extent that he could not even see the shotgun, let alone be intimidated by it. The Council Leader moved closer and pushed the twin barrels up under his captive's chin, then forcibly tilted his face up so that they were looking at each other. McMinn sighed and closed his eyes. After what he had been through since his capture he regarded death as a welcome release.

"Don't do it! Jesus – don't do it!" someone shouted from further down the row of cells. Radley shrugged, and pulled the trigger.

The sound of the twelve-bore discharging was like a thunderclap in the confined space, and the gun's recoil snatched it upwards so that the smoking barrels were pointing almost at the ceiling, leaving Radley's arm tingling painfully. McMinn's body jerked with the impact and the two Special Council Workers let him fall into a twisted heap which rapidly became surrounded by an expanding pool of dark crimson blood. The gunshot reverberations echoed from the hard walls of stone and concrete, then died away until once again there was silence.

Radley addressed his captive audience. "You can chant at me as much as you like, ladies, but let me tell you this: next week the people of Wirral vote on whether we should bring back the death penalty, and I suspect the outcome will almost certainly be that we should..." He smiled maliciously. "I doubt very much whether any of you will be alive by Christmas."

He walked slowly and smugly towards the exit, pausing in the doorway to look back at the cells.

"Sweet dreams, ladies."

That afternoon, the French made another bold offensive move which put the procrastinating English to shame. Radley had just returned to the executive suite in the town hall, and was awaiting the arrival of several officials for yet another meeting. He was describing to Terence McCarthy how he had dispensed lethal justice to the man who had shot him, and was wielding the sawn-off shotgun as a prop in his re-enactment of events.

"Is that thing loaded?" McCarthy asked nervously.

"Oh, I don't think so," Radley replied dismissively, annoyed at having his story interrupted. To placate the chief executive, he fumbled ineptly with the gun until it broke open. A single empty cartridge case was ejected across the room. McCarthy, who was an experienced clay-pigeon shooter, peered at the other chamber and was outraged.

"Jesus, Gerald – there's a live one in there! You could've blown my head off!"

"Calm down, Terence – the safety catch was on!"

"I don't give a damn! You never point a loaded gun at anyone... unless you want to kill them, that is. It's basic common sense!" He regained his composure. "Seriously, Gerald, if you're going to carry that thing around you should at least know how to handle it safely. And if it goes off under your coat it'll blow your hip off...or your balls." He looked suddenly startled and turned towards the window. "What the hell's going on?"

From outside the building came a series of noises in quick succession - the droning of an aircraft, people shouting, several loud *bangs!* and then, incredibly, the unmistakable rattle of a machine gun. The two men rushed towards the window but Simms, who was already looking out, waved them back in alarm.

"Get down, sir! Looks like we're under attack!"

They threw themselves onto the carpet as several bullets struck the masonry of the outside wall with a *thwack!* and one of the windows shattered. Then there was a loud detonation somewhere nearby which made the floor shake and toppled a slender statuette on Radley's desk. Simms drew his pistol – a ridiculously futile gesture – and hazarded a quick glance out of the window in time to see a twin-engined aircraft disappearing from view, flying north along the Mersey. Radley and McCarthy hurried through one of the adjoining rooms to a balcony overlooking the river, from where they caught a fleeting glimpse of the plane as it passed the prison fort at Perch Rock and headed out to sea.

"Why aren't the soldiers in the lighthouse firing at it?" Radley asked in frustration.

"They're probably as surprised as we are," McCarthy replied.

"And they don't want to shoot down a friendly plane by mistake," added Simms.

"Oh well, never mind." Strangely, the Council Leader was beaming with delight. "This is excellent. An air raid! Well I never... This is better than I'd imagined!"

The French air raid, it emerged, had caused only limited damage. Improvised incendiaries dropped out of the open door of the plane had set alight some vehicles in the town hall car park, while a stray bomb had destroyed the roof of a house nearby; the strafing had been a purely symbolic gesture intended to shock rather than inflict injuries. In total, Wirral suffered five casualties, none of them serious, but the psychological impact of the attack far outweighed the physical destruction it caused and was, ironically, a perverse Godsend for Gerald Radley: air raids added a whole new dimension to the war and its influence on everyday civilian life, ushering in a wealth of exciting possibilities. Air raids meant blackouts, wardens, anti-aircraft batteries, shelters dug in back gardens, the Spirit of the Blitz and, most importantly, civilian casualties which would help maintain public support for the war by giving ordinary people an ongoing reason to hate the French. Air raids united citizens in adversity and were inextricably linked to bygone British greatness.

Without delay, Radley sent a coded message to Monsieur Lebovic, his French counterpart in Normandy:

'*Congratulations on your wonderful air raid. May there be many more.*'

He received a confusing yet intriguing reply:

'*A pleasure. Two-nil to us, I think.*'

One morning, Robert Taylor arrived at his school to find a double yellow line painted along the entire length of the road outside the building, and new 'pay and display' ticket machines installed in the car park. He cursed the Council and its devious fund-raising tactics, and resolved to defy them by cycling to work the following day. In the meantime, however, he did not have sufficient money for the unexpected expense of parking at his own place of work. A large sign reassuringly informed him that this was not a problem, as the fee would simply be deducted automatically from his salary, with an additional fifty percent penalty surcharge levied in respect of 'administrative costs'.

"Bastards!" he exclaimed to himself. He was beginning to regret voting for Gerald Radley.

Feeling rather conspicuous in his army uniform, Robert entered the building to find a hand-written notice on a flip-chart in the foyer, which informed all staff that there was to be a meeting in the school hall at the end of the day. He sighed: no doubt Clive Hanrahan, the head teacher, would be announcing more cost-saving redundancies. Since the imposition of the SCW-enforced discipline system, which had admittedly transformed the standard of pupil behaviour in the school, the Council had reviewed staffing levels and decided that ten non-teaching posts should be axed. It was widely believed that members of the highly-paid Leadership Team would be the next casualties in the cost-cutting process, and after that ordinary classroom teachers would be vulnerable.

As it turned out, the meeting was not about job cuts, but rather the content of a new Council-produced document entitled '***Learning*** *to Win the War: A Strategy for Success*,' which outlined a complete overhaul of Wirral's secondary education system.

Clive Hanrahan stood impatiently at his lectern while the ICT technician fiddled around with a computer and projector, until eventually a huge image of the front page of the Council document shone onto the screen behind. The headteacher waited for the last stragglers to sit down and for the rumble of conversation to die away, then thanked everyone for attending and apologised for calling the meeting at such short notice. A Council stooge sat on the front row, silent and ostracised, recording proceedings with a camcorder so that the authorities could check that the school was embracing the latest reforms in a suitably positive manner.

"A copy of this document will shortly be issued to all Heads of Department," Hanrahan announced, referring to the image on the screen while holding up a copy of '***Learning*** *to Win the War*' for added emphasis. "I haven't had time to study it in great detail, but I wanted to speak to you about it now so you're all aware of its implications...and I don't think I'm exaggerating when I say that the proposed changes represent the most radical reforms I've ever encountered during my thirty years in education."

"Not more changes!" someone exclaimed.

Hanrahan nodded apologetically and glanced uneasily at the Council representative. "It's going to mean large scale restructuring and retraining, with all of us having to learn new skills. Basically the National Curriculum will be swept aside and replaced by a new curriculum devised by the Council, which is intended to increase the contribution made by our young people to society and the War Effort."

Martin Higgins leaned close to Robert and whispered subversively, "They're going to turn the school into a munitions factory..."

The hall was echoing to the sound of disgruntled murmurs and Hanrahan had to wait for silence before continuing.

"As I said, I haven't gone through this with a fine tooth-comb, but I have extracted the key points to be able to give you an idea of how the new curriculum will look."

He pressed a button on his remote control unit and the following information appeared on the screen:

Core Subjects to be Taught to all Pupils Under the Proposals Outlined in 'Learning to Win the War: A Strategy for Success'

English (emphasis on grammar and spelling)
Maths (emphasis on basic arithmetical skills)
Science (emphasis on experimental science relating to weapons and warfare)

Technology (emphasis on design, development and construction of military technology)
French (emphasis on written and conversational French)
Humanities (emphasis on geography of Wirral and Normandy, and the historical importance of war with the French)
Citizenship (emphasis on fostering patriotism, social respect and obedience, personal standards, teamwork, and an appreciation of a code of ethics based around 'The Four Cs' – Council, Church, Children, Community)
Community Service (emphasis on pupils performing tasks of benefit to society and the War Effort)
Martial Studies (emphasis on singing, marching, drill, slogan painting and other unifying activities)
Physical Education (emphasis on personal fitness and competitive team games)

There were gasps and exclamations of disbelief.

"Is this some sort of joke?" was one teacher's response.

"How does the Council propose to consult with schools over these rather, erm, drastic proposals?" enquired Malcolm Carlisle, who was head of the science department and a union representative.

Hanrahan fidgeted uncomfortably and tried desperately to avoid looking in the direction of the Council stooge with the camera. Eventually he said: "Er, these are not proposals. There will be no consultation process. The Council wants all schools in the Authority to be following this new curriculum by the end of the month..."

Robert was fuming when he returned home after the meeting. Preparing the lessons and teaching materials needed for such a massive re-design of the education system would be a huge and immensely time-consuming task, and he simply did not have any spare time available. It seemed that life was determined to break his spirit and that, no matter how hard he worked, there would always be some additional task demanding his attention and sapping his last vestiges of youthful exuberance.

Salvation arrived the following morning, in the unlikely form of an envelope bearing the Council franking stamp. Inside was a letter informing all members of the Territorial Army that, due to a perceived increase in the threat level, their services would henceforth be required full-time. Robert kissed the letter gratefully – in four lines of text it effectively absolved him from the onerous task of contributing to the Council's educational reforms. Suddenly he was no longer a school teacher, he was a full-time soldier.

In the aftermath of the French air raid, Radley and his military commanders came under great pressure to retaliate. Colonel Hogan was given the task, and assured by the Council that, within reason, finance would not be an issue: the overriding priority was to satisfy the public's demand for revenge, at almost any cost. In areas such as Tranmere, Birkenhead and the North End there was tangible frustration - even anger - at the apparent lack of offensive action from British forces since the start of the war. People felt that Wirral was taking punches without giving any in return, and they accused the Council of complacency. An increasing number of calls were being received by the town hall's answerphones demanding Gerald Radley's resignation and replacement by a more proactive and aggressive leader.

Hogan decided that a retaliatory air raid would be an appropriate response, and enquiries were duly made in respect of leasing an aircraft to carry out the attack. Unsurprisingly, no-one in the aviation world was willing to hire out a plane for use in a war, leaving the Council with no alternative but to buy one. After further deliberation it was decided that a helicopter would offer greater versatility than a fixed-wing aircraft, so Steven Saunders was tasked with procuring a suitable machine, while the Human Resources department made enquiries pursuant to recruiting a pilot to fly it.

Saunder's staff in the Procurement Executive used the Internet to locate an affordable second-hand Agusta A109 in reasonable condition and, conveniently, the dealer selling the helicopter recommended a freelance pilot by the name of Tom Brotherton. Brotherton was an ex-Fleet Air Arm veteran of the Falklands War, who had been working on the fringes of legality for the past twenty years, flying as a mercenary in assorted unsavoury hotspots around the world. He agreed immediately to fly for Wirral because, to him, Gerald Radley's war with the French seemed an intriguingly twee and civilized little adventure compared with what he was used to - with the added bonus of an enemy who was unlikely to dismember and burn him if he were shot down and captured.

Major Hubbard from the Engineers tasked a team of his more talented personnel with the job of producing improvised bombs to be dropped from the helicopter. In peacetime such a requirement would have taken years to meet and cost the taxpayer vast sums of money, but it was amazing how quickly and cheaply effective solutions to problems could be found by innovative people during a war. A mixture of incendiary and high explosive devices were produced, designed to detonate either on impact or on a time-delay fuse to cause maximum mayhem. The bombs were to be released from a specially designed rack of vertically stacked tubes fitted beneath the helicopter, with a primitive sighting system employing mirrors to enable the bombardier in the cockpit to see the ground directly below without having to lean out of the door. Initial trials on the Hoyle sandbank in the Dee estuary were promising, with most of the bombs landing on or very near to the old dinghy used as a target, and the majority detonating satisfactorily. However, these results were achieved with the helicopter stationary, hovering directly above the target, which concerned Brotherton.

"I'd be happier if we could improve the sighting system so we could release the ordnance without having to stop," he commented to Hogan after the trials. "We'd be a lot less vulnerable. I mean, are we expecting 'triple A' on this mission or not?"

"I can't answer that," Hogan replied. "I'm afraid all I can say is, you'll find out when you get there. As for the sighting system, we can refine it later on, but right now the priority is to take this war to the French. For this first mission you'll have to hover, but if you prefer you can always go in at night..."

"It's tempting, Colonel, but won't the Frogs have blacked-out Caen?"

"Apparently not. One of our people flew over it on a scheduled flight the other day, and said the whole place was lit up like a Christmas tree. And if they do turn the lights off you can always fire a few Schermully flares out of the cabin once you're over the city. We might even be able to get you some infra-red kit by the time you go..."

"Okay, let's go at night then. When?"

"As soon as the weather and moonstate are suitable. Hopefully that means the day after tomorrow."

Two days later, towards the end of the afternoon, the helicopter took off from Wirral on a supposedly routine flight to Hampshire. In due course the machine would be painted in a camouflage pattern of green, grey and black, but for this mission it remained largely white, with a crude layer of black spray paint hurriedly applied to the underside. No bombs were aboard. They were in the process of being transported by unmarked white van to the south coast, in an attempt to circumvent a potential problem arising from the helicopter's limited range. The Agusta could not fly directly from Wirral to Caen and back, so it would have to refuel during the mission. If it landed at an airfield on the south coast, it might be inspected by officials from HM Revenue and Customs, who would undoubtedly impound the aircraft if they found weapons onboard. So the plan was to refuel first and then, when it was dark, land in a field somewhere to rendezvous with the white van and load up the bombs, before flying south over the English Channel. During the rendezvous, all external lights on the helicopter would be blacked-out using thick tape, to prevent the machine being easily spotted from the ground.

Much to everyone's surprise – and Radley's delight – the audacious mission was a resounding success. At just after midnight, Brotherton took the helicopter over the city of Caen, which remained illuminated and oblivious, and dropped his bombs on the Hotel de Ville and the Headquarters of the Gendarmes. Both buildings caught fire and there was considerable peripheral damage to the surrounding area. A bomb containing plastic explosive, nails and bolts blew-in the window of a bar, blasting those inside with glass and shrapnel, while an incendiary turned an old man and his dog to skeletal ashes. Such was the level of surprise and confusion that no retaliatory shots were fired up at the helicopter as it hung in the night sky like an invisible angel of death. As soon as the last bomb had been released, Brotherton dipped the aircraft's nose and headed for home, leaving the good people of Caen reeling with shock and seething with rage. The attack reopened an old wound, for it had been the British who had ordered the destruction of the city by heavy bombers back in 1944, during the stalemate following the D-Day landings. To the Normans, the use of a helicopter at night seemed somehow despicable, dishonourable and ungentlemanly...It was like employing peasants with crude bows and arrows to massacre noble knights. How typical of the accursed English!

The war had entered a new phase. It was no longer a whimsical figment of Gerald Radley's warped imagination. People had started dying.

CHAPTER 12

For Those of You Who Do Not Know Me...

It's implausible, outrageous, ridiculous, irreverent, and it may well be shite - but I loved it!

Wayne Surferdude
Chillout Magazine

Mr Roberts replies:
Now, that's the kind of review I like!

Ironically, although he had undergone a transition to full-time soldier, Robert Taylor was still teaching. Within days of the complete mobilisation of Charlie Company, he and several other NCOs - including Brabander and Gorpe – were seconded as instructors to the Regimental Recruit Training Team, or RRTT. Their job was to help select and train the first batch of new recruits, who were urgently required in order to get the Army up to strength and ready for war on the scale envisaged by Gerald Radley. As predicted by Colonel Hogan, there was no shortage of applicants, and the steady stream of young men visiting the recruiting offices increased noticeably after the French air raid.

The recruit selection and training programme was run along similar lines to the system previously employed by the TA before war was declared. Interviews and a medical examination were followed by a selection weekend featuring fitness tests, written exams and, if these were successfully passed, issue of basic kit. The recruit - conspicuous by his lack of beret badge - then spent several weekends training with one of the regiment's three operational arms – Infantry, Engineers or Logistics Corps. This provided the potential soldier with a useful insight into army life, and also represented a valuable stage in the selection process; if serving soldiers were not impressed by the potential new recruit, he was simply given his marching orders before any more time or money was wasted on him. And there were plenty of other hopefuls queuing up to take his place...

Having survived the initial selection process, the would-be soldier then embarked upon a three-week basic training programme, along with around seventy other hopefuls who collectively formed a 'company' which, for administrative and competitive purposes, was divided into three platoons. It was to this twenty-one day training cadre which Robert was seconded, and he found himself appointed to Waterloo Platoon under the overall supervision of Sergeant Pete Collins, his own platoon sergeant from C Company. Usually, a lieutenant would have fulfilled this role, but the chronic shortage of personnel meant that many officers and NCOs were being assigned positions of responsibility one or two ranks above those which they actually held. Robert was pleased to be working with Collins, who was an easy-going and approachable man.

Robert's role in Waterloo Platoon was to deliver lessons from the military syllabus to all twenty-four recruits, and to act as mentor to the eight men of One Section. The other two sections were under the supervision of Gorpe and an engineer corporal called Stanton. Prior to the arrival of the first intake of recruits, Collins and his three corporals met with Mike Protheroe, the erstwhile C Company Permanent Staff Instructor who had been promoted to Regimental Sergeant-major, to decide how best to conduct the training. The meeting was held in a portacabin at the makeshift training barracks which had been established on the site of a former school near Noctorum. Several months previously, the Council had relocated the pupils before closing the school and selling the land to a developer for a hefty sum. Now, despite the fact that construction work had commenced on a new housing development, the Council had claimed the site back under emergency wartime legislation which authorised the seizure of any assets required to support the War Effort. The shells of some half-finished houses occupied part of the old playing field, but fortunately the school buildings themselves had not been demolished by the developers. Workmen were in the process of refurbishing the hall, classrooms, canteen and offices for military use, but until this work was complete, the training centre and recruit barracks would consist of a collection of stark portacabins, arranged in rows on the muddy grass around the old tarmac playground which now served as a drill square.

"As I see it," Collins said, "there are two basic approaches: we either hit them hard and bugger them about from the very start, or begin fairly relaxed and steadily increase the pressure. The first option might enable us to weed out unsuitable candidates early on, but on the other hand if we beast them too severely from day one we might lose people who would have made good soldiers if given half the chance."

"And remember, gents," the RSM interjected, "getting soldiers is what this is all about. At the end of the day, we need more men in the field. Lots more men – and quickly."

Sergeant Collins turned to Robert. "What do you think, Corporal Taylor? You're a teacher, after all."

"I think we need a balance," Robert replied. "There's got to be a certain amount of fuck-about-factor, because they'll get that anyway and we need to make sure we end up with people who are useful to us in the sections. But on the other hand, these guys have volunteered, so I reckon they deserve to be treated with some respect and consideration. We should be here to teach them, not piss them off and humiliate them."

"What's the current practice in the regulars?" Collins asked the RSM quickly, before Gorpe could contribute his no-doubt lengthy opinion.

"Firm but fair. The days of making them stand on the drill square stark bullock naked at three in the morning just to mess them about have gone. If they're going to be buggered around it should be for some justifiable reason...So by all means bug them out in the middle of the night, or beast them as a punishment if they're not working hard enough, but don't make them cut the grass with nail scissors or clean the heads with cotton buds just for the sake of it. That achieves nothing, other than to make them resentful, and then they won't work so well for you or learn as much."

So the 'firm but fair' principle was adopted as the training cadre's ethos, and when the first intake of apprehensive recruits arrived at the depot one Saturday morning in late July - many of them quivering with National Service horror stories told by their grandfathers - they were treated with greater respect and consideration than they had expected. Learning was the key aim of the course. As Collins pointed out, his team only had three weeks in which to train these men to a standard which would enable them to join their units as assets rather than liabilities. There was no time to waste on gratuitous degradation, and in any case, the men would be put under enough pressure by the demands of the course. However, the overriding need to impart knowledge and skills did not prevent the instructors from having some harmless fun at their students' expense.

"Every time you hear a whistle blast from any of us," Collins told the trainee soldiers as they stood at attention on the drill square, "it means there's incoming artillery fire and you must hit the deck immediately. Last man to take cover gets The Log."

'The Log' was, quite literally, a log – a large chunk of tree trunk with the bark removed, painted fluorescent yellow. Any recruit who messed up and was spotted by an NCO had to write his name on The Log and carry it with him wherever he went, guarding it like his rifle until some other unfortunate soldier committed a blunder and became its new custodian. Carrying The Log was a sign of incompetence, an inverse status symbol to be avoided at all costs.

Robert was careful not to blow his whistle too casually or indiscriminately. When the recruits were wearing their filthy combat clothing he would make them dive for cover anywhere, including thick mud or deep puddles. But if they were dressed smartly for drill practice or classroom lessons he refrained from blowing the whistle unless they were on surfaces such as tarmac which would not ruin their uniform; he had heard the grumbles of resentment in the canteen after Gorpe had made the entire platoon throw itself into the quagmire of the sports field as they returned from inspection parade, resplendent in their pressed uniforms and highly polished boots. With that single impetuous whistle blast, the gauche corporal had effectively sentenced twenty-four men to hours of unnecessary scrubbing, ironing and polishing, in addition to all of their other chores that night. As a consequence, many got virtually no sleep and were too tired to learn properly the following day.

And learning, after all, was what it was all about.

When the novelty value of the 'taking cover' game wore off, Collins proposed a variation on the theme to give it a new lease of life.

"Right, gents," he declared solemnly while addressing the platoon at morning muster, "today we're going to try something different. Every time you hear the dreaded whistle blast, you have to get yourself off the ground as quickly as possible. Last man to do so gets The Log."

Later that day, the sergeant blew his whistle as the men were marching in formation around the drill square, practising their "le-eft turn!" There was pandemonium as they scattered in every direction, competing to stake a claim on any structure strong enough to take their weight. Within seconds, men were balancing precariously on car tyres and litter bins, or hanging by their fingertips from portacabin window ledges. One of the funniest spectacles Robert witnessed during his brief secondment to the training team was that of two recruits clinging desperately to a tiny sapling - little more than a twig - which bent and twisted under their weight, miraculously without snapping.

The first few days of the training programme were based entirely in the classroom or school grounds. Each morning began with reveille at 5.30am, followed half an hour later by fitness training under the harsh supervision of Corporal Dwyer, the Physical Training Instructor, or PTI. After breakfast the men fell-in on the drill square for inspection by their hyper-critical NCOs before lessons commenced at 8.30. Recruits were taught weapon handling, drill, marksmanship principles, battlefield first aid, fieldcraft theory, map reading, nuclear, biological and chemical warfare skills, and essential facts about army life such as badges of rank and who to salute in different circumstances. One man dropped-out after day two of the training programme, but the remainder of the platoon struggled on, and gradually began to display a pleasing cohesion and *esprit de corps*.

Towards the end of the first week, the trainee soldiers were taken to the range complex on the north coast to fire live ammunition, first with .22 rimfire weapons and then with the standard issue SA80 automatic rifle. All skill-at-arms training at this stage was based on the SA80, although the Council was awaiting delivery of four hundred M16 rifles from America. The M16 had been the obvious choice for Wirral's new army, and Hogan had been pleasantly surprised when the US government had granted its export to the peninsular. Originally known as the Armalite, the rifle was a tried and tested design which had been used by American forces for forty years and was also favoured by the British SAS. It was a generally more robust and reliable weapon than the SA80 and, conveniently, the magazines for the two rifles were interchangeable and they could, in an emergency, fire the same ammunition.

Collins and his team maintained their ethos of 'firm but fair,' and only once during the first week were the recruits subjected to what could genuinely be considered gratuitous 'fuck-about-factor'.

This occurred on Thursday evening, when the instructors noticed a general lowering of standards and motivation amongst their students, with several men arriving late to parades, and lower-than-expected standards of uniform.

"They need a good kick up the arse," Collins told his NCOs. "And here's how we'll give it to them..."

The recruits had dinner at five o'clock, followed by an evening lesson on basic infantry tactics from Lieutenant Evans between six and seven-thirty. Half an hour of drill completed the scheduled training programme for the day, and the men retired wearily to their portacabins to iron their uniform, polish their boots and do homework tasks before finally collapsing into bed. Collins waited until eleven, when all the lights were out and the sound of blissful snoring drifted from the dormitories, then sent his corporals in like terriers to rouse the men from sleep and tell them to be outside in full uniform within five minutes. Dazed and dejected, the recruits formed up in sections on the drill square and were inspected ruthlessly by torchlight.

"Look at those boots – they're covered in shite!"

"There's half a fucking sheep on that beret!"

"Ever thought of using a razor?"

"You should take those trousers down to the Transport Museum so one of their trams can ride along the creases. One fucking crease – how many times do we have to tell you?"

After this harsh scrutiny the recruits were dismissed, but told to fall-in again three minutes later wearing their PT kit. They were then subjected to another inspection and judged on the basis of some ludicrously comical criteria including 'degree of sock symmetry' and 'straightness of shorts'. Someone muttered querulously, but would not own up to it, so the whole platoon did press-ups as punishment. Then they were allowed back to their dormitories. The instructors waited an hour before turfing them out of their beds once again to parade in full combats with helmet and webbing...The ordeal continued through the night. As the hours passed, the dress requirements became progressively more bizarre.

"Five minutes, gents," Collins said sternly, "then I want you back out here in boots, PT shorts and T-shirt, with your bergen and helmet..."

By three o'clock in the morning the recruits were swaying unsteadily in the dark wearing full nuclear, biological and chemical warfare kit from the waist up and PT shorts and trainers from the waist down. Collins decided to call it a day. The process had achieved its intended purpose of nipping complacency in the bud and making the recruits painfully aware of how harshly they could be treated if they did not perform as expected.

Standing in the darkness next to his disgraced section, Robert could not stop himself from grinning as he listened to Sergeant Collins' final admonitory speech of the night, which contained some of his favourite army clichés:

"Right, gents, you seriously need to start sorting your lives out. It's your own time that you're wasting now. How can you be expecting to be treated like professional soldiers when many of you are looking like a bag of shite, with gopping boots and minging berets? You're acting like a bunch of Muppets with your thumbs up your bums! Start switching on! At six o'clock – that's three hours from now – I want you out here in pressed combats, and you'd better be immaculate. Then I think a good hard tab might do you all some good...Get a grip and start impressing us, big-style, or what we've just done will be a nightly fixture."

At six o'clock in the morning, a subdued Waterloo Platoon paraded on the drill square, minus three of its number, who were standing outside the instructors' portacabin wearing civilian clothes and with their suitcases packed. Corporal Gorpe escorted them to the gate and they were banished - in shame but with considerable relief - back to civilian life.

"It's worse than prison," one of them muttered resentfully as they walked away. "At least in prison they leave you alone in your cell for a while. Here they bugger you around twenty-four hours a day."

The remaining recruits stood bleary-eyed on the drill square until called to attention by the duty student when Sergeant Collins appeared to conduct the obligatory inspection. Collins moved slowly along the ranks, scrutinising not only the standard of uniform but also the expression on every tired face, which would give a good indication of each man's suitability as a soldier. The borderline cases, who might fail at some later stage in the course, looked demoralised and sullen - even bitter. Other recruits, although clearly fatigued, had an air of humbled fortitude about them, and these men were likely to go on to make perfectly satisfactory soldiers. A few - those showing early promise as future NCOs or even officers – wore an expression of perceptible defiance, as if to say, "I can hack it. Do your worst. You won't break me."

Collins completed the inspection and addressed the whole platoon. "Right gents, remember what I said last night. *You* determine how *you* are treated, by the way in which *you* conduct yourselves... Now, the PTI will be here in five minutes to give you what he probably calls a challenging physical training session but I call a good beasting. You'll need your helmet, webbing and day sacks, with at least thirty pounds of weight in them – that's about fifteen kilos under the old metric system. I suggest you use the gravel from the drainage channels - shove it into plastic bags to make up the weight. We'll be weighing your kit at the start and finish, so don't go ditching stuff half way through unless you want to do the whole thing again with sixty pounds..."

The depleted platoon continued training with a reduced ORBAT and finally made it to the end of the first week. On Saturday the camp commandant, Captain Anderson from the Logistics Corps, decided to reward the surviving recruits with some free time, although they were not allowed out of camp. To compensate, a DVD projector and several crates of beer were brought into the barracks and a makeshift mess was set up in one of the newly refurbished classrooms. Most of the men were so tired that they spent their rest and recreation time sorting out their kit and sleeping, which left more alcohol for a minority of hardened beer monsters who were paralytic by the time they fell into bed, and suffered terribly for it the following morning.

During the second week of the course, less emphasis was placed on inspections, parades, PT and drill, as the training team focused on infantry fieldcraft. This involved practical lessons outside the barracks in areas such as Thurstaston Common or Bidston Hill. The recruits learned how to survive in the field - sleeping, eating and fighting from within the shelter of a two-man 'shell scrape' which they dug with their folding entrenching tools. They were taught patrolling techniques, moving in formation during day and night, and how to set up ambushes and observation posts. They also learned the basic skills involved in carrying out section-level attacks against small enemy positions such as trenches and bunkers.

On several occasions during the course, Colonel Hogan or Major Blundell arrived unannounced, to observe the training and get an impression of the quality of the recruits. Fortunately for Robert, these informal visits always seemed to coincide with his most successful lessons, and consequently the officers received a very favourable impression of him which was perhaps a little unjustified. In the Army, entire reputations could be built or destroyed on the basis of unrepresentative snapshots of an individual's performance, glimpsed fleetingly by senior staff. Mark Conrad, for example, was in reality an excellent soldier but had once, in the pre-independence Mercian battalion, been branded an insubordinate fool by the Regimental Sergeant-major as the result of a single careless comment. The RSM had criticised the state of Conrad's scruffy combat jacket during a marksmanship coaching course, whereupon the irreverent lance-corporal had jovially responded, "I've never seen a crease that would stop a bullet, sir!" The RSM had been distinctly unimpressed, and reported the incident to Major Blundell at C Company; three days later, Conrad was standing nervously outside the OC's office awaiting a disciplinary interview. Thereafter he had always been regarded unfavourably by the battalion's higher echelons, and no amount of good work on his part could ever restore his tarnished reputation.

One morning, in a fenced-off area of woodland near the disused observatories on Bidston Hill, Robert was taking a lesson on camouflage and concealment. All army lessons were supposed to start with the phrase, "For those of you that do not know me, my name is..," which made sense if the students were strangers but seemed a little ridiculous considering Robert had taught these recruits for over a week now.

"There are four main principles to think about when trying to achieve effective camouflage and concealment," he explained wisely. "It sometimes helps if you remember them as '*The Four Ss*': Shape; Shine; Shadow; and Silhouette. Any one of these can give away your position. Have a look at this handout..."

He passed around some sheets, photocopied from the official instructional pamphlet, which illustrated good and bad examples of personal camouflage and concealment. The trainees were given a few minutes to study the images and identify as many faults as possible. After discussing the salient points, Robert moved on to his favourite part of the lesson.

"It's important to realise that, with camouflage, you need to get a balance between too little and too much. Here we have a soldier who clearly hasn't put enough effort into his personal camouflage..."

From the undergrowth appeared one of the 'general duties' soldiers, or 'GD men', who assisted the training team in whatever capacity was required of them; GD men were often members of the 'Dole Patrol' and were sometimes referred to as 'general dogsbodies'. The soldier – a private from the Logistics Corps – had one streak of camouflage cream across his otherwise clean face, and a single token bracken frond stuck in his helmet. A torch with a red filter was clearly visible clipped to his webbing and was almost as conspicuous as the white handkerchief protruding from a breast pocket next to a shiny whistle.

"As you can see," Robert commented, "this soldier is easy to spot because he hasn't thought about the principles of camouflage. There's no base layer of cam cream on his face to get rid of the shine, and there aren't enough stripes on his face to break up the shape. Because of the lack of vegetation his outline is a familiar human silhouette which would be easily seen against most backgrounds...On the other hand, you can overdo personal camouflage..."

There was a rustling in the woods behind and a second GD man came into view like a walking bush, staggering under the weight of vegetation which he was carrying. For added comic effect a small tree had been uprooted and hooked onto his webbing so that its branches dragged along behind him.

"Now, you might think this is good camouflage," Robert continued, "because if he stood still he would be hard to spot. But he's got so much cam cream on his face it's a perfect Al Jolson silhouette, and with so much foliage hanging off him he can barely see or move, let alone fight. So, try to get a balance, like this guy."

A third GD man stood up only a few metres away and the recruits realised that he had been lying there unnoticed throughout the lesson, and were suitably impressed.

"This is good personal camouflage," Robert explained. "He's used a mixture of cam cream and spit to get a base layer which takes the shine off his face, and he's broken up the outline with just the right amount of dark streaks. There's enough vegetation on his helmet and webbing to make his silhouette irregular but he can still see, move and open his pouches. Most of the ferns and grass are on his back because in battle he's going to be lying down most of the time. So, overall, he's hard to see but most importantly he can still fight effectively, which is what it's all about. Any questions?"

No-one responded, and Robert noticed glazed expressions on the faces of several students. This was understandable, as it was a warm afternoon, they were all physically and mentally tired, and were probably reaching information saturation point. Practical activity was required if learning was to continue.

"Right, gents," he declared, "what I want you to do now is to go off into the woods in pairs and cam each other up. Then conceal yourselves as well as you can, but you must be in a firing position – we're not playing hide and seek here. I'll then come and find you. You've got ten minutes…Off you go."

He watched them hurry away into the woods and was about to relax against a tree when he noticed Sergeant Collins standing in the dappled shadows.

"Hello Sergeant, I didn't see you there. How long have you been lurking in the bushes?"

"Only a couple of minutes. Looks like it's going well."

"It's going fine. They're not a bad bunch, really. In fact, I reckon some of them will make much better soldiers than some of the Muppets we've got in Charlie Company at the moment."

"You're probably right. Anyway, what I wanted to see you about is that we've just been informed that the assault course is finished. The commandant wants us to take the platoon down there now and try it out."

A party of Engineers had been constructing an assault course on the reclaimed refuse tip at Bidston Moss. They had laboured industriously to complete the project before the start of the first recruit training cadre, but had been thwarted by a frustrating shortage of wooden beams and scaffolding poles. Bidston Moss covered a large area which included within its spiked perimeter fence a vegetated artificial 'hill' of topsoil-covered refuse, a small lake which had once been part of the docks, and an expanse of concrete, tarmac and rubble where the municipal incinerator had once stood. The Engineers had built the assault course on flat, grassy ground next to the lake, and incorporated several ponds and water-filled channels into the design.

Escorted by the PTI and training team NCOs wearing fluorescent jackets, the men of Waterloo Platoon speed-marched from Bidston Hill to the assault course in full kit. When they arrived, Robert was impressed by the sappers' handiwork. They had created a fearsome array of obstacles which would challenge even the fittest soldier. The platoon walked around the course with the PTI, who demonstrated the correct techniques for overcoming the most difficult or potentially dangerous structures. Then the recruits were let loose on the seemingly never-ending succession of walls, pits, ropes, tunnels, wire entanglements, beams and deviously utilised lorry tyres. As the men hauled themselves and each other over, under and through the obstacles, their instructors shouted encouragement or berated them as appropriate.

All was going well, until a white van with 'H&S Patrol' painted on the side pulled up on the hard-standing and parked fastidiously. A bespectacled man of about forty-five wearing a high-visibility waistcoat over his grey suit climbed out and looked disapprovingly at the activity on the assault course. He reached back into his van for a hard hat and clipboard, then strode purposefully to where Robert and Sergeant Collins were standing.

"Who's in charge here?" he asked brusquely.

Collins glanced at Robert and then stared suspiciously at the man. "I am. Who are you?"

"Donald Rawlings, Health and Safety." He proudly flaunted an identification badge bearing a photo which looked nothing like him and the impressive holographic logo of the Council.

"What's the problem, Mr Rawlings?" Collins asked impatiently.

Rawlings gestured at the assault course. "Am I right in thinking that this, er, facility, has just been constructed?"

"You are. We're the first ones to use it."

"In that case, does it have an appropriate inspection certificate stating that it has been built by qualified persons, and checked and tested, and confirmed as safe and suitable for use?" There was the faintest hint of a smug, victorious smile in Rawlings' expression: he *knew* that the structure was not covered by such a certificate, as he would have been the official who issued it.

Pete Collins was generally an easy-going man but now he sighed bitterly, put his hands in his pockets and stared defiantly at the horizon with narrowed eyes. "I don't know, that's not my problem, Mr Rawlings. My problem is that we're at war and we urgently need more troops, and they need to be trained and this assault course helps me train them."

"But it might be a death trap!"

"It looks alright to me. The Engineers do a good job."

Rawlings hesitated, then declared, "I'm afraid I cannot allow you to continue using this facility unless you can show me a valid inspection certificate. It'd be more than my job's worth..."

Collins subjected him to a look of utter contempt. "Excuse my French, Mr Rawlings, but I don't give a steaming pile of shit what you say. My orders – which come from my commanding officer, not you - are to train these soldiers. They will continue using this assault course until I'm instructed otherwise by an appropriate military authority. Now, if you'll excuse us..." He turned away and resumed watching the men on the obstacles.

Rawlings turned a deep puce. “You’ll regret this, sergeant…?”

“Collins.”

“Collins. Not only are you knowingly violating Council health and safety regulations by defying my instructions to stop using this facility, but I believe you also made your men run down here wearing boots. On roads! I trust that you will be happy to pay from your personal finances the compensation claims which these men might submit in twenty years’ time when they develop arthritis!”

He stormed back to his van, outraged by what he perceived as the sergeant’s impudent defiance and lack of respect. Rawlings was unaccustomed to such treatment. Usually he was king of his domain, able to shut down entire factories for days with a single signature.

“Let’s see what Mr Silverlock has to say about this,” he muttered as he drove hurriedly away. His powers *would* be enforced, of that the sergeant could be certain…the process would just take a little longer than usual.

Less than an hour later, Captain Anderson contacted Collins by mobile phone and ordered him to bring the platoon back to camp. Use of the assault course was suspended until further notice.

“It’s ridiculous,” Collins fumed as he and Robert queued for food in the canteen. “Don’t people like that realise that war is an inherently unsafe thing?”

“They get paid not to realise.” Robert commented. “Changing the subject, why is it that the cooks are always so stingy when ladling out cheap stuff like rice? Rice costs virtually nothing, but the way they begrudgingly spoon out a poxy little portion and then spread it over the plate to make it look more, you’d think we were depriving their own kids of food…”

Collins nodded. “And I bet they throw shed-loads away at the end of the day.”

From out of the corner of his eye, Robert noticed Gorpe making his way across the canteen towards them, no doubt intending to subject them to tedious anecdotes about the day’s training. Collins remained unaware of Gorpe’s approach, so Robert slapped him on the back, smiled sadistically, and said, “And now, sergeant, if you’ll excuse me, I’m off for a shit!”

The final week of the course culminated in an ‘advance-to-contact’ exercise intended to put into practice all of the skills which the recruits had learned, in a challenging and realistic scenario. Up until now the cadre’s three platoons – Waterloo, Agincourt and Talavera – had been either training independently or in friendly competition, each trying to beat the others in certain key skill areas. Agincourt had attained the highest aggregate score on personal weapons tests and had won the drill competition, while Waterloo had dominated the march and shoot and the infantry combat fitness test; Talavera had failed to win anything, although it had achieved some creditable second places. During the final exercise, all rivalries would be put aside as the platoons operated together as a company, advancing in tactical formation from the beach at Thurstaston until they were engaged by enemy positions, which they would attempt to attack and destroy.

By this stage in the course the recruits had achieved a reasonably high level of competence in many basic infantry skills. Certain fundamental codes of conduct, such as always having their weapon within arms reach, or unpacking the bare minimum of kit at any time in case of sudden attack, were now second nature to them. They still had a great deal to learn, but at least they had started to think like soldiers and operate as a cohesive unit. Several students had emerged as natural leaders and the instructors had identified them as candidates for a 'Potential NCO Course' planned in the near future. These individuals had been put in charge of sections for the final attack, to test their leadership abilities in a tactical situation.

During the penultimate day of the course, Waterloo Platoon dug-in in a wood near Thurstaston village and conducted reconnaissance patrols under the tutelage of their instructors. The patrols continued into the early hours of the following morning, when the exhausted men returned to the platoon harbour to receive their orders for the impending final attack. They were then finally allowed to get some sleep, albeit with an hour's sentry duty, or 'stag', thrown-in at some point during the night to make sure they did not get too comfortable.

At four o'clock in the morning the instructors quietly arose, packed their kit and crept stealthily to the edge of the wood for a pre-arranged rendezvous with some GD men, who stood waiting like conspirators with thunderflashes and rifles loaded with blanks. The two recruits on sentry duty at the time saw the instructors leave, and realised that the platoon was about to get 'bugged out.'

Sergeant Collins handed Robert a pack of mini-flares and gave Gorpe a larger 'Schermuly' illumination rocket. "Start setting these off as soon as the firing starts," he whispered. Corporal Stanton from the Engineers hooked his finger around the ring-pull of a smoke-grenade, while the GD men got ready with their thunderflashes. They all waited expectantly for Collins to give the command. It was at times like these that Robert was very glad to have completed his recruit training years ago.

"Now!" Collins hissed, and the wood erupted in an extravaganza of light and sound. Gorpe's Schermuly hissed up into the sky above the treetops and initiated with a 'pop', lighting up the landscape as the burning flare slowly descended on its parachute, spinning erratically as it fell and creating a crazy drunken world of lurching shadows beneath the latticework of branches. Robert's mini-flares shrieked overhead in burning streaks of green and red, while eerie white smoke spewed like supernatural fog from Stanton's smoke-grenades, and the GD men's thunderflashes exploded with enormous thuds that literally made the ground shake. The pyrotechnic display was accompanied by bursts of automatic gunfire and Sergeant Collins's screams of "Stand to! Stand to!"

In the shattered darkness, men who had been asleep only moments before were fumbling frantically as they tried to pack away their kit as quickly as possible without the aid of torchlight. Those who had foolishly removed their boots or combat jackets before getting into their sleeping bags struggled wretchedly with uncooperative laces or infuriatingly snagged sleeves, and realised with hindsight that they had made a mistake which they would not repeat.

Robert had been 'bugged-out' on numerous occasions and rated it as one of the most unpleasant aspects of training. An infantryman tended to enjoy precious little sleep at the best of times, so to be jolted out of it so harshly and abruptly was cruel indeed. Robert had learned from past experience that it was advisable to sleep fully clothed, with boots on, when 'in the field'. If he believed there was a particularly high likelihood of being bugged-out, he would even sleep in his helmet and trade comfort for convenience by leaving his foam roll-mat attached to his bergen, rather than lying on it. That way, if an attack did occur, all he had to do was stuff his sleeping bag and bivvi-bag into his bergen, clip on his webbing and pick up his rifle; from unconscious to combat-ready in less than a minute.

The instructors advanced into the wood, firing indiscriminately and casually tossing thunderflashes at their exhausted, abject students.

"Return fire, you Muppets!" shouted Gorpe into the flickering blackness, and a few hesitant shots were let off by a couple of the more alert recruits – probably the ones who had been on sentry duty at the time of the attack.

It took the platoon over four minutes to vacate the wood and assemble on the adjacent road, where they were instructed to fall-in and 'listen up'.

"Not good enough, gents," admonished Sergeant Collins. "If that had been for real, half of you would not have made it out alive and the rest would've left so much kit in there that the Forestry Commission could open an army surplus shop, while you could not have continued operating effectively as soldiers. Right, you've got five minutes non-tactical time to go back in there with your torches and find all the stuff you left behind...Oh, and has anyone lost this?" He held up a rifle which had been surreptitiously taken from a sleeping recruit during the night. The guilty man sheepishly shuffled over to reclaim it, realising dejectedly that his chances of winning the coveted 'best student' trophy at the end of the course were now well and truly dashed.

Shortly before dawn the platoon moved down to Thurstaston beach, proceeding tactically in a single file which stretched for almost three hundred metres and wormed its way through the early morning landscape like some giant elongated snake. Upon arriving at the strip of flotsam-strewn silt and sand, the men of one and two sections formed-up into an extended line along the base of the crumbling clay cliffs, while three section was positioned to the rear, in reserve: this was evidently going to be a 'two-up' attack. Further along the beach, Agincourt and Talavera platoons were also getting into formation, ready to advance. Lieutenant Evans was to be in overall command of the operation, acting as company commander, while the three sergeants took on the role of platoon commanders. This situation was hardly ideal, but it was not actually making unreasonable demands of the personnel concerned, as the Army required that each rank was capable of doing the job of the one immediately above. As Lieutenant Grudge often reminded Pete Collins, "A sergeant is only one bullet away from being a platoon commander."

Colonel Hogan arrived with Gerald Radley just as the company started its advance. The first enemy position, manned by two GD men, opened fire on Waterloo platoon in the vicinity of the Wirral Way, and the recruits' initial response was impressive. They returned fire in the general direction of the enemy, took cover, and tried to locate the position - exactly as they had been taught, to the delight of their instructors. Then the attack lost momentum. The GD men, hidden in a bunker made from turf slabs stacked around a shallow trench, continued firing blank rounds in abundance, but for a while none of the recruits could locate the enemy, and as a result they failed to return fire.

"Don't just lie there!" Collins shouted. "If you can't see them, move to a position where you can... *But stay in cover!* You don't stand up in a firefight!" He shook his head in frustration. "Jesus!"

"I can see them!" shouted Recruit Molloy from Robert's section. "They're over there!"

"Then give a target indication!" Robert urged. "Come on, Molloy, remember what we've taught you!"

"Er," floundered the recruit, desperately trying to extract the correct sequence of commands from the stultifying mass of information which he had struggled to assimilate during the preceding three weeks. In his memory, target indication had become inextricably tangled with section battle drills, fire control orders, preparation for battle, marksmanship principles and a whole host of other skills, featuring a baffling array of initials, mnemonics and acronyms.

Eventually, Molloy shook his head in defeat and Robert took over in order to restore the impetus of the attack. "Section!" he shouted, "Two hundred metres, quarter left of axis – tree in hedgerow. Two knuckles right of base of tree – enemy bunker! Rapid fire!"

While Robert's men put down covering fire on the enemy position, Gorpe moved his section round to the left in a flanking manoeuvre. In the process, several of his recruits ran in front of Robert's section and were screamed at.

"Not in front! Do you want to get shot by your own side? Go behind for Christ's sake!"

To the rear, Lieutenant Evans exchanged a despairing glance with Colonel Hogan, while Gerald Radley watched proceedings with great interest. These were the men who would make possible his war, and the social change which it would be used to justify.

The recruit who had been put in charge of Gorpe's section was a twenty-three year old builder called Sam Clarke, who had distinguished himself as a competent student during the course. He now led his men along a hedgerow which provided a covered approach towards the enemy bunker.

"Hedges won't stop bullets," advised Gorpe, "but the mound of earth along the bottom of it might. You'll have to crawl."

Squirming on their bellies through the coarse grass and nettles in the hot sunshine, the recruits grunted and panted and sweated and cursed. Gorpe was in his element here, as he walked self-importantly alongside his toiling disciples, deriving a sense of vicarious satisfaction from their exertion. As they neared the bunker, he instructed six men to take up positions along the base of the hedge to provide additional covering fire, while Clarke and a recruit called Baker continued crawling laboriously onward until they finally reached the line of trees and bushes concealling the enemy position, which lay a mere twenty metres away.

The GD men in the bunker were aware of the recruits' approach but deliberately ignored them, choosing to continue trading shots with Robert's section in the distance. Eventually, the two-man assault team reached the bunker and Baker, the grenadier, posted a fizzing thunderflash inside. As soon as it detonated he leaned over the edge of the turf parapet to spray the interior with fully automatic fire, but his SA80 jammed after the first few shots.

"Take over!" Gorpe urged Clarke, who dived past Baker and emptied an entire magazine at the cowering GD men, who obligingly pretended to be dead.

"Now bayonet them!"

Clarke let out a battle cry, leapt down into the bunker and went through the motions of bayoneting the enemy 'corpses'. His eyes were wide with aggression and exhilaration and his chest heaved from the physical demands of the assault.

"What now?" Gorpe asked him.

Clarke loaded a fresh magazine into his rifle. "Er, re-org?" he panted hesitantly.

"Go on then. Tell them the position's clear."

"Position clear! Re-org! Re-org!"

Through his binoculars, Colonel Hogan watched as the remainder of the assault section followed the route taken by Clarke to re-group around the captured bunker. "Well that didn't look too bad," he commented approvingly to Lieutenant Evans. "You've done a good job with these boys."

"I shouldn't speak too soon, sir," Evans replied with a grin.

No sooner had the platoon started moving beyond the captured position than it came under fire from two 'depth' positions further up the slope, and the whole laborious process had to be repeated. Clarke's section would now give covering fire while the other two sections would attack the bunkers from the flank, using a ditch to cover their approach. This time, however, Lieutenant Evans told his corporals to be less involved in directing proceedings, largely leaving the recruits to their own devices. Almost immediately, things began to go wrong.

Somehow, the trainees managed to manoeuvre themselves into a situation in which the assault group was advancing across open ground directly in front of their own fire support team, while the third section had strayed so far off to one side that they came under fire from Agincourt Platoon, which mistook them for enemy. The instructors intervened briefly to steer proceedings back on course, but shortly afterwards the recruit in charge of the lead section seemed to forget all of the tactical doctrine he had been taught, and led his men in a chaotic charge reminiscent of the First World War. In a real battle none of the attackers would have survived, but the GD men duly stopped firing and played dead as the apparently indestructible recruits swarmed onto their position. To consummate the debacle, the order to regroup was given too early, with the result that sixteen men were crowded together around the bunker as yet another depth position opened fire.

Lieutenant Evans sighed and shook his head despairingly. "It's a clusterfuck," he declared wryly. "That's great – a single mortar round could wipe out two-thirds of a platoon..."

"Don't forget," Colonel Hogan reminded him, "these men were civilians only a few weeks ago..."

"I think they've done splendidly," announced Gerald Radley, whose ignorance of infantry tactics prevented him from recognising the plethora of mistakes. He nodded enthusiastically. "Four more of these training courses and we've got our army..."

By the time the order 'End-ex" was given at the end of the afternoon to bring the glorified war-game to a close, the three platoons of the training company had attacked almost twenty enemy positions between them, and every man was physically and mentally exhausted. After unloading their weapons and giving the customary declaration that they had no blank rounds, empty cases or pyrotechnics in their possession, they lined up in a field near the *Dungeon* and were collectively addressed by Colonel Hogan. He congratulated them on passing the course and welcomed them into the ranks of the Regiment's trained soldiers, before presenting each man in turn with the coveted beret badge which was the symbol of graduation. A convoy of four-tonne trucks arrived to take them back to camp to clean weapons, wash, and pack away their kit before heading into Birkenhead for a celebratory Friday night piss-up with the instructors.

The following morning the men departed with a proud sense of achievement and, in most cases, a severe hangover. They were granted a weekend's leave before joining their allocated units on Monday morning. Robert and his colleagues started preparing for the next course, but were informed on Saturday afternoon that it would be postponed until further notice, due to computer failure in the Council-run recruitment and selection centre which had delayed the processing of the next batch of applications. He and his fellow instructors were told to return to their parent units on Monday, but to be prepared to resume their duties with training team at short notice.

Robert returned home to find Ben Spencer and the Mullah watching television in the living room, while Mark Conrad was in the small back garden, digging a large pit for an air-raid shelter. He was referring to a diagram in a mud-spattered Council pamphlet entitled *'Air Raids: What You Should Know and Do'*. Piles of corrugated iron and empty sandbags lay on what remained of the lawn.

"Aha, a mudfest," Robert remarked with a grin. "What *are* you making? Your very own private pillbox? You could sit in it and shoot the neighbours' cats with your air rifle!"

"Save it for the judge. You'll be begging to come in when the bombs start falling."

"Where did you get all this stuff?"

"Council depot. If you've got Army I.D. you get priviledged status and go to the front of the queue. *And* I got rolls of anti-blast tape for the windows, *and* a free bag of seed potatoes...the Council wants us all to become more self-sufficient. Apparently we can keep chickens now as well."

"How did you get it all home?"

"Spencer's bought a car."

Robert shook his head in disbelief. "How can he afford a car when he owes money to everyone in the entire world, including a pygmy in the Congo who lent him three shrunken heads? So what's he bought?"

"A Capri."

Robert chuckled. "Oh – I saw that as I was parking. I thought someone had dumped it. And what happened to the wheelie bin?"

"Someone torched it last week, along with about ten others in the road. We need to ask the Council for a new one. And you're going to have to pay for a parking permit like the one Spencer's just got. It costs ten quid. Anyway, enough of this idle banter, you malingering fop – grab that spade and give us a hand...Unless, that is, you'd rather go and sit with those sad losers in there doing bugger all."

Robert jumped down into the hole, picked up a spade, and quoted from one of his heroes, Captain Edmund Blackadder: "I think bugger all might be rather more fun..."

CHAPTER 13

A Busy Day for Gerald Radley

Mr Roberts's story was factually inaccurate before it was even published, as the Historic Warships tourist attraction in the East Float dock closed several years ago. He really should try to be more up to date if he's to appeal to local readers.

Cornelius Fitzpatrick
Merseyside Review

Mr Roberts replies:
You are right, the Historic Warships were closed to make way for luxury flats, but I decided to ignore that regrettable development in my story, partly because to do so suited the plot, but also because I wanted to commemorate the now defunct visitor attraction and what it represented. Anyway, the character of Wirral is changing so fast that I could never hope to keep pace with developments, as major landmarks such as Liscard Hall, Woodside Hotel, the church of Saints Peter and Paul and the Historic Warships disappear or are redeveloped, all in the name of progress or economy...

It was to be a busy day for Gerald Radley. His hectic schedule commenced at eight in the morning, when he arrived at the town hall for the customary daily meeting in which he and his coterie of selected 'inner circle' colleagues discussed significant developments, formulated policy and 'brainstormed' new ideas. Then, at nine, he was due to visit the dry docks at Cammel Laird with Terence McCarthy to see how refurbishment work was progressing on the warships *Plymouth* and *Bronington*. Following that engagement, he would proceed to the roll-on, roll-off ferry terminal with Steven Saunders from the Procurement Executive to inspect the first shipment of weapons and equipment which had just arrived at the docks. A quick lunch would follow, after which he would return to the town hall for a succession of brief interviews with each of the six Heads of Department, to discuss their contribution to the War Effort. The final engagement of the day would be a meeting of the entire Council cabinet, held in the conference suite.

Terence McCarthy and Duncan Silverlock arrived at the town hall well before their illustrious leader, in an attempt to remain an integral part of the decision-making process. The two men - who had been such key players during the early stages of Gerald Radley's radical new administration - had been feeling rather left out since the outbreak of war. Military matters were currently occupying the majority of the Council Leader's time and attention, with the result that Blundell and

Hogan had become his principal advisers and confidantes. Policy issues relating to the general running of the borough had slipped in priority and largely faded into the background, leaving the two subordinate members of the 'Senior Executive Committee' with progressively less and less to do. This did not concern McCarthy greatly, as Radley had put him in charge of organising the nascent navy, which was likely to assure him an instrumental role in the near future when the refurbished ships became operational. But Silverlock had not been given any vital new duties recently and was becoming increasingly paranoid that he might soon be surplus to requirements. Tasks which had been his responsibility during the regime's infancy, such as creating the SCW or restructuring the Council's budget, were now largely complete and only required minimal supervisory input from him to keep them ticking over. He yearned to be indispensable again, and had been frantically wracking his brains for new initiatives with which to impress his boss and restore his status as one of the 'Big Three.'

The Council Leader arrived with Simms and his two SCW bodyguards shortly after eight o'clock. He was in a foul mood.

"And I thought our social improvement programme was working!" he declared angrily. "Well, it seems that people are just as rude and ignorant as ever!"

"What's the matter?" enquired McCarthy in a soothing, avuncular voice, as if he were addressing a child who was having a tantrum.

"Bloody Low Quality People in white vans!" Radley spat. "We had one sitting right on our tail for practically the whole journey just now, with three uncouth types sitting in the front glaring aggressively at us. They carried on along the motorway when we pulled off, and they were making obscene gestures at me, and blowing their horn! The impudence!"

"Did you get the registration?" Silverlock asked quietly. "We could make life very difficult for them."

"No – that's the annoying thing. The bloody van was so filthy you couldn't read the number plates. That should be illegal!"

"It is."

"Well, from now on that law's going to be enforced. A thousand pound fine for unreadable number plates! And as for white bloody vans..."

Radley picked up the phone and dialed the extension for George Lawton at SCW Headquarters.

"Ah, George, good to talk to you... No worries. Look, George, I need a job doing... Tonight...Yes, I appreciate that...Anyway, I want your boys to go out and do some damage to white vans - you know, the big buggers. I want tyres slashed, mirrors and headlights smashed, bricks through windows, that sort of thing...No, no fires - I don't want them destroyed, I just want the people who drive them to be messed around like they mess everyone else around, you know, a taste of their own medicine...Dog shit on the seats? Hmmn, yes, I like the sound of that...Okay, erm, how about fifty? At least fifty vans, then, all over Wirral... Be discrete, obviously. Tell the lads there's a bonus in it for them if they do a good job. Oh - and I should have some more toys for them to get their hands on this afternoon. I'll be in touch...Sure. Thanks then, George...Goodbye."

He put the phone down with a satisfied sigh and turned to McCarthy and Silverlock. "It really is so much better now, don't you think? I mean, if you want something done, it gets done, straight away. Not like in the old days when you had to fart around for months putting every trivial little thing through endless committee meetings...Right, let's make a start. Anything important I need to know about today?"

McCarthy shook his head. "As far as I'm concerned there's nothing that we can't discuss on our way to the docks in a few minutes."

"There's something I'd like to discuss with you, Gerald," said Duncan Silverlock eagerly, producing some sheets of paper from his briefcase.

"Fire away, Duncan. But please try to make it quick - I've got a lot to do today."

"Of course...Right, erm, I was thinking the other night about what we can do to occupy all those people we're in the process of taking off benefits and putting back to work. Now, as we discussed, we can usefully employ teenage mothers or the elderly or disabled in local workshops doing various tasks to help the War Effort, but many young men aren't going to be happy sewing uniforms or assembling ammunition. So, we need something to occupy unskilled men in a manual capacity..."

Radley fidgeted a little impatiently. "And?"

"Indulge me. And the same evening I was thinking that we - the Council - should be making some kind of permanent mark on the landscape of Wirral, something that will last and endure, a physical reminder of what we - in particular you, Gerald - have tried to achieve. We should create some form of a grand structure, like the Pharaohs did in Egypt, as our legacy to future generations. And then I thought we could kill two birds with one stone. We can use our surplus people to build a modern day equivalent of the pyramids..."

Radley was genuinely intrigued. "So what are you actually suggesting, Duncan?"

"A canal. A canal in a huge cutting, running all the way along the southern boundary with Cheshire, connecting the Dee with the Mersey and effectively cutting off Wirral from the rest of the country, which is how it should be now that we're a self-governing region."

He passed Radley some computer-generated concept designs. "It would be a statement of our independence, and a great security asset. There would only be three access points into the borough from Cheshire in the south: the M53, the A41 and the A540, and they could be easily guarded. We could even have patrol boats moving up and down the canal. And with all the sandstone we dig out we can build a huge amphitheatre or arena in Birkenhead Park for Council rallies, or perhaps a massive new Council building. Here, I had someone in Regeneration produce these illustrations…I rather like the idea of a terraced stone pyramid, virtually impregnable…"

Radley studied the artist's impressions, which superimposed grand structures onto existing views of contemporary Birkenhead. He was simultaneously impressed, tempted and sceptical. "I like the idea, Duncan, but the costs would surely be prohibitive…"

"But that's the beauty of it! There'd be no labour costs – we're paying for these people to sit around on their arses at home at the moment, so why not pay them to dig a canal?"

Like most dictators, Radley had a weakness for grandiose projects, imposing edifices and hopelessly ambitious schemes. He took one last lingering look at the canal images before passing them back to Silverlock. "Okay, consider it provisionally approved by me, but we'll need to discuss it this afternoon in the cabinet meeting. There'll have to be a feasibility study and I'll need forecasts of costs and timescales, obviously."

"Of course."

Radley donned his heavy leather trench-coat, which had been custom made for him and featured protective Kevlar panels and a special internal holster sleeve to accommodate his sawn-off shotgun.

"Right, if that's all for the time being, we'll be off." He turned to Simms. "To the docks, my good man, and don't spare the horses!"

Robert Taylor was not required to report to the TA Centre until ten o'clock on Monday morning, so he decided to use the available time productively by endeavouring to resolve the problem of the burned wheelie bin, and applying for a parking permit, before he departed. He searched the telephone directory but, to his disbelief, could not find a suitable phone number for the Council. When he looked-up 'Council', the directory instructed him to 'See Local Authorities'; when he followed this advice and looked-up 'Local Authorities,' he was advised to 'See Councils'. Muttering with exasperation, he threw the directory at the wall and asked his housemate Simon if he could use his computer to access the Council website. Eventually, having used up half of his spare hour, he found a phone number for a division of the local authority called 'Streetscape', and dialled it eagerly. His call was answered by a recorded voice message.

"Thank you for calling Streetscape. In order to help us to help you, we need to know your name, address and Wirral citizen identity number. If you wish to proceed with this call, please provide these details after the tone. Calls may be recorded for training and monitoring purposes."

"But I'm supposed to be finding something out from *you!"* Robert exclaimed. "So how come suddenly *I'm* the one answering questions? Jesus Christ!" But he duly provided his details as required.

"Please repeat that information, speaking slowly and clearly," instructed the recorded voice.

"Just let me speak to a human being and there won't be a problem!" He was really angry now, but repeated his details in the slowest, clearest voice he could manage under the circumstances.

"All of our operators are busy. Please hold. Your call is important to us. You are number sixteen in a queue. This call is being charged at the standard local rate with an additional War Effort surcharge. Thank you for helping Wirral win the war."

The voice was replaced by classical music and Robert punched the wall in frustration. If, at that moment, he had been granted one wish, it would have been to inflict upon the creator of automated phone systems a particularly unpleasant demise. He calculated that, if only one caller was dealt with at a time, and each enquiry lasted a conservative five minutes, it would be around an hour and a half before he spoke to a human being who might or might not be able to help him. But he only had half an hour…

Five minutes later he was still number sixteen in the queue, so decided to hang up and redial the same number, in the hope of finding a quicker route through the system. To his despair, the recorded voice informed him that he was now number eighteen in the queue. He lost his temper.

"Well screw you then!" he shouted into the handset. "Screw all of you! All I want is to find out how to get a new sodding bin because some bastard's burned ours, but no, that's asking too much of you bunch of desk-polishing office-dwelling arsewipes who –"

Suddenly there was a clicking noise on the other end of the line and a woman's distraught voice could be heard. "What – oh, there's no need for that language, oh-oh-oh!" Her sobbing was replaced by another click, followed by a dialling tone and then a new recorded voice:

"The Council will not tolerate verbal abuse towards its staff. Your call has been recorded and may be used as evidence against you in court. This offence carries a three hundred pound fine or three year prison sentence. You may settle out of court and save yourself one hundred pounds if you pay voluntarily by credit or debit card in the next three working days. If payment is not received within this timescale you will receive a court summons by post. If found guilty you will be required to pay legal costs in addition to the fine."

The line went dead and Robert put the phone down with an expression of combined fury and disbelief. He was beginning to really despise the Council, and would have despised it even more had he known the truth about the burned bin, which had in fact been set alight by Special Council Workers masquerading as random arsonists in one of Duncan Silverlock's devious fund-raising schemes. Residents were charged two hundred pounds to replace bins which cost less than fifty pounds to produce, making the Council a tidy one hundred and fifty pounds profit per household, all of which went to fund the War Effort.

When Gerald Radley and Terence McCarthy arrived at the site of the former Cammel Laird shipyard they found *HMS Plymouth* and *HMS Bronington* in the drydocks, supported somewhat ignominiously by a latticework of timber props and struts while work proceeded to make them seaworthy. From under *Plymouth*'s grey bulk showered sprays of golden welding sparks, but none were visible around the minesweeper *Bronington*; her hull had been constructed from wood as protection against magnetic mines, which would have been attracted to steel. Large patches of red priming paint on both ships made them appear shabby and decrepit.

"Shall we go aboard?" suggested Terence McCarthy, gesturing at the gangway leading across the gaping void of the dock onto *Plymouth*'s deck.

They wandered around the frigate, talking to the workmen and inspecting their labours. Radley was impressed by the size of the vessel, which he had driven past on numerous occasions but never deigned to visit when it had been merely a humble tourist attraction.

"We really are very fortunate to have these," he declared smugly. "I bet the French haven't got anything like this. They'll be sick with envy..."

They descended a ladder onto the foredeck and walked beneath the barrels of the two 4.5 inch guns which protruded menacingly from their box-like turret.

"Can we get these working?" the Council Leader enquired hopefully.

McCarthy shook his head. "I don't think so. For a start, we haven't got any shells for them, and even if we could get hold of some we'd need to have the guns inspected to find out if they're safe to fire. Otherwise they might blow up or something..."

"Can't we pay someone to come and look at them? Surely anything's possible for the right sum..."

"That's the problem, they're so old we don't know who to approach. They were built by Vickers originally."

Radley looked disappointed. "Pity. Seems a shame to waste such an asset, and it kind of defeats the object of having warships if they haven't got guns that work."

"The Oerlikon cannons up there should work," McCarthy reassured him, pointing to the pair of slim black barrels protuding from each side of the superstructure. "We've got some people coming over from Sweden to advise us on how to restore them to working order, and to negotiate ammunition sales. The same applies to the Bofors gun on *Bronington* – we should be able to get that working as well. In fact, we've got another Bofors which used to be part of the dockside display next to the warships... A pair of forty millimeter guns and a pair of twenty millimeter ones – that's not to be scoffed at, Gerald. And we're also working at getting the anti-submarine mortar at the stern operational. Several school technology departments are working on the design of the bombs..."

Radley nodded approvingly. "How long before these ships can go to sea?"

"Hopefully about two weeks. Most of the work is done. They're just finishing off now."

"Excellent. And is your sailing club friend still prepared to be the skipper?"

"He is. In fact he can't wait to get back in command of a warship. Used to be a destroyer captain."

"What about the submarine?"

"*Onyx*? She's still over in the East Float. I honestly don't think we can do anything with her. Submarines are a completely different kettle of fish to surface ships – much more specialised and complicated."

"Pity..." Radley was disappointed. He loved the romantic idea of a submarine landing raiding parties or spies at night on the French coast, in a manner reminiscent of SOE operations during that supreme example of British greatness, the Second World War.

"Right," he declared with satisfaction, "I've seen enough. Good work, Terence, you've done well here. I look forward to seeing these proud vessels heading out into the Mersey to take the fight to the French. Now, let's go and see what Steven Saunders has to show us..."

Leaving the docks in his armoured BMW, Radley travelled the short distance to the roll-on, roll-off freight terminal where the head of procurement, Steven Saunders, was waiting to greet him at the entrance to one of the warehouses. The floor of the building was littered with a multitude of boxes and crates which were in the process of being opened, inspected and catalogued by a small army of Council minions. A considerable number of armed Special Council Workers were standing around on guard, looking menacing.

"Good to see you, Council Leader," Saunders said, extending an obsequious hand. He was a relative newcomer to the Radley clique and still felt a little uneasy about his status and responsibilities.

"Good morning, Steven. How's it going?"

"Fine, as far as I'm aware. We're still in the process of checking items on the delivery manifests against our records of orders placed... some of the clothing doesn't appear to have arrived, but all of the important items seem to be here."

"Show me."

"Of course. Follow me."

Saunders led Radley, McCarthy and Simms through piles of boxes containing items such as ration packs, sleeping bags and boots, to a heavily guarded corner of the warehouse where the newly arrived weapons had been stored. Radley, in the true tradition of psychotic megalomaniacs, had a fascination for military hardware, and his eyes lit up when he saw the crates of M16 rifles, General Purpose Machine Guns and the four 81mm mortars.

"Fantastic," he declared quietly. "Now we can really achieve something..."

"Where is all this stuff going now?" Saunders enquired. "A Council depot, or straight to the Army? I think we should shift it from here as soon as possible."

"Virtually all of it's going to the military," Radley informed him. "I'll tell Colonel Hogan to send some vehicles over to pick it up. But I want one mortar and six of the machine guns put aside for personal collection by George Lawton, who'll take them back to SCW headquarters..." He paused, then added furtively, "But I don't want anyone else to know about it, okay?"

When Robert Taylor, Mark Conrad and Ben Spencer reported for duty at C Company headquarters on Monday morning, they were promptly told to go home again.

"We need your spare items of uniform," the Company Quartermaster-Sergeant (CQMS) told them brusquely. "Combat jackets, trousers, boots, socks, shirts, lightweights – the lot. There's been forty new soldiers joined the regiment and they've taken all the reserve kit. No new guys can be recruited because there's not enough clothing for them. So we need your spares." He grinned cynically. "And you're not going to believe this, boys, but if the supply situation doesn't improve, the Council have decided you'll be 'hot uniforming'. That means sharing your clothes - giving everything except your underpants to someone of the same size when you go off duty. Needs must, lads!"

"Thank God we bought our own kit," Robert said to Conrad as they drove home. Both men had spent their own money on hooded SAS combat smocks and tropical-issue trousers, which were thinner and therefore dried quicker than the standard temperate-issue ones. "Presumably even the Council can't take stuff from us that we've paid for ourselves..."

"I'm beginning to think," Conrad replied cynically, "that they can do whatever they like. You know how it is: if you're not Council, you're little people."

After a hurried lunch at one of his favourite restaurants in Wallasey, Council Leader Radley returned to the town hall for a series of brief meetings with the directors of the six Council departments and their associated elected representatives. These meetings were ostensibly intended to discuss how each department could maximise its contribution to the War Effort, but they served another, more sinister purpose: by interviewing each director in isolation, and applying subtle psychological pressure in the form of generous praise and veiled threats, Radley hoped to stifle the emergence of unified dissent in the full cabinet meeting scheduled for later in the afternoon. "Divide and conquer – that's the key, Duncan," he had told Silverlock confidentially. Ideally he would have liked to have abolished the monthly gathering of the whole cabinet entirely, but to do so would have involved blatantly sweeping aside the last vestiges of democracy which served to lend respectable legitimacy to his regime, and were all that protected him from accusations of totalitarian dictatorship.

Despite his considerable power, Gerald Radley did not enjoy complete support or unchallenged authority. In fact, had the people of Wirral, or even the staff of the Council itself, been asked anonymously whether they were in favour of him or his policies, the majority would have replied nervously that they were not. But that was largely immaterial. The masses were no longer important to him. Radley's skill lay in ruthlessly eliminating his opponents and cultivating as his allies the principal figures of influence within the borough. He knew that, if he controlled the significant minority, the insignificant majority would fall onto line and be powerless to oppose him.

Of the six brief preliminary meetings that afternoon, the only one which caused him any concern was with the two representatives from the Regeneration Department: Brian Salter, the permanent non-elected Director, and Sylvia Fadden, the elected councillor with whom he worked closely. Neither could be counted as Radley's allies, which troubled him. Salter was a competent director, a little undynamic but highly experienced and shrewd in his particular field of expertise. There had been occasions in the past when he had voiced opposition to some of Radley's policy proposals on ethical grounds, although he had never expressed outright hostility. The Council Leader regarded him as an inconvenience rather than a serious threat to his authority, but nevertheless would have liked to have replaced him with a more malleable official, an unequivocal 'yes' man. This was easier said than done, partly because Salter was wilier than he appeared, but also because he enjoyed the protection of Sylvia Fadden.

Although he would never have admitted it, Radley was intimidated by Ms Fadden. She had been a councillor for years, and had even served as temporary leader for a short period between the unexpected resignation of one incumbent and the appointment of his successor. Sylvia Fadden was respected for her eloquence and outspoken honesty, which could make her a fearsome adversary during debates. In contrast with the slightly shabby Salter, whose dowdy suits somehow managed to look old-fashioned even when new, Ms Fadden always appeared stylish and sophisticated; today her outfit consisted of a chic business suit with skirt and knee-length boots. One of the reasons why Radley found her so hard to deal with was that she was a woman, and an attractive one at that. He lacked an effective personal strategy for responding to a mature, articulate yet undeniably sexy female who was not impressed by him and who treated him at times like a wayward schoolboy. They had known each other for almost twenty years, and during that time had enjoyed an ambivalent relationship, attacking each other in heated arguments one minute and almost flirting the next. Radley admired her as a worthy opponent, secretly lusted after her, and would never directly target her for elimination, yet at the same time he wished she would go away, thereby leaving Salter isolated and vulnerable. For a long time he had hoped that pregnancy and the subsequent demands of bringing up children might hamper her career aspirations, or even cause her to abandon them completely, but now that she had reached her mid-forties and remained unmarried, that possibility grew ever more unlikely with each passing month.

Brian Salter was the last director to be interviewed that afternoon, and he and Sylvia were ushered into Radley's office at three-thirty. They found themselves confronted by the intimidating triumvirate of Silverlock, McCarthy and the Council Leader himself, sitting in a row behind the large mahogany desk. Simms lurked discretely in a corner of the room with pen and paper, supposedly as minute-taker, although there was no real need for him to take notes as the entire meeting was being recorded by hidden cameras.

Sylvia looked amused. "You boys look like the three wise monkeys – you know, 'See no evil, Hear no evil, Speak no evil'..."

Radley granted her a token smile but otherwise ignored the remark. "Have a seat please, Sylvia – and Brian. Thanks for coming. Right, to business. The reason for these informal chats with all the department heads is to avoid wasting everyone's time discussing specific department-related matters during the cabinet meeting. What I really want to do is to establish what each department is doing, or could do, to maximize its contribution to winning this unpleasant war. So, can you tell me what the Regeneration Department has been doing?"

"To help win the war?" Salter asked hesitantly, a trace of defiance in his voice.

"Yes."

"Not a lot, to be honest, Gerald."

"May I ask why not?"

"Because it's not within this department's remit and no-one asked us. Until now. Oh – we did identify the land for military training areas, and we were involved in the appraisal stages of the Mockbeggar Wharf rifle range project. But apart from that, it's been business as usual, although obviously we've had to reschedule a few things and cancel a few others due to the spending cuts you announced to help fund the War Effort..."

"That was inevitable," said Silverlock defensively. "In wartime you have to prioritise and make sacrifices."

Sylvia Fadden looked distinctly unimpressed. "Wartime?" she scoffed. "So far, 'Wartime' for Wirral has consisted of a single plane dropping a few bottles of petrol on the town hall! Hardly the Blitz! Surely it's more important that we continue with our existing regeneration programme, rather than abandoning everything over some ridiculous disagreement with Normandy which will probably all be resolved in a few weeks' time...Honestly, Gerald, sometimes it's as if you think you're Winston Churchill or something!"

Radley regarded her with a condescending expression and spoke in a patronising voice. "I'm sorry to hear you're so *negative* about the situation, Sylvia. We're a team here, with a common purpose. Everyone else who has been in here this afternoon has been very positive about things. This is a challenging time for Wirral. I need team players who are proactive, committed, reliable and eager to make a contribution. It really disappoints me to hear you being so *negative*..."

'Negative' was a favourite buzz-word of Radley's. He used it frequently when trying to verbally manipulate subordinates by making them feel that their grievances were actually the result of a deficiency in their character, rather than the unreasonable or frankly ludicrous demands being placed on them. The Council Leader had learned this technique at a one day seminar entitled *Psychological Tools for Effective Management*, held at a Manchester hotel by a private consultancy firm which charged over six hundred pounds per delegate. The course had included an impressive dinner, a glossy booklet and a CD-Rom to accompany the 'powerpoint' presentation. Even Radley had to admit it was a complete rip-off, but that did not concern him: he was not paying, Wirral's tax payers were.

"Advise us, then, Gerald," Salter said dourly. "What do you want my department to do?"

Radley looked pleased. The dissidents were finally falling into line. "Well, for a start, Colonel Hogan and the Defence Committee want a survey of all the non-built up areas of Wirral. They want information and photos detailing every grid square outside the main towns so they can better plan military operations. They also want the location and condition of every pillbox dating from the Second World War marked on a map. Can you do that?"

Salter nodded, surprised at the nature of the request, which was actually a completely reasonable and appropriate task for his staff. "No problem. I've got an assistant planner who'll jump at the chance to get out of the office and do some survey work. Is that all?"

"Er, no, Duncan's got a proposal, although I think it might be best if he explained it."

"Actually, Brian's already aware of it, Gerald," Silverlock said hurriedly. "It was one of his staff who produced the images I showed you this morning."

"Oh, the canal thing..." Salter said.

"What canal thing?" asked Sylvia Fadden.

Silverlock produced his portfolio of artist's impressions and proudly showed her the illustrations. "I'm proposing we build a canal along the boundary with Cheshire. Labour would come predominantly from currently redundant members of the workforce and the whole scheme would be run by Regeneration. Technical Services have got too much on at the moment, although obviously they'd be closely involved. What do you think?"

"I think it's completely preposterous!" she scoffed. "A canal across

Wirral? What, an anal canal? It's like some mad scheme of a deranged Roman Emperor. You'll be telling me it'll be dug by hand by slaves in togas next…"

"That's the idea," said Radley without any trace of humour. "Once again you're being *negative*, Sylvia! And we haven't even finalised the details. What we really need at this stage is a feasibility study. Can your department at least produce that, Brian?"

"We can, provided you're happy for staff to be taken from other duties.'

"This takes priority…"

"In that case we can start right away – tomorrow, in fact."

Sylvia Fadden glanced at her colleague in disappointment, feeling that he had capitulated too readily and become a collaborator too willingly. In fact, Salter was as cynical of the whole situation as she was, but appreciated that it was in his own interest and that of his department to be as useful as possible to the new regime, for the time being at least. The fact that Radley was even considering such a ludicrous project as Silverlock's canal was an indication that his mental state was deteriorating, in which case his days in office might hopefully be numbered. Producing a feasibility study would be a convenient and morally uncontroversial way of keeping Regeneration Department staff occupied, and the lunatic appeased, until sanity was restored.

Radley smiled. "Then that's all sorted, good. Now – *mission statements.* As you know, mission statements are vital these days and I've issued each department with a revised one to reflect their wartime role. From now on yours will be: *To promote the regeneration of Wirral from both a military and civilian perspective, thereby improving the quality of life for residents, enhancing the attractiveness of the peninsular to visitors and investors, and enhancing our ability to win the war.*"

He passed a photocopied sheet bearing the new mission statement to both Salter and Fadden. "You'll need these in the cabinet meeting later. Read and inwardly digest, please."

"Oh Gerald, you spoil us!" declared Sylvia sarcastically.

It was comments like these which Radley found so hard to respond to, lacking as he did a sense of humour of any significance. McCarthy came to his rescue. "We try to, Sylvia - don't say we never give you anything!"

Radley looked at his watch – a gesture he performed unconsciously whenever he wanted to bring a particular situation to its close. "We're pushed for time, so I suggest we move next door and start the cabinet meeting straight away…"

They adjourned to the conference suite, where the other directors and councillors were congregating around the coffee urn and plates of biscuits. Radley's distrust of even his most senior officials caused him to insist that no-one arrive more than five minutes early, thereby denying them the opportunity for social interaction which might evolve into unified dissent by the time the meeting commenced. As soon as everyone was seated, the Council Leader drew the meeting to order.

"We'll make a start," he declared impatiently, glancing again at his watch. "Right, firstly, on behalf of the Senior Executive Committee - Duncan, Terence and myself - I'd like to thank you for coming and also for your participation in the preliminary meetings earlier this afternoon. I've already discussed most of the parochial matters with individual directors, so we should be able to keep this fairly short, especially as there are no items under Any Other Business."

Sylvia Fadden wrote discretely on her pad so that only Brian Salter could see: '*Were you asked if you had anything for AOB? I certainly wasn't!*'

"I'd like to say," Radley continued, "how encouraging I found those meetings earlier – everyone is working so hard and being so proactive and supportive in these difficult times. We really are working as a team and singing from the same hymn sheet. I think we should all share some of that collective positive energy, so I'd like each director to tell the rest of us what their department is doing at the moment and also what their new mission statement is. Jonathon – you can start."

"Thank you Gerald," said Jonathon Powell, who was head of Technical Services and one of Radley's staunchest allies. "We've been heavily involved in constructing coastal defences and other military facilities during the past couple of months, as well as providing advice and distributing materials for air raid protection. We've raised a lot of funds for the War Effort by carefully, er, how can I put it? – *managing* the planning system, and we've also assisted in the work being carried out on the Historic Warships. Oh – and there's the obvious contribution made by George Lawton, who works for us, and his Special Council Workers, in combating anti-social behaviour in the borough. So overall we've been pretty busy. And our new mission statement is: *To provide high quality technical services to the civilian and military authorities, thereby ensuring the efficient operation of the borough's infrastructure and enhancing its ability to win the war.*"

Radley nodded appreciatively. "Thank you, Jonathon – a very impressive contribution. Peter, can you go next please?"

One by one, the senior officials delivered their summaries with varying degrees of enthusiasm. Peter McMahon relished informing everyone of how Corporate Services had been responsible for producing new legislation and recruiting the large number of military and SCW personnel required by the borough, while simultaneously saving considerable sums by pruning surplus administrative posts within the Council. Tony Williams, who had taken over from Duncan Silverlock in Finance, bored them all with an overly detailed account of his department's devious means of generating additional income for the War Effort, which had included selling Council-owned land to developers at premium rates six months previously and then either sequestering it under the Emergency Powers Act or buying it back at a fraction of the purchase price now that the property market had slumped. The director of Adult Health and Social Care, Simon Beatty, explained with a hint of regret how 'social improvements' under the new regime had made possible huge savings in the provision of Council-funded care and benefits payments, while Margaret Daniels from Children and Young People extolled the virtues of the radical changes to the education system.

When all of the brief verbal reports had been delivered, Radley sat back in his chair with an expression of pompous satisfaction.

"Well, I think we should all congratulate ourselves. It really is a remarkable achievement. Wirral has undergone a miraculous transformation from an insignificant, largely unheard-of peninsular – always the poor relation to Liverpool – to an orderly independent region which has proved itself perfectly able to stand on its own two feet. We've got more people in work, fewer people on benefits and a far lower crime rate than at any time in the past fifty years. We've banned the hooded top…Anti-social behaviour has almost ceased – in fact, George was telling me the other day that gangs of youths are so scared of the SCW that they scatter in terror at the merest sight of a white van, even if it's not a Council one! Apparently the local plumbers and builders find it hilarious!

"Discipline, respect and consideration for others have been restored in schools and in the wider community. We've got our own army and navy, which men are queuing up to join. The apathy of benefit and compensation culture has been swept away, and pride restored to the Wirral…

"All of these improvements have been the result of your efforts and your positive attitudes, and I'm very aware of how much hard work you've all had to do to make it happen. The SEC has therefore decided that all of us here should be awarded a thirty percent pay rise with immediate effect. Pension benefits will be adjusted accordingly, and you'll be pleased to know that shrewd financial management in recent months has enabled us to pay significant extra sums into the fund. I'm sure you'll all appreciate this gesture in recognition of your outstanding performance, but just to keep things democratic we ought to put it to a vote. Does anyone oppose the motion?"

Sylvia Fadden almost raised her hand but thought better of it. She decided that the best way to oppose Radley was to avoid attracting attention to herself, thereby preserving his attitude of ambivalent tolerance towards her. If she antagonised him too blatantly, she had no doubt that he would somehow remove her from office… And only by remaining a key Council player could she hope to oppose him effectively in the future. She would bide her time, discretely collecting evidence of his impropriety and looking for fellow conspirators amongst her colleagues. Then at some point, perhaps, an opportunity might present itself…

Radley's gaze passed from face to face, looking for opposition to his pay and pension proposal, but finding none.

"Good, the motion is carried, then. Let's face it – we deserve it!

That night, the Special Council Workers went out in force on Radley's van-wrecking spree. After four hours of wanton vandalism they had achieved their target of fifty damaged vehicles, although next morning it emerged that two of the vans actually belonged to the Council.

At the same time as George Lawton's men were slashing tyres and smashing windows, the French mounted another air raid. It was considerably more ruthless than the first attack, featuring bombs of greater destructive power which were intended for the town hall but mostly fell on nearby houses. There were twenty-six casualties, including nine deaths.

The following day, supposedly in response to public demands for increased protection, the Council announced the creation of a number of anti-aircraft gun emplacements across Wirral. There were already three small army detachments positioned at strategic points along the north coast - on Hilbre Island and at the lighthouses at Leasowe and Fort Perch Rock. Each was armed with a machine gun intended primarily for defence against seaborne invasion, but equally capable of firing at aircraft. On Radley's instructions, an additional six anti-aircraft positions would be created to augment these existing defences. The locations would be the disused observatory on Bidston Hill, the trig point on the sandstone ridge above Thurstaston Common, the roof of Wallasey town hall, the SCW Headquarters in the old clock tower by the docks, and atop the two huge structures which housed the ventilation shafts for the Mersey tunnels. The height of the ventilation towers and their strategic location made them ideal platforms for gun emplacements, but their tops were exposed to the elements and represented a harsh environment for people to occupy for any length of time, especially in winter. To improve conditions for the machine-gun crews, the Council helicopter was used to transport large quantities of sandbags and two complete garden sheds to the top of each shaft. Heavy paving slabs were then placed over the floors of the sheds to prevent them being blown away in a gale, and a circular sandbag wall constructed to provide additional shelter from the wind as well as protection from enemy fire. On the top of the sandbags was fixed a curious arrangement of bent wire which looked odd but fulfilled a vital purpose: it was designed to control the traverse of the machine guns and make it impossible for them to fire in a direction which might result in bullets falling on Liverpool.

Radley was adamant that the new gun emplacements should be manned by Special Council Worker crews, against the wishes of Colonel Hogan.

"I'm just a simple soldier, Council Leader," the officer argued, "but it's traditionally the Artillery who provide AA defence. *Surely* it's an army responsibility..."

"I respect your opinion, Colonel, but don't you think it's a waste of trained soldiers to have them sitting around doing nothing for most of the time on top of the ventilation shafts? I mean, it's a simple job – all that these men have to do is fire a machine gun at a plane when told to do so. That's it. After all, they're really only there to keep the public happy – I certainly don't expect them to hit anything! The fact is, each position will need at least four men, and be able to remain operational twenty-four hours a day, so that's six times four...twenty-four men in total. Isn't that almost a whole platoon? Can you really afford to lose that many? The way I see it, we can replace twenty-four Special Council Workers a lot more easily than twenty-four trained soldiers."

Hogan was persuaded, although Radley had withheld the true motive behind his desire to have the AA guns operated by SCW personnel rather than soldiers. Like many tinpot autocrats before him, Radley both admired and distrusted the military. He depended upon them to make his dreams of a purifying war a reality, yet at the same time the existence of a large force of armed men, over whom he did not have complete control, made him distinctly uneasy. If there were to be machine guns positioned on strategic high points overlooking Birkenhead and the town hall itself, he wanted to be damned sure that the men operating them owed their allegiance to him, and to him alone.

CHAPTER 14

The Girl in Black

My advice to female readers is that this is clearly a man's book. We have to wait until Chapter 14 before encountering a female character of any significance - and she turns out to be a blatant male fantasy creation! Be warned, girls, unless you're into stories about macho men with guns, this is not a book for you.

Sandra Bithell
Health, Beauty and Holistic Therapy Magazine

Mr Roberts replies:
This is a man's world. But it wouldn't be nothing – nothing! – without a woman or a girl...

Gerald Radley was not unduly concerned by the French air raids - indeed, they were entirely consistent with his vision of Wirral at war - but he remained perplexed and troubled by Lebovic's 'two-nil' comment. It was some time before the British finally began to suspect that they had already been infiltrated.

The French reconnaissance team had done a remarkable job, although their methods were somewhat unorthodox. Unlike conventional military intelligence-gathering operations, which typically lasted a few days at most, the French unit was active in Wirral for several weeks – a truly epic achievement. During that time the men operated mainly at night, slipping out from Thurstaston Common in pairs or as a complete four-man team to covertly reconnoitre the British positions along the west coast. They also carried out some highly audacious work during daylight hours, demonstrating tremendous courage and temerity, and obtaining much valuable information in reward for their bold exploits. Each soldier had packed in his bergen a tracksuit and a pair of trainers, and every few days one or two of them would go for a jog. With so many young Wirral men out training in preparation for their army selection tests, the foreigners were inconspicuous, provided they kept their mouths shut. On several occasions they ran blatantly along the Wirral Way, making mental notes of the coastal defences and ending up at the supermarket at West Kirby, where they bought provisions. Their biggest worry was being engaged in conversation by local people, so the large, busy and impersonal supermarket was the only shop they dared visit.

Some of the information gathered by the patrol was relayed back to Caen by mobile phone, but more detailed intelligence such as maps and sketches was placed in envelopes and posted to an address in Holywell, just across the Dee estuary in neutral Wales, where two

French corporals masquerading as tourists were renting a holiday cottage. From Holywell the information was simply posted or e-mailed back to Normandy. Using Wirral's own postal service to smuggle out information was a stroke of genius, a cunningly parasitical technique which worked perfectly and exploited the great British tradition of not taking a security threat seriously until after the event. It was not until much later in the war that Radley's security staff finally identified and closed the loophole, by which time it was too late.

The first indication that French special forces were operating on the Wirral came one night when a farmer, out hunting foxes in fields near Frankby, noticed the shadowy figures of an army patrol moving along a hedgerow in the darkness. This was not the first time he had encountered troops on his land, and he called out to them in a friendly manner. On previous occasions, soldiers had always returned his greeting, and sometimes even stopped for a chat, but this particular patrol stopped abruptly, hesitated, and hurried away into the night as if guilty of some crime or trespass. The farmer thought their behaviour sufficiently strange to report the incident to the authorities the following morning. Captain Aldridge checked the patrol reports from every unit which had been 'in the field' the previous night and could not account for the mysterious men, although the farmer was of course informed that they were a team of elite troops training for special operations, and told to keep the sighting secret.

Immediately, a poster campaign was launched which instructed the public to report all sightings of troops on exercise. To avoid provoking panic or paranoia, the policy was justified on the grounds that it would sharpen the soldiers' patrolling skills and encourage the civilian population to be vigilant as part of the Council's '*Defence Begins at Home*' initiative.

Charlie Company was expanding. The first Combat Infantry Training Cadre, to which Robert had contributed as an instructor, had produced almost sixty new soldiers, the majority of whom were posted to C Company for 'continuation training'. However, their addition to the ranks had less impact than might have been expected, due to the fact that Seven and Nine platoons had always been severely under-manned and the new troops were largely swallowed-up in simply bringing these units up to strength, leaving only about thirty 'extra' men for the planned Alpha and Bravo companies.

Colonel Hogan was confident that the recruit selection and training programme would, in due course, provide sufficient men to fill the ranks of the battalion-sized force envisaged by Gerald Radley, but he remained concerned about huge deficiencies in the command structure. There was little point in recruiting hundreds of new private soldiers without sufficient officers and NCOs with the necessary experience to lead them. In recognition of this, Hogan and his 'head shed' of senior officers frantically sought ways of providing suitable training for those men with the potential to carry rank or, in the case of existing officers and NCOs, be promoted to higher grades. After some negotiation with the UK MoD, it was agreed that soldiers from Wirral would be allowed to attend courses run by the British Army at Sandhurst or Brecon, although they would be classed as 'foreign' students and charged at premium rates.

At the same time as this urgent training programme was taking place, the recruitment office was gratefully receiving applications from ex-British Army officers and NCOs who were currently living outside the borough but were prepared to fight for Wirral in return for citizenship. As the MoD in Whitehall refused to disclose any information from its military personnel records, Hogan's team were forced to use their own methods to validate the credentials of such applicants. If they passed basic fitness tests and could perform elementary skills such as stripping an SA80 rifle or demonstrating competent radio voice procedure, they were then subjected to a gruelling interview conducted by the RSM. This featured a long list of specially selected questions relating to specific details of the ex-soldier's military career including his training, periods of active service and the names of his commanding officers, as well as testing his response to various hypothetical scenarios appropriate to the rank he claimed to have held. The process exposed a number of charlatans, but most of the applicants proved to be genuine and the Wirral Regiment benefited from the addition to its ranks of a number of competent ex-regular and TA officers and NCOs, which contributed significantly to alleviating the leadership crisis.

As part of the urgent programme to build-up the combat strength of the infantry, men from the C Company nominal roll who had not attended training during the previous three months were contacted and told to report for duty immediately or risk being arrested for desertion. This was a perfectly justifiable procedure in wartime, but Hogan and Blundell were unsure as to whether they really wanted such reluctant soldiers in their new army.

"Perhaps we should just get their kit off them and tell them to go away," Blundell suggested. "If we're actually going to do some fighting, as seems likely, do we really want men who aren't keen?"

"I understand what you're saying, Alistair," Hogan replied, "but beggars can't be choosers. Let's get them back into their units and get them training again. I'm sure then some of them will prove to be useful soldiers. And those that turn out to be a waste of rations can then be booted out or relegated to a reserve list or something. But right now we need every man-jack we can get, in the field..."

Charlie Company underwent a restructuring process, with changes being made to the composition of the three platoons and their respective sections. Robert reluctantly said goodbye to Mark Conrad, who was given temporary promotion to full corporal and transferred against his will to Nine Platoon as a section commander.

Jason Farrell took over from him as second-in-command of Robert's section, but would hold only the notional rank of 'acting lance-corporal' until he passed a potential NCO course. Also transferred to 9 Platoon was Hughes 42, one of Robert's most experienced soldiers. To compensate for his section's losses, Robert received two newly-trained men fresh from the recruit training cadre which he had helped to run. Both were competent, but one of them - a twenty-nine year old ex-regular from Cardiff called Gwyn Thomas – had won the 'best student' award on the course and was rumoured to have served in the SAS. Robert was always wary of men who claimed to be ex-special forces, as they frequently turned out to be sad frauds who inhabited a fantasy world of imaginary military derring-do. And there were many of them about.

"It should be a diagnosed medical condition," he had once remarked to Mark Conrad. "*SAS-itis: 'A psychological state in which the patient suffers delusions of having been in the Special Air Service*'. You find them everywhere – on trains, at bus stops, in museums...fat old duffers with thick glasses who might once have done National Service or the TA or something, but were most likely car park attendants or shop security guards, who spend their lives boring people shitless with their made-up stories about when they were in the Regiment. In fact, if you added up all the people who say they were in the SAS it'd come to hundreds of thousands...Wouldn't be a very *special* air service then, would it? God, I hope I don't become like that..."

"I reckon Gorpe's a likely candidate," Conrad had commented wryly.

What convinced Robert that Thomas might genuinely have been an SAS trooper - apart from his conspicuous military competence and impressive fitness level - was that he refrained from discussing his background in any detail. All he would disclose was that he had 'done a few years in the Fusiliers' and had left following an injury. He proved to be a valuable addition to the section, although Robert remained disappointed at having lost Conrad and Hughes 42 while retaining the likes of Spencer and Harding, who were, quite frankly, liabilities.

In the absence of actual combat, the company occupied itself with tedious home defence duties and repetitive training exercises. Robert's section spent three days manning pillboxes along the western shore, then took part in a large-scale exercise which involved Eight Platoon acting as a quick reaction force to repel an invasion at New Brighton. The 'enemy' force – a motley band of cadets, engineers and drivers – was duly repulsed, and the civilian spectators went home reassured that they could sleep soundly at night, safe from the threat of French invasion. A day's leave passed in the blink of an eye and then the soldiers were back in the pillboxes, desperately bored as they stared out to sea and reported 'nothing seen' to headquarters every hour. It was September, and there was a faint chill in the air which heralded the arrival of autumn. The weather was overcast and grey, reflecting the soldiers' moods and denying them the pleasure of sunbathing during their monotonous vigil.

During one period of guard duty in the pillboxes, Robert learnt through the army grapevine (or rather, a logistics corps driver who seemed to know all the latest news) that the Council had managed to process the backlog of recruit applications and, at the same time, a long awaited consignment of uniforms, boots and equipment had finally arrived at the docks. The upshot of this was that the recruit training courses would almost certainly be restarting in the very near future. Robert fidgeted impatiently in his cold, draughty pillbox, hoping that, at any moment, he might be summoned to headquarters and told to resume his duties as an instructor. Anything was preferable to this soul-destroying inactivity.

Eventually, much to his relief, he was rescued from the tedium of home defence duties but, surprisingly, his new assignment did not involve training recruits.

"The Council are conducting a survey of the Wirral," Alistair Blundell informed him as he stood 'at ease' in the major's office. "Apparently they want to gather information about all the grid squares outside the built up areas – I'm not really sure why, but there it is. I think they said it was for 'military and strategic planning purposes', or something like that. Anyway, they're going to send someone out to survey these areas and take photos, but she'll need a military escort… You're probably not aware of this, Corporal Taylor, but we have reason to believe that there may be French agents operating on our soil even as we speak, although we don't have definite proof. So, we can't have some poor woman with a clipboard wandering around in the woods on her own, can we?"

"No, sir," Robert agreed, a little ridiculously.

"Now, I'd like you to accompany this lady while she does her survey work. I've picked you because I know you'll conduct yourself in an appropriate manner and be a good ambassador for the company. It should be an interesting change for you."

"Thank you, sir. How long will this survey take?"

"I think my answer to that has got to be 'as long as it takes'. I would have thought a good few days. Obviously if something drastic happens you'll be recalled immediately. In the meantime, enjoy the break. You are to collect this girl – Susan Fletcher is her name – tomorrow morning at nine hundred hours, at her home address. You'll need to sign-out your weapon, and I've arranged for you to use the hard-top Land Rover."

When Robert arrived at the address in Upton the following morning he found a young woman in her mid-twenties waiting for him outside a block of smart apartments. She was dressed entirely in black – black coat, trousers, boots, gloves – and Robert found her immediately attractive. She reminded him of a beautiful female Russian spy from a clichéd espionage movie. He had been expecting someone older and uglier, and was pleasantly surprised to find that Susan Fletcher was young and pretty…Usually life had a habit of not working out that way for him. They introduced themselves to each other, a little awkwardly, and then she climbed into the Land Rover so that they could discuss the day's work ahead.

"Where are we going to start?" Robert asked, trying desperately not to look at her in a way which might appear lecherous.

"I'll show you on the map," she replied. But when she unfolded the Ordnance Survey sheet it was upside-down, and the sight of the blank paper provoked an almost involuntary response from Robert.

"By God, it's a bland, featureless desert out there!" he blurted out, then realised with regret that he had probably made himself appear foolish.

"Aha – a *Blackadder* fan," she remarked approvingly, turning the map over with a smile that made him tingle all over. "So, Baldrick, what we need here is a cunning plan…"

They decided to start the survey work in the south of the peninsular and gradually work their way northwards, so Robert drove to where the borough bordered Cheshire, in the vicinity of Hooton and Raby. Susan's brief was to record the landscape character and general features of interest within every rural grid square. This was to be achieved by annotating an enlarged map of each area and taking video footage and still photos from different viewpoints. Robert's job, in addition to acting as her bodyguard, was to add to the survey map any information of specific military relevance, such as potential locations for platoon or company harbours, existing pillboxes dating from World War Two, areas of dead ground, and features which could be easily defended if the need arose. Radley had also requested that the survey identify a suitable location for an emergency Council headquarters for use in the unlikely event that that he had to abandon the town hall; the requirement was for a piece of isolated woodland in an area not frequented by the public, but which was accessible by a track of some kind.

For Robert it really was an extremely cushy assignment, and for once he had to acknowledge a sense of gratitude towards Major Blundell. All he had to do was drive around the Wirral with an attractive, intelligent girl, take a few pictures and make some notes, and enjoy a pub lunch at the Council's expense. And get paid for it! The war receded from his mind and he became carefree and lighthearted - immature, even. It was like being a student again. He and Susan got on well from the outset and discovered that they shared common interests and a similar outlook on life. What really catalysed their burgeoning relationship was a mutual predilection for certain television comedy classics from the nineteen seventies and eighties, including *Blackadder*, *Fawlty Towers* and *The Young Ones*.

Robert and Susan were too young to have seen these programmes when they were originally broadcast, but both had watched them as cult late-night viewing on repeat channels while students at university. So impressed was he by her that, when she asked the inevitable question, "So what made you join the TA?" he spared her his usual "I just wanted to kill people" response and instead replied: "I'm not sure, really. I guess I wanted a challenge, and the extra money came in handy at college..."

The day passed very quickly – too quickly, from his point of view – and at six o'clock he dropped her off at the flat which she shared with another girl from the Council, and drove home tingling with excitement and desire and lustful longing, his stomach feeling as if it were filled with helium gas. So intoxicating was her effect upon him that it was not until he was standing at his own front door, trying to find the key while staring vacantly at the crosses of bomb-blast protection tape which Conrad had stuck to the panes, that he suddenly realised he had forgotten to return the Land Rover or his rifle to the TA Centre.

What he had *not* forgotten – indeed, the one fact of which he was all too painfully aware – was that he still had a long-term girlfriend. That evening he went for a five-mile run in an attempt to purge, through physical exertion, the turmoil raging in his mind. When he returned he lay on his bed, staring at the ceiling, unable to stop thinking about the girl he had met that day. Then, as if to twist the dagger of guilt which was already stuck firmly in his heart, the phone rang downstairs and 'The Mullah' shouted up to inform him that it was Linda on the line. He simply could not speak to her at that moment. It would not have been fair - to either of them.

"Tell her I'm in the shower and I'll call her back," he said miserably, hating himself for lying, then went out for another run. By the time he got back it was too late to phone her, so he went to bed. Sleep eluded him and he fidgeted wretchedly for hours, his mind filled with thoughts of Susan Fletcher.

The following morning he collected her again and they continued with their survey work, like a pair of truanting schoolchildren out on a spree in a parental car borrowed without permission. Robert felt guilty about leaving his comrades to their tedious duties, and also about enjoying Susan's company so much when his loyalties should have been with Linda. But his sense of guilt did little to detract from the intense vivacity and exuberance he experienced as they proceeded from one grid square to the next, annotating maps and taking photos.

At midday they patronised a pub in the village of Thornton Hough, and were standing at the bar perusing the lunchtime menu when she suddenly asked, "So, Robert, do you have a girlfriend?"

He knew that this was a pivotal moment, a turning point at which his life could change direction for the better or, if the opportunity was not seized, trudge wearily along as before. After what seemed like an eternity, but was in fact only a few seconds, he replied:

"No. Do you? Have a boyfriend, I mean?"

"No..."

They looked at each other in awkward expectation.

"Are you ready to order?" interjected the jovial barman, and the moment was lost – not forever, but for the time being at least. Robert could have punched the man.

When, at the end of the day, the time came to part again outside her flat, there was a tangible sense of unfinished business between them. As she climbed out of the Land Rover and was about to walk away, he plucked up all of his courage, swallowed hard and asked: "Susan, do you want to go out for a drink or something tonight? If you've not got other plans, that is..."

She thought for a moment. "Yes, Robert, I would. What time?"

"How about eight o'clock? I'll come and pick you up."

"Okay, I'll see you then."

He drove to C Company headquarters to return the Land Rover and his weapon, then hurried home to wash, change and – most importantly – phone Linda. No matter how smitten he was with Susan, it was essential for his own piece of mind and the preservation of his personal code of ethics that he acted in an honourable way with regard to the girl who had been his partner for so long. When Linda answered the phone she sounded distant and unimpressed.

"Robert. How are you? I thought you were going to call me back yesterday..."

"I know, I'm sorry about that..." He sighed desperately and summoned all of his courage for the second time that day. "Look, Linda, I don't really know how to say this but...I don't want to be with you anymore."

With respectful, regretful firmness he told her that their relationship was over. She was surprisingly distraught, and begged him to reconsider the situation, to give her another chance. But he knew that, if the conversation was to have any purpose, he had to be uncompassionate – merciless, in fact.

"Linda, I have to go," he declared resolutely. "I'm sorry it's worked out like this. I'm sorry I've wasted your time, but I know we'll both be happier in the end. Let's face it, we haven't been happy for quite a while now, have we?"

"That's my fault," she sobbed. "I've been a real wet weekend. But I'll really try, if you'll only let me..."

'Yeah, and then as soon as you get a better offer you'll dump me, won't you?' he was tempted to reply. Instead he simply said: "Take care Linda, and thanks for all the good times. Goodbye." Then he put the phone down, and went downstairs to ask The Mullah to tell any callers that he had gone out.

Robert felt as if a huge weight had suddenly been lifted from his shoulders, and a massive python of self-doubt – which had been constricting his chest for years – released its grip and slithered away. At the same time, gravity weakened and he became a light, buoyant, airy being. To add a final touch of liberated delight to the occasion, his humble Vauxhall seemed like a low, sleek, high-performance sports car in comparison with the clumsy Land Rover he had become used to driving, and the short journey to collect Susan was a pleasure to be savoured and which he would remember for the rest of his life. Fortune had smiled upon him, and he felt like the luckiest man in the world.

They spent an enchanted three hours at the Irby Mill pub, engrossed in each other's company, and at closing time they held hands briefly as they walked to the car.

"Do you want to come back to mine?" she asked, then added with a chuckle, "For a coffee?"

Despite every instinct telling him to accept the offer, Robert was determined to create the impression of being a courteous and considerate suitor – of hopefully being different to the unscrupulous majority of men, who would take whatever they could without compunction or commitment. So he replied, "I'd love to, Susan, but maybe we shouldn't go too fast – I mean, we've only known each other since yesterday, although to use a cliché it seems like much longer... You are the most wonderful person I've ever met, and being with you is the most fantastic experience of my life so far, and I don't want to rush things and spoil it."

She smiled, put her hands on either side of his head, pulled his face to hers and kissed him tenderly. "You're a very special man, Robert Taylor."

When he saw her waiting for him outside her flat the next morning, a scintillating shudder of excitement rippled through his body and left him tingling all over. She was still dressed completely in black, but today was wearing a skirt instead of trousers. They kissed rather shyly, unsure as to who might be watching from behind the net-curtained windows of the flats.

"Where did we decide we'd start today?" Robert asked.

"Er, Brimstage wasn't it?"

"I think you're right. Brimstage it is!"

The Land Rover protested as he tried to wrestle it into gear. Like many TA vehicles, it was long past its prime and featured a number of idiosyncrasies which the driver had to learn to accommodate. One of these was a reluctance to willingly engage first gear, which forced Robert to experiment with various crunching and grinding gear-stick positions before he and Susan were finally on their way.

Leaving behind the suburban houses of Bebington, they drove along Lever's Causeway towards the village of Storeton. Suddenly, without explanation, Susan unclipped her seat belt and shrugged off her coat, despite the fact that it was cold in the cab.

"Are you okay?" he asked with surprise.

"I'm fine – just keep driving."

In his peripheral vision he could see her squirming awkwardly in her seat, as if in extreme discomfort, or performing some kind of contortionist trick. Then, with female deftness, she teased her bra - which was of course black - from the sleeve of her jumper, and draped it seductively over his arm. He almost swerved into the oncoming traffic.

Such was his combined confusion, excitement and embarrassment that all he managed to say in response was a pitiful, questioning "Err...?"

She smiled and said boisterously: "Come now, Robert, we're both *men of the world*...we make *two* cups of coffee in the morning..."

He relaxed a little and grinned, recognising the quote from *The Young Ones*. "But we don't drink both of them, do we?"

She turned to him, feigning sudden seriousness. "Now then, lover-boy, find us somewhere secluded..."

After passing through Storeton they proceeded downhill along a sunken country lane with hedgerows on either side. As the slope leveled out and they approached a fork in the road, Robert noticed an open gate leading into one of the fields, on the far side of which lay a dark, gloomy conifer plantation. The small wood seemed at once forbidding yet strangely familiar, and he realised that it had been the location of the C Company harbour during the night preceding the infamous Arrowe Park 'joyrider' mission. Somewhere under the branches of the pines would be the remains of the shell scrapes which the soldiers had dug and slept in for a few short hours.

Robert drove across the field and tucked the Land Rover in at the edge of the wood, in the shadow of the overhanging trees. He turned off the engine, climbed out, and stood for a while, scanning the surrounding area and listening for sounds of activity nearby. When he was satisfied that the location was as private as could reasonably be expected, he opened the door, leant inside the cab and said, "This looks okay, but we'd better be quick."

In a plastic sack on the back seat he found a musty camouflage net, which he draped over the Land Rover and then stretched into an irregular shape using fallen branches placed above and beneath. Meanwhile, Susan laid out his roll-mat and sleeping bag in the rear of the vehicle. He climbed in to join her.

"So how do you want to do this, then?" he asked, in a voice trembling with nervous excitement.

"Well, for a start, you can take off all that horrible army stuff..."

She insisted on undressing him completely but kept most of her own clothes on, which made him feel as if she were somehow taking advantage of him. Pushing him gently down onto the sleeping bag, she enveloped him in her coat and made love to him very tenderly and very beautifully. Afterwards they lay in a motionless embrace, their faces pressed cheek to cheek, lost in their separate thoughts. He pulled her against him, feeling her heartbeat against his chest, intoxicated by her soft feminine warmth. The war and everything associated with it faded into blissful insignificance.

"Can I stay here forever, please?" he asked childishly.

"Of course you can."

Suddenly – shockingly, from nowhere – there was a loud banging on the window, and raucous laughter could be heard outside the vehicle. Robert jerked upright, reaching for his rifle, but at the same moment Susan clamped herself around him in terror, effectively pinning him down and preventing him from wielding the weapon. A helmeted face, streaked with brown and green, peered in at the window, and for a horrifying moment Robert felt certain that he and his lover were both about to be killed - or worse. Then the face at the window grinned and spoke.

"So that's what you've been doing these last few days, Tayl, you lucky bastard."

It was Karl Brabander. The rest of his section were standing behind him in the gloom of the woods, shaking their heads. He smiled at Susan. "Hi, I'm Karl, I don't think we've met, have we?"

Robert relaxed, but his face turned red with embarrassment and indignation. He was simultaneously incredulous at being discovered yet relieved that it had not been by French special forces. He was also pleased that Susan had kept her clothes on, thereby limiting Brabander's voyeuristic satisfaction. After a few moments he said, "Brab, do us a favour and go away please. Oh – and would you mind keeping quiet about this?"

"I'll do my best." Brabander turned to his men. "Come on lads, let's give the man some privacy. Nice to meet you, er...?"

"Susan."

"Susan. Right, Tayl, I'll catch you later...Don't you worry about us, tabbing away all day, oh no - you enjoy yourself, mate..."

Three section vanished from view to continue their patrol, leaving a crestfallen Robert to apologise humbly to his lover. It was, of course, hopelessly naïve to think for a moment that Brabander or his men might keep the incident secret, and within days Robert had been nicknamed 'Corporal Trousers Down' because, as Brabander put it, "That's how we caught him." Robert was not unduly concerned about his new reputation; in the Army, men were congratulated, envied and admired for their sexual exploits. Carnal encounters with the opposite sex were almost considered a soldier's primary motivation in life, a fundamental prerogative to be grabbed at any opportunity. No-one in Charlie Company would ever be genuinely ridiculed for making love with a beautiful girl in a Land Rover while on duty, and Robert's nickname - unlike Gorpe's - was a term of endearment rather than derision, and carried considerable kudos.

The only person who Robert really did not want to find out about the incident was Major Blundell, who would have regarded it as a betrayal of trust and a violation of C Company honour. So when, at the end of the afternoon, the sheepish corporal signed his rifle back in at the armoury and returned the Land Rover keys and documentation to the company stores, he gave the OC's office a wide berth and scurried furtively back to his car.

That evening, Robert and Susan had dinner at a restaurant situated on the shoreline of the River Dee near Heswall, and when she invited him back to her flat after the meal he accepted the offer without hesitation. In contrast to the chaotic squalor of his all-male household, with its festering floor-covering of cigarette butts, food fragments and rancid crockery, Susan's apartment was the epitome of female cleanliness and order. Everything was neat and tidy and beautifully civilised, with delightful 'girly' touches such as vases of dried flowers, bowls of pot-pourri, tasteful pictures, and the occasional soft toy. Unlike his rented cesspit, which was essentially a temporary lodging for transitory students and layabouts, Susan's flat felt like a proper home – a place to relax and enjoy life, rather than simply survive.

She made hot chocolate in the spotless kitchen and they retired to her room. He had expected her to wear black nightclothes and was surprised when she changed into a long pink T-shirt which, at some point during the night, ended up in a heap on the floor. Robert slept little, so consumed with wonder was he by the magical beauty of his lover. It seemed incredible that, only three days before, he had been unaware of her existence, yet now she was the centre of his universe.

At seven o'clock the following morning he prised himself from her and reluctantly climbed out of bed. His army identification discs jingled as he slipped them over his head, and she looked up at him sleepily.

"What are those?" she asked.

"Dog-tags."

"What are they for?"

He hesitated. "They're to identify me if...if anything happens."

"Do you mean if you get killed?" She looked distraught. "Oh – Robert!"

With a shudder he climbed back into bed and held her again. It was only just beginning to dawn on him that perhaps this ridiculous, abstract war, which no-one had ever believed would ever amount to anything, might actually involve a genuine risk of injury or death. The dog-tags were usually kept in a filing cabinet at the TA centre, guarded by a possessive clerk who only issued them, with great reluctance, when the company deployed overseas, or if individual soldiers were engaged in especially hazardous duties which might potentially result in them being so badly mutilated as to be unrecognizable. Recently, all soldiers had been told to wear them the whole time, which implied that the perceived threat level had increased significantly. Suddenly, Robert experienced the same sense of foreboding which he had felt on Hilbre Island. Susan pulled him tightly to her breast, as if protecting him, and at that moment he wanted nothing more in life than to spend the duration of the war in this bed, with this girl, holding her close and never letting her go.

During the night, while Robert and Susan were enjoying the enchantment of sleeping together for the first time, the authorities received undeniable proof that a French unit was operating on Wirral soil. The warden at Thurstaston Country Park had set up an infra-red camera to film badgers in the vicinity of the Wirral Way, and next morning, when playing back the tape, he noticed the legs and lower bodies of what were clearly two soldiers, patrolling across the camera's field of view. He immediately phoned the emergency number displayed on one of the Council posters, and within an hour the recorded images were being viewed by Radley, Silverlock, Hogan and Blundell. The downward angle of the camera lens prevented it from capturing the mysterious soldiers' upper bodies, but Hogan and Blundell gasped when they saw the unmistakable outline of French FAMAS rifles, with their distinctive built-in carrying handles and bipods. Lebovic's two-nil comment was instantly explained, and once again it seemed that the enemy had shamed the British by demonstrating greater courage and initiative.

Radley was furious, and expressed his outrage to Hogan and Blundell. "Two immediate priorities, gentlemen, which are to take precedence over all else...One: find, capture or kill these Frogs. Two: get some of our boys on French soil immediately – I don't care what they do there, I just want them there... Oh – and three: start making preparations for a full-scale offensive operation against Normandy without further delay. We've fannied about for too long...I want an invasion within six weeks."

CHAPTER 15

Firefight on Thurstaston Common

Yet another war novel by someone who has never experienced war. This irksome author purports to know everything about combat, yet apparently he's never fired a gun in anger...If readers want to know about real combat, they need look no further than my latest book, 'Travels with a Kalashnikov.'

Hugh Hardnut
Mercenary Monthly

Mr Roberts replies:
I don't intend to purport anything! All I wanted to do was write a book, for the sense of satisfaction it would bring me and, hopefully, for the interest and enjoyment of whoever chose to read it.

Enthralled by the rapture of their blossoming relationship, Robert and Susan were desperate to prolong their survey assignment. They were painfully aware that completion of the task would see him returned to ordinary military duties and her back at her desk in the town hall - an inevitable situation, but one which they were eager to postpone for as long as possible.

"If we carry on at our current rate of progress," he told her, "I reckon we'll be finished in two or at most three days. Which doesn't seem that great to me. How can we spin this thing out?"

She looked at him with a devious expression which made him tingle. "How about looking for Council Leader Radley's headquarter locations? I reckon we can justify at least a day or two on that, and no-one will dare query it because it was at the request of the Great Man himself..."

He nodded approvingly. "I'll go with that."

So they spent the morning investigating areas of woodland in the vicinity of Storeton which appeared to meet Radley's criteria, approaching the task with meticulous and time-consuming attention to detail. But then, as they were walking happily along a track near the village of Landican, Robert's mobile phone rang like a harbinger of doom and he was instructed to return immediately to C Company. A depressing cloud passed across the beautiful sun which had been shining so pleasantly on his world for the past three days.

He dropped Susan off at her flat and drove in forlorn misery to the TA Centre, which was a hive of activity. All C Company personnel had been temporarily relieved of their coastal defence duties by engineer and transport soldiers, enabling the three platoons to muster at full strength in the crowded drill hall. Robert found Lieutenant Grudge and saluted. The officer returned the salute.

"Ah, Corporal Taylor, good to have you back after your, er, 'gruelling' assignment. Nice work if you can get it, by the sound of it... You've already got all of your personal kit signed-out haven't you?"

"Yes, sir. Oh - I haven't got a radio."

"Right, then get one from the stores, find your section and make sure it's sorted out and ready for orders at twelve hundred hours."

Ten minutes later the three platoons, in full kit, were seated in rows on the drill hall floor, facing a hurriedly erected screen onto which a digital projector shone an aerial photograph of Thurstaston Common. Lieutenant-colonel Hogan and Major Blundell stood next to the screen, and on a chair to one side sat Gerald Radley, watching proceedings like a spectating hawk.

Hogan stepped forward with his hands on his hips, and the background murmur of conversation died away.

"Good afternoon Charlie Company," he began. "I'll keep this short, as you'll be receiving detailed orders from your platoon commanders directly after this briefing...Right - to business." He pointed a laser pen at the image of Thurstaston Common and waved the red beam over it.

"Ground. The woods and heathland of Royden Park and Thurstaston Common. Most of you will be familiar with this terrain from exercises we've conducted there, and needless to say it's not an easy area to work in. Woodland of varying density, large areas of bracken and heather, sandstone outcrops and marshy pools, all leading up to the sandstone ridge of Thurstaston Hill.

"Situation. Friendly forces: none. The nearest other 'friendly' units are the B Company troops manning the defences along the Dee shoreline, so you can assume there are no other friendly forces in the Thurstaston Common area. However, there are likely to be civilians in the area, although we've asked the warden to close the car parks and clear as many people out as possible before we arrive. Now, the important bit. Enemy forces: intelligence indicates there are French special forces operating as two or possibly four-man reconnaissance patrols in this area. We don't know how many of these units are active in Wirral at the moment – there may be just one, there may be several. They are dressed in French DPM style clothing and are armed with FAMAS automatic weapons.

"Mission. The Company will conduct cordon and search operations in the area of Royden Park and Thurstaston Common in order to find and destroy enemy reconnaissance units believed to be operating from there. I say again, the Company will conduct cordon and search operations in the area of Royden Park and Thurstaston Common in order to find and destroy enemy reconnaissance units believed to be operating from there.

"Execution. After the preparation phase, which must be completed asap, platoons will travel to the search area by troop carrying vehicle. Eight and Nine platoons will de-bus at the edge of Royden Park and advance through the area in extended line, like a sweep net. The plan is that they will flush-out the infiltrators and kill or capture them, or else drive them towards Seven Platoon, which will be positioned along the sandstone ridge on the western edge of the common, here-." He pointed with the laser. "Seven Platoon will be deployed in a line consisting of a series of two-man 'stops', strategically positioned to spot and engage any enemy who try to break-through. There will also be vehicles continually patrolling the roads around the area as backup Quick Reaction Forces, in case any infiltrators manage to slip through the net.

"During the sweep of the area, Eight Platoon will be on the left and Nine Platoon on the right. The axis of advance will be a magnetic bearing of 3200 mils, which obviously is due south. Major Blundell and Company HQ will be located between the two platoons, I will be with Seven Platoon on the ridge. Good communications at all levels will be vital here, gentlemen. If comms are below par, then the whole advance will go pear-shaped and, at best, we'll have wasted our time and possibly alerted the French that we know they're there. At worst we'll end up with blue-on-blue contacts and friendly fire casualties. There's to be no unauthorised movement and it's essential that you confirm targets and follow standard rules of engagement before opening fire. Think before you shoot - before you kill your mate by accident. And at the end of the operation, whatever the outcome, it's vital that Eight and Nine platoons stop short of the ridge and no-one goes up onto the top until they get the all-clear from me personally."

The Colonel paused for a moment to check his notes. It had been several years since he had briefed a large body of men for a real operation, and even before his retirement from the Regulars the orders he issued related to artillery operations rather than infantry ones. He was not particularly satisfied with his own performance, but looking around the drill hall he saw men nodding thoughtfully and NCOs taking notes, which indicated that he was not doing too badly. His gaze caught Gerald Radley's eye for a moment and he realised that he had neglected to mention a crucial detail – probably because he disapproved of it so strongly.

"Oh – there's something else I need to tell you, gentlemen, which I suppose should really be under *attachments and detachments...* Because the area to be covered is relatively large, and in places is densely vegetated, Council Leader Radley has used his authority to get us some extra, er, 'help'. As part of the 'Community Service' element of the curriculum, over a hundred children from Greasby Boys' School will be filling-in gaps in our extended line..."

The operation to flush-out the French recce patrol began shortly after two o' clock in the afternoon along the northern boundary of Royden Park. Coordinating the advance of two platoons through the dense woodland would be difficult enough, but the officers and NCOs also had to contend with the additional challenge of incorporating into their extended line five classes of pupils from the local boys' school, aged eleven and twelve. The idea – Gerald Radley's idea – was that the boys would fill-in gaps between soldiers to ensure that a thorough sweep of the area was achieved.

"Think of it this way," the Council Leader had reasoned in an effort to pacify Hogan and Blundell. "We need to involve the wider community in local military operations if we're to retain popular support for the war. And if your men go tramping through the woods with twenty metres between them, how will you know the enemy aren't hiding in the gap? These boys will be like little terriers – they'll worm their way into all sorts of inaccessible places which your men won't be able to get at."

"Councillor Radley", the Colonel protested, "we can't have schoolchildren taking part in an advance to contact against a potential real enemy! There's live ammunition involved, for heaven's sake! These French soldiers are clearly very professional and it's unlikely they'll surrender without a fight...Are you really prepared to have schoolboys caught in the crossfire when the lead hornets start flying?"

Radley looked at him sternly. "I'm prepared to do whatever it takes to win this war. Like you yourself said, Colonel, victory will depend on us being more determined, aggressive, resourceful, and prepared to make greater sacrifices than the enemy. Anyway, the French might be less likely to shoot at you if they see there are children around...It might give you an advantage."

Hogan remained unconvinced. "Council Leader Radley," he declared through tight lips, "I'd like you to know that I'm completely against the idea. I certainly wouldn't be happy if my son was involved. And what's next? Getting children to wear big boots so they can clear minefields for us?"

"Don't be ridiculous, Colonel Hogan, this is completely different and you know it!"

"I don't know it, Council Leader Radley, and I'll hold you responsible if it all goes tits-up..."

Alan Hogan was swiftly moving towards membership of an expanding fraternity which did not approve of Council Leader Gerald Radley or the way he was running the war.

Eventually, after much shouting and fraying of tempers, Eight and Nine Platoons began to advance slowly southwards through Royden Park in extended line, with the soldiers in front and the hyper-active schoolboys forming a skittish second row behind them. Initially they made reasonable progress, moving with relative ease through open conifer woodland featuring little or no understorey vegetation. The troops walked with their rifles at the ready, nervously scanning the landscape ahead for potential hiding places, while the boys scurried back and forth to their rear, squirming under fallen tree trunks and wriggling into clumps of bushes which might conceivably have concealed a French fugitive.

Lieutenant Grudge hurried busily to and fro behind his three sections, trying with commendable energy to make sure that they remained in a reasonably straight line and no-one fell too far behind or advanced too far ahead. At the same time he maintained continual radio contact with Major Blundell in Company HQ, located somewhere off to the right between the two platoons.

On several occasions, parts of the extended line encountered thickets of holly or brambles, and the whole advance had to halt while the vegetation was carefully searched. To help deal with such obstructions, Robert and several other NCOs had army-issue machetes, but they were so blunt that their blades would have been challenged by soft butter, let alone briars like barbed wire.

When the troops progressed out of the conifers and entered deciduous woodland their rate of advance slowed dramatically. In this terrain it was far more difficult for every man to maintain visual contact with his comrades on either side, which in turn made it almost impossible to advance as a large formation in a straight, unbroken line. At one point, Robert received orders by radio to halt his section and wait until further notice, although no explanation was given as to the reason why. For over half an hour nothing happened and the men grew bored and restless as they crouched expectantly in the damp leaf litter and became steadily colder in the cool autumnal breeze. Robert listened intently to the radio traffic and ascertained that some of Nine Platoon, under the command of Lieutenant Evans, had drifted off the axis of advance and had to be steered back on course before the company could proceed again. The main culprit within Nine Platoon seemed to be Three Section, which, Robert realised with a grin, was commanded by Mark Conrad.

While the soldiers waited for the order to continue, the schoolboys behind started fidgeting with the frustration of inactivity and were soon messing around. They threw sticks at each other, traded insults and began play-fighting. Their teacher, a man in his mid-forties, tried valiantly to calm them down, with limited success. Robert empathised with the man, who he was sure he recognised, probably from a training course at the teacher's centre at Acre Lane. His own teaching career seemed a dim and distant memory, although he realised with surprise that it was actually less than two months since he had last taught a lesson in school. It seemed far longer ago than that.

At last Blundell's voice came over the radio, instructing Eight and Nine platoons to resume their advance. Eventually, the formation moved onto Thurstaston Common and the number of enforced halts increased considerably. By listening to voice traffic over the company radio net, Robert was able to keep a mental tally of the number of times each of the six sections was responsible for a hold-up, and he formed a league table ranking them from best to worst. Initially his section was in joint second place, just behind Karl Kavaner's, having caused only one delay since the start of the mission. Then it dropped to third place when Harding became entangled in a gorse thicket and had to be physically dragged out by Stevenson.

Towards the end of the afternoon the temperature dropped as the light faded, and Robert began to suspect that the entire operation would turn out to be a futile waste of time. The wooded sandstone ridge of Thurstaston Hill – the finishing line of the advance - could be glimpsed above the vegetation ahead.

Suddenly there was the sharp crack of gunshots somewhere off to the right. The soldiers instantly dropped to the ground, leaving the schoolboys standing like startled rabbits, staring around uncertainly to try to see what was happening.

"Get down!" Robert screamed. "Get down now! And stay down!" Further along the line he could hear Farrell and Stevenson shouting the same instructions, although he could not see them from where he lay. The boys dropped down into the heather and there was more firing from the direction of Nine Platoon's area, accompanied by frantic shouting.

"*Contact, wait out!*" came over the radio net, but the sender forgot to mention their callsign, so no-one knew who they were or precisely where the contact was taking place.

Blundell's agitated voice crackled over the airwaves. "*Callsign in contact, this is Zero, identify yourself.*"

"*Er Zero, this is Three-one Charlie, contact wait out,*" replied the hesitant voice of Corporal Shilton from Nine Platoon. He sounded extremely stressed.

Robert heard several short bursts of automatic fire which were immediately answered by volleys of single shots in quick succession, followed by some longer automatic bursts which probably came from Nine Platoon's Light Support Weapons (LSWs). Evidently a gun battle was taking place somewhere in the dead ground off to Robert's right. Then several bullets cracked directly overhead, and for a terrifying moment he thought that his section was coming under effective enemy fire. After a moment's panic he realised that no rounds were striking the ground nearby and those passing through the air above were much too high to have been deliberately aimed at him and his men. They were probably stray shots from Nine Platoon's firefight, although they served as a sobering reminder that this was not an exercise and potentially lethal live rounds were flying around indiscriminately. Keeping low to the ground, Robert peered up over the heather to his front, quickly scanning the landscape ahead but seeing no sign of enemy soldiers. Glancing to either side, he could see Thomas crouching in the vegetation to his left but was concerned that Spencer – who should have been about ten metres to his right – was nowhere in sight.

"Spencer!" he hissed urgently. "Spencer - where the hell are you?"

The sheepish face of Ben Spencer, framed by a lopsided helmet with most of its vegetation camouflage hanging off, rose miserably out of the heather. He looked as if he had just woken up.

"Switch-on, Ben, for fuck's sake!"

At that moment a voice shouted from behind. "Corporal Taylor!" Robert turned around with a start. It was Lieutenant Grudge, crawling through the heather towards him. "Corporal Taylor, go firm here until I get back. I'm going to find out what's going on. Tell your section to watch and shoot now, but make sure they're certain of their targets, okay?"

"Okay, sir."

Grudge slithered away and Robert passed the message down the line that his section was to remain where it was until further notice. They waited, lying in the heather and bracken, listening nervously to the sporadic crackle of gunfire and the frantic radio communications. Then there was a lull in the firing, and Lieutenant Evans, commander of Nine Platoon, spoke to Blundell over the radio net.

"*Hello Sunray this is Three-Zero...er, have engaged at least two enemy infiltrators... they are moving towards the ridge...we are in pursuit and are moving round to cut them off from the right flank...we have one casualty, I say again -*"

Another burst of firing cut the lieutenant off in mid-sentence and the radio went dead for a few seconds. Then the muffled sounds of heavy breathing, more gunshots and urgent shouting could be heard in the headsets of everyone in the company who possessed a radio – evidently Evans must have been leaning on his prestle switch and broadcasting without knowing it.

"No – *that* way!" he was shouting. "Corporal Shilton – go left flanking! Corporal Conrad – go firm where you are!" Evans's voice lowered to a private whisper. "Jesus – talk about a piss-up in a brewery!"

The radio went quiet again, presumably as Evans altered his position and released the switch on his radio. Robert crouched apprehensively, watching, listening, waiting, his body quivering with tension and fear, his intestines icy cold. For a short period there was no noise apart from the rustling of leaves in the birch trees. Then from Nine Platoon's area came more shouting, followed immediately by a crackling cacophony of gunfire which built to a crescendo like popcorn bursting in a pan, and then stopped abruptly.

Lieutenant Evans's voice came over the radio once again.

"*Zero, this is Three-Zero, we have one enemy dead here. Be advised that a second infiltrator may be moving towards Two-Zero's location, over...*"

Robert shuddered. Two-Zero was the callsign for Lieutenant Grudge and for Eight Platoon generally, which meant that the enemy was heading his way. He glanced around at the men of his section who were visible to either side – Spencer and Stevenson to his left, Thomas, Harding and Farrell to his right – and shouted a quick warning:

"Two section – possible enemy heading this way! Watch and shoot – but check your targets!"

In front of where Robert lay, the heathland was level for about thirty metres before it dropped away into a shallow valley from which the branches of birch saplings reached skyward, wafting like tentacles in the breeze. Such terrain, which could not be seen into from an observer's position, was referred to in the army as 'dead ground'.

Robert considered the feature to be a possible escape route for the enemy, so he decided to move his section forward so they could look down into it. He stood up tentatively and was about to move forward when, suddenly, a soldier appeared out of the dead ground, like a hunted animal. The man's face was heavily camouflaged, accentuating the white of his wide, staring eyes. For a moment the two men stared at each other in mutual surprise. Then, before Robert had time to react, the enemy soldier had ducked back down into the valley and disappeared. His image lingered on Robert's retina even after he had vanished from sight.

"Two section – move up!" Robert yelled to his men, uncertain as to whether any of them had seen the Frenchman. He was disappointed with himself for not having reacted swiftly enough to shoot the enemy soldier, although when he reflected upon the incident later he realised that he was actually very fortunate not to have been shot himself. His mind was racing as he tried to decide how best to proceed. On the one hand, undue caution and hesitation would enable the enemy to escape, but on the other, he was acutely aware that a careless, impetuous error of judgement on his part could have potentially fatal consequences for himself or his men; right at that moment the enemy was most probably fleeing, but he might conceivably be leading the British into an ambush.

Robert quickly informed his section that an enemy infiltrator had been sighted ahead, and told them to advance in alternate pairs. As they waded through the heather and bracken towards the ridge of Thurstaston Hill, progressively more of the dead ground became visible. The heathland sloped gently down into a shallow valley featuring a marshy pool surrounded by birch saplings. Beyond the pool, a wooded hillside with sandstone outcrops rose up towards the ridge. Robert glimpsed the French soldier running uphill amongst the trees, zig-zagging erratically to make himself a harder target to hit. Thomas dropped to one knee and took aim. Robert, in the spirit of fair play and the much vaunted rules of engagement, shouted:

"Army! Halt or I fire!"

The Frenchman glanced around, tripped on a tree root and stumbled forward. He turned the stumble into a dive, rolled over and fired several shots in the direction of his pursuers. Robert dived for cover as Thomas fired back – three rounds in quick succession. The enemy soldier rolled down the slope and disappeared behind a clump of bracken.

"Two-Two Charlie - contact, wait out!" Robert said into his radio microphone, to keep Lieutenant Grudge quiet for a minute or two at least. Then he instructed Stevenson and Spencer to provide covering fire if necessary, while he and Thomas cautiously approached the vegetation into which the Frenchman had tumbled. They moved alternately, one dashing forward five or six metres while the other kept his rifle aimed at the bracken.

Robert's boot struck something small, round and hard, which

bounced along the ground in front of him. Glancing down, his heart missed a beat when he saw that it was a hand-grenade...Then he realised with immense relief that the pin and fly-off lever were still in place, so it could not detonate. The enemy soldier had most probably dropped it as he ran. Robert kicked the grenade away into the heather and moved on. His heart was pounding as he gestured for Thomas to move around and approach the clump of bracken from the other side.

The Frenchman, it turned out, was not in the bracken. They found him a short distance away on the grass beneath some trees, lying face down with one arm outstretched and the other bent under his body. He appeared to be dead.

Robert mouthed the words "search him," and Thomas nodded slowly. Following the standard, well-rehearsed procedure for searching an enemy casualty, Thomas placed his rifle on the ground next to Robert and then circled round to approach the soles of the Frenchman's boots. Robert aimed at the man's head while Thomas, with sudden speed, darted forwards, snatched-up the FAMAS rifle and tossed it away into the bracken. Then he dropped down onto the motionless figure, driving his knees into the man's kidneys; if the enemy soldier was playing dead, it would be extremely difficult for him to maintain the pretence when assaulted in such a way. He showed no signs of life.

The next stage in the searching procedure was potentially the most dangerous. It involved Thomas lying on the enemy's back and rolling the body onto its side to enable Robert to look for booby-traps beneath. A possible last act of a dying soldier might be to pull the pin from a grenade and then lie on it...when his body was moved, the fly-off lever would spring away and the grenade would explode.

Thomas gripped the sleeve of the Frenchman's combat jacket and signalled to Robert that he was ready.

"Now!"

Thomas rolled to one side, pulling the Frenchman's limp shoulder and torso up off the ground. The man's head lolled grotesquely. Robert glimpsed a grenade.

"Grenade!" he shouted, and shot the Frenchman through the head. A red mist sprayed out onto the grass as Thomas, his teeth clenched and his eyes tightly shut, let the corpse roll back onto the ground and clung to it tightly. Contrary to the impression created by Hollywood, hand-grenades contained very little explosive, and a human body would smother and absorb most of the blast and shrapnel. With the added protection of his body armour, Thomas should escape serious injury.

The two men waited for what seemed like an eternity while a stream of blood poured from the side of the Frenchman's skull and formed a dark scarlet pool on the ground. There was no explosion. Thomas opened his eyes. At least ten seconds had elapsed since Robert had fired his shot – if the grenade was going to detonate it should have done so by now.

"Try again," Robert said quietly. Thomas pulled the body up further this time, and it became apparent that the grenade was actually clipped to the Frenchman's webbing, and was not a booby trap after all. Robert could not bring himself to look at the man's face, or at the huge exit wound on the other side of his head. He felt nauseous, hollow and ashamed. Susan would not be proud of him.

Fortunately, Lieutenant Grudge arrived at the scene and took charge of the situation. He was clearly pleased that Eight Platoon had 'bagged' one of the infiltrators. Thomas, who was evidently less squeamish than Robert, searched the Frenchman's body and found personal documents, a mobile phone and a map of Wirral with feint pencil annotations.

By now it was getting dark, and Colonel Hogan gave permission for the schoolboys to go home. He would later visit their school in person, without Radley's knowledge, to apologise to the headteacher for exposing the pupils to danger and to offer assurances that such an outrageous situation would never arise again. The men of Eight and Nine Platoons waited in the fading light for Land Rovers to reach the sites of the two separate firefights and transport the dead and wounded to ambulances parked on a nearby road. Both Frenchmen were pronounced dead on arrival at Arrowe Park hospital. British casualties were one dead and three injured, all from Nine Platoon.

The final advance up the slope to the top of the ridge took place in virtual darkness, but no-one's heart was in the operation after the stress of combat, and it became something of a token gesture. Unlike the blinkered Blundell, Hogan could sense when his men were no longer functioning effectively, and he was acutely aware that fatigued, nervous and switched-off soldiers blundering around in the darkness with live ammunition was a recipe for friendly-fire disaster, so as soon as the two platoons were lined up along Thurstaston Hill with every man accounted for, he declared the operation suspended until the following morning.

Seven Platoon, which had enjoyed a relatively easy and uneventful day, was allocated security duties that night while Eight and Nine Platoons, exhausted from their baptism of fire on Thurstaston Common, returned to the TA Centre to relax and rest. The CO put a hundred pounds of his own money behind the bar to fund celebratory drinks, but warned the men not to over-indulge, as a follow-up mission would commence at first light to search the common for the French recce team's hiding place and equipment.

Robert sat with his usual social crowd of Conrad, Murphy, Brabander and Spencer. They laughed and joked and discussed the day's events, while Brabander drank too much and became infuriatingly argumentative, as usual. It was all reassuringly familiar, but Robert remained tense and unsettled; the red mist spraying from the Frenchman's skull was a recurring image, which he could not banish from his mind. It would haunt him for the rest of his life.

During the night, a pair of fugitives made their way furtively across the Wirral peninsular. The two surviving members of the French reconnaissance patrol had escaped death or capture as a result of the diversion created by the death of their comrades, and also by the timely descent of darkness. Initially they tried heading south, intending to cross the border and rendezvous with the two corporals in Wales, but found their escape route blocked by British forces occupying Thurstaston Hill. In desperation they headed north across the fields of a rural corridor about a kilometer wide which stretched between the built-up areas of Newton and Greasby. Their immediate priority was to put as much distance between themselves and Thurstaston Common as possible; although they had thoroughly camouflaged the entrances to their underground sleeping cells, they had to assume that the British would discover them in due course, and deduce that the recce team had comprised four men. Then every copse, barn, field and wood in the vicinity would no doubt be thoroughly searched.

The map showed a large expanse of undeveloped land between the residential areas of Hoylake, West Kirby and Saughall Massie, which initially looked promising but turned out to be mostly open farmland which was largely devoid of cover. Farms were unsuitable refuges for fugitive soldiers, as farmers knew their land intimately and would swiftly spot anything unusual. They also tended to have dogs...

As the night wore on, the two men became increasingly tired and desperate for somewhere to sleep. It was a cold, clear night with plenty of stars but, to their relief, no moon. Over to the east, searchlight beams waved around like glowing silver lances in the sky as the SCW anti-aircraft positions searched for possible night intruders. The two weary soldiers, who had demonstrated tremendous courage, endurance and determination during the preceding weeks, dejectedly discussed giving themselves up, but their French pride made them decide to try one last bold and audacious move. Instead of avoiding the built-up areas, as the British would expect, they would head into the heart of the urban sprawl and hopefully throw their pursuers off the scent.

They crossed the railway line between Meols and Moreton, then swung east until they reached a stream which, according to the map, was called 'The Birket'. This flowed along a sunken channel for much of its length and provided a concealed conduit leading toward their final goal, the reclaimed refuse tip at Bidston Moss, which looked a promising feature on the map. It was gone four in the morning by the time the men arrived at the spiked perimeter fence which surrounded the artificial hill. Peering through the galvanized railings, they could see plantations of trees swaying in the darkness, the gentle rustle of the autumn leaves beckoning like a siren's call. Using their foam roll-mats to protect them from the vicious prongs of the palisades, they climbed over the security fence and trudged up into the welcoming shelter of the trees. Within minutes, both men were asleep.

CHAPTER 16

In a French Bush

During Chapter 16 I began to lose the will to live! I can't remember when I last endured such a tiresome piece of writing. Page after page of tedious detail about living in a bush...Ploughing through this chapter is arguably a more challenging ordeal than the one it describes.

Elizabeth Plomptom
Nihilist Weekly

Mr Roberts replies:
It was supposed to be tedious, to convey the discomfort and monotony of such an operation. Empathise, empathise!

At first light the next morning, the soldiers of Charlie Company climbed stiffly aboard a fleet of four-tonne trucks and once again headed for Thurstaston Common to conduct a follow-up search of the area in which the firefights had occurred. Robert Taylor did not go with them. He had been told by the CSM shortly after reveille to report to the OC's office at 7.00am. His initial suspicion was that Major Blundell had found out about his exploits with Susan and intended to reprimand him, but when he learned that five other soldiers – including Mark Conrad, Gwyn Thomas and Sergeant Carter from Seven Platoon - had also been summoned, he realised that the interview must be for some purpose other than to slap him on the wrist for indulging in amorous antics with a girl in a company Land Rover while on duty.

When the six soldiers entered the room they found themselves confronted by an impressive line-up of influential personalities: Colonel Hogan, Major Blundell, the Regimental Sergeant-major, and, incongruous amongst the camouflaged fatigues in his black leather trenchcoat, Council Leader Radley himself. Robert and the other soldiers saluted the officers before being stood at ease by the RSM.

"Good morning, gentlemen," Blundell began. "I've brought you here because the CO and Council Leader Radley have asked the Company to carry out a special mission, and I believe you are the right men for the job..."

It was to be a clandestine reconnaissance mission into French territory, with the aim of gathering intelligence to inform the planning of a large-scale invasion in the near future. A four-man team would be flown-in at night by helicopter from *HMS Plymouth* and spend several days reconnoitering an area of coastline north of Bayeux. Sergeant Carter would lead the operation, which was fine by Robert, as Carter was arguably the most professional and competent NCO he had ever met.

The two men knew each other well, having been part of the same team in the Cambrian Patrol competition two years before. With Lieutenant Grudge in charge and Sergeant Carter as second-in-command, the team had won a creditable silver medal and restored battalion honour after a succession of disappointing performances in previous years. A telecom engineer by trade, Dave Carter was the sort of ultra-dedicated TA soldier who caused those who served with him to wonder why he had not joined the regular army and excelled. He even possessed the appearance of the archetypal British Army NCO, with short, thinning hair, a thick neck, tattooed forearms and the obligatory moustache.

Due to the top-secret nature of the mission the selected team – which included two reserves – would henceforth be isolated from the rest of the company and all contact with the outside world was strictly forbidden. The operation would commence as soon as weather conditions in Normandy were sufficiently poor to conceal the team's insertion by helicopter. Long-range forecasts predicted wet and windy weather reaching the region in about a weeks' time, so this became the provisional date on which the men would land on French soil. It was estimated that three days would be required for *HMS Plymouth* to steam down to Normandy, which left just four days for training and the preparation of equipment.

Warrant-officer Protheroe, the Regimental Sergeant-major, drew-up a training programme which focused on honing the team's reconnaissance skills. "Look on the bright side, lads," he told them jovially, "you'll be able to wear your woolly hats!" This was a standing joke in the company, as regular army Protheroe had always been amused and bewildered by what he regarded as an obsessive desire amongst TA soldiers to wear commando-style knitted skull-caps. "I don't understand you boys," he would remark during exercises, "the Army issues you with a perfectly good helmet to protect your head, yet at every opportunity you put on these bloody woolly hats! What is it with the TA and woolly hats?"

The six men practised rapid helicopter boarding and disembarkation drills, initially in daylight and then by night, with Brotherton flying them in low over the River Dee and touching down fleetingly on a patch of heathland in the Heswall Dales nature reserve. They became adept at setting up observation posts in patches of dense gorse or bramble, cutting their way into the spiky vegetation with secateurs and leaving no external signs of disturbance. During the evenings, the men studied maps and aerial photos of the objective area, and were given lessons in essential French by a school teacher from Paris who had married a Wirral man and been placed under house arrest since the declaration of hostilities. The hours of darkness were spent patrolling across the peninsular, refining night navigation skills using map and compass or hand-held Magellan GPS.

A considerable proportion of time was allocated to skill-at-arms training at the Mockbeggar Wharf firing range complex, zeroing weapons and rehearsing 'breaking contact' drills using live ammunition. The rest of Charlie Company were in the process of re-equipping with the newly-arrived American M16 rifles, but it was decided that the recce team would retain their SA80s for the mission, partly for reasons of familiarity but also because it was a shorter, more concealable weapon. After zeroing the rifles during the day and making a note of their sight settings using a device called a collimator, the men repeated the process at night with CWS image-intensifying sights fitted. In addition to rifles and bayonets, the team would also be armed with two Browning pistols and one of the confiscated civilian guns – a .22 Ruger carbine featuring a shortened barrel, folding stock and silencer.

"This may be useful for taking out dogs or anything else which might be in danger of compromising you," the RSM explained, passing the compact weapon around for the team to handle. "But, at the end of the day, if it all goes pear-shaped, you may find yourselves having to use your bayonet on someone, so you need to know how to do it..."

Watching Protheroe's gruesome demonstration, Robert seriously doubted his own ability to kill a man in cold blood with a knife. To shoot an enemy who was shooting at you from two hundred metres away was one thing – an almost abstract concept – but to hack out a man's throat while clamping a hand over his mouth to stop him screaming was something altogether different...Not for the first time, he was incredulous at the speed with which this preposterous little war had suddenly become such an obscene, out-of-control reality, and was dismayed that events seemed determined to escalate and embroil him ever deeper, when all he wanted in life was to be with Susan. On several occasions his mind replayed the image of the red spray erupting from the French soldier's head, and he shuddered at the realisation that the impending mission would put him in real danger of having his own brains blown out in the very near future.

While the six men experienced the luxury of no-expense-spared training conferred by their elite status, all around them Wirral's war machine was coming to life, like a mighty creature awakening from dormancy. The recruit courses started up again and began training a company of men at a time. A mile off the north coast, *Plymouth* and *Bronington* were undergoing sea trials, being put through their paces by crews composed of erstwhile sailors from the Royal and Merchant navies, new recruits, and specialists such as cooks and engineers. At the same time as Robert and his comrades were zeroing their weapons at Mockbeggar Wharf, the newly formed Sustained Fire (SF) platoon began test-firing its General Purpose Machine Guns on an adjacent range and, beyond them, the fledgling mortar platoon was conducting 'dry' training using inert bombs dropped into special practice barrels. Dai 'Taff' Jones, the C Company Sergeant-major, had been a mortar NCO in the Regulars and was assisting Lieutenant Monty in the task of training the new platoon, which largely consisted of volunteers poached from the technically-minded engineers. Mortars were essentially the infantry's own artillery, so it was hardly surprising that Colonel Hogan - an ex-gunner - took a keen interest in the new platoon's progress. Both he and Monty were outraged at having to accommodate within the training programme a group of six Special Council Workers, who turned up on the first day with their own mortar and a letter from Council Leader Radley, which decreed that they be allowed to join the course.

"They're not soldiers," Hogan had muttered resentfully. "Why are we wasting our time - *and* a valuable mortar - on *them*? I mean, what are they going to do with a bloody mortar?"

As the pre-operation training continued, Robert became increasingly desperate to speak to Susan. He prayed that their nascent relationship would survive this cruel interruption, and harboured doubts about his own mental suitability for the mission ahead. A week ago, before he had met her, he would have embraced wholeheartedly the challenge presented by the reconnaissance operation, and dedicated himself to the task without any reservations. But now his excitement was tinged with a growing sense of foreboding and a fear that something infinitely precious - for which he had waited his entire life – might be in danger of slipping from his grasp forever.

A day before the team were scheduled to depart for France, Robert unexpectedly encountered Paul Murphy in the toilet at the TA Centre.

"Paul!" Robert exclaimed with surprise. "What are you doing here? I thought you'd been sent to train recruits."

"I have, but I needed some pamphlets from the RSM. What are you up to?"

Robert grinned. "If I told you I'd have to kill you. *Need to know* and all that, very hush-hush...Mum's the word - in fact, I'm not even supposed to be talking to you, or anyone else."

Murphy was aware that a team had been selected for a special operation, so he refrained from questioning Robert any further. Instead he asked, "Have you heard from your bird?"

"No. Like I said, I'm not allowed to contact anyone."

"Well, you'll like this. They gave the job of looking after her to Stanley. You should've seen him – it was like he'd won the lottery! He was strutting around telling everyone how he was going to be shagging all week in the Land Rover…then as soon as he made a pass at her she gave him a slap and put in an official complaint about him. The stupid twat's been put on a charge…"

Robert smiled. Lance-corporal Stanley was second-in-command of Brabander's section. A short, stocky man with a bald head and moustache, Stanley was an old-style NCO who held rank due to time served rather than aptitude, and whose idea of leadership was to shout ever louder and use ever more foul language. He was not particularly bright, and struggled with some of the more technical and intellectual duties required of a modern infantry corporal, such as writing a set of orders or completing a patrol report, so he would probably never be promoted beyond lance-jack. Robert suspected that Stanley was the sort of man who would act impetuously in battle and either save the day or get everyone killed, depending on the circumstances. A tacit animosity existed between the two men. Stanley had always disliked Robert, whom he regarded as a stuck-up college boy, while Robert considered Stanley an ignorant oaf who was a weak link in the Eight Platoon ORBAT. Susan's response to the lance-corporal's advances both amused and reassured him. He hurriedly scribbled a note to her which Murphy agreed to deliver, and returned to his training with renewed optimism.

When soldiers from Seven Platoon eventually discovered the camouflaged French sleeping cells on Thurstaston Common, it became apparent from the hidden parachutes that the enemy team had comprised four men - which meant that two were still at large. Further searches of the area proved futile and the British troops returned to their coastal defence duties, although they were kept on a higher state of alert in case the Frenchmen were sighted. Intelligence officers from the Council's War Department studied all of the reports received during the previous months which might possibly have related to the enemy patrol's activities, and concluded that the French team had operated on Wirral soil for several weeks at least. This raised the question of how they had been supplied. By air? By boat? By local agents or sympathisers? It was a perplexing and vexatious mystery. Then someone suggested that perhaps the men had simply bought food from shops, and when the CCTV footage from the supermarket at West Kirby was studied this was confirmed: sure enough, there was one of the now-dead Frenchmen, wearing a tracksuit, paying for groceries at a checkout. The British realised that they had been duped. In response, Council officials visited every food shop on the peninsular and issued till staff with a list of questions designed to expose imposters. The questions – of which a random three were to be asked of every adult male customer – related to subjects as diverse as football, local knowledge and contemporary British music and television programmes.

From then on, the British had to assume that French spies were watching Wirral, and efforts were made to conceal all military activities and in particular the movements of the warships *Plymouth* and *Bronington*. Henceforth, they left the docks under cover of darkness and came and went erratically without following any routine. In fact, the Frenchmen on Bidston Moss had observed the ships through binoculars and reported their existence by text message, but the British deception plan was partly successful in that the spies were never sure of the vessel's whereabouts at any particular time. So, when *Plymouth* slipped her mooring one night and ventured out into the murky darkness of the Irish Sea, the enemy soldiers hiding on the reclaimed rubbish tip were not even aware that she had left port, let alone that she was heading for their own beloved homeland.

Colonel Hogan came to the dockside to see the British reconnaissance team off and wish them luck. He had deliberately not informed Gerald Radley of the departure time, as he believed the Council Leader interfered excessively in army affairs and was generally bad for morale. Hogan knew that many of his men regarded Radley unfavourably, with attitudes ranging from mild distrust to unmitigated loathing, so any farewell speech by him to the recce team was likely to be counter-productive.

"Remember," the colonel told them, "gather as much intelligence as you can, but don't get compromised. You don't need me to tell you how important this mission is and how much depends on its successful outcome. For the next few weeks, you represent our Main Effort in this war. Good luck, gentlemen – I look forward to your safe return..."

For two days the ship steamed south. The new crew became steadily more proficient at handling the elderly vessel, which in turn seemed proud and grateful to be back at sea, and eager to please. Robert and his fellow team members spent much of the time in the ship's wardroom, studying maps and aerial photographs, and running-through the various tactical procedures over and over again until they knew every stage of the mission off by heart. They also packed and re-packed their equipment, test-fired their weapons, exercised on the helicopter deck, and fidgeted impatiently with a combination of frustrated boredom and nervous excitement. Unable to relax or settle, Robert wrote an emotional letter to Susan which was only to be read 'in the event of my death', and passed it to the RSM for delivery to her if he did not return.

When *Plymouth* was about forty miles from the Normandy coastline, Protheroe advised the members of the recce team to make their final preparations. Two of the six men learned, with a combination of relief and disappointment, that they were now definitely reserves for the mission and would be staying on the ship. The chosen team would comprise Sergeant Carter, Robert, Mark Conrad and Gwyn Thomas. To save weight, they decided not to take helmets or body armour, much to the amusement of the RSM. "What'll you wear on your heads then, lads?" he chortled. "Don't tell me – woolly hats! TA habits die hard!"

They loaded their bergens onto the helicopter but were then informed that weather conditions were not yet suitable and departure would have to be postponed. A low pressure system was moving into the region, bringing the desired wet and windy conditions which would help disguise the helicopter's noise and hopefully reduce the number of local people 'out and about' who might see or hear the machine land. The four men of the reconnaissance team cursed inconsiderate meteorological forces which were beyond their control, as they went slowly insane with the agony of waiting. Even Robert, unenthusiastic as he was, wanted nothing more than to get the green light and go.

Finally, at one o'clock in the morning, just as Robert had drifted into a fragile sleep, the men were shaken awake by the RSM.

"Time to get up, gents," he said quietly. "You're off."

On *Plymouth*'s helicopter deck, the Agusta's protective tarpaulin had been removed, along with the pieces of plastic sheeting taped over the air intakes, exhausts and other openings vulnerable to the ingress of salt water. Brotherton was conducting pre-flight checks by red torchlight, and the support crew was carefully fitting bombs into the rack on the machine's underbelly. The plan was that, once the recce team had been dropped-off, the helicopter would fly onwards to Caen and drop some bombs as a deception tactic. Any French citizens who saw or heard the helicopter that night would, it was hoped, attribute its presence to the bombing raid rather than to clandestine operations.

Intermittent squalls of rain lashed the elderly frigate and gusts of wind whipped the sea into a foaming black swell which made the deck pitch and roll and rise and fall. These were ideal weather conditions for the mission – not so severe as to make flying dangerous, but sufficiently inclement to mask engine noise which would have carried for miles on a still night.

With the four soldiers and their kit on board, Brotherton took off and piloted the Agusta down the west coast of the Cherbourg peninsular towards St Malo, before swinging eastwards and heading inland. By approaching their objective from the landward side via neutral Britanny, the British would avoid overflying coastal defences and would hopefully enter Norman airspace undetected. The unbroken cloud cover left so little ambient light that Brotherton had to pilot the helicopter following instructions from his co-pilot, who was equipped with an infra-red night-sight.

The landing zone had been selected using aerial photographs downloaded from the Internet, and consisted of an expanse of rough grazing land two miles south of the coast. As soon as the helicopter touched down, the recce team disembarked and sprinted away from the machine in an X-shaped formation. They threw their bergens onto the grass and lay on them as the Agusta lifted into the night sky and, in a blast of rotor downwash, clattered away to inflict some diversionary misery upon Caen.

The men lay motionless for several minutes, peering over their rifles, watching, listening, and generally becoming accustomed to their new environment. Through their CWS night-sights the landscape appeared as a mosaic of green and black shapes, but nothing hostile materialised from the darkness to challenge their presence in enemy territory. Without a word, Sergeant Carter rose silently to his feet, shouldered his heavy pack, and led his patrol northwards into the cover of some trees. The overriding priority was to put as much distance between themselves and the landing site, so they moved quickly towards the coast, negotiating their way around the edge of fields, through hedgerows and across roads, dodging the occasional car. It was difficult terrain to traverse stealthily, as in places the network of walls, fences, hedges and settlements formed an ensnaring net which threatened to trap the men in situations from which there was no easy escape. On several occasions they found themselves caught in sunken lanes, hemmed in by the steep sides and very vulnerable to being compromised by any vehicles which might suddenly appear and illuminate them in the harsh glare of headlights. Progress was slow, and Robert could appreciate why the British and American forces had found this dense countryside so difficult to fight through in the weeks following D-Day.

After an hour they had travelled about a mile and a half from the landing zone and the landscape became more open as they approached the coast. Field sizes increased and, rather than becoming entangled by the terrain, the men struggled to find sufficient features to conceal their movement. The French evidently did not have a blackout in place, as all vehicles still had their headlights switched on; the beams cut through the darkness for hundreds of metres in this exposed landscape. Fortunately, many of the fields contained maize with stems higher than a man, which offered a welcome refuge to the fugitive soldiers.

Carter navigated his team towards the 'lying-up point', or LUP, which had also been pre-selected using aerial photos and map studies. Several potential sites had been identified, but final selection would have to be made 'on the ground'. The requirement was for a clump of dense vegetation in a relatively remote area away from roads, buildings, footpaths or other features likely to attract people. The site had to permit mobile phone communication with *Plymouth*, and a nearby source of water was essential if the men were to operate effectively for any length of time.

Finding such a site proved more challenging than anticipated, as human habitation seemed to be everywhere. The location which had appeared most promising from the aerial photographs turned out to have a campsite close by, so the weary soldiers trudged on. A quarter of a mile away they found a second site, consisting of a bank of dense brambles and bushes at the edge of a wood. It seemed ideal, but as they prepared to occupy the location, a car appeared, seemingly from nowhere. Headlight beams cut into the wood, creating a whirling kaleidoscope of shadows as the vehicle bumped along a track – unmarked on the map and hidden by foliage on the aerial photos – a mere ten metres from where the soldiers lay. Tired and disappointed, they moved on with an increasing sense of urgency; it was imperative that they were concealed in a suitable LUP by daybreak.

Carter consulted the map and led his team west, navigating by GPS, until they reached a stream flowing towards the coast. Initially this brook trickled through farmers' fields, but as the men followed it northwards they entered a wooded valley with some encouragingly dense thickets of gorse, bracken and bramble.

"This looks good," Carter whispered, shrugging off his heavy bergen and letting it fall into the overgrown grass. "All round defence, here."

They lay in a cruciform formation with overlapping legs for several minutes, listening intently and scanning through their night sites in case they had been followed. Seeing and hearing nothing of concern, Carter sent Robert and Mark Conrad out on a clearance patrol to check the immediate environs, while he attempted to establish communications with *Plymouth* by sending a four-digit text code. A coded reply came back almost immediately, so the sergeant selected a suitable thicket of gorse and bramble and instructed Private Thomas to start cutting his way in using secateurs. By the time Robert and Mark returned with nothing to report, Thomas had carved-out an obliquely angled passageway the length of his body, and was about to change direction to create a dog-leg in the tunnel which would prevent anyone outside being able to see directly into the hiding-place.

Until Thomas completed the access tunnel into the mass of vegetation, there was little for the other team members to do, so Carter sent Robert and Mark down to the stream to fill bottles and a large collapsible plastic cube with water. They returned to find that the passageway was complete and Thomas was in need of assistance to enlarge the interior space. Robert removed his webbing and squirmed on his belly through the narrow tunnel, scratching his face on numerous cut stems and spiky branches. Deep within the mound of gorse and bramble, the criss-cross lattice of stalks became less dense, presumably due to lack of light, and Robert found himself inside a sort of low-ceilinged cave with an earth floor, littered with rabbit droppings and dead gorse needles. The roof above consisted of intertwined branches and briars, supported by woody stems of varying thicknesses. Wriggling up alongside Thomas's boots, Robert began cutting away selected stems, trying to achieve the conflicting aims of enlarging the space whilst ensuring that the ceiling of branches did not collapse on top of him.

Conrad squeezed his way in and the three men worked as fast as they could to create a sufficiently large void to accommodate the whole patrol and its equipment. The cut branches and stems were disposed of by simply pushing them into the surrounding vegetation. It began to rain again, and although the dense layer of foliage above formed a reasonably protective roof, enough drops found their way through to torment the soldiers with dripping water-torture as they struggled in the claustrophobic, earthy-smelling darkness to complete their refuge. Gorse spines speared their heads through their woolly hats, and brambles snagged their clothing and tore at their hands, but at last the nest-like shelter was finished.

The next task was to transfer four sets of webbing and bergens into the hiding place. Robert crawled outside so he could pass items down the tunnel to Conrad. When everything had been dragged in, he asked Carter for permission to go to the toilet.

"Then make sure you go a decent distance away," the sergeant told him, "and be quick!"

Carrying only his rifle, Robert hurried away to urinate, savouring the cool night air and the opportunity to stretch his legs; he was not eager to consign himself to the confines of the bramble womb. As he relieved his bladder, his nervous mind spawned visions of enemy soldiers converging on him from every direction, and at any moment he expected the night to erupt with the dazzling light of flares and the harsh shouts of search parties. But nothing happened, and he returned to the bramble thicket as the first vestiges of dawn manifested themselves in the form of a forlornly singing bird and a faint lightening of the sky to the east.

Sergeant Carter was the last one into the hiding place. He entered feet-first so that he could straighten the flattened vegetation at the tunnel entrance and conceal the opening with a gorse branch. Then Conrad was put on sentry duty while the others sorted themselves out. With great difficulty they pulled out their sleeping bags, which were sheathed inside waterproof bivvi-bags, and tried to squirm inside - an almost impossible task in the extremely restricted space. Robert became frustrated almost immediately, as his muddy boots refused to slide down into the quilted cocoon – they simply pushed the entire sleeping bag further and further down towards the bottom of the bivvi-bag. Desperate for warmth and rest, he became increasingly annoyed and impatient, which served only to exacerbate the situation. Sergeant Carter, meanwhile, had succeeded in entering his sleeping bag and was using his bivvi-bag as a light-proof shelter from which to send a text message to inform *Plymouth* of the patrol's location status, or 'loc-stat'. Mobile phones represented the team's only means of communication, as the standard army radios were too bulky, unreliable and limited in range and battery duration to be suitable for the mission. The phones issued to the four men were old models, deliberately selected for their discrete, dimly-lit screens and keypads, and their general lack of fancy, battery-draining features; all that was required of the devices during this operation was that they be capable of sending and receiving ordinary phonecalls and text messages. Using phones at all was potentially risky, as in theory they could be traced, but it was unlikely that the autonomous Normandy possessed the technical ability to locate a phone which had only been switched on for a few seconds.

Eventually, Robert gave up struggling and resigned himself to being only partially covered by his sleeping bag, and consequently cold and miserable. He pulled the flap of his bivvi-bag over his head so that he was completely enclosed and his red torchlight would not escape, then wrote-out a stag-list on waterproof paper to allocate sentry duties for the next twenty-four hours. He copied the list three times onto separate sheets and passed them to his comrades, so that each would know when they were next on duty.

Having established themselves in the gorse and bramble thicket, the recce team began operating according to 'hard routine' - an ascetic existence featuring a long list of forbidden activities which included cooking, shaving, smoking, talking, teeth-cleaning or washing with soap. No-one would exit the lying-up position during the hours of daylight, and the men would have to subsist on cold rations and water, while urinating into containers and defecating into plastic bags. It was a miserable existence combining boredom with austerity in an insanely frustrating union which was made all the more unpleasant by the cramped conditions of their hiding place. Robert felt as though he were trapped and suffocating within a barbed wire tomb. He could not get comfortable, and needed the toilet again despite having been only a few hours previously. This was probably psychological, but it prevented him from sleeping and became an all-consuming preoccupation. When it was light enough to see without a torch, he summoned the motivation to search his bergen for something to piss into.

With excruciating slowness, he partially unzipped the nearest side pouch, feeling like someone in a cinema trying to discretely unwrap a boiled sweet during a quiet scene in a movie. He slipped his hand into the pouch and groped around for the small plastic 'pee-pot' bottle which he had packed for just such an eventuality. His fingers located a folded waterproof jacket, a pair of binoculars, two hesian sandbags and an entrenching tool, but could find no trace of the bottle. That meant it had to be in the other pouch, on the opposite side of his bergen. '*Typical!*' he thought bitterly. '*Why is it that, in the Army, the outcome of fifty-fifty situations never seems to work out in my favour?*' As he struggled to rotate the rucksack, its fabric scratched across the prickly ceiling, and a chastising "Shhhh!" hissed from the direction of Carter's bivvi-bag. A cursory tactile search of the second side pouch failed to find the elusive bottle, forcing Robert to begrudgingly remove every item until it was completely empty and he knew for certain that he was looking in the wrong place. By now his bladder was crying-out for relief and he was rapidly loosing his temper. Trying to remain calm, he carefully repacked the second pouch and then searched the first one again in a more methodical manner. Removing the entire contents, he finally found the bottle hidden in a fold of his Gore Tex jacket.

The actual act of going to the toilet necessitated wriggling out of his sleeping bag, thereby loosing all of the hard-won ground which he had gained during the struggles of the previous few hours. Shivering wretchedly, he lay on his side in the rabbit droppings, carefully positioned the bottle...and accidentally urinated over his fingers. He had only been in the hiding place for a few hours yet already he hated it, and sincerely hoped that this mission was not going to be a long one.

The day passed with interminable slowness and the men became desperate to get out of the confined space and conduct their first reconnaissance patrol during the hours of darkness. Communicating in whispers, sign language and written notes, Robert and Sergeant Carter worked out their patrol routes and finalised their objectives. The plan was that, at ten o'clock that night, a pair of two-man teams would set-out from the lying-up position and head for the coast. Each team would find a suitable location for an observation post, which afforded a good view of the potential invasion beach, and be established and fully concealed before dawn. The following day would be spent in OP routine, watching the beach and the area immediately inland. When darkness fell the two parties would rendezvous back at the LUP in the bramble thicket.

Robert ate a meal of cold boil-in-the-bag chicken pasta and a chocolate bar, washed down with water, then took over from Thomas on sentry duty. The Welshman handed him the silenced Ruger carbine, a range card and a short stick attached to a piece of comms cord which stretched back along the entrance tunnel; the other end of the cord was looped loosely around Carter's neck, and the sergeant had given instructions that he was to be notified of any potential problem immediately with three firm tugs on the string. Robert placed his SA80 rifle next to the Ruger, checked that both weapons had their safety catches on and a round 'up the spout', then settled down on his elbows to commence his hour-long vigil. During that time, a jogger and a woman walking a dog passed along a small footpath down by the stream about a hundred metres away, but neither suspected that they were being watched.

At the end of the hour he was relieved at the sentry position by Carter, and crawled back to his bivvi-bag to try to get some sleep before the night's mission. He lost consciousness almost immediately, only to be jolted awake again a few minutes later by a sharp shove from Conrad.

"You're snoring, mate," his friend whispered.

"Shit. Sorry..." Robert was genuinely contrite, as the sound could easily betray the patrol's location. He rolled miserably onto his side, closed his eyes, and fidgeted for a while before drifting into an uneasy sleep featuring a succession of bizarre dreams. In one of these he was in bed with Susan but got up, naked, to shoot at a Frenchman who was cutting the grass outside. The apparently bullet-proof Frenchman simply smiled and told him jovially to go back to bed. This he did, but when he lifted the covers it was Linda, not Susan, who waited expectantly for him. Despite his disappointment, he climbed into bed with her, and awoke from the dream feeling guilty and confused. For a while he lay with his eyes open, re-living the moment when he had shot the French soldier in the head, and wondering fearfully what calamity would befall him as retribution for his sin. Then he fell asleep again and had a terrible nightmare in which hordes of murderous French locals carrying flaming torches surrounded the bramble thicket and doused it with petrol before setting it alight. He woke with a whimper, convinced that a drop of petrol had just landed on his face. But it was only water from another dismal shower of drizzly rain, so he pulled the flap of his bivvi-bag further up over his face and decided to abandon the idea of sleep altogether, as it was proving too unsettling an experience. Instead, he occupied his mind with wholesomely erotic thoughts of Susan, which passed the time pleasantly enough until it was his turn to do sentry duty again.

At last the light began to fade. The wind dropped and the sky cleared, which was not good for the intended night operations; it was generally preferable to conduct clandestine missions in inclement weather, when the enemy was more concerned with surviving the elements than maintaining military vigilance. Droves of midges and mosquitoes materialised in the hideaway and added to the soldier's misery and their desire to get outside. Robert was susceptible to insect bites, and suffered miserably from the murderous airborne onslaught during his period of sentry duty. Unable to use any form of insect repellant due to its tell-tale odour, he protected himself as best he could by applying an extra thick layer of camouflage cream, pulling the hood of his smock tightly around his face, and putting his gloves on. Despite these measures, some of the maddening insects succeeded in getting through his defences and biting him voraciously. Something – presumably a mosquito of some kind – proved capable of penetrating the thin material of his tropical-issue trousers and feasting upon his legs, so it was with great relief that he completed his hour's sentry duty and crawled gratefully back to the protection of his bivvi-bag, to rub and scratch his infuriatingly itchy skin.

To consummate his sense of persecuted degradation, his stomach began to churn and he realised with frustration that he could not delay the inevitable any longer. If only his intestines could have waited another hour – it would have been relatively easy to relieve his bowels when out on patrol... Cursing, he found a plastic bag and tried to defecate into it. He had performed the procedure successfully during training, but on this occasion only half of the sloppy, stinking excrement ended up in the bag and he had to scrape the remainder from the ground using a piece of waterproof paper and his penknife. Tying up his own warm faeces in the transparent plastic bag, he smiled with bitter amusement at his bizarre situation, and wondered if it were possible to feel any more abject.

At ten o'clock that night, the two patrols left the shelter of the bramble thicket and headed north towards the coast. Robert and Mark Conrad were the first to emerge, like furtive prey animals leaving their burrow to feed. As soon as they were outside, the two men moved off quickly into the night. Carter and Thomas waited a few minutes to check that it was safe before they too crawled out through the bramble tunnel and set off on their nocturnal mission. Both pairs travelled light, carrying only their weapon, webbing and a day-sack, containing essential items such as food, waterproofs and warm clothing. The bulky bergens were left hidden in the gorse bush but contained no maps, note books or other items with any intelligence value.

As the two separate patrols made their way stealthily across the landscape, Robert began to appreciate the importance of what they were undertaking that night. Cutting out a glorified den in a tangle of gorse and brambles might have made him feel like a member of the SAS, but it provided no useful intelligence about the all-important coastline. By contrast, tonight's operation might, by identifying beaches suitable for amphibious landings, determine the outcome of the entire war. It was a heavy responsibility to bear...

CHAPTER 17

Recce Patrol

The author really should try to view his work from the reader's perspective. We're interested in the overall story and the development of the characters, not the minutiae of military operational procedures... Do we really need to know about every detail of tactical defecating?

Cuthbert Billberry
Viewpoint magazine

Mr Roberts replies:
Of course the real issue here is the incredible surfeit of critics and reviewers out there, all voicing their opinions in a desperate attempt to avoid doing some real work. We've become a nation of natterers, it would appear.

Robert and Mark Conrad made their way north-west towards the coast, using hedgerows and woods for concealment as they traversed a rural landscape of farmland interspersed with scattered villages. They made good progress, skirting around settlements and walking with a casual gait in the hope that, if glimpsed as silhouettes, they might pass as locals returning home after a few beers. The countryside here was relatively open and exposed, and on several occasions the two men were forced to lie motionless in the furrows of ploughed fields to avoid being illuminated by the headlights of cars passing in the distance. In several meadows they walked amongst the motionless shapes of cows, which sat in eerie silence on the grass but did not stir as they passed. Robert assumed that the majority of French troops would be deployed along the coast, so he and Conrad proceeded more cautiously as they sensed a damp, salty feel to the air, which suggested that they were nearing the sea. Every fifty metres or so they halted and scanned the ground ahead through their night-sights, but saw no signs of enemy activity.

Their objective was stretch of coastline to the north of the village of Longues-sur-Mer, which maps and aerial photographs had suggested might provide a suitable location for the planned British landing. Unlike the shoreline further east - which generally featured wide, exposed beaches directly adjacent to towns and major roads - the area under consideration had crumbling cliffs and was only accessible by a minor country lane. Colonel Hogan and his military planners hoped that the cliffs might shield an approaching invasion fleet from view and provide cover for the troops once they had landed, while the limited access would impede the movement of French reinforcements to the area and delay any counterattack. The British had gleaned a considerable amount of information about the area from the Internet, but there remained gaps in the available intelligence which it was the job of the reconnaissance team to fill. The most significant unknown quantities requiring clarification related to the numbers and dispositions of enemy forces in the vicinity, the suitability of the beach for landing men and equipment, and whether the cliffs could, realistically, be scaled by soldiers attacking in daylight or darkness.

Approaching Longues-sur-Mer from the south-east, the two British soldiers skirted around the village, scurried across the main coastal road, and crept towards the cliffs through a field of maize. The crops were clearly past their best but the tall stems in neat rows provided much-appreciated cover, and enabled Robert and Mark to creep unseen to within thirty metres of the cliff-top. They paused for breath at the edge of the plantation and peered cautiously out from the maize. Alongside the ploughed field in which they were hiding was a track of some kind, beyond which lay a strip of overgrown grass and brambles which presumably marked the edge of the cliffs. The smell of sea air was fresh and strong, and waves could be heard breaking in the darkness below.

Robert had studied pictures on a tourism website prior to the mission and knew that, somewhere over to his left, was the 'Batterie de Longues', an old German gun battery from the Second World War. He was aware that the fortifications comprised a large concrete observation bunker perched on the edge of the cliffs, with four huge gun emplacements located in a field about two hundred metres further inland. According to the website, the massive concrete structures still retained their original guns, although after nearly seventy years they would presumably be too badly rusted to ever be fired again. Nevertheless, if French troops were present along this stretch of coastline, it seemed logical that they would occupy the existing fortifications rather than go to the trouble of building new ones, so the two furtive British soldiers decided to give the battery a wide berth.

"We need to get ourselves into those bushes before it gets light," Robert whispered to Conrad, gesturing towards the brambles beyond the track. "But we'll give it a couple of minutes to make sure no-one's around. You take the right arc, I'll take the left."

They lay between the maize stalks, looking through their night-sights for the presence of enemy troops. Seeing none, they crawled stealthily across the track into long grass and tried to force their way into one of the patches of bramble. Just short of where the ground dropped away sharply at the edge of the cliffs, Robert found a place where the tangle of briars could be lifted sufficiently to give access into the interior - a cramped, dismal space not dissimilar to the lying-up point which they had gratefully vacated earlier that night. There would be little opportunity for movement once inside, so the two men quickly emptied their bladders, drank some water and donned warm clothing before crawling in. They made themselves as comfortable as possible and waited for daylight.

Within minutes of settling down inside their new observation post, they were alarmed by voices nearby, and watched with baited breath as a group of men came into view and loitered on the rough grass by the cliff edge. One of them - identifiable as a soldier by his helmeted silhouette - walked slowly over to the bramble patch and stopped within two metres of where the British men were hiding. For a terrible moment, Robert feared that his mission had been compromised almost before it had begun, but then there was the reassuring sound of a fly being unzipped and urine splashing onto vegetation. Someone shouted something in French, the urinating man responded in an agitated voice, and the four-man patrol sauntered off eastwards along the track, moving noisily in the direction of the stretch of coast being reconnoitered by Carter and Thomas.

Not long afterwards, distant voices could be heard coming from the direction of the battery, and just before dawn a vehicle approached and descended the cliffs to the beach; this represented a particularly valuable observation, as it confirmed that the track shown on the map remained usable by vehicles. Robert decided it was too risky to use any form of light, but he opened his notebook to a blank page and, in the almost total darkness, blindly scribbled down a few brief details relating to each event as it occurred; these abbreviations and hieroglyphs would to form the basis of an incident log, to be written-up more legibly later on.

When dawn broke the confusing patchwork of shadows around them materialised into a coherent landscape and they found that their hiding place offered a limited view of the beach. The tide was out, revealing a mixture of sand, shingle and lumps of rock running in bands along the shore. This was precisely the sort of information that the military planners required. Robert drew an annotated panoramic sketch of the scene and made a note of the time and the magnetic compass bearing from his location. He also estimated the width of the beach at low tide, and wrote a comment to the effect that it looked a long distance for attacking troops to cover quickly, especially if they were under fire.

Throughout the day Robert and Mark operated a 'two hours on, two hours off' roster which enabled one of them to get some rest while the other watched the beach. The duties of the observer included filling-in the observation log and taking a photograph every half-hour to record the position of the tide, using an old and completely manually-operated SLR camera which had been specially selected because it was more robust than newer digital models and lacked the flashing lights, brightly-lit screens and infernal beeping noises which might potentially have betrayed their location. They also took some video footage at intervals using a similarly outdated camcorder with a small black and white viewfinder hidden deep inside the cowl of a rubber eyepiece. To stave off boredom, Robert zoomed-in on any feature of interest he could find, including ships, aircraft, women walking dogs on the beach, and some curious dark shapes forming a broken arc in the sea several miles to the east. They were clearly very large structures, and when magnified through the camcorder it became apparent that they were the remains of the Mulberry harbour, assembled after D-Day in 1944 to enable huge quantities of supplies to be brought ashore at Arromanches.

As well as the French patrols, which wandered past at irregular intervals looking bored and indolent, there were civilians using the cliff-top: joggers, dog-walkers, families and couples. The closest that Robert and Mark came to being discovered that day was when a labrador dashed up to their hiding place and began sniffing around excitedly, as if following a scent. Conrad aimed the silenced Ruger at the dog, but it suddenly bounded away and disappeared from view, much to the relief of the two British soldiers. Both men had cricks in their necks from peering through binoculars and cameras while lying in the same position, and were finding it increasingly difficult to remain vigilant as the day dragged on with excruciating slowness. As another tedium-alleviating tactic, Robert diligently completed the 'route out' section of his patrol report while details of the journey were still fresh in his mind. He also drew a sketch plan of the area and started to neatly copy every entry from his untidy observation log onto a fresh sheet. Every incident was recorded, no matter how trivial, because even a seemingly insignificant piece of information might turn out to be of vital importance to the planners and intelligence staff back in Wirral. In addition to details of observed French military activity in the area, Robert and Mark Conrad also recorded all civilian movements, any vehicle noises in the near vicinity, and the numbers and types of boats passing across their field of view. Towards the end of the afternoon, Robert began to experience an almost overwhelming desire for a cup of tea, while Conrad was tormented by an intense craving for "an ice-cold bottle of lager with condensation on the outside."

Eventually it grew dark again, but Robert decided not to head back to the lying-up point until well after midnight, for two reasons. Firstly, most of the local population would hopefully be in bed by then, reducing the risk of being spotted. Secondly, it was important to record as near to a full twenty-four hour cycle of activity in the area as possible, which would mean remaining in the OP until around three o'clock in the morning. Men's voices, vehicle engines and the sound of a generator continued to originate from further along the clifftop, and he became convinced that French troops were occupying the old German observation bunker. Ideally Robert would have liked to have crept up close to the building and conducted a 'close target reconnaissance' to determine how many men were occupying it, but he dismissed the idea as too risky. He thought back to his *Junior Brecon* corporal's course two years previously, when he had been severely reprimanded by his instructor for taking a reconnaissance patrol too close to an 'enemy' position manned by the Ghurkas. "It's not the job of the ordinary infantryman to go creeping into the enemy's house and stealing his underpants," the Colour-sergeant had told him sternly. "It's too dangerous. If you play the hero you'll compromise your mission and get you and your mates killed. You've got binoculars and night-sights: you observe from a *distance*."

These words returned to him now and persuaded him to forget any audacious exploits and remain within the realistic parameters set for the mission. He reminded himself that this was not a TA exercise: the enemy here was real, and the purpose of the operation was to covertly gather information and get out undetected. If he and Conrad were compromised then the entire mission would be for nothing. Colonel Hogan had emphasised this very strongly prior to the team's departure from Wirral. "Remember, gents," he had warned, "that if the enemy even *suspect* you've been in the area, we can't risk using it for future operations. Make sure you're not seen, or caught on CCTV, or overheard talking in English...if you so much as accidentally drop a British sweet wrapper we've got to start again from scratch with a completely different area and your mission will have been an expensive waste of time."

As he contemplated leaving the observation post and heading back to the lie-up point, Robert became concerned that the nature of the cliffs still remained a mystery, and in this respect he had failed to achieve one of the mission's primary objectives. After much deliberation, he decided that it was essential to obtain more information before leaving the area. When it was properly dark, he and Conrad emerged from the bramble patch, crawled towards the cliff edge and tried peering over to ascertain whether it was a sheer drop or a climbable slope. But in the darkness it was impossible to tell, even through night-sights. Without a rope it would be foolhardy to attempt to climb down into the unknown, so they decided to try something audacious: they would sneak down the track leading to the beach and then attempt to scale the cliffs from the bottom.

Both Robert and Mark carried a small piece of camouflage netting in their day-sacks and they spent a few minutes entwining bramble, ferns and grass into the mesh to form a cloak of vegetation under which to hide from enemy patrols. Then, very cautiously, they crept slowly towards the top of the track. Once, on exercise, Robert had spent over an hour crawling unseen along a small stream towards an enemy bunker, only to set off a trip flare within twenty metres of the objective. Now, as a precaution against such a calamity, he dangled a long stalk of dried bracken vertically in front of him to detect any wires before he blundered into them.

They crawled through the long grass, staying close to the cliff-top bramble and bracken which would provide concealment if enemy troops appeared. Kneeling in the vegetation and peering through his CWS sight, Robert found himself looking at the top of the track which led down to the beach. It appeared to be unguarded, although a makeshift barrier of poles and barbed wire had been constructed across the tarmac to control access. After a few minutes of precautionary observation, the two men crept forward, slipped silently around one end of the barrier, and began descending the track in the dark shadows of overhanging trees and bushes. About halfway down there was a hairpin bend, after which the track sloped straight down towards the beach and disappeared into the shingle. The end of the track was blocked by another barrier, consisting of two concrete bollards with a steel pole fixed between them. There were also some coils of razor wire and a large, angular structure which perplexed Robert for a while until he realised that it was a pillbox, guarding the exit from the beach. To his surprise, no enemy soldiers could be seen in the vicinity.

Robert peered up at the silhouette of the cliffs which rose above them to the right of the track, but could not estimate their gradient. He began to feel uneasy, scarcely able to believe that they had made it this far, but wary of 'pushing their luck' by proceeding further. One option would be to conceal themselves in a clump of vegetation and wait until daylight to get a good view of the cliffs, but that would necessitate spending another full day hiding in an observation post without food or water, which was not an attractive proposition. Alternatively, they could attempt to climb the cliffs immediately and then return to the lying-up point as swiftly as possible. After a whispered discussion, they opted for the latter course of action.

Along the base of the cliffs were some overgrown scree-slopes which had been colonised by grass, nettles and other plants. Robert and Mark clambered up one of these slopes, dodging thickets of nettles, bracken and brambles until they came to a buttress of cold, crumbling rock which rose almost vertically and disappeared into the inky-blackness above.

"This doesn't look good..." Conrad whispered, running his hand along the rock. Robert agreed, but they persevered, and after exploring further it became apparent that the cliffs consisted of sheer, rocky buttresses interspersed with steep grassy slopes which might just be climbable. Robert's first attempt to reach the cliff-top via one of these slopes ended in failure, as the clumps of grass came away in his hands and sent him sliding back down into Conrad, who was crouching below. He tried a second time, with the same result, and had to admit that the gradient was simply too steep. They moved on, clambering around the base of another crumbling rock outcrop until they reached a grass-filled gully which looked promising through the night-sights. Robert slung his rifle tightly against his back, then borrowed Conrad's bayonet and began to climb on all fours, grasping clumps of wiry grass with his hands and making good progress. The gradient steepened and he used the bayonets like ice-axes, stabbing them deep into the soil and pulling himself up on the handles. Then, to his surprise and relief, the slope became less steep, until suddenly it leveled out and he found himself crouching in the grass at the top of the cliff. He congratulated himself for having discovered that, at certain points, the cliffs could be climbed with relative ease, at night-time, by soldiers without specialist training or equipment. All he and Conrad had to do now was return safely to the lie-up point and share the information with Carter.

They made it back to the wooded valley without incident and stopped several hundred metres short of the LUP to mount a 'snap ambush' in case they were being followed. After a few minutes they proceeded again, but in the darkness one bramble thicket looked very much like another and they could not find their hideaway. By now, both men were extremely tired and were on the verge of 'switching off'. They were desperate for rest and warmth, and the knowledge that their sleeping bags were lying somewhere nearby but could not be located was immensely frustrating and soul-destroying. Eventually, Conrad recognised a familiar pattern of trees which helped guide them back to the correct bramble thicket. Unsure as to whether Carter and Thomas had already returned, Robert cautiously approached the entrance with his rifle at the ready and whispered "Foxtrot Alpha."

"Romeo Tango," came the reply, and the gorse branch 'door' was moved aside to let the two men in.

"Glad you're back," whispered Sergeant Carter as they crawled wearily into the confined space and groped around to locate their personal kit. "I need your patrol report asap."

Robert sighed despondently, but knew that Carter was right: army good practice dictated that patrol reports were completed immediately upon returning from a mission, while events were still fresh in soldier's minds. He climbed clumsily into his sleeping bag, pulled the Gore Tex flap of the bivvi-bag up over his head and reluctantly began filling-in the document by red torchlight. The quilted cocoon was blissfully snug and soporific and he struggled to keep his eyes open, repeatedly drifting into unconsciousness for varying amounts of time, ranging from seconds to minutes. He was glad that he had already completed some of the task earlier in the day, although the remainder of the form took over an hour to fill-in and left him with a mere fifteen minutes of relaxation before it was his turn to take over from Conrad on sentry duty. It began to drizzle again and he lay shivering in the bramble tunnel, feeling very tired and very dejected as he fantasised about Susan, and wished that this miserable mission would be over as soon as possible.

The news that British forces were finally operating on French soil reached Gerald Radley during a garden party held at his home in Heswall for selected friends, colleagues and people of consequence whose acquaintance he was eager to cultivate. Colonel Alan Hogan arrived in mid-afternoon and was ushered into the garden by a Special Council Worker. The tall, weather-beaten officer in camouflaged fatigues looked out of place and slightly uncomfortable amongst the lounging bureaucrats in their sports jackets, who were standing around in small groups, chatting and sipping drinks. Upon noticing Hogan, Radley detached himself from his conversation and walked over to welcome the colonel with an unctuous smile.

"Alan, nice to see you. To what do we owe the unexpected pleasure?"

"I've got some news which I'm sure will interest you, Council Leader." No matter how hard he tried, Hogan could not bring himself to like Gerald Radley – there was something unsavoury about him, which the colonel could not precisely define. The two men were set apart from each other and made incompatible by a fundamental difference: Alan Hogan was a gentleman, and Gerald Radley was not.

They walked a discrete distance away from everyone else and Hogan gave Radley the latest update on the reconnaissance mission in France, as communicated in code by Sergeant Carter earlier that morning. The Council Leader looked pleased.

"Alan, this is excellent news, I'm delighted things are going well over there. Let me get you a drink – what will you have?"

Hogan shook his head in polite refusal. "Er. No thank you, Council Leader, I need to get back to my duties, if you'll excuse me…"

"Well, thanks for keeping me informed – I appreciate it. It's wonderful news that we're finally on their turf. Pity we can't inform the public that we're finally taking the fight to the French…"

Hogan's expression changed suddenly to one of concern, almost hostility. "Councillor Radley, I've come here to tell you about this in person because of the highly sensitive nature of the operation. We've got four men in the field over there and their safety must be our primary concern. Under no circumstances must news of this mission enter the public domain, even when our men have been brought back - you must understand that."

"Of course, of course, you're right – I wasn't suggesting for a moment that we start shouting about it. It's just that I get the feeling that the public don't regard the Council as being sufficiently, er, *proactive* in conducting the war at the moment."

"Let the public think what it likes, Council Leader, while we get on with the job of winning this war."

Radley gave a sagacious nod. "Wise words from the military, as ever. And how are preparations in general going at the moment, Colonel? Will we be able to mount a large-scale invasion soon?"

"We're doing everything we can. It's recruiting personnel that takes time. At this very moment there are over a hundred new recruits undergoing basic training. In another month we should hopefully have the basis of three infantry companies, which is the minimum strength needed to achieve what we've discussed…"

"Excellent. And the invasion strategy?"

"Being refined every day, although obviously we need to incorporate the new intelligence from the team in France."

"Good, good. Now, you're sure you won't have a drink? Come on

Alan – take a few minutes off, relax...there are a few people I'd like you to meet..."

During his career as a regular army officer, Alan Hogan had attended his fair share of tiresome social functions, but he objected to being paraded around like one of Radley's stooges. Fortunately, at that moment, fate intervened and spared him the awkwardness of having to extricate himself from the situation. A jet airliner roared overhead, drowning out all conversation as it climbed into the sky from Liverpool's John Lennon Airport. Radley glared up at the plane with an expression of loathing, providing Hogan with the perfect opportunity to slip quietly away. The engine noise rolled across the Dee estuary and washed back from the Welsh hills on the opposite shore, producing a rumbling reverberation which lingered for a considerable period. By the time the sound finally died away, the aircraft that had created it was a distant speck in the sky.

Radley strode over to McCarthy and Silverlock, his face as thunderous as the aircraft noise. He was seething. "It's bloody outrageous! In the last few years we've had a steady increase in the number of those bloody things flying over Wirral and deafening us. Not to mention all the atmospheric pollution they're pumping out. And for what? Just so the plebs can have their cheap flights to the Costa Del Prole to get a sunburned beer belly and wear ridiculous shorts!"

"Ah," said McCarthy, with a gleeful twinkle of provocation in his eye, "but think about all the tax revenue they bring to the economy..."

"Whose economy?" asked Silverlock. "Certainly not ours. Wirral doesn't get a penny of revenue from cheap flights going out of Liverpool...The government in London rakes in the cash while we put up with the noise and pollution. I bet the Prime Minister doesn't live directly under a major flight-path..."

"I know what we'll do," Radley announced with great excitement. "We'll contact the Civilian Aviation Authority, and John Lennon Airport, and tell them that, due to the war, our airspace is an exclusion zone which may not be entered, and any aircraft which does so is at risk of being shot down." He thought for a moment. "Do either of you know if we've got anything that could shoot down one of those buggers?"

"The Bofors gun on *Bronington* could probably give them a good scare," replied McCarthy.

"Good, then that's what we'll do. Either they divert the flights or we'll fire at the first plane that comes over. Let's see how they like *that!*"

Radley's mobile phone started ringing to the tune of 'Jerusalem,' and he glanced at the screen to find that the caller was Brian Salter from the Regeneration Department, whose absence from the party had definitely not been an oversight. The Council Leader answered the call with an irritated expression.

"Brian, I'm in a meeting right now – is it urgent?"

"Sorry Gerald," came Salter's undynamic voice at the other end of the connection. "I just wanted to run something by you. We've just received confirmation from the contractors that the hostel for under-age mothers has just been completed, and the building needs a name. Sylvia and I thought '*The Haven*' might be appropriate..."

Radley considered the suggestion for a moment. "Yes, that would be touching..." He smiled wickedly. "But let's call it...*Slappers*."

In Normandy, the four British soldiers were enduring the privations of their mission with reluctant stoicism. They were quickly adapting to the routines of reconnaissance operations against a 'real' enemy, patrolling at night and laying-low throughout daylight hours, either within the bramble thicket of the lying-up point or else concealed in an observation post somewhere within sight of the coast. Robert found the long periods of inactivity in confined spaces particularly challenging, and hungered for relaxed walks in the open air, and hot, satisfying food and cups of tea. Cold boil-in-the-bag meals washed down with sterilised water tasting of chlorine may have satisfied his body's nutritional requirements, but they did little for his morale. It was also very difficult to remain concealed and quiet all the time. Every cough, sneeze and fart had to be stifled and suppressed, zips had to be undone a tooth at a time, and Velcro fastenings painstakingly teased apart to avoid making tell-tale noises which might betray their position.

After a mere two days, the men were struggling to remain sane and motivated, and they began to regard with increasing admiration the achievements of the French patrol which had parachuted into Wirral and operated successfully for several weeks.

Ironically, just as the British finally succeeded in establishing a token presence in Normandy, the epic French mission in Wirral came to an end. After living as vagrant fugitives and evading detection for an incredible total of five weeks, the two surviving soldiers had reached the limit of their endurance and were desperate to get home. However, unlike their British counterparts in Normandy, the Frenchmen did not enjoy the reassuring luxury of a support ship offshore with a helicopter ready to extract them on request. They alone would be responsible for their own escape from Wirral. And it would not be easy. The peninsula's coastline was too exposed, well guarded and treacherously tidal to permit escape by boat, although the corporals in Wales were willing to attempt such a rescue and had made enquiries about obtaining a suitable craft. The problem was that, realistically, even if the two fugitives managed to pass undetected through the trenches and barbed wire entanglements and somehow reach a boat, they would almost certainly be intercepted by the Hoylake lifeboat – now painted grey and armed with a machine gun – which loitered on permanent picket duty out in the estuary.

An alternative possibility which the two men considered was to hide their military kit, change into their tracksuits and try to board a

Mersey ferry which would take them across to neutral Liverpool. But a precautionary jog to the Seacombe ferry terminal revealed that the boarding jetty was heavily guarded by armed SCW personnel who were conducting thorough checks of passengers' identity documents, so the idea was immediately abandoned. In desperation, they decided to head south at night and attempt to cross the border into Cheshire, where the two corporals could collect them by car and take them back to Wales.

Travelling undetected from Bidston Moss to the Cheshire border might potentially take several days, especially if they were forced to lie-up somewhere due to unforeseen circumstances, so they decided to mount one last mission to the local supermarket in order to replenish their severely depleted provisions in readiness for the journey. The more senior of the pair, a lance-corporal, volunteered to go. In the early hours of the morning, when it was still dark, he changed into his tracksuit, climbed the palisade fence which surrounded the reclaimed tip, crossed the river and railway line, and skirted around the supermarket car park using a belt of trees for cover. He emerged from the vegetation at a large roundabout and jogged along the main road leading towards Birkenhead until he reached a pillar box, into which he posted his final patrol report. From there he jogged along a residential street and entered the woods of Bidston Hill, where he hid until it was light and he knew that the supermarket would be open. Then he ran casually out of the woods and back down to the store. The car park was almost full and the shop itself was crowded with customers, which would benefit the Frenchman – it was easier to be inconspicuous in a busy place than an empty one.

The lance-corporal quickly filled his basket with bananas, pasties and chocolate bars and joined a queue at one of the checkouts, trembling with anxiety as he desperately tried not to look suspicious. A Special Council Worker walked along the row of tills, carrying a shotgun and staring menacingly at the customers. The Frenchman caught his eye for a moment before glancing away with casual indifference, although he felt guilty and conspicuous. To his relief the SCW man continued walking, engrossed in his own self-importance, although he then stopped and loitered by the exit. The queue shuffled forward and more shoppers accumulated behind the Frenchman, effectively trapping him between the checkouts. Tiny beads of sweat emerged treacherously from the pores on his forehead and he wiped them away with his sleeve, hoping that people would attribute them to his jogging. Finally it was his turn to pay. He avoided eye contact with the woman on the till as she scanned his purchases and put then into a bag, but suddenly – much to his alarm – she engaged him in conversation.

"Making the most of it while you can, eh love?" she asked jovially, then noticed his confused expression and added: "They're talking about rationing if this war continues."

The lance-corporal had perfected a few English phrases, but

his command of the language was too weak to enable him to hold a conversation. He had no idea what this woman was talking about, so he just shrugged and smiled in a friendly and innocuous manner. She finished scanning his purchases and, to his relief, the total cost was displayed on the till for him to read. He handed her a twenty-pound note, but while the receipt was being printed she reached languidly for a clipboard and declared, "Now, love, I've just got to ask you a few of these questions – it's company policy I'm afraid...Let's see, er...*Do you know how much they're going to increase the tunnel toll by?"*

He stared at her blankly, recognising only the phrase 'how much'. Unable to answer the question, he decided that the time had come to play the trump card which he held in reserve for just such an eventuality. He pointed apologetically to his throat, shook his head sadly, and handed her a piece of paper upon which was written: *Sorry. Have had throat operation. Can't speak.*

The cashier smiled kindly. "That's okay, love – don't worry about it. Here's your change and receipt, and here's your War Fund coupons. Bye love, take care."

He smiled back at her, picked up his bag of groceries and hurriedly walked away, while she discretely pressed a hidden alarm button with her foot.

Immediately, supermarket security staff and the Special Council Worker converged upon the lance-corporal before he reached the exit.

"Just hold it there," the SCW man barked, his finger on the trigger of his pump-action shotgun.

The Frenchman sighed wearily and put down his shopping. Escape was totally out of the question – he was far too tired to even contemplate that possibility. So he stood obligingly still as a pair of store security guards wearing tan uniforms reminiscent of the Foreign Legion searched him for weapons. After spending so long enduring the privations of a fugitive existence, surrender almost seemed a welcome relief. There would be no more hiding like a vagrant criminal on the run. For him, the war was over.

Within hours of the lance-corporal's capture, every available British soldier on the Wirral had been mobilised and organised into search parties to comb the entire area within a two mile radius of the supermarket. Even new recruits were put to good use, being temporarily withdrawn from their basic training programme to provide additional manpower, supplementing the trained soldiers as they searched woods, waste land, allotments and anywhere else which might possibly have concealed enemy infiltrators.

When his comrade did not return, the remaining Frenchman on Bidston Moss realised that something must have gone wrong. He sat down forlornly on his bergen with his head in his hands, desperate to flee but aware that, realistically, he could do nothing until nightfall. Then, from the far side of the artificial hill, he heard distant shouts which sounded to him like military commands. He quickly made his way up through the trees to the brow of the hill, from where he could see down towards the lake and the assault course; at the bottom of the slope, a large number of troops were forming up into extended line, although they had not yet started to advance.

Like a hunted fox, the Frenchman returned to the plantation near the perimeter fence where he and his comrade had made their camp. On the other side of the spiked railings lay a large retail park, and he briefly entertained the notion of scaling the fence and fleeing through the yard of the large DIY store. Realistically, however, he knew that he would not get far in broad daylight wearing army uniform. No, he decided, he had done enough for Lebovic, Normandy and French honour. For weeks he had endured extreme hardship and lived like a wretched animal. It was time to give himself up, with dignity.

He quickly stripped the two FAMAS rifles and rendered them useless to the enemy by burying the internal parts in notches cut into the earth with his bayonet. Then he tossed one rifle into the bushes, picked up the other and shouldered his bergen before trudging up the slope to meet the British.

At the top of Bidston Moss's artificial hill was a sculpture known locally as 'The Stargazer' – a huge earth figure lying on its back, staring up at the heavens. The French soldier climbed up onto the crumbling face and stood silhouetted against the sky, his rifle held above his head with a white handkerchief tied to the muzzle. He was seen by acting-sergeant Paul Murphy, who studied him closely through his binoculars and radioed back to Company HQ that an infiltrator had been sighted and appeared to be trying to surrender. Fearing it might be a trap, Murphy sent a section around in a wide arc through the trees to approach the man from the left flank, from where they could give covering fire if necessary. He waited until they were in position before moving cautiously up the slope with the remainder of his men in extended line, advancing by alternate fireteams until they were within a hundred metres of the silhouetted figure. Then he and a private slowly approached the man. They snatched away his rifle and made him kneel down with his hands on his head, to be searched for weapons and items of interest to the intelligence staff. Murphy glanced around nervously and asked, "Are there any more of you?"

The Frenchman shook his head. He was shaking slightly and looked immensely tired. Murphy felt sorry for his prisoner and treated him sympathetically, as one soldier to another, recognising that someone who had been through what this man had endured deserved respect and consideration.

A few hours later, both Frenchmen were securely behind bars at Fort Perch Rock prison, which was relatively empty following the latest round of Radley-sanctioned executions. In comparison to what the two men had experienced during their epic reconnaissance mission, incarceration in the prison seemed almost like a stay in a luxury hotel, although it was not to remain that way for both of them. The private who had surrendered to Murphy on Bidston Moss enjoyed a comfortable imprisonment for the duration of the war, but his comrade was rather less fortunate. When Radley learned that the lance-corporal had been captured wearing civilian clothes, he frowned and declared, "Then that makes him a spy, and the penalty for spying in wartime has always been death..." Blundell and Hogan pleaded for clemency, but the Council Leader would show no mercy and so, only two days after his capture, the poor man was taken from his cell, blindfolded and tied to a post on the roof of the fort, in full view of the public on the beach below.

"Vive la France!" he shouted, as the SCW firing squad loaded their shotguns. People walking along the promenade looked up in the direction of the shout, then flinched as the twelve-bores roared, and the body on the post went limp.

No-one admired the achievements of the French reconnaissance team more than their British counterparts operating out of the bramble thicket in northern Normandy. After only three days in the field, Robert and his comrades could fully appreciate the physical and mental stamina demonstrated by the French patrol, which had operated effectively for so long.

The British mission was proceeding well. Several night patrols and daytime observation posts had yielded detailed information about the beach and the area immediately inland, with most of the intelligence appearing to confirm that the stretch of coastline was a promising potential invasion site.

Robert was disappointed with himself for feeling so overwhelmingly tried despite having opportunities to rest during the day. For some reason he found it almost impossible to sleep in the hollowed-out bush, and spent much of his relaxation time fidgeting in claustrophobic misery, with the result that, when darkness fell, he was in a zombie-like state which impaired his performance. What he really needed was a cup of tea, but unfortunately that was out of the question.

Tonight, he and Conrad had been tasked with reconnoitering the roads approaching Longues-sur-Mer, with a view to identifying potential ambush sites. The two men left their hiding place just before midnight and made their way slowly and cautiously towards the objective area. As they patrolled through the dark landscape, Robert could not exorcise from his mind the chorus of a song which repeated itself endlessly, like background music in his subconscious. The song, by Billy Joel, dated from Robert's youth in the Nineteen Nineties, and featured the lyric, *'In the middle of the night, I go walking in my sleep...'*

It was Lieutenant Grudge who first noticed the article in the *Wirral Herald.* Under the headline *Our Boys on French Soil*, the text referred to an interview with Gerald Radley in which he had been asked why it always seemed to be the French who were taking the initiative in the war. The Council Leader had been distinctly rattled by what he interpreted as accusations of inactivity on his part, and his response was impetuous and ill-considered: "The media seem obsessed with criticising the Council for not doing enough, but you should remember there's a war on. For reasons of security, we cannot publicise details of all of our current military operations. Just because we haven't informed the press that our forces are operational in France doesn't mean that such operations don't exist..."

The lieutenant was so appalled by the article that he took it straight to Colonel Hogan, who read it with an expression of disdain, which quickly turned to anger.

"I don't know who I'm more annoyed with," the CO declared, "the Council Leader for making the comments or the newspaper for publishing them. We have to assume, of course, that the French will read this."

Grudge nodded gravely. "In which case, I think we should bring our men out immediately, sir. It's not fair to leave them there – who knows what classified information Mr Radley will blurt out next."

"You're right, Lieutenant, and that's precisely what we'll do. Thank you for bringing this to my attention."

"I had to, sir."

"Oh, just one thing, Lieutenant Grudge..."

"Yes, sir?"

"Why did you come to me about this, rather than Major Blundell?"

Grudge stared blankly at the colonel, who was studying him keenly with the faint trace of a smile. The lieutenant shuffled awkwardly.

"I-I thought it was so important that I should go straight to the top, sir, and I knew you'd take it seriously."

"And Major Blundell wouldn't?"

"I'm not saying that, sir..." Grudge replied defensively, reluctant to speak his mind, although both men were tacitly aware of the reality of the situation: Blundell had connections with the Council, and the Council was not to be trusted.

The coded text message came through on Sergeant Carter's mobile phone shortly after six o'clock in the evening. Level-headed and professional as always, he calmly communicated the information to the rest of his team by passing around a piece of paper on which was written: *Extract tonight 02.00hrs. No move before 23.00hrs. Stag roster continues till then. Make sure your area is sterilised. STAY SWITCHED ON – WE'RE NOT HOME YET!*

Robert read the note and smiled. It was the best news he could have hoped for.

The men left the bramble thicket in the early hours of the morning and headed for the designated pick-up point two miles away. As well as the sense of elation at the mission's unexpected curtailment, they also harboured an uneasy, almost superstitious feeling that success might be cruelly snatched from them in the final few hours. This looked like a very real possibility as they moved in single file around the edge of a large field and Thomas, the scout, spotted an enemy patrol in the darkness ahead, climbing noisily over a gate into the same field. There was sufficient ambient light from the half moon to prevent the British team simply turning around and retracing their steps without the risk of being seen, so they ducked down into the shadows at the base of the hedge and quietly squirmed backwards into the long grass and nettles. With his heavy bergen still strapped to his back, Robert felt like a vulnerable, ungainly tortoise which had been flipped over onto its shell, and he prayed that the French patrol would not notice him or his comrades.

Robert was the last man in the line and he watched anxiously as the lead Frenchman reached the point where Thomas hid in the darkness of the hedge. The enemy scout continued on silently past Carter, then Conrad, then Robert himself, apparently without noticing any of them; it was surprising how effectively a soldier could conceal himself at night simply by lying motionless in the shadows. Robert repeatedly moved his index finger from the trigger of his SA80 to the safety catch, to make sure it was set to 'off'. Never in his life had he experienced such an intense combination of fear, tension and excitement. A total of eight men filed past in the moonlight, all apparently unaware of the British soldiers hiding only a couple of metres away.

As soon as the French patrol had disappeared from view, Carter's team got up and hurriedly vacated the area, in case the enemy had in fact noticed them and were organising an attack at that very moment. Once again, Robert had visions of the red spray erupting from the French soldier's head, and shuddered with dread. He was desperate to get aboard that helicopter.

They reached the large ploughed field of the landing zone with an hour to spare and hid in a small copse while waiting for time to pass, which it did with cruel slowness. Five minutes before the helicopter was due to arrive, Carter and Thomas crept out into the middle of the field and dug a small pit, into which they placed a luminous chemical glow-stick which would only be visible from the air.

Eventually the sound of rotors became audible and grew steadily louder, until the black silhouette of the Agusta appeared in the night sky and hovered momentarily above the glow-stick before descending. As part of the deception plan, the helicopter had come directly from another diversionary bombing mission, this time over Bayeux.

"Let's go!" Carter urged, and the four men ran out to meet the noisy machine as it touched down on the furrowed earth. The co-pilot helped secure the patrol's bergens while Thomas braved the strong rotor downwash to retrieve the glow-stick and kick soil back into the pit. Less than a minute after the helicopter had landed, all four soldiers and their equipment were securely on board.

"Is that everyone?" Brotherton shouted from the cockpit.

Carter responded with a thumbs-up.

"Then, as the shepherd said, let's get the flock out of here!"

As they lifted off into the cool night sky with the door of the helicopter still open, Robert could scarcely believe that they had actually managed to complete the mission successfully without a shot being fired. His naturally pessimistic nature found this hard to accept and he expected, at any moment, to see glowing rods of tracer arcing up at them from the dark landscape below. But then, looking down, he could just make out the white flecks of waves breaking on the beach, and after that only the rolling ocean lay beneath them, from which no hostile fire would come. They were safe. Conrad pulled the door shut and they began to relax for the first time in four days, while Brotherton piloted the helicopter to rendezvous with *HMS Plymouth*, which was already steaming towards Land's End.

CHAPTER 18

A Momentary Pause for Breath

How can you have a book about a local authority which makes no reference to the Mayor? This ignorant and arrogant author clearly doesn't know a thing about local government.

Adrian Hermitage
Ex-Mayor

Mr Roberts replies:
You're right, I know very little about the organisation I help to fund with my monthly council tax payments, which is worrying. I can easily find out about the workings of central government from the national media, but the structure and operation of my local authority remains shrouded in mystery. Is this intentional, I wonder?

During the voyage back to Wirral, the four members of the reconnaissance patrol were subjected to a merciless debrief by a team of Council officials who were waiting like vultures with clipboards to pounce on them the moment their helicopter touched down on *Plymouth*'s rolling deck. All that Robert and his weary comrades wanted was to have a shower, eat a substantial hot meal and sleep while the adrenalin dissipated from their veins, but their interrogators were intent on extracting as much information as possible while it remained fresh and undistorted in their minds. So they found themselves sitting around the table in the frigate's wardroom, filthy, stinking and fatigued, resentfully recalling details of the mission with the aid of their notes, sketches and annotated maps.

After three hours, Sergeant Carter's eyelids began to flicker heavily, whereupon the Council official who had been interviewing him promptly declared, "Of course, you'll be including all of this information in your patrol report, which we really do need as soon as possible..."

"We'll do it tomorrow," Carter said sternly, "after we've sorted ourselves out." He turned to his comrades. "Right lads, we're off to bed." The four men stood up defiantly and walked out, leaving the Council intelligence vultures to pore-over and assimilate the large quantity of information which the mission had yielded.

When *Plymouth* came within helicopter range of Wirral, the Council team was flown back to the War Office so that the mission's findings could be incorporated into the invasion strategy without delay. On Colonel Hogan's instructions, the Agusta then returned to the ship to collect the four men of the reconnaissance team and bring them back to the TA Centre in style, in recognition of their commendable efforts in Normandy. As the helicopter approached the peninsular, Brotherton changed course slightly to give his passengers an aerial view of the colossal canal workings which were being excavated along the borough's southern boundary. Below, dwarfed to insignificance by the sheer scale of the huge cutting, men and women toiled like ancient Egyptian slaves, labouring under the Council's 'Idle Hands' programme, which had been created to transform Wirral's unemployed into a productive workforce.

"They reckon it won't be long before it's finished," Brotherton shouted back from the cockpit. "Although they're going to have to do a lot of dredging to reach the deep water channel in the Dee...Tell you what, we'll go over the park so you can see the Arena."

He piloted the helicopter in a sweeping arc which took them across Birkenhead Park, where some of the stone excavated from the canal workings was being used for the construction of a massive circular arena, which dominated the landscape and towered over the surrounding trees and houses. No-one could deny that it was an impressive structure, rendered awe-inspiring by its sheer size.

The Agusta A109 touched down within the wire perimeter fence of the TA Centre and Colonel Hogan and Major Blundell came out to welcome their men back. The CO was aware that the recce team had been debriefed during the return voyage, so he refrained from asking them detailed questions about the mission. Instead he offered them tea in his office, chatted about their personal welfare and rewarded them with two days' leave. He reminded them of the necessity for complete secrecy regarding the operation, and warned them that Gerald Radley had expressed a desire to congratulate them the moment they arrived back on Wirral soil.

"So, gentlemen," Hogan advised cynically, "unless you want to find yourselves telling our illustrious Council Leader all about your adventures in France, I suggest you go home now..."

They got up to leave and the CO, who had long ago learned the importance of praise in maintaining morale, called after them: "Well done, gents – a very good effort. You've done yourselves and your company proud."

Robert was desperate to see Susan but knew that she would be at work, so he and Conrad returned to their rented house in Rock Ferry. During their absence there had been further air raids, and several houses and cars at the end of the street had been damaged by fire.

The Mullah, who seemed to spend his entire life lounging on the sofa watching television, looked up with surprise as Robert and Mark entered the living room.

"Where have you guys been?" he asked, without any real interest.

"If I told you I'd have to kill you," Conrad replied. This was one of the standard quips from his repertoire of glib remarks, and it had the desired effect: the Mullah nodded absently and asked no further questions.

Robert trudged wearily up to his room, dumped his kit on the floor and lay on the bed for a few minutes, thinking. Then he showered and set about trying to remove the residual traces of camouflage cream which gave his face a dirty, ashen, almost cadaverous complexion. The greasy green and brown cream penetrated and clogged-up skin pores and always proved particularly hard to dislodge from the hair follicles on his jaw, chin and neck. Repeated wet shaving with a sharp razor was the only effective way of removing it, although this resulted in a multitude of tiny abrasions and made his skin red and inflamed.

He changed into a shirt and jeans, which felt reassuringly clean and casual after a week in stinking combat clothes, then drove to Susan's flat via a greengrocer's which sold flowers. She had just returned from work when he arrived, and her expression upon answering the door was one of surprise, delight and relief.

"Robert!"

They made love with almost desperate passion before getting dressed and going out for a meal at a local restaurant. She knew from the note which Murphy had passed to her that Robert had been involved in a secret military operation and, suspecting that it might have been a traumatic experience, treated him with respectful sensitivity. After the waiter had brought drinks and taken their order for food, she leaned over the table towards him and quietly said, "Robert, I know you've been away somewhere on army business, and I'm not going to ask you about it, but do tell me if you want to..."

"Thanks." He smiled at her gratefully, appreciating how fortunate he was to be with this girl. They talked about her work, the war, and the situation in the borough, but Robert soon began to feel restless and uncomfortable in the restaurant. It was as if he were an alien imposter from a different world, detached from the mundane surroundings and prosaic humdrum of everyday life which existed around him. A fat and slightly drunk man at a nearby table, who was showing off his party trick of removing a cork from inside a wine bottle using a napkin, seemed to Robert to epitomise irritating civilian inanity, and he had to resist the urge to shout abuse at him. Susan sensed his mood and suggested they go home.

Walking along the high street in the early evening, Robert found himself regarding passers-by as lesser mortals, although he was aware that his aloof attitude was completely unreasonable. After all, he reminded himself, these people were simply relaxing and enjoying themselves with family or friends, which surely had to be a more worthwhile pastime than lying in a bush for several days. Nevertheless, such had been the intensity of his experience in Normandy that he found it difficult to relate to ordinary people doing ordinary things.

Susan noticed his sullen introspection with unease and wondered whether becoming involved with this man had been a mistake. Less than three weeks had passed since they had first met, and she could easily have ended the relationship before it developed further, but the fact was that she had fallen in love with Robert Taylor and already cared for him deeply. If the war was dragging him into some dark chasm which might change his personality forever, then it was her duty to pull him back from the abyss before he descended too far. She had taken it upon herself to become the custodian of his soul, to nurse him through any unpleasantness and reap the rewards at the end. Robert Taylor, she believed, was her soul mate, and she was not prepared to let the war take him from her.

Back in her flat they went to bed early and lay side by side, holding hands. She could tell that he was trying to act as if nothing was wrong, but the façade was a poor one.

"Robert," she said eventually, unable to bear the silence any longer, "you're not yourself. What's the matter? Can you tell me?"

"I don't know..."

"Is it something to do with me?"

"No."

"Is it something that's happened to you?"

"Yes."

"Tell me. Please - it might help."

"I don't want to drag you into it. Don't worry - I'll be alright... Anyway, I'm not really sure what the problem is, so I think I'll have to try to figure it out myself."

During the night, Susan had to endure the legacy of Robert's week-long diet of 'compo rations,' as he produced the most foul-smelling and noxious farts in his sleep. Then, suddenly and without warning, he sat up with a quiet whimper, and when she hugged him he was damp with sweat.

"What is it, Robert?" she persisted.

Reluctantly, he told her about the firefight on Thurstaston Common, and how he had shot a man in the head and was unable to dismiss the recurring image from his mind. She listened in silence, deeply troubled by what he was saying. Eventually she asked, "Did you *really* have to shoot him?"

"That's what's bothering me. But it's what we're trained to do."

"But if he was just lying there..." She wanted to be on his side, but was appalled that her lover had committed such a barbaric act. People did not do that sort of thing in the civilised world with which she was familiar.

I couldn't take a chance," he said defensively. "I thought he had a grenade. I thought he was trying to trick Thomas and me into thinking he was dead."

"Then it seems to me your conscience is clear. It just seems so horrible, though..."

"I know. But that's war."

She shuddered in the darkness, wondering whether perhaps his humanity had already slipped away and she had lost him forever.

Gerald Radley was disappointed to have missed the reconnaissance patrol's return to Wirral, and decided as a compensatory gesture to welcome home the crew of the *Plymouth* when she docked in Birkenhead. He toured the ship with her captain, chatting to the sailors about their first operational voyage.

"Very impressive, Captain," he declared with satisfaction at the end of the tour. "Just think – a few months ago she was a rusting museum piece and now – a proud fighting ship once again, just returned from a successful mission! My congratulations to all concerned."

"How long before we go out again?" the captain asked.

"As soon as possible. Within two or three weeks, I would hope. I'd like you to make a list of anything that needs sorting out before then – any repairs or modifications which need doing, that sort of thing."

"Already done, Council Leader."

"Excellent." Radley looked disapprovingly at the sailors disembarking from the frigate's gangway. "But I'm not sure I like those overalls your crewmen are wearing. Makes them look like mechanics, not sailors."

"They're comfortable and practical, Council Leader..."

"Hmm, nevertheless, they should look the part as well. They need a uniform of some kind...British sailors should wear white jumpers, like what's-his-name in *The Cruel Sea*. I'll put an order in for you..."

When Robert Taylor heard on the military grapevine that Radley had insisted all sailors wear white crew-neck jumpers, he laughed out loud.

"Whatever will he think of next?" he asked Conrad rhetorically. "Issuing us with Lee-Enfields or something?"

"These modern rifles may be effective, but they don't have any *character,*" Radley complained to Duncan Silverlock as they entered the town hall and the two soldiers of the ceremonial guard stood to attention with their odd-looking SA80s.

"The .303 Lee-Enfield," he declared, "*that's* the rifle which made Britain great. I'll speak to Alistair, see if he can get hold of any..."

Fortunately, there were several Lee-Enfield No.4 rifles amongst the confiscated civilian guns in the C Company armoury. They were duly cleaned and oiled and issued to the town hall guard, who were also ordered to wear smartly pressed 'number two' dress uniforms instead of their usual camouflaged combats. Radley was the sort of man who derived disproportionate pleasure from whimsical touches such as his personalised car number plate or the *Jerusalem* ring tone on his mobile phone, so the sight of the gleaming Lee-Enfields each morning was a source of great delight to him, of which he never tired.

On the second day of his leave, Robert found himself with nothing to do. Susan had to go to work – ironically, to produce large-scale annotated maps and computer models from the data gathered by the recce team in France – so he lounged around in her flat until the inanity of daytime television made him restless and angry.

He drove back to his house in Rock Ferry to see Mark Conrad, but he had gone out also, leaving Robert feeling like a little boy with no-one to play with. Sorting out his kit occupied a few hours, and then suddenly he remembered some unfinished business.

Equipped with a small rucksack containing some carefully selected items, he cycled on his mountain bike to Thurstaston Common, heading for the area in which the firefight had taken place. When he was quite close he hid his bike in some bushes and made his way carefully through the heather, until the view ahead matched the one in his memory – the view he had seen as he led his section during the advance to contact. It was not long before he came to the small valley in which the French soldier had been killed. He glanced around furtively with a combination of guilt and nervous excitement, almost expecting to see the man's corpse still lying by the stream. It was gone, of course, but something else was still there. After a surprisingly quick search, he found the grenade which the Frenchman had dropped and he had kicked into the undergrowth. For a few minutes he crouched in the heather, making sure that no-one else was in the vicinity, before pulling on a pair of disposable rubber gloves and scooping the grenade into a sealable transparent plastic bag. This was then wrapped in an ordinary carrier bag and placed in his rucksack. What he was doing was highly illegal, and he would face a severe penalty if caught, but his actions were driven by some inner sense of foreboding about Gearld Radley's regime, which told him that the grenade might be useful in the future. Now all he had to do was hide it somewhere.

It was too risky to take it home, so he jogged through the woodland to the edge of the common, where the trees and bushes ended abruptly at a wooden fence bordering a road. He found a secluded spot with a particularly distinctive triple-stemmed birch tree, and used his folding entrenching tool to dig a small but deep hole at its base, carefully placing the turf and soil onto a piece of plastic sheet. Then he donned a fresh pair of disposable gloves and put the grenade, still wrapped in its plastic bags, into the bottom of the hole and carefully replaced the soil and turf. Within a day or so it would be impossible to tell that the ground had ever been disturbed.

His chosen location was just out of sight of the road but he pushed through the gorse and bracken to reach the boundary fence, where he used his penknife to cut a small notch in one of the wooden posts, to help him locate the site in future. Then he jogged back to his bike and cycled home.

On his way through Prenton he came across a group of agitated-looking people who were partly blocking the road. Several citizens were shouting angrily and throwing assorted missiles at one of the houses, while another man was crudely painting the words 'anti-social scum' across the garage door of the property. From behind the shattered pane of an upstairs window, a youth was shouting abuse down at the crowd, ducking out of sight every few seconds to avoid the stones and bottles being hurled at him.

The crowd ignored Robert and he cycled on without looking back. As soon as he had turned the next corner and was out of sight of the mob, he used his mobile phone to contact the police. Eventually, after a series of exasperating recorded voice messages, he got through to a human being – a pleasant-sounding woman - and explained what he had just witnessed. She put him on hold while she checked her computer.

"It's alright, sir," she declared reassuringly, "we know about that. In fact, an officer has just left the scene. I'm not sure whether you're aware, but under new legislation, anyone convicted of more than one offence automatically loses their right to the protection of the law. It's what Council Leader Radley calls *community justice*. That house belongs to a family with multiple convictions for anti-social behaviour, so they are not entitled to assistance from the police if they become the victims of anti-social behaviour such as vandalism or abuse. But thanks for calling..."

Robert began to suspect that the whole world had gone mad, and felt vindicated in hiding the French grenade.

It was around this time that a new and terrifying threat appeared to menace the people of Wirral. Up until this point, French air raids had been sporadic and small-scale, inflicting relatively few casualties and causing only limited damage. Suddenly, the nature of the raids changed dramatically. They began taking place every night, and the improvised incendiaries and home-made bombs were replaced by high-explosive munitions of devastating power. The trend was for between three and five of these new bombs to be dropped onto a residential area in the early hours of the morning, and, despite large quantities of tracer being pumped into the night sky by the SCW air defence gunners, the enemy aircraft always seemed to escape unscathed.

In reality there were no enemy aircraft. The explosions which rocked Wirral nearly every night came not from the French but from the SCW mortar, concealed in the back of a white panel van with no roof which was driven to various firing locations around the peninsular. Its targets were the homes and workplaces of anyone who had got on the wrong side of Gerald Radley and his Council. Dissident intellectuals, uncooperative businessmen, obstructive lawyers, critical journalists, disapproving clergymen - basically any citizen who had dared to defy the authority of the Council Leader - all were regarded as real or potential threats and as such were fair game. Each night, just as the mortar unleashed its first shot, the AA gunners were ordered to start firing into the air to create the impression of a genuine air raid. The mortar bombs were directed onto their target by SCW spotters in an unmarked car, who observed the fall of shot and advised the mortar crew accordingly, so that adjustments could be made if necessary. Usually, a few preliminary rounds were required before the target was hit, and this trial-and-error process caused a lot of collateral damage to neighbouring houses. Radley regarded these 'innocent' casualties as an acceptable consequence of war, and believed that the process, though regrettable, would contribute towards the strengthening of Wirral's stoicism and resolve. It certainly hardened people's attitudes towards the French and increased their fear of air raids; those who had previously not taken the threat seriously now hurriedly taped up their windows, stockpiled supplies and built shelters, which they scurried into whenever the warning siren wailed - much to Gerald Radley's satisfaction.

Across the river Dee in Wales, the two French corporals had bought a small rowing boat and some fishing gear. On several occasions when the tide and weather were favourable, they rowed out into the channel and sat fishing from their boat in the vicinity of the Hoyle sandbank, from where their binoculars gave them a good view of Hilbre Island and the men defending it.

Robert and Mark Conrad returned to a Charlie Company which had changed considerably during their absence. The unit was now up to full strength, although many veteran privates and NCOs had been transferred to the fledgling A and B companies to redistribute the level of experience within the regiment. They were replaced by novices fresh from basic training whose inexperience was often compensated for by their enthusiasm and willingness to learn, which made a refreshing contrast to the indolence of 'old sweats' like Spencer and Harding. Robert was disappointed to learn that these two slovenly soldiers remained in his section while at the same time he had lost Finnegan and Thomas, both of whom had been posted to A Company as section second-in-commands. Jason Farrell remained as his own 2ic and had been officially promoted to lance-corporal, while three new recruits – Donnelly, Armstrong and Norman – had joined the section. Eight platoon's sergeant, Pete Collins, had been transferred to Nine Platoon and Paul Murphy had been promoted to replace him, much to Spencer's amusement: "When they present you with your three stripes," he said, with a titter of childish laughter, "will they also give you a little box containing your regulation issue moustache? I mean, everyone knows that all sergeants *must* have moustaches..."

The most obvious change which Robert noticed upon reporting for duty was that the SA80 rifle had been replaced by the American M16. He and the other three members of the Normandy patrol were each issued with a weapon and given an introductory lesson on it by the company armourer, who also furnished them with a training pamphlet to 'read and inwardly digest'. Then, in recognition of their special status, they were allowed to travel by civilian car to the Mockbeggar Wharf range complex and spend the remainder of the day 'zeroing' the new rifles at ranges varying from twenty-five to four hundred metres. Robert missed the short length and magnifying SUSAT sight of the SA80, but was impressed by the M16s robustness and ease of cleaning; it disassembled into just three main components, compared with the thirteen strippable parts of the SA80, some of which were tiny. When the four men had used up their quota of ammunition, they set about becoming as familiar as possible with the weapons by repeatedly practising the various drills until they could literally perform them blindfolded; as NCOs it was essential that they demonstrate complete proficiency in handling the new rifle, especially in front of new recruits, who would have trained with the M16 from the outset.

There followed a period of platoon level training which served to assimilate the new arrivals into their units and refine individual skills in preparation for a battalion level exercise to be held over three days. The intensity of training increased noticeably, and the soldiers began to suspect that they were being prepared for imminent action. As Hughes 42 put it, "Something's going to happen soon, lads."

Then, just as Robert was enjoying being back within the familiar brotherhood of Eight Platoon and Charlie Company, he, Conrad and Carter received notification that they were to transfer to A Company immediately.

"Major Aldridge will explain everything to you when you arrive," Blundell said simply. "Just remember that you carry the reputation of Charlie Company with you – I expect you to impress the hell out of those numpties."

With a growing sense of foreboding, the three men were driven over to Alpha Company's headquarters, located in one of the primary schools which the Council had sold to developers and then repossessed. An earth embankment had been bulldozed up against the walls as protection against air attack, and trenches dug around the building to complement the high razor-wire fence. Two sandbag 'sangars' guarded the entrance to the compound, and from their firing slits the barrels of LSWs traversed menacingly, pointing at the C Company Land Rover as it pulled up at the barrier. A sentry emerged and approached the vehicle.

"Good afternoon gents," the soldier said in an officious voice, before exclaiming, "Rob, Mark, Sergeant Carter – good to see you!"

"Finnegan!" Robert exclaimed. "Or should I say, '*Lance-corporal* Finnegan!' How goes it?"

"Not good. It's just been announced that the entire company is confined to barracks. No leave, no contact with anyone outside until further notice. I reckon we'll be off on a foreign holiday very soon..."

Major Aldridge, the erstwhile C Company second-in-command, greeted them cordially when they entered his office. He also expressed appreciation that they had 'volunteered' to be seconded to A company, as if they had any choice in the matter. Thomas was already present, sitting casually in a chair, chatting to the RSM. Glancing around the room, Robert noticed that the scene bore a striking resemblance to the initial meeting in Blundell's office prior to the reconnaissance mission, and it was with no great surprise that the four soldiers learned that they would soon be returning to France.

"When we land we'll need your knowledge of the ground for the first few days," Aldridge told them. "You'll be spread throughout the company to provide advice as and when required, until we build up an intelligence base ourselves. Then we'll get you back to Charlie Company as soon as possible, except of course for you, Lance-corporal Thomas – you're with us for the duration, I'm afraid."

"What a fantastic reward for our efforts over there," Robert muttered bitterly to Mark Conrad, after they had left Aldridge's office and were walking to their accommodation. "We did so well, we get to go back! It's just fucking typical!" He was utterly resentful that, for the second time in a month, the Army was snatching him away from Susan against his will, without even allowing him the opportunity to say goodbye.

The following day, Alpha Company commenced a five-day 'offensive operations' training package which included a night-time amphibious assault on the coastal defences at Thurstaston. As the soldiers launched their attack using blank ammunition and thunder-flashes, Robert realised that the scenario had been deliberately created to mimic Longues-sur-Mer. There was even a mock-up of a concrete fortification which resembled the German observation bunker perched on the cliff-top in Normandy. By now, all of the men knew that they were destined for France, although only officers and selected NCOs had been officially informed. The Council's 'Military Committee' had decided that detailed briefings and full orders would take place on board the ships during the voyage south, to prevent breaches of security which might have led to sensitive information being leaked to the press.

While A Company rehearsed amphibious landings from small boats, the regiment's other units were occupied with defensive duties around the peninsular. Two platoons from B Company were permanently dug-in along the Dee coastline, with a third in reserve. Charlie Company was responsible for guarding the north coast, from West Kirby to Fort Perch Rock, while the engineers and transport troops protected the Mersey shore from possible attack. Everyone could sense that the tempo of the preparations was steadily increasing, but they were of course unaware that Radley and Lebovic had been engaged in secret discussions and that a date had already been set for the invasion.

Then, one dismal October night, the men of A Company were roused quietly from their beds and taken by coaches and four-tonne trucks to the East Float dock, where they boarded the ships which would carry them south into battle. Company Headquarters, One Platoon and various support troops embarked upon the frigate *Plymouth*, while the requisitioned ferry *Royal Daffodil* accommodated Two and Three Platoons. Tethered to the stern of each ship were the small boats which would carry the troops ashore, and amongst these diminutive vessels floated some crude landing craft, hurriedly constructed from welded steel plate to transport the company's vehicles and heavy equipment. Two of the landing craft contained large and mysterious tarpaulin-covered *somethings*. These were the Trojans, the British secret weapon for securing a beach-head on the Normandy coastline.

Colonel Hogan had studied the Allied landings of 1944 and was aware that British and Canadian forces had benefited enormously during D-Day from what had been referred to as 'The Funnies' – purpose-built armoured vehicles which were specially designed to breach coastal defences such as sea walls, ditches, barbed wire entanglements and minefields. He had therefore requested that similar machines be produced to support A Company, and the Trojans were the result. They were basically bulldozers with waterproofed engines, a smoke generator fitted behind the blade and armour plate welded at angles over vulnerable areas such as the radiator grille and windscreen. The driver steered the vehicle using vision slits and a periscope, and behind the cab was a protected platform on which several soldiers could shelter in relative safety from incoming fire. On either side of the machine, above the tracks, were steel coffin-like compartments with slits at the front ends, through which a rifle or machine gun could be fired by a soldier lying inside. A total of four bulldozers were converted to Trojans and camouflaged in black and green; two were destined for France, while the others remained in Wirral to help protect the Motherland.

In utmost secrecy, the troops filed aboard their respective vessels and made themselves as comfortable as possible. Much to Hogan's annoyance, Gerald Radley insisted upon accompanying the invasion force, and took up residence in the captain's cabin aboard *Plymouth*.

In the early hours of the morning, while it was still dark, the *Plymouth* and *Royal Daffodil* slipped their moorings and sailed discretely out into the Mersey, with their small boats and Trojans bumping along in their wakes like tin cans behind a newlywed couple's car. The war was about to begin in earnest.

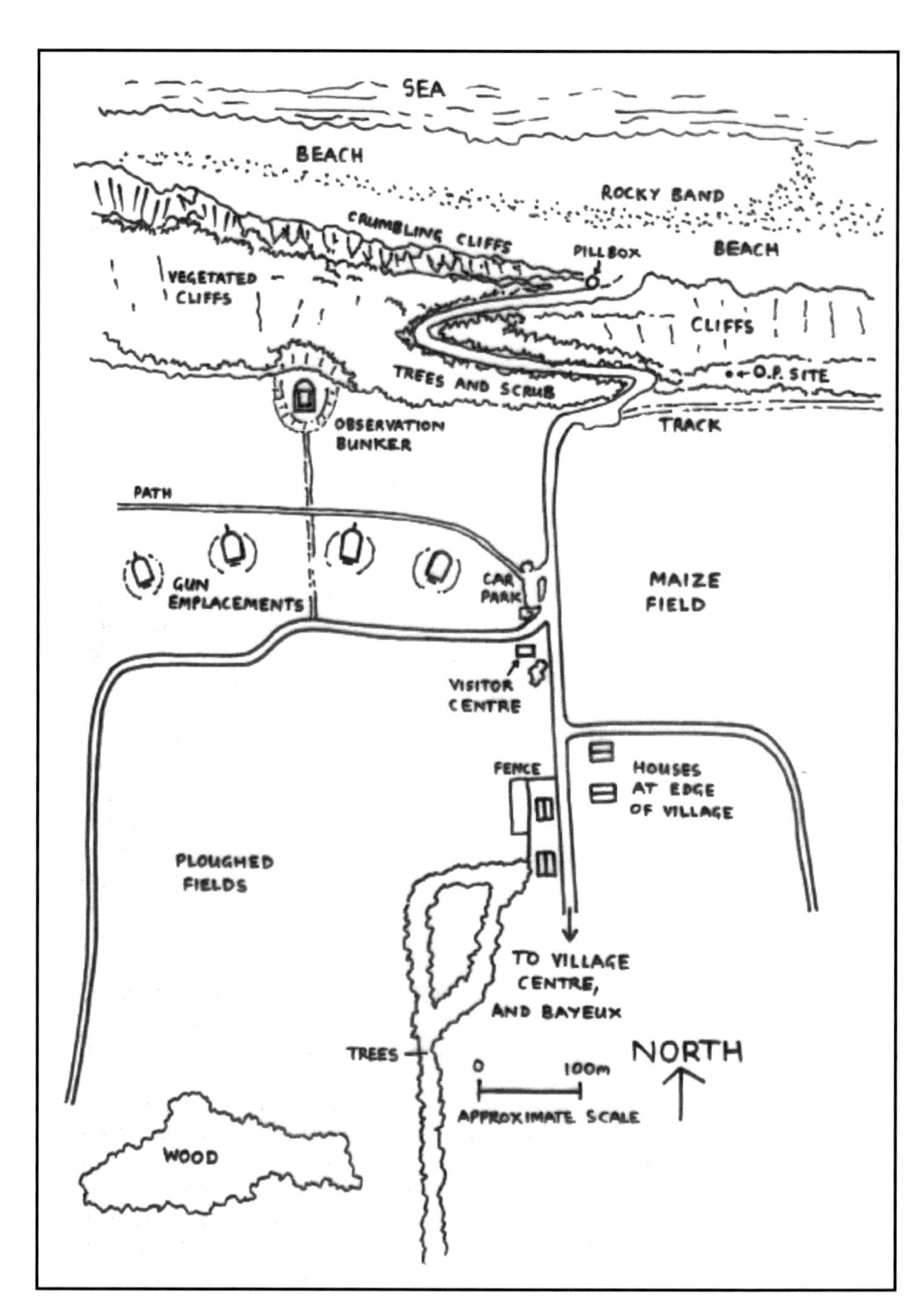

Robert Taylor's sketch map of Longues-Sur-Mer coastline

CHAPTER 19

D-Day

My advice to readers is to temporarily suspend disbelief and enjoy this book for what it is – a slice of pure, escapist hokum.

Joseph Chopicalqui
Amateur Yachting Monthly

Mr Roberts replies:
Hokum shlocum!

And so it came to pass that Robert Taylor found himself aboard the twenty-eight foot yacht *Sea Vixen*, a kilometre off the French coast in increasingly choppy seas. The yacht, which was being used as a motor boat without sails, lurched and rolled unpredictably, and in the dark confines of the cabin he felt nauseous despite the precautionary sea-sickness tablets he had swallowed earlier.

The shadowy bulk of *Plymouth*, barely visible in the blackness, towered above the flotilla of small craft as they formed up into a line along the frigate's port side. It was essential that, as far as possible, the vessels set off in a straight line so that they arrived at the beach simultaneously; to help them orientate themselves in the darkness, each boat had been fitted with a pair of small lights – green for port and red for starboard – which were recessed deep within protective cowls so that they could only be seen when viewed directly from the side. *Sea Vixen*'s skipper – a civilian volunteer – stood on tiptoes in the cockpit and looked from left to right along the line of lights to check his position. Deciding that he was a little too far forward, he put the engine briefly into reverse and nudged the boat back into alignment.

Major Aldridge peered out from the rear hatch and tutted impatiently when he realised they were still alongside *Plymouth*, rather than heading towards the shore. He immediately got on the radio to find out the cause of the delay, and was informed that a man had gone overboard from *Royal Daffodil*, which had held up the embarkation process.

The boat rolled unexpectedly, causing Aldridge to lose his balance and fall against Robert. There were eight men and their equipment crammed into the confined space of the cabin, and all that the soldiers could see of each other in the almost total blackness was the tiny luminous green glow-stick which they all wore on the rear of their helmets to make them visible from behind and, hopefully, prevent them from being shot in the back by their own comrades during the night assault.

"Just hang on in there, gents," the major told them reassuringly. "It'll be a few more minutes before we're off, I'm afraid."

"Don't worry, sir," someone responded in the claustrophobic gloom. "We're not in any great hurry, to be honest."

"Why was H-hour brought forward, sir?" Robert enquired, aware that he was perhaps being impertinent but feeling that, given the circumstances, he was entitled to ask any question he liked.

"Because the weather's changing, Corporal Taylor," Aldridge replied. "It was supposed to stay calm all night, but the sea's getting rougher and there may be a storm on its way. We need to get ashore as soon as possible."

Robert's bowels felt as if they were about to explode, so he pushed his way apologetically through the press of bodies to the yacht's forward compartment in the hope of finding a toilet. To his surprise, his groping hands touched a pair of legs, which flinched with startled irritation.

"Keep your hands to yourself, mate," said an indignant voice from above. It was the boat's LSW gunner, positioned in the front hatch to give covering fire as they approached the beach. The Light Support Weapon was not an ideal gun for the job, as it was magazine-fed and therefore limited in firepower. A request from Hogan that it be replaced or supplemented by the superior belt-fed 'Minimi' machine gun had been turned down by Gerald Radley in a fit of pique; on the day that the he received the written request from the colonel, the Council Leader had been in an anti-army mood and had suddenly decided to spend the money on submachine-guns for an elite squad of one hundred Special Council Workers which would form his personal guard. This extravagant expenditure was completely unjustifiable, as the SCW had only fired a couple of shots in anger since being issued with firearms, but logic and common sense did not always prevail in Gerald Radley's decision-making process. So the Special Council Workers got their trendy and expensive Heckler and Koch MP5s to pose with on street corners, while the infantry had to make do with the less than ideal LSW as they went into battle against the French.

"Sorry, mate," Robert called up to the gunner, "but I'm absolutely busting for a shit. Is there a toilet in here?"

"I'm standing on it. Wait a minute."

Begrudgingly, the man moved his feet to one side and Robert located a foul-smelling chemical toilet buried under a pile of bergens. He fumbled to untie his life-jacket and drop his trousers, then lent back against the sandbags which had been stacked in the bow as protection against bullets, and sighed with relief as he finally emptied his bowels.

"That's disgusting," commented the LSW gunner, as a horrendous stench drifted upwards, and Robert had to agree. Moments later, the yacht's engine rumbled into life and the boat surged towards the shore.

At the same time as the invasion fleet was finally unleashed, the Agusta helicopter took off from *Plymouth* on a very important mission.

On board the aircraft were Sergeant Carter and five other heavily armed soldiers whose job it was to set up ambushes on the main routes leading to the invasion beach – the routes along which French reinforcements were most likely to come. The helicopter clattered over Robert's boat in the darkness and swung away to the east, giving the landing beach a wide berth so as not to alert the defenders.

The flotilla was halfway towards the shore when suddenly, from behind the boats, came three enormous detonations and flashes of light in quick succession. This was *Plymouth*'s mortar, firing enormous canister-like bombs at the French coast. The huge munitions were of three types – high-explosive, illuminating and smoke – and had been developed by the science and technology departments of several Wirral secondary schools. After successful trials, large-scale production had been carried out by pregnant teenage girls and former benefit claimants working in converted church halls and community centres under the Council's 'Idle Hands' programme.

One bomb dropped onto the beach, another fell slightly short into the breaking waves, and the third landed with a *thud* in a field just behind the old German observation bunker. For several seconds nothing happened, then thick black smoke began to pour from two of the canisters; the third had evidently malfunctioned. Immediately, the French responded by firing up several rocket flares which initiated with a *pop!* and hung in the sky on parachutes, illuminating the invasion fleet as it wallowed in the heavy swell. From several points along the shore came streams of tracer, gliding out towards the British boats and sending up spurts of water as they hit the sea. *Plymouth* returned fire with her Oerlikon cannons, aiming for where the French fire seemed to originate from. The frigate's huge mortar fired another salvo, and shortly afterwards three tremendous explosions shook the coastline as the high-explosive fragmentation canisters blasted out a lethal hail of nuts, bolts and stone chippings.

Major Aldridge stood in the cockpit and shuddered as he watched the mortar bombs explode. Then he leaned into the cabin and shouted "Corporal Taylor - on me if you please. I need your advice."

Robert was only too glad to get out into the fresh air and he climbed eagerly up into the cockpit. Standing next to the OC, he peered over the top of the cabin towards the dim silhouette of the French coast, which rose and fell in the darkness ahead.

"Do you recognize anything?" Aldridge asked, as a stream of glowing tracer swung towards the yacht but fell mercifully short. "The GPS reading is right, the bearing's right, but I'd still like to be certain we're heading for the right place."

Robert squinted through his CWS night sight, but spray on the front lens made it impossible to identify any features clearly. Then the French obligingly fired up two more rocket flares, and in their eerie, flickering light he recognized a distinctive piece of cliff-top. Suddenly the panorama made sense to him.

"Can you see that point on the cliffs where there's trees and bushes to the right but to the left it's flatter?" he shouted to the major.

"Seen."

"I'm fairly sure that's about where the track from the beach comes up onto the cliff-top. The tracer we can see coming from the right over there is probably from the observation bunker. The other tracer from way over on the left is from a trench on the cliff-top, and the firing coming from lower down must be from the pillbox on the beach."

"Good. So we should hit the beach about two hundred metres from the pillbox..."

Three more fragmentation canisters exploded on the shore and pieces of shrapnel whined through the air and splashed into the water a short distance ahead. The French flares burned out and once again it was almost completely dark, apart from a few small fires burning on the cliffs. Robert watched in fascination as tracer rounds from *Plymouth*'s Oerlikon cannons drifted through the blackness to his right, appearing to move with impossible slowness before striking the cliffs like a series of mighty hammer blows. Then there was another salvo from the frigate's mortar, which this time sent shrapnel raining down onto the boat. Aldridge decided that the risk of casualties from these munitions was becoming unacceptably high as the flotilla neared the beach, so he quickly made radio contact with *Plymouth*.

"Hello Neptune this is Zero, message, over."

"*Neptune, send, over.*"

"Zero, no more HE, er, smoke only from now on. I say again, no more Hotel Echo, smoke only, over."

"*Neptune, roger out.*"

Then, as Robert watched in horror, the French gunners struck lucky and scored a direct hit on one of the boats. Tracer bullets started a small fire which swiftly grew into a large blaze, and presented the enemy defenders with a clearly visible target. From the shore came three vengeful streams of tracer, which converged on the stricken craft like light rays focused by a convex lens. Shouts and screams were audible above the sound of the waves, and in the light of the flames, figures could be seen jumping into the sea. Robert shuddered. They were still a considerable distance from the beach.

It was a horrific spectacle but Aldridge, to his credit, remained composed throughout. He calmly informed *Plymouth* of the situation by radio and requested that a rescue boat be dispatched immediately. Then he issued an 'all callsigns' command for the gunners in the invasion fleet to open fire.

"What am I firing at, sir?" shouted the LSW gunner from *Sea Vixen*'s front hatch.

"Anything you can see - wherever the enemy fire is coming from," the major replied. "It doesn't really matter – just start putting rounds down in the direction of France!"

At that moment, the gunners in the other boats began to open fire, and the soldier on *Sea Vixen* forgot his concerns about the lack of clearly identifiable targets and followed suit. The LSW might not have been the best light machine gun in the world, but sixteen of the weapons firing simultaneously could lay down an impressive volume of fire. Every fifth round fired was a tracer bullet, which enabled the gunners to see where their shots were going; most of the bullets simply disappeared on impact, but a few lay burning on the cliffs like glowing embers, and a considerable number ricocheted into the air in all directions – some even came spinning back towards the invasion fleet, which was rather unnerving.

Yet more smoke canisters from *Plymouth* landed in the vicinity of the beach and added to the dark veils already swirling around the cliffs. Then, to everyone's amazement, a stream of tracer materialised out of the night sky and poured down onto the French defences. It took Robert a few seconds to realise that this was not divine fire support from the heavens, but rather the Agusta helicopter, strafing the cliff-top with its door-mounted machine-gun as it returned from dropping-off the ambush teams.

From his privileged position in the boat's cockpit, Robert watched proceedings with a combination of fear, excitement and almost voyeuristic wonderment. He was thrilled to be part of the momentous proceedings, yet at the same time felt strangely detached from it all, as if he were watching live coverage of the event on television.

No more flares had been sent up by either side, but even in the darkness it was possible to make out the white foam of waves which were starting to break around the boat, indicating that the water was getting shallower.

"We're getting close, gents," Aldridge shouted. "Prepare to move."

The LSW gunner continued firing bursts blindly into the veil of black smoke, although there seemed to be very little tracer coming back from the French positions. Waves were breaking against the stern of the yacht, carrying it in towards the shore like a surf board. The skipper opened the throttle fully to ensure that they hit the beach as fast as possible and ran aground firmly to prevent the craft from being dragged back out again as each wave retreated. According to the invasion plan, the moon should have provided sufficient ambient light to guide the boats ashore, but the unexpected cloud cover had denied the British any significant natural illumination. Aldridge considered the pros and cons of using flares during the final approach, and decided that the risk of men drowning in the dark probably out-weighed the risk of French gunfire. He fired up a single Schermuly, and suddenly the beach and cliffs were visible through the smoke - much closer than expected.

"Private Pearce!" the major shouted down into the cabin, "Get ready!"

Pearce, a large man from Company HQ, made his way precariously along the boat's handrail to collect an anchor attached to a length of thick rope, tied to the prow. He crouched next to the LSW gunner and held onto the front hatch to steady himself as the yacht lurched and rolled like a bucking bronco. At that moment the flare burned out and it was dark once more. *Sea Vixen* surged forward and there was a sudden jolt as her twin keels struck submerged rocks and brought her to an abrupt halt.

"Stop! Stop firing!" Aldridge shouted at the LSW gunner. "Pearce – go now!"

Clutching the anchor and coil of rope, Pearce leapt from the bow into the swirling black water below, and waded towards the shore. Another wave broke around the yacht, carrying her in a little further and engulfing Pearce in white foam. He stumbled, braced himself as the surf sucked back, then ran through the shallow water and up onto the beach above the tide line, which consisted of sand and shingle strewn with large, rounded boulders. As soon as the rope went tight he flung himself down, wedging the anchor into a crevice between two barnacle-covered rocks and lying on it with his full weight to prevent it from being dislodged.

"Go go go!" shouted Aldridge, and one by one the men aboard *Sea Vixen* jumped down into the turbulent knee-deep water and headed for dry land, frequently faltering as their boots struck unseen rocks in the darkness. No enemy fire greeted them, much to their surprise and relief, although tracer could be seen flashing across the beach some distance away to their right, where the pillbox guarding the cliff road was evidently still holding out.

When everyone was ashore they lay in a line amongst the rocks, nervously pointing their rifles in the direction of the dark outline of the cliffs ahead. Robert squinted through his night-sight, but was unable to see very much at all due to the smoke and almost total absence of ambient light. All along the beach, spaced at irregular intervals, the other craft of the invasion fleet were running aground and their occupants struggling ashore. He took advantage of the momentary lull in the proceedings to shrug off his life-jacket and check his webbing pouches and other items of equipment.

Major Aldridge was doing his best to remain calm and composed but was finding the darkness and general confusion of the situation very stressful. To make matters worse, the company signaller was experiencing radio problems, which were making it impossible to contact prominent personnel such as the CSM or the three platoon commanders.

"Company Sergeant-major!" Aldridge yelled in the direction of a group of shadowy figures who were just visible a short distance away. "Sergeant-major Blackburn! It's the OC here... Has anyone seen the CSM?"

No-one answered, and Aldridge swore under his breath. The key figures in the company had been deliberately dispersed throughout the flotilla as an insurance against them all being wiped-out simultaneously, but now that the troops were ashore it was imperative that the command structure re-formed and began operating effectively as soon as possible. It was in circumstances such as these that the discrepancy in experience between a senior-ranking TA officer and his regular army equivalent became starkly apparent; the assault had been planned and rehearsed in considerable detail but, lying on the beach 'for real', Aldridge was struggling to act decisively for fear of possibly disastrous consequences. He was aware that the main priority was to get his men off the exposed beach without delay, and to maintain the momentum of the assault, but at the same time he did not want to lead the company impetuously into an ambush or similar disaster. His mind was racing, and as he frantically considered the various courses of action open to him, he could hear the words of one of his instructors at Sandhurst echoing sternly in his mind: '*Whatever you do, do **something**. Doing nothing is not an option!*'

Aldridge crawled up alongside Robert. "Corporal Taylor! Where's the wire?"

"On the other side of this band of rocks, I think, sir!"

"Go forward with Pritchard and cut it."

"Right, sir."

Keeping as low to the ground as possible, Robert and Private Pritchard made their way awkwardly across the treacherous, ankle-twisting band of boulders and rock pools, then crawled over an expanse of sand and shingle until they reached the single coil of razor wire. They had just started to go to work on it with their wire-cutters when, from further along the beach, there came a sudden flash of light and the loud *thud!* of an explosion, as an anti-tank missile was fired at the French pillbox. The structure began to spew pale smoke, and there was a sudden crackle of smallarms fire, which petered out until the only sounds were those of men shouting above the breaking of the waves. Then there were several muted detonations as grenades were posted inside the smouldering fortification, followed by bursts of automatic fire, before all went quiet again.

Meanwhile, Aldridge had got on the radio to ascertain how many of his men were ashore and what they were doing. He needed to know whether he currently commanded a company, a platoon or a fragmented rabble. Much to his relief, as the various callsigns responded, it became apparent that the operation had gone remarkably well. Apart from the boat which had caught fire, the entire invasion fleet had succeeded in reaching the beach - albeit with a number of casualties - and now almost a hundred soldiers were lying or crouching just above the tide line while their officers and NCOs frantically tried to marshal them into fireteams and sections so that they could start operating effectively. Several sub-units had already sorted themselves out and, acting on their own initiative and in accordance with the orders they had received the previous evening, were breaching the wire and advancing towards the cliffs.

Robert and Pritchard finished cutting out a section of razor-wire, and used their rifles to drag it aside and open up a gap. Moments later, the men from *Sea Vixen* dashed through the breach and headed towards the base of the cliffs. This area was something of an unknown quantity, as Robert and Mark Conrad had been unable to see it clearly during their reconnaissance patrol. Abruptly, Aldridge's men found themselves standing against a sheer face of crumbling sandstone. They were disappointed not to have found a climbable slope, but on the positive side, at least they were off the exposed beach and in an area of good cover. The major pulled the radio handset out of the signaller's bergen and finally succeeded in making contact with the CSM to arrange a rendezvous.

"Is Major Aldridge around here?" shouted a silhouetted figure, stumbling towards them out of the gloom. "Major Aldridge?"

"Foxtrot Romeo," Robert challenged.

"Oscar Golf!"

"Who is that?" Aldridge asked, intrigued.

"The cameraman," answered the mysterious figure. "I was hoping you could tell us how it's all going - for the viewers back home?"

Aldridge was aware that Gerald Radley wanted the landings filmed and had brought along a reporter-come-cameraman for that specific purpose. The major also knew that the Council Leader had deliberately restricted the media presence during the invasion to this one man, so as to increase the exclusivity of his reports and inflate their value when sold to the highest bidding external news agencies, to generate additional Council income.

"So, Major Aldridge," the reporter said, "Can you tell us how the operation is going at this stage?"

"Wait a minute," Aldridge said suspiciously, "are you filming me?"

"Er, yes. Sir."

"How?'

"I've got an infra-red facility on this camera..."

Aldridge exploded. "You're illuminating me with an infra-red light on a *battlefield*? Are you mad? Turn that bloody thing off and go away now! If I see you again tonight I'll shoot you myself!"

The reporter scurried sheepishly away as more troops accumulated at the base of the cliffs on either side of Aldridge's group. Some began making tentative attempts to scramble up the crumbling sandstone rock face, without success. Meanwhile, down at the water's edge, the two landing craft containing the Trojans had just hit the beach and were lowering their ramps to release the machines. What no-one could believe was the lack of French resistance. Everyone had been expecting – dreading – a murderous hail of fire from the cliffs above which would turn the beach into a killing ground, but instead there was nothing. No machine-gun fire, no mortar bombardment, no illuminating flares – nothing.

"Corporal Taylor," Aldridge said, "where's the place where you climbed up the cliffs during your recce?"

"Er, way over there, sir – beyond the pillbox. But that doesn't mean there aren't other places we can get up..."

Several figures emerged out of the gloom and Robert challenged them. "Foxtrot Romeo!"

"Oscar Golf! Who's that?"

"The OC," replied the major indignantly. "Who's that?"

"The CSM, sir."

Aldridge was greatly relieved. If anyone could bring order to the confusion on the beach it was the Company Sergeant-major. In fact, due to the chronic shortage of senior officers within the battalion, Aldridge was currently without a commissioned second-in-command and was unofficially relying on the CSM to fulfill that role. "Ah, thank God – Sergeant-major Blackburn!" he declared affectionately. "I was wondering where you'd got to..."

"We ended up landing near the pillbox sir, with Two Platoon..."

"Not to worry. I've been having some intermittent comms trouble, Sergeant-major, so I'm not entirely sure what's going on. Can you give me a sitrep?"

"Well it could be a hell of a lot worse, sir, to be honest. Most of the men are pretty much where they should be. Three Platoon are over to the right, Two Platoon are in the middle and One Platoon appear to be around here with you – I just bumped into Corporal Watts's section just now, trying to get up the cliffs."

"Any luck? Is it like this all the way along?"

"No, thank God. There's quite a long stretch between here and the pillbox where the cliffs slope right down to the beach, without this sheer bit like you've got here. Several sections are trying to make their way up with ropes."

"What's the score with the cliff road? Is the pillbox out of action?"

"Yes sir. Two platoon are getting ready to advance up the road, but they're still sorting themselves out and are waiting for one of the Trojans, which I think is just on its way up now, by the sound of it."

"Good. It sounds like everything's going about as well as we could have hoped for. The main effort now must be to get as many men onto that cliff-top as quickly as possible, then sweep the area for enemy and advance inland before the French counter-attack. I need to get up there myself, while you get things organised down here. Three Platoon are staying here to secure the beach and act as our reserve. They'll need a section dug-in on each flank in case the enemy try counter-attacking along the beach. One Trojan can stay down here to clear the wire out of the way and help construct defences, the other needs to be up at the top of the road."

"Right, sir. Where do you want the Company Aid Post – and the Command Post for that matter?"

"I haven't decided definitely about the CP yet, but the CAP needs to be roughly in the centre of the beach, at the base of the cliffs - how about just this side of the pillbox – or even in the pillbox, once it's been checked?"

"Sounds good to me, sir."

"Oh – one other thing, Sergeant-major. Make it a priority that the mortar team get set up asap, and let me know the moment they're operational. We need fire support in place ready for any counter-attacks."

"Right, sir. I'll crack on, then."

The CSM hurried away into the night, taking with him most of the HQ personnel and leaving the major with just Robert and the company signaller. Aldridge finally succeeded in making radio contact with each of his platoon commanders, and was delighted to learn that his company was in a better state of organisation than he had dared hope. A climbable route to the cliff-top had been discovered by a section from One Platoon, while soldiers from Two Platoon were advancing cautiously up the cliff road behind one of the Trojans. Satisfied that events were proceeding as planned, Aldridge passed the radio handset back to the signaller. "Come with me, gents!" he announced suddenly, and strode away in search of the route up to the cliff-top.

After seeking directions from various shadowy soldiers on the beach, and blundering around for a while amongst waist high gorse, bracken and bramble, the three-man party of Major Aldridge, Robert and the company signaller spotted a faint green glow in the darkness and headed for it, tripping and cursing on the way. The glow turned out to be a shrouded luminous glow-stick, fixed to a flare picket to mark the beginning of the route up. A small group of soldiers were loitering by the marker light, while others were dimly visible in the darkness above, ascending a grassy gulley with the aid of a rope in which loops had been tied at regular intervals to act as handholds. One of the shadowy figures at the bottom turned out to be Lieutenant Whitham, commander of One Platoon.

"Ah, Angus, glad you made it," Aldridge said, as if he were welcoming the lieutenant to a social function in the officer's mess. "How many men have you got up there? Your whole platoon?"

"Only two sections of it, I'm afraid, sir. It was one of our boats that got hit on the way in."

"Oh, I'm sorry…Right, we need to get up there now…"

One after another, they climbed up the gulley using the rope for assistance. Robert reached the hammered-in steel spike to which the top end of the rope had been attached and scrambled through rough grass and brambles to where Whitham's men were lying in all-round defence on the wet ground. The surroundings had a familiar feel, and he realised that the bush in which he and Conrad had concealed themselves during the reconnaissance mission must be nearby, somewhere off to the right.

"What now, sir?" asked Whitham. "Do you want us to start digging-in?

"Not yet. I want you to leave one section here, covering the left flank. Corporal Taylor thinks there's an enemy trench over to the left, but we're not going to deal with it now – we'll wait until we've got more men up here. I want your second section to advance along the cliff edge and make sure the French haven't got any nasty surprises for Two Platoon as they come up the road."

While the two officers were talking, Robert crouched next to the silhouette of a large man whom he guessed - correctly - to be Mark Conrad.

"How goes it, M.C.?"

"Robert! Not good, not good, R.T....Actually, I suppose at least we've made it this far. Miracles will never cease..."

Robert shielded his watch and pressed the button to illuminate the display. He was surprised at the time.

"Guess how long it's been since we started heading in towards the beach?"

Conrad thought for a moment. "Two hours? Three?"

"Just over forty minutes."

"Jesus! Doesn't time drag when you're not having fun!"

Lieutenant Whitham interrupted the conversation. "Corporal Conrad, I need you to go with One Section and lead them to the top of the road, okay?"

"Right, sir."

Conrad departed, leaving Robert lying in the cold, wet grass with Aldridge, Whitham and the company signaller. Robert scanned the landscape through his night-sight and found that he could see reasonably clearly now that the smoke had cleared and a feint glow from the moon was penetrating the clouds. Directly to his front lay the large maize field through which he and Conrad had approached the cliff-top during their reconnaissance mission, although the crop had since been flattened and left to rot. By kneeling up he was able to see over the broken stems and could just discern the shapes of the houses at the edge of the village, as well as a clump of small trees which he knew surrounded the toilets and visitor centre associated with the tourist attraction of the old German gun battery. Silhouetted against the skyline over to his right were the huge mounds of the gun emplacements themselves.

It was not long before Conrad and One Section reached the top of the cliff road and rendezvoused with Two Platoon. The French had made a token effort of blocking the road at that point with a barrier of telegraph poles and barbed wire which the clattering, lumbering Trojan swiftly bulldozed aside. Two Platoon then swung to the right and advanced across a field until its lead section came across the massive German observation bunker which lay like a great brooding beast in a hollow at the top of the cliffs. At the base of the bunker's rear wall, the British soldiers discovered a paralysed Frenchman, surrounded by spent rocket-flare tubes. He could neither move nor speak; the most likely explanation for his unfortunate situation was that he had been leaning out from beneath the bunker's concrete roof to fire-off the flares, when one of *Plymouth*'s mortar bombs had detonated nearby and caused him to fall onto his back.

Men from Two Platoon cautiously cleared the huge bunker by throwing grenades into each room and following-up the explosions with bursts of automatic fire. They found various items of equipment inside, but no living or dead enemy personnel; the defenders had evidently abandoned the position in haste during the invasion. Meanwhile, soldiers from One Platoon conducted a sweep of the left flank of the cliff-top and came across a trench containing a damaged machine gun, hundreds of fired cartridge cases and the decapitated body of a French defender.

Major Aldridge crouched at the top of the cliff road and listened with satisfaction to the radio reports coming in from One and Two Platoons. So far, everything seemed to be proceeding more or less according to plan – in fact, there had been less French resistance than expected – but he could not understand why the enemy showed no sign of counter-attacking. Then, as if in response to his perplexity, the radio crackled into life and one of Sergeant Carter's ambush teams reported "*Contact, wait out*."

The two-man team had set up its ambush on the main coast road about a mile south of the beach, and had spotted a convoy of what appeared to be military vehicles, approaching from the direction of Arromanches. They waited until the lead lorry was about one hundred metres away before firing an anti-tank missile straight into the front of the cab. The missile exploded and the vehicle swerved off the road into a farmer's field and came to rest in flames. Survivors from the back of the truck leapt to the ground and fled into the night. The driver of the second lorry slammed on his brakes only moments before he was killed by a long burst of automating fire from the British team's Light Support Weapon. French troops jumped from the rear of the stricken truck in a well-executed anti-ambush drill and began returning fire. The two British ambushers beat a hasty retreat and headed back towards the coast.

Aldridge decided to recall the other two teams, as it was now too dangerous to leave them isolated in enemy territory. They had served their purpose by delaying the French and making them wary and tentative, gaining the British a few more precious hours in which to consolidate their beachhead and advance further inland. However, tragedy struck an hour later, when Carter's team approached the German gun battery and stumbled into a clearance patrol from Two Platoon. In the darkness and confusion a brief firefight ensued before the company signaller, who could hear all of the radio traffic, realised what was happening and, acting on his own initiative, told each group to cease fire. They did, but by then it was too late: Sergeant Dave Carter lay in the mud, cursing at the irony of being shot in the abdomen by one of his own comrades.

By daybreak, Alpha Company had advanced a considerable distance inland without opposition. The lead unit – One Platoon – had occupied a small wood close to the edge of the village of Longues-sur-Mer, about half a kilometre from the beach. Major Aldridge decided that this would be the forward extent of their incursion into enemy territory, known as the Limit of Exploitation, or LoE. Any advance beyond this point would risk overstretching the company and make it vulnerable to attack from either flank.

With the sky beginning to lighten, he issued the command "Stand to," which marked the transition from night routine to day routine. Every member of the company stopped whatever they were doing and lay shivering on the dew-soaked ground, staring bleary-eyed over their weapons as dawn broke. There was an on-going debate in army circles as to whether the widespread use of night vision equipment had rendered the stand-to procedure obsolete, as an enemy could in theory attack effectively at any time during the hours of darkness, and certainly did not have to wait until dawn. Aldridge, however, liked the tradition of stand-to, believing that it afforded soldiers the opportunity to adjust their senses to the changing conditions and take stock of their situation, which was beneficial regardless of the likelihood of actually being attacked.

Even the first meagre traces of daylight were sufficient to banish much of the confusion which had hampered the night-time phase of the operation. Men could now just about see each other with the naked eye, and the baffling mosaic of shadowy shapes materialised into a comprehensible three-dimensional landscape in which it became possible to judge distance and recognise features such hedgerows, trees, walls and ditches. As the amount of daylight increased, disorientated units which had blundered around blindly during the night and deployed in the wrong locations were able to sort themselves out and move into the correct position.

The company remained at stand-to while Aldridge hurried between the three platoons, discussing the deployment of each with its commander before giving the order to start digging-in. It was a cold, grey morning, and the exhausted soldiers – many of whom had been civilians only a few weeks previously - wanted nothing more than to climb into their sleeping bags and rest for a few hours. Fear and adrenalin had sapped their energy and their offensive spirit, leaving them enervated husks of men, as if sucked dry by a giant spider. Many were frankly amazed to even see the dawn, having feared that daybreak would find them amongst a multitude of bullet-riddled corpses lying on the beach or floating in the surf.

The company position was to be semi-circular in plan, with the beach forming the base and a perimeter of shell-scrapes following an arc which curved inland to the small wood before returning to the cliffs. Shell-scrapes were essentially shallow rectangular trenches, large enough to accommodate two men lying side by side, excavated to a minimum depth of at least half a metre so as to provide basic shelter from artillery fire. In due course they would have to be replaced by much deeper battle trenches with full overhead protection, but right now the officers and NCOs had enough of a challenge on their hands trying to motivate the cold and weary men to get their entrenching tools out and do any digging at all.

"Listen, lads," Three Platoon's sergeant said in a scornful voice to a couple of disaffected privates who were sitting dejectedly on their bergens. "It's no use monging it now, there's work to be done. If we get DF'd you'll feel pretty stupid if everyone else is safely below ground but you're not, and then soon after that you'll feel pretty dead. So start digging."

Shortly after dawn, the French twin-engined aircraft flew over the beach to film the British positions with a camcorder. It was greeted by a ruthless barrage of small-arms fire and hurried away trailing a thin plume of smoke. The British troops cheered.

Major Aldridge had decided to establish the company command post, or CP, in the huge German observation bunker. A ladder of iron rungs gave access to the structure's upper observation deck, which was protected by a concrete slab roof and provided good views out to sea and back inland. In the main bunker below, a shielded doorway led into a dungeon-like interior of stark concrete chambers which would be completely impregnable to anything the French might conceivably throw at them.

A few hundred metres further inland from the observation bunker lay the four equally massive gun emplacements. Each was partially buried beneath a grassy mound, and behind the gun casemate were two concrete rooms, which the British put to good use as troop shelters, ammunition stores, workshops and dressing stations. General Purpose Machine Guns, mounted on tripods and protected by sandbags, were quickly sited on top of the emplacements, from where they had excellent fields of fire over the surrounding landscape.

Robert accompanied Major Aldridge on a visit to One Platoon's position in the small wood at the forward edge of the front line, where he once again encountered Mark Conrad. They chatted briefly while Aldridge and Lieutenant Whitham discussed the situation.

"Bloody typical!" Conrad muttered bitterly. "How come I end up in the most dangerous and exposed position on the whole sodding front line?"

Robert grinned smugly. "Life's a shit sandwich and you've just taken a bite..."

"Well, all I can say is enjoy yourself, Rob, in your fancy bunker... Don't you worry about me..." There was a trace of genuine resentment in Conrad's voice.

Suddenly Aldridge turned to Robert and announced, "Corporal Taylor, I've decided we need a secondary CP in this wood, so I need you to start digging us a shell-scrape over by that tree if you don't mind. Oh – and a brew would be much appreciated, while we've got the chance..."

"Unlucky, mate!" Conrad whispered with delight, but Robert was not amused; he had been secretly hoping to spend most of his time in France in the relative safety of the observation bunker. In dejected silence he set up his hexamine stove to boil a mess tin of water, then unfolded his entrenching tool and thought longingly about Susan as he started to dig.

On board *Plymouth*, Gerald Radley was in a state of barely controlled ecstasy. At daybreak, the ship had moved further offshore so as to be clearly outside the official one kilometre exclusion zone, but this had left the Council Leader feeling detached from the action and desperate to join the troops ashore. Resplendent in his full-length leather trench coat, worn over his usual expensive suit and tie, Radley approached the frigate's captain and asked for a boat to take him ashore immediately.

"Certainly, Council Leader," the captain replied. "The Land Rovers and generators are about to go ashore now – you can go with them if you like."

In fact, the captain was only too glad to be rid of Radley, who had spent the entire duration of the invasion in the ship's operations room, listening to the radio traffic and generally making a nuisance of himself by demanding continual progress reports and information updates. From the captain's point of view, it was definitely time for the Army to take responsibility for the Council Leader.

In a ludicrously histrionic gesture – which made the captain dislike him even more – Radley pulled out his sawn-off shotgun, broke it open and checked that it was loaded, as if he and the absurd weapon might somehow make a decisive contribution to events ashore. Then he snapped the gun closed, returned it to its holster and declared, "Right, Captain, thank you for your hospitality - I shall see you later. You deserve to be very proud of yourself, your crew and your ship. The operation has been a resounding success, by all accounts. I feel we've put the *Great* back into *Great* Britain - it's definitely one-nil to us now. I mean, we've got almost a hundred men on French soil, and how many have they got on ours? Precisely *none!*"

This happy state of affairs was to last just under one hour.

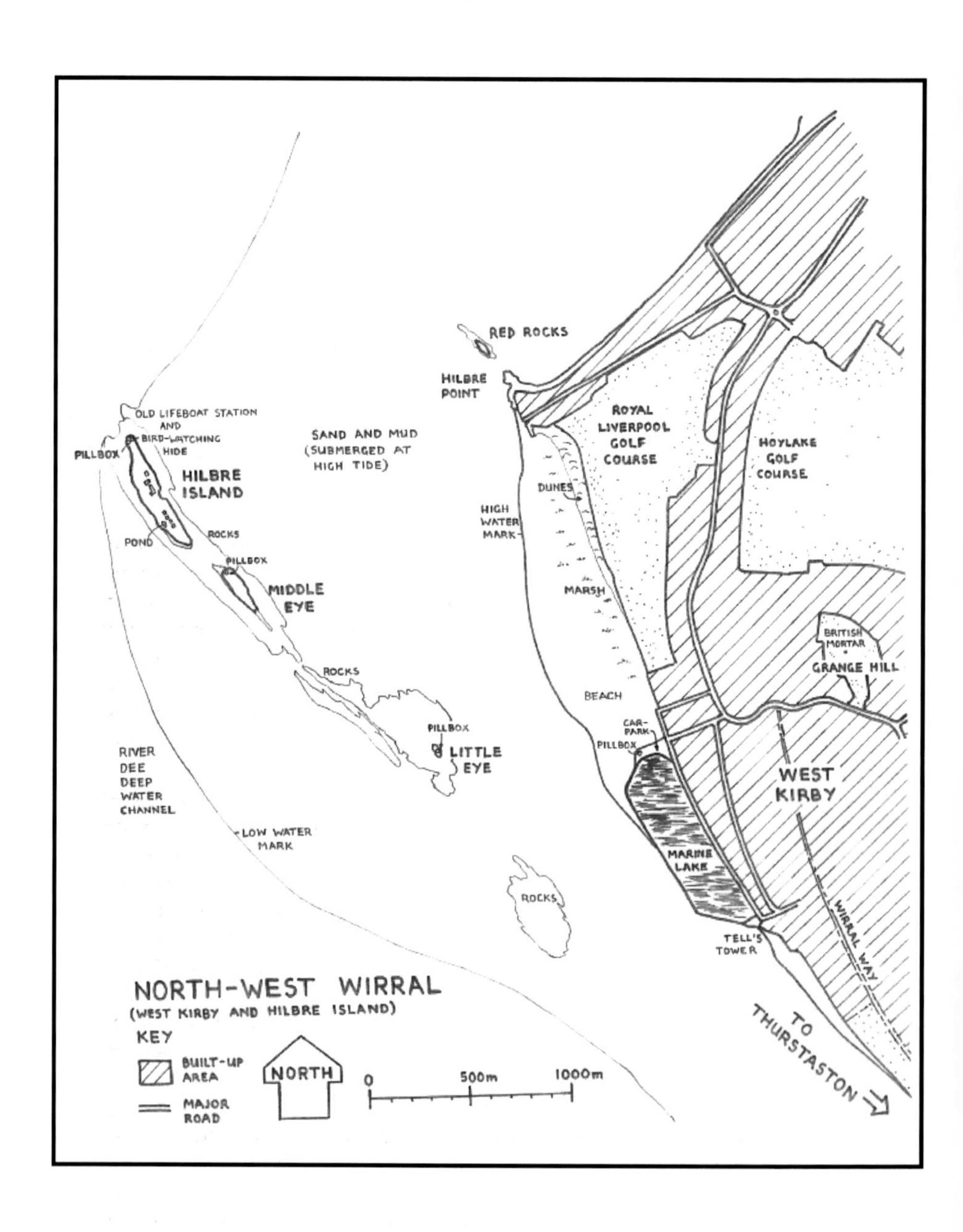
RED ROCKS
HILBRE POINT
OLD LIFEBOAT STATION AND BIRD-WATCHING HIDE
PILLBOX
HILBRE ISLAND
POND
ROCKS
SAND AND MUD (SUBMERGED AT HIGH TIDE)
PILLBOX
MIDDLE EYE
ROCKS
PILLBOX
LITTLE EYE
RIVER DEE DEEP WATER CHANNEL
LOW WATER MARK
ROCKS
ROYAL LIVERPOOL GOLF COURSE
HOYLAKE GOLF COURSE
DUNES
HIGH WATER MARK
MARSH
BRITISH MORTAR
GRANGE HILL
BEACH
CAR-PARK
PILLBOX
WEST KIRBY
MARINE LAKE
TELL'S TOWER
WIRRAL WAY
TO THURSTASTON
NORTH-WEST WIRRAL
(WEST KIRBY AND HILBRE ISLAND)
KEY
BUILT-UP AREA
MAJOR ROAD
NORTH
0
500m
1000m

CHAPTER 20

The French Strike Back

Quite simply the best novel I've read all year!

Hunter Hillman
Projectile and Edged Weapons Review

Mr Roberts replies:
Thanks for the accolade, but I'm always rather sceptical of such praise. I mean, whenever I go into a bookshop, virtually every title I pick up is lauded as 'The novel of the year.' But they can't all be, can they? And the date of the review must surely be pertinent. Presumably, the only reviews worth taking notice of are those written at the end of December. Unfortunately, Mr Hillman, your much-appreciated comments were printed in the first week of January...

As dawn broke over Hilbre Island off the north-west corner of Wirral, Sergeant Paul Murphy conducted his early morning rounds to inspect the small garrison at stand-to. He checked that no-one remained asleep or malingering in the bunkhouse accommodation, then visited the bird-watching hide, the pillbox and the various sandbag bunkers which formed the island's defences. The Hilbre detachment under Murphy's command comprised twelve soldiers, plus four ornithologists who helped with observation duties in return for being allowed onto the island to watch birds.

When there was sufficient daylight to see the offshore wind turbines, Murphy issued the command 'stand down' so that his men could wash, eat breakfast and generally sort themselves out for the day. He then returned to the bird-watching hide to check communications with the mainland and use a powerful torch to flash 'good morning' in Morse code at the minesweeper *Bronington* as she sailed past the island. The ship returned his salutation before turning around in a wide arc at the mouth of the River Dee and heading back towards the Mersey. *Bronington* was Wirral's naval sentry, patrolling ceaselessly along the north shore and up and down each estuary to protect the peninsular from seaborne threats.

It was one of the birdwatchers who first noticed the strange vessel which materialised out of the early morning haze and appeared to be heading straight for Hilbre. Initially the ornithologist paid it little attention, as many large ships followed a similar course before veering off towards Liverpool, but when it had clearly passed the wind turbines and showed no sign of altering its course, he notified Murphy. The sergeant climbed up into the hide and studied the approaching craft, which seemed to change shape as he watched, appearing to expand

and contract like a strange mirage, and reminding him of the famous camel-rider scene from the film '*Lawrence of Arabia*'.

"Perhaps we should get *Bronington* to go and check it out," he mused casually, glancing out through the hide's vision slits in search of the minesweeper. But *Bronington* had disappeared from view and was probably, by now, rounding Fort Perch Rock and sailing up into the Mersey at the far end of her patrol corridor. Suddenly it occurred to Murphy that the speed and direction of the approaching unidentified vessel would result in it reaching Hilbre when *Bronington* was about as far away as she could possibly be. It also occurred to him that this might not be coincidence. And, with the tide in, the island was cut-off and could not be reinforced from the mainland for several hours…If the enemy intended to attack, now would be the perfect time.

Gripped by a growing sense of unease and foreboding, Murphy stared through the binoculars again, willing his eyes to discern greater detail. After a while he realised why the dimensions of the mystery craft seemed to change: it was not a single vessel, but rather a smaller ship towing a larger one.

He immediately made radio contact with Lieutenant Grudge at platoon HQ in West Kirby and notified him of developments. Grudge advised him to alert the duty officer at the Council's War Office, which he duly did. The Council official studied the images being relayed by Hilbre's web-cam and decided that the approaching vessels definitely constituted a potential threat. Murphy was assured that *Bronington* would be sent back to Hilbre forthwith, and was advised in the meantime to prepare for possible attack. His orders were to hold the island for as long as possible so that reinforcements could be sent out by boat.

"Stand to! Stand to!" the sergeant shouted from the hide. "This might be for real, lads!" He turned to the birdwatchers. "You're not expected to stay for this, gents. Find your two mates and get to the slipway. Take the dinghy, okay?" The two ornithologists nodded and hurried off. Murphy squinted again through his binoculars.

The approaching vessels were much closer now and it was obvious that *Bronington* would not arrive in time to intercept them. Through the binocular lenses, the sergeant could make out what appeared to be a tug, towing a much larger, slab-sided ship – possibly a barge of some kind. Two speedboats were following along behind, wallowing in the big vessel's wake.

Murphy descended the ladder from the hide with such speed that he slipped and twisted his ankle. Cursing, he hobbled to the concrete pillbox which had been constructed on a prominent sandstone outcrop next to the hide. A soldier lay alongside the structure, aiming a LAW94 anti-tank missile at the distant vessels; the weapon's back-blast prevented it from being fired from within confined spaces such as pillboxes, so the man had to lie out in the open with only a low concrete ridge for cover. Murphy gave him a reassuring pat on the shoulder and limped inside the pillbox, where the two occupants – Lance-corporal Kilby and Private Brady – were peering nervously out of the firing slits at the oncoming ships. As they watched, the tug began to drift sideways, diverging from the larger vessel like a dividing cell, so that two distinct craft were now clearly visible, approaching head-on. By now they were perhaps six hundred metres away and figures could be seen on the deck of the tug and in the accompanying speedboats. There was no doubt in Murphy's mind that this was an invasion force, and Hilbre was its objective. He sent a brief situation report to Grudge over the radio net, then leaned out of the pillbox doorway and shouted to all of his men who were within earshot, "Don't fire until I give the order! Wait for my command!"

Murphy ducked back into the pillbox and aimed his rifle through the firing slit with hands that were trembling. Never in his life had he been so intensely excited and afraid. He was in the process of trying to clarify his thoughts sufficiently to decide what to do next when suddenly, as he was later to describe it, 'all hell was let loose'.

From the approaching ships came a barrage of gunfire so intense it completely overwhelmed the British defences. Tracer came pouring onto the island, striking the sandstone with a *thwack!* and ricocheting into the air with a high-pitched whine. Bullets hammered against the outside of the pillbox like angry hail, dislodging flakes of concrete from the interior walls and causing the men inside to duck down and cower on the floor. Murphy hazarded a glance out through the firing slit and saw muzzle flashes all over the front of the tug and on the prow of the larger ship – certainly too many weapons to count, producing what was referred to in army parlance as a 'leadfest'. Then, above the crackle of machine-guns came a much louder *crack!* of a larger-calibre weapon. Its first shot must have gone high, but the second punched straight through the layer of sandbags inside the bird-watching hide and showered the occupants with sand and splinters.

The island's defenders began returning fire with their rifles and LSWs, but their efforts seemed puny and ineffectual in comparison with the ferocious display of firepower coming from the French force. Murphy peered out of the doorway at the soldier with the anti-tank weapon, wondering why he had not fired the missile. The man lay slumped on the ground, killed by a bullet which had penetrated his helmet, but the LAW94 appeared undamaged. Murphy reached out, grabbed the rear of the tube and dragged it into the cover of the pillbox. He checked that it was prepared for firing, then leant around the concrete doorway and sighted on the larger ship, which was now less than four hundred metres away. There was no time for the luxury of spotting rounds, so he pushed the selector lever forward and fired the armour-piercing warhead directly into the bow of the vessel. The blast left him reeling and concussed, but the men in the pillbox cheered and he realised that he must have scored a hit. Looking out, he was disappointed to see that, apart from a small amount of smoke coming from the bow, the ship showed no obvious sign of damage, and kept on coming.

In formulating their invasion plan, the French had adopted a different approach to that employed by the British in Normandy. A company of troops had travelled from France in relative comfort aboard the *Dauphin*, a requisitioned ferry similar in size to *Royal Daffodil*. Then, just outside Wirral's one-mile coastal exclusion zone, the soldiers transferred to a large dredging barge, towed from Normandy by the tug *Bastille*. The barge was an expendable vessel with the sole purpose of getting the troops ashore. To this end it had been specially modified with doors cut into the side of the hull above the waterline and a thick layer of concrete poured into the bow for protection, which was counterbalanced by a useful ballast of fresh water stored in tanks at the stern. The plan was that, once released from the tug, the barge would rely on a combination of momentum and three outboard motors to reach Hilbre, where it would be run aground in the small bay beneath the pillbox. *Dauphin* would not participate in the actual invasion, but would remain permanently stationed in neutral waters just outside the exclusion zone to provide support for the troops once they were ashore. Most of the covering fire during the final approach would come from the *Bastille*, which had been equipped with a multitude of machine-guns and a Second World War vintage German 20mm canon taken from a museum in Bayeux. With typical Gallic ingenuity, the French had not only re-activated the weapon but had also succeeded in making ammunition for it by painstakingly machining individual cartridge cases from solid brass.

The canon fired again, blasting a chunk out of the corner of the pillbox just as several machine-gun bullets entered the vision slits and killed Lance-corporal Kilby. Another LAW94 missile flashed overhead, fired from one of the sandbag bunkers further back on the island, but it missed the French tug by a few metres and struck the sea in a harmless plume of spray. It was painfully evident to Murphy that his position was completely untenable. From the rear door of the pillbox he could see tracer rounds streaking through the air like swarms of angry fireflies, demonstrating beyond any doubt that the French had definitely won the firefight. The token British force was clearly not going to repel this invasion, nor even delay it, so Murphy decided his priority now was to minimise his own casualties and conduct a tactical withdrawal as soon as an opportunity presented itself. However, the pillbox and bird-watching hide were situated at the end of a rocky promontory protruding out into the sea, so the sergeant and his comrades would face a long dash up an exposed, uneven slope before they reached any sort of worthwhile cover.

Lieutenant Grudge was demanding a situation report over the radio and it occurred to Murphy that he had not even sent the obligatory "*Contact wait out*." He did so immediately, then pressed a switch in the pillbox to ignite a battery of crude smoke generators. Across the seaward side of the island, piles of old car tyres burst into flames and began pouring acrid black smoke into the air. While waiting for the smokescreen to thicken, Murphy and Private Brady crawled from the pillbox to the rear of the old lifeboat station. Cowering behind the thick sandstone walls was young Private Reid, his eyes wide and staring, his face streaked with sweat and blood.

"Where's Stevens?" Murphy asked.

"Dead – up there, sergeant," Reid replied wretchedly, pointing up at the bird-watching hide, which had been set alight by tracer. He had only completed recruit training a fortnight ago and was clearly very shaken.

Murphy hesitated, wondering whether he was supposed to check bodies to ascertain death before leaving each corpse. What if he abandoned men who appeared dead but later turned out to have been merely injured? Would they or their families hold him personally responsible if they later died, or were captured and mistreated? This issue was something that he had not previously considered, and it had never been covered during training. He looked up at the blazing hide and asked Reid, "Are you sure Stevens is definitely dead?"

The young soldier nodded abjectly and gestured at his combat jacket, which was spattered with dark red patches. "It's his blood all over me, sergeant."

Suddenly, for no apparent reason, the intensity of the French gunfire abated. The smokescreen was still developing, resembling a torn black curtain with numerous holes in it, but Murphy decided that it was now or never.

"Go go go!" he shouted, and the three men sprinted up the rocky slope towards the higher ground in the middle of the island. By a miracle they arrived unscathed at the first of the sandbag bunkers, where they collected its two occupants before continuing on. The next position, near the island's crest, was firing bursts of tracer at the French barge and seemed unaware of the retreating soldier's presence as they approached through the intermittent smoke. Murphy's party scrambled over the rocks on one side of the slope to avoid the stream of 'friendly fire' and crawled around the bunker's flank. At that moment, the smoke cleared for a few seconds and the men inside finally spotted them. One of the bunker's occupants was Corporal Kingsley, the detachment second-in-command. "Sergeant Murphy, good to see you!" he declared, then grinned: "It's like the three little pigs!"

Murphy was in no mood for humour. He ducked down next to the LSW gunner and peered out at the smoke-obscured panorama beyond the firing slit. "Oh," he declared sarcastically, "here comes *Bronington*. You're too late, you stupid featherspitters!"

The reason why the French barrage had lessened now became apparent. Off to the right, steaming at full speed along Wirral's north shore, came the minesweeper, firing its Bofors gun at the enemy vessels. Unfortunately, the weapon had been originally intended for anti-aircraft use, and its barrel would not point low enough to engage surface targets at relatively close range; consequently, the potentially decisive 40mm shells were all going high, landing harmlessly in the sea several miles beyond the French ships. But *Bronington*'s intervention saved the soldiers on Hilbre, as it caused *Dauphin* to swing around to face the new threat. The two French speedboats had been unleashed like hunting dogs and were racing towards the minesweeper, machine guns ablaze. Suddenly they swung out to sea, leaving a wide arc of foam equidistant between *Dauphin* and *Bronington* and depositing a trail of liquid – presumably fuel – in their wake. Flares were fired into this liquid and a sheet of flame swept across the surface of the sea, creating a burning barrier which was a real threat to the wooden-hulled minesweeper. As if acknowledging defeat, *Bronington* turned about and steamed away apologetically, to retire to a safe distance from where she might be able to use her gun effectively.

Meanwhile, the French barge had continued its slow yet inexorable progress towards Hilbre. From Murphy's position inside the bunker, the vessel was starting to disappear from view behind the rock outcrop with the pillbox on top, so it would only be a matter of time before enemy troops swarmed ashore. The sergeant considered the various options open to him and decided that the best course of action was to leave Hilbre immediately, withdrawing to the neighbouring island of Middle Eye, from where mortar fire could be directed onto the invaders. The only problem with this plan was that, with the tide in, a considerable stretch of water separated the two islands.

Murphy used the radio to inform Grudge of his intent and issue the order for all surviving members of the detachment to withdraw immediately. As his group ran along the path which led to the slipway at the southern tip of the island, they were joined by other soldiers who had abandoned their positions and were escaping through the motley collection of houses, huts and bungalows. One man had evidently been hit and was being dragged over the coarse grass by two of his comrades, his head lolling limply from side to side.

"Who's that?" Murphy asked.

"Palmer. Hit in the back, Sergeant."

"Is he alive?"

"I think so..."

"I'm alive," groaned Private Palmer through clenched teeth.

Panting and exhausted, they reached the bottom of the slipway, where a Land Rover was parked just above the lapping tide. Middle Eye, separated from them by about two hundred metres of turbulent, murky water, looked so near and yet so far away.

"Where's the fucking boat?" exclaimed Corporal Kingsley with dismay.

"The birdwatchers took it," Murphy replied, staring at the expanse of rippling sea. He was not sure how deep the sediment-filled water was, but believed it to be waist-height at most. "Right, Willoughby and Mountjoy – you're coming with me and Palmer in the Rover. Kingsley – you and the rest of the lads are wading across. Remember there's lots of rocks and shit under there, so watch your footing and hold onto the rope. As soon as you reach the other side, get the jimpy set up and start giving the Frogs the good news while we get a fire mission sorted out, okay?"

Kingsley nodded and led his group down the slipway and into the brown water. A rope had been fixed between the two islands for just such an eventuality, and provided a much-appreciated handrail for the men as they struggled across the channel against the pull of the tide, which was now receding. Meanwhile, Murphy's group lifted the injured, grimacing Palmer into the rear of the Land Rover. Willoughby hurriedly tore open some field dressings and held them against Palmer's blood-soaked wounds, while Mountjoy injected the casualty with morphine and fumbled around trying to find a pen with which to mark an 'M' on his forehead. Murphy started the engine and they drove cautiously down into the turbid waves.

The Land Rover lurched on the uneven, rocky seabed and the water level rose higher around the vehicle. It had been fitted with a snorkel attachment for the air intake and a specially modified exhaust pipe, but Murphy was concerned that the depth was still increasing and soon they would be swamped. Lieutenant Grudge pestered him over the radio, demanding a situation report and wanting to know whether Murphy and his men had left Hilbre yet.

"Affirmative, I can confirm we are off Hilbre, over," Murphy informed him.

"*Go firm on Middle Eye until a boat comes out for you. Be advised that a fire mission against the lifeboat station is imminent, over.*"

"Roger, out." Murphy turned and shouted back to warn the men in the rear. "There'll be incoming any minute now, lads – we need to be quick."

The sergeant glanced over his right shoulder to check on Corporal Kingsley's party. They were wading through waist deep water and making good progress, following the guide rope which led across the channel at its narrowest point. Murphy could not follow their route in the Land Rover due to the uneven nature of the seabed at that point, which forced him to take a detour off to one side where there were fewer rocks and crevices. Suddenly, the vehicle lurched forward and dropped down, striking something hard and unyielding which brought it to an abrupt stop. "Shit!" Murphy exclaimed, grinding the gear-stick into reverse and flooring the accelerator in desperation. The Land Rover began to move backwards just as an unusually large wave broke over the bonnet and water flooded in. Then, to his dismay, the engine spluttered and died. "Bollocks!" He tried repeatedly turning the ignition key, to no avail, and looked anxiously back at Hilbre, almost expecting to see French soldiers taking aim at him from the top of the cliffs. To his relief there was no sign of enemy troops, but it could only be a matter of time before they appeared...

"We're sitting ducks here," he decided. "Time to abandon ship."

"What about Palmer?"

"He's coming with us."

The men jumped down into the cold, swirling water, which was flowing past at considerable speed. The Dee was notorious for its idiosyncratic currents, and as the soldiers clung to the Land Rover and felt the relentless tug of the retreating tide they began to doubt their ability to wade to Middle Eye without the aid of a rope.

Murphy felt that he had lost control of the situation. "Shit shit shit! If we're not careful we're going to get swept out to sea!" There was a trace of panic in his voice.

A mere fifty metres away, Kingsley and his bedraggled companions were climbing out of the water and scrambling up onto the rocks of Middle Eye. A small pillbox had been constructed on the northern tip of the island, and the corporal positioned his machine-gun team next to it to cover the arcs towards Hilbre. From the pillbox he could see Murphy's party clinging to the swamped Land Rover about fifty metres away, and shouted across to them. "Hang on in there lads – there's a boat on its way!"

Moments later, the first French soldiers reached the grassy crest of Hilbre and started advancing cautiously down towards the slipway. They were immediately engaged by Kingsley's GPMG team on Middle Eye, and took cover along the skyline to return fire. Fortunately, the enemy troops could not see the stricken Land Rover, which was hidden from view in the 'dead ground' between the two islands, so Murphy's group were safe - for the time being at least.

Suddenly, a huge plume of water erupted from the sea about a hundred metres from the lifeboat station, as the first British mortar round landed. It was followed by two further shots in quick succession. Kingsley advised the mortar team, which was dug-in by the war memorial on Grange Hill above West Kirby, to make adjustments which would hopefully place the bombs onto the centre of the island.

"Four Three Alpha, this is One One Charlie, left one hundred, add two hundred, over..."

Kingsley flinched as bullets thudded into the pillbox and gouged furrows in the thin soil around it. He was not confident in his ability to issue mortar fire control orders using the correct voice procedure, so hunted in the inside pocket of his combat jacket for the laminated 'aide memoire' which Grudge had given him. As a TA soldier, Kingsley was familiar with the process of directing artillery and mortar fire, but it was certainly not second nature to him; fire support tended to be largely ignored during the majority of TA exercises, as it interfered with the orderly manoeuvre of men on foot, and forced infantry commanders to acknowledge the uncomfortable truth that it was artillery and air power that ruled the modern battlefield, not men with rifles.

Corporal Kingsley found his aide memoire, but before he had the chance to consult it, a mortar bomb landed near one of the bungalows on Hilbre. It exploded with a terrific *thump*, followed shortly afterwards by the sonic howl of the projectile's descent through the sky. Kingsley looked out from the pillbox and saw the French troops fleeing in panic, desperate to find cover before the next round landed. There were two more explosions near the centre of the island, so he advised the mortar team that they were "On target" and instructed them to "Neutralise for two minutes". Bomb after bomb rained down on Hilbre, blasting its surface with fragments of rock, soil and shrapnel, and throwing the French force into disarray. It was every man for himself, as soldiers jumped into the sea or took shelter in caves or rock crevices. Several men, caught in the open on the exposed upper part of the island, threw themselves into the reed-filled freshwater pond which represented one of the few worthwhile pieces of cover in the vicinity. At the same time, the minesweeper *Bronington* reached a position from which she could use her Bofors gun effectively and began firing 40mm shells at the French, further adding to their demoralised state. At a distance of almost two kilometers the shelling was inaccurate, but after about twenty shots *Bronington*'s gunner scored a hit on the stern of the French barge, sending precious fresh water cascading into the sea.

Sergeant Murphy and his companions were shivering violently in the swirling water, but dared not expose more than just their helmeted heads above the surface due to the shrapnel showering down around them. Injured Private Palmer, lying in several inches of sloshing water in the back of the Landrover, had lost consciousness. Murphy was beginning to wonder for how much longer they could remain in this position, when the mortar fire stopped abruptly and in its place could be heard the sound of an outboard engine, approaching from the direction of West Kirby. A rigid-raider boat nudged cautiously around the side of Middle Eye and then sped towards the stranded men, slowing down at the last minute and bumping gently against the side of the Land Rover. Karl Brabander jumped from the prow onto the vehicle's bonnet and used a length of rope to tether the boat and prevent it from being dragged away by the tide.

"Come on, Murph," he said in his usual disparaging voice, "we need to get you out of here..."

At Hilbre Point on the north-western corner of the mainland, Colonel Alan Hogan watched through his binoculars as explosions erupted silently on Hilbre Island, followed some three seconds later by the sound of each detonation. Deployed in the sand dunes which stretched south along the edge of the Royal Liverpool golf course was a hurriedly assembled force, comprising a platoon from each of B and C companies. Hogan had also moved B Company's mortar up from Thurstaston to join the C Company weapon at the war memorial site, and positioned tripod-mounted machine guns from the Sustained Fire

(SF) Platoon at intervals along the dunes. One of these guns was dug-in a short distance from where Hogan now stood, firing bursts of tracer in a graceful arc to harass the French on Hilbre.

The colonel was confident that he had sufficient assets at his disposal to not only halt the French invasion but also to repulse it with an immediate counterattack. However, Council protocols dictated that he could not launch such an operation without prior approval from the Senior Executive Committee, the members of which had insisted on being referred to as 'The War Cabinet' when dealing with military issues.

"We can keep them pinned-down with mortar fire while we move more men onto Middle Eye," he told Terence McCarthy over the phone. "All I need is the green light from you and we can drive them into the sea!"

McCarthy replied that Hogan could take whatever defensive action was necessary to prevent the French from reaching the mainland, but should wait until Gerald Radley had been consulted before mounting any counterattack. The conversation ended, leaving Hogan fuming at what he regarded as inexcusable interference in army matters by civilian bureaucrats who knew nothing of warfare, and whose procrastination might jeopardize a golden opportunity.

Ten minutes passed without word from the War Cabinet, so Hogan decided to walk south through the sand dunes to West Kirby and discuss the situation with Alistair Blundell. Accompanied by his radio operator and the Regimental Sergeant-major, the Colonel made his way behind the men of Nine Platoon, who lay in the dunes, staring nervously at distant Hilbre. Many of the soldiers were unaware that their commanding officer had just passed by, as Hogan was the sort of officer who gained the respect of his men by always wearing a helmet and carrying a rifle when 'in the field'. This was in stark contrast with his predecessor in the pre-autonomy regiment, who had been known to turn up on exercise sporting a Barbour jacket and beret and looking as though he were about to lead a grouse shoot rather than a battalion advance to contact. Hogan's soldierly approach was partly due to his high personal and professional standards, but was also born out of experience gained in Ulster and Iraq, where he had learned that appearing in any way different to the rank and file increased the likelihood of being targeted by snipers.

A considerable number of civilian spectators had gathered along the esplanade at West Kirby, despite the megaphone instructions from a prowling Council van telling them to go home immediately and stay indoors. To keep the crowds at bay, the car park next to the marine lake had been cordoned off with lengths of mine-tape and was guarded by soldiers with fixed bayonets. Hogan stepped over the token barrier and strode across the tarmac to the large pillbox where Major Blundell had based himself.

One of the Trojan bulldozers was parked next to the pillbox and

Hogan found Blundell leaning against it, steadying his binoculars as he gazed at the smoke-shrouded island which lay over two kilometres away. The mortars had ceased pounding Hilbre for the time being and the dominant sound was the distant buzzing of an outboard motor, as the boat carrying Brabander and Murphy slowly made its way back from Middle Eye. Lieutenant Grudge emerged from the pillbox carrying the radio, map and compass which were the essential tools for directing mortar fire missions. He looked surprised to find the CO standing outside.

"Oh – hello, sir."

"Lieutenant Grudge, good to see you." Hogan watched the boat draw nearer across the expanse of choppy water, and turned to Alistair Blundell. "Is that carrying all of our men from Hilbre?"

"No sir. Corporal Kingsley and, I think, about five others are still on Middle eye."

Hogan frowned and looked at his watch. Almost half an hour had elapsed since the conversation with McCarthy, yet still he had received no reply regarding the matter of a counter-offensive.

"Shall we get them off?" Blundell asked.

"It all depends on what the War Cabinet decides," Hogan replied. "If they want us to counter-attack, we could really do with keeping those men on Middle Eye to help direct the mortars. If we're not going to counter-attack we need to get them off as soon as possible. I just don't see why it's taking so long for them to make a decision…What's the matter with your Council colleagues?"

When the rescue boat arrived at the slipway a few minutes later, paramedics quickly lifted the unconscious Private Palmer into an ambulance and rushed him away to Arrowe Park hospital. Privates Mountjoy and Willoughby, who were both soaked, shivering and close to hypothermia, were taken to a second ambulance to warm-up and be checked over by medical staff. Murphy was in no better state, but he insisted on giving an account of events to the officers inside the pillbox as he changed into some dry clothes which Grudge gave him. Suddenly Karl Brabander appeared in the doorway, looking agitated.

"Shall I go and get Kingsley and the others?" he asked tetchily.

"Just wait a minute, Corporal," Blundell told him. "We're still waiting for advice from the Council."

From the direction of Hilbre came the sound of distant explosions, and Kingsley's voice crackled over the radio. He sounded very scared. "*Hello Two Zero this is Two One Charlie, we have enemy incoming, over…*"

"Fuck the Council!" Brabander spat with contempt, and he strode back toward the boat. The three officers hurried after him.

"Corporal!" Hogan shouted. "You can go and get them, but I need you to drop off some men at Little Eye on the way." He turned to Blundell and Grudge. "We can afford to lose Hilbre and Middle Eye, but not Little Eye. It's much too close to home…"

A few minutes later, Brabander set off again in the motor boat, carrying Lance-corporal Farrell and three men, equipped with a general-purpose machine gun. Farrell's team was dropped off at Little Eye, the tiny wart of grass-covered sandstone which protruded from the sea about a kilometre from West Kirby. Little Eye was the southernmost island in the string of three, and its proximity to the mainland made it strategically more important than Middle Eye and Hilbre to the north. For this reason another pillbox – intended only to be occupied in an emergency – had been constructed on the grassy platform which was barely above the waves during high tide. Farrell's team hurried inside, set up their machine gun, and watched Brabander's boat creep nearer to Middle Eye, which remained under French mortar attack.

At West Kirby, Colonel Hogan contacted Lieutenant Monty, the officer in charge of the British mortars on the high ground by the Grange Hill war memorial. Having spent over twenty years of his life as an officer in the Royal Artillery, the colonel felt completely comfortable with this kind of long-range, high explosive warfare. He ordered Monty to bombard Hilbre with the highest possible rate of fire, to enable Kingsley and his men to retreat across the open ground of Middle Eye and meet Brabander's boat at the southern end of the island.

"Use as much ammunition as you can," Hogan told Monty over the radio. "Stonk the bastards – I want them well and truly stonked!"

In response, each three-man mortar crew began operating like automata, feeding bombs into their barrels at such speed that, for a brief period at least, there were almost twenty rounds in the air at once, and the French on Hilbre prayed to God for salvation, cursed Claude Lebovic, and wished more than anything else in the world to be somewhere else.

As Hilbre shuddered under the merciless barrage of high explosive and shrapnel, which quickly caused it to vanish beneath a swirling maelstrom of smoke and dust, Kingsley and his men made a frantic dash across Middle Eye and rendezvoused with Brabander's boat. They arrived safely back at West Kirby just as Colonel Hogan received a call from Terence McCarthy at the War Office informing him that, for the time being at least, there was to be no counter-attack.

CHAPTER 21

Beach-head

I do wish these modern authors would be more considerate and consistent with their chapter lengths! In my day, a competent and disciplined author was able to limit each chapter to a convenient, reader-friendly length. In this frustrating work, we plough through some interminable chapters before being suddenly presented with a pathetic four page effort that's barely worth getting the book mark out for. What's the literary world coming to?

Milicent Lavender
Powder Puff Ladies Journal

Mr Roberts replies:
And when was your day, dear? I rather fancy it's been and gone...

On the beach at Longues-sur-Mer in Normandy, Gerald Radley was proudly watching supplies and equipment being brought ashore when his mobile phone rang with its distinctive *Jerusalem* ringtone. It was Terence McCarthy, informing him that the French had invaded Hilbre. The news came as no great surprise to the Council Leader, as he and Lebovic had planned for simultaneous invasions, but he pretended to be dismayed.

"Oh dear," he declared gravely to the nearest soldier to him, the Company Quartermaster-Sergeant, who was trying to sort out the multitude of ration packs, ammo boxes and crates of miscellaneous stores which were arriving in a steady stream from *Plymouth* and *Royal Daffodil*. The CQMS ignored him, but Simms knew what was expected of a loyal aide, and obligingly asked, "What is it, sir?"

"The French have invaded Hilbre Island and are threatening West Kirby," Radley announced solemnly. "We need to tell Major Aldridge..."

Escorted by a couple of soldiers from Company HQ, Radley and Simms made their way up the cliff track to the observation bunker, within which Aldridge had established his command post. They found the major in one of the dungeon-like rooms, engaged in an 'O' group with his three platoon commanders. Radley broke the news about the Hilbre invasion, and declared his intention to return to Wirral sooner than originally intended – ideally within the next two or three days.

"That would probably be for the best, Council Leader," Aldridge agreed. "Things will probably start hotting-up here very soon..." The major was eager to be rid of Radley, whom he regarded as an interfering liability whose presence had a detrimental impact on morale.

Aldridge resumed talking to his lieutenants, outlining the tasks to be carried out by each platoon in order to achieve the overall company mission. Radley sat listening, nodding with approval at the purposeful military activity being discussed, although most of the army jargon meant nothing to him – especially the baffling array of abbreviations, initials, nicknames and acronyms. In the adjoining room, Robert Taylor was starting work on a model of the Company Tactical Area of Responsibility. He inadvertently caught Radley's eye through the doorway and for a fleeting moment a pulse of recognition passed between the two men, before Robert looked away.

Suddenly, from outside the bunker came several ground-shaking *thumps* in quick succession, followed by the muted rattle of machine gun fire. Urgent voices crackled over the company radio net, with several callsigns reporting contacts or incoming mortar fire.

Aldridge turned to Radley and said, "I think you'd better get back to *Plymouth*, sir – for the time being at least. They're probably only probing our defences, but we can't take a chance with your safety... Corporal Taylor will take you back."

Crouching low to avoid stray bullets, Robert, Radley and Simms scurried across open ground towards the top of the track which led down the cliffs to the beach. A machine gun opened fire in the distance and they threw themselves down onto the muddy grass.

"We've met before, haven't we, Corporal?" Radley asked, as they waited for the firing to abate.

"We have, Council Leader."

"You're a teacher, if I remember rightly..."

"I was." Robert rose to his feet. "Come on, Council Leader, we need to get down onto that track. We'll be in cover then."

A mortar bomb exploded in a field some distance away, blasting smoke and soil high into the air. Radley was delighted to be experiencing the reality of battle. Already he was picturing himself back in Wirral, describing to reporters how he had suffered alongside the troops under fire, and winning the admiration and adoration of his colleagues and the public alike.

They reached the beach without mishap, and a short time later the Council Leader was ferried back to *Plymouth* aboard one of the small supply boats. He watched as further explosions burst on the plateau at the top of the cliffs, and smiled with satisfaction. British troops had gained a foothold in Normandy. French troops had invaded Hilbre...Everything was proceeding as planned.

Gerald Radley remained with the invasion force for three days, during which time he flitted back and forth from *Plymouth* to discuss developments with Aldridge and appear in as many publicity photos and video sequences as possible. Meanwhile, the soldiers consolidated their positions by digging proper battle trenches to replace their shallow shell-scrapes. The Trojan bulldozers worked ceaselessly, piling up earth into ramparts and excavating alcoves in the crumbling cliffs for the storage of ammunition and supplies.

The expected French counter-attack failed to materialise, although there was almost continual harassment from small-arms and mortar fire, and the enemy sent out frequent patrols to probe the perimeter defences. In response, Aldridge dispatched his own reconnaissance and fighting patrols to gather intelligence and dominate the strip of no-man's land beyond the British barbed wire. Where possible, these operations involved Robert, Mark Conrad and Gwyn Thomas, whose knowledge of the area made them valuable guides for the patrols. During one such mission, the patrol to which Robert had been allocated observed a French section moving into a small copse about three hundred metres from the British lines. A mortar fire mission was requested immediately and the exploding bombs drove the enemy out of the wood and into open ground, where they came under machine gun and rifle fire and suffered several casualties. Such operations were valuable in denying the enemy freedom of movement in the immediate vicinity of the British salient, but Robert found them extremely stressful; for him they were without doubt the most nerve-wracking - and at times totally terrifying – experiences of the war so far.

On another occasion, his patrol came under mortar and small-arms fire whilst returning from an observation post mission, and they were forced to make a desperate dash to safety with bombs bursting behind them like the footfalls of a pursuing titan. Back in the relative safety of the British lines, Robert discovered a jagged shard of shrapnel - the length of his thumb - which had gone right through his daysack before mercifully being stopped by his body armour...Had it been a mere six inches higher it would have struck the base of his skull and almost certainly killed him. The incident made him appreciate more than ever that his survival in this environment depended as much upon luck as upon his own skill or judgement.

In addition to guiding patrols and acting as Aldridge's unofficial batman, Robert's other significant contribution to the proceedings was the construction of a model depicting some two square kilometers of French terrain which formed A Company's Tactical Area of Responsibility, or 'TAOR'. Every infantry NCO was required to have their own model-making kit, and Robert's was something of a legend within C Company. Wrapped-up inside an old ammunition bandolier, it included items such as laminated card squares, coloured ribbon, cocktail sticks, assorted pieces of chalk, small wooden blocks, and 'puffer' bottles filled with red, yellow and blue powder paint which could be used to draw rivers, tracks and boundaries onto a model landscape. Robert had even included sixteen tiny plastic soldiers retrieved from a toy box in his parent's loft. Upon seeing the figures for the first time, Karl Brabander had snorted with contempt and called Robert a 'sad bastard', but within a week he had added some to his own model kit, and frequently used them to illustrate troop formations while delivering his orders.

Robert took great pride in his model of the area around Longues-sur-Mer, which occupied an entire room in the observation bunker.

A layer of sandy soil had built up over the years on the floor of the chamber, and he sculpted this with his entrenching tool into the contours shown on the map. His assistant for the task, the company clerk, was sent on a quest to gather gravel, sand, empty ration-pack boxes and small-leaved vegetation. He returned after an hour carrying a bulging poncho filled with a cornucopia of useful materials. The hardest part of model-building was always transposing from the map to duplicate the correct overall layout, but at a much larger scale. Once this was achieved, the details could be added, which was the enjoyable part of the task. Blue powder paint was used to colour the sea, a sprinkling of sand represented the beach, and miniature woods, copses and hedgerows were created using fern fronds and moss. Roads, tracks, streams and boundaries were drawn on with powder paint, lines of gravel represented walls, and laminated labels showed the location of significant features such as the Company HQ and aid post, the three platoons, the mortar pit and the rear echelon. Robert carefully cut card from the ration boxes and stuck it together with electrical tape to make the significant buildings within the TAOR. Finally, he stretched comms cord across the model and pegged it down to represent the grid squares from the map, then used sticks to make a north point and scale bar.

He enjoyed building the model. It was certainly easier and less stressful than trench-digging, patrolling, or accompanying the OC on his visits to the forward positions, and it provided a welcome distraction which focused his mind upon a tangible, achievable task rather than dwelling upon futile, obsessive thoughts. He was concerned that he was becoming increasingly withdrawn and introspective, preoccupied with three main areas of thought: recurring fantasies about Susan; the haunting memory of the French soldier's exploding head; and imaginary subversive plots, in which he succeeded in bringing Gerald Radley and his regime crashing down.

When Major Aldridge saw the finished model he was delighted. "Oh good effort, Corporal Taylor!" he exclaimed appreciatively. "Absolutely magnificent...this is just what I need for my briefings and orders." He looked suddenly apologetic. "And as you've put so much effort into it, I suppose you'd better be the one to destroy it in the event of an enemy attack..."

Robert nodded wearily. "Right sir. What shall I do now?"

"Go and give the boys a hand with the trenches outside. Oh – and a brew would be much appreciated, if you don't mind..."

Robert left the bunker, climbed up out of the hollow and walked dejectedly to where several battle trenches had been partly dug in the field between the cliff top and the four German gun emplacements. The trench excavations were deserted, so Robert jumped down into the nearest one and unfolded his entrenching tool. He set up his hexamine cooker to heat water and, while waiting for it to boil, surreptitiously used his mobile phone to send a text message to Susan that simply read, '*Still alive, luv u loads*.' Only officers and NCOs were allowed to have mobile phones 'in the field' and they were strictly for use as a back-up means of communication to supplement the standard army radios, which were bulky and notoriously unreliable. By sending his message to Susan, Robert was committing an offence and would face disciplinary action if caught, but he did not really care, as there could be no punishment worse than everyday life on the front line.

The sky was overcast and a cold wind blew across the dreary landscape, carrying with it a fine, drizzling rain. He donned his Gore-Tex jacket and started to dig with his diminutive spade, while reminding himself of the importance of remaining 'switched-on'. But it was hard to maintain personal morale in a muddy hole in a foreign field when, at home in Wirral, a beautiful girl was going to waste, growing older every lonely second without being hugged or admired or loved as she deserved.

That night, in her empty bed, Susan Fletcher dreamt of her lover calling out to her, then glimpsed a rigid, charred corpse being rolled stiffly into a shallow grave, and woke up in tears, calling Robert's name.

CHAPTER 22

The Thurstaston Front

This is supposedly a local novel by a local author, but Mr Roberts is evidently not intimately acquainted with Wirral...The idea of an attacking force moving on foot from Hilbre Island to Thurstaston via the Dee Estuary is frankly absurd – they would find themselves mired in some of the stickiest mud on the planet!

Rowan Gladstone
Local History Enthusiast

Mr Roberts replies:
You are right, of course. Thurstaston mud is indeed one of the most glutinous substances known to man.

The French could not remain confined to Hilbre indefinitely and they knew it. For a start, their military commanders were aware that occupying an uninhabited island would never satisfy public demand for a military achievement of sufficient magnitude to compensate for the British landings at Longues-sur-Mer. Then there was the problem of potable water. Hilbre possessed no streams, and its marshy freshwater pond was too small to meet the needs of an infantry company for any length of time. But the most serious issue related to the island's vulnerability to British mortar bombardment. There was only a thin layer of soil overlaying the sandstone bedrock, which prevented the invaders from digging-in and caused mortar bombs to explode on the surface, which maximised the lethal radius of their shrapnel. Every day the British harassed their foe with a string of bombs, fired in quick succession at completely random times. The explosions demoralised the occupying force and inflicted casualties which, the French knew, could not be sustained in the long term.

Claude Lebovic, unlike Gerald Radley, had not accompanied his troops to Wirral, preferring instead to remain in Caen and leave the military to its own devices. However, his telephone calls to the invasion force commander, Major Vassort, made it clear that he expected further significant progress to be achieved in the very near future. The military planners had always intended that Hilbre be merely a springboard from which to launch an invasion of the mainland, but the speed with which their troops' position on the island became untenable caused them to accelerate the preparations for the next phase of the operation.

Vassort had scrutinised the stretch of Wirral coastline directly opposite Hilbre through binoculars and realised that the exposed mudflats and strong British defences would make any attack by his forces in that area a foolhardy undertaking. He therefore decided to invade the mainland further south, bypassing the enemy troops dug-in between Red Rocks and West Kirby, and hopefully breaching the coastal defences where they were weaker. However, there was one small but significant obstacle in the way which could potentially jeopardize the speed and surprise needed for such an operation to succeed: the British outpost on Little Eye. Eliminating this irritating thorn in his side became Vassort's immediate priority.

At that time, the most stressful assignment for any British soldier on the Wirral was, without doubt, a period of sentry duty on Little Eye. Each four man team was required to spend twenty-four hours guarding the isolated lump of rock out in the estuary, nervously watching neighbouring Middle Eye for signs of French activity. During the day, with good visibility and the tide out, the men could relax a little, but when darkness fell and the advancing sea cut them off from the mainland, they felt isolated, vulnerable and subject to all of the primordial nocturnal fears experienced throughout history by human beings at night in dangerous places. False alarms were commonplace, with jittery soldiers firing at waves, seagulls or drifting pieces of flotsam, and triggering panic on the mainland as stand-to was called and anti-invasion drills initiated. The drills became increasingly lacklustre as the number of spurious incidents steadily accumulated and the soldiers ashore grew frustrated and angry at being repeatedly roused from their sleeping bags, although few of them blamed the men on Little Eye.

Three days after the invasion, it was the turn of Lance-corporal Stanley and his men to occupy the pillbox. They were taken out by boat at noon when the tide was high, relieving Corporal Brabander's team, and spent the first few hours cleaning the GPMG, listening to the radio and keeping watch. One soldier had even brought a fishing line, which he cast out into the Dee in the hope of catching bass or plaice. By mid-afternoon the tide had receded sufficiently for Stanley to venture out onto the wet sand to check the dual rings of razor wire encircling the island, and it was then that he heard the sound of an engine approaching from the direction of Middle Eye. He immediately alerted the mainland, then watched through binoculars as a single vehicle drew steadily nearer. After a while he could see that it was a quad bike, towing a trailer and flying what appeared to be a Red Cross flag. It stopped midway between the two islands, and the driver and another figure began unloading heavy objects onto the sand. Then the quad bike headed back towards Middle Eye and disappeared. Stanley relayed the information to Lieutenant Grudge and a Land Rover was sent out from West Kirby to investigate. The objects which had been left on the sand turned out to be the bodies of the three British soldiers who had died defending Hilbre.

By early evening the tide was coming in again and it was dark and growing cold, so a stove was lit inside the pillbox for warmth and brewing tea, and Stanley started the portable generator which powered the island's floodlights. These were mounted on pylons located just inside the outer ring of razor wire, and used a system of polished aluminium reflectors to prevent the bulbs being shot at and destroyed. After the men had eaten, Stanley drew up a 'stag roster' for the night's sentry duty, based on a 'two on, two off' system. Usually, full corporals were exempt from stag duty, but with only four men occupying the pillbox, Stanley would have to do his stint like everyone else. Shivering in the damp concrete chamber, he lit a cigarette, put a warm top on under his body armour, and squinted through the CWS night-sight at the grainy silhouette of Middle Eye, which was just visible across the expanse of turbulent black water.

That night, a team of French soldiers in full scuba gear made their way slowly and painstakingly up the estuary from Middle Eye to Little Eye. They timed their approach to exploit the flow of the tide, which ushered them towards their objective with the last vestiges of its inbound energy before it turned and started to recede again. The divers were heavily weighted to prevent them being carried off course by the currents, and were able to walk on the sand and rock of the river bed for much of their journey, concealed from view by the darkness and the waves. Initially they headed for the British floodlights, but when they got nearer they skirted around Little Eye with only their snorkels showing above the water, and approached their target from the rear. After some cautious probing, the frogmen located the gap in the outer wire which had been deliberately left to allow access by small boats, and slipped through. They jettisoned their weight belts and shrugged off their buoyancy control devices and air cylinders, which they then used as floating rifle rests as they approached the rocky shore of the island.

The black outline of the pillbox could be seen silhouetted against the floodlit-brightened sky, but there was no sign of the British defenders. Three of the divers remained in the water to give covering fire if necessary, while the fourth slipped up onto the rocks like a black, glistening seal with murderous intent, and cut through the inner coil of wire. He slithered stealthily across the sandstone to the pillbox and, scarcely able to believe that he had made it so far without being spotted, pulled the pin from a grenade and posted it through the nearest vision slit.

From within, a voice shouted in alarm and a British soldier leapt from the entrance just as the grenade detonated. He threw himself into the sea then stumbled to his feet and waded obliviously towards the three divers, who gunned him down without mercy. The French grenadier by the pillbox posted another grenade inside and, after it had gone off, pointed his rifle muzzle around the edge of the doorway and sprayed the interior with automatic fire.

On the mainland, Hogan and Blundell heard the gunfire and grenade explosions, and immediately tried to contact Stanley by radio, without success. Fearing the worst, the two officers set about preparing their defences for a major French assault, which they assumed would take place in the vicinity of West Kirby.

About an hour before dawn, French mortar bombs began falling on the estuarine mud in front of the British positions along the sand dunes bordering the Royal Liverpool golf course. The Frenchmen manning the mortar on Hilbre must have been steadily lowering the elevation of their weapon after each shot, increasing the range of the bombs by a small increment every time they fired. The British troops watched apprehensively as the explosions advanced inexorably towards them in what was known as a 'creeping barrage'. When the thunderous detonations – visible only as a sudden flash in the darkness – were so close that the ground was shaking and the men of Seven Platoon were being sprayed with sand and chunks of mud, the order was given to abandon those positions which lay directly in the path of the advancing bombardment. Shortly afterwards, the barrage passed across the dune defences and started churning up the fairways of the golf course. Then it ceased abruptly. Minutes later, the bombs started falling once again onto the mudflats in front of the dunes, but this time they were smoke projectiles rather than high explosive ones.

Hogan responded by ordering a counter-bombardment of Hilbre, in the faint hope of neutralising the French mortar. The sky was beginning to lighten, but it was still frustratingly dark and little could be seen of the enemy-held island, even through image-intensifying equipment. The colonel, convinced that an offensive was imminent, mentally reviewed his defensive preparations. The two platoons which were dug-in from Red Rocks to West Kirby had been stood-to and were bracing themselves for a major attack, while a third platoon was on stand-by as a mobile reserve. Both mortars up on Grange Hill had a good supply of ammunition, and more was on its way from the docks. All of the troops had rehearsed the anti-invasion drills and knew what was expected of them. For the time being there was nothing more to be done, except wait, and watch, and wait…

Just before dawn, the French mortar started dropping smoke bombs progressively further south, until they were falling between West Kirby and Little Eye. Hogan stood in the pillbox by the marine lake, watching the smokescreen develop, and became convinced that he could hear vehicle engines coming from the direction of Hilbre. He turned to Major Blundell.

"This is it, Alistair. They're coming – I'm sure of it. Clever buggers – with the wind in this direction, the smoke's blowing right over onto our positions. The first we'll see of them will be when they reach our wire – and that's only a hundred metres away!"

The tide was right out now, and from somewhere within the curtain of smoke which drifted across the estuary came the distant but unmistakable sound of engines revving. French smoke bombs continued bursting softly on the wet sand, creeping even further south along the shoreline towards Caldy, while British bombs hammered Hilbre in retaliation. For the British troops dug-in along the sand dunes it was an agonising time, as they stared intently into the smoke in anticipation of a French assault. Several men opened fire out of sheer nervous expectation, convinced that they could see enemy troops crawling up to the single coil of razor wire which stretched along the shore.

The engine noise remained audible, but it was impossible to ascertain the direction in which the vehicles were moving. Hogan and his men waited – excited, scared and frustrated, almost *wanting* the French to attack, so as to relieve the stressful pressure of anticipation. Then, strangely, the engine noise started to die away, as if the vehicles were moving south past Little Eye, and shortly afterwards a radio message was received from a corporal in one of the B Company trenches at Caldy Beach, who reported that men and vehicles were moving across the mud flats in front of his position, heading south. Hogan gasped and his insides turned cold, as he realised that he might have been duped.

"Oh God," he said quietly to Blundell, shaking his craggy head with bitter dismay. "Maybe they're not going to attack us here after all..."

He immediately contacted Major Hubbard, the ex-Engineer officer who now commanded B Company and was responsible for the defence of Wirral's entire western shoreline from West Kirby southwards. Hogan warned him to expect an attack in the very near future somewhere along his TAOR. It was advice which proved unnecessary, as during the conversation the French launched an assault on the B Company defences at Thurstaston, less than a kilometre from Hubbard's headquarters in the country park visitor's centre.

The French had demonstrated a high degree of resourcefulness and tactical acumen by deceiving the British and moving troops quickly from Hilbre to Thurststaon. Major Vassort knew that his men would be vulnerable to machine gun and mortar fire as they crossed the mud flats between the two locations, and therefore it was imperative that they covered the distance as swiftly as possible. He had two light utility vehicles – the equivalent of the British Land Rover – at his disposal, but decided not to risk losing them on the potentially hazardous estuarine mud at such an early stage in the operation. Instead, he opted for a pair of quad bikes, towing flat-bed trailers with balloon tyres which could carry essential supplies such as ammunition, food and water. The soldiers themselves, relatively unencumbered with kit, would then travel on foot across the expanse of sticky mud, staying as far out in the estuary as the water level permitted. As the force advanced southwards under cover of darkness and smoke, small units would break off and provoke firefights with British positions at different points along the shore to create panic and confusion.

While the main body was accompanying the quad bikes on foot, an advance party consisting of two speedboats towing soldiers in rubber dinghies was dispatched to mount a preliminary assault on the defences in the vicinity of the Dee Sailing club. This particular location was of great strategic significance, as it was the only point along a five kilometre stretch of coastline where vehicles could easily access the cliff top from the beach, courtesy of a steeply sloping tarmac ramp. The French had studied maps of the area, and knew that they ought to be able to get quite close to this ramp by following a serpentine channel which cut through the estuarine mud from the deep water of the main river.

Evidently the luck of battle was with the French that day, for their audacious plan succeeded. While diversionary firefights raged further north, the speedboats and their towed inflatables slipped quietly up the channel and managed to get to within three hundred metres of the sailing club at the top of the ramp before being spotted. Three sections of French troops scrambled out of their dinghies and took cover behind the natural parapet of mud at the edge of the channel, supported by machine gun fire from the speedboats. In an impressive display of well-executed fire and movement drills, featuring great courage and aggression, the Frenchmen dashed across the slippery mud and began breaching the barbed wire. A bunker atop the crumbling boulder clay cliffs put up stiff resistance before it succumbed to a determined grenade attack, and the surviving British defenders – shocked and demoralised - conducted a fighting withdrawal back along the Wirral Way towards company HQ in the visitor centre of the country park.

Major Edward Hubbard listened to the sound of gunfire, and tried to make sense of the contact reports coming in over the company radio net. When it became apparent that the French were attacking the sailing club, he began frantically formulating an appropriate defensive strategy. There had, of course, been a well-rehearsed procedure in place for many months, but recent events had left that plan in tatters by stripping B Company of the assets needed for the task. Hubbard should have had at his disposal a reserve platoon to act as a quick reaction force, together with both direct and indirect fire support in the form of a mortar and some medium machine guns, but these resources had been moved to West Kirby to counter the perceived threat of invasion there. All of his remaining troops were deployed in two-man battle trenches which stretched right along the coastline, and it would take too long to assemble them into an effective force for a counter-attack. The major decided that the best strategy would be to pull his men back from the confusion of the coastal strip, and regroup along a secondary line of defence on the higher ground further inland. He contacted Hogan by mobile phone and requested permission to withdraw.

"My concern is that they will roll-up my positions from the flank, sir," he told the colonel. "If we pull back, they'll have to attack us head-on, in daylight, fighting up hill across open ground..."

Hogan agreed, and not only approved an immediate withdrawal but also promised to send reinforcements which would include the company's own mortar and machine gun assets, together with a party of Engineers to help construct emergency defences.

While not quite a rout, the British withdrawal was confused and chaotic. The troops had been dispersed along the cliff top in widely separated trenches and bunkers, and when the order came through to abandon the positions and regroup at Thurstaston village, they began heading inland in small, uncoordinated groups. In such a situation, 'blue-on-blue' contacts were almost inevitable, and several casualties were caused by spontaneous firefights between men of the same side, although miraculously no-one was killed.

By about ten o'clock in the morning the drama was largely over. A curious state of equilibrium established itself between the opposing forces, with neither side demonstrating any inclination to disrupt the status quo. Hubbard's men, reinforced by their returned third platoon and additional soldiers from Charlie Company, the Engineers and the Logistics Corps, had taken up new positions along a broadly semi-circular line which stretched from Caldy golf course in the north and reached Thurstaston village at its most easterly extent, before curving past the Dungeon and returning to the coast just above Heswall in the south. Within this defensive perimeter, the French invasion force was effectively contained, for the time being at least. Three machine gun teams from the Sustained Fire (SF) Platoon took up positions on the high ground overlooking the area, and the company's mortar was quickly set up on Thurstaston Hill and began bombarding the French-occupied coastline. Logistic Corps trucks rumbled back and forth delivering construction materials to the ever-dependable Engineers, who rose magnificently to the occasion and worked frantically to close the single road leading from the enemy-held beach. They also created bunkers, embankments and razor wire fences. Initially, the Engineers were assisted in this construction work by Special Council Worker units which arrived with diggers and other equipment, but when the French began harassing them with desultory machine gun fire, the SCW downed tools and declared that, as civilians, it was not their job to operate in a war zone. Before they departed back to the comforting security of their white vans, cups of tea and tabloid newspapers, Hubbard implored them to leave some of their equipment behind, as a couple of his men had been qualified JCB operators in civilian life. The SCW reluctantly relinquished two machines, but their refusal to help exacerbated the growing animosity between the army and the paramilitaries, which was to reach a state of mutual loathing by the end of the war.

Throughout the day, the British soldiers took it in turns to dig trenches or peer over their weapons towards the Dee, in nervous anticipation of further enemy attacks, although none came. The truth of the matter was that the French were exhausted, both physically and mentally. They were relieved and elated that their bold plan had succeeded, but lacked the offensive energy to push further inland against an enemy which had clearly regrouped and reinforced itself. Besides, Major Vassort was quite satisfied with the progress achieved during the past few days. His forces now occupied three British islands and a sizeable area of mainland territory, which would be sufficient to appease the public back home. French honour had been restored.

Colonel Hogan left Alistair Blundell in charge at West Kirby and hurried to Thurstaston village to assist Hubbard in his defensive preparations. The two officers were studying the landscape from the stone church tower when they were joined by Duncan Silverlock, who arrived in Gerald Radley's bullet-proof BMW to show Council support for the troops. Hogan had never liked Silverlock, whom he regarded as a fastidious, weasel-like character with a disturbing resemblance to Heinrich Himmler.

"So what's the situation, Colonel?" Silverlock asked in his usual peremptory tone, as they surveyed the enemy-held territory from their vantage point. From the high ground behind them poured streams of tracer, which glided gracefully overhead before being swallowed up by the landscape, and down near the coast, plumes of black smoke were rising from where British mortar bombs fell periodically to remind the French that they were not welcome.

"The French have broken out from Hilbre and secured a beach-head down by the sailing club and the golf course," Hogan explained. "We've conducted a tactical withdrawal to a new line of defence, and I'm confident we can make sure they don't make further progress inland."

Silverlock looked displeased. "Council Leader Radley will be most disappointed", he declared solemnly. "He was very keen to keep the enemy off mainland soil."

Hogan was tempted to remark that perhaps the Council Leader would like to get in a trench and repulse the attack himself, but instead he remarked, "Well, Mr Silverlock, with your permission, I believe I can defeat the entire French invasion force in less than a month."

Silverlock raised his eyebrows sceptically. "Oh yes? How?"

"Well, we estimate the French have about seventy or eighty men down there," Hogan said, gesturing down towards the Dee. "That means they can't have many left on Hilbre. If we recapture Hilbre, it'll be very difficult for them to resupply their forces here – they'll be cut off. Then all we have to do is grind them down in a war of attrition which they cannot win, until they run out of food and ammunition and either have to surrender or be driven into the sea."

Silverlock nodded approvingly. “Sounds logical, Colonel. But I'm afraid I can't authorise such action myself – as you know, Council Leader Radley insists on exercising full control over all major strategic decisions. I spoke to him this morning when we first heard the French had attacked the mainland, and he said he would be returning from France immediately.”

Hogan frowned. “But that might mean we don't get a decision for several days! I'm just a simple soldier, Mr Silverlock, and I don't want to get involved in politics, but you must understand that the longer we delay, the more time we give the French to dig-in, build-up their supplies, and strengthen their position…”

“I see. I'll try to contact him again today if you like. In fact I'll go and do it now…”

Silverlock hurried away to his car but returned a few minutes later, shaking his head sadly.

“I'm afraid that Council Leader Radley's instructions are to hold the French here until he gets back. He'll advise you then.” He looked at his watch. “Right, Colonel, I must be getting back to the town hall.”

Hogan watched him drive away and then turned to Major Hubbard. “Sometimes, Edward,” he declared grimly, “I get the distinct impression that those office jockeys in the town hall really don't want us to win this war…”

The Town Hall

Old Pump House at Four Bridges (SCW HQ)

TA Soldier with SA80 rifle

Infantry patrol. Note LSW in foreground, and TA woolly hats!

Historic warships in the East Float Dock
(Photograph by Frank Smith)

Mersey Ferry 'Royal Daffodil'

HMS Plymouth and HMS Onyx

HMS Bronington
(Photograph by Ted Rodden)

Longues-sur-Mer coastline, with the remains of the Mulberry harbour visible in the distance

Thurstaston coastline

Hilbre Island from Middle Eye, with the tide out

The old lifeboat station, Hilbre Island

German gun emplacement, Longues-sur-Mer

German observation bunker, Longues-sur-Mer

Norman farmhouse

Jagdpanzer 'Hetzer'

81mm mortar in action

Trying out the M16

View towards Storeton from the top of Rest Hill Road, with Storeton Wood on the right and Mount Wood on the left

Thurstaston Common

Storeton Wood in winter

View towards Storeton from Mount Wood

One-man 'shell-scrape', with no overhead protection

Front view of two-man trench, with full overhead protection

CHAPTER 23

Home Front

Implausible and ridiculous as it is, there's something intriguing about this portrayal of Wirral at war. Rationing, seizure of property, blackouts and air raids...I'm sure there are some would-be political leaders out there who get turned-on by such things.

Barry Dovetail
Sanity Fair magazine

Mr Roberts replies:
Yes, I'm sure there are...

Upon hearing the news that the French had invaded mainland Wirral, Gerald Radley left Normandy immediately aboard the requisitioned Mersey ferry *Royal Daffodil*, and headed for home. Accompanying him on the voyage were nine corpses, a number of wounded soldiers including Sergeant Carter, and Robert Taylor.

Gazing back at the French coastline as it receded into the distance, Robert felt relieved to be returning home, yet simultaneously guilty at leaving behind his friend Mark Conrad, whose worst nightmare had cruelly come true the previous evening. A corporal from One Platoon had been badly injured, and Lieutenant Whitham had immediately requested that Conrad temporarily take over the wounded man's section until a permanent 'battle casualty replacement' could be sent from Wirral. Major Aldridge had agreed, on the grounds that Alpha Company's need for trained NCOs was greater than Charlie Company's. So Conrad remained on the front line in Normandy, while Robert sailed for home in the company of the unscrupulous megalomaniac whose perverted lust for glory and *greatness* had been the very cause of the war in the first place. Unable to distance himself from the Council Leader within the confines of the relatively small vessel, Robert adopted a polite yet detached persona which was courteous without being amiable. Radley, by comparison, was exceedingly cordial towards Robert, and treated him like an old friend and trusted confidant.

"It really is strange don't you think, Corporal Taylor," he kept saying, "how you and I keep bumping into each other during this war? It's as if destiny intends our paths to cross or something..."

After a three day voyage the *Royal Daffodil* approached Wirral, giving the area around the wind turbines at the mouth of the Dee a wide berth so as to avoid the French support ship *Dauphin*, which loitered just outside the one-kilometre exclusion zone.

"That really would be quite a coup for the Frogs, wouldn't it?"

Radley declared with a self-indulgent smile. "I mean - to capture this ship and find me on board!"

An hour later, they moored in the East Float dock close to the submarine *Onyx*. It was gone ten o'clock at night and Birkenhead was in darkness. Ambulances were waiting to rush the wounded to Arrowe Park hospital, and two SCW vans were ready to transfer the dead to the Council morgue. Radley's BMW was parked by the gangway, courtesy of Duncan Silverlock, who had driven over from the town hall to collect his beloved leader. Robert had been expecting a C Company Land Rover to take him back to the TA Centre, but no army vehicles were in evidence at the dockside. He felt rather forlorn and dejected as he watched the injured men being helped onto the ambulances, and stood awkwardly like an unwanted child as Silverlock strode over to welcome Radley with an uncharacteristically affectionate embrace.

"Gerald, good to see you…Glad to have you back in one piece. A lot has happened during your absence, I'm afraid."

"Don't be afraid, Duncan," Radley replied reassuringly. "It sounds like you've got everything under control and have coped magnificently… But tell me all about it anyway…" Suddenly the Council Leader noticed Robert standing on the dockside a short distance away. "Is there no-one here to collect you, Corporal Taylor?"

"It doesn't look like it, Council Leader."

"Where should you be going now?"

"I don't know, to be honest. I suppose back to the TA Centre."

"Well, have the night off. We'll give you a lift home and you can report for duty tomorrow morning. If anyone says anything, tell them I gave you permission, and if they're still not happy, refer them directly to me. How does that sound?"

Robert hesitated. On the one hand he was reluctant to accept favours of any kind from this man, whom he found morally repugnant, but on the other he was desperate to see Susan, and time was ticking away…

"What's the problem?" Radley asked, unable to understand Robert's indecision.

"Er, I've still got my rifle, Council Leader…"

"So what? A soldier should have his rifle with him at all times – I learned that in France! Just don't shoot anyone with it tonight. Unless, of course, they're French!" Radley and Silverlock both laughed heartily. "Come on, Corporal Taylor – my generous offer expires in five seconds…"

Robert made up his mind. On this occasion, moral rectitude would have to take second place to his physical and emotional needs. He heaved his heavy bergen onto one shoulder and said, "What the hell – let's go."

Ten minutes later he was standing outside Susan's apartment block, pressing the intercom button by the communal door and praying that she would answer. She did, and five minutes later they were making love.

During the night, air-raid sirens began to wail and crisscrossing lines of tracer streamed into the starry sky from the SCW anti-aircraft positions around Birkenhead. A short while later there was a terrific explosion which started a colossal fire at the Rock Ferry oil terminal. Several huge fuel storage tanks were set ablaze, and such was the magnitude of the conflagration that fire crews were barely able to contain the flames, let alone extinguish them.

Next morning, Radley visited the scene on his way to the town hall. All of the buildings in the vicinity of the terminal had been evacuated and a vast cloud of black smoke hung over the area. The Council Leader spoke briefly to firemen and local residents - ensuring that his presence at the scene was thoroughly recorded by the media - before resuming his journey to work.

At a junction near Hamilton Square, a large Mercedes four-by-four vehicle with tinted windows pulled out suddenly from a side road, forcing Simms to slam on the brakes and screech to a halt. The Mercedes stopped momentarily, blocking the road, and Simms subjected it to a blast from his horn. The front window of the four-by-four slid down and the driver - a fat man wearing a leather jacket - leaned out, raised two fingers at Radley's car, and shouted some abuse. Then the large vehicle swung around and accelerated away, with the driver making obscene gestures out of the window.

"Shall I go after him, sir?" Simms asked, jotting down the offending vehicle's registration and other identifying features.

Radley was outraged, but retained his composure. "No, I've got more important matters to attend to. We'll deal with him later..."

McCarthy and Silverlock were already present in the executive suite when Radley stormed in with a face like thunder. "It's outrageous!" he announced angrily. "With this fire at Rock Ferry we're likely to have a fuel crisis in the near future, and the Army is crying-out for vehicles, yet we've got oinks like that driving around in enormous gas-guzzling four-by-fours! *And* behaving like yobs at the same time! To think, the English used to be renowned and admired around the world for their manners and politeness and sense of fair play. Now it seems they're just a bunch of fat, ignorant gits! I think we'd better add 'Etiquette and Manners' to the school curriculum..."

He reached for the phone. "This is most definitely a job for George Lawton..."

Within minutes, the fate of the Mercedes driver had been sealed. He would be identified, arrested, found guilty of sexual offences against children, and sent to the Fort, where he would probably be murdered by other prisoners before the Council had the opportunity to execute him. DNA evidence would form the basis of his conviction. Radley frequently resorted to DNA as a convenient means of establishing the guilt of people he wanted 'out of the way'. He extolled its virtues thus: "It's irrefutable, we call the shots, and the defence can't argue against it, no matter how clever their lawyers are. All we need is to present the jury with a few images of blurred black and white lines, and have a boffin tell the court how the suspect's DNA precisely matches that found at the crime scene, and *bingo!* – we've got our conviction! We don't even need to bribe witnesses. It's a real Godsend!"

To lend credibility to the charade, he had even authorised the creation of Wirral's very own 'forensic science centre,' which supposedly specialised in DNA analysis. From the outside the new brick-built facility appeared convincing – through the windows, men in lab coats could dimly be seen peering down the barrels of microscopes, or loading samples into large white machines resembling those used for gel electrophorysis. But it was all a façade. In reality the scientists and technicians were simply SCW ruffians recuperating from injuries, and the large white machines were old industrial top-loading washing machines. Inside the building, the facility's most important pieces of equipment were a computer and printer used to produce the fake DNA matches needed to secure a conviction in court...Those who fell foul of the Council, for whatever reason, stood little or no chance against its legal, financial and technological might.

Having addressed the specific issue of the rude man in his big car, Radley set about rectifying what he perceived to be the root cause of the wider social malaise.

"It all comes down to people theses days having too much, and not appreciating it," he declared. "I think the time has come for some austerity measures. We are at war, after all."

The three men thrashed-out the new policies in a matter of minutes. With immediate effect, any privately-owned four wheel drive vehicle with an engine capacity above two litres could be requisitioned by the Council under wartime 'Emergency Powers' and donated to the Army or SCW. No compensation would be paid to the rightful owners, because the vehicles would, supposedly, be returned to them after the war. Other 'donations' required from the population in support of the War Effort would include iron and steel gates and railings, aluminium pans, gardening tools, and mobile phones. In order to reduce electricity consumption, distribution of the supply would be controlled so that each region would be without power for two hours per day. And to deter decadent extravagance while simultaneously generating further revenue for the Council, VAT on 'luxury' goods would be increased to thirty percent.

While Radley and Silverlock discussed each austerity measure with great relish - knowing full well that they would not be personally affected by any of them - Terence McCarthy seemed rather less enthusiastic.

"Don't go too far, Gerald," he warned. "I mean, the situation isn't dire enough at the moment to really warrant any of this. The public will go ballistic if they realise you've introduced these measures just for the sake of it."

"But it's in their interests!" Radley insisted. "Deprivation builds strength of character, we all know that, and strength of character is what we need to win this war. And deprivation makes for a healthier lifestyle. Take food, for example. Did you know that the British population was never healthier than during the Second World War? There certainly weren't all these fat porkers lounging around in tracksuits then. I think we should seriously consider introducing rationing!"

"Gerald, the supermarkets are full!" McCarthy declared in disbelief. "You can't be serious!" The chief executive was a man who enjoyed his food.

"I don't see why not, Terence. Like I said, it'd be good for the slobs. They'd thank us in the long run."

"But didn't you say you wanted everyone eating roast beef and Yorkshire pudding for Sunday dinner?"

Radley nodded thoughtfully then shrugged. "So we don't ration the ingredients for the traditional Sunday roast. And bread and potatoes were never rationed, even in the Second World War. But everything else...If it's modern or foreign, I say ration it! And if we ration fuel as well, we might get a few more people to walk and lose some of those surplus pounds." Noticing the scepticism on the faces of his colleagues, he added, "Of course, the essential nature of our duties will exempt us from rationing of any kind..."

So the new 'austerity package' was implemented without delay, although as the measures took effect it soon became apparent that they were not altogether impartial: a few days before its offices were conveniently destroyed in an 'air raid', the *Gazette* newspaper observed ironically that the residences belonging to the members of the Senior Executive Committee still flaunted their grandiose gates and railings, while the homes of most of their political opponents did not.

By the time Robert rejoined C Company, the unit was no longer reinforcing Hubbard's men at Thurstaston and had returned to its former duties of guarding the north coast and acting as a mobile reserve. Intelligence reports suggested that the French had insufficient men on Hilbre to mount a second attack on the mainland from there, but the company mortar and a platoon of soldiers were permanently deployed in the vicinity of West Kirby as a precaution.

Further south, B Company now had sole responsibility for containing the French within what had become known as the 'Thurstaston Bulge'. Both sides had consolidated their positions and were now well and truly dug-in, but, although they kept a watchful eye on each other from observation posts, and mounted numerous reconnaissance patrols, aggressive operations had all but ceased. Neither side was eager to do anything rash which might result in further casualties. This situation seemed to satisfy Council Leader Radley when he ventured out from the town hall to visit the troops on the front line.

"The forward French positions are along that hedgerow," Colonel Hogan explained, passing Radley a pair of binoculars and pointing to a line of bushes in the distance. "The intervening ground is fairly open and exposed, but if we attack at night I'm sure we could break through their defences…Shall we start planning an offensive?"

"Good gracious no!" Radley replied, then hurriedly added, "At least, not until I've tried to establish some sort of dialogue with Lebovic. I'd like to avoid further bloodshed if at all possible – perhaps we can resolve this conflict through diplomatic means after all."

The colonel appeared unconvinced. "Perhaps. But please be aware that, while you're talking and negotiating, those French troops will be improving their defences and making themselves harder and harder to dislodge..." He subjected Radley to a piercing stare which made the Council Leader feel uncomfortable. "But you must do what you consider best, of course, Council Leader. I'm just a simple soldier, after all."

Radley looked unimpressed. "I know. So you keep telling me."

One evening, Robert and Susan were preparing their evening meal in her small but immaculate kitchen when she suddenly announced, "Oh – I forgot to tell you. Council Leader Radley came round to my department today."

"Lucky you," he replied, chopping carrot with sudden aggression. "I really don't like that man, as you know. What did he want?"

"He's looking for girls – well, women, you know – to work in the War Office. Moving things on maps or something, he said."

Robert grinned and raised his eyebrows. "How bizarre. What sort of maps?"

"Well, apparently they've got some big maps of Wirral and Normandy on the walls and some big models of the invasion areas, and he wants a couple of girls to move symbols or labels or whatever to keep everything updated. He needs quite a few volunteers because it'll only be for a four-hour shift, twice a week. What do you think?"

"Are you tempted?"

"I'm not sure. It'd be paid as overtime, and the extra money would come in handy. I also thought about what you said – about how he'll only be brought down from within - and I thought it might be useful to know a bit more about what's going on, from the inside, so to speak."

"Hmm. I'm not sure it's a good idea to deliberately get any closer to that man than you have to. But you're right, it might be useful." He shrugged. "It's up to you."

"I think I'll go for it then. *And* you'll get to see me in uniform."

"What sort of uniform?"

"A tan-coloured blouse, dark green tie and dark green A-line skirt – below the knee of course. And some *very* sensible shoes."

"Sounds saucy. Susan – just one thing…"

"What?"

"If you do end up working there, don't let Radley know we're an item. He knows me, and I don't think it'd be a good idea for him to make a connection between us. I'm not really sure why, it's just gut instinct. And whatever you do, don't trust anything he says or does. He's an evil weasel."

Two weeks after the invasion at Thurstaston, the military situation along the Dee Estuary remained unchanged. The media used terms such as 'stalemate' or 'deadlock' when reporting upon the lack of progress made by the opposing forces, although 'voluntary inertia' might have been more accurate. The French knew that they could not realistically advance further inland without seriously overstretching their supply lines, while the British were content to sit in their trenches and make the most of the lack of orders instructing them to take offensive action. Neither side wanted further casualties. Gerald Radley, of course, was entirely satisfied with the situation, which had developed exactly as envisaged, and he used it to justify some of his more extreme social policies. For example, when a prominent local businessman publicly objected to having his BMW four-by-four vehicle seized by the SCW under a compulsory requisition order, Radley berated him thus:

"I am frankly appalled by your selfish attitude. Here we are, with French forces dug-in only five or six miles away at Thurstaston – within striking distance of the town hall - and you're bleating about having to temporarily give up the use of what is essentially a luxury toy. I hope you appreciate that, if we lose this war, you're likely to lose a hell of a lot more than your expensive car. You could well lose everything. Desperate times call for desperate measures, and we all have to make sacrifices..."

Other drastic measures made possible by the French invasion included a substantial rise in the basic rate of Wirral Tax and a night-time curfew from ten until six. Special Council Worker powers were increased to the point where the organisation could do practically anything it wanted, from searching individuals, their vehicles and homes, to arresting suspected subversives and detaining them indefinitely without charge, all in the name of homeland security and the War Effort.

One morning in November, Radley was relaxing on a sofa in the lounge area of the executive suite when Duncan Silverlock approached him, a little tentatively.

"Good morning Duncan," the Council Leader said, without looking up from the document he was perusing. "I keep meaning to ask – how's your canal?"

Silverlock was by nature a humourless man, but even he was amused by the potential for comedy offered by Radley's question, and he was tempted to reply in a facetious manner. It was evident, however, that he did not have Radley's undivided attention, and therefore any attempt at turning the unintentional double entendre into a joke would probably fall on deaf ears. So he simply replied, "Oh, er, it's proceeding well, Council Leader."

"What happened to 'Gerald', Duncan?"

"Sorry – Gerald, yes, the canal's going well, but progress has been a bit slower than expected and the completion date's slipped again. I'm afraid Technical Services underestimated the sheer quantity of material that would come out of the cutting. They're at a bit of a loss as to what to do with it all..."

"Build more events arenas of course!" Radley exclaimed, becoming suddenly animated. "I went past the one in the park yesterday on my way home and was immensely impressed – a wonderful piece of architecture, and an excellent original idea from you. My congratulations to all concerned. All we need to do now is organise some events to take place inside it. How about a 'Community Day' every Sunday? We could encourage people to 'take the air' with a stroll in the park after their Sunday dinner - to celebrate the sense of identity and community which comes from being a Wirralian. And perhaps we could lay on some kind of entertainment for them..."

Silverlock nodded weakly. He had not intended the conversation to stray down this route. "A good idea, Gerald..."

"I thought so, Duncan. And how about this for another good idea? I was so inspired by your events arena that I've been trying to think of an equally magnificent project myself. And I thought, why not bring shipbuilding back to the Wirral by commissioning Laird's to build a battleship? Imagine the sense of pride we'd all get from watching a mighty vessel, built in our own shipyards in the great tradition of Cammel Laird's, sliding down the slipway into the Mersey, ready to take the fight to the French!"

Silverlock swallowed hard and declared quietly, "Gerald, I really don't think we can afford it, I'm afraid..."

"What?"

"Tony Williams and I have been reviewing finances. The economy has stagnated in the last couple of months, and the war and other projects are costing more than we forecast."

"Can't we hold another golf tournament?" Radley asked. "We did very well out of The Open the other year."

"I'm not sure that the world's elite golfers would be queuing up to play in a war zone...Anyway, the measures we agreed last week, such as increasing Wirral tax and VAT, should generate sufficient additional revenue to balance the books, but until they start having an impact I think it would be wise to restrict spending to essential items only."

Radley nodded soberly. "Of course. We must all tighten our belts in these difficult times – including the Council. I'll speak to Personnel later today and instruct them to identify superfluous staff for the next tranche of redundancies. All remaining employees will have to accept a cut in their pay and pension entitlements – shall we say ten percent, for now? We can always cut it again in the future if need be. Obviously the cuts won't apply to anyone of director level and above."

"Obviously. Oh – on the subject of golf, are you playing this afternoon?"

"No. Well, actually, I might if I've got time, but I want to pop over to the East Float to see how *Onyx* is coming along."

Ever since the surface ships *Plymouth* and *Bronington* had been refitted and sent out to fight the French, the third vessel in the historic warships collection – the submarine *Onyx* – had remained forlornly in the dock, a once proud veteran of the Falkland's War, now seemingly devoid of purpose. Until, that was, Gerald Radley had ventured aboard out of pure curiosity and become fascinated by the cramped conditions and claustrophobic atmosphere. He fell in love with the space-saving craftsmanship of the wooden furniture and fittings, which to him seemed so redolent of British naval tradition, seafaring stoicism and general *greatness*. Determined not to allow the vessel to remain completely redundant during Wirral's finest hour, Radley adopted it as his secret hideaway. Through cash-in-hand payments to George Lawton, he had the wardroom and captain's cabin completely refurbished to create a small but luxurious suite for himself and a few of his most trusted staff. Large quantities of supplies were brought aboard secretly at night, and heating, air conditioning and communications systems were discretely installed by men who asked no questions if paid the right sum.

Sitting in a chilly bunker overlooking the beach at Red Rocks on the north-west corner of the peninsular, Robert Taylor exhaled steaming breath into the cold night air and looked at his watch. It was just before midnight.

"Right, lads," he announced, "five minutes to go. Start getting your kit packed away so we can get out of here as soon as the wagon arrives."

He climbed stiffly out of the bunker and walked along to the other positions occupied by men of his section, making sure they were ready to leave. Out in the estuary, French-occupied Hilbre was invisible in the darkness. It had been a quiet and uneventful shift – indeed, Charlie Company had seen no further action since the initial invasion, and rumours were circulating that men from A and B companies now joked that the 'C' in C Company stood for 'cushy'.

At just after twelve, a Bedford four-tonne truck came rattling along the access road to the beach, bringing Three Section to take over from Robert's men in the bunkers. As soon as he had handed-over command of the position to Karl Brabander, Robert and his section climbed aboard the truck and were taken back to the TA Centre, where they were officially off-duty as soon as they returned their weapons to the armoury. Robert had arranged to meet Susan at her flat, and was preparing to leave, when the Company Quartermaster Sergeant handed him a crumpled letter from Mark Conrad, which he slipped into a pocket of his combat jacket.

With petrol now rationed and all vehicle lights prohibited due to the black-out, Robert tended to use his bike for transport, especially at night. He hurriedly put his kit away in a lockable cabinet in the Eight Platoon storeroom – even in wartime there were unscrupulous soldiers who would steal whatever they could find – before signing-out at the guardroom and pedalling madly towards Oxton. The orange glow created by Liverpool's streetlights and the burning oil tanks at Rock Ferry provided just enough ambient light to see by, although on several occasions he cycled into invisible pot-holes which lurked like landmines in the darkness and almost sent him head-first over the handlebars.

On the road ahead he could dimly make out a white van with several dark figures standing next to it, and as he approached nearer he was illuminated by a number of red-filtered torch beams.

"Stop there, mate," one of the figures said sternly, stepping into his path as he braked to a halt. In the meagre red light, Robert could just make out some black-uniformed men with sub-machine guns, loitering next to a striped barrier which partially blocked the road, and he realised that he had cycled into a Special Council Worker checkpoint.

The SCW commander shone his torch into Robert's face with one hand, while pointing his gun at him with the other. "Keep perfectly still and keep your hands on the bike," he instructed. "Don't you know there's a curfew? You should've been indoors two hours ago! Right, very slowly, I need to see your Wirral passport or identity card."

"I'm Army," Robert declared, with a hint of contempt. "I've just come off duty. That's why I'm in uniform."

The SCW man seemed unimpressed. There was no love lost between his organisation and the military. "Then I'll need to see your army I.D. card. Anyone can go around in a set of combats."

"Can I take my hands off the handle bars to get it?"

"Go on. But do it slowly, or I might just blow a hole in you by accident."

Robert produced his army-issue I.D. card, which bore his photo and an anti-forgery hologram. The SCW man examined it by torchlight, then said, "Wait here while I check it out." He walked over to the white van and began conversing with someone over the radio, presumably verifying the details on the card and checking that Corporal Robert Taylor existed and had not been killed or sent to France.

Shivering with cold and nervousness, Robert stood motionless astride his bike, simultaneously impressed yet dismayed by the level of technological sophistication evidently possessed by the SCW. He suddenly felt anxious and vulnerable: his army I.D. card was all that granted immunity from the brutality of these men – without it he was as powerless as any other ordinary nobody. What if the SCW commander took the card and denied ever having seen it? Or dropped it down a drain out of sheer malice? Conrad's words echoed in his mind, acquiring new relevance and wisdom: "*If you're not Council, you're little people...*"

After what seemed like a very long time but was probably only a few minutes, the SCW commander returned and, much to Robert's relief, handed back the precious I.D. card.

"There you go. Cheers, mate."

"Can I go now?"

"You can, but not through here. You'll have to find another way." He chuckled.

Robert sighed. Evidently he had suffered the misfortune of being stopped by a small-minded man, who derived pleasure from abusing his powers and inconveniencing people unnecessarily. For such men – little men made big – the SCW was their dream come true, the apogee of their entire lives. Suddenly, without the requirement for lengthy training, or study, or persistent hard work, this particular breed of thugs had found themselves in control of society, able to command respect which they had not earned and did not deserve. It was all very corrupt and unjust, but under the circumstances there was absolutely no point in arguing with such people. Robert turned around and cycled away without looking back. His heart was still pounding when Susan met him at the main entrance to her block of flats and they embraced passionately.

"How long have you got?" she asked, leading him up the communal stairs to her flat.

"Twenty-four hours. Good, eh?"

She frowned. "Typical. I've got to work in the morning. Why can't you get your leave at the weekend?"

"Why can't you phone in sick?"

"Normally I would, but I'm at the War Office. If I have any time off they'll sack me."

"How's that job going?"

"Not bad," she replied, opening the door to her flat and ushering him inside. "Actually it's quite interesting. Mind you, I only hear little snippets of information about what's going on. That's probably why we only do four hour shifts – so none of us ever learn too much."

"And Radley? How do you find him?"

She thought for a moment. "He's okay, I suppose. I mean, he's always polite, and he tries to be charming, but I can see what you mean about him...Oh, you'll never believe what he gave me today!" She reached for a slender packet on the sideboard and held it up for him to see.

"What is it?"

"Black silk stockings with seams up the back. You know - like women used to wear in the old days. He wants all the girls to wear them as part of their uniform."

"With suspenders?" he asked hopefully.

She gave him a coquettish smile. "If it would please you, darling."

"Oo-er!" For a moment there was silence, then he asked, "Is he a pervert, do you think?"

"The Council Leader? I don't know. I don't think so, but it's weird..."

"What is?"

"The whole situation. The war. Everything."

"In what way?"

"Well, I know I've only done a few shifts in the ops room, but I almost get the impression that Council Leader Radley *likes* there being a war on, and enjoys all this stuff about air raids and rationing and what-have-you. And sometimes it almost seems as if he knows what the French are going to do before they even do it..."

Next morning, Susan departed for work at the War Office wearing her old-fashioned uniform, leaving Robert lingering unashamedly in bed. He had intended to catch up on some much-needed sleep, but found himself restless and fidgety. Eventually, he gave up trying to sleep and listened to the radio instead, savouring the relaxed comfort and tranquility of his clean, civilized surroundings. Then he remembered Conrad's letter, which he retrieved from his jacket pocket and read in bed. It quickly became apparent that the war in France was being prosecuted with far greater energy and ferocity than was the case on the Wirral:

So, how's it going, R.T.?
(Obligatory response of 'Not good, not good M.C.'!)

Greetings from the Muppets Road Show, which this month is visiting Normandy. Actually that's not strictly fair – the A Coy boys are doing their best, but there just isn't the same esprit de corps here that we've got in Charlie Company, I suppose because the lads haven't been together for so long and most are so inexperienced. Mind you, they're having to learn pretty fast, or get their heads blown off! It's pretty fucking grim here – the Frogs are probing our defences the entire time, and as you know, I've never been a man who likes being probed!

I'm writing this from inside one of the German gun emplacements, having just got back in from a recce patrol. We've been given four hours' rest time, so I thought I'd drop you a quick line in the grand old British tradition of writing letters in harsh circumstances. Aldridge is running us ragged at the moment – it's an endless succession of O.P.s and patrols, and everyone is completely chin-strapped, but I don't think it's his fault. The real problem is there simply aren't enough of us here to do the job. You should think yourself very lucky that you got out when you did, as they certainly wouldn't let you go now if you were still here. And because we're not getting enough sleep, a lot of the boys are switching off and becoming careless and then becoming dead. We've had four killed in the last week and nine wounded, two seriously, so morale is plummeting. Wally Whitham doesn't help matters – he really is a liability and doesn't seem to be learning from his mistakes or close escapes. Someone suggested fragging him, but to be honest I reckon he'll get it anyway – you know, sometimes I can just look at a guy and I know that guy's not gonna make it, there's no fucking way...

Fortunately, the platoon sergeant's an ex-Para who knows his stuff and is pretty much running the show. I've also got Finnegan as my 2ic, which is a bonus. Oh – I bumped into Thomas yesterday, being escorted to the HQ bunker by the CSM. Apparently he had an argument with another lad, which ended up in a fight. Tom hit the guy in the throat so hard he had to be casevac'd back to Plymouth and won't be coming back. There's talk of a court martial, but to be honest we need men in the field so badly here that I reckon they'll decide it was self-defence and send Tom back to his section. I doubt anyone will be arguing with him again! Mind you, tempers are fraying a lot because everyone's so tired and pissed-off, and we feel like we've really picked the short straw and got the shitty end of the stick, if you get my drift. How's things back in Wirral? Someone said you've got food rationing! Whatever next – Vera Lynn songs on the radio – or the crystal set? Hope you enjoy your bread and dripping, you won't believe this, but after countless meals of it, my love affair with chicken pasta boil-in-the-bag is officially over! I'd do anything for a proper decent dinner on a china plate, with an ice-cold beer in a green glass bottle with condensation on the sides...

Right, I'd better stop here and sort my life out before we have to venture out once again into the Big and Dangerous Wide World. Hope to see you soon, mate – I'm keeping my fingers crossed that they'll send me back to Charlie Company, but if the situation here doesn't improve I reckon you'll be out here with me by Christmas!

Keep your pecker hard and your powder dry and remember – adventure, excitement...a Jedi craves not these things! Cheers,

Mark.

PS If anyone from the Council censors this letter, I just want you to know that I've put a curse on it and I hope you all die horribly you bastards!

After reading the letter, Robert felt guilty to be lounging around in idle luxury while his friend was enduring such terrible privations. He decided that physical exercise might help purge his sense of unworthiness, so went out on his bike and cycled east until he reached the Mersey, then headed north along the edge of the river. Approaching the Egremont Ferry pub, he saw a crowd of people standing around the large lump of rock which bore a plaque designating it as a 'speakers' corner' – a place where any citizen could air their views to anyone who would listen.

Robert could not recall ever having seen anyone using the stone for its intended purpose, but as he cycled nearer it became apparent that today a man was exercising his right to free speech. He looked like an ex-soldier - unshaven and with long straggly hair and a combat jacket. Robert stopped and looked at the man, half expecting to recognise him, but decided it was not someone he knew. He began to listen to what the speaker was saying, but remained astride his bike, just outside the edge of the crowd. Parked a short distance away was a white van, its SCW occupants watching events with interest. One of them was filming the crowd with a camcorder. As Robert watched, a second van drew up quietly behind the first and stopped. It featured an unusual turret on the roof, from which protruded a tube of too great a diameter to be a normal gun; Robert guessed it was probably a water canon. The speaker at the stone spotted the vans and pointed at them.

"And these white vans!" he exclaimed angrily. "They seem to get everywhere, making sure we all stay in line. Talk about Big Brother's watching you! Did anyone here vote to have white vans patrolling our streets, with armed men inside who've been chosen on the basis of no other criteria than they're loyal to the Council Leader and are prepared to do anything he asks them to, however outrageous or unethical? I know I didn't. Was anyone here consulted on the matter? I know I wasn't. And here's something really disturbing: a friend of mine is a lawyer, and a couple of months ago he was asked to represent a construction company which wanted to take legal action against the Council for reneging on a contract for one of the school playing fields which our dear Mr Radley so gaily sold off. Anyway, as my friend delved deeper to gather evidence for the defence, he uncovered all sorts of examples of misconduct, incompetence and general impropriety concerning Council Leader Radley and his administration. Some of it was very disturbing. Then my mate disappeared. A neighbour reported seeing him being bundled into the back of a white van and I haven't seen or heard of him since. The Council deny any knowledge of him, and I can't find any legal firm on the Wirral who're prepared to take the case on…

"So, people of Wirral, I ask you this: watch this regime carefully – for it is a regime, an evil and self-serving regime – and do not trust it. Question it, challenge it, express discontentment at its conduct if you're not happy. I urge you not to be intimidated or coerced or threatened by it. Don't give it any more authority and claw back some of the power it's acquired so deceitfully. Demand, en-masse – for Radley and his cronies will never take individuals seriously – that it demonstrates integrity and is accountable to the People rather than merely itself. And always think back to the time of the vote for autonomy, and remember the principles and ideals that you voted for, and ask yourselves whether they still exist now." He paused, peering through the crowd to see Special Council Workers climbing out of their vans. “Here they come now – don’t let them through! People power – only that will preserve our freedom!”

He turned and fled past Robert, running south along the riverside esplanade as the Special Council Workers pushed their way through the crowd in pursuit. Many of the bystanders were uncooperative, deliberately turning their backs on the SCW men and blocking their path.

“Let us through please!” the SCW commander shouted. “Stand aside please!” When this failed to produce the desired response, he drew his baton and screamed, “Get out of the way or you’ll all be arrested!”

Still the crowd failed to part. One SCW man tripped and fell, and people laughed and jeered. Other paramilitaries demanded, “Move aside!” to the backs of an impenetrable phalanx of citizens who seemed totally deaf and oblivious to their presence. Meanwhile, the protester in the camouflaged jacket had disappeared up a side street leading into Wallasey’s labyrinth of terraced houses.

“Right, lads – back to the vans!” the SCW leader shouted, and his men disengaged themselves from the crowd and returned to their vehicles.

Robert, who was detached from events by a distance of about thirty metres, decided that it was time to leave the scene of the disturbance. He swung his bike around and began cycling south towards home, while behind him the SCW van with the strange turret sprayed the crowd with a highly staining purple dye. As Robert passed the side street up which the protester had disappeared, he heard vehicle doors slamming and turned to see a white van accelerate away with a screeching of tyres. Of the man in the combat jacket there was no sign. Robert shuddered, and pedalled home as fast as he could.

CHAPTER 24

A Walk in the Park

I tell ya, if I see this Roberts fella in the park, I'll set me Rotty on 'im and that'll learn 'im good!

Name and address supplied

Mr Roberts replies:
No comment.

Gerald Radley was furious when he heard about the display of public defiance outside the Egremont Ferry pub.

"As if we haven't got enough challenges fighting the French," he snarled angrily, "without having to contend with treachery from our own people! Honestly, what's the matter with these plebs? Have they no sense of patriotic duty?"

"Most of them have," remarked McCarthy thoughtfully, a note of caution in his voice, "but you shouldn't take too many liberties with them, Gerald."

"Why not? They voted for me."

"Some of them did..."

Radley eyed the chief executive suspiciously. "Whose side are you on, Terence?"

"Yours, Gerald. But every great leader needs someone to play Devil's advocate to them, and help keep their feet on the ground, and I've always regarded that as my job with you. I just think that you had overwhelming public support a few months ago and now there's a danger you're losing it. And it's not just the public who are showing signs of disaffection. I'm starting to hear murmurs of discontentment within the Council itself."

Radley was horrified. "What do you mean?"

"Well, I was in the toilet the other day, in one of the cubicles, and I heard two men talking outside. I couldn't recognise their voices or hear everything they were saying, but one of them was comparing you to Adolf Hitler."

Radley smiled smugly, then realised that the remark had probably not been intended as a complement, and quickly changed his expression to a concerned frown.

"Our own employees?" he said in disbelief.

"Yes," contributed Duncan Silverlock, "I'm afraid Terence is right. I've overheard admin staff in the canteen criticising the SEC and SCW. Lunchtime's a prime breeding ground for conspiracy and dissent – it's an ideal opportunity for subversives to get together and gossip."

"What do you suggest we do?" Radley asked. He was frankly appalled.

McCarthy answered first. "Ease off for a while, and tell George and his SCW boys to do the same. Make sure there's no repetition of the incident at speaker's corner, which if you ask me was dealt with far too heavy-handedly. Focus your attention on the war, which is where you definitely *do* have popular support at the moment."

"I'd like to suggest a few measures we can take to keep our own people in line," added Silverlock with a deviously sinister smile.

"Go on..."

"Well, for a start, make the staff lunch break as short as possible, say twenty minutes. Justify it as a productivity measure necessitated by the War Effort. The idea would be to give people just enough time to get their food and get back to work, without any opportunity to chat and whinge and conspire against us."

"Sounds sensible. What else?"

"Introduce a new offence of propagating negativity and defeatism, and ban the public and private expression of all anti-Council sentiment. Increase CCTV around the building and randomly check staff e-mails, internet use and personal computer files. Also, if we replace conventional keys with electronic ones, we can monitor where everyone goes and identify unusual activity. We can then easily remove from the system anyone we regard as a security threat – we simply cancel their key code and hey presto! – they can't even access the building! Oh – and I recommend tapping a few select phones and possibly hiding microphones at strategic locations to see what they pick up."

McCarthy looked sceptical. "Duncan, we can't possibly keep our entire staff under continual surveillance – we'd need hundreds of people to monitor them all effectively."

"We don't need to monitor everyone the whole time," Silverlock replied. "All we do is keep watching and listening until we catch someone doing something they shouldn't be, then make an example of them to everyone else. After that, the entire workforce will be paranoid that they're under constant surveillance, and no-one will dare step out of line. Trust me, the vast majority of our employees are a bunch of sheep."

The Council Leader nodded enthusiastically. "All good suggestions, Duncan. Consider them approved. Take the necessary finance from the SEC contingency fund, and fast-track these measures through - I want them in place immediately. I don't think we need bother putting the matter before Cabinet for discussion on this occasion..."

On the morning of the last Sunday in November, Gerald Radley looked out of his bedroom window and scowled.

"What is it?" his long-suffering wife asked sleepily.

"Next door's bloody cat – on the roof of the Porsche convertible again! If it damages it I swear I'll have the wretched thing skinned and presented to Deirdre as a nice pair of mittens." He banged on the window and the cat looked up at him indifferently, which only served to rile him still further.

"Right, that does it!" he declared, opening his wardrobe and reaching inside for his leather trenchcoat. "I mean, if I wanted a cat on my property I'd buy a bloody cat!" He pulled out his sawn-off shotgun, checked that it was loaded and strode purposefully to the window, only to find it locked. Cursing, he searched for the key but by the time he found it the cat had disappeared.

"Next time…" he growled menacingly, putting the gun away. "You stay in bed, dear; I'm off to church and then the park. Time to mingle with the Great Unwashed."

He met Sean Simms in the breakfast room downstairs and they discussed the day's schedule over coffee and cereal. Then the two men ventured outside onto the gravel drive, where a pair of stocky SCW guards waited by the car, having spent the night taking turns to patrol the garden and check the CCTV monitors. As Radley climbed into his armoured BMW he noticed something on his shiny shoe, and swore aloud. "Oh bugger it!"

"What is it, sir?" Simms asked in alarm.

"Bloody cat shit! The worst kind of shit!" He sighed, wiping the excrement off onto the lawn. "Right, my good man – get me to the church on time!"

Radley was not a religious man – indeed, he only believed in God when it suited him – but he liked the sentimental idea of the public attending church every Sunday, and knew that he had to set an example. To this end, Paul Ryder in Public Relations had arranged for representatives from the local press and radio station to be present when he arrived at St Augustine's for morning worship. Radley regarded it as an ideal opportunity to show-off his spiritual credentials and demonstrate his commitment to '*The Four Cs*' – Church, Children, Community, Council – each of which would be celebrated in different ways during the day.

After the service, he posed for photos with members of the congregation and gave a live radio interview, before returning to his car and heading for Birkenhead Park to participate in Wirral's first 'Community Day' – a concept which had been his brainchild. The idea was that the public should visit the park en masse to walk, converse, exercise, play and generally appreciate being members of Wirral's unique community. At midday, a programme of Council-organised entertainment would take place in the new Events Arena, after which it was intended that everyone would drift happily home for their traditional family dinner of roast beef and Yorkshire pudding, glowing with a newfound sense of social well-being.

It was a cold, bright day and people huddled inside thick coats and exhaled clouds of steaming vapour. Most citizens walked around briskly to keep warm, and, perhaps unsurprisingly, were less than enthusiastic about patronising the programme of entertainment scheduled to take place in the arena that afternoon - during which they would be seated in the open air, at the mercy of the chill breeze. To ensure that the event was well attended, George Lawton had instructed teams of Special Council Workers to roam the park like intimidating sheepdogs, herding people towards the arena.

Radley entered the Council box and found Duncan Silverlock waiting for him with a thermos of mulled wine and a hip flask of brandy. Terence McCarthy had elected not to attend. At one o'clock, with the venue virtually full, a Council 'Master of Ceremonies' walked out into the centre of the arena and announced, "And here, to open our feast of free entertainment for your delight, is our very own Council Leader, so please stand and show your appreciation to Council Leader Gerald Radley himself..."

Prompted by the Special Council Workers, the majority of the audience rose to their feet and clapped, but there was also some jeering which resulted in several people being dragged from their seats and forcibly ejected. Radley stood up and took the microphone a little hesitantly, unprepared for a speech which he had not expected to have to make. Unlike his heroes - Winston Churchill and Adolf Hitler - he was not a great public orator.

"Good afternoon, everyone," he began, sounding awkward and unconvincing. "Firstly, er, I'd like to welcome you to this, our first Wirral Community Day, which incidentally is also the first event to be held in this magnificent arena – hopefully the first of many events to be held here...I'd like to thank you all for coming here on this cold November Sunday and, in doing so, showing your loyalty and commitment to that special brotherhood of which every Wirral citizen is a privileged member. I'd also like to take this opportunity to thank you for your overwhelming support for me and the Council, during what has been a very difficult past few months for all of us. I'm afraid I can't offer any immediate solutions, or promise a drastic improvement in the situation in the immediate future, but I'm confident that we'll enjoy a decisive military victory before Christmas, which will bring the possibility of peace nearer in the New Year. In the meantime, thank you for your fortitude and sacrifice, and I hope you enjoy the afternoon's events."

He sat down to applause which was less than rapturous, congratulating himself on his ability to extemporize. The entertainment began with a series of performances by local schoolchildren and youth groups who sang, marched, acted and danced fairly ineptly but with great enthusiasm. They were followed by several adult bands and choirs singing a mixture of new and traditional songs, with the common theme of solidarity and courage in the face of adversity. A rousing rendition of *'You'll Never Walk Alone'* - accompanied by the SCW brass band - rounded off the musical section of the programme, before an announcement came over the loudspeaker system which politely instructed all children under the age of sixteen to leave. People looked enquiringly at each other, intrigued and uneasy and suddenly curious as to why a high mesh fence separated the circular floor of the arena from the seats surrounding it. A squad of armed Special Council Workers took up positions around the fence as the Master of Ceremonies informed everyone that the 'Gladiatorial Contest' was about to begin.

Six men wearing the plain grey overalls of 'The Fort' walked out onto the stone floor of the arena, looking rather bewildered. The MC introduced them as convicted criminals from death row, who had been offered the opportunity to have their sentences commuted to life imprisonment by fighting for public entertainment. Only two of the six would be granted this reprieve, the other four would die, either in the arena or on the prison gallows. Three of the prisoners were very young - teenagers of sixteen and seventeen, who had been found guilty of beating a pensioner to death in the park for no other reason than pure sadistic gratification. A relatively well-groomed individual in his late twenties was in fact a local drugs dealer and small-time gangster, convicted of shooting a neighbour who threatened to testify against him in court. And finally, there were two brutal-looking characters in their forties with shaved heads covered in scars – genuine hard men from the North End of Birkenhead, whose long history of violent crime included extortion, assault, arson and attempted murder; they had put several Special Council Workers in hospital while resisting arrest.

As it dawned on the audience that they were about to witness a gladiatorial fight, many people attempted to leave, but found their exit blocked by SCW 'ushers' who told them politely but firmly to return to their seats. "The Council Leader wants everyone to stay and enjoy the show," the SCW men said, casually pointing their sub-machine guns at the incredulous citizens, who duly did as they were told.

The Master of Ceremonies 'named and shamed' each of the six men in turn and revealed details of the crimes they had committed. Members of the crowd jeered and booed, while the two shaven-headed men snarled back at them, raising two fingers in defiance. Then a Special Council Worker appeared with two large axes and a pair of carving knives, which he threw over the fence into the arena.

The two North-Enders decided to work as a team to eliminate their opponents one by one and win the contest, and soon it was all over. Some of the audience cheered and applauded, while others were physically sick or buried their heads in their hands in revulsion. Radley had watched proceedings from the edge of his seat, enthralled by the display of savagery, and seemingly oblivious to the disapproval and repugnance of many spectators. As the two victors were disarmed at gunpoint and led away to start their life-sentences, he turned to Simms and commented, "I reckon we might have a use for those two, don't you? I'll speak to George Lawton..."

Leaving the arena, Radley and his entourage went for a stroll around Birkenhead Park to, as he put it, "Meet the people and take in the air". They had completed a circuit of the lake and were heading back to the car, when they heard the sound of a dog barking, and turned to see a Rottweiler bounding across the grass towards them, with its owner in hot pursuit a considerable distance behind. For a few anxious moments it seemed that the animal was about to attack the Council Leader's group, but at the last minute it stopped short and stood snarling at Radley, with slimy trails of foam dangling from its barred teeth. One of the SCW bodyguards raised his sub-machine gun, but the Council Leader extended a restraining hand, and without averting his eyes from the growling dog, declared, "I'll handle this..."

The dog's owner, an overweight, bullet-headed man in his forties, was still some distance away. "It's alright mate," he shouted as he lumbered nearer, "he won't hurt you. Just stand still and he won't hurt you."

Radley pulled out his sawn-off twelve-bore and shot the dog in the head. It dropped like a stone, but he discharged the second barrel into it for good measure, just as the owner finally arrived at the scene with an expression of horrified disbelief.

"By Jove you're right!" Radley exclaimed gleefully. "He won't hurt me...*Because he's dead!* Now, I suggest you take the fucking thing away and put it in a bin somewhere, before I have you arrested for the double offence of threatening my personal safety *and* littering a public place."

He turned to Simms. "I think we need some legislation to prevent this sort of thing. I mean, it's outrageous – what's the point in banning people from carrying guns or knives if they can parade around in a public place with a dangerous animal the size of a leopard? What if I decided I wanted to walk around my neighbourhood with a lion – should that be allowed? Of course not!"

They returned to the car, but once again events had sown in Radley's mind the seeds for an eccentric scheme. Later that afternoon, he telephoned Steven Saunders in the Procurement Executive and made a very unusual request, which resulted in an extensive and ultimately successful internet search for a rare and bizarre commodity. The ensuing transaction was conducted in total secrecy, for although Radley's grip on reality was beginning to falter, he remained sufficiently aware to realise that, with the Army lacking crucial equipment and the civilian population living under austerity measures, no-one would be impressed to learn that a yacht had been dispatched to Senegal to collect a pair of leopards, purchased at great expense as personal pets for the Council Leader.

A few days after the incident in the park, yet another Council-produced leaflet was posted through the letterboxes of the peninsular. Entitled *'Keep Your Pet to Yourself'*, it promulgated new legislation concerning the private ownership of cats and dogs. With immediate effect, the new laws required all dogs to be on a lead in public places and made it illegal for any breed considered especially dangerous – including Rottweilers, Dobermans, Alsatians and bull-terriers – to ever leave private property. Ownership of such animals would henceforth require a licence, purchased from the Council, and if any were ever seen in public they would be shot on sight by the SCW, and their owners arrested. Similarly Draconian measures would be taken against anyone failing to clear up their dog's excrement. Cats were also subject to the new legislation, with owners being required by law to prevent their pets straying onto neighbouring properties, and severe penalties for anyone whose animal was deemed to have caused human health problems such as the child-blinding disease *toxo-plasmosis*, which was transmittable through feline faeces.

Radley read the leaflet in his office and sighed with satisfaction. He was delighted by the speed with which he was now able to bring about meaningful change, without all of the irritating and time-consuming consultation and discussion which democratic protocols had once demanded. "I go out into society," he proudly announced to Terence McCarthy, "I identify a problem, and within days the matter's been resolved. Now surely that's a man of action!"

He walked over to the window and looked out through the lattice of bomb-blast tape which criss-crossed the panes. On the balcony outside was a SCW anti-aircraft gun emplacement, its GPMG pointing skyward, and down below at the main entrance, the Army guards in their immaculate uniforms stood with their polished Lee-Enfields, bayonets gleaming in the winter sunshine. Out on the Mersey, the minesweeper *Bronington* sailed slowly past the town hall, while out of sight in the surrounding streets, people were rationing their food, growing vegetables and digging air-raid shelters in their gardens. And only ten kilometers away, British and French forces faced each other on the front line at Thurstaston, and provided an ever-present reminder that Wirral was at war and had to be a stoic and cohesive society if it was to ultimately prevail. Radley smiled to himself: this was exactly what he had envisaged. *Greatness* had returned - if not to England as a whole, then at least to that small part of the Green and Pleasant Land over which he exercised authority. He decided that the time had come to start work on his autobiography.

CHAPTER 25

Things Turn Nasty

I was undecided about this book, until I reached Chapter 25. Then I stopped reading it.

Muriel Timson
Landed Gentry Quarterly

Mr Robert's replies:
That's your prerogative. Provided you bought the book and paid good money for it, I don't mind if you don't like it or even read it. I've got a family to feed...

At the Batterie de Longues in northern Normandy, Mark Conrad tried to rest, but found himself unable to stop looking repeatedly at his watch, as if he were afflicted by some form of obsessive compulsive disorder. The waterproof diving watch had served him well over the years, but now he resented the moving hands and the inexorable passage of time they represented. Conrad's section had been granted six hours' respite from frontline duty, and was taking advantage of the sanctuary offered by a chamber situated to the rear of the rusting artillery piece in one of the huge German gun emplacements. There were two such rooms in each emplacement, protected by a thick layer of concrete and soil, and they represented the safest refuges within the entire A Company Tactical Area of Responsibility, or TAOR. Conrad was aware that he needed to make the most of the opportunity to relax his mind and body, but he was so preoccupied with his imminent return to duty - and the sense of dread that accompanied it - that he could not 'switch off' and appreciate the break. He remained tense and fidgety for the entire six hours.

It was bitterly cold inside the room, the thick concrete walls ravenously sucking heat from sleeping bags, cups of tea and the bodies of the soldiers themselves. Conrad looked around at the men with whom he shared the dark, dungeon-like chamber. Despite having referred to them as 'Muppets' in his letter to Robert Taylor, he had to admit that they were not a bad bunch – no different, in fact, to his comrades in C Company. In frustrating contrast to him, the remainder of his section seemed able to enjoy the opportunity to relax, temporarily free from the threat of mortar bombardment or small-arms fire. Lance-corporal Finnegan, the section second-in-command, who had once served with Conrad in C Company, was writing a letter to his girlfriend. Private Gibbs lay asleep within the cocoon of his bivvi-bag, snoring loudly. Conscientious Private Dalton was cleaning his rifle yet again while listening to music through an earphone, and Privates Daniels and Mordecai were playing cards in the light of their headtorches. A corpulent soldier whose real name was Squibb, but who was only ever referred to as 'The Beluga', or 'Bel' for short, sat on his roll-mat and lugubriously spooned a boil-in-the-bag meal into his mouth. There should have been an eighth soldier, but the section had been under strength since Private Buckley had been wounded in the shoulder by what everyone hoped was a random machine-gun bullet fired from the French lines, rather than a deliberately aimed shot from a newly-arrived sniper.

Such was Conrad's restlessness that he was almost relieved when, an hour before the section was due to return to its trenches, the platoon sergeant entered the bunker and presented him with a 'warning order'. The purpose of warning orders was to give soldiers advance notice of impending operations, so that they could start making the necessary preparations in good time. This particular warning order, written in 'Lumocolor' pen on laminated card, contained the following information:

SECTION WARNING ORDER

A SITUATION/COMMANDER'S INTENTIONS
No change enemy or friendly forces. Intent – to mount fighting patrol for offensive operations outside the TAOR.

B PROBABLE MISSION/TASK
Helicopter insertion/extraction. Ambush grid 918956. Mission - to destroy enemy vehicles in transit.

C TIME OF TASK/DEGREE OF NOTICE TO MOVE
No move before: 21.30hrs
Time out: (heli pick-up) 22.00hrs
Ambush set: 00.00hrs
NTM: 30 mins

D TIME/LOCATION OF O GROUP
Model room 17.15hrs

E ADMIN
CQMS to provide meal at 18.30hrs. Section to prepare personal kit for ambush - PAWPERSO, to include 3xCWS and 2xLAW94. Water/rations for 24hrs.

After reading the warning order, Conrad carried out a mental 'time appreciation' exercise, working backwards from the departure time to estimate how long he had to prepare his section for the mission. Assuming that the orders group with Whitham or Aldridge was finished by six o'clock, he would have three and a half hours to get everything ready. The final half hour before departure would be occupied by rehearsals, inspections and kit check, while the half hour before that would be taken up by the delivery of his own set of orders to the men of his section. Experience advised him to allow a contingency of at least fifteen minutes to accommodate unforeseen developments, which effectively left him two and a quarter hours to plan the details of the mission and write his orders. While he was thus occupied, Lance-corporal Finnegan would take care of administrative arrangements such as distributing rations and ammunition, in accordance with the time-honoured army principle of 'concurrent activity'.

Conrad climbed out of his sleeping bag and swung his arms around vigorously to warm up. He looked at his watch again and found that it was almost five o'clock. The walk from the gun emplacement to the model room in the observation bunker would take about ten minutes, so he put on his webbing, helmet and radio, picked up his rifle, handed the warning order to Finnegan, and set off to receive his orders for the night's unpleasantness.

Five hours later, Conrad and his men were lying in 'all round defence' in the mud of a farmer's field, staring apprehensively into the darkness as the sound of the helicopter receded into the distance and was swallowed by the cold, wet wind. It was a foul night, the miserable weather serving to exacerbate the soldiers' sense of being unwelcome trespassers in the hostile, forbidding territory beyond the relative security of their own lines. They were all extremely scared.

It took longer than anticipated to patrol to the ambush site in a small wood and move tactically into position, with the result that Conrad finally gave the order 'ambush set' well after midnight. Once the men were in position, it was simply a matter of watching, waiting and exercising extreme self-discipline in the struggle to endure the cold and discomfort and boredom and, most importantly, to stay awake.

In theory the plan for the mission was straightforward. The ambush site overlooked a narrow lane leading to some farm buildings about a kilometre away, which intelligence suggested might be an enemy command post. A British observation post, or OP, had been set up to watch the farm, and earlier in the day it had spotted two French light utility vehicles arrive and park outside. Several figures had hurried into the farmhouse, escorted by what appeared to be bodyguards, so it seemed reasonable to presume they were personnel of some importance. It also seemed reasonable to assume that, at some point during the next twenty-four hours, they might leave in their vehicles. The location was out of range of A Company's mortar on the beach, so Aldridge had decided to deploy Conrad's section to mount an ambush on the only road leading to or from the farm. Conrad could not actually see the buildings from where he was hiding, but the OP would contact him by radio and inform him if the vehicles were on their way.

The plan for the ambush was to destroy the vehicles with maximum firepower, including anti-tank missiles if necessary, then vacate the area immediately and move rapidly to the helicopter pick-up point for extraction back to company lines.

The section remained in position all night, fidgeting and shivering but seeing and hearing nothing. Every man fell asleep at some point, although they generally only lost consciousness for a few seconds at most. At one point, Private Daniels even began to sleepwalk out of the ambush site, before Finnegan dragged him back and slapped him awake. Eventually, the sky to the east began to lighten and Conrad prayed that a message would come through on the radio from Aldridge, ordering him to collapse the ambush and head for the helicopter pick-up point. As dawn broke, a poor quality message was received, but instead of telling the section to withdraw it instructed them to remain in position until further notice. Conrad sighed bitterly, then told his men to apply their safety catches while he ventured out to check that the ambush remained well camouflaged as the concealing cloak of darkness receded.

An hour later, another radio message was received, this time from the OP: "*Be advised, there is a large enemy force approaching your location from the south-west, ETA figures 10 minutes, over...*"

Conrad shuddered. Had the enemy somehow become aware of his ambush and sent a fighting patrol to deal with it? Or was the observed force simply passing through by unlucky coincidence, on some unrelated task? He decided not to take a chance, and crawled over to Finnegan. "There's enemy heading this way – lots of them. Time to get the hell out of Dodge City. Now."

With a sense of urgency which verged upon panic, they quickly disarmed and packed away the trip-flares and improvised claymore mines, and dismantled the ground spike antennae which gave the radio greater range. Conrad checked that the site bore no traces of having been occupied, then hurriedly led his men north through the wood in single file. As they moved, he tried informing Company HQ of the situation by radio, but could not make contact, probably because they had dropped down into a valley. He did, however, succeed in establishing communications with the OP, which promised to relay his message to Aldridge.

The section made its way out of the wood and ran swiftly downhill across a field of rough grass which was partly overgrown with clumps of brambles and bracken. In the bottom corner of the field was a rusting plough and some oil drums, and beyond these lay a gate opening onto the lane which led back to the enemy-occupied farm. Conrad squeezed through the gate and peered cautiously up and down the narrow road, which was bordered on either side by high hedgerows. Seeing no signs of activity, he ushered his men across the crumbling tarmac towards another gateway on the opposite side. This gave access to a grassy meadow which sloped upwards quite steeply towards a wooded ridge at the top of the valley. Conrad decided to make for the wood, hoping to find a suitable landing site for the helicopter on the far side.

They were toiling up the slope using a sparse hedge for cover, when the OP suddenly made radio contact again: "*Hello One-Two Charlie, this is Three-Three Charlie, message, over.*"

"One-Two Charlie, send, over," Conrad replied wearily.

"*Three-Three Charlie, be advised that the enemy force has turned away from your location. I say again, enemy force is no longer heading towards you. Also be advised that enemy personnel are getting into vehicles at the farm. If you are still in position you may still be able to achieve your mission as planned, over.*"

Conrad tutted as he slogged up the hill. He was no longer in the mood for the mission. "One-Two Charlie, er, roger your last, let me know if they depart, over."

There was a brief period of radio silence, then the OP announced, "*Three-Three Charlie, vehicles are leaving now. I say again, you have figures two vehicles heading your way, over.*"

Conrad stopped and looked despairingly up at the heavens. "One-Two Charlie, roger, out."

With a weary sigh, he turned and gazed back down the hillside towards the sunken lane, which was largely obscured by overgrown hedges. Despite his lack of enthusiasm, a sense of professional pride convinced him that he really should try to achieve the original mission.

So Lance-corporal Finnegan and Private Daniels were sent back down to the gate at the bottom of the slope, armed with one of the LAW94 anti-tank missiles, while Conrad hurriedly arranged the remainder of the section into an ambush 'killer group' to pour bullets down onto the lane. Already the sound of vehicle engines could be heard, approaching from the direction of the enemy farm.

Down by the gate, a mental countdown was ticking away in Finnegan's head, matching the pounding beat of his heart, as he frantically pulled the polystyrene end caps from the LAW94 and, with trembling hands, prepared the weapon for firing. The task seemed to take an age as he fumbled ineptly, his fingers rendered clumsy by fear and stress, but eventually the missile launcher was ready. Crouching behind some dead bracken by the gate, he aimed towards a bend in the lane about a hundred metres away. There would be no time for the luxury of spotting rounds – he would have to fire as soon as the lead vehicle came round the corner, otherwise the missile would not have time to arm itself in flight, and would therefore fail to explode. Finnegan pushed the selector lever to 'main armament' and waited, as the engine noise grew steadily louder.

On the hillside above, Conrad scanned the landscape in an attempt to spot the approaching vehicles, without success. Then, suddenly - nearer than expected - something blue flashed across a gap in the hedgerows down in the valley, and he became gripped by a terrifying panic. "Finnegan!" he shouted, leaping to his feet and running down towards the gate, "Finnegan – wait!"

In the sunken lane, Finnegan and Daniels were shivering almost uncontrollably with fear as they stared intently at the bend in the road and listened to the engine noise, which seemed to be reaching a crescendo. Then a vehicle came round the corner and Finnegan fired, almost as a nervous reflex action. There was a flash and a deafening *thump!* and the lane became filled with smoke. The vehicle swerved into the overgrown embankment on one side of the road and burst into flames. But it was not, as expected, a military light utility vehicle carrying enemy soldiers. It was a blue Renault people carrier, driven by a mother on the morning school run. In the back were five children, aged between four and eleven.

Finnegan dropped the smoking rocket tube and ran towards the blazing vehicle to try to rescue those inside, but the intense heat drove him back. He stood, paralysed by an all-consuming anguish, staring in horror at the inferno and the human silhouettes fleetingly visible through the roaring flames.

At that moment, the French military convoy came round the corner and screeched to a halt, almost colliding with the rear of the burning people carrier. Soldiers leapt out and gazed at the terrible sight with expressions of despair, which turned quickly to rage. A sergeant peered past the burning vehicle, saw Finnegan standing in the road, and gunned him down, firing burst after burst into him even after he had collapsed onto the tarmac and lay still.

Conrad reached the gate and looked along the lane just in time to see Finnegan fall. Young Private Daniels was still crouching by the roadside, obviously in deep shock. Conrad grabbed his webbing straps, pulled him to his feet, and dragged him back up the slope towards the rest of the section.

Encumbered by their body armour and equipment – which included the remaining LAW94 – the six British soldiers ran up into the wood at the top of the slope, desperate to distance themselves from the scene of the appalling catastrophe. Conrad was eager to call-in the helicopter, but knew that this could only be done from a safer location; it would take time to find a suitable landing site, contact Company HQ with a grid reference, and then wait for the machine to arrive. And then, of course, they had to be able to get on board and take off without being shot-down…

On the other side of the wood lay a fairly flat landscape of fields, intersected with fences and hedgerows and interspersed with the occasional small copse or reed-edged pond. In the distance the roofs of some farm buildings were visible above the hedges. Conrad checked his compass to make sure they were still heading north, and led his disgraced and guilt-ridden team across the fields in the general direction of the British lines.

News of the atrocity swiftly reached Colonel Delbonnel, the French commander. He immediately alerted his troops at Longues-sur-Mer to be on the look-out for a renegade British patrol trying to get back to their own lines, and mobilised all available rear-echelon soldiers to hunt down the fugitive murderers, who were to be shot on sight.

"The gloves are off now," he told his second-in-command. "I think it's time we unleashed the *Hetzer*."

Although the French might not have enjoyed the benefits of historic assets to match the British warships *Plymouth* and *Bronington*, they did possess some valuable items of military hardware, courtesy of their turbulent past. These included a number of World War Two vintage tanks and other armoured fighting vehicles on display at the D-Day beaches and various museums around Normandy. One such vehicle, taken from the museum at Bayeux and brought back to life by skilled French mechanics, was a small, wedge-shaped German self-propelled gun known as a 'Hetzer'. This squat machine, camouflaged in stripes of green, brown and sand-colour, mounted a 75mm gun, but in trying to get the weapon operational the French encountered the same problem which had prevented the British from using the main armament aboard *Plymouth*: it was simply not possible to obtain worthwhile quantities of suitable ammunition. So, as a compromise, a team of French engineers fitted a pair of tubes inside the Hetzer's gun barrel and connected them via compressors to cylinders of fuel and oxygen, to create a flame-throwing tank. Trials of the vehicle showed it capable of projecting a devastating jet of fire to a range of a hundred metres. It was perhaps not surprising that Colonel Delbonnel considered this fearsome weapon an appropriate response to the British ambush atrocity.

Mark Conrad and his band of desperate fugitives were running for their lives, but were beginning to tire. They had become increasingly spread out, with the fittest men way ahead and the stragglers dropping further and further behind. Away to his left, across the fields in the distance, Conrad could see the canvas top of a military truck moving behind the hedgerows and then slowing to a halt, presumably to allow troops to de-bus. In order to give the vehicle a wide berth, he decided to alter his course slightly and head towards the cluster of farm buildings and an adjacent area of woodland. Perhaps, he hoped, they might be able to use the concealment of the trees to shake-off their pursuers, and find a suitable helicopter landing site on the other side of the wood.

They ran along the edge of a very large field of mud and straw stubble, with super-fit Private Dalton leading the way despite carrying the heavy LAW94. Close on his heels was Private Daniels, followed by Conrad himself. The corporal glanced over his shoulder. Gibbs and Mordecai were lagging behind, while the Beluga was a long way back and clearly struggling.

"Head for the farm, we'll regroup there!" he shouted to Dalton and Daniels, before dropping back to encourage the stragglers. At that moment, a group of French soldiers appeared at the far side of the field and opened fire. The shots missed, but they were sufficiently close for Conrad to throw himself down into one of the muddy furrows. "Get on the other side of the hedge!" he yelled at Gibbs and Mordecai. "Then get to the farm!"

He fired a few shots back at the enemy to keep their heads down, then crawled to the hedge and tried to find a way through, as bullets *thwacked* into the field around him. The hedge's latticework of stems and branches formed a dense, thorny barrier, but he found a gap and started to squirm through, rifle first. His daysacks and webbing caught on the snagging branches, so he shrugged them off, wriggled through the opening, and reached back to retrieve them. Then he was up and running again, heading for the stone farm buildings which were still several fields away. There was no time to wait for the others – it was every man for himself now. If they waited for the likes of the Beluga, they would surely all be captured or killed.

Sporadic firing continued on the other side of the hedge, but suddenly a new sound became audible in the distance: the revving of a powerful engine, combined with a squeaky metallic clattering. Conrad recognised it at once and felt very afraid: an armoured vehicle of some kind, without a doubt. He had worked with armour during training exercises in the past, and always found the experience highly nerve-wracking. On several occasions, he and Robert Taylor had spent stressful nights in shell-scrapes on Salisbury Plain, while Challenger tanks roamed around them in the darkness like predatory prehistoric monsters; even though the huge machines were not firing live ammunition and had no genuine hostile intent, the risk of soldiers being accidentally crushed under their oblivious tracks was very real.

Conrad stopped running and looked around frantically, trying to work out where the sound was coming from, without success. All he knew for certain was that it was rapidly growing louder. Behind him, Mordecai and Gibbs were doing their best to catch up, but the Beluga was nowhere in sight. He was lying in the mud several fields further back, fatally wounded by several bullets.

There was one final field for Conrad to cross before he reached the farm buildings. Dalton had already reached them, and had disappeared around the corner of a high stone wall. Daniels was clearly exhausted and had stopped running. Conrad caught up with him and dragged him towards the farm, just as Dalton reappeared from around the corner and shouted, "There's a gateway here, Corporal."

By now the revving and clattering were very loud indeed, and Conrad was certain that the vehicle – whatever it was – was approaching from the right and would emerge into view at any moment. With heaving chests and wildly pounding hearts, he and Daniels followed Dalton around the corner of the high stone wall. They found a wide gateway leading into a rustic farmyard, where startled chickens darted under a derelict tractor and an ancient chained dog barked half-heartedly at them. Dalton dashed over to the open doorway of the large farmhouse and disappeared inside, still carrying the LAW94. A moment later, an elderly farmer emerged. He looked at Conrad and Daniels with an expression of stern disapproval, then walked off towards one of the barns.

Conrad left Daniels panting in the farmyard and hurried back into the field to make sure that Gibbs and Mordecai knew where to go. Meanwhile, Private Dalton had made his way into an upstairs bedroom of the farmhouse. He opened the shutters of a large window, and prepared his LAW94 for firing.

The Hetzer had been fitted with steel prongs under the hull, and it used them to bulldozer its way through a final hedgerow and enter the field across which Gibbs and Mordecai were stumbling, delirious with exhaustion. They saw the tank burst into view, and their terror gave them renewed energy, enabling them to run for the relative safety of the farm.

"Come on boys!" Conrad shouted, as the Hetzer commander traversed his machine in a sweeping arc and activated his compressors.

There was an ear-splitting noise, like the squeal of a tortured banshee, and a huge jet of fire belched out from the tank's barrel and billowed across the field, catching and consuming the two men as they fled. Conrad leapt back behind the corner of the wall as a searing blast of heat washed past him. He ran back into the farmyard in a state of shock, completely at a loss as to what to do next. Surrender seemed the most attractive option, but he was not sure that these vengeful French troops would allow him and his men the luxury of giving themselves up.

Then - horror of horrors - a soldier on fire came staggering through the gateway and collapsed in front of Conrad and Daniels, his entire body consumed by a mass of flames. Unable to identify whether it was Mordecai or Gibbs, Conrad watched the tragic figure writhing in silent agony and then, grimacing with revulsion, he shot the burning soldier several times until he lay still.

Up in the bedroom, Private Dalton watched as the Hetzer growled and clattered towards the farm across the burning stubble of the field. Enemy troops were advancing behind the tank, using its armoured bulk for protection, but Dalton was standing well back from the open window in the gloom of the bedroom and they failed to see him as he took aim with the LAW94. He had witnessed the Hetzer incinerate his two friends, and was so determined to exact revenge that he completely forgot that anti-tank missiles could not be fired from within enclosed spaces such as rooms.

Dalton fired a single tracer spotting round, which scored a direct hit, then immediately switched to main armament and pressed the trigger. The back-blast of the missile's ignition blew him head-first out of the window, while at the same time a shower of sparks erupted from the Hetzer and it shuddered to a halt. An instant later, burning fuel flooded out from the tank and engulfed everything around it in a cataclysm of fire. On the earth beneath the farmhouse window, brave Private Dalton lay on his back staring up at the sky, paralysed from the neck down.

In the farmyard, Mark Conrad heard the *thump* of the missile being fired, together with the sound of glass shattering as several windows were blown-out. Above the stone wall he could see black smoke pouring into the sky from the field on the other side, and noticed grey smoke drifting from the door and windows of the farmhouse.

Leaving Daniels to cover the gateway, Conrad ran up the farmhouse stairs to the bedroom from which the smoke was originating. He noticed the empty missile tube lying on the floor, and peered cautiously from the window. There was a huge pool of fire in the field, with the black silhouette of the Hetzer blazing away in the centre of the inferno. Seeing no sign of Dalton, Conrad assumed that he had made his way out of the building, and hurried back down the stairs. The Hetzer's destruction would generate a lot of confusion amongst the enemy troops, and this might hopefully provide the British fugitives with an ideal opportunity to slip away unnoticed. But they would have to be quick…

Meanwhile, at the gateway, Private Daniels was nervously aiming his rifle out into the field, on the look-out for advancing enemy troops. He did not notice the elderly French farmer who emerged from the barn and strode purposefully towards him carrying a 'Sten' sub-machine gun. The farmer's father had been a member of the resistance movement during the Second World War and, ironically, the Sten had been issued to him by the British Special Operations Executive for use against the Nazis. The farmer aimed at Daniels and fired a short burst, before the archaic gun jammed. Daniels rolled forward onto the ground, clutching his arm, while the farmer tried to clear the stoppage. He was in the process of re-cocking the Sten when Conrad emerged from the farmhouse and killed him with a three-round burst from his M16.

Daniels's life had been saved by his body armour, but one bullet had struck his unprotected upper left arm and he was in great pain. Conrad helped him to his feet and together they hurried across the farmyard to a door in the far wall. This opened onto a narrow lane, beyond which lay a large, dark wood which beckoned invitingly to the two soldiers. They closed the heavy wooden door behind them and scurried across the lane into the welcoming concealment of the trees.

For a while they stumbled blindly through the wood, before stopping to catch their breath and take stock of their situation. Daniels was losing a lot of blood, so Conrad applied a field dressing to the wound on his arm. The long-range radio had been incinerated with Private Gibbs, so Conrad used his mobile phone to contact Company HQ and request immediate extraction by helicopter. A short while later, the two men were crouching in a large glade, watching with relief and gratitude as the irreverent yet dependable Brotherton brought the Agusta down into the clearing to, as he so eloquently put it, "Pull the Infantry out of the shit yet again."

CHAPTER 26

French Anger

Why must the author insist on subjecting his readers to such a relentless bombardment of foul language throughout his book? This, together with his irritating over-use of the comma, spoiled for me what is otherwise an interesting story.

Benedict Linctus
Philatelist Gazette

Mr Roberts replies:
But that's how real people speak – especially soldiers. Sorry, about, the, commas, though.

The repercussions of the bungled ambush were not confined to Normandy. On the Thurstaston Front in Wirral, French troops learned of the atrocity and began fighting with greatly increased determination and aggression. This passionate expression of outrage might have subsided after a few days, had it not been for the fact that some of the troops were related to the children who had died in the people carrier. The officer commanding Five Platoon, Lieutenant Maurice, had lost his niece in the tragedy, and became consumed with anger, hatred, and an all-pervading lust for vengeance. A gendarme in civilian life, Maurice was a conscientious and professional officer, and for a while now he had been growing increasingly frustrated by the apparent reluctance of his superiors to demonstrate any significant offensive spirit or initiative which might have broken the stalemate. Upon hearing of the appalling death of his niece, he could tolerate this inertia no longer, and strode to his commanding officer to demand action.

"Sir, they are burning our babies!" he declared with obvious emotion to Major Vassort. "We cannot allow this war to continue - we must defeat the English by Christmas! I have a plan..."

Vassort listened sympathetically to the lieutenant's proposal, nodding in agreement while simultaneously squirming uncomfortably and looking apologetic.

"But Philippe," he said awkwardly, when Maurice had finished speaking, "what you are proposing is a major operation, which may even break the rules of engagement. I cannot authorise it - you know I can't, no matter how much I'd like to...You know that all major strategic decisions can only be taken by Monsieur Lebovic himself..."

"Lebovic is a politician and a fool!" the lieutenant spat. "And every soldier knows that politicians and fools should never be allowed to meddle in the affairs of the military during a war. And as for rules of engagement – what rules were the English following when they burned our children? We have to act, sir! If you will not support me, then you must arrest and court-martial me now, because if you don't I'll go myself with as many of my men as will follow me – and I think you may find it's quite a few!"

The major looked around furtively, clearly struggling with his conscience. Then he sighed reluctantly and said, "Alright, I'll support you – unofficially, of course. Just make sure you succeed, or they'll resurrect the guillotine just for me. When do you want to go?"

"As soon as possible. Tonight, if we can. The rain will help us."

"Then be quick. Take what you need, and may God be with you."

At five o'clock in the morning, Lieutenant Maurice and three of his men slipped stealthily out through the French lines in the southern sector of the Thurstaston Front and crawled along a hedgerow until they reached a small copse in no-man's land, where they stopped and waited. A few minutes later, the French mortar began bombarding the northern sector of the front with smoke and high explosive bombs, accompanied by rifle and machine-gun fire, to divert attention away from Maurice's activities in the south. The lieutenant knew from reconnaissance patrols that the southern stretch of line was something of a backwater, a quiet sector which had seen little fighting and was weakly defended by both sides. A single British bunker and two coils of razor wire were all that stood between him and the top of the ridge.

On Maurice's signal, the mortar began working its way southwards, until eventually the bombs were falling around the British bunker. In the copse nearby, the lieutenant and his team watched and waited, keeping their heads down as shrapnel peppered the trees above. Then the mortar fire marched north again, and in the smoke and confusion Maurice's team attacked and destroyed the bunker with ruthless efficiency, killing the two men inside. Major Vassort had granted the lieutenant a light utility vehicle and a quad-bike, each with a trailer, and these now drove through the breach at speed, laden with supplies and equipment which included a mortar and as much ammunition as could be spared. The men of Five Platoon ran alongside the vehicles as the breakaway force made its way uphill, moving rapidly across fields, through gateways and along tracks until it reached the main road running along the top of the ridge. This road lay some distance behind the British lines and was consequently still used by civilian traffic. In accordance with the Council's blackout regulations, all vehicles were required to drive with specially shrouded sidelights only, which limited their speed at night to a virtual crawl and made them easy prey for the band of French desperados. Maurice's men began hijacking every car which came their way, forcing the startled occupants out at gunpoint and confiscating their mobile phones, then keeping them captive behind a hedge in the pouring rain. There was not a great deal of traffic at such an early hour, but within ten minutes the French had seized four cars and a people carrier – sufficient transport for the entire platoon. They released their civilian prisoners, climbed aboard the commandeered vehicles, and headed towards Heswall with grim determination.

Maurice's plan was to launch a desperate and highly aggressive attack on the town hall, in the hope of capturing or killing Gerald Radley. He was aware that his chances of achieving such an ambitious goal were remote indeed, but took encouragement from several audacious operations from the annals of military history, which had succeeded against the odds simply because the enemy had not expected such a bold move. Even if Radley eluded him, Maurice was confident that he could capture the town hall temporarily, which would severely ruffle the feathers of the English Council and be a major propaganda coup for the French. Unfortunately, however, he mistakenly believed that the town hall was located in Hamilton Square, when in fact it was further north in Wallasey, so his plan would have failed even if he had managed to break through to Birkenhead.

On the map, the most direct route to Hamilton Square involved heading north along the ridge road, but this would have taken the French through the village of Thurstaston, which was known to be occupied by British troops, so Maurice was forced to go south towards Heswall. His intention was to swing north at the first opportunity and make a frantic dash for Birkenhead, hopefully outwitting the enemy commanders, who would probably take a while to figure out what was going on.

One of the civilians whose car had been hijacked ran along the road to B Company HQ in Thurstaston village and raised the alarm. Within minutes, the entire British military command was in panic. Roused from sleep by an urgent phone call, Colonel Alan Hogan reached for a map and, with bleary eyes, tried to guess the French intentions and predict where they might be heading.

Gerald Radley was asleep in his house in Heswall at the time of the French break-out and, ironically, Maurice's men passed within a kilometre of his home without realising just how close they were to their quarry or how easily they could have seized him. When Hogan phoned to inform him of the emergency, Radley immediately assumed that the French had somehow discovered his home address and were on their way to get him. He quickly scurried with his wife, two daughters and Sean Simms into the secret hideaway which had been constructed in the cellar using money siphoned from the Council's 'Miscellaneous Expenditure Fund'. The tiny room, which was barely the width of a person, had been created by building a false wall adjacent to the real one, leaving a narrow cavity in between. It contained a chemical toilet, blankets, food and water, and communications equipment. Once safely inside, Radley pulled out his mobile phone. He was outraged by this unexpected turn of events, which violated the code of conduct and military rules of engagement agreed between Lebovic and himself, so he immediately sent a blunt text message to the French leader.

"*What's going on?*"

The reply, when it came, simply added to his vexation: "*What do you mean?*"

Meanwhile, Colonel Hogan had acted swiftly, alerting all army units to the new threat posed by the unexpected French break-out. In Thurstaston village, Major Hubbard readied his men to repulse a possible attack from the rear, while on the other side of the peninsula, engineers and transport troops moved from their defensive positions along the Mersey to form a protective cordon around the town hall. At the same time, Hogan ordered Charlie Company's Quick Reaction Force to move south from their holding locations on the north coast to intercept the maverick French unit before it reached Birkenhead. The QRFs, consisting of troops in Land Rovers and four-tonne trucks, drove down the M53 motorway in a state of ignorant impotence, unable to take effective action until they received information regarding the enemy's whereabouts. Then a message came through from a SCW surveillance team which had been keeping watch on the house of a suspected dissident in Thingwall: the French force had just driven past their white van, heading in the direction of Arrowe Park.

The C Company convoy left the M53 at Prenton and was in the process of deploying on the bridge above the motorway when the French vehicles came down the hill towards them. By now it was getting light, and Maurice could dimly see the British trucks forming a roadblock ahead of him. He ordered his vehicles to swing around in a u-turn and head back up the road to a junction at which they could either go north or south. Maurice believed that the British would probably expect him to go north, so he decided to head south and cross the M53 at the village of Storeton. From there, it was only a short drive to the outskirts of the urban sprawl which covered most of the east side of the Wirral. If his force could reach the labyrinth of residential streets, it might be able to evade the British and strike at the town hall. However, unknown to Maurice, his chosen route to Storeton took his convoy past the SCW surveillance van in Thingwall for the second time, so the British learned of its whereabouts and direction of travel almost immediately.

Controlling proceedings by radio from the War Office, Hogan sent Seven Platoon in pursuit of the French vehicles, while dispatching Alistair Blundell and the rest of C Company in the opposite direction, with orders to proceed with haste to Storeton and block the enemy advance.

Unfortunately for the British, traffic congestion in Prenton delayed Blundell's column, and the French arrived in Storeton first - just in time to see the C Company vehicles thundering down Lever's Causeway towards them. Maurice glanced at his map: two other roads led from Storeton into the built-up area of Bebington, so there was still a chance that his plan could succeed. He left six men at the end of Lever's Causeway to ambush the British, then took his remaining vehicles in the opposite direction to find one of the alternative routes.

As the British vehicles carrying men from Nine Platoon approached the houses of Little Storeton at the end of Lever's Causeway, they came under fire from French soldiers who were lying in wait behind hedges and garden walls. The lead Land Rover swerved across the road and collided with a tree, while the driver of the Bedford truck behind it took evasive action, bumping over the kerb and crashing through a barbed-wire fence into the safety of a field. The other vehicles in the convoy followed suit, peeling left and right between the avenue of trees and beating a hasty retreat out of the French killing area. As they sped away, the surviving soldiers from the wrecked Land Rover began crawling to safety under the cover of smoke grenades, leaving two of their comrades dying in the cab.

The battered British force regrouped at the opposite end of Lever's Causeway, out of range of the French guns. A rather shaken Alistair Blundell climbed out of his Land Rover and ran over to Lieutenant Evans, the officer in charge of Nine Platoon.

"Set up a roadblock here to make sure they can't get through," the major said. "If we can block Rest Hill Road and Red Hill Road, we'll have them trapped."

Blundell shouted over to Lieutenant Grudge, who was sitting in the cab of one of the Eight Platoon lorries. "Andrew, take your platoon and block the other two roads coming out of Storeton. We mustn't let them reach Bebington! I'll catch you up."

As the vehicles carrying Eight Platoon sped away, Blundell jumped back into his Land Rover and peeled in amongst them. When they reached the crossroads by the Traveller's Rest pub, where the lane from Storeton known as Rest Hill Road climbed up out of the valley and joined the main road running along the ridge, the convoy halted. Grudge sent Sergeant Murphy and Three Section further along the ridge road to block the last remaining route from Storeton, then ordered One and Two Sections to de-bus next to the pub. While corporals Brabander and Taylor quickly deployed their men in ambush positions, Grudge and Blundell drove cautiously down Rest Hill Road, between Storeton Woods on the right and Mount Wood on the left, to see if they could spot the French. The two officers had just nudged their Land Rover out from beneath the bare branches of the overhanging trees, when they saw the French convoy emerge from Storeton, heading towards them at speed. It would take about a minute for the enemy to drive down into the shallow valley and climb up the other side to where Blundell and Grudge were now sitting, so there really was no time to lose. They reversed quickly back up the hill to the pub, abandoned the Land Rover, and sprinted back down the slope to take charge of the welcoming committee which would show the French the same brand of hospitality traditionally displayed by the English towards invaders from the Continent.

Suddenly Blundell's mobile phone rang. It was Gerald Radley, demanding a situation report.

"I'll have to call you back, Gerald – they're on their way!" was all the major could say.

"Just make sure they don't get through, Alistair!" the Council Leader told him, his voice trembling with anxiety. "You *must* stop them reaching Birkenhead!"

Lieutenant Grudge had instructed Robert Taylor to deploy Two Section to the left side of the road, and Karl Brabander to position One Section to the right. There had been insufficient time to select ideal firing positions for every man, but Robert had managed to place his two LSW gunners in prime locations with an uninterrupted view down the hill, to where the lane turned a corner between two houses in the bottom of the valley, about two hundred metres away.

Suddenly, the French vehicles screeched around the bend in the road and came speeding up the hill towards the British troops. Rather bizarrely, the lead vehicle in the column was a red Citroen estate car, with a soldier aiming a machine gun from the sunroof.

Now it was the turn of the British to be merciless. Grudge waited until the Citroen was only about a hundred metres away before giving the order to open fire, and within seconds the car was riddled with bullets. It swerved erratically, clipped a stone wall, and spun around so that it completely blocked the road. The British continued firing as the next car in the convoy – a Ford Focus, which was unable to stop in time - ploughed into the side of the Citroen. Trapped in the narrow lane, with a wall on one side and a dense hedge on the other, the remaining French vehicles had no option but to reverse out of the killing area. The car, people-carrier and quad-bike at the rear of the column managed to withdraw back around the corner to safety, but the third vehicle in the convoy – the military jeep – became stuck when its trailer jack-knifed, effectively blocking the escape route of the Ford Focus in front. French troops crawled from the trapped vehicles and began returning fire. One soldier threw a smoke canister over the Citroen in an attempt to create a smokescreen, but it rolled back down the slope and began spewing smoke from under the jeep.

At the top of the hill, Alistair Blundell crouched behind a projecting piece of sandstone wall and watched the battle as bullets cracked past him or ricocheted off the tarmac and went whining through the air. The enemy vehicles which had escaped from the ambush had now retreated to the opposite side of the valley, and their occupants were engaging the British at the extreme limit of their weapons' range. Blundell's mobile phone rang, and he tutted with irritation when he saw on the screen that it was Gerald Radley - again. At that moment, with the phone buzzing in his hand and the battle raging all around him, Alistair Blundell experienced a sudden and irreversible metamorphosis of character. He saw the men around him as if in slow motion: young Private Phillips, clearly terrified but resolutely firing burst after burst with his LSW; Private Howarth, his face contorted in grim revulsion as he struggled to apply a field dressing to a wounded comrade; Corporal

Brabander, screaming fire control orders from the edge of Storeton Woods; and Corporal Taylor, desperately trying to drag injured Private Wynne off the road and into cover. Sharing their fear and courage, their desperate camaraderie in the face of extreme stress and danger, Blundell underwent a dramatic change in allegiance. He stopped being Alistair Blundell, Assistant Director of Housing, part-time TA soldier and compliant military lackey in Gerald Radley's warped Council, and became instead Major Alistair Blundell, Officer Commanding C Company, The Wirral Regiment, whose loyalties lay first and foremost with his men. He stared resentfully at the vibrating phone, then pressed the button to answer it and simply said, "Contact, wait out," before switching it off completely. Radley would damned well have to wait.

Down the hill, the French had set off more smoke grenades to cover their withdrawal, and the British were now firing blindly into a swirling grey-white mist.

"Roll grenades down at them!" shouted Lieutenant Grudge to the men nearest to him. Most of the grenades bounced off course and exploded in the roadside verges, but one detonated under the Citroen and set it alight. The burning vehicle began to produce a choking curtain of acrid black smoke, under the cover of which the French managed to unhitch the trailer from the jeep and roll it down the hill and around the corner. The remaining men helped their wounded into the back of the jeep, which then reversed to safety with a shattered windscreen, leaving behind two wrecked cars and five dead or dying soldiers.

"Stop!" shouted Grudge, as the French vehicles fled across the valley and disappeared into Storeton village. "Watch and shoot! Watch and shoot!"

Robert Taylor peered over his rifle at the carnage on the road, watching for signs of life. The Citroen was burning fiercely, belching out huge plumes of black smoke, and anyone inside must surely be dead. He glanced at his watch and was amazed to find that the engagement, which had seemed to go on for ages, had in fact lasted a mere ten minutes.

In Storeton village, Maurice and his men regrouped behind a large farmhouse at the top of the hill. They were all physically and mentally exhausted, and in varying states of shock following the trauma of the ambush.

"What now, Lieutenant?" asked the platoon sergeant, using his sleeve to wipe sweat, camouflage cream and blood from his stinging eyes.

Maurice looked at the map and sighed, shaking his head wearily. His plan had been thwarted. "I don't know. It seems that the English are not as slow and stupid as we thought. There are three roads out of this village which go in the right direction. The English have certainly blocked two of them and will no doubt have blocked the third by now..."

"Then we must go back?"

Maurice thought for a moment. "I don't think that's an option, sergeant. No, we won't go back…We'll stay here."

The sergeant was perplexed. "For what purpose, sir?"

"To be a thorn in their sides - a pain in the arse of the English! We'll hold this village for as long as possible, and tie-up as many of their troops as we can in the process. They'll have to commit a lot of men to make sure we don't break-out again."

So the French soldiers spread out through the village and took up defensive positions around the outskirts. One squad was in the process of deploying amongst a cluster of houses known as Little Storeton, in the north-west corner of the village, when they noticed a white van driving towards them along a muddy track between the fields. It appeared to have come from an area of woodland about a quarter of a mile away. Intrigued, the French watched from behind a sandstone garden wall as the vehicle stopped at the gate blocking the end of the track, and two black-clad paramilitaries carrying sub-machine guns jumped out and hurried to undo the padlock. One of the men noticed the French soldiers, and raised his weapon in alarm. The troops opened fire, killing both men. Moments later, two other black-clad figures leapt from the rear doors of the van and tried to run away. They did not get far before they, too, were shot and killed.

It was not long before the civilian population of Storeton began heading out of the village along Lever's Causeway, encumbered by bags and babies and pets. Some were in tears, or looked shocked and bewildered, while others wore expressions of bitter outrage. All were on foot, as the French had prevented any vehicles from leaving the village. The stream of refugees reached the British roadblock at the end of Lever's Causeway just as Colonel Hogan and the Regimental Sergeant-major arrived to take charge of the situation. With Eight and Nine Platoons blocking all roads out of the village to the east, and Seven Platoon cutting off escape routes to the west, the French were effectively trapped in Storeton, at least as far as movement by vehicle was concerned.

"We need to make sure they can't break out on foot," the Colonel told Major Blundell. "So we'll form a cordon of shell scrapes right around the village, spaced closest together from eleven o'clock through to six o'clock, which is where they're most likely to try to break out. I'm not so worried about the western sector – they'll be heading away from Birkenhead if they go in that direction."

A short while later, as the British troops were deploying to form a cordon around Storeton and the stream of refugees slowed to a trickle, Gerald Radley arrived in his armoured BMW, clearly displeased by this unexpected turn of events. He glanced reproachfully at Blundell for a moment, then turned away from him and spoke in a peremptory voice to Alan Hogan.

"Colonel, this really is a most unsatisfactory state of affairs! I want you to rectify the situation immediately and get those Frogs out of there. I mean, we can't have them sitting in one of our villages, cocking a snoot at us from within striking distance of the town hall, can we?"

"Don't worry, Council Leader," Hogan replied calmly. "I can assure you we'll have them out of there as soon as possible. But we can't rush things. Until we know the enemy's strength and dispositions we can't go charging in there..."

"Then we must use siege tactics," Radley declared proudly, congratulating himself on his knowledge of military strategy. "We'll cut off the gas, electricity and water, and stop any supplies going in." He chuckled deviously. "They won't last long without water!"

"I shouldn't count on that, sir," the RSM remarked soberly. "There's a stream flowing through the valley."

"Then we'll poison it!"

"Not allowed under the Geneva Convention, I'm afraid, sir," the RSM replied, shaking his head apologetically. "Anyway, they'll have water in the tanks in the houses, and they'll collect it with ponchos and plastic sheeting whenever it rains..."

"How about food then? Surely we can starve them into surrendering?"

The RSM gave a wry smile. "Well, sir, there's a farm over there packed with cows, plus a good few horses in the riding stables – and you know how Pierre likes to chomp on Dobbin! Add to that a few cats and dogs, some frogs in the ditches, and all the slugs and snails in the gardens, and I reckon you've got enough scoff to keep your average self-respecting mollusc-muncher happy as a pig in shit for a considerable time to come..."

Radley looked disappointed. "Then it seems that you'll just have to go in there and remove them by force, Colonel."

"We will, Council Leader, we will. But I suspect our best bet will be to engage them in a war of attrition and force them to use up their ammunition, which they can't replace. Then they won't be able to put up much of a fight when we launch a full-scale assault. In fact, this whole situation could work to our advantage and present us with a golden opportunity to win a decisive victory. The French have allowed a significant force to put itself in a very vulnerable position. If we play our cards right, we should be able to capture or kill the lot of them. But it'll take time..."

And so, as November slipped into December and the weather became increasingly foul, a second front was established on the Wirral – a front which was referred to by the military as 'The Storeton Pocket,' and by Gerald Radley as 'The Storeton Abscess.'

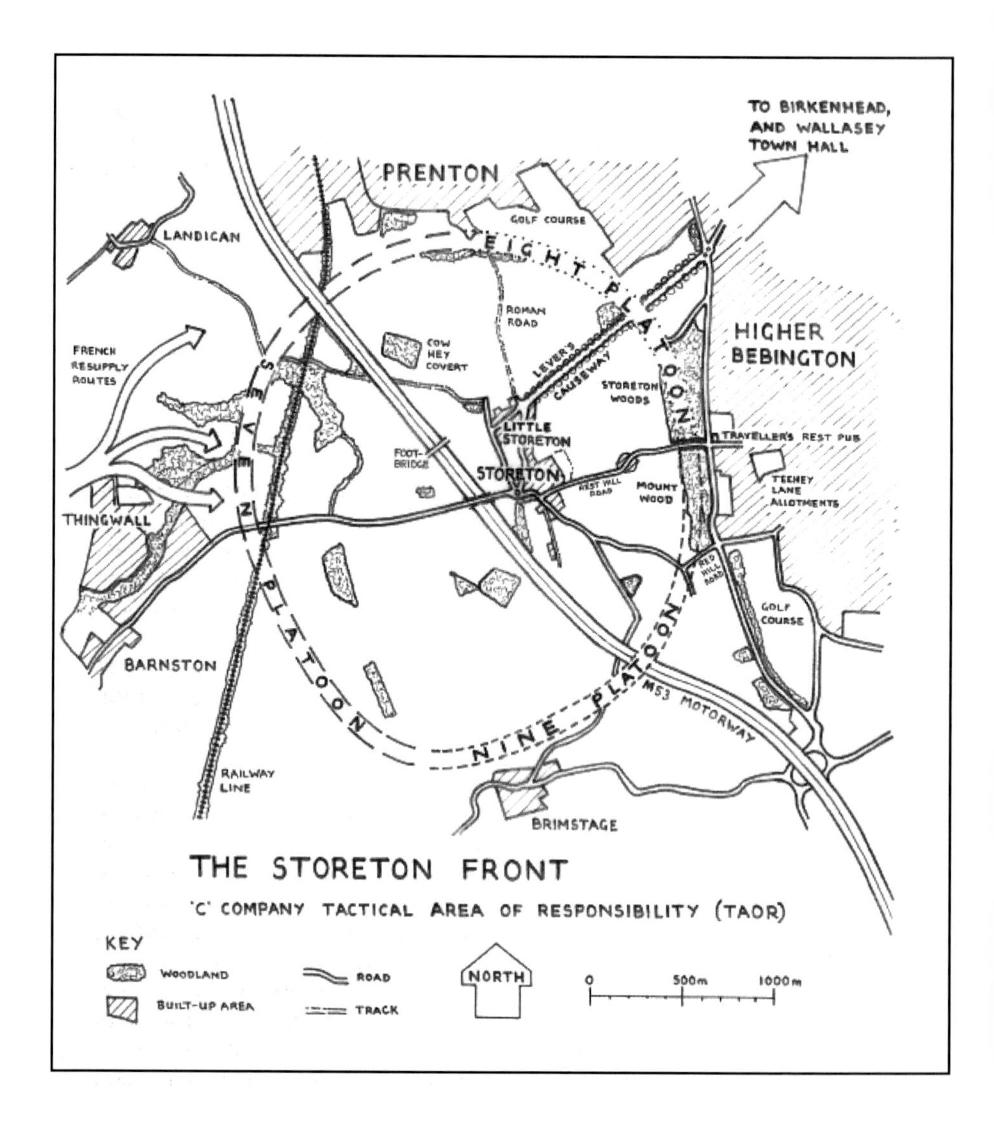

THE STORETON FRONT

'C' COMPANY TACTICAL AREA OF RESPONSIBILITY (TAOR)

CHAPTER 27

Digging-In

I love Wirral, it is my home, and I personally object to someone superimposing this vile work of fiction upon our beautiful, peaceful peninsular. Why couldn't the author set his horrible story somewhere else?

Beatrice Stubbs
Letter to the Wirral Herald

Mr Roberts replies:
I just wanted to try to put Wirral on the map…

The British began digging-in around Storeton, encircling the French within a ring of positions consisting mostly of two-man 'shell-scrapes'. These were sited a minimum of five hundred metres from the edge of the village, creating a defensive cordon with a large circumference. Manning this line stretched Charlie Company to its limits. Responsibility for the southern and western sectors – where the enemy was least likely to attempt a breakthrough – was given to the men of Seven Platoon, and their shell-scrapes and observation posts were relatively widely spaced apart, with large expanses of terrain covered by a single position. By contrast, Eight and Nine Platoons were deployed in an arc covering the northern and eastern sectors to protect Prenton and Bebington, where the threat was considered greatest, and their shell-scrapes were by necessity much closer together.

Within hours of the brief battle with Maurice's men, Robert's section started digging-in along the raised embankment known as 'The Old Tramway' in Storeton Woods, but found the task difficult with their short, collapsible entrenching tools. The woods had been created decades before on the site of an old quarry which had been filled-in with spoil excavated from one of the Mersey tunnels, and the ground contained large quantities of rubble which defied spades. After several hours of wrist-jarring, back-breaking frustration, the Company Quartermaster-Sergeant turned up with some pick-axes, crow-bars and full-sized shovels, which made the job easier. He also provided the soldiers with piles of sand-bags to fill with earth and stack around their shell-scrapes to form a parapet.

There were numerous tasks to be completed as a matter of urgency, in order to create a defensive line which was capable of stopping any further French advance, so the men worked at a frantic pace without rest. Robert rushed around, feeling like the proverbial 'headless chicken' as he tried to discharge a multitude of responsibilities at platoon, section and individual level. His immediate priority was to ensure that his section became properly dug-in as soon as possible, and began operating as an effective defensive unit. This involved not only supervising the digging of the shell-scrapes, but also the distribution of ammunition, pyrotechnics, food and water, and ensuring that his men prepared range-cards and were confident of details such as their arcs of fire, sentry-duty roster, stand-to procedure, passwords, and the location of key features. The most important features to be aware of were the sentry posts, neighbouring positions, company and platoon command posts, and the 'shit pit'. It had to be assumed that the platoon would be occupying the woods for a considerable period of time, so for reasons of hygiene, a deep hole was dug to the rear of the shell-scrapes as a receptacle for the soldiers' excrement. Next to the hole lay a pile of soil and a shovel with which to cover each layer of faeces. As time went by, the 'shit pit' became a 'shit mound', into which unfortunate Private Miller stumbled one night in the dark and sank up to his thighs, earning himself the unenviable nickname 'Private in the Shit'.

As well as organising his own eight-man section, Robert was also given the task of establishing the platoon 'track-plan' within the wood. This involved clearing the vegetation to create a pathway connecting all of the platoon positions, including each shell-scrape, Grudge's HQ location, and the shit pit. The purpose of the track-plan was to enable every soldier to find his way around in the potentially confusing wood, especially at night. To aid nocturnal movement, Robert looped green 'comms cord' around the trunks of trees adjacent to the path. During the day, this cord was slackened so that it lay on the ground, but when darkness fell it was raised to waist height and formed a valuable handrail to guide disorientated soldiers, who might otherwise have blundered around blindly for hours trying to find their way back to their own shell-scrape.

While trying to discharge section and platoon level duties, Robert also had to find time for 'personal admin' such as weapon cleaning, checking his camouflage, annotating his map, changing radio batteries and frequencies, and recording or updating passwords and other crucial pieces of information. The Army worked on the principle of 'lead by example', so he could not very well expect high standards from his men if he did not demonstrate them himself. But there was simply so much to do – an impossible amount, it seemed, and he felt himself approaching overload. No matter how frantically he tried to discharge his manifold responsibilities – and despite delegating as many tasks as possible to Farrell – he could not keep pace with the never-ending list of demands avalanching down upon him....

"Corporal Taylor, I need your section ammo state now."

"Corporal Taylor, the comms cord's broken – see to it, please."

"Corporal Taylor, have all your men eaten a hot meal today?"

"Corporal Taylor, send someone to collect your section's rat-packs."

"Corporal Taylor, have both your section LSWs been cleaned

since the engagement earlier? Remember – only one weapon to be stripped at a time…"

"Corporal Taylor, there are some new nick-numbers for you to add to your map."

"Corporal Taylor – that shell-scrape over there is definitely not eighteen inches deep!"

"Corporal Taylor – stand-to rehearsal in five minutes okay?"

"Corporal Taylor, I just asked your sentry position what the password and method of relief were and they didn't know! Not good enough - there's a real enemy over there! Come on – get a grip and make sure your boys start switching-on!"

And so it went on, to the point where he began to have what Mark Conrad would have referred to as 'a sense of humour failure'. Exhausted and exasperated, he sat down angrily on the edge of his half-finished shell-scrape, and flinched with pain as his buttocks were punctured by the fang-like thorns of a hidden bramble.

"Oh fucking hell!" he exclaimed to Ben Spencer, with whom he shared the shell-scrape. "It's official – Corporal Taylor's thrown his teddy in the corner! He doesn't want to play this game any more!"

But before he had time to wallow any longer in his own disgruntled self-pity, Lieutenant Grudge shouted down to him from somewhere further up the slope: "Corporal Taylor – the wire's arrived. Come up with three of your lads and get some."

Two logistics corps trucks laden with 'defence stores' were parked on the ridge road next to the wood, and soldiers were busy unloading coils of wire when Robert arrived. He stared at the materials in sullen silence, ashamed by his own lack of enthusiasm.

"There's razor wire and barbed wire," Grudge told him. "Run the barbed wire along the edge of the wood – tangle it into the vegetation so it's hard to see. The razor wire we'll do tonight, out in the field about fifty metres from the tree-line. Make sure you take some reinforced gloves, plenty of pickets and a thumper."

While making his way back down through the wood with the coils of wire, Robert encountered Karl Brabander, coming up the slope in the opposite direction. They exchanged a look of mutual fatigue.

"It's a lovely fucking war!" Brabander remarked.

"Too right. I'm bollocksed already!"

"I tell you mate, we're living on fumes!"

Robert left Spencer to finish digging the shell-scrape, while he led a working party to create a barbed wire barrier amongst the trees and bushes just inside the wood's margin. The idea was that attacking enemy troops would be hampered by the concealed entanglement, and then be gunned-down by soldiers manning the defensive positions along the top of the embankment, deeper within the wood.

It was a cold and damp beneath the trees, but Robert was sweating from exertion and could feel himself becoming progressively more dehydrated as the day wore on with relentless intensity. The stress, trauma and excitement of the morning's battle had sapped his energy reserves, leaving him cold and enervated, and unless he replaced some fluids and glucose he was at risk of 'going down'. So he granted himself a moment's respite to gulp down a few mouthfuls of water and eat the Kendal mint cake from his ration pack. Initially this made him feel nauseous, but after a few minutes his energy levels began to rise and invigorate his weary body. The engagement on Rest Hill Road had been the most violent experience of his life, and in his mind he replayed events over and over again, analysing what had happened and trying to decide whether he had acquitted himself well or not.

In the early afternoon, Colonel Hogan and the Regimental Sergeant-major walked along the Old Tramway to see how work was progressing. Robert was busy tangling barbed wire around the trees and bushes at the foot of the embankment, when Hogan called down to him.

"Corporal Taylor – come up here a minute."

Robert climbed up the steep earth slope to where the CO and RSM were standing. The Colonel pointed out through the bare branches of the trees towards Storeton.

"Corporal – have a glance over there. What can you see?"

Robert duly gazed across the valley. In the distance, some French troops were visible, digging-in on the top of a large embankment next to the riding stables.

"Have a crack at them," the Colonel said keenly.

Robert still retained some of his civilian squeamishness, and felt a little uneasy about firing at men who posed no immediate threat to him. But he reminded himself that the enemy soldier he spared today might kill him tomorrow, so quickly organised his section into two firing parties. His four-man group – Charlie fire team – would target the Frenchmen on the left, while Farrell's Delta fire team would go for the men on the right. With the CO and RSM standing behind like spectators at a sporting event, he took aim at one of the distant figures with his M16, and pulled the trigger. The rest of the section opened fire simultaneously an instant later, the riflemen firing single shots while the LSW gunners unleashed short bursts of four or five rounds. As the reports rolled across the valley, the enemy troops dived for cover and Hogan lowered his binoculars with a satisfied smile.

"Well, I don't think you hit any of them – they're out of range really – but you certainly gave them a scare! Keep an eye on them, Corporal Taylor – if you see them starting to dig again, have another crack at them. Keep harassing the beggars!"

The Colonel and RSM moved on down the line, and it began to rain. About an hour later, a sergeant and two soldiers from the Sustained Fire (SF) Platoon appeared, with orders to set-up a general purpose machine-gun at a suitable location somewhere along Robert's stretch of line. Robert and the sergeant walked up and down the tramway embankment, and selected a position where the gun would command wide arcs of fire without interfering with any of his section's shell-scrapes. The sergeant then departed to site another gun elsewhere in the wood, leaving his two men to hack away at the stubborn ground to create an emplacement for the GPMG.

While the men of Charlie Company toiled away at constructing their defensive perimeter, staff at the town hall were grappling with the problem of cutting-off services to Storeton, which proved rather more difficult than expected. The first challenge was to establish which of the manifold private utility companies were actually responsible for services in that part of Wirral. Once this had eventually been ascertained, the Council made the appropriate requests for water, gas and electricity supplies to be cut-off immediately. However, most utility companies were little more than glorified cash-collection agencies, skilled at milking lucrative franchises to facilitate the transfer of large sums of money from the public purse to the accounts of their directors and share-holders, but rather less keen to get involved in the vulgar business of buried pipes and wires. Incensed by what he perceived as incompetence, Radley flew into a rage and ordered George Lawton to deal with the matter personally. Lawton arrived at Lever's Causeway with a gang of Special Council Workers equipped with detection apparatus, which they used to scan the roadside verges and locate a buried cable. This was unearthed, and severed with blasts from a shotgun. However, it soon became apparent that they had cut the wrong cable, as several hundred houses in nearby Bebington were left without electricity, while the power supply to Storeton remained unaffected. It was two days before all services to the enemy-held village were finally cut-off, by which time the French had recharged their radio batteries and mobile phones, filled baths and every other conceivable container with water, and used gas ovens in the occupied houses to cook meat from several slaughtered cows.

By late afternoon on that first day, Robert was utterly exhausted, and had to summon all of his reserves of energy and determination in order to remain what Farrell cynically referred to as 'a leader of men'. At times like these he frankly envied the ordinary private soldiers, who simply followed orders and whose prerogative it was to cut-corners, shirk and generally 'look after number one' wherever possible. The light faded, and 'stand-to' was called at dusk. The men lay in their shell-scrapes, watching and listening as day turned to night; it was the first significant opportunity to rest that Robert had been granted all day.

After stand-to, the company moved into night routine. Work on the positions continued, but with all artificial light forbidden it had to proceed at a slower pace. Then, just as Robert began to perceive a welcome relaxation in the intensity of activity, he was summoned to the company command post, located in a tent at the top of the wood, near to the Traveller's Rest pub.

"Ah, Corporal Taylor," Major Blundell said when he arrived, "I'd like to call upon your creative talents and ask you to build me a model of the company TAOR..."

Robert would not have minded this task, had he been excused his usual section commander's responsibilities while he performed it. But he knew that building the model was essentially an extra duty, and he would still be expected to somehow command his section while simultaneously complying with Blundell's request. If an inspection was held during the night, and his section compared unfavourably with Brabander's or Kingley's, it was highly unlikely that his model-building efforts would be taken into account as extenuating circumstances. He was reminded of a quote from the film *Platoon*, which went something like: "*Excuses are like arseholes: everybody's got one.*"

Fortunately, he encountered Paul Murphy, the platoon sergeant, and explained his predicament to him. Murphy was sympathetic, and responded by shanghaiing two men from the other sections to act as helpers. Robert put one of them to work digging a large rectangular pit, rather like a shallow shell-scrape, in which the model would be built, and tasked the other with gathering construction materials. Then he hurriedly followed the cord 'handrail' back along the track-plan to his own section, so that he could delegate a list of tasks for Farrell to supervise in his absence.

It would have been impossible to construct a worthwhile model in the near total darkness which pervaded the wood, so Robert tied string between surrounding trees and draped ponchos over it to form a light-blocking screen. Sergeant Murphy checked its effectiveness by watching from a short distance away, while Robert used a small red-filtered torch to illuminate the area of the model pit. Murphy was satisfied that no light was escaping towards Storeton, and Robert was left to proceed with his work. After an hour he had sculpted the main landform, and was in the process of adding the roads using powder paint when Murphy reappeared out of the darkness to interrupt his creative endeavours.

"Okay you three," he said to Robert and his helpers, "come with me. You need your weapon and CEFO."

Robert's heart sank. CEFO stood for '*Combat Equipment, Fighting Order*,' and referred to the basic items such as rifle, helmet and webbing which a soldier took into battle. Perhaps, he thought with a shudder of dread, the company was going to assault Storeton that very night...

He blundered blindly through the upper reaches of the wood behind Murphy, following the high sandstone wall which ran along the boundary with the main road. After much stumbling and tripping over invisible tree roots, they reached a gate in the wall and emerged from the claustrophobic blackness of the wood onto the tarmac of the road. Robert had expected to find a four-tonne truck there, waiting to take him and his section to a drop-off point somewhere, ready to attack the village. Instead, he was greeted by Colour-sergeant Morris, the Company Quartermaster-Sergeant, or CQMS. Robert liked Morris, who had once been a highly competent platoon sergeant and now brought the same degree of professionalism to the job of satisfying the company's logistical and catering requirements.

"Who's that?" the CQMS asked, as Robert trudged towards him in the darkness.

"Corporal Taylor."

"Ah, Corporal T, glad you could make it. How's it going for you?"

"Oh, mustn't grumble I suppose, Colour – as long as you've got your health and all that..."

"Good man. Get your mess tin and diggers out. There's hot scoff over there by Dudley, and a Norgie of tea, and one of soup..."

Robert experienced a sense of overwhelming gratitude, and could almost have hugged the CQMS; for the first time that day, someone had treated him with a modicum of friendly consideration, and shown concern for his welfare.

Of course, the period of blissful respite did not last long. Shortly after midnight, he was told to stop work on the model and rejoin his section. The night was cold and blustery and very dark, and he reached his shell-scrape largely by trial and error. Spencer was snoring in his sleeping bag, and Robert was annoyed to notice the slovenly soldier's rifle propped against the parapet, from where anyone could have taken it. Had this been an exercise, Robert would have hidden the weapon, and then delighted in Spencer's panic next morning when he woke up and realised it was missing. But this was no time for practical jokes, so he checked that the M16's safety catch was on, then tucked it under Spencer's arm. He was desperate for sleep but knew that, before he allowed himself the luxury of rest, he must first visit Farrell to check how work had proceeded in his absence.

The lance-corporal was still awake, having only just squirmed into his own sleeping bag. Shivering with the cold, Robert crouched next to him and went through the list of delegated tasks, which he was pleased to learn had nearly all been completed. Most importantly, Farrell had implemented a 'stag roster,' and two soldiers were currently occupying the sentry position at the edge of the wood. Satisfied that the main priorities had been attended to, Robert was about to return to his shell-scrape for some much-needed sleep, when Sergeant Murphy found him yet again and handed him a laminated warning order card.

"Tayl – Lt Grudge wants you for an O group at the CP – now!"

Robert sighed with exasperation and buried his head in his hands. "It never ends!" he groaned quietly.

"What's that?" asked Farrell, who had not heard Murphy's comment.

"Orders. Now."

"Hors d'oeuvres?" exclaimed the lance-corporal joyously. "Hors d'oeuvres - which must be obeyed at all costs!"

Robert could not help grinning. "It's all very well for you, you facetious bastard – you don't have to go to the bloody things!" He held the warning order card down in the bottom of Farrell's shell-scrape and read it by the light of his red-filtered 'Maglite' torch. "Anyway," he declared with satisfaction, "it says here that the company commander's intent is to mount night-time operations at section level – so that includes you. No Move Before zero one-thirty hours. And what is it now…?" He looked at his watch. "Quarter to one. I shouldn't get too comfortable if I were you, mate…"

CHAPTER 28

Incoming!

All Mr Roberts has done here is cobbled together a tacky necklace composed of scenes pilfered from numerous clichéd movies, threaded onto a flimsy string of plot. At times his plagiarism is so blatant he's forced to come clean and acknowledge the original source. Be under no illusions – this is pulp fiction, not quality literature.

Herman Gok
Erudite Voice magazine

Mr Roberts replies:
It's a fair cop, guvnor!

Stumbling like a blind man in the darkness, Robert groped and shuffled along the comms cord to platoon HQ, where he found Lieutenant Grudge crouching by a fairly crude and hurriedly-constructed model of Storeton and its environs. Corporal Kingsley was already there, so Robert sat down next to him to wait for Brabander, whose section lines were farthest away.

Grudge's orders for the platoon's work that night covered two distinct tasks. Of these, the priority was the construction of a line of razor wire in the fields beyond the edge of the wood, which had to be completed before dawn. The job would be carried out by a work party consisting of each section's Delta fire team, under the supervision of the platoon sergeant. At the same time, the three section commanders would lead patrols out into no-man's land, to 'dominate the ground', as Blundell put it. They would place trip-flares and wire obstacles at strategic locations such as gateways, footpaths or gaps in hedgerows, to deny the French freedom of movement and make it difficult for them to approach the British lines undetected.

When Grudge had finished delivering his orders, Robert hurried back to his shell-scrape to prepare for the patrol mission, but got lost on the way and wandered around pathetically for a while, until he fell into one of Three Section's shell-scrapes and was pointed in the right direction by the disgruntled soldier he had so rudely awakened.

There was insufficient time to write a full set of orders, so he resorted to modifying the notes he had taken during Grudge's 'O' group by embellishing them with useful phrases such as 'follow Standard Operating Procedures' (which basically meant 'do what we usually do in this situation'), or 'await my snap orders' (which was Armyspeak for 'I'll decide what to do when the time comes'). As it was not possible to build a proper model in the time available, he used coloured chalks to draw a simplified map onto a piece of green plastic sheet which he kept specifically for that purpose. He had just finished the drawing when a light drizzle began to fall, threatening to ruin his work. The solution was to turf Spencer out of his shell-scrape, and use bungee cords to fix a waterproof poncho over the top of it, forming a makeshift roof. The briefing was conducted with the soldiers lying on their bellies with their heads and upper bodies beneath the poncho, studying the chalk map by faint red torchlight.

Robert's patrol left the relative safety of their own lines at two o'clock in the morning and trudged reluctantly out into the forbidding darkness of no-man's land. He felt decidedly unprepared for the mission, and was convinced that he had forgotten something of vital importance which would have dire consequences later. While conducting a radio check at the edge of the wood, he realised that he was still wearing a warm top which he had intended to take off before setting out. It was only a trivial matter, but it frustrated him out of all proportion – there was no chance of removing it now from under his body armour, jacket, radio, webbing and helmet, but it would cause discomfort and excessive sweating during the mission.

With Stevenson in the lead as scout, the patrol moved stealthily along various hedgerows towards the first location where a trip flare would be placed. The black silhouette of Storeton was just visible against a slightly lighter sky, and Robert was careful to keep a safe distance from the village at all times. The patrol cut across Lever's Causeway and skirted around a large field towards Prenton Golf Course. Robert experienced a moment of panic, when it suddenly occurred to him that he had forgotten to update his 'next of kin' records to include Susan. In the event that he was killed or injured during the patrol, the Army would notify his parents...and Linda. He gritted his teeth and resolved not to become a casualty that night.

Interrupted only by the occasional parachute flare fired up by nervous sentries on both sides, the patrol reached its main objective - the strategically important footpath known as 'The Roman Road.' There they placed several trip-flares and wire obstacles, before heading back towards Storeton Woods. With arms outstretched to indicate they were 'friendly forces,' the four soldiers re-entered British lines through a sentry position manned by men from Brabander's section. This outpost was very isolated, very dark and a very long way from the other positions, so it quickly became known as 'The Dark Side of the Moon', and was the least desirable posting along the entire front line.

Robert reported to Grudge for the customary post-mission de-brief, before finally struggling into the blissful cocoon of his sleeping bag at around five in the morning. He was so tired that sleep eluded him, and for a while he simply lay in the shell-scrape, savouring the opportunity to rest his body while he thought longingly of Susan, who, by cruel irony, was lying in her bed only a few miles away, longing to be with him.

An hour later, the pre-dawn stand-to was called and the working day began again. He climbed resentfully out of the warm sleeping bag and shivered in the chill air as he donned his damp helmet and webbing. Spencer remained asleep like some enormous bloated khaki maggot, and had to be kicked a few times to wake him up. Robert felt giddy and itchy with tiredness, and his eyes throbbed and were sore and unwilling to focus. He and Spencer leant on the muddy shell-scrape parapet, pointing their rifles in the general direction of Storeton, and watched as night gradually turned to day and the familiar landscape materialised from the gloom.

Meanwhile, Corporal Karl Brabander had been presented with an unexpected problem in the form of young Private Fisher, who refused to get up. It was quite common for soldiers to be unenthusiastic about leaving the comfort of their sleeping bags – especially after cruelly brief periods of rest – but they could usually be persuaded, cajoled or threatened into cooperating. Fisher would not respond to any such methods, much to Brabander's vexation. The private pulled the draw-cord of his bivvi-bag tight around his neck, and stubbornly declared that he would not be going anywhere that day.

"Come on Fisher, get your lazy arse out of there and start getting a grip!" Brabander told him sternly.

"No Corporal, I'm staying here."

"Think again. Either you get out of your gonk bag voluntarily, or I'm going to have to kick you out."

"If you kick me then I'll sue you for assault, Corporal."

Brabander thought for a moment. "Whatever. I'm going to give you one last chance to get up. After that you'll just have to take what's coming to you."

"Then I'll take what's coming to me," Fisher insisted defiantly, "because I'm not getting up. I just told you, Corporal."

"So you're completely refusing to follow orders?"

"Yes, Corporal."

"Okay." Brabander reached down and snatched Fisher's rifle from under him. He unloaded the weapon and slung it over his shoulder, then turned to dependable Privates Kelly and Porter.

"Here, Kell, Porter - give us a hand with this sack of shit."

Together they picked up Fisher in his bivvi-bag and carried him with some difficulty to Company HQ, where they dumped him in front of the Company Sergeant-major, Dai 'Taff' Jones - an ex-regular from the Royal Welsh Regiment. Within minutes, Fisher had been emptied out into the mud like a piece of refuse, stripped of his kit, handcuffed, and taken under armed escort to the prison at Fort Perch Rock to await court-martial. A week later he was excavating stone as a member of the penal labour gang working on Duncan Silverlock's canal project, which was nearing completion.

While Brabander was dealing with Fisher, Robert and his section lay silently in their shell-scrapes, fidgeting and shivering. Eventually, the platoon runner came round to tell them to 'stand down', and they set about their usual early morning routine. Robert unfolded his hexamine stove in the bottom of the shell-scrape and began heating water in his mess tin. He carefully placed a boil-in-the-bag meal into the water and, while waiting for it to heat up, applied polish to his boots using a cut-down toothbrush. When the water boiled, he used most of it for a cup of tea, but poured some into a packet of rolled oats to make glutinous porridge, and left the remainder in the mess tin for washing and shaving. One of the reasons for soldiers shaving 'in the field' was so that, in the event of a gas attack, their respirators would make an air-tight seal against the smooth skin of their necks, but even in the absence of any Nuclear, Biological or Chemical threat, it was still an important daily procedure. Robert always found that washing and shaving helped wake him up and maintain his all-important personal morale. He also made sure that he regularly cleaned his teeth, and rubbed a 'wet-wipe' over his body under his clothes, in the interests of hygiene.

At the same time as eating his breakfast, Robert 'battle cleaned' his rifle by pulling a cloth patch through the bore and oiling the working parts. He also had to clean the greasy black hexamine residue from his mess tin before putting it away – a task which had once involved copious tiresome scrubbing with an abrasive pad, until Murphy had shown him how the exudations from a warm tea bag instantly dissolved away the soot by some miraculous chemical process which seemed almost too good to be true.

Robert glanced across at Spencer and was concerned to see that he was still cooking, and had items of kit strewn all over the shell-scrape. "Come on Ben," he urged, "start switching-on. You're an old sweat compared with some of the lads, but you left your weapon lying around last night and there's a kit explosion all over the place. I'm going to check the other positions, and by the time I get back I expect to see all this stuff packed away, your weapon cleaned, some polish on your boots, and you having washed and shaved - and had some scoff, okay?"

Spencer nodded sullenly, like a reprimanded schoolboy. "Okay... Corporal." He looked really miserable.

Robert conducted a brief tour of the other three shell-scrapes and the sentry position at the edge of the wood, and was relieved to find that all of the other men were in a better state of preparedness than Spencer, with the possible exception of Harding the Invertebrate, which came as no great surprise. When he returned to his own position he found that Spencer had packed his kit away, but his boots appeared untouched and there was mud in the muzzle of his rifle.

"Ben, have you cleaned that weapon and put some polish on those boots?"

Spencer stared at the ground wretchedly. "I've shaved..."

Robert lost his temper and censured his friend severely. He liked

Spencer, and felt guilty about scolding him, but his unsatisfactory conduct risked endangering the lives of his comrades.

Throughout the morning, the British added the finishing touches to their hurriedly prepared defensive line. The police and SCW closed the M53 motorway at the junctions north and south of Storeton, and all roads leading to and from the village were blocked with felled trees, scaffolding poles and razor wire. People living in the houses along the ridge road behind Storeton Woods were told to evacuate their homes due to the danger of stray bullets and shrapnel, but one resident was a personal friend of Radley's and insisted on staying, as did many of his neighbours. They were concerned that their homes might be looted if left unoccupied, and Radley had to acknowledge that their fears were not entirely unfounded, as it had emerged recently that certain criminal elements within Wirral had started taking advantage of the blackout to perpetrate crimes at night. It was agreed that the residents could stay in their homes, at their own risk. To provide a degree of extra protection, Council workmen raised the height of the sandstone wall along the eastern boundary of Storeton Woods by almost a metre. This would prevent French bullets from hitting the ground floor of the houses, although the trajectory from the enemy positions a kilometre away meant that the first floor rooms remained vulnerable, so residents were advised not to go upstairs. The Council workers also created some extra openings in the wall, to improve access into the woods for the delivery of supplies or the evacuation of casualties. British troops, unlike their adversaries in Storeton, were fortunate to enjoy the reassuring presence of three ambulances, which were parked behind the Traveller's Rest pub on permanent standby, ready to rush casualties to Arrowe Park hospital. Colonel Hogan had been most impressed by the ambulance crews, who, in stark contrast to the Special Council Workers, were willing to enter the danger zone of the wood in an emergency, provided that the Army issued them with helmets and body armour.

Just before midday, a figure carrying a white flag emerged from Storeton and began walking along Lever's Causeway towards the British lines. He was spotted by a sentry from Brabander's section, who immediately informed Alistair Blundell by radio. The major hurried over from his command post in the woods and crouched next to Brabander in one of the roadside shell-scrapes, as the lone soldier came steadily nearer. Suddenly Blundell became alarmed.

"Quick, Corporal Brabander – grab something white and walk down to meet him!"

"But sir, he'll be here in a minute or two..."

"Exactly – and by then he'll have an excellent view of our positions! So get down there!"

They searched frantically for something white, and settled for a grubby handkerchief which was hurriedly tied to a stick to make a crude flag. Brabander left his rifle with Blundell and walked briskly down the road to intercept the French emissary. The major watched through binoculars as the two men met and stood facing each other. Then the Frenchman began to speak and gesture with his hands, although no words were audible from Blundell's position. Brabander nodded several times, before heading back towards his own lines; the French soldier remained standing in the road, waiting.

"What did he want, Corporal?" Blundell asked eagerly, hoping against all hope that the enemy had offered to surrender en masse without further fighting.

"They want a ceasefire for half an hour to sort out the dead and wounded, sir," Brabander replied. "They want to remove the bodies from the cars on Rest Hill Road and give us the chance to get our lads out of the Rover they ambushed yesterday. They've also got two badly injured men who'll die if they don't get proper medical treatment, and they want to hand them over to us so we can get them to hospital."

Blundell was unimpressed. "Oh they do, do they now? Surely that's their problem!" He sighed. "But they're right about the bodies... Did he suggest a time?"

"Half twelve till one."

The major looked at his watch. "Okay, tell him we agree...But also make it clear that we might not be so accommodating in the future."

So the bodies were removed by teams of soldiers who had the misfortune to be selected for arguably the most unpleasant work detail of the entire war. The French team grimaced as they struggled to extricate the remains of their comrades from the charred shell of the Citroen on Rest Hill Road...They buried the corpses in a garden in Little Storeton. At the same time, a group of British soldiers drove down Lever's Causeway to retrieve the bodies from the ambushed Land Rover, and also to collect two injured Frenchmen, who were taken to Arrowe Park hospital for treatment.

When Alistair Blundell returned to the company command post in Storeton Woods, he found Lieutenant Monty from the Mortar Platoon waiting for him. In many respects, Monty did not 'look the part' – he was diminutive in stature, had a boyish face and wore glasses. But he was a competent officer who knew his job well and executed his duties with ruthless energy. He did not suffer fools and was totally intolerant of anyone whom he regarded as unprofessional. Robert Taylor had once witnessed Monty's peremptory nature in action, during a training exercise in the pre-autonomy days of the Mercian Regiment. A signaller was having difficulty establishing communications with battalion HQ, through no fault of his own. "I can't get this GSA to work," he told Monty apologetically. Army radio equipment was notoriously unreliable, but the mortar officer was totally unsympathetic. "That's your problem," he said brusquely, "sort it out!"

Monty had brought C Company's mortar down from the north coast and was eager to get it into action against the French, so he and Blundell set about choosing a suitable location for the weapon.

"Your mortar is absolutely crucial for providing the fire-support we need to win this campaign," Blundell told Monty, "so it's vital the Frogs don't find it. I suggest we hide it somewhere within the built-up area."

The lieutenant nodded and studied the map. "Makes sense. Now, it's got a range of just over four K. Let's say Storeton's a K away from here, and we need to be able to put bombs down at least a K beyond the village...That means we can basically site it anywhere in Prenton or Bebington, provided it's within two kilometers of here."

After some deliberation, they found an ideal location in the Teehey Lane allotment gardens, half a kilometre to the east. The allotments were fenced-off and accessible only through lockable gates, and there were sheds in which to store ammunition, or use as sleeping quarters. Without further delay, Monty established his team at the site. A large pit was dug and reinforced with sandbags, then the mortar was set-up at the bottom and aligned along a compass bearing in the direction of Storeton. The crew could not see their target, so a striped 'aiming post' was stuck in the ground a short distance away to provide a fixed reference point against which to make sight adjustments.

Under Monty's direction, the NCO commanding the mortar team used his hand-held targeting computer to obtain the necessary data to enable the sights to be set for initial firing, with the correct propellant charge fitted to the bombs. When Monty was satisfied that everything was in order, he and his radio operator hurried back to C Company and moved into one of the sentry positions at the edge of the woods, which offered a good view of Storeton and the surrounding landscape. He established radio contact with the mortar team in the allotment, made himself comfortable with his map and binoculars, and issued the order to commence firing. The first two shots exploded in a field some distance from the village and were disregarded, as they simply served to 'bed-in' the mortar as it recoiled into the ground; only when the weapon's baseplate had firmly embedded itself in the earth could worthwhile adjustments be made.

The soldiers of Charlie Company watched with satisfaction and awe as Monty guided a succession of bombs progressively nearer to Storeton. Viewed from the shell-scrapes in the woods, each detonation appeared as a large fountain of soil, erupting silently from the landscape; the sound of each explosion reached the British lines about two seconds later. The seventh round exploded at the base of the riding school embankment, atop which the French had been digging-in the previous day, and several enemy soldiers could be seen abandoning their positions and fleeing back into the village. The British infantry in the woods opened fire on them as they ran, while Monty calmly used his radio to inform the mortar team of the amount of adjustment required.

"Just a gnat's cock more..." murmured the 'Number One' mortar crewman in the allotment, as he made tiny adjustments for elevation. Then he checked that the sight's spirit-level bubbles were centralised, and the crosshairs were correctly aligned on the aiming post. The next bomb exploded on top of the embankment, right on target, and Monty recorded it as 'X-Ray One'. He then spent the next half-hour building up a collection of 'x-ray' numbers, each of which related to a key feature in the landscape. The x-ray system enabled targets to be engaged rapidly at any time in the future, with minimal trial and error. If, for example, British soldiers spotted French troops in the vicinity of the lone oak tree in the valley, they simply had to contact the mortar team and request a fire mission against 'X-Ray Six', without having to waste time working-out bearings and grid-references, and sending them in code.

When a total of fifty bombs had been fired, Monty closed his map case, radioed the mortar crew to tell them to cease fire, and sat back with a satisfied sigh. The men of Eight and Nine Platoons, who had watched events from their shell-scrapes, felt a renewed smugness and confidence. With such formidable firepower at their disposal, they would dominate the ground and defeat the enemy by Christmas. It never occured to them that the French in Storeton might possess a mortar of their own...

Robert Taylor was sitting on the edge of Lieutenant Grudge's shell-scrape at platoon HQ, copying x-ray numbers from the officer's map onto his own, when he heard a succession of loud reports originating from Storeton. The bangs were followed by a rumbling in the sky, rather like the sound of a jet aircraft flying overhead at altitude. Grudge immediately stopped writing his orders and looked at Robert with an expression of alarm.

"Shit – incoming!" He leapt to his feet, cupped his hands around his mouth, and shouted down the slope towards the platoon lines: "Incoming! Take cover – incoming!" Then he dived into the shell-scrape, along with Robert and the radio operator.

Throughout the wood, men threw themselves into shell-scrapes and curled-up like hedgehogs, trying to leave as little of their bodies exposed as possible. A few of the more experienced soldiers pulled their bergens over themselves as extra protection. Seconds later, the first French mortar bomb landed in one of the fields beyond the edge of the wood. The next two rounds crept nearer to the British lines until, suddenly, there were explosions shaking the ground amongst the trees within the wood itself. Each concussion was deafeningly loud and sent debris raining down onto the cowering soldiers, who felt terrifyingly vulnerable in their 'bare-minimum' shell-scrapes, and regretted not having dug proper battle trenches with full overhead protection. Their failure to do so was partly due to the rubble-ridden earth and a shortage of time, but it was also attributable to the fact that, as the RSM put it, they 'still had their TA heads on,' and shell-scrapes were what they were used to. However, the shallow excavations would probably have provided adequate protection, had not one of the French bombs exploded in the branches of a tree and blasted the British with shrapnel from above.

The bombardment ceased after a mere eight rounds, although had the French known the havoc their bombs had wreaked they would have fired many more. The terrified soldiers of C Company lay cowering in their shell-scrapes and listened anxiously for further incoming bombs, but none came.

"Sounds like that's it for now," Lieutenant Grudge said to Robert. "You'd better get back to your section, Corporal T – the Frogs might be about to attack..."

Robert ran down through the woods as fast as he could, following the track-plan so that he could jump into the nearest shell-scrape if the enemy mortar fired again. Reassuringly, he knew that bombs fired from Storeton would follow a trajectory which arced thousands of metres up into the sky, and was far longer than the line-of-sight distance separating the French and British lines. The practical upshot of this was that the sound of the enemy mortar firing would reach Storeton Woods several seconds before the bombs actually landed, giving the British a modicum of early warning; provided they remained alert and did not stray too far away from their shell-scrapes, they should be relatively safe from all but a direct hit.

As Robert approached his section's location he could hear cries for help coming from one of the positions, and discovered that two of his men had been wounded by shrapnel from the tree-bursting bomb. Their names were Donnelly and Armstrong, but they were only ever referred to within the section by their nicknames: 'The Scoffmeister' and 'Sweet-thing'.

The Scoffmeister's left arm was bleeding profusely and he was struggling to get at his field dressing, which was in a small pocket on his uninjured arm and could not be reached without causing great pain to his wound. Sweet-thing lay shivering in the bottom of the shell-scrape, clutching his left thigh, from which blood was literally pouring. His teeth were clenched tightly together and he was clearly in absolute agony.

For a moment, Robert stared dumbly at the wounded men, paralysed by indecision and the sight of so much blood. The Scoffmeister looked up at him. "Give us a hand with this bastard wound dressing will you, Corporal?" he asked.

The request snapped Robert out of his mesmerised state. He shouted up the slope for a medic to provide assistance as a matter of urgency, then stepped down into the shell-scrape between the two casualties, and pulled The Scoffmeister's field dressing out of its pocket. "Thanks, Corporal," the soldier said through gritted teeth, "I can put it on, you need to look after Sweet-thing - he's hurt worse than me."

Robert tried to stay calm as he turned his attention to the younger man. "Don't worry, mate, you're going to be all right. Is it just your leg that's hurt?"

"Ye-yes, Corporal," Sweet-thing moaned, staring at him like a rabid dog, while clutching his upper leg tightly with both hands. Blood was trickling through his fingers. Robert fumbled for his *Battlefield First Aid* booklet, a small 'aide-memoire' issued to all soldiers to ensure that they treated casualties correctly and did not overlook some vital procedure in the stress and trauma of the situation. But Robert's booklet was buried somewhere inside his combat smock, wrapped in a waterproof plastic bag secured with a rubber band...By the time he got it out, found the relevant page and followed the flow-chart for guidance, Sweet-thing would have lost a lot more blood, so he decided to rely on his memory and past training instead. He quickly raised Sweet-thing's leg and placed the boot on the edge of the shell-scrape to elevate the injury. The wounded soldier cried out in pain.

"Sorry mate," Robert said guiltily. "You're going to be all right – trust me. Just keep applying pressure while I get a dressing sorted out."

At that moment Spencer arrived on the scene, looking pale and apprehensive. He asked if he could help.

"Well, you can tie this bastard dressing off around my arm," The Scoffmeister declared frustratedly, "cos I'm buggered if I can do it!"

While Spencer helped The Scoffmeister, Robert tried to remove Sweet-thing's field dressing from the pocket on his arm, but it was so tightly wedged-in that he could not pull it out. Feeling clumsy and slow, he fumbled for his penknife and used the blade to slit the pocket. Then, when he had removed the dressing, he sliced open its waterproof wrapper, which he knew from experience could be difficult to tear. The fluffy white pad expanded in his hand, and he was about to apply it to Sweet-thing's leg when it suddenly occurred to him that he did not even know the extent of the injury, as it was hidden beneath the young soldier's clutching hands and the blood-soaked trousers beneath.

"You're going to have to let go for a minute so I can get this on you," Robert told Sweet-thing, who nodded and released his grip on his upper leg. Robert cut open the trouser material and was horrified to find a huge oozing gash, crimson and slippery with blood. Sweet-thing saw it, closed his eyes in misery and began to cry. He was only a young lad, fresh from recruit training, and with an innocent-looking face – hence his nickname, which had been Farrell's idea.

Blood started pouring from the wound and Robert glanced around in panic. Spencer had secured The Scoffmeister's dressing in place and was staring in paralysed fascination at Sweet-thing's leg.

"Ben! Get your boot in his crotch to stop the bleeding!" Robert shouted. "Not on his bollocks! Against his inner thigh!"

While Spencer tried to push his foot onto the pressure point in Sweet-thing's groin to slow the flow of blood, Robert gritted his teeth and grimly placed the absorbent pad of the field dressing over the wound.

"Hold tight there, mate," he told Sweet-thing, in as reassuring voice as he could muster under the circumstances. The sight of the injury was making him feel faint and nauseous, and his hands were weak and tingling with squeamishness. "Don't worry, we'll soon have you out of here – you're going to be alright..."

He began unrolling bandages around Sweet-thing's leg, tightly wrapping layer upon layer over the pad to keep it securely in place. Blood continued to pump from the gash and Robert could feel it flowing, warm and sticky, into the numerous small cuts and abrasions on his hands and fingers.

"You haven't got AIDS or anything, have you Sweet-thing?" he asked without thinking. It was a ridiculous remark, and he regretted it immediately.

"I did have, Corporal, but I got over it..."

Robert flinched in alarm. Then he noticed the grin on Sweet-thing's face, and a wave of admiration swept over him which brought a lump to his throat. Despite being only seventeen years old - and horribly injured – the lad had cracked a joke. Robert felt humbled.

Colour-sergeant Morris, the Company Quarter-Master Sergeant, arrived with Lance-corporal 'Duffer' Dudley and several other members of Company HQ, including the clerk and two cooks, who were carrying medical packs and stretchers.

"Have you given him morphine, Corporal T?" the CQMS asked, gesturing towards Sweet-thing.

"No, Colour."

"Right, I'll do it."

Morris took a morphine auto-injector and jabbed it into Sweet-thing's thigh. He then tilted the injured man's helmet back and used a black marker pen to write the letter 'M' on his forehead, together with details of when the dose had been administered. "Right, son," he said in a fatherly voice, "that'll have you feeling better in no time. Let's get you to an ambulance."

"Do I get any morphine, Colour-sergeant Morris?" asked The Scoffmeister, in a voice like that of a hopeful child.

Morris grinned and shook his head. "No, but you can have an extra large pie when you get back from hospital." He turned to his assistants. "Okay lads, let's get these boys onto the stretchers."

Listening anxiously for more incoming mortar rounds, the CQMS led his stretcher party uphill through the woods towards the main road. Several walking-wounded from other positions joined the procession, assisted by able-bodied comrades. Miraculously, the French salvo had not caused any fatalities, thanks to the combined protection of shell-scrapes, helmets and body armour - plus a degree of sheer good fortune.

When Colour-sergeant Morris and his party reached the main road, they were met by a team of civilian paramedics who transferred the injured men to wheeled stretchers and rolled them at speed towards the ambulances parked behind the Traveller's Rest. Morris accompanied them, determined to see his comrades safely on their way to hospital. He was rather taken aback when, just as the ambulance doors swung open to receive the wounded, a man in a suit appeared and accosted the casualties.

"You'll need to complete Form Triple-Six before we can take you," he announced briskly, thrusting a clipboard into Sweet-thing's face. "It's Council Primary Health Care Trust policy that all potential patients complete Section A of Form Triple-Six before entering a CPHCT vehicle or receiving treatment, so I just need to ask you a few short questions, if that's okay. The first one relates to initial patient satisfaction, so, can you tell me: How would you rate the performance of your ambulance team in getting you from the site of injury to the vehicle? Would it be: a) Excellent; b) Good; c) Satisfactory; or d) Unsatisfactory? There's a space below for you to add any additional comments if you wish..."

Sweet-thing stared at the man in the suit with a blank expression of bewilderment, and said nothing.

"He's on morphine," Morris remarked in disbelief. "And he needs to get to hospital now!"

"I'm sorry, but CPHCT policy states that Section A of Form 666 be completed before the patient receives further services," the man in the suit insisted. The paramedics looked at Morris and shook their heads in silent despair, evidently as exasperated by this ridiculous administrative procedure as the CQMS was. Meanwhile, The Scoffmeister had completed his form and was being loaded onto an ambulance. "Just sign it, Sweet-thing!" he shouted as he was wheeled aboard.

Eventually, when all of the necessary documentation had been completed to exacting Council standards, the ambulances departed, leaving the soldiers of Charlie Company to work at improving their defensive positions as a matter of urgency. The priority was to replace the inadequate shell-scrapes with two-man battle trenches featuring full overhead protection. But battle trenches were six feet deep, and their excavation would involve far more work than digging the shell-scrapes had done. Colonel Hogan contacted Gerald Radley to ask for SCW assistance, but his request was turned down.

"Council workers are not paid to work on battlefields," Radley told him bluntly. "I'm afraid that's the Army's job – that's what you're paid for."

Hogan responded by arguing that the average Special Council Worker actually got paid considerably more than the average soldier, but Radley would not be swayed; he was adamant that none of his precious paramilitaries would be put at risk by entering the woods to help dig trenches. He did, however, make concessions by agreeing to loan some Council excavation equipment to the Army, and authorised funding for the purchase of the large quantities of timber and corrugated iron which would be needed to shore up the sides of the trenches to stop them collapsing.

Once again, it was the engineers and transport soldiers who came to the infantry's aid in its hour of need. Leaving only a skeleton force to guard the Mersey shoreline, they hurried to the woods to dig alongside C Company with picks, shovels and mechanised equipment. None of Blundell's men needed any persuasion to put their backs into the work...With the trauma of the mortar attack still fresh in their minds, they were eager to dig down as deep as possible, in the interests of their own self-preservation. By the time darkness fell, all of the basic trenches had been excavated, and several had been roofed with timber, plastic sheeting and eighteen inches of soil. The soldiers moved in, and resigned themselves to a long, unpleasant winter in the woods.

CHAPTER 29

Chin-Strapped

A nasty novel written by a jingoistic misogynist and full of unpleasant men with guns...Horrid horrid horrid!

Felicity Pleasant
Domestic Bliss magazine

Mr Robert's replies:
Well, if you don't like it, rather than getting all het-up about it, simply throw it away, sit down on the sofa with a café latte, and watch a nice mediocre cookery programme on your widescreen telly.

Robert Taylor was so tired he could barely function. His eyes were red and sore, and a painful pressure had developed beneath his throbbing temples which made his head feel as if it were being slowly crushed in an invisible vice of fatigue. At times he swayed drunkenly, and during one of Grudge's 'O' groups, he repeatedly drifted into sleep and had to force himself awake by slapping his jaw and inhaling deep breaths.

During the initial phase of the Storeton Campaign, the soldiers spent most of their time patrolling, working at improving the defences, or manning sentry or observation posts. This gruelling routine – imposed by Major Blundell according to his '*The side which works hardest will win*' philosophy – allowed little opportunity to eat or sleep. On a number of occasions, the CQMS prepared meals for the troops which they did not get the chance to eat, and the OC's demands for round-the-clock 'aggressive patrolling' resulted in some sections going without rest for several days. The demanding regime was clearly unsustainable, and the men's performance began to deteriorate through sheer exhaustion, to the point where the Regimental Sergeant-major, Warrant Officer Protheroe, took Blundell aside and diplomatically suggested that perhaps he was being a little over-zealous.

"Sir, the boys are chin-strapped. They can't keep this up, and if you expect them to we'll have serious problems, believe me. This isn't a weekend TA exercise where you run them ragged for forty-eight hours and then send them home to have a rest. We could be here for months. Soldiers need food and sleep. With all due respect, sir, if you send men out on patrols or ambushes who haven't slept for two days, the only thing you'll achieve will be to get them killed."

Blundell said nothing. He stared silently into his mug of tea while assimilating the RSM's words, and initially considered telling the regiment's highest-ranking NCO to keep his opinions to himself. But he was aware that Protheroe, as an ex-First Battalion soldier, had nine years' regular army experience under his belt, including several operational tours of duty in war zones. By comparison, Blundell's own TA background only amounted to about two years of accumulated service, none of it involving actual combat. After a pause, the major nodded slowly, and looked a little ashamed.

"You're right, Sergeant-major, I'm demanding too much of the men. I just have high standards and expectations, that's all...But now that the trenches are finished, I suppose we can adopt a slightly more, er, relaxed routine..."

The situation on the front line improved slightly after that, although it remained a dismal, arduous and stressful lifestyle. Every day the French mortar fired a few harassing bombs at random intervals to keep the British on their toes, and there was the ever-present threat from machine-gun and sniper fire. Lieutenant Monty helped maintain morale with his retaliatory policy of always firing three times as many bombs back at the French as they fired at the British. It was hoped that this tactic would not only inflict casualties as part of the war of attrition, but might also make the enemy realise that, logistically, it was a one-sided contest which they had no chance of winning.

Less than a week after the initial digging-in, the heavens opened and torrential rain lashed the woods and continued unabated for almost three days. The muddy ground quickly became saturated, and turbid torrents flowed downhill into the British battle trenches. In a few hours the positions were flooded to a depth greater than a man's boots. Using planks, pallets, bricks and milk crates, the soldiers hurriedly constructed makeshift platforms in the dank, miserable confines of their trenches, to elevate themselves above the rising water table. Robert had the idea – which was swiftly emulated by many of his comrades – of wearing his rubber NBC overboots on top of his normal leather boots, thereby sparing himself the morale-lowering discomfort of permanently wet feet and the associated possibility of 'trench foot'. Once again, the maxim *'Any fool can be uncomfortable'* rang true.

In an attempt to improve conditions in the trenches, Major Blundell requested Council assistance, and two days later a pair of diesel generators was delivered to the woods, along with pumping gear and large coils of flexible plastic piping. But, by the time the equipment was operational, the rain had abated and the water levels had subsided, leaving the trenches slimy and stinking – especially those downslope of the 'shit-pit'.

A week after the initial French mortar bombardment which had left Robert's section under strength, two new soldiers arrived from recruit training cadre as 'battle casualty replacements,' or BCRs. They were both very young, and one of them looked familiar.

"What's your name?" Robert asked suspiciously, fairly certain that he knew what the answer would be.

"Smythe, sir."

"Don't call me 'sir' - I work for a living! It's 'Corporal' to you! Did you go to Ridgefield School?"

"Yes, sir – I mean, *Corporal*."

Robert's suspicions were confirmed: it was Ryan Smythe, the scrawny youth whom he had watched being dragged from the Green Bar by bouncers before the war. He sighed with despair, turned to Farrell and muttered, "Of all the sections in all the platoons in all the world, why did he have to walk into mine?"

"Is he a waste of rations, Corporal T?" Farrell asked loudly, walking over to Smythe and staring at him with disdain. "Jesus!" he exclaimed with exaggerated revulsion. "He makes the banjo player from *Deliverance* look handsome! Squeal like a pig, boy!"

Smythe, who had never seen the film *Deliverance* but could sense that he was being ridiculed, did his best to look proud and defiant. Farrell began to play an imaginary banjo and make pig noises, until Smythe grinned awkwardly and told him hesitantly to "Piss off."

Farrell became suddenly serious, and leaned forward to speak to Smythe with quiet malice. "Smythe, you are what happens when cousins breed. Listen, you'd better watch your attitude, or you'll last about as long as a snowball in hell. And in future, it's piss off *Corporal!*" The lance-corporal walked away in disgust, and from then on always referred to Smythe as '*The Banjo Player*.'

Robert shook his head. "Not a very good start, was it Smythe? That's your section 2ic, so it's not a good idea to get on the wrong side of him. Listen, this isn't like school where you piss around and get away with it. If you're a pain in the arse here, you'll probably get yourself fragged."

Smythe stared at him blankly. "What does that mean, Corporal?"

"Someone will shoot you in the back during a night patrol and dump you in a ditch, and we'll claim it was an ambush. So, start making a good impression. Your section should be like your family. Basically our motto is 'Fit in or fuck off.'"

The section had no such motto, of course, but Robert wanted to make it clear to Smythe from the outset that any form of unsatisfactory conduct would not be tolerated. However, to his amazement, Smythe turned out to be a surprisingly good soldier. He worked hard, followed instructions, and generally did his best to 'fit in'. Perhaps, in the final analysis, that was what he had been seeking throughout his troubled life: somewhere to 'fit in.'

In these difficult winter days, one of Robert's few consolations was that, as an NCO, he was allowed a mobile phone as a back-up means of communication in case his army radio let him down. This privilege conferred the enormous benefit of enabling him to speak to Susan. He kept the calls brief, partly for reasons of discretion (personal calls were, technically, forbidden, although everyone with a phone made them), but also because the soft tenderness of her voice threatened to erode his capacity to endure the privations of life on the front line. At the end of each conversation he had to suppress the urge to abandon his post and run to her for a night of passion.

While Robert abused his mobile phone privilege in order to make discrete phonecalls to Susan, Farrell went one step further and audaciously arranged to meet his girlfriend Kirsty on the main road one night for a clandestine assignation. In addition to affection, she brought him sweets, toiletries and an MP3 player. Other soldiers followed his example, and such illicit rendezvous' became a valuable means by which the men in the trenches were kept supplied with morale-boosting supplies of non-issue items, including 'comfy-bum' toilet paper, cigarettes and pornographic magazines.

One night, when the woods were quiet and most of the men who were not out on patrol were sleeping peacefully in their positions, a single muted gunshot was heard, sounding as if it had come from inside a battle trench. Bewildered and scared, the men of Charlie Company squirmed out of their warm sleeping bags as 'stand to' was called. They aimed their rifles through the firing slits of their trenches, as senior NCOs rushed around trying to discover the origin of the report. They suspected a negligent discharge from an incompetent soldier, but found instead young Private Halliwell, lying close to death in his sleeping bag. A large piece of his face had been blown off by a single shot from his own rifle, leading to speculation that it had been a suicide attempt. He died shortly afterwards, so the truth was never discovered, but the most likely explanation was that he had put the weapon in his sleeping bag, as instructed during training, but had forgotten to leave the chamber empty and the safety catch on; it had subsequently fired accidentally and killed him. No-one put their rifle in their sleeping bag after that.

During the early stages of the Storeton Campaign there was very little close-quarter contact with the enemy, although the two sides regularly exchanged mortar and machine-gun fire and sniped at each other across the valley. Radley visited the British lines every few days and, seeing little evidence of actual fighting, complained to Colonel Hogan about what he perceived as a lack of offensive spirit.

"Well, Council Leader," the Colonel replied defensively, "when we see any enemy troops we fire at them, although to be honest they're really out of range."

"Then perhaps you should consider moving your line forward to bring them into range. The only way we're going to remove this abscess is by inflicting casualties on the enemy, and I'm afraid I don't see much evidence of that at the moment, Colonel."

Hogan struggled to keep his temper. "Council Leader Radley, the purpose of our defensive cordon is to contain the French in Storeton and prevent them advancing further. If we move our positions down into the valley we'll be much more exposed to enemy fire than we are in the woods – and much less effective as a defensive line."

Radley reluctantly accepted this argument and departed in his

BMW, leaving the Colonel feeling relieved to have won a victory for common sense on behalf of his men. Their welfare was his primary concern, and he was determined to keep casualties to an absolute minimum during the campaign. From Hogan's point of view, the longer he could maintain the long-range stand-off the better. Signs of simmering discontent amongst the civilian population made him cautiously optimistic that regime change might be on its way, bringing the possibility of a diplomatic rather than military solution to the Storeton problem, and obviating the need for a full-scale assault, with all of its associated misery.

In Storeton village, Maurice's men were steadily using up their limited supplies of ammunition, so after ten days an attempt was made to resupply them by air. The French twin-engined aircraft had come close to being shot down by ground fire in Normandy, and as a result its pilot was unwilling to risk a daylight mission, preferring instead to fly-in at three o'clock in the morning under the cover of darkness. Maurice's beleaguered soldiers lit small fires in pits in the centre of the village to mark the drop zone, but a strong wind blew the parachute-retarded canisters off course and they landed in the valley beyond the French lines. A patrol rushed out to retrieve the precious supplies but was beaten back by an eruption of gunfire from Storeton Woods and a salvo of mortar bombs, courtesy of Lieutenant Monty. The British fired up rocket flares to illuminate the scene so that the two SF machine guns could let loose on the canisters with tracer rounds. The containers absorbed a surprising number of hits before they eventually exploded, to the delight of the British and despair of the French.

Life in the trenches followed a fairly grim routine for the men of C Company, but there were little moments of humour to alleviate the misery and monotony, and help maintain morale. One such incident occurred when Lieutenant Grudge came across Private Spencer, crouching in the mud, with his waterproof jacket spread out on the ground next to him and a worried expression on his poorly camouflaged face.

"What's the matter, Spencer?" the officer asked, intrigued.

"Sir – it's my rifle. I think it's gone down!" Spencer declared, pulling back the jacket to reveal his M16. The weapon appeared to be 'shivering' thanks to a clever arrangement involving an elastic bungee cord and a length of string, which was being repeatedly tugged by Harding the Invertebrate, who was hiding behind a nearby tree. Grudge generally had little time for either Spencer or Harding, whom he regarded as 'weak links' in the platoon ORBAT, but on this occasion he could not help but be amused, and decided to indulge them.

"Well," he said, unable to suppress a grin, "you know what you need to do, Private Spencer: put it in a sleeping bag immediately! Oh – and put another weapon in with it, so they can share body heat..."

Although he never went out on patrol, Grudge worked tirelessly to ensure that Eight Platoon remained a disciplined and effective fighting unit and did not succumb to the slovenliness which could be cultivated by boredom and routine. He was forever touring the platoon positions, inspecting trench construction and checking details such as range cards, arcs of fire, stag rosters, weapon readiness and the soldiers' knowledge of essential information. If any man did not know the password or have a basic idea of what tasks were to be performed that day, Grudge would hold the relevant section commander responsible and be harsh in his criticism. Robert Taylor approved of being 'kept on his toes' in this way, believing it maintained high operational standards which would hopefully ensure they all stayed alive, but others were less appreciative of the Lieutenant's ardent leadership style. Farrell, for example, had never liked Grudge, and even composed a derogatory song about him, based on the theme tune from *The Mickey Mouse Club*:

"Who ate all the pies and cake
In Charlie Company?
L-t-A n-d-y G-r-u-d-g-e
Andy Grudge (Andy Grudge!)
Andy Grudge (Andy Grudge!)
Forever will he chomp on cake and pie...

"Who's so fat his webbing won't fit
Around his big belly?
L-t-A n-d-y G-r-u-d-g-e
Andy Grudge (Andy Grudge!)
Andy Grudge (Andy Grudge!)
Forever will he hold his mess tin high..."

After the first two verses the song petered out, as Farrell and his fellow anti-Grudge conspirators guffawed with laughter. They never tired of singing it, and derived much amusement from humming the tune disrespectfully in the Lieutenant's presence, delighting in the fact that he was unaware of its connotations.

In mid-December, the weather became bitterly cold and added a new dimension of hardship to life in the woods. Each night, the ground froze like granite and the men shivered in the sentry posts and even in their sleeping bags. The early morning landscape looked picturesque beneath a layer of thick frost, while the weak sun, when it finally rose behind the British positions, bathed the icy scene in misty, golden light and picked out the delicate sparkling threads of every spider's web. In happier circumstances the soldiers would have considered the view from their trenches a beautiful sight, but right now all they wanted was to go home in time for Christmas.

Robert found himself struggling to keep warm, especially during periods of relative inactivity or while trying to sleep at night. His usual clothing – comprising T-shirt, Norwegian shirt and combat smock – was simply not providing sufficient insulation, so he searched in his bergen and found a thermal 'Helly-Hansen' top and an army-issue woollen pullover, which made a big difference. There was also a quilted jacket liner – often referred to by the men as a 'Chinese fighting suit' – but he could not get it on under his body armour. Besides, he was reluctant to wear too many layers, in case circumstances suddenly demanded extreme physical activity and caused him to sweat excessively and overheat. Encumbered as he was by webbing, helmet, Kevlar vest and radio equipment, it was not easy to remove surplus clothes in a hurry. As a consequence, he spent much of his time being either too hot or too cold.

The one part of Robert's anatomy which he really struggled to keep warm was his hands. His leather 'Northern Ireland' gloves looked warry, and their padded knuckles provided good protection, but they were not especially warm under normal conditions and were worse than useless when wet. In desperation, he phoned Susan and gave her a shopping list of items to buy from shops in Liverpool. She brought them to him one night when his section was being fed by the CQMS on the main road outside the Traveller's Rest. The purchases included a pair of black Goretex gloves, waterproof socks, thermal underwear, a clockwork radio and a meths-burning camping stove. This latter item enabled him to quietly heat food or water from within the safety of his battle trench, without the risk of sterility posed by using army-issue hexamine cookers within confined spaces. He knew that, if possible, he would like to have children with Susan at some point in the future, so it was important to protect his reproductive assets.

Robert used the wind-up radio to tune-in to the local radio station, Wirral FM, which kept him informed of the latest developments on the battlefields and the home front. Regrettably, the service was Council-sponsored and therefore heavily biased, and was used by Radley to broadcast daily political speeches to the masses. These typically involved his rhetorical response to questions or criticism originating from some nebulous and undoubtedly imaginary party, which he referred to simply as '*people*'.

"Greetings, good citizens of Wirral," Radley began one morning. "I trust the day finds you all in good spirits and keeping the home fires burning. I hope also that you remain committed to the Great Struggle and have faith in the righteousness of our cause and the inevitability of our ultimate victory. Unfortunately, not everyone shares your fortitude and determination, and sadly there are those among us who remain concerned only with their own self-interest – those whose negative attitude is frankly defeatist. People often ask me: 'Council Leader Radley, why must we continue fighting this war? Why must we go without luxury and endure the hardship and the bombing?

The French are not our enemies,' they say, 'why can't we negotiate for a peaceful settlement?' Well, to them I say this: What if Winston Churchill had sued for peace in Nineteen Forty? What if the people of Britain, in those dark days, had put personal comfort before patriotic duty and moral obligation? Had we acquiesced then, our great nation would never have dared hold its head up high and look the world in the eye again! Do not be fooled! The alternative to war is not peace. The alternative to war is capitulation, subjugation and humiliation! Know your enemy! We must continue, undaunted, along the road to victory and greatness. We must endeavour to follow in the footsteps of our forebears and keep alive the tradition of individual sacrifice for the common good. War puts the stamp of nobility on those with the courage to face it! Now folk rise up and storm break loose! *I* shall not falter, nor waver in my conviction – there will be no compromise or concessions from me. We *will* triumph, of that you can all be sure, but unless we all remain united and committed to the cause, the journey to victory and glory will be a long and painful one…"

"Just like his bloody speeches!" snorted Spencer, exhaling a cloud of vapour into the freezing interior of the claustrophobic battle trench. "Jesus – doesn't he go on?"

"He does," agreed Robert. "Still, it's good to know that our esteemed leader is sharing in our hardship and sacrifice. It must be hell in that cosy office over at the town hall…"

At that moment the Company Sergeant-major, 'Taff' Jones, stuck his head into the dug-out. "Corporal T," he said, "make sure your section's in good order – we're having a visit from 'The Hulk,' any time now…" The CSM was referring to Colonel Hogan, who had been nicknamed 'The Hulk' by soldiers old enough to remember the American wrestler and TV personality 'Hulk' Hogan.

"I wonder if he'll ask us about the food…" said Spencer, who cherished several theories about army stereotypes. One was that all platoon sergeants had to have moustaches. Another was that high-ranking officers always and without fail enquired about the quality of the catering when visiting soldiers in the field. "I'm sure it must be part of their Sandhurst training," he once joked. "You know – *Rule number twenty-five: When talking to the men, always ask how the food is…*"

A few minutes later the two soldiers were summoned outside by the CSM, and found the CO waiting for them in the dog-legged entrance to their battle trench. As usual, Robert was impressed to see that Hogan's face was thoroughly camouflaged and he was equipped with rifle, helmet, webbing and even a radio – a true example to his men.

"And here we've got Corporal Taylor and Private Spencer," the CSM announced, by way of introduction. As they stood to attention, Robert hoped that Spencer would remember that, as they were in a battle zone and everyone was wearing helmets, the colonel was not to be saluted. To his relief, his slovenly friend kept his hands firmly down by his sides.

Hogan evidently remembered Robert from previous encounters, for he extended a friendly hand and said, "Ah, Corporal Taylor, we meet again. So how are you finding life here in the woods?"

For a moment Robert was tempted to give a truthful answer, but instead he simply replied, "Fine, sir, everyone's coping well."

"And how's the food?"

Spencer almost wet himself with barely suppressed laughter and had to turn away, while the CSM glared at him. Fortunately, Robert diverted attention away from his friend by responding with an audacious dose of simple honesty: "Well, sir, since we came off the ration packs, all we seem to be getting is all-in stew, and the lads are getting rather fed up with it."

Hogan scowled. He despised 'all-in stew' - which was usually made from the left-overs of previous meals - and regarded it as indicative of lazy cooks. "I'm not surprised they're fed up with it, Corporal – they deserve better rations than that!" He turned to the CSM. "Why are the men being fed all-in-bloody-stew, Sergeant-major?"

"According to the CQMS, that's all the cooks are being provided with. We reckon it's left-overs from the Council canteens, sir..."

The CO was furious. "Well, it's totally bloody unacceptable!" He turned to Robert. "Corporal Taylor, if you and your men can continue doing your job properly, as I'm sure you are, I'll go and make sure that others do their job properly, as it seems they are not..." And with that he stormed off, presumably to berate the cooks, or their suppliers - or both.

That night, when the patrols had gone out and the majority of British soldiers remaining in the woods were asleep in their trenches, a sentry from Nine Platoon noticed large-scale movement down in the valley and immediately alerted Lieutenant Evans, the platoon commander. Evans peered through his night-sight and decided to rouse Major Blundell from his camp bed in the command post.

"What's going on?" the major asked.

"Have a look, sir."

A herd of Friesian cows was moving tentatively downhill from the farm in Storeton towards the British lines.

"It must be some kind of trick," Evans decided, squinting suspiciously through his image-intensifying sight. "I reckon the cunning buggers are using the cows as cover to sneak up on us without being seen. I think we should open up on them, sir – give them the good news before they get any closer..."

Blundell gave the order for the entire company to stand-to, but was reluctant to tell the men to open fire on the cows. He was surprised by his own squeamishness, and a little ashamed; for days now he had been exhorting his men to suppress feelings of compassion and show the enemy no mercy, yet now, here he was, finding himself unable to order the slaughter of a herd of cows. It struck him as strange - and even disturbing - that he had fewer reservations about sanctioning the massacre of men than of animals.

As the cows plodded nearer, Blundell sent a patrol down into the valley to investigate, and fired up some Schermully rocket flares to provide illumination. The patrol found no evidence of enemy troops hiding amongst the livestock, and by daybreak it became apparent that the French had in fact performed an honourable deed. Realising that it would be impossible for their small force to ensure that the animals were milked, fed and generally looked after in a humane way, Maurice had decided to release the majority of the herd. A few select cows were retained in the village to graze the gardens and verges, providing milk and meat as required, but the rest were set free. It was a noble, gentlemanly gesture, which met with the approval of the British soldiers and helped engender a growing sense of respect and admiration towards the enemy in Storeton, at a time when such feelings towards the Council were rapidly diminishing.

CHAPTER 30

In the Bleak Mid-Winter

So many literary clichés and unconvincing use of hackneyed imagery! There's even a white Christmas in Chapter 30. I can't even remember the last time it snowed at Christmas on the Wirral...

Erma Harlett
Wirral Monarch magazine

Mr Roberts replies:
Neither can I. Does it matter?

December dragged on interminably, a seemingly never-ending succession of patrols, work parties and futile ambushes, interspersed with brief periods of relaxation which were usually interrupted or cut-short. It was these continual interruptions which Robert found particularly soul-destroying. At times it seemed that he was the unfortunate plaything of some cruel, omnipotent being that delighted in his misery. Whenever he tried to grasp a moment to himself in which to eat, rest, sort out his kit or even defecate, some factor beyond his control always materialised to sabotage his plans. During one especially infuriating afternoon he tried three times to empty his bowels, without success: the first two attempts were scuppered by the call of 'stand to' as he made his way to the 'shit pit', while on the third occasion he had actually dropped his trousers and partly relieved himself, when the enemy mortar in Storeton inconsiderately fired three rounds, and the cry of "Incoming!" reverberated through the woods. The exasperating interruptions became such a recurrent phenomenon for all soldiers that Farrell devised his own terminology to classify them. There was 'dossus interruptus' (interrupted sleep); 'scoffus interruptus' (interrupted eating); 'chattus interruptus' (interrupted conversation); and, of course, 'shitus-interruptus' (self-explanatory).

During the night of the fourteenth of December, an observation post manned by men from Seven Platoon spotted a French working party removing barbed wire from a fence to the west of Storeton, presumably for use in their own defensive positions closer to the village. A quickly assembled fighting patrol was sent out immediately and caught the enemy by surprise, inflicting several casualties. The following night, French troops were once again seen foraging for barbed wire, and another fighting patrol was dispatched. However, this time the wire-gathering party was in fact acting as bait, to lure the British out of their trenches and into the open; the men from Seven Platoon came under effective mortar and machine gun fire, which killed one man and wounded several others, including the hard-to-replace section commander.

Mid-December saw the first of many Council-spawned directives, which were to bedevil the military during the following months. Soldiers already picked-up most of the empty cartridge cases (known as 'brass') from their trenches and returned them in sandbags to the CQMS so that they could be reused, but the new edict decreed that, from now on, all fired brass was to be rigorously collected. The front-line positions would be regularly inspected by officials from the Council's *Efficiency and Savings Unit* and, if any empty cases were found in the vicinity of a particular trench, the occupants would be reprimanded and fined twenty pounds, with all proceeds going to fund the War Effort. Such policies served only to lower morale still further.

Major Blundell had 'eased-off' a little since the RSM's intervention, but he continued to impose upon his soldiers a demanding schedule involving 'aggressive patrolling' and intelligence-gathering missions. One bitterly cold and forbidding night, Robert was ordered to lead a four-man reconnaissance patrol to look for signs of enemy activity in the vicinity of a track, which passed through a tunnel beneath the silent M53 motorway and was believed to be used by the French to re-supply their beleaguered force in Storeton. Buffeted by the icy wind, and feeling distinctly unenthusiastic, the four men left the safety of C Company lines through the Dark Side of the Moon sentry position, and trudged out across the frozen furrows of a ploughed field until they reached the edge of Prenton golf course. Staying close to hedgerows for concealment, they made their way cautiously towards the Roman Road bridleway, which was a prime location for the French to mount an ambush. With hearts pounding, the British patrol cautiously crossed the feature without incident, and hurried on across another field, heading for an isolated wood identified on the map as 'Cow Hey Covert'.

As the black, sinister silhouettes of the trees loomed ahead in the darkness, Robert realised that the wood had been one of the sites identified by Susan and himself as a potential Council headquarters location during their survey of Wirral. In fact, it had fulfilled all of Gerald Radley's criteria: fairly isolated, large enough to conceal a building, and with vehicular access along a nearby track.

Approaching the wood, Robert became convinced that his patrol would be ambushed before it reached the treeline, and he began trembling with fear. At any moment he expected an eruption of muzzle flashes from the shadows ahead, so he mentally rehearsed his response, in preparation for the worst case scenario. But then the gloom of the trees enveloped the patrol, and he realised with relief that they had entered the wood unscathed.

In the almost total blackness, Cow Hey Covert was a forbidding, scary place, and with the wind howling through the bare, skeletal branches overhead, thoughts of werewolves and demons momentarily dispelled those of enemy soldiers. The four men shuffled nervously through the trees towards the far side of the wood, from where it ought to be possible to observe the tunnel under the motorway. They had gone about halfway when Robert's heart missed a beat, as he became aware of a strange silhouette through the trees to his left – a large, angular shape which definitely did not belong in this wood. He tried looking through his night-sight at the mysterious object, but there was so little ambient light that it was virtually useless: the image consisted of an incoherent mosaic of shimmering green and black, which actually revealed less than the naked eye.

Intrigued, he told the others to stay where they were and crept slowly toward the strange silhouette, taking great care with each step to avoid snapping twigs. With his rifle raised in readiness, he edged steadily nearer until the large, almost prehistoric shape loomed silently above him. Suddenly, as he lowered his front foot, there was no ground on which to place it, and he lost his balance and tumbled forward. The frozen ground rasped his knees as he slid down into some sort of pit, his helmet striking against something solid and unyielding. He steadied himself, then reached out and touched the object, groping around its contours until the mystery was explained. It was the steel bucket of a mechanical digger – a JCB of some kind. Puzzled, he climbed slowly to his feet, but his rifle strap snagged on something at the bottom of the pit, and he was forced to crouch down and grope around in the darkness to try to free it. His probing fingers felt something hard yet strangely familiar, and he shuddered with dread. Trembling, he pulled out his small 'Maglite' torch, and shrouded the beam with his fingers, so that only a faint red glow escaped to illuminate the familiar object and confirm his initial suspicion: it was a human hand, protruding from the side of the pit, its frozen fingers curled and stiff and partly decomposed.

Close to panic, Robert scrambled out of the hole and stumbled back to the others.

"What did you find?" asked Stevenson, shouting above the wind.

"A digger."

"A what?"

"A digger – a JCB, you know."

"French?"

"I don't know. Come on –let's go."

As they moved on through the trees, Robert tried to work out why the French would use a digger to bury bodies in this wood, which lay well outside their perimeter defences. Then it occurred to him that maybe the pit had nothing to do with the French. Perhaps Gerald Radley had not been interested in a headquarters site after all. Perhaps he had been looking for a suitable location for a mass grave. Robert wondered how many corpses were buried in the wood. The use of a digger suggested it was more than one.

The patrol set up an observation post at the edge of the covert and spent four miserable hours peering through their night-sights, seeing nothing of consequence as they slipped slowly towards hypothermia. Robert could not concentrate on the surveillance task. His imagination became usurped by nightmarish thoughts of the violated dead rising from the pit and creeping towards him. No amount of rational thinking could dispel the fear that, at any moment, ghostly skeletal hands might grab his ankles and drag him back into the darkness...

A week before Christmas, Mark Conrad returned from France and rejoined Charlie Company as a section commander in Nine Platoon. During a lull in activities he came to find Robert, leaning into the rear entrance of his battle trench and catching him unawares.

"Robert?"

"Mark!"

Robert was about to launch wholeheartedly into their customary "How goes it, M.C.?" routine, but Conrad's expression and the look in his eyes made him think better of it. He knew enough about what had happened in Normandy to be aware that his friend would have to be treated with sensitivity and cautious respect, and their brief reunion confirmed this. It was immediately apparent that the Mark Conrad who now stood before him was a very different man to the one he had said goodbye to in France a month before. He seemed to have aged, and the cheerful, irreverent exuberance had been replaced by bitter cynicism and a deeply ingrained sadness. Robert hoped that the change could be reversed. Perhaps, he thought, Conrad's old personality could be coaxed back into existence with the help of friendship and the familiar company of people who cared about him.

Conrad was only able to stay for a few minutes before he had to return to Nine Platoon's lines in neighbouring Mount Wood, but the two men resolved to meet up whenever circumstances permitted. Robert took it upon himself to try to reintroduce a modicum of humanity to his friend on every occasion, with the ultimate aim of rebuilding his damaged soul.

In the days leading up to Christmas, the Council distributed leaflets warning about what it described as 'festive traditions incompatible with the War Effort'. These included any form of extravagance or excessive luxury, drunkenness, 'merriment at the expense of vigilance or productivity' and practices which compromised the blackout – including putting up external decorations or illuminations of any kind. A resident of Bebington, who tried inflating a huge, glowing snowman on his roof, found himself confronted by armed and humourless SCW men, who clearly did not believe in the festive spirit. They immediately burst the snowman with blasts from their shotguns, and fined the householder five hundred pounds, with the money going to help fund the War Effort.

Christmas came, bringing with it flurries of snow from the Arctic which blew through the woods in swirling, spiraling vortices and coated the north-facing side of every tree trunk with a white crystalline crust. Across the peninsular, children celebrated the white Christmas with snowball fights and sledging, while the soldiers on the front lines cursed the snow for invading their trenches, rendering their personal camouflage ineffective, and betraying their patrol routes with tell-tale lines of footprints.

The Council had decreed that Christmas this year would be a modest, sombre affair – which was almost inevitable under the restrictions imposed by blackouts, curfews, rationing and other austerity measures. But citizens resented this enforced frugality during the festive season, and their discontentment combined with a growing sense of pessimism about the outcome of the war. With casualties steadily mounting and no sign of victory or peace in sight, a wave of despair and melancholy swept across Wirral, which was darker and more turbulent than the clouds bringing the snow.

Then, on Christmas morning, something remarkable happened: the people went to church. From West Kirby, Wallasey, Birkenhead and Bebington they came, united by an urge to somehow connect with their fellow citizens in this desperate hour and share the burden of their sorrow. Many Wirral churches had always been well supported, but on this Christmas day even those with a normally scant congregation were filled to capacity. The petrol shortage prevented most people from driving, so they donned their scarves and gloves and overcoats, and walked along pavements which many of them had used little in their car-dominated lives. Across the peninsular, sombre crowds converged on the churches as if gathering for some mass uprising. During the walk, people encountered familiar faces from their neighbourhoods, and felt a new empathy towards them. Even the bullet-headed men, who typically regarded the world with hostility and contempt, were somehow humbled, their usually aggressive eyes softened with a sudden humility which seemed to say, "I'm a human being, and I'm hurting inside – are you?"

All over Wirral, vicars and priests struggled to accommodate the unexpected crowds within the walls of their churches. By this stage in the conflict there were very few members of the population fortunate enough to be completely untouched by war-related grief or anxiety. Many had friends or relatives in the Army, or else knew people who had been killed, injured or made homeless in 'air raids'. Everyone came to pray for the souls of the deceased, and for the safety and salvation of the living.

At All Saints church in Oxton, Susan Fletcher – dressed in black as usual – knelt at a pew and prayed for Robert. During one of the hymns she noticed a large, well-dressed man with white hair standing two rows ahead of her, and thought he looked vaguely familiar. Later in the service, when the man turned around to shake hands with others in the congregation and bid them 'peace be with you', his identity was confirmed. It was Terence McCarthy - chief executive of the Council, and Gerald Radley's right-hand man. McCarthy had not told Radley that he was going to church that morning, or why. He was there to pray for his twenty year old son Darren, who had had joined-up without his father's knowledge and was now with A Company in Normandy, fighting for his life.

Meanwhile, on the front lines at Thurstaston and Storeton, the soldiers huddled in their trenches and quietly froze. Recently, the intense cold had become their principal enemy, and they made fires of hexamine blocks, ration boxes and twigs in order to keep warm. Each man had received a special 'Christmas Box', containing gifts donated by the public, but much of the contents consisted of items which people evidently thought soldiers might want, rather than things they actually wanted. Included in the parcels were letters from local primary school children bearing messages such as 'Daer Solder, thank you for keeping us safe,' and illustrated with crayon drawings of stick men with guns. Robert cursed the Council for its unforgivable manipulation of the peninsula's youth, then added the letters and the cardboard packaging from the Christmas Box to the merry little trench fire around which he and Spencer huddled.

Later that morning the padre delivered two identical services, one after the other, which were attended by soldiers from alternate trenches respectively, to ensure that the front line remained evenly manned. Robert was not religious, but he went along to one of the services because he felt compelled to engage in some form of spiritual acknowledgement of the suffering and sacrifice of the war. Shortly after the service, Colonel Hogan visited each position to thank the men for their continued stoicism and hard work, and to wish them a happy Christmas. Then, at midday, the CQMS treated the troops to a roast turkey dinner, which they ate from their mess tins. The remainder of the day was occupied with the usual defensive routine, although no patrols were sent out. Robert passed the time listening to the radio inside his trench, but was dismayed to discover that, at Radley's insistence, Wirral FM was only playing hymns, carols and stirring songs from the nation's glorious past - including such classics as *'We'll Meet Again,' 'Lilly Marlene'* and *'Jerusalem'*. One particular hymn struck a chord in Robert's mind, and two lines from it reverberated there throughout the day:

In the bleak mid-winter, frosty wind made moan,

Earth stood hard as iron, water like a stone...

The one tangible benefit of Christmas was that the festive spirit brought about a tacit, temporary cessation of hostilities. On either side of the front line, British and French troops kept a watchful eye on each other, but maintained a respectful policy of non-aggression, and although the sense of goodwill to all men did not result in any comradely football matches in no-man's land, not a shot was fired that day.

CHAPTER 31

Unhappy New Year

This novel is frankly an outrage, an insulting, slanderous, poorly-written and thinly veiled attack upon the integrity of Wirral Metropolitan Council. And believe me, we shall be taking robust action against the author. When our legal team get their teeth into this impudent upstart he'll wish he'd never put pen to paper...

Gavin Muntrot
Wirral Metropolitan Borough Council

Mr Roberts replies:
Forgive me if I've created the wrong impression, but I honestly think there's been a misunderstanding. You've confused my fictitious organisation, which I've nebulously named 'Wirral Council', or just 'The Council', with your real organisation – Wirral Metropolitan Borough Council – which does such sterling work for the borough. And in any case, an administrative body of such undoubted integrity as your own would surely be far too dignified and assured of it's own propriety to be in any way riled by an insignificant, impudent, council tax paying rascal like myself...

Fighting resumed as usual on Boxing Day and was accompanied by fresh snowfalls across Wirral, as temperatures dropped well below freezing and dragged the soldiers' spirits to new depths of despondency. In response to a request from Colonel Hogan for arctic warfare clothing to help the men operate effectively in the harsh conditions, the Council delivered several large containers to Bravo and Charlie companies which, when opened, were found to contain piles of white bedsheets. Included in each crate was a crude photocopied drawing suggesting how the sheets might be tailored into white oversuits. Some rudimentary templates were also provided, but any form of sewing kit was conspicuous by its absence.

"They really are adding insult to injury," Robert remarked to Farrell, as they prepared to go out on patrol. He stared contemptuously at his section's allocation of sheets. "My hands are so cold there's no way I can sew anything. Where's global bloody warming when you need it?"

"Maybe we should just cut eye holes in them and go around like ghosts from Scooby-Do," remarked the lance-corporal wryly. "So, where are we bimbling off to now, oh glorious leader?"

Robert removed his bulky Gore-Tex gloves so that he could show Farrell the map and set a compass bearing for the first leg of the route. He stuffed the gloves into his combat smock, but one slipped out and dropped to the ground. When he picked it up, he was dismayed by the quantity of powdery snow which had somehow managed to enter the glove in a matter of seconds. Even shaking and banging it against his leg failed to dislodge a stubborn residue of fine crystals. These melted as soon as he put the glove back on, leaving his hand damp and cold, and further adding to his sense of hard-done-by misery.

Robert's patrol that night passed without incident, but Corporal Dixon from Nine Platoon was not so lucky. His section had the misfortune of stumbling upon the first of the French 'pipe bombs' to be encountered in the fields around Storeton. These simple booby-traps were made by attaching a trip-wire to a grenade, then removing the pin and inserting it into a short length of snug-fitting pipe. The pipe prevented the grenade's fly-off lever from detaching, so it would lie dormant until pulled out by a tug on the trip-wire. About five seconds after being dislodged from the tube, the grenade would explode.

It was the scout in Dixon's patrol who walked into the tripwire and unwittingly pulled the grenade out of its hidden pipe, but it was the corporal behind him who bore the brunt of the explosion. Dixon received a face full of shrapnel, which permanently blinded him in both eyes. Robert had just returned from his own patrol when the injured NCO was rushed through the woods on a stretcher, his face covered in blood-soaked field dressings. The terrible sight made Robert think of a verse from a poem by Siegfried Sassoon which he had studied at school, and he spontaneously blurted it out to Spencer in the darkness of the trench:

Does it matter? – losing your sight?...
There's such splendid work for the blind;
And people will always be kind,
As you sit on the terrace remembering
And turning your face to the light.

Witnessing or hearing about the horrific injuries suffered by his comrades caused Robert great stress and trauma, which progressively and insidiously eroded his confidence and sapped his personal morale. To him, it seemed that there was a neat finality about death – an abrupt transition from real existence to noble memory. Death brought closure. But major injuries - from which men would never recover - mocked the living by providing ghastly, enduring reminders of man's inhumanity to man. Whenever Robert saw a fellow soldier with terrible wounds, he instinctively pictured himself as the victim, and shuddered with dread as he imagined the impact that being maimed would have upon his life. Would Susan still love him? Would he expect her to? Would he even want her to look at him if he was severely disfigured?

One day, poor Private Cotterell triggered a pipe bomb containing a phosphorous grenade, and sustained terrible burns. For weeks afterwards, Robert had nightmares about being similarly injured, and became increasingly paranoid about going out on patrol.

On New Year's Day, British morale suffered a major blow when news was received of heavy casualties on the French Front in Normandy. Under the cover of a diversionary attack, the enemy had managed to advance with a Sherman flame-throwing tank into the wood occupied by A Company's forward platoon. At least ten men had been incinerated, and the survivors were caught in the open by a mortar barrage as they fled. It was the biggest single disaster suffered by the Wirral Regiment since its formation, and as the clocks struck midnight, the only thoughts in the minds of the soldiers on all fronts were that the New Year might see an end to the senseless and increasingly bloody conflict.

In Storeton village, Maurice and his men clung on with grim determination, their resolve fortified by messages of support and encouragement from home. Initially, Monsieur Lebovic had been furious at the renegade Lieutenant's actions, and had contacted Major Vassort to demand that Maurice withdraw from Storeton immediately. Vassort had pretended to be unable to establish radio contact and had not passed on the order, which was just as well, as Lebovic rescinded it a day later in response to overwhelming public opinion; the people of Normandy were elated by the news of the audacious advance, and Maurice became a hero and household name overnight. Lebovic was left with no choice but to allow the maverick lieutenant to remain in Storeton, although his weekly communiqué to Radley gave the impression that he was doing his utmost to persuade Maurice to abandon his campaign and surrender.

As predicted by Warrant Officer Protheroe, the French troops in Storeton had sufficient food to survive almost indefinitely, but were gradually running out of ammunition. Two daring foot patrols from Thurstaston succeeded in slipping through the British blockade at night, carrying rucksacks full of smallarms ammunition, but the most pressing supply problem related to mortar bombs. These were too heavy and bulky to man-pack in worthwhile quantities, so resupply by vehicle was the only option. This was achieved one night during a snowstorm, when a courageous patrol escorted a quadbike and trailer laden with mortar rounds out from the French lines at Thurstaston. They moved stealthily across Wirral, using footpaths, farm tracks and hedgerows for cover, and finally rendezvoused with a patrol sent out by Maurice to guide them into Storeton. Approaching the village from the west, the Frenchmen faced the challenge of crossing the M53 motorway undetected. Although the motorway had been closed to traffic since the start of the campaign, it remained a serious obstacle due to its steep, vegetated embankments and the searchlight-equipped machine gun emplacements which the British had created to cover the carriageways. The French solution was to go under the motorway using a drainage tunnel which was just large enough to accommodate the quadbike and trailer. Once through the conduit, a quick dash across the snowy fields brought the patrol safely into Storeton with its precious cargo. A British observation post reported hearing what might have been engine noise that night, but no follow-up action was taken, and Maurice gratefully took possession of a hundred additional mortar bombs with which to battle Lieutenant Monty.

On New Year's Day, the Council's Senior Executive Committee held an informal progress meeting in the lounge of the executive suite, to discuss the latest developments in the war and formulate future plans and policies. As usual, Sean Simms was the only other attendee and no official minutes were taken, as officially the meeting did not exist.

"We'll start with the military situation," Radley began, "and I'm afraid I must confess to being rather dissatisfied with how things have turned out. As you know, I find the continued presence of enemy forces in Storeton quite unacceptable. I simply cannot understand why Colonel Hogan does not launch an all-out offensive and lance the wretched abscess once and for all."

"I was talking to him about it the other day," McCarthy remarked. "He's biding his time, wearing the enemy down and building up intelligence in preparation for an assault. But he also feels we're better off leaving them where they are and concentrating on re-taking Hilbre. He's adamant that if we do that we can cut their supply line and end the war in a matter of weeks..."

"But we don't want it to be over in a matter of weeks!" Radley exclaimed crossly. "We want an ongoing stalemate, which is what we had before this damned Storeton affair. At the moment the French have two fronts on our territory – three if you count Hilbre – whereas we've only got one on theirs. In the eyes of our public they're winning, which reflects badly on us..."

For a moment there was silence, then McCarthy said, "Changing the subject slightly, Gerald, are you aware of how many men we're losing in Normandy? We're having real problems recruiting replacements..."

Radley looked taken aback. "What do you mean? I thought they were queuing up to fight for Council and country."

"They were, but they're not now. Not with the death toll rising, and more and more crippled young men hobbling along the streets on crutches or in wheelchairs. And let's face it, Gerald, public opinion is changing. I don't think people are as supportive of the war as they were at the start. You've read the letters coming in to *The Herald*..."

Radley scowled. In recent weeks, the Council-controlled newspaper had been receiving an increasing quantity of correspondence from disaffected citizens, demanding his resignation and an immediate cessation of hostilities. Radley had given the editor strict instructions not to publish any of these 'defeatist' letters in order to maintain the specious impression that all was well in the borough and public morale remained high. But before each letter was destroyed, it was scanned by the Council and stored on a secret database containing the personal details of all potential dissidents. The database had a rapidly expanding number of entries.

"Honestly!" the Council Leader declared, shaking his head despairingly. "Here we are, living through the most momentous events in recent history, and people haven't got the backbone for the struggle! The negative whingers! Whatever happened to the Dunkirk spirit?"

"I suspect," replied McCarthy soberly, "that if it ever existed, it died with the Dunkirk generation. Times have changed I'm afraid, Gerald. The British people have changed. They like their comfortable lives and consumer goods. They want to drive around the corner to the supermarket in their four-by-fours and watch soap operas and eat their microwave ready-meals. They want to put up huge inflatable snowmen at Christmas! These are the things that matter to them, Gerald, not some vague concept of noble struggle or patriotic glory or whatever you call it. People these days aren't used to hardship and they don't like it, which is understandable. And they certainly don't like having bombs dropped on them..."

Gerald Radley turned a deep puce colour and his body trembled with tension, as if he might explode with rage at any moment. Duncan Silverlock, who had been quietly watching Terence McCarthy with suspicious interest, quickly intervened in an attempt to calm the situation.

"If we're having problems recruiting, perhaps we should consider conscription," he suggested. "It might also have cost benefits at a time when we really do need to save money..."

"Oh yes?" asked Radley. He was always interested in cutting costs, provided of course that the savings measures did not impact upon him personally.

"What I mean is, we could probably set a lower rate of pay for conscripts. All soldiers at the moment are on pre-autonomy British Army salaries, which I must say seem rather generous in the current economic climate. In fact, we could even consider 'contracting out' the Army. I made some enquiries the other day, and we could hire some absolutely fanatical fighters from the Balkans or Somalia for half the cost of indigenous troops, without the financial headaches of sick-pay, national insurance, death-in-service benefits or pensions. What do you think?"

Radley considered the suggestion for a moment then shook his head. "It's tempting, but I don't think it'd be in the spirit of this war..." He looked at his watch. "Anyway, we might as well move on, because we seem to have inadvertently jumped to the next item on the agenda, which is finance. So it's over to you again, Duncan. How's the economic situation?"

"Not good, I'm afraid, Gerald. Here, look at this..." Silverlock rotated his laptop computer so that the Council Leader could study the graph displayed on its screen. "The green line represents income, the red line's expenditure, and the blue is a forecast of what I believe we'll need to implement projects planned for the next six months. As you can see, there's a significant shortfall, which may mean some deferments or even cancellations..."

The Council Leader frowned with concern. "Well, I trust that it won't impact upon what we discussed yesterday, Duncan..." He was referring to two issues of personal concern to him - namely the replacement of both his official vehicle and his beloved shotgun. His BMW saloon car was unable to accommodate the pair of leopards which had now been trained and were ready to be paraded in public, so a 'Hummer' vehicle seized from a local drugs dealer was in the process of being converted into a suitable replacement. The work, which involved full bullet-proofing and the installation of a cage for the leopards, was costing the taxpayer tens of thousands of pounds. In addition, Radley was eager to replace his shotgun, which was not 'top of the range'. "These Cogsworths are all very well," he had commented to Silverlock, "but a man in my position should have the best, and that means Purdey..."

The erstwhile head of finance assured him that these two projects were safe, the funds for them having been 'ring-fenced'. But other schemes were definitely in jeopardy, and a cunning combination of prudent financial management, creative accounting and some ingenious revenue-generating schemes would be required during the coming months if economic catastrophe was to be averted. Radley appeared surprisingly unconcerned.

"Surely we just sell more Council war bonds and raise Wirral tax again by a few percent, like we've done before. That'll bring in a few million, won't it?"

Silverlock shook his head sadly. "I really don't think we can raise taxes again, at least not for a while, Gerald. We've had six increases in the past five months, and at the moment the basic rate is fifty-two percent, and VAT's at forty percent. I don't think the public will stomach any further rises. What we need here are some more imaginative solutions – I've come up with some ideas for your consideration and, hopefully, approval."

"Fire away, my trusty money-maestro, fire away."

"Okay, in no particular order, then...Wheelie bins are still making us money, not only from the replacement of ones the SCW destroy, but also from the recycling programme, which is proving to be a double earner. We're generating revenue for the War Effort through the sale of recyclable materials such as steel and aluminium, and we're also bringing in some extra cash by sending random letters to households informing them that they've put forbidden items in their recycling bins - which carries a fifty pound fine. Money in the bank!"

Radley nodded enthusiastically. "I like it! What else?"

"I think we should review the parking policy again. Resident parking permits are too cheap – they should be at least a hundred quid. The way I see it, if people can afford a car, they can afford to pay to park it."

"Absobloodylutely!"

"And," Silverlock added, "we should modify the parking restrictions. At the moment, most areas are permit-parking only, which means non-residents don't park there and we don't collect any revenue from fines. We've had a trial scheme running in Prenton where non-permit holders can park for limited periods, but we use multiple signs which are deliberately confusing so people think they're okay to park there when in fact they're not – so they get fined. It's proving quite lucrative. Shall we extend the scheme?"

"Definitely, if it's making money. After all, making money's what it's all about. Anything else?"

"Oh yes. Licences. We should introduce a new licensing system for anything we conceivably can – dogs, radios, bikes, airguns – the more the merrier. Of course, the Council would issue the licences. At twenty pounds a go, they should bring in a fair amount – plus there'd be revenue from a punitive system of fines for people who don't buy the appropriate licence. Another suggestion is that we use the existing CCTV network more effectively to catch people committing minor offences – you know, dropping cigarette ends, spitting, riding bikes on the pavement, not wearing a seat belt, that sort of thing. I'm not sure how much it'd bring in, but I reckon it'd be worth a try. And on the subject of cameras, it's my belief that speed cameras could be earning us a lot more money if we used them more effectively."

"Explain, please, Duncan."

"Well, we drop the speed limit on certain roads, and set a new limit at an odd number of miles-per-hour. For example, if a road is currently forty, we change it to, say, twenty-eight. We only put up one sign per mile to inform drivers of the new limit, and we install hidden speed cameras. I bet hardly anyone under the age of eighty will drive at twenty-eight miles per hour, which means plenty of fines. As you know, I consider fines to be the way forward. The way I see it, prison costs us money, fines make us money. And as you said, Gerald, making money's what it's all about."

"Splendid, Duncan – well done! Is that it now?"

"Just one more idea: education."

"Oh yes?"

"We conduct a review of workplaces across Wirral – including our own Council offices – and we come to the conclusion that employees are under-qualified or under-trained for the jobs they're doing, with potential health and safety consequences. We then provide, through the existing system of schools and colleges, appropriate training courses which people must attend - at their own expense - in order to retain their job. Of course, we'd ensure that the courses make us a tidy profit..."

Radley leaned back in his chair like a replete diner after a large and particularly gratifying meal. He sighed with satisfaction. "Congratulations, Duncan – you've outdone yourself! All excellent suggestions – you have my whole-hearted support to implement them right away. Right – is that it for the financial situation?"

"Just one more thing, Gerald," Silverlock added hurriedly. "Have you ever thought of privatising the Special Council Workers?"

"No, I can't say I have. Why?"

"Well, it occurred to me the other day that we could sell-off the organisation to a private firm, and not only generate some extra cash but also reserve for ourselves some valuable executive positions, which might come in handy in the future. I mean, we can't run the borough forever, and it's only prudent to make arrangements for the time when we have to relinquish command, so to speak..."

Radley nodded. Under Silverlock's guidance, all three members of the SEC had been discretely accumulating secret reserves of wealth to safeguard their future financial security. Considerable sums of public money had been siphoned-off into Swiss bank accounts and various British accounts opened by underlings on behalf of Radley, McCarthy and Silverlock. Each man had invested substantial sums in stocks and shares, and had purchased gold Krugerrands. They had also bought investment properties in Liverpool, London and – ironically – France. These nest-eggs would preserve the high standard of living to which they had become accustomed, but all three enjoyed being men of influence as well as affluence, and were eager to remain salaried decision-makers when they no longer held their current posts. To this end, they endeavoured wherever possible to cultivate connections and engineer opportunities which might yield lucrative executive positions in the future. By selling the SCW as a profitable franchise, they would be able to reserve for themselves three places on the board of directors.

Radley considered Silverlock's proposal. He was tempted by it, but eventually he said, "I'm not sure, Duncan. Carry out a feasibility study, by all means, and maybe test the water to see who might be interested and how much they'd be prepared to pay. But my gut feeling is that we need the SCW under our direct control. Also, as we created the organisation, I feel a certain parental affection towards it...I'm not sure I like the idea of handing our baby over to someone else."

The Council Leader drank some water and turned to the next item on his mental agenda. "Right, if that's it for the financial situation, we'll move on to the Home Front. Overall I'm pretty satisfied. The canal and events arena are complete, we've got zero immigration apart from military volunteers, and the Wartime Emergency Powers legislation continues to produce a very disciplined, united society with virtually no unemployment or anti-social behaviour. The war has united people in the common struggle against the French, and Wirral's a better place – a *greater* place – as a result. Am I right?"

"Oh, most definitely," Silverlock agreed subserviently, but McCarthy looked sceptical. "Gerald," he said slowly, "I'm concerned, I really am. I know you think I've become overly negative recently, but it's not to antagonise you, it's because I care about you as a colleague and a friend..."

Radley looked rather bored and a little patronised, but he indulged the chief executive.

"Go on, Terence, what is it now?"

"Well, I really think you should ease off the initiatives for a while, otherwise there's a danger we may push our luck, so to speak. In fact, I'm worried that maybe we already have. Most people I've spoken to were initially in favour of the 'Punishment Fits the Crime' initiative, but they feel the lifebelt thing was definitely going too far. It sickened a lot of people."

The incident to which McCathy was referring involved two boys who, for reasons known only to themselves, had decided to stretch a lifebelt rope across the esplanade at Seacombe, apparently with the aim of garroting passing cyclists. They had been identified using CCTV footage and punished in what Radley considered an ironically appropriate manner in front of a crowd of spectators, which included their own parents. Special Council Workers re-attached the lifebelt rope at neck height once more, exactly as the boys had done, then tied the two miscreants to a specially constructed cart and drove them at speed along the promenade until they struck the rope. They sustained severe throat injuries from the impact, and Radley then ordered that they be thrown into the Mersey. Their parents were invited to rescue them but, of course, the lifebelts had been vandalised...Both boys drowned.

Radley was unrepentant. "Nonsense, Terence! That was my finest piece of poetic justice to date! If people can't take the heat they should damned well get out of the kitchen, the negative whingers!"

For a moment, McCarthy buried his face in his hands, then dragged his fingertips down across his cheeks in a gesture of exhausted patience. "Gerald, you don't seem to understand what I'm saying. If you go too far too often, you piss people off. If you piss too many people off too many times, they'll get rid of you. And trust me, people are getting pissed off."

"Honestly, Terence, I'm disappointed to hear even you being so negative," Radley scoffed. "Who, then, am I 'pissing off', as you so eloquently put it?"

McCarthy sighed. "Ordinary people – the people who voted for you in the first place. They feel that the Council has become preoccupied with the war and grand schemes but is neglecting the issues that concern them. My wife overheard a woman in the post office complaining that the Council workers are too busy standing around on street corners with guns, when they should be sorting out the pot-holes in the roads and the broken benches in the parks and the overflowing bins. She reckoned the only reason we have a blackout is so no-one knows how many streetlights don't work."

Radley scowled. "Could your wife identify this woman? There's bound to be CCTV footage of her in the post office – perhaps we should prosecute her for dissent..."

"Gerald, you're missing my point. It *matters* what people think of you."

"Well, quite frankly, I don't really care about thc plebs."

"Then you should! And you certainly should care about the Army. You're becoming unpopular with the soldiers as well."

Radley's eyes narrowed to suspicious slits. "How do you know? Who've you been talking to, Terence?"

McCarthy had not told Radley about his son, who sent him desperate, bitter, traumatised letters each week from the battlefield in Normandy. So he simply said, "I have my sources..."

"Oh yes? It wouldn't be Colonel Hogan would it? I've always doubted his loyalty."

McCarthy shook his head. "No, it's the troops themselves who are unhappy about things." There was a note of persuasive pleading in the chief executive's voice. "Gerald, I *talk* to people – people with sons or brothers or friends who are soldiers. And the men don't think you care about them."

"I see." Radley thought for a moment. He would not have tolerated such criticism from anyone else, but McCarthy had been his friend, colleague and adviser for a long time, and his opinions deserved acknowledgement. During Radley's ascent of the career ladder, there had been a number of occasions when cautionary words from the chief executive had spared him the humiliation of making a complete fool of himself in public. Radley was concerned that McCarthy was drifting out of his close circle of trusted confidantes, and was keen to retain his support and loyalty. So, as a conciliatory gesture, which turned out to be one of his last ever concessions to compromise, he made a suggestion: "Alright, then, Terence... if the men are unhappy and don't think I care, why don't we pay them a visit - you and me? How about first thing tomorrow morning?"

That night, Robert Taylor received orders to lead a patrol to reconnoitre the enemy positions around Storeton's northern perimeter, in the vicinity of the Roman Road. As he prepared to leave British lines through the Dark Side of the Moon sentry position, Karl Brabander hurried over.

Tayl," he said, glancing around furtively, "you've been into Cow Hey Covert, haven't you?"

Robert trembled with unease. "I have..."

Find anything, er, unusual?"

"I found a JCB. Why d'you ask?"

"I was in there this afternoon, and I found a JCB as well. It's a Council one. And I found a pit with at least seven bodies in it."

"Shit. I only saw one, but it was dark and I didn't hang around.

There's definitely something rotten in the state of Denmark."

"In the state of Wirral, more like. So what are we going to do?"

"I don't know. But I do know that we need to be very careful, or we might end up in a pit ourselves somewhere. I suggest we keep our heads down for now and bide our time. But something's got to be done." He peered at the dimly illuminated screen of his digital watch. "Right, I need to go. Don't tell anyone about this, Brab – don't you be no fool! I'll see you later."

Clad in their ridiculously flimsy bedsheet oversuits, Robert and his section trudged out into the snow-covered fields of no-man's land and headed for the line of dark vegetation bordering the golf course. They would give Cow Hey Covert a wide berth that night.

The following morning, Terence McCarthy got to work early and found himself alone in the executive suite, awaiting the arrival of Gerald Radley. Even the secretaries were not yet at their desks, so he made a cup of coffee, checked his in-tray and sat down meditatively to worry about his son. Recently, McCarthy had found himself existing in an almost permanent state of nervous anxiety, dreading every phone call or official-looking letter in case it brought terrible news from Normandy and confirmed that his worst nightmare had come true.

He switched-on his computer and, while the start-up scripts scrolled across the screen, wandered over to Radley's desk and glanced curiously at some of the documents which were stacked in a neat pile, awaiting the Council Leader's attention. Under the fifth revision of the Education Strategy and a glossy brochure for Purdey shotguns lay a collection of artist's impressions depicting a new statue, recently commissioned for the Mersey waterfront. Radley had decided that the 'speaker's corner' stone outside the Egremont Ferry pub was a 'breeding ground for dissent, sedition and treason', and had ordered it to be dumped it into the Mersey by the SCW. In its place would go a new bronze statue depicting the three members of the Council's Senior Executive Committee – Radley, Silverlock and McCarthy – in suitably heroic poses. McCarthy had already seen preliminary pencil sketches of the proposed design, but the colour images on the desk in front of him were altogether more refined. Radley had ruined several of the pictures by thoughtlessly scrawling comments onto them. McCarthy could not help but smile when he noticed one particular annotation, which read: *Make me taller than Chief Exec – otherwise he seems more important.*

McCarthy almost shook his head in despair, but remembered the CCTV cameras which kept the room under twenty-four hour surveillance, and instead nodded approvingly before returning to his desk. The situation beggared belief: social unrest was beginning to simmer, the economy was in terminal decline, and an ever-increasing number of young men were being killed or maimed every week on the battlefields, yet the Council Leader seemed more concerned with the minutiae of a statue's design! This disregard for matters of great gravity, coupled with an obsession with the trivial, was just one of a number of bizarre character traits exhibited by Radley in recent months. He had become increasingly dogmatic, volatile, deluded, extravagant and inhumane, leading McCarthy to suspect that he was slipping towards complete insanity.

Radley arrived just before nine o'clock, accompanied by Duncan Silverlock and Sean Simms.

"We have to think of the future," the Council Leader was saying, "both for the sake of the borough and for ourselves. That's why I'm really keen to get more big business on board." He glanced a little reproachfully at McCarthy. "I know Terence here is adamant that we shouldn't forget the masses, but my attitude is that the people will always be there, so we can take them for granted. But big business has to be *attracted.* It's like fishing – you have to convince them to bite, then reel them in and stop them escaping. With a couple of big corporations moving into Wirral, our financial worries would be over. Now, Terence, what time are we meeting Colonel Hogan?"

"Half past nine."

Then what are we waiting for – let's go and visit those squaddies!"

CHAPTER 32

Change for Change's Sake

I was vaguely amused by this book, until I reached Chapter 32. It's one thing to lampoon fictitious Council officials, but to suggest that our public servants deliberately make work for themselves to justify their salaries is definitely going too far! My concern is that gullible readers might be taken in by this scurrilous calumny...

Percival Poncenby
Ex-Council Chief Executive

Mr Roberts replies:
I, personally, believe that a great many policy decisions are being made at local and national level simply to keep policy makers and administrators in lucrative employment. And most people I know feel the same way.

Colonel Alan Hogan was a man under stress. At times he felt as though he were shackled to some medieval torture machine, which was pulling him apart from every direction simultaneously. As the regiment's Commanding Officer, he bore ultimate responsibility for the military situation on all fronts – a workload which, it had become evident, was frankly impossible for one man to adequately fulfill. How, he asked himself, was he supposed to support and direct the forces under Aldridge in France, Blundell at Storeton, Hubbard at Thurstaston and Myers along the coastal defences, while simultaneously being expected to spend an increasing amount of time at the War Office as Radley's principal military adviser?

Hogan was especially concerned by the situation in Normandy, and had a nasty suspicion that Aldridge was out of his depth there. The problem stemmed from the unforeseen aggression demonstrated by French forces in the aftermath of the Renault people carrier tragedy, which had plunged A Company into a desperate battle for survival and left no latitude for errors caused by leadership deficiencies. However, the colonel hoped that salvation might be at hand, in the form of a thirty-three year old ex-major from the Royal Marines, who had moved to Wirral and volunteered his services. Hogan had been tempted to employ him as his own second-in-command, but had decided that he would make a more valuable contribution in Normandy, where he might take some of the pressure off the beleaguered Aldridge.

While waiting at the sandbag sangar which guarded the entrance to Storeton Woods, Hogan fidgeted restlessly and cursed Gerald Radley. As if he did not have enough on his plate at the moment, without having to provide a guided tour of the trenches for the Council Leader and his fawning lackeys. It had been a particularly bad night, during which the French mortar had fired a creeping salvo of five rounds at Nine Platoon's positions in Mount Wood. The fourth bomb had scored a direct hit on the sentry bunker at the edge of the wood, leaving only a smoking crater. Daylight had revealed body parts scattered in a wide radius around the hole, including several limbs lodged high up in the branches of trees, which had a devastating impact on morale.

The Council Leader arrived slightly late, as usual, presumably to emphasise his own importance by making others wait for him. Before entering the woods, Radley, McCarthy and Simms were kitted-out with camouflaged clothing, helmets and body armour.

"It's important you don't stand out from the rest of us," Hogan explained, "in case there's a French sniper watching..." He paused, then asked, "Have you thought any more about my request for leave for the men, Council Leader Radley?"

Caught of guard and slightly taken aback by the Colonel's aggressive tone of voice, Radley hesitated momentarily before regaining his composure. "Er, I'm still considering the matter...I'm waiting for feedback from Finance and Personnel, and apparently their computer's crashed at the moment...It really comes down to staffing levels and costs, I'm afraid. Remind me, what was it you wanted?"

"Two days off every two weeks."

Radley shook his head regretfully. "I very much doubt that we can accommodate that. The budget's very tight at the moment..."

"I'm not asking for anything extra," Hogan replied, barely able to conceal his irritation. "We'll cover it within the platoons. But these men have been in the trenches for almost a month now – they deserve a break. And the Council and the War Effort will benefit, believe me. Morale will improve and the lads will work harder for us."

"But if we start allowing men to take leave, surely the line will be more weakly defended? And what if they don't come back?"

"A couple of men missing from each platoon at any one time won't make a difference to whether we hold the line or not, Council Leader. But if we don't give them some official leave, they'll be far more likely to take it unofficially by going AWOL."

Radley sighed, annoyed by the colonel's persistence. Eventually he said, "I can't give you a decision now. I'll let you know in due course. Now, if you'd be so kind as to show us the front line?"

They visited the collection of tents, trenches and sandbag bunkers which formed the company command post, and found Major Blundell delivering a set of orders to his three platoon commanders. Radley listened with interest for a while, before indicating to Hogan that he had seen and heard enough. Accompanied by the Company Sergeant-major, the party wandered down through the wood towards Eight Platoon's positions along the old tramway. Snow lay on the ground and gusts of icy wind dislodged showers of fine, powdery flakes from the black skeletal branches of the trees above. There were no signs of activity as Radley's group approached the trenches at the lower edge of the wood – indeed, the entire scene was remarkably peaceful.

The first battle trench they arrived at belonged to Corporal Kingsley from One Section. He had evidently received no prior warning of Radley's visit, and was sitting on a folding camping chair, his sleeping bag pulled up around his waist for warmth, and a mess tin of cooked breakfast on his lap. The radio was on and a 'pocket rocket' gas stove was boiling water for tea in an alcove cut into the wall of the trench. In fact, Kingsley had been served his breakfast at six o'clock that morning, but circumstances – including several emergency stand-tos – had denied him the opportunity to eat it until now, almost four hours later. Radley, of course, had no way of knowing this; to him, the trench looked remarkably cosy and inviting.

Upon seeing the CO and CSM, Kingsley rose abruptly to his feet and his sleeping bag fell to the floor. He sheepishly put his mess tin aside and stood to attention, hurriedly swallowing a mouthful of food and trying not to choke. Radley chatted to him for several minutes. The majority of the conversation related to living conditions on the front line and the general level of morale. In response to several questions, Kingsley hesitated and glanced enquiringly at the CSM, as if seeking guidance before answering. The corporal seemed nervous and uncomfortable, but did not express any major complaints, leading McCarthy to suspect that he was saying what he believed was expected of him, rather than what he actually felt.

The dignitaries moved along the line of trenches, briefly speaking to the occupants of each, until they came to Robert Taylor's position. Ben Spencer was on sentry duty at the edge of the wood, so Robert was alone in the trench, preparing a set of orders for a reconnaissance patrol to be conducted that afternoon. Radley, as always, greeted him like an old friend.

"Corporal Taylor, we meet again!" He extended a chubby hand, which Robert duly shook, then looked around the trench and smiled. "Looks like a cosy little den you've got here…And there was me thinking it was all mud and bullets!"

Robert could not think of a suitable reply and shrugged awkwardly. Radley stepped past him and peered through the firing slits at Storeton in the distance. "You've certainly got a good view of the enemy from here, Corporal. Have you managed to kill any of them yet?"

"I don't know. We've fired at them quite a few times…"

"Splendid, splendid…"

Radley stayed in the trench for about ten minutes, talking to Robert about his duties as a section commander, and expressing great interest in the various administrative processes and associated documentation including written orders, casualty and ammo cards, patrol reports and such like. Eventually the Council Leader looked at his watch and said, "Gosh! Is that the time? We'd better move on.

Thank you, Corporal Taylor, a most informative chat." With that, he shook Robert's hand vigorously and ducked out of the trench, with his entourage in tow.

The tour group did not visit Brabander's section, as the line of trenches stretching out from the woods along Marsh Lane and beyond was considered too exposed and dangerous for someone of Radley's importance. Instead, the party headed towards neighbouring Mount Wood to visit Lieutenant Evans and Nine Platoon, but on the way, the wind picked up and Radley and Simms began shivering, so the visit was cut short by common consent. The dignitaries returned their helmets, clothing and Kevlar vests to the guardroom sangar at the entrance to the woods, just as the CQMS was preparing to serve lunch from a line of folding tables placed on the road in the shelter of the wall. Radley watched with interest as the first four soldiers appeared at the entrance and crouched with their mugs and mess tins ready for 'tactical feeding'. His attention was then drawn to a group of women who were peering around the corner of the Traveller's Rest pub, in a state of considerable excitement. The Council Leader's interest turned to incredulity as one of the women suddenly ran across the road and began passionately kissing a young lance-corporal.

"What's going on here?" he asked Hogan in amazement.

"Some of the wives and girlfriends come up to try to grab a few moments with their men when they come out for their food," the Colonel explained, matter-of-factly.

"And that's acceptable to you?"

Hogan shrugged. "I don't have a problem with it, provided it doesn't interfere with operational effectiveness. The way I see it, the boys don't get any official leave, and if they can grab a quick snog while getting their scoff, well, good luck to them. After all, some of them may not live to see their next meal or their next snog. Like those poor lads last night..."

Radley and McCarthy arrived back at the town hall in time for a lunch of Dover sole and new potatoes, prepared especially for them by the executive suite's resident cook. Duncan Silverlock joined them for the meal.

"So, how did you get on?" he asked, fastidiously tucking a napkin into his collar and placing another carefully over his lap.

"Most interesting," Radley replied, thoughtfully chewing on a mouthful of fish. "Most interesting..."

"In what way?"

"Well, it all seemed rather relaxed to me. In the two hours we were there I didn't see any evidence of actual fighting at all. Just lots of squaddies sitting around smoking and drinking tea and generally keeping their heads down at the taxpayer's expense. No wonder they've made so little progress in ejecting the bloody Frogs from Storeton!"

"That's not strictly fair, Gerald," interjected McCarthy with a hint of annoyance. "I was talking to a couple of those lads and they were saying that the morning's always quiet. Most operations take place at night."

Radley ignored him. "And what I found really staggering was how archaic it all was. I thought we were supposed to have a Twenty-First Century army, but all I saw was men in holes and lots of notebooks and pieces of paper flying around. It was almost like something out of the First World War. They're clearly very set in their ways. It's outrageous really – the Army is employed by us, the Council, and all of those soldiers are Council employees, but they seem to operate in a world of their own. I saw no evidence of our standard management systems in operation, and there wasn't a computer in sight!"

Like many senior officials, Radley possessed only a limited working knowledge of computers, but was convinced that they were inextricably linked with progress and should feature everywhere in the modern workplace. He had been disappointed to find that the only computer directly involved in fighting the French was a small hand-held device used by the mortar team for obtaining targeting data.

"So what do you propose?" asked Silverlock keenly, rubbing his hands and almost salivating at the prospect of a bureaucratic feeding-frenzy.

"Well, I've decided I'm going to grant the Colonel's request for a day's leave every two weeks, but in return there will have to be a major shake-up of the way the Army operates. We need to bring those guys into the Twenty-First Century – bring them out of their comfort zone and start making them think 'outside the box'."

"I don't think any soldier is in a 'comfort zone' at the moment, Gerald," said McCarthy quietly, thinking of the horror stories described by his son in his letters from Normandy.

"Well, it certainly looked that way to me just now," Radley replied indignantly.

McCarthy sighed with exasperation. "Gerald, you're not seriously suggesting that we start telling the Army how to do its job, are you? Believe me, they know what they're doing – they've been doing it for years..."

"Precisely, my dear Terence. And do you know what happens when people resist change and keep doing the same thing year after year?"

"They start doing it well?"

"They become complacent! Initiative and innovation are stifled! Only with fresh ideas from independent contributors can the impetus be regained."

"But let's face it, Gerald, we don't know the first thing about military operations."

"Ah, but we have something far more valuable to offer," Radley said excitedly. "We have *management skills*. We're facilitators, innovators, system changers...We don't get bogged down in parochial details or specific areas of expertise – it's the *Big Picture* we're interested in - the *Strategic Vision*. We take proactive decisions at a strategic level and let the positive effects percolate downwards through the management structure like fine coffee..."

"Very eloquent. But I really think we should leave the military alone to do their job. If it aint broke don't fix it."

"I'm not saying it's 'broke', Terence, I'm saying that it's not demonstrating the dynamic and proactive approach we expect from all our staff. And besides, if the Army's allowed to rest on its laurels, then sooner or later it'll start *plotting* against us..."

McCarthy sighed wearily, his patience exhausted. In recent weeks, Radley's paranoia had swollen to the point where he trusted no-one, and had become convinced that everyone was conspiring against him, or 'plotting,' as he called it. The Council Leader believed that he had identified four distinct sources of potential dissent and insurrection, which he referred to respectively as 'The Gutter Threat,' 'The Intellectual Threat,' 'The Internal Threat' and 'The Military Threat.'

The 'Gutter Threat' related to ordinary citizens who might conceivably try to attack him, either as determined individuals such as Jeffrey McMinn, or as part of a riotous or rebellious mob. Radley considered this threat to have been largely neutralised by measures such as disarming the people and recruiting the SCW from within the very communities which posed the greatest threat to him, thereby ensuring that the gossip grapevine provided early warning of nascent conspiracies. The 'Intellectual Threat' involved educated citizens with the potential to oppose him through discussion groups, letters to the press, leaflets or websites, while the 'Inside Threat' related to treacherous colleagues within the Council itself. But it was the 'Military Threat' which caused him the greatest worry. He no longer trusted his two most senior officers, Hogan and Blundell, and believed that a coup d'etat organised by them was a genuine possibility in the future. One solution, which he was seriously considering, was to send Blundell to France, then remove Hogan from the equation with a Council-arranged accident of some description. Radley would then personally take over command of the Army. It was only the very real threat posed by the French at Storeton that prevented him from exercising this option, as he needed the expertise of the two officers to ensure that the enemy were contained in the village and ultimately defeated. The French breakout from Thurstaston, and their subsequent occupation of Storeton, had further exacerbated his insecurity by making him suspicious that perhaps Lebovic had secretly authorised the operation and was actually seeking victory in the war, rather than the ongoing stalemate originally agreed between the two leaders.

McCarthy remained unconvinced. "I still think we should avoid meddling in matters outside our own areas of expertise. We should get on with running the borough, and leave the Army to fight the war."

Radley snorted contemptuously, then asked pointedly, "Terence, how much do you earn?"

"You know precisely how much I earn, Gerald."

"I do. And how much do you think those boys in the woods are being paid to get shot at? About a tenth of your salary. Okay, so you don't want to change anything. But change is what we're about – it's what we do, our very *raison d'etre*! If we're not seen to be changing things, then people like those soldiers we just met will start wanting to know why we earn the salaries we do."

"Well, if you ask me, it's change for change's sake."

Radley stared at him sternly. "Then in that case, perhaps you should consider very carefully your own suitability for the position you hold..."

Sharply dressed Damon Dickinson stood in the executive suite, patiently sipping water while waiting to start his presentation. On a desk beside him was a laptop computer connected to a digital projector which shone the words '*Integrated Battle Management System*' onto a specially erected screen. His small audience that day consisted of the three members of the Senior Executive Committee, plus Steven Saunders from Procurement. Sean Simms sat in a corner as usual, keeping a watchful eye on proceedings over the top of his men's magazine.

Dickinson worked for a company called 'Integrated Information Solutions'. The identity badge on his lapel described him as 'Marketing Director', but essentially he was a salesman, and his mission at the town hall today was to persuade Radley to part with large sums of public money in exchange for the goods and services offered by his firm.

The Council Leader sat down with his coffee and gave the salesman an encouraging nod. "Right, Mr Dickson, when you're ready."

"Thank you, Council Leader. Right, good morning, my name is Damon Dickinson, from Integrated Information Solutions, and I'm here today to tell you about the Integrated Battle Management System, or IBMS as we'll call it from now on for ease of reference."

He pressed a button on a tiny remote control and an image of a soldier 'in the field' appeared on the screen, crouching next to a computer. McCarthy, cynical as ever, thought there was something unconvincing about the photo; the man's hair and clothing looked too neat, and his weapon and equipment had a strangely artificial appearance – it was as if he were a model in uniform rather than a real soldier.

Damon Dickinson commenced his sales patter. "IBMS is a computerised management system", he declared proudly. "It features advanced hardware and software, designed to enable all aspects of combat-related administration to be amalgamated into a single integrated and user-friendly package. It permits the user to access and manipulate management data at all levels, from administrators at a strategic level, such as yourselves, right down to junior officers and NCOs on the front line..."

Radley and Silverlock nodded approvingly, while McCarthy picked languidly at the quicks of his fingernails. Dickinson delivered a very slick presentation, suitably embellished with visual aids and numerous quotations from existing IBMS users such as the mysterious 'Soldier X' or 'Officer Y', all of whom, of course, sang the system's praises. There was also a glossy brochure and, for some reason, a hand-out containing photocopies of all the 'powerpoint' slides used in the presentation, complemented by a DVD and CD-Rom. Radley was impressed by Damon Dickinson and the wares he was peddling. The Council Leader admired the salesman's expensive suit, his well-oiled sales patter and the top-of-the-range BMW he had parked outside. Gerald Radley liked Damon Dickinson because he recognised in him a kindred spirit – a man whose career depended more on image than actual substance, but who succeeded in carrying off the whole performance with style and panache. In short, Radley liked Damon Dickinson because the salesman reminded him of himself.

"Are there any questions?" Dickinson asked when he had finished his presentation.

A sceptical Terence McCarthy raised his hand. "I'm afraid I really can't see what's so special about it. To me it just looks like a bog-standard laptop, loaded with the usual admin software, and plonked onto the battlefield. For a start, is it soldier proof?"

Dickinson gave a supercilious smile. "Oh yes, most definitely. Every computer comes in a tough waterproof case which even floats. And for a small additional cost we can supply the units with a camouflaged finish..."

McCarthy remained unimpressed. "I still don't see how this is going to help us win the war..."

Radley spared the salesman the effort of responding by answering the question himself. "It will streamline the Army's administrative procedures and bring them into line with the rest of the Council, which will improve accountability. We'll all be singing from the same hymn sheet. Terence, you saw how they're doing things over there in those woods. It's archaic! The problem is, most of the corporals and lance-corporals don't regard themselves as managers, but that's what they are – managers on the Council payroll. Yet they don't keep records of what they do, and it would appear that they're not subject to any form of official performance management. The taxpayer is entitled to know they're getting value for money, and with this system we can better ensure that. We can monitor Corporal Bloggs to make sure he's doing his orders properly, or keeping his ammunition records up to date or whatever. We can e-mail every officer and NCO directly, at any time, with instructions from the War Office, and we can request information electronically rather than having to drive over to the trenches to ask for it. Overall, I think the system's an excellent idea. It'll bring our army into the Twenty-First Century."

"Shouldn't we consult Colonel Hogan or Alistair first?" asked Duncan Silverlock, who was worried about the frightful cost of the project.

"Definitely not. The military are so set in their ways they'd almost certainly oppose any radical changes. No, this is a decision we must make ourselves, and present it to the Army as a *fait accompli*...It'll be a key component in a wider programme of modernisation which we'll call the *Army Administration Initiative*."

McCarthy glanced up at the salesman and waved to attract his attention. "Just one more question, Mr Dickinson."

"Fire away."

"We saw some quotes and interviews with existing users of the system, who were obviously very satisfied customers. I wondered whether you could tell me which army they were from? Who else is using the system at the moment?"

Dickinson faltered for a moment, then looked apologetic. "I'm afraid I can't answer that, Mr McCarthy, without breaking confidentiality clauses in the sales contracts. But believe me, we have a great many contented clients, who are only too happy to endorse our products and services." In truth, there were no such satisfied customers and Dickinson's firm was on the verge of bankruptcy, but he had no qualms about lying if it helped secure a lucrative deal giving access to taxpayers' money. There were many such businesses in Britain – private companies supposedly generating revenue for the national economy through skilled enterprise, yet in reality simply exploiting the golden goose of public finance.

"I've made my decision," Radley declared emphatically. "We will buy your system, Mr Dickson. I've calculated that we'll need five sets per platoon...let's call it twenty sets per company, to include some spares...So I reckon that's a total of one hundred sets, plus ancillary equipment and a technical support contract for maintenance and repair..."

Silverlock looked worried. "Gerald, can we really afford to do this?"

"My dear Duncan, the question is, can we afford *not* to do it! If necessary we'll take the funds from other areas of the military budget. I'm sure your masterful creative accounting skills can save the day once again..."

CHAPTER 33

Computers, and Other Embuggerances

The author is clearly another 'let's un-invent the wheel' technophile who dislikes computers. He is also a hypocrite: I bet he didn't use a typewriter or a John Bull printing set to produce his novel.

Corey Dweevlish
IT Monthly magazine

Mr Roberts replies:
I'm not completely anti-computer, but I believe they are massively over-rated and over-used in modern society and, in some cases, are causing more problems than they are solving. I mean, if you want to send a rocket into space or de-code digital signals, fine, use a computer, but don't store every conceivable piece of information electronically simply for the sake of it. And no organisation should ever use the excuse 'the computer's crashed' – they decided to use computers, not me, so why should their problem become my problem?

The first indication of the tsunami of change about to engulf the military came in early January, when a party of engineers arrived at Storeton Woods with instructions from the Council to construct two new concrete bunkers. These structures, which were much larger and better protected than the trenches and dug-outs occupied by the soldiers, were situated close to the company command post near the road, where they would be less likely to be hit by enemy mortar fire. Ever since the people carrier tragedy in Normandy, the French had regarded themselves as occupying the moral high ground in the war, and were determined not to lose it by inflicting British civilian casualties. As a consequence, their mortar team in Storeton always allowed a large safety margin when firing across the valley at the British lines in the woods, so as to avoid hitting the houses behind; to date, no bombs had fallen within fifty metres of the company command post.

As the combat soldiers watched the new bunkers taking shape, there was much speculation as to their purpose. Most of the men assumed that they would be occupied by Blundell and his staff from company HQ, which naturally gave rise to grumbles of resentment along the lines of, "Oh, so it's not enough to be a hundred metres back from the front line – he needs a Gucci custom-built bunker as well!" When the major became aware of these comments he was so indignant that he personally visited every trench to set the record straight: the new bunkers had nothing to do with him. This assertion was confirmed the following day, when office furniture and computers began arriving, along with heaters, de-humidifiers, kettles and a microwave oven.

Upon completion, the larger of the two bunkers was immediately occupied by a Council official who looked suitably ridiculous in body armour and helmet, worn over a suit and tie. He was a fastidious, humourless and reclusive man, who busied away within the gloomy concrete womb of his bunker and only emerged occasionally to scurry, mole-like, across to Blundell's trench, clutching sheets of paper or computer discs. The soldiers soon nicknamed him 'The Admin Gimp'.

The second bunker became home to the 'Information Technology Network Administrator', whose job it was to oversee the introduction and operation of the Integrated Battle Management System within Charlie Company. His sobriquet amongst the soldiers was 'The Computer Geek'.

While the Council was busy extending its bureaucratic influence into military operations, life in the trenches went on as usual. Robert hated the miserable routine, which featured varying degrees of discomfort, boredom, exasperation, excitement, melancholy, despair and, occasionally, pure terror. Underlying it all was a perpetual sense of unease - a constant background fear that the enemy might attack at any moment - which kept every soldier permanently on edge and made true relaxation impossible. Thoughts of Susan, together with the camaraderie engendered by shared hardship, were all that sustained Robert through these difficult times.

Robert's second-in-command, Lance-corporal Farrell, was especially 'good value' when it came to maintaining morale. Much of Farrell's humour was based on a repertoire of dirty jokes and endlessly repeated quotes from films and television programmes, which soon entered trench parlance and became much-loved catchphrases. One of Farrell's favourite films was the 1964 classic *Zulu*, starring Michael Caine and Stanley Baker as rival lieutenants at the battle of Rorke's Drift in 1879. Farrell's favourite scene involved Infantry officer Bromhead, played by Caine, discovering that Royal Engineer Chard had been using men from his platoon to build a dam, and asking, in a preposterously exaggerated upper-class voice, "*Who said you could use my men?"* Farrell knew the dialogue for the entire scene off by heart, and frequently re-enacted it for the entertainment of his comrades.

For some reason, the line "Who said you could use my men?" stuck in Robert's mind and gave rise to an on-going joke between him and Farrell, which lasted until the end of the war. It began one day when Robert accosted Farrell in his trench and suddenly asked, for no apparent reason, "What did Bromhead say when he found that Chard had taken his light machine gun – the one with the curved magazine on the top?"

Farrell stared at him blankly and shook his head in utter bewilderment. Robert grinned mischievously and explained, "Who said you could use my *Bren?!"*

A smile of enlightenment appeared on Farrell's face. He

immediately responded with a retaliatory question of his own. "Okay, what did Bromhead say when he found that Chard had taken his World War Two sub-machine gun – the one with the magazine on the side?"

"Who said you could use my *Sten?"*

"Bastard!"

Robert chuckled. "How about this one, then: what did Bromhead say when he found that Chard had borrowed his female chicken?"

"Er, 'Who said you could use my *hen?*'"

"Too easy, I suppose."

And so it went on, progressing through *pen*, *ten*, *Ben*, *den* and *Glen*, until Farrell suddenly declared, in his Monty Python voice, "Stop that – it's silly! You're a very silly man and I'm not going to talk to you!"

From then on, the challenge was to try to think of suitable one-syllable words ending in 'en' and then construct an amusingly cryptic question to act as the clue. Robert was particularly proud of this one:

"Farrell, what did Bromhead say when he found that Chard had taken his Buddhist spirituality while working on a Harley Davidson?"

Farrell thought about it for a while but finally shook his head in defeat. Robert punched the air victoriously. "Yes – one nil! You'll kick yourself: Who said you could use my *Zen!*"

It was all rather pathetic and puerile, but it kept them amused, and helped to alleviate the depressing reality of trench life, on the front line, in winter...

Shortly after the completion of the two bunkers, every officer and NCO, from Major Blundell down to the corporals commanding the sections, was issued with an Integrated Battle Management System computer in a camouflaged case. The Network Administrator, or 'Computer Geek', scurried from trench to trench, connecting cables and helping the recipients of the machines to 'log-on' to the new system. In addition to their camouflaged laptop, each IBMS user was also allocated an electronic 'notepad' to replace the old-fashioned paper notebooks which were anathema to Gerald Radley. When the Computer Geek had finished wiring-up the machines in the trenches, he trudged back uphill though the snow to check that they were all communicating properly with the main server unit located in his bunker, which formed the nerve-centre of the entire system.

Robert stared resentfully at his newly-installed computer and wondered how much it had all cost. He simply could not understand the rationale behind the whole system. "I often wonder why the Powers That Be seem so obsessed with bringing computers into every aspect of life," he remarked to Spencer. "I mean, I spent years at school learning to write, but no-one's ever taught me to type...Yet now they want me to throw away my pen and use a keyboard instead. It doesn't make any sense."

The Council's '*Army Administration Initiative*' demanded that, from now on, every piece of ephemeral infantry paperwork, including sets of orders, patrol reports, ammunition record cards, warning orders and replenishment requests, must be completed electronically on computer and sent by e-mail. All e-mails and personal files would be randomly scrutinised by 'Milcheck', the recently formed inspectorate set up by the Council to 'ensure high operational and administrative standards within the armed forces'. Milcheck was staffed by an esoteric group of individuals, all of whom were personal acquaintances of Gerald Radley's. During the Milcheck recruitment process, nebulous qualities such as 'administrative acumen', 'personal background', 'political orientation' and 'general loyalty' were considered to be of far greater importance than any in-depth knowledge of military matters. Indeed, candidates with army experience were told not to apply, as they were considered too likely to exhibit sympathetic tendencies towards the soldiers they were employed to scrutinise. There had been no shortage of applicants for the six Milcheck jobs, which commanded generous salaries and numerous perks.

Robert begrudgingly switched-on his computer and waited. A main-menu screen materialised, featuring numerous icons superimposed over a satellite image of Wirral. In the centre was a grey box which requested that he enter a password. He cursed: no-one had mentioned passwords. Typing the word 'password' had no effect, so he tried several other possibilities, including his surname, initials, army number, forename and surname together and, finally, 'fuckinghell'. All were similarly unsuccessful. Next, he consulted the weighty guidance manual which accompanied the hardware and software, but it simply advised that, 'Your network administrator will provide you with your approved individual password which, for security reasons, is required to log-on to the system.'

"That's just great," he sighed to Spencer. "As if I haven't got enough to do, without having to go and ask that Computer Geek for help."

After informing Farrell and Sergeant Murphy by radio that he was leaving his post, Robert jogged up to the ICT bunker, zig-zagging as he went in case a sniper was watching. The most recent snow had fallen several days ago and had turned crystalline and crunchy, although temperatures remained too low for it to melt, and a bitter wind continued to howl through the trees. Robert descended the steps leading down into the warm ICT bunker and startled its occupant, who was sitting at a desk, staring intently at a flat-screen monitor. The bespectacled Network Administrator was slightly younger than Robert and, in contrast to the 'Admin Gimp' in the neighbouring bunker, wore a full set of combats as well as helmet and body armour, presumably because his duties involved frequent visits to the front line, where he might be spotted by the enemy.

"I need a password," Robert said impatiently.

"Of course. Can I have your name, rank and the last four digits of your army number, please?"

"Corporal Taylor. 1830."

"Okay...Right, Corporal Taylor...your password is *Saladin*. You have the option to change it if you wish."

"It's alright, thanks."

"No worries."

As Robert turned to leave, the Network Administrator called after him, a little awkwardly.

"Oh - Corporal Taylor? Next time, can you make your request by e-mail rather than in person? It's Council policy under the AAI – the whole point of the new system is to cut down on paperwork and unnecessary journeys."

"I'll try to." Robert was tempted to reply sarcastically that, on this occasion, he could hardly have sent an e-mail when he had been unable to even log-on to the system without a password, but refrained from doing so; he suspected that he might need the computer man's assistance again in the future, in which case it was probably unwise to offend him.

The full implications of the Army Administration Initiative and its bastard child, the Battle Management System, became apparent within hours of its implementation. Soon after the computers had been installed, Lieutenant Grudge summoned corporals Brabander, Kingsley and Taylor to the platoon CP to receive their orders for operations that night, but, when they turned up clutching their old paper notebooks, he promptly sent them back to their trenches to fetch their new electronic 'palmtops'.

"I know it's a pain in the arse, gents," Grudge said when they returned, "but we're going to be expected to be using this kit sooner or later, so it might as well be sooner. From now on, everything you do should be on these things, or your main laptop computer. Every time you do orders, cas/ammo cards, range cards, patrol reports, whatever - make sure you save it and e-mail a copy to the admin bunker. I also recommend that you print a hard copy for yourselves and put it in a ring-binder file, so you've got proof that you're doing your job properly and are following correct procedures. That's what I'm going to do. I call it my *evidence file*. At some point in the future we're bound to get inspected..."

"What if we just don't do it, sir?" Robert asked peevishly. "Will they sack us?"

Grudge ignored him. "Right. Orders for night patrols and platoon defensive operations...Corporal Kingsley, what's the matter now?"

"I can't turn the bastard thing on, sir!"

"Let's have a look..."

Grudge fiddled around with the device and eventually located the cunningly hidden on/off switch, but neither he nor any of the others were able to access the note-taking software. The palmtop stubbornly refused to cooperate, informing them in no uncertain terms that it had locked itself 'for security reasons'. All attempts to unlock it failed, so the Network Administrator, or 'Computer Geek,' was summoned to solve the problem.

"Did you try pressing control-hash-enter at the same time on the keyboard before entering the username and password?" the Network Administrator asked.

Grudge looked at him as if he were mad. "No. How the bloody hell was I supposed to know that?"

Eventually, all of the electronic notepads were functioning correctly, and Grudge was able to deliver his orders. But almost an hour had been lost, significantly reducing the amount of time available to the three corporals for preparing their men for the night's missions. Robert hurried back to his trench to write his own set of orders for the reconnaissance patrol his section was to conduct that night. Prior to the arrival of the palmtops, each corporal had his own preferred method of writing orders. Brabander had perfected a technique using a 'nirex folder' of transparent plastic pockets, while Robert's preferred system employed waterproof notebooks, which could be written on with rain-impervious pencil. The purpose of orders was, to quote the instructors at Brecon, '*To ensure that every soldier is sent into battle knowing what he is to achieve, how he is to achieve it, and what fire support he can expect to receive.*' To write a comprehensive set of orders quickly, and achieve the right balance between too much and too little detail, was a skill which only came with experience.

Back in his trench, Robert immediately encountered yet another ICT-related problem: the screen of the hand-held 'palmtop' was simply too small to legibly display more than one page at a time, preventing him from referring to Grudge's orders while he wrote his own. Instead, he was forced to flick repeatedly from one screen to another, which was both time-consuming and frustrating, especially when time was a commodity in such short supply. He considered trying to down-load Grudge's orders onto his main computer, which had a bigger screen than the palmtop, but no leads had been provided to link the two machines together and he knew that a wireless system had not been adopted due to the risk of signals being intercepted by the French. In desperation, he groped around in the inside pocket of his combat jacket and fished-out his trusty notepad...

Two section's mission that night was to patrol in an arc to the north of Storeton, looking for signs of French activity and checking various strategically-placed trip-flares and sections of razor wire. The mission was uneventful, although a valuable piece of intelligence was gathered when Robert noticed a faint speck of light coming from the gable end wall of a house overlooking the Roman Road bridleway. He knew that there were no windows in the upper part of the wall, so the most likely explanation was that the French had removed a brick or two to create a firing slit to cover the northern approaches to the village.

The section returned to their own lines at three o'clock in the morning. Robert left Farrell to sort out sleeping and sentry duty arrangements, while he groped his way along the comms cord and informed Grudge that his patrol was safely back in and had discovered something of significance. Then he stumbled further up the slope for the customary debrief in the company command post. Major Blundell listened to his verbal account of the mission with interest, then said, "Good work, Corporal Taylor. I'll need your full patrol report asap – and remember it has to be done electronically now. But I'd like a hard copy as well, for company records."

Robert arrived back at his trench to find Spencer asleep in the shelter bay, snoring loudly. Giddy with tiredness, he switched on his laptop computer and scrolled through various menu screens until he located the patrol report template on the network. It was different to the one he was used to, and his fatigued brain struggled to adapt to the new format. To make matters worse, several of the boxes on the form were too small to accommodate the information he wanted to type into them. Unable to find away of enlarging the cells, he simply omitted some of the key facts until the text fitted. After two hours he had completed a fairly mediocre patrol report, but when he tried to save his work so that he could e-mail it, the following message appeared on the screen: '*Read-only document. Cannot save*'.

Robert swore profusely and went in search of the Network Administrator, who was asleep on a camp bed in his bunker. Despite having to be shaken awake, he was surprisingly amiable, and obligingly followed Robert through the darkness to his trench. By the time they arrived, the computer appeared to have switched itself off.

"It was working when I left it," Robert said despairingly, gazing at the machine with pure loathing.

"Oh dear," said the computer man sadly. "Did you save your work?"

"It wouldn't let me save it – that's why I came to see you! Why has the bloody thing turned itself off?"

"I don't know. The only thing I can think of is that there's been a power failure. If the mains supply is cut off, the computer will work on its internal battery for a few hours, but at these temperatures it won't last long...You were probably working on internal power without realising it."

"Why wouldn't it let me save my work?"

"You were typing onto the original template file on the network. You should've copied it onto the clipboard on your machine before attempting to add text."

"Nobody told me that."

"We assumed you'd know how to do it. Are you familiar with the 'Gimbal' software package?"

"No. Are you familiar with leading an eight-man infantry section?"

"Point taken. I'm sorry, Corporal Taylor, all I can do is go and check the power supply and then get back to you. We should be able to recover your data, but I can't promise anything."

Robert sighed and looked despairingly at his watch. It was almost five o'clock. In another hour or so everyone would be roused from sleep, and the daily routine would begin again.

After he had escorted the computer man back to his bunker, Robert called-in at the company command post to tell Blundell that his patrol report had disappeared into the ether.

"Oh well, Corporal T," the major said casually. "Just do it on paper as usual."

In the days that followed, some of the computer system's teething troubles were rectified, but it remained intensely unpopular with the soldiers who were forced to use it. They resented the burden of additional administrative procedures, which simply added to their already demanding workload and appeared to have little or no relevance to actually fighting the French. For example, under the old, time-honoured system, a corporal who was asked to confirm the ammunition status of his section simply wrote the information onto a pre-printed laminated card, using a felt pen or 'chinagraph' pencil, and handed it to the platoon sergeant. After each mission, the card was wiped clean and used again. Under the Battle Management System, the same procedure was rather more complex and time-consuming: the corporal had to access the relevant computer file (assuming his machine had not 'crashed', which they often did), type-in the information, then e-mail it to the admin bunker for storage in the network archives. The 'Admin Gimp' would then print-out two 'hard' copies of the document. One of these was filed in the company records, while the other was laminated and passed to the platoon sergeant. If any of the details changed, only two 'unofficial' alterations were allowed to be made by hand before the entire laborious process had to be repeated. After the mission, the corporal had to put the laminated form in his personal 'evidence file', which would be used to prove that he was doing his job properly in the event of a Milcheck inspection.

Colonel Hogan was furious at having what he described as "This absurd electronic embuggerance" foisted upon his men without consultation. "How is this supposed to help us win the war?" he demanded of Alistair Blundell. "It's just a glorified admin system in camouflaged clothes – totally inappropriate for the way we operate. And what's all this about 'performance management interviews?' I have confidence in my men, and I trust them to do their job properly – I don't need to see every bloody ammo card or warning order they produce, and I certainly don't need to see it on a computer! It's just yet more bureaucratic meddling from those fools in the town hall. If the Council really is serious about us winning this war, then they can forget this electronic gimmickry and give me the freedom to do what needs to be done – which basically means re-taking Hilbre Island..."

Like Hogan, Robert despised the Battle Management System, but he grew to like the Network Administrator, who shared many of the same risks as the troops and was hard-working and approachable. In recognition of this, Robert encouraged his comrades to change the man's nickname from 'the Computer Geek' to 'the Computer Man.' Unlike the 'Admin Gimp', who was clearly a Council stooge, the Computer Man had no ulterior motives or hidden agendas; his purpose in life was to serve his electronic mistress, ensuring that her every need was attended to and she performed as required.

One day, Robert was trudging down towards his trench from the company command post when he noticed the computer man on his hands and knees in the snow, checking one of the many cables which snaked through the wood. So engrossed was he in his task that he seemed completely oblivious to Robert's approach, or to the distinctive sound of the French mortar firing from across the valley in Storeton. Robert glanced around frantically. The nearest refuge was an unoccupied battle trench, which had been dug partly as a 'depth' defensive position but also to serve as an emergency shelter for anyone caught in the open during just such a situation.

"Quick – over here!" he shouted urgently.

Startled, the computer man looked up at him with a blank expression, and remained crouching in the snow. Robert dashed over to him, grabbed the epaulet of his combat jacket, and dragged him towards the trench. "Quick, mate – incoming!"

They dived through the narrow doorway and threw themselves down into the layer of snow which had accumulated on the floor. Moments later, there was a tremendous explosion outside, which sent debris showering into the confined space of the shelter and shook the ground so severely that Robert feared the roof might collapse on top of them. There were four more blasts in quick succession, none of them as close as the first, but terrifying nonetheless. After the bombardment had ceased, the two men lay cowering in the snow, until eventually they dared open their eyes and remove their fingers from their ears. The trench was full of smoke and dust, and there was a strong smell of burning.

Robert looked at the computer man, who stared back at him with a shell-shocked expression. "I think we were very lucky there."

"I should say!"

Robert laughed - a nervous, tension-relieving laugh, and the computer man started laughing too. Within moments both men were in hysterics, and only restrained themselves when they saw the Company Sergeant-major coming down through the trees to see if anyone had been killed or injured.

Robert quickly regained his composure. "Get to know that sound," he advised the computer man. "Listen out for the bangs in Storeton, and if you hear them, take cover immediately. You've got about six seconds. Okay?"

"Sure thing. Thanks, Corporal Taylor. I think you probably just saved my life."

"No worries."

CHAPTER 34

R 'n' R

When the author submitted this book to me for possible publication, I turned it down on the grounds that it was too long and too preposterous to appeal to the general reader. It is not a decision I regret.

Hannibal Slocum
Nexus Publishing

Mr Roberts replies:
It is not a decision I regret, either, Mr Slocum.

The French mortar attack had not caused any British casualties, but it did have an unexpected consequence which several soldiers found far from amusing. A number of cables connecting the computer bunker with front line trenches were severed by the blasts, and as a result, some men in Corporal Kingsley's section did not receive the e-mails informing them of their day's leave until after the date had already passed.

Robert eagerly awaited his own day-off, and when he received the confirmatory e-mail he immediately phoned Susan in a state of great excitement. She, however, sounded subdued.

"When, Robert?"

"Tuesday."

"Which Tuesday?"

"Next Tuesday."

"But I'm on duty in the War Office!"

"Oh you're joking me!" His disappointment was overwhelming. "Can't you change it?"

"No, no more than you can change when you're on duty. And I can't even swap with anyone – one of the girls is sick and another was killed in an air raid last week, so there's only four of us here to do everything."

He swore copiously, then apologised. "I'm sorry, My Love, it's just so unfair. I've been looking forward to it for so long."

"Me too. When's your next day?"

"Two sodding weeks. I'm not sure I can wait that long..."

"I can't see what else we can do."

He thought for a moment. "When do you come off duty?"

"Six am, on Wednesday morning."

"Well, my leave finishes at midday. How about this: I'll see if I can get my day changed, or see if anyone will do a swap with me. And if that doesn't work, we'll meet up as soon as you come off duty on Wednesday morning – even a few hours are better than nothing. How does that sound?"

“It sounds better than nothing. Do what you can, Robert - I can’t wait to see you.”

Robert went to see Dai Jones, the Company Sergeant-major, to ask if it would be possible to change the date of his leave, but was told that the matter was outside Company control and could only be dealt with by the Council’s Personnel Department. Unsurprisigly, all of his attempts to contact the relevant people in the Council failed - thwarted by the impenetrable barrier of telephone answering machines and automated voice response systems. Fuming, he marched to the admin bunker to ask the Admin Gimp for help, but the man refused to speak to him on the grounds that it was ‘against Council policy’ for soldiers to have direct access to Council staff. None of Robert’s comrades were prepared to swap dates, so he resigned himself bitterly to spending a few meager hours with Susan on the morning his leave ended.

A minor consolation was that, by coincidence, Mark Conrad’s day-off coincided with his own, so the two friends returned together to their rented house in Rock Ferry. Robert had not been there for almost two months, although it felt like much longer. Entering his own room after such a long period of absence was a slightly eerie experience, almost like uncovering a tomb; a half-drunk cup of tea festered on the window ledge exactly where he had left it, clothes lay in an untidy heap on the floor, and a book remained face-down on the table, open to the page he had last been reading.

Many soldiers chose to spend their leave getting fantastically drunk, but this did not appeal to Robert. He knew that, for him, large quantities of alcohol would lead to a predictable sequence of events: initially, he would be relaxed and garrulous, then his behaviour would probably become loud and argumentative before entering a sullen and sentimental phase, after which he would be consumed with fatigue and nausea, and finally fall asleep. The following morning he would wake up with a frightful hangover and have little recollection of how he had spent his precious twenty-four hours of freedom. As this was his first day-off in over two months, he was determined to make the most of it and savour every second.

The two men tossed a coin to decide who would use the bathroom first. Robert lost, so performed some essential body maintenance while waiting for his turn to have a bath. He started with his feet. During the past two months he had only removed his boots on a few occasions, and then only for a couple of minutes at a time in order to change his socks, apply foot powder or dress a blister. When he finally prised off his footwear, the skin beneath looked wrinkled, pale and unhealthy, so he decided to remain barefooted for as much of the remaining twenty-three hours as possible and allow his feet to ‘breathe’.

He sat contentedly on his bed, cutting his toenails and listening to a favourite CD while relishing the peaceful cleanliness of his surroundings and enjoying the simple fact that no-one was trying to kill him. Of course, after being on edge for so long, it was impossible to completely relax and slough-off the stress of active service. This was emphasised when, through the open window of his bedroom, he heard the distant crump of mortar fire. He immediately stiffened in terror and looked around frantically for somewhere to take cover, before realising that the reports were too loud to have come from the French in Storeton, and therefore must have originated from 'Monty's Mortar' in the Teehey Lane allotment, so he was in no danger whatsoever.

When both Robert and Mark had completed their ablutions, they sat in the living room, momentarily at a loss as to how to spend their precious time. While in the trenches, they had frequently experienced desperate cravings for unobtainable items, ranging from bottled beer to "those flying saucer things with sherbet in which you used to have as a kid." To pass the time, they visited their local convenience store on a mission to procure as many of the desired items as rationing permitted, although when they took their booty home, none of it quite lived up to expectations.

A new Council-produced pamphlet entitled '*Licensing to Win the War*' had just been delivered, and Robert glanced idly through it while lounging on the sofa. "According to this," he told Conrad, "we're now going to have to pay twenty quid for a licence to own any of these things: dog; mobile phone; airgun; camera; radio; computer; canoe or boat; bicycle; central heating boiler."

"Doesn't surprise me. How else are They going to pay for Themselves?"

Robert had treated Conrad with respectful caution since his return from France, being unsure of the extent to which his mental scars had healed. He knew that his friend's re-integration back into Charlie Company was not going well – in particular, Conrad resented being posted to Nine Platoon, which he referred to scornfully as '*Special Needs Platoon*.' Conrad was critical and intolerant of the men in his section and they, unsurprisingly, objected to his insensitive attitude, and demanded that he be replaced with a more approachable and considerate NCO. To make matters worse, Conrad's girlfriend had ended their relationship within days of his return from France, and since then he had become increasingly misogynistic and introverted.

Later in the afternoon they bought takeaway curry with numerous side dishes, and gorged themselves while watching pointless television.

"How are you finding this computer system thing?" Robert asked between mouthfuls.

"A right royal pain in the arse."

"Me too. And are you building up your 'evidence file'?"

"No. What's the point?"

"Isn't it in case we get a sudden Milcheck inspection? Oh – and for performance management. Have you had your interview yet?"

"No. Have you?"

"No. I think mine's next week."

"I don't really know what it's all about..."

"Well, if it's the same as we used to have when I was a teacher, it's all about justifying your job."

"Why on earth do we need to justify our jobs? If they don't think we're necessary, let them send us home. Then, after the French have captured the town hall and slotted that dickhead Radley, maybe they'll appreciate what we do."

"Exactly. It's my theory that the whole performance management thing was dreamt up by corporate executives in London, who suddenly realised that their staff were being paid big money for sitting at computers, sending e-mails to their friends, looking at internet porn and having long lunch-breaks. It certainly shouldn't apply to real jobs like ours."

Conrad scowled bitterly. "Then why are we having to do it? And why do all these bloody administrators get paid more than us? I reckon it's harder to be an infantry corporal on the battlefield than it is to go around with a clipboard ticking boxes to check that we're jumping through all their bloody hoops."

"So do I. But that's how it is, and it'll never change."

"Why not?"

"Because, my friend, the only people with the power to change the system are the people who benefit from it, and they're hardly going to vote themselves out of very lucrative jobs, are they?"

"Well, I think it stinks. All those desk jockeys are going to be the first against the wall when my revolution comes."

Robert grinned. "Do you remember at Crickhowell camp, before it closed, there was a range warden who printed out amusing quotes and stuck them on the wall? I always liked '*The Floggings Will Continue Until Morale Improves*', but there was another good one, which I seem to remember came from an ex-head of the KGB. It went something like: '*I can't stand this proliferation of paperwork, and it's useless to fight the forms. You have to kill the people producing them.*' Wise words, I reckon."

"Absolutely."

They sat in silence for a while, sipping beer and crunching pappadums. Then Conrad asked, "How's Spencer getting on?"

Robert shook his head despairingly.

Conrad smiled – the first time Robert had seen him do so since his return from France. "D'you think he'll make it?"

Robert shook his head again.

Conrad nodded wisely and said, "You know – that's precisely what I saw. Sometimes I can just look at a guy and I know, that guy's not gonna make it – there's no fucking way!" This was a quote from the film *Platoon*, and it delighted Robert, as it was evidence that the spirit of the old Mark Conrad had not died completely in Normandy.

"How about a bit of *Platoon*, while we're here?" Robert suggested, climbing out of his armchair and rummaging through the chaotic slag-heap of video cassettes piled beneath the television.

"Fine by me, but didn't we wear out the tape we had?"

"Oh yeah, I think we did...Spencer's got a DVD of it in his room, though."

"Then we'll watch that." Conrad rose to his feet and went upstairs. There was a crashing sound as he kicked Spencer's door open, and a few moments later he returned to the living room carrying a DVD player and disc of *Platoon*.

"The best war film ever made, in my humble opinion," Robert declared as they watched the opening credits. "It's the only one I can think of that shows soldiers being physically exhausted, rather than Hollywood actors running around with guns that never run out of ammo, like it's all a jolly game."

In some respects it was ridiculous to be watching a war film during their day's leave from the front line, but *Platoon* was reassuringly familiar, and they could empathise with the characters far more than with the people appearing in the various mediocre television programmes being broadcast that evening, such as '*Celebrity Farm*', or '*Obesity Challenge Revisited*.'

When the film ended, Conrad flicked despairingly through numerous channels until he came across a repeat of the classic documentary series *The World at War*, narrated by Sir Laurence Olivier. Tonight's programme focused on the decisive battle for Stalingrad.

"This series seems to have followed me through life," Robert remarked. "I remember watching it with my Dad when I was a kid, then again when I was a teenager, and again when I was at university. And now, again. And the funny thing is, there are twenty-six episodes but I always seem to see this same one about Stalingrad..."

Watching the black and white images of wretched-looking men struggling to stay alive in the freezing depths of the Russian winter, a thousand miles from home, Robert felt almost fortunate to be a twenty-first century soldier fighting a small-scale war with the benefit of modern clothing and medical facilities. He had no particular fondness for Hitler's Wehrmacht, but could not help feeling a certain pity for the starved and frozen figures, recorded on film being dragged from their bunkers and marched in huge columns to almost certain death in Siberia.

"What I've never been able to understand," he remarked to Conrad, "is why the ordinary German soldiers put up with it. I mean, it wasn't as if they were defending their country or anything. When the conditions got really bad and they were literally freezing to death, why didn't they just say 'sod it' and go home?"

Conrad shrugged and looked at him philosophically. "Why don't we?"

The next day, Robert drove to Susan's flat at six o'clock in the morning and intercepted her just as she arrived back from the War Office. They went straight to bed and slept in each other's arms for four blissful hours, until awoken by an alarm clock which Robert had deliberately set to enable them to have some conscious time together before he had to return to duty at midday.

"I don't want to go back there!" he moaned childishly, nuzzling into her neck. "I don't like it there! Robert doesn't want to play this game anymore – he wants to stay at home!"

"Can't you leave?" she asked. "Resign from the Army, I mean?"

"Unfortunately not. If we were allowed to do that, there'd be no-one left to fight the French. Everyone wants out – well, everyone except a few psychos who'd kill their own grandmothers given half the chance. We've been told that no-one goes back to civvy street until the war's over."

"What if you just don't go back?"

"Then I'll be classed as AWOL, and could even be shot as a deserter. Besides, there's personal honour involved – I couldn't abandon the lads and live with myself afterwards."

She tutted with frustration. "How about if you deliberately start doing everything badly, or pretend to be mad or something? Surely they'd get rid of you if you're incompetent...?"

"They'd probably promote me. Seriously, though, the Council have thought of that one as well – and got it covered. They've invented a new offence called 'malingering'. The penalty, if found guilty by court-martial, is to be sent to the French Front indefinitely. And that's a place you really don't want to be..."

"It's just so corrupt," she declared, shaking her head in despair. "In my department, everyone's watching their backs and keeping quiet about all the injustice, because they're scared about hidden cameras and microphones. You can't be too careful – two people from my department are in The Fort right now because a bug in their office recorded them making negative comments about the Council Leader. After that happened, everyone was given a copy of a leaflet called '*The Door's That Way*,' which advised us that we should resign unless we're completely committed to the Council. But everyone knows there aren't any other jobs to go to now, with the economy in such a dire state."

"Why do we all put up with it?" he declared, with a bemused frown.

"Because of the SCW. Everyone's terrified of them. There're rumours of people being bundled into white vans and never seen again, although I'm not sure I believe it. I mean, where would they go?"

"I think I know where they go," he said quietly. "They end up buried in a wood somewhere. Do you remember when we had to find suitable sites for a headquarters for Radley?"

"How could I forget!"

"Well, one of the places we identified was a wood called Cow Hey Covert, near Storeton. I took a patrol through there one night and found a pit with bodies in it."

"You mean the Council are killing people?"

"That's what I think. Anyone who threatens Radley's regime is given the smoky hole and dumped in a wood."

For a while they lay in silence, then Susan said, "What can we do? We can't just let it carry on – we've got to do something."

Robert whispered very quietly. "The best thing to do would be to slot that bastard boss of yours. With him gone, everything would return to normal, I'm sure. But killing him is going to be easier said than done…"

When Robert returned to his trench, he found Farrell and Spencer sitting at the computer, gazing excitedly at lurid images on the screen.

"What are you doing?" he asked in a voice intended to convey that he was distinctly unimpressed.

"Looking at internet porn, Corporal T," replied Farrell sheepishly, quickly exiting the forbidden website.

"So I see. Why?"

"Well, surely the only point in having a computer is to look at low-grade grot? That's what the internet was invented for, wasn't it?"

Robert sighed and stared at the machine with an expression of loathing. "Well I hope you two realise that, when my user records are checked by the Council, as they will be, I'll be officially reprimanded and fined five hundred quid. Thanks a bundle, boys."

"Sorry, boss."

Farrell looked suitably ashamed as he sloped off back to his trench, but he did not offer to pay the fine.

Later that afternoon, Robert encountered the computer man in the woods, and explained the situation to him.

"No worries," the computer man said cheerfully, clearly amused by Robert's predicament. "I'll access your files and alter the entry to a legitimate site. No-one will ever find out what you've been up to."

"What my men have been up to, you mean."

"Of course."

"Thanks."

"No worries."

A short while later, Lance-corporal Farrell came to Robert's trench looking subdued and apologetic. "Sorry about what happened earlier, Rob," he said. "I'm going to go to Blundell and the Computer Geek now and explain that it was me who logged-on to the grot site. I don't see why you should carry the can."

Robert was touched, but decided to let his second-in-command sweat for a while. "That's very noble of you, Jason, but do you realise that, not only will you have to pay the fine, but you'll also get busted down to private?"

Farrell looked horrified. "You're joking! I can't go back to being a tom!"

Robert found himself unable to continue the pretence, and started laughing. "It's alright, don't worry about it. You don't need to see anyone or pay anything – I've sorted it out. At the end of the day, it's not what you know, it's who you know."

CHAPTER 35

Inspections

I was frankly disgusted by the way in which Mr Roberts belittles and pillories health and safety regulations and the people involved in enforcing them. I should like to remind him of how fortunate he is to live in an era in which the workplace is no longer the dangerous environment it used to be. Would he like to return to the times when employees were killed or maimed in their thousands by indifferent and unaccountable employers? Of course not! The rights enjoyed by modern workers did not appear by chance, they were the result of dedicated efforts from people like the 'Donald Rawlings' character so disgracefully ridiculed in this preposterous novel.

Aldond Glinswar
H & S Review

Mr Roberts replies:
You are right, of course. My intention was not to demean or dismiss the principle of health and safety. I just think that sometimes the idea can be taken a little too far...

To the south of Storeton Wood lay Mount Wood, where the men of Nine Platoon were dug-in under the command of Lieutenant Evans and Sergeant Collins. Located amongst the trees near the top of the ridge was a huge telecommunications mast, festooned with dishes and aerials, which had been put to good use by the British as an observation tower. Young Private Festive was sent, like a bespectacled monkey, up into the metal latticework to a point just above the top of the trees, from where he had an excellent panoramic view over the entire landscape around Storeton. Festive always volunteered for the task because it made him feel important and indispensable for once in his mediocre life. He was too slow-witted to provide accurate verbal descriptions, so instead was issued with a camcorder, linked to a monitor in the company command post, and given instructions by radio about where to point it. In the absence of specific orders, Festive simply panned the lens slowly across the field of view from left to right, using what little initiative he possessed to zoom-in on anything which appeared unusual.

One day in early February, when the snow had finally melted and the woods were an ugly quagmire of churned-up mud, Sergeant Pete Collins was sorting ammunition into piles, ready for distribution to the sections, when he noticed a bright object moving in his peripheral vision. Looking up, his heart sank: it was a high-visibility waistcoat, worn by none other than Donald Rawlings of the Health and Safety Patrol, who was marching purposefully towards him carrying his trademark clipboard. Collins pretended not to have noticed the inspector, and continued with his duties right up until the moment when Rawlings stopped next to him and said briskly, "Good morning. I'd like to speak to whoever's in charge here."

"That'll be Lieutenant Evans," Collins replied, relieved that Rawlings appeared not to have recognised him. "I'll go and get him, but you'll need to take off that hard hat and fluorescent jacket before someone puts a bullet through them."

Suddenly Rawlings realised that they had met before. "Wait a minute, aren't you ...?" he began, but the sergeant had disappeared before he could finish the sentence. Collins informed Lieutenant Evans that Rawlings wanted to see him, then laid low until the Health and Safety Inspector had departed. "When I met him last year at the assault course, I didn't have live ammunition," Collins mumbled to his platoon commander. "I'm worried about what I might do to him now..."

Rawlings presented Lieutenant Evans with an official-looking document which, he explained rather pompously, gave him the authority to inspect Nine Platoon for the purpose of ensuring that all relevant health and safety policies were being adhered to. He exchanged his hard hat and high-visibility waistcoat for a combat jacket, helmet and body armour, before accompanying Evans on a tour of the lines.

At the first trench they came to, Rawlings requested that the occupants remove their boots. "I need to check that they've got their names in them," he explained. "Otherwise there's the risk of people putting each other's boots on by mistake, leading to cross-contamination with things like verucas and athlete's foot."

"Not much chance of that," Evans said with a smirk. "They've hardly taken their boots off at all in the past two months!"

Rawlings looked horrified. "Well, that's completely unacceptable, Lieutenant. They should remove them for at least six hours in every twenty-four hour period, then clean their feet and apply foot powder. You should know about basic foot hygiene, surely..."

"And what if the French suddenly launch an attack?" Evans scoffed. "What are they supposed to fight in – their socks?"

Rawlings ignored the remark. Instead, he checked to make sure that each man was wearing body armour and helmet, then stared dubiously at the construction of the battle trenches. "Hmm. These don't look like they were built by qualified engineers... You're going to have to do some more work on these access passageways – they need to be wider and more gently sloping to allow wheelchair access. It should be a one-in-twelve gradient, minimum."

Unsure as to whether the inspector's comments were to be taken seriously, Evans followed him around the platoon position, trying not to laugh when, for example, Rawlings asked why there was no soap or water available at the 'shit pit'. At one point, the lieutenant commented cynically that, if the Council was so concerned about the soldiers' health and safety, why did it not simply send them all home? Again, Rawlings chose to ignore the remark. Then, as they walked beneath the telecommunications pylon, Private Festive shouted down from above: "How much longer d'you want me up here for, Lieutenant?"

Rawlings stopped abruptly in his tracks like a predatory lizard which had just sniffed a scent. He stared accusingly at Evans. "You're not going to tell me you've sent a man up there, are you?"

"Well, not really a man..."

"That's a functioning transmitter, Lieutenant! It's giving out very high levels of radio and microwaves. God knows what they're doing to him – especially to his reproductive system!"

"But it's only Private Festive... He shouldn't be allowed to reproduce anyway. We're doing humanity and the gene pool a favour by irradiating his gonads!"

Unsurprisingly, Rawlings failed to find the remark amusing. "Get him down – immediately! Does Major Blundell know about this?"

"He suggested it."

"Then I hope you're all aware that this is such a serious breach of health and safety regulations that I may have to press for a prosecution." With a dramatic flourish, Rawlings made some more notes on his clipboard. "Right, Lieutenant, you'll be hearing from me in due course. In the meantime, you are absolutely forbidden to send anyone up that mast, do you understand? Good-day!"

The following day, Major Blundell received an e-mail from Rawlings which censured his command for 'exposing employees to unacceptable levels of unnecessary risk'. The inspector also warned that Private Festive's health would be closely monitored, and if he developed any medical problems which might be attributable to exposure to high levels of electromagnetic radiation then Blundell, Evans and possibly even Colonel Hogan would face prosecution. Ironically, the hapless Festive was killed in an ambush the following week, rendering Rawlings's threats null and void. However, Charlie Company had not seen the last of the health and safety inspector. He returned without warning one rain-drenched night to bedevil the soldiers yet again with his well-intentioned but totally inappropriate regulations.

Sergeant Paul Murphy was about to lead two sections from Eight Platoon on a fighting patrol to ambush a French working party which had been spotted digging a new position on the edge of Storeton. Blundell had suggested a fighting patrol rather than a mortar strike, because he wanted to capture enemy personnel and gauge their level of morale and health after two months besieged in the village. Speed was essential, as the French might disappear at any moment, so the patrol was assembled very quickly and given details of its mission in a hurried briefing rather than a full 'O' group. The two section commanders, corporals Taylor and Kingsley, were dashing around in the darkness trying to organise their men, when Rawlings appeared out of the gloom, accompanied by Major Blundell and the Company Sergeant-major, Dai 'Taff' Jones. The Company Commander regarded the whole situation as ridiculous, but Council policy forced him to cooperate with Rawlings and allow him to conduct his random inspection.

"Is there a possibility that these men might be firing live ammunition tonight?" Rawlings asked.

"That's the idea," Blundell replied tersely.

"Then in that case I'd like to check their hearing protection."

"Their what?"

"Their hearing protection."

"But this is a real operation! We don't wear ear defenders during combat missions!"

"And who's going to pay all the compensation claims when these men get tinnitus or lose their hearing in ten years' time? You, Major?"

So the CSM slipped and slithered back up the muddy slope to Company HQ to fetch packets of ear plugs for those soldiers who were without them, while Rawlings went from man to man, checking that they were wearing body armour and possessed first field dressings and morphine. Meanwhile, Sergeant Murphy fidgeted impatiently, eager to start his mission and aware that the window of opportunity might close at any time. His frustration increased when the observation post which had originally spotted the enemy working party reported by radio that two Frenchmen had already gone back into Storeton village.

When 'Taff' Jones had distributed the last of the earplugs, Blundell turned to the Health and Safety Inspector and said, "Well, Mr Rawlings, if you're happy now, I hope you'll allow my men to proceed with their mission."

"Of course, Major. All I need to see now is the risk assessment."

"The what?"

"The risk assessment. All potentially hazardous activities undertaken by Council employees must have a risk assessment, to comply with health and safety policy. So I need to see your risk assessment for this operation. Blundell's fingers clenched with exasperation on the plastic stock of his rifle. "It's on the computer at the CP," he lied, "so if you'd like to accompany me there we can have a look at it while these men get on with their job."

"I'm sorry, Major Blundell, but I can't let the mission proceed until I've seen the risk assessment. It'd be more than my job's worth."

Blundell finally snapped. "Mr Rawlings, I'm trying to be reasonable with you, but I'm fast losing my patience. These men are leaving now, and there's nothing you can do to stop them. It's your choice – you either come with me to the CP and we can discuss the situation in a civilized way, or I'll have the Sergeant-major here remove you from this wood at bayonet point."

So Blundell and Rawlings retired to the company command post to argue about risk assessments, while Sergeant Murphy finally led his grim-faced patrol out into the hostile night. But before the patrol reached the site of the intended ambush, the observation post reported that the French had stopped work and returned to Storeton, rendering the mission a waste of time.

Blundell was furious when he heard the news. "If that meddling fool hadn't delayed everything, we might have got them!" he remarked angrily to Lieutenant Grudge. "How on earth are we supposed to fight a war like this, Andrew?"

Robert and his fellow corporals were struggling to get to grips with the Battle Management System, until Lieutenant Grudge came to their rescue by producing some generic documents which he downloaded onto each section commander's laptop. There were pre-prepared sets of orders for standard missions such as ambushes or reconnaissance patrols, as well as risk assessments, warning orders and patrol reports. From Robert's point of view, Grudge's material was a Godsend. Instead of having to start typing from scratch, all he had to do now was select the relevant document and tailor it to his particular requirements by inserting grid references, timings and other details specific to the mission. It remained a laborious process, but the generic document templates definitely made life a lot easier for the three corporals in Eight Platoon, and Grudge's efforts were very much appreciated.

Two days after the infamous health and safety inspection which had scuppered Sergeant Murphy's ambush, Robert was sitting in his trench trying to access risk assessment forms on his computer but, for some inexplicable reason, the entire system was failing to respond. It was raining heavily and a strong, cold wind blew droplets of water onto the screen of his laptop.

The Company Sergeant-major, 'Taff' Jones, squelched down the muddy accessway and stuck his head into the confined space. "It's your lucky day, Corporal T," he said jovially in his thick Rhondda Valley accent. "Now, don't you go saying that we never give you anything... Spoil you rotten we do, you lucky lads!"

The CSM reached into a camouflaged rucksack and, for a hopeful moment, Robert thought that he was about to receive an item of mail – perhaps a letter from Susan, or his family or friends. But he sighed with disappointment when all that 'Taff' presented him with was a copy of the Council's own internal magazine, '*Excelling at Excellence*,' which was distributed free to every employee each month. Robert had glanced through previous issues of the publication and knew that it was essentially a piece of Senior Executive Committee propaganda, containing articles about wonderful new initiatives and how Council officials were meeting or exceeding their self-imposed targets. Robert scowled, and added the magazine to his store of combustible items. To him, it epitomised the organisation it glorified – outwardly wholesome and impressive, but in reality diseased and lacking in substance. The Council had become a specious edifice built upon a foundation of solid bullshit, in which highly paid executives patted themselves on the back, awarded themselves meaningless accolades, and worked tirelessly to convince the public that they were doing a fantastic job and thoroughly deserved their impressive salaries. After two months on the front line, Robert had come to the conclusion that what he hated most in life was bullshit, and the type of bullshit he despised above all others was bullshit for which someone had been handsomely paid. He turned to the CSM with a peevish expression.

"Sir, does it ever seem to you that the people who do the least often seem to be the ones who blow their own trumpets the loudest?"

"It does, Corporal Taylor. And that's why I personally always get my wife to blow my trumpet, if you get my meaning. I like the tune she plays, see." He winked lewdly.

Robert grinned. "Any idea why I can't access my files on this sodding thing?" he asked, pointing an accusing finger at the computer. "The whole system seems to have frozen."

'Taff' Jones shook his head. He was an old-style soldier, an ex-regular from the Royal Welsh Regiment, and computers had nothing to do with the Infantry as far as he was concerned. "You know what you need for that?" he said, peering at the computer screen with a puzzled frown.

"What, sir?"

"A great big fuck-off sledgehammer, right through the bastard screen. That'd sort it out!"

Robert laughed appreciatively at the CSM's irreverent humour. "Do 'Fuck Off' still make sledgehammers, sir? I thought they went out of business about the same time as Champion Sparkplugs."

The Sergeant-major nodded sadly. "They did, but you can still get hold of them – all made in China now, of course."

Suddenly, Lieutenant Grudge appeared. "Has your computer frozen, Corporal Taylor?"

"Yes, sir."

"So has everyone else's, from the OC downwards. It probably means that we're about to get a Milcheck inspection, any time now. Apparently they freeze the system two days before they arrive, so that we can't change anything retrospectively."

Robert looked dismayed. "Great. As if I haven't got enough to worry about already."

"Then don't worry about it, Corporal," Grudge said reassuringly. "They can take us as they find us. Oh – and don't forget your performance management interview on Friday, in the admin bunker. Bring your evidence file in case they want to see it..."

The Milcheck Inspector was a dour, officious man with a beard who looked frankly bizarre wearing a Kevlar vest over his smart suit. He spent two days assessing Charlie Company, and seemed more concerned about the extent to which the Army Administrative Initiative had been implemented than with how well the soldiers were actually fighting the war. In particular, he wanted to scrutinise copies of the myriad forms which the troops were now required to fill-in under recent Council directives. During his first day in the woods, the inspector's baleful eye focused upon Major Blundell and Company HQ. Then he turned his attention to the lower strata of the command structure.

Robert was checking the razor wire in front of his section's positions when the inspector accosted him and requested an interview.

"Right, Corporal Taylor," the Milcheck man declared briskly, as they sat down on camping chairs in the confines of the battle trench. "I need to check that certain systems are in place, and are being used by yourself and your men to ensure that standards are being met and you're fighting the war in accordance with Council administrative policy. So, firstly, can you please show me a copy of the risk assessment you completed for the patrol you led two days ago, on the night of the third of February..."

"Do you want to see it on the system, or a hard copy?"

The inspector thought for a moment, as if choosing an appetiser at a restaurant. "Erm, a hard copy please."

Robert dug-out his 'evidence file' from a plastic bag in his bergen and presented the inspector with a copy of the requested document.

"Hmm," the man said, perusing it with an expression of mild disapproval. "Is this a generic risk assessment, which you've adapted for the mission?"

"It is."

"Oh. We'd prefer you to produce individual ones for each mission, really. That way we know you've considered all of the issues yourself. The problem with generic documents is that people just print them off without really looking at them, which rather defeats the point of having them."

"And what exactly is the point in having them?"

The inspector looked as though he had just been slapped in the face. "Are you seriously questioning the need for mission risk assessments, Corporal Taylor?"

"I am if they don't change anything. I mean, if I assess the risk to myself and my men of going out on patrol tonight, I'd come to the conclusion that it's too dangerous and we should all stay in our trenches. But we're not allowed to stay in our trenches! So what's the point in doing a risk assessment, if we've got to go anyway? It's just yet another bureaucratic embuggerance."

The Milcheck Inspector was unimpressed. "Council policy is that a risk assessment is carried out for all potentially hazardous activities, it's as simple as that. I don't make the rules, Corporal Taylor, I just check they're being followed. Now, I'd like to see a copy of the orders you prepared for your patrol on the night of the twenty-seventh of January..."

Robert leafed through his evidence file again, but realised with dismay that the date in question had been when the Battle

Management System had first been introduced, and he had been unable to produce his orders on computer. But the inspector was not interested in excuses, and simply put a cross in one of the boxes on his form, beneath which he wrote '*Failed to provide evidence*.' Then he stood up to leave.

"Thank you for your time, Corporal Taylor. The inspection report will be posted on the Council website next week for you to look at."

Robert was incredulous. "Is that it? Don't you want to see me commanding my section, or leading a patrol or something?"

"No, I've seen enough, thank you. Besides, I don't have the military expertise to know whether you're doing that part of your job well or not. It's mainly administrative procedures I'm interested in, and whether you're keeping adequate records."

"Can I just ask why you're so obsessed with records? Surely it's what we're doing now to fight the French, or what we're going to do in the future, that's more important than what we did three weeks ago - and whether we kept a record of it...?"

The Inspector gave a condescending sigh. "Well, Corporal Taylor, look at it this way: suppose you get hit by a bus – or shall we say a mortar bomb – tomorrow, and are killed. Someone will then have to take over your section. Without adequate records how will they know what you've been doing?"

"Well, all I can say is, if I'm going to get hit by a bus or a mortar bomb tomorrow, do you honestly expect me to give a shit about how good my records are?"

"Good day, Corporal Taylor."

After the inspector had left, Robert sat down on his camping chair, feeling like a failure and cursing the whole farcical system. How could his competence be judged on the basis of two pieces of paperwork? He was furious that all of his consistent diligence and hard work seemed to have been ignored, and he had been assessed on relatively trivial criteria. To add insult to injury, he later learned that Brabander and Kingsley had been asked for copies of orders dating from after Lieutenant Grudge had provided his computer templates, and had both received glowing reports.

Robert's interview may not have done justice to his talents, but at least it had remained reasonably civil, unlike the inspector's encounter with Mark Conrad. In an outburst of bitter rage, Conrad told the man, in no uncertain terms, where he could stick his clipboard and checklist. Blundell had to write a letter of apology to Milcheck, but that did not solve the thorny problem of what to do with embittered and traumatised Corporal Conrad, whose re-integration back into the company had not been a success. Then the major had an idea which, he hoped, might resolve the issue.

On a number of occasions, French soldiers had been seen moving around Storeton, just beyond the effective range of the standard British 5.56mm calibre M16 rifles. It was almost as if the enemy was taunting the men of Charlie Company, in the same way that crows know the lethal range of a farmer's shotgun and loiter mockingly just beyond it. Blundell decided to remove Conrad from Nine Platoon and give him a new role as a sniper, armed with the company's 7.62mm Accuracy International rifle which, in trained hands, was capable of hitting targets out to eight hundred metres and beyond.

Conrad accepted the role, and was given time to zero the rifle and make himself a 'ghillie suit' by sewing strips of sandbag hessian and camouflage netting onto his spare combat jacket and trousers. Snipers usually operated with an observer as a two-man team, but Conrad insisted on working alone, and Blundell was only too happy to let him.

Conrad spent the first week in his new role operating throughout the eastern sector of the Company TAOR. During that time he fired three rounds of ammunition, and achieved one confirmed kill and a possible wounding. When Colonel Hogan proudly reported this to Radley at the twice-weekly progress meeting, the Council Leader raised his eyebrows superciliously and said, "One kill – is that all?" The colonel refrained from mentioning that, during the same period, C Company in its entirety had fired over two thousand rounds, and failed to kill anyone.

CHAPTER 36

Performance Management

Having already sullied health and safety policy, information technology and local authorities, it is perhaps unsurprising that the author turns his attention to performance management in Chapter 36. The truth is, of course, that this valuable process has streamlined British working practices and made the nation far more competitive, efficient and productive.

Gertrude Garter
Corporate Policy Journal

Mr Roberts replies:
With British manufacturing in seemingly terminal decline and the economy largely funded by unprecedented debt, the only thing we seem to be producing more of is bureaucracy. Performance management is part of that trend.

"Come in please, Corporal Taylor," called a female voice from inside the admin bunker. Robert, who had been waiting behind the concrete blast wall which protected the entrance, descended the steps and ducked through the low rectangular doorway. The interior was surprisingly plush, considering the environment outside. Most of the space contained the computers, printers and filing cabinets used by the resident 'Admin Gimp', but one corner had been arranged into an interview area with a desk and comfortable chairs. Behind the desk sat a woman in her late forties, with dyed hair and a smart trouser suit. A plaque stated her name as 'Ms Angela Cartwright'.

"Good morning," she said pleasantly, "please take a seat."

Robert placed his rifle on the floor and sat down. He glanced discretely at Ms Cartwright's computer screen in an attempt to see what personal information the Council held about him, but reflected light made it impossible to read. They shook hands.

"Right, Corporal Taylor, before we start, I'm required to inform you that this performance management interview is being recorded by webcam for security and training purposes."

"But not for reasons of totalitarian control?"

"I'm sorry?"

"Nothing, it doesn't matter."

"As I was saying, Corporal Taylor, the interview will be recorded. Are you happy with that?"

"No."

She looked a little startled, having evidently expected a different answer. "Well, it's Council policy that all performance management interviews are recorded and kept in the data archive. The interview cannot proceed if you're not prepared to cooperate and agree to it being recorded, I'm afraid."

He feigned disappointment. "Oh well, I'll be off then."

"But it's mandatory that, as a Council employee, you participate in the performance management process! You don't have a choice in the matter, Corporal Taylor!"

"Then why ask me whether I mind or not?"

She stared at him sternly in a way which made Robert wonder if she had ever been a schoolteacher, or perhaps wanted to be one. There was an awkward pause, then Ms Cartwright said, "Corporal Taylor, I *do* hope we're not going to get off to a bad start...This whole process can be easy or difficult, it's up to you...Now, will you please allow me to start the interview?"

He nodded begrudgingly.

"Thank you. I'd like to start by asking, where do you see yourself in a year's time?"

"That's an easy one. Anywhere but here, I hope!"

"I see." She sighed. "Well, if you're going to display a negative attitude towards everything I say, we might as well dispense with the pleasantries and get on with the priority task. Now, as you're no doubt aware, the performance management process is primarily for your benefit. I'm here today to try to help you make sure you get the most out of your career as a soldier, and also to confirm that you're satisfying the Council's performance criteria."

He leaned back defiantly on his chair like a naughty schoolboy. "If you don't think I'm doing a good job, sack me."

She gave him a patronising smile. "No-one's saying you're not doing a good job, Corporal Taylor. It's just that the public has a right to expect value for money from the Army. After all, soldiers' salaries are paid from Wirral Tax revenue."

"So are yours. And if you're so concerned about value for money, perhaps you should start by looking at the highest paid people in the town hall. Or do they simply dream up this bullshit without having to go through it themselves?"

"Corporal Taylor! I must warn you that your comments are completely inappropriate and unacceptable, and if you continue in this vein I shall have no choice but to report you! Whether you like it or not, performance management is here, it's here to stay, and you must comply with the process like everyone else. Do you understand?"

Robert shrugged indifferently, a gesture which Ms Cartwright evidently chose to interpret as one of compliance. "Good," she announced warily. "Now, what we have to do is agree three targets for you to meet over the coming year, in order to increase your contribution to your job, to the Council and to the War Effort. The first target has to involve Continuing Professional Development, as the Council is keen for the Army to get the *Investors in People* award."

"Can you send me on a two-year sabbatical to study erotic art at the Institute of Sex in Stockholm?"

"I shall ignore that remark. The Council has decided that all NCOs should achieve a basic health and safety qualification to ensure correct procedures are followed on the battlefield. That will be your first target."

Robert was intrigued. "So how will that work? Will it be day release or something?"

"I'm afraid not. We can't afford to lose you from the front line. You'll have to study during your periods of leave, or whenever you've got any spare time in the evenings. It's a distance learning course, but you'll have a facilitator at the college to mentor you by e-mail or phone. Oh – the cost of the course will be two hundred pounds, deducted directly from your pay."

"A bargain," he said sarcastically. "And when do I have to start?"

"It doesn't matter, anytime after this interview. The important thing is to get the qualification by the time we meet again to review your progress...You don't look happy. Surely it's to your benefit to increase your range of qualifications?"

"But I've got qualifications! I've got GCSEs, A-levels, a degree, a PGCE...I've got my NBC Instructor's qualification, Battlefield First Aid, TA Radio User, Range Management One-to-Three, Advanced Map Reading, AFV Recognition, Section Commander's Battle Course...I bet I've got more qualifications than you!"

"Corporal Taylor, this isn't helping either of us! Target one of your performance management interview will be '*To obtain a basic health and safety qualification*'. Now, target two...As you're aware, the Council wants the military to move towards paperless management, using the new Battle Management System which was introduced under the groundbreaking Army Administration Initiative."

Robert sighed impatiently. "Go on, put me out of my misery. What's my second target?"

"To show that you've embraced the new procedures and systems. We want to be confident that you're using the Battle Management hardware and software as intended, to ensure efficient use of time and resources. Proof that you're using the system effectively will be in the form of the evidence file which I know all officers and NCOs are compiling. The file should contain copies of all documents you produce during your day-to-day duties as a section commander, from full sets of orders through to rangecards and attack estimates. We'd like typed evaluations for each mission you lead or take part in – ideally mentioning how the Battle Management System contributed to the success of the operation."

"And what if it contributed to the failure of the mission?"

"We don't want to know. Positive comments only, please. So, to sum-up, target two is..." she wrote on her pad while reading the words out loud. "*To develop and demonstrate competence in the use of IBMS, and compile an evidence file as proof*."

By now, Robert had realised that it was futile to try to resist the whole process or even be openly cynical of it. So he nodded seriously and asked, "And target three?"

"Right, this has to relate to your performance on the battlefield, and the way the Council has decided to do it is to set a bodycount target for you individually, and also for your section."

"A bodycount target?"

"Yes, we've calculated what we believe to be a reasonable number of casualties for you to inflict upon the French. Our figures are based on past data from the two Gulf wars, the Falklands Conflict, and the battle of Arnhem in World War Two. Based on these previous case studies, we reckon you should be killing or seriously wounding an average of two-point-seven French soldiers a week, with your section target being twenty-one-point-six. Evidence will of course be required, in the form of authenticated photos of corpses, or items taken from them such as weapons, insignia or identification documents. And you'll achieve extra credit for achieving your bodycount target using less than your allocated allowance of ammunition..."

Robert stared at her as if she were completely mad. "But there's only an estimated hundred French troops on the Wirral!"

"And?"

"Well, there's over four hundred of us! How can we possibly each kill two enemy soldiers a week?"

Ms Cartwright sighed. "It's a pity to hear you being so *negative*. It's a target. It gives you something to aim at."

"I'd like to aim at your bloody head!" he was tempted to retort, but restrained himself. "But it's impossible! Any sane person can see it can't be achieved!"

"With that sort of negative attitude you'll certainly never achieve it, Corporal Taylor! Anyway, that's your third target: '*to meet or exceed an individual bodycount score of 2.7 and a section score of 21.6, within ammunition allocation*'. Oh – and if you don't achieve the target, your ammunition allocation will be cut."

"Jesus!" he muttered under his breath.

Ms Cartwright looked disappointed. "You seem to be harbouring a lot of very negative thoughts, Corporal Taylor, which is a pity, as it's positive workers who are going to win the war for Wirral. But I may be able to help..." She typed something on her computer keyboard and studied the screen with a satisfied expression. "Ah, yes – there's a one-day course on '*Challenging Negative Thinking*' next week at the Victoria Hotel. It's run by Jobie Silver, who's excellent – he does a lot of motivational work in industry. I'm going to put your name down for it, as part of your continuing professional development."

"Sounds good. Anything's better than a day in a cold, wet trench."

"Oh, I'm afraid you'll have to use one of your leave days – the

Council can't afford to send troops on courses by taking them off operational duties. But then, we've all got to make sacrifices if we're going to win the war!"

"But I only get to see my girlfriend for one day every two weeks!" he protested. "You can't take that away and send me on some poncy bloody workshop!"

"I've already signed you up for it – it's on the system, so it's out of my hands now. Besides, I'm sure you'll feel differently after the course – Jobie Silver's an expert on changing people's perspectives and making them see things in a more positive light...Right, Corporal Taylor, we'll meet again in six months to review your targets and set some new ones..."

The ice and snow had melted, but February remained cold, wet and bleak. Every day, British forces exchanged gunfire with their French adversaries across the valley, and Lieutenant Monty sent over his daily delivery of high explosive, but apart from occasional confused clashes between patrols at night there were few close-quarter encounters between the opposing forces. As a result, the British officers and NCOs failed in spectacular style to meet their Council-imposed bodycount targets.

One night, just as Robert had finally wriggled into his stinking sleeping bag and was drifting into an uneasy sleep, there was a burst of static in his radio headset and Private Smythe's voice came over the net, reporting from the sentry position at the edge of the wood.

"Trip flare! Trip flare! In the valley!"

Cursing, Robert stood up in his sleeping bag and peered, bleary-eyed, through the firing slit of the battle trench. In the blackness of the valley below, a single trip-flare was burning brightly, illuminating a small patch of ground around it. He was still half asleep, and struggled to think coherently. Surprisingly, the rest of the British lines remained silent, as if no-one else had seen the flare. Smythe, alarmed at having received no acknowledgement of his first message, repeated it with additional urgency. Robert responded by telling him to fire up a Schermully flare. There was a hiss as the rocket climbed swiftly into the night sky, followed by a *pop!* as the flare initiated. Robert contacted platoon HQ on the radio and got through to Lieutenant Grudge, who instructed him to keep watch but withhold fire until it could be confirmed that no 'friendly' patrols were operating in the valley. Moments later, the CSM called "Stand-to," and every soldier in the woods was roused from sleep.

Like a miniature star, the Schermully flare drifted serenely over the valley on its parachute, burning with a brilliant white light which lit-up the landscape of fields and hedges. In its harsh glare, several distant black figures could be seen, fleeing back towards Storeton. The light faded as the wind carried the flare away, so Robert told Smythe to fire up another. He was fully awake now, and invigorated with nervous excitement. Ducking down behind the parapet of the firing bay, he used his red-filtered torch to identify the location of the trip-flare and check whether it had been allocated an X-ray reference code. It had, so he relayed the information to Grudge, who could then pass it on to Lieutenant Monty if mortar fire was required.

The period immediately following the initial sighting of the trip-flare had passed very slowly, but suddenly time seemed to accelerate as multiple events occurred simultaneously. It was confirmed over the radio net that no British patrols were in the area of the flare, so all callsigns were instructed to fire at will. Meanwhile, Monty's mortar sent up some illuminating rounds, which deployed on parachutes and turned night into day. Confused birds began to sing, while in the trenches the NCO's yelled target indications to their sections, and, moments later, all sound was drowned out by the incredible din of multiple small-arms opening fire simultaneously. Streams of tracer poured down onto the unfortunate men in the valley, and shortly afterwards, high-explosive mortar bombs began to descend from the heavens and detonate with earth-shaking flashes. Robert's exhilaration turned sour as he suddenly felt sorry for the distant Frenchmen, who could no longer be seen running. Some mediocre retaliatory fire started coming back from Storeton, and a few rounds cracked harmlessly through the air above Rober's trench, but it was too feeble to cause serious alarm.

Suddenly, Lieutenant Grudge scrambled down into Robert's trench and squeezed between him and Spencer. "I can't see from my position," he explained, squinting through his binoculars. "Can't see anything moving – I reckon it's time we stopped firing. Give the order to your section – watch and shoot!"

Robert tried shouting, "Two section – STOP! Watch and shoot!" several times, but his voice was lost amidst the cacophony of gunfire. He resorted to passing the message on to Farrell by radio, and in his headset he heard other section commanders doing likewise. Gradually the firing lessened, but there were two positions in each section which were not equipped with radios, and their occupants continued firing obliviously.

"You'll have to go and tell them in person," Grudge advised, so Robert reluctantly left the safety of the trench and made a dash for the nearest neighbouring position, instinctively weaving from side to side and ducking low, despite the fact that the enemy could not see him, and therefore he had as much chance of swerving *into* a bullet's path as out of it. He followed the comms cord to the first trench and told its occupnts to cease firing, but when he was half-way to the next position there was a huge explosion out in the fields beyond the edge of the wood. Robert dropped to the ground in terror as shrapnel rained down around him and the pressure wave from the blast made his eardrums ring. Evidently the French mortar was repaying Monty's compliments. He crawled behind a tree and curled up into a ball, like a scared hedgehog, trying to make himself as small as possible. Three more bombs fell in quick succession, but to his relief, none of them exploded any closer than the first.

Eventually the firing on both sides petered out, and there was silence. Monty fired up some more illuminating rounds, but no signs of human activity could be seen in the valley below.

"I'm sure I can see at least two bodies down there," Grudge declared with satisfaction after a long squint through his binoculars. This was confirmed the following morning, when a French stretcher party bearing white flags emerged from Storeton and made its way solemnly down through the bomb craters to collect their dead. The British watched as three bodies were rolled onto makeshift stretchers and carried back up into the village.

For Charlie Company, the incident was a bureaucratic Godsend, as each soldier naturally decided that his personal marksmanship had been responsible for the French casualties. Consequently, when the end-of-week bodycount report forms were issued, every man declared that he had killed three enemy soldiers, and the company met its target for the first time. Blundell was aware of the farcical nature of the situation, but chose to ignore it. The Council, of course, was overjoyed – so overjoyed, in fact, that Paul Ryder, head of public relations, invited the *Wirral Herald* to report on the outstanding success. A few days later, when the article was published, Robert and his comrades snorted with contempt at the headline: '*Army Target-Setting Drives-Up Standards. French Suffer Unsustainable Casualties. War Over By Easter?*'

Lieutenant Andrew Grudge was not having a particularly satisfying war. No significant offensive operations had occurred at platoon level since the start of the Storeton Campaign, with the result that he had spent his time growing increasingly frustrated within the confines of Storeton Woods. Every night, the lieutenant watched enviously as patrols led by corporals, or occasionally the platoon sergeant, ventured out into no-man's land, and he longed to go with them. His role had become almost one of platoon administrator and caretaker, rather than commander, and he was becoming increasingly worried that he might never get the chance to lead his men into battle.

Dissatisfied as he was, Grudge remained determined not to let professional standards slip, and he worked tirelessly at ensuring that Eight Platoon maintained – and justified - its reputation as arguably the best unit in the entire regiment. To this end, he insisted that his three section commanders attended a lesson each week which would enhance their knowledge of tactical doctrine and give them greater awareness of 'The Bigger Picture'. Today, they were going to learn about something called a 'combat estimate', which was usually taught to junior officers but, as Grudge had a habit of reminding his corporals, "Any one of you is only two bullets away from being platoon commander..."

Robert enjoyed Grudge's lessons, as they stimulated his mind and provided welcome relief from the monotony of defensive routine in the trenches. He had found the previous week's session particularly interesting, as it had considered the merits of departing from the tradition of dividing platoons into three sections, each comprising eight men. Grudge had been impressed by an article he had read in an army journal, which advocated platoons composed of five sections, each comprising only five men, but heavily armed with belt-fed Minimi machine-guns to provide greater firepower. The lieutenant had even tried to persuade Major Blundell to allow him to experiment with such formations within Eight Platoon, but had been told firmly to "Stick with what we know, Andrew, for Christ's sake."

Robert was usually a keen and attentive student, but today he was so tired that he kept drifting momentarily into sleep. He apologised for performing poorly on Grudge's customary end of lesson test, and was about to slope off back to his trench for a cup of extra-strong tea, when Alistair Blundell appeared.

"Good afternoon, gents," the major said, addressing the three corporals. "I know you've got a lot on your plates at the moment, but I'm afraid I've got to ask you to do something else. I've just received another Council directive, and this time they want you – the section commanders – to be in charge of your own ammunition, pyrotechnics and spare parts. Effectively you'll each have a 'budget' which you'll have to manage – from now on, you'll have to predict your requirements for each week, in advance, and that'll be your allocation. You'll no longer be able to just go and get some more ammo from your platoon sergeant or the CQMS."

Brabander rolled his eyes back into his head in despair. "Just one question, sir: *why?"*

"Oh, it's all part of the latest streamlining initiative from *The Efficiency and Savings Unit.* They want you lads to be more accountable for your ammunition use. I think they're worried that we're being given more than we need..."

Robert was genuinely perplexed. "But sir, how can we predict how much ammunition we're going to need next week? Surely that depends on what the French get up to, which is completely beyond our control..."

Blundell nodded sympathetically. "I agree, Corporal Taylor, and I said exactly the same thing to the Council, but they didn't want to know. They said I was being unreasonably negative and we – the Company - should at least give the new system a try."

"Well," said Corporal Kingsley, "surely the thing to do is over-estimate, so they give us more than we need. It's better to be safe than sorry."

"They've thought of that, I'm afraid," the major replied. "The new system's going to operate on a 'use it or lose it' basis. They want you to collect and return all fired brass in special sealed bags as proof that you're using your allocation of ammo, otherwise it'll be reduced. And if you can't retrieve the empty cases for some reason, the Council will require a written report explaining the circumstances. Any questions?"

"Where do babies come from?" muttered Brabander.

Blundell ignored him. "Right then, the forms for estimating your ammo requirements can be downloaded from the network – look under '*Admin Updates*.' Oh - Corporal Taylor, the performance management wench asked me to remind you about a course you're attending tomorrow. She said you'd know what it's about, but recommended you look at the CPD section of the Council Intranet to confirm the timings and venue..."

CHAPTER 37

Blue Sky Thinking

I run management training courses designed to improve motivation within the workplace, and I object to the way they are portrayed by Mr Roberts in Chapter 37. The feedback I receive is always very positive.

Roland Backcomb
Mind Gym Training

Mr Roberts replies:
People are always positive at the end of a cushy course, when they are about to go home.

Robert Taylor left his trench at 8.30am, half an hour before the 'Challenging Negative Thinking' course was due to start at a hotel three miles away. He handed-in his rifle at the sandbag 'sangar' which guarded the entrance to the woods, and was driven to the venue in a company Land Rover, arriving with about ten minutes to spare. As a protest against having to attend the course on what should have been his day off, he had deliberately refrained from washing, shaving or changing his uniform. Surprisingly, his combat smock and trousers were not as filthy as might have been expected, considering they had not been washed for over two months; it was almost as if the clothes cleaned themselves after reaching an apogee of filthiness. The caked mud dried and flaked off, and oil and grime gradually faded, leaving the disruptive pattern material a mottled, dusty brown colour, and smelling of stale biscuits.

There were no other soldiers on the course and Robert received some strange looks from the other attendees, who were mostly dressed in suits or 'smart-casual' attire. His presence seemed to make the other delegates uneasy, perhaps because he represented a physical embodiment of the war, a conscience-jerking reminder of something unpleasant which was taking place on their own doorstep but which they preferred to ignore. He poured himself a tiny cup of tea from an urn in the corner of the function room, pocketed as many biscuits as possible (they would have considerable currency value when he returned to the trenches), and sat down. Unsurprisingly, no-one seemed eager to sit next to him.

Robert had attended similar courses during his previous life as a teacher, and knew that they were generally regarded as 'jollies' – a relatively easy and relaxed day at the employer's expense. They usually started late and finished early, and featured plenty of coffee breaks and a decent lunch. He regretted arriving early, as many of the other delegates seemed to know each other and had formed small cliques. Isolated and alone, he felt like a social leper, until a man in his mid-fifties, wearing a rather dowdy suit, shuffled along the row of chairs and asked, "Is this seat taken?"

Robert shook his head. "Help yourself."

"Brian Salter," the man said, extending a friendly hand. He seemed unconcerned by the camouflage cream and general dirt which covered Robert's hand, or by the multitude of cuts, abrasions and strips of filthy zinc oxide tape. "I work for the Regeneration Department of the Council. I oversee new projects designed to revitalise Wirral – oh, and help win the war, of course."

"Pleased to meet you. I'm Robert Taylor, and I work for the Infantry. I live in a muddy hole and try to kill people - and they try to kill me."

Salter grinned. "And do you enjoy your work, Corporal Taylor? Is it a satisfying job?"

Robert gave a cynical shrug. "It pays the bills, I suppose."

"So how come you're here at this gathering of work-dodging shirkers, who are only interested in a free lunch, courtesy of the Wirral taxpayer?"

"Well, given the title of the course, I suppose I must have some negative thoughts which need challenging."

Salter feigned shock. "Not another subversive thinker of negative thoughts! And I thought I was the only one!" He glanced around furtively. "I wonder how many people here are fellow dissidents, and how many are Council stooges...Oh – it looks like we're about to start..."

Jobie Silver was a stocky forty-five year old with dyed black hair and fashionable glasses. He sauntered smugly over to one end of the room and stopped next to a screen, onto which was projected an image of a bottle of red wine and a single empty wine glass on a silver tray. It was only when he moved past the screen to a small table in the corner that his audience realised that the bottle, glass and tray were actually in the room and were being filmed by a small camera on a flexible stalk. Reveling in his clever use of technology, Jobie Silver slowly poured some wine into the glass and carefully checked the level before holding it towards the camera, so that its image filled the screen. Robert tutted quietly to himself, unimpressed by the digital theatricals.

"Good morning, my name is Jobie Silver, and I hope you're all here to learn how to challenge negative thinking in the workplace. If that's not what you're here for, please leave now, as you're not entitled to lunch!"

There was a titter of laughter from some of the more sycophantic attendees, which evidently pleased Jobie Silver, for he smiled self-indulgently before becoming suddenly serious. "Now, I haven't poured this wine so that I can have a quick tipple while I talk to you. I've poured it for a *purpose*, to illustrate an important concept in challenging negative thinking...I want you to look at the glass, and in particular I want you to look at the amount of wine in it. Can you all do that now for me please? In case you're wondering, I've filled it exactly half-way." He paused, holding the glass as steadily as he could in front of the camera. "Okay, now, I want you all to ask yourself this question: is the glass half empty, or is it half full?"

He pointed a remote-control unit at a nearby computer and the wine glass vanished from the screen, to be replaced by the question he had just asked: *Do you see the glass as half empty or half full?*

"Now," Jobie Silver continued, "I'm going to spare you the embarrassment of telling me what you think in front of everyone, as people tend not to give the their honest answer. But I bet that, if I asked you to write it down, some of you – most of you, in fact – would say that you see the glass as half empty. I'm hoping that, by the end of this course, all of you will see it as half full."

Robert scowled and raised his hand.

"Yes," said Jobie Silver, seeming a little unsettled at having been unexpectedly asked a question at such an early stage in the proceedings. "Question from the man in green!"

"Presumably," Robert said, "what you're going to do today is get us to look at everything with air-headed optimism so we don't complain, no matter how shit things are. But surely, with your half full or half empty cliché, the way you look at it depends on the situation. I mean, if my rifle magazine only has fourteen rounds in it when it should have twenty-eight, that's bad, because I need it to be full, and if it's not full I'm entitled to be pessimistic and say it's half empty..."

Jobie Silver looked at him uncertainly. "Okay...er, I'm not sure I see your point..."

"My point is that there are times when people are perfectly entitled to be pessimistic, and no amount of philosophical corporate bullshit can change things."

Jobie Silver fidgeted uncomfortably, unable to show how irked he was without contradicting the very ethos of his training course. "An interesting point, which we can discuss over lunch. But right now we need to press on, so, without further ado, here's the programme for today..."

The morning session followed a fairly standard format involving the obligatory 'powerpoint' presentation, a 'thought shower' syndicate exercise which resulted in the creation of some spider-diagrams on large sheets of sugar paper, some role-play, and finally a group discussion. A couple of protracted coffee breaks helped soothe the painfully slow advance towards lunch.

"Okay, that's it for session one," Jobie Silver declared, rubbing his hands with satisfaction. "Are there any questions?"

"How much do you get paid for this crap?" Robert asked, eliciting a few laughs from the group.

For a moment, Jobie Silver appeared visibly riled. Then he grinned, looked Robert in the eye, and said, "Enough to drive a

Porsche. Right – we'll stop for lunch now. We'll meet back here in an hour's time, at half one..."

Robert sat with Brian Salter during lunch. As they discussed the war, the Council, and the general situation in Wirral, Salter gradually began to suspect that he was talking to Susan Fletcher's boyfriend. At one point in the conversation he tried to confirm this by casually remarking, "I hear a bit about what's happening on the front line from a girl in my office whose boyfriend is at Storeton. Maybe you know him. The girl's name is Susan Fletcher, but she's never told me her boyfriend's name..." He stared keenly at Robert, watching for a response. Robert caught his gaze and held it for a moment, then shook his head blankly and looked away. "There are a lot of guys in C Company – I don't even know all of their names, let alone their girlfriend's names..."

For a while they sat eating in silence. Then Salter said quietly, "And what do the troops think of the Council Leader? Is he popular amongst the men?"

In accordance with his personal policy of not trusting anyone from the Council, Robert's response was once again vague and evasive. He gave a non-committal shrug. "Most of us try not to think about the politics behind it all – we just concentrate on getting on with the job."

Salter nodded slowly. "That sounds like exactly the sort of answer he'd like to hear. But I'll tell you this, Corporal Taylor, not everyone in the Council is a 'yes man'. I don't approve of Council Leader Radley, or his policies, or his war. And he knows it." He laughed. "That's why he sent me on this course!"

A few minutes later they were joined by none other than Jobie Silver himself, who sat down at their table with his vegetarian lasagne and engaged them in friendly banter, probably in an attempt to win over his most troublesome cynics before the afternoon session began. He was certainly jovial, but Robert resented his presence because it reduced the dialogue to mere small-talk; before Silver's arrival, Robert had been increasingly intrigued by the subversive tone in Salter's voice, and he was left wondering where the conversation might have led had it not been interrupted.

The afternoon session began with a syndicate exercise in which groups had to create a poster displaying catchy sentences designed to foster positive attitudes within the workplace. Then the various groups had to evaluate and discuss each other's work, although Jobie Silver decreed that all feedback had to be '*positive and constructive*'. Robert found the whole laborious process tiresome and inane. While the course was certainly preferable to being on the front line, it compared most unfavourably with sleeping with Susan, which was what he should have been doing at the time.

Jobie Silver remained irritatingly ebullient throughout the afternoon, copiously praising even the most banal and mediocre efforts, and becoming very excited whenever anyone used phrases such as *'Leaving the negative comfort blanket at home with mum,'* or *'Opening the mind envelope of positive thoughts'*. At around three o'clock he announced that such good progress had been made by the group that he would be able to finish early. Robert regarded this as the most worthwhile statement that Silver had made all day.

"To finish with," Jobie Silver announced, "I'd just like to consolidate what you've achieved here today. Firstly, you've all been great and worked really hard, so give yourselves a great big pat on the back – go on, well done! Secondly, does anyone remember the phrase '*Blue Sky Thinking*' from a few years ago?" A few delegates raised their hands. "Okay, well for those of you that haven't come across it, blue sky thinking is all about positive attitudes and mindsets. It's about being the sort of person who thinks the sky will be blue tomorrow and anything is possible, rather than someone who assumes it's going to rain so doesn't make any plans. So, to finish with, I'd like all of you to think of a 'blue sky thought' to share with the rest of us, so we can all leave here in a really positive frame of mind, okay?"

Jobie Silver waited for a few minutes before choosing people to share their thoughts, and was rewarded with offerings such as '*No task is too big because you're as big as you feel*,' or '*Remember – the sun is shining somewhere*,' or '*There's no such thing as problems – only challenges and opportunities to excel*.' He deliberately left Robert until last.

"And finally, Corporal Taylor, can we have a blue sky thought from you, please?"

Robert stared at him and nodded slowly. "My blue sky thought is that hopefully I won't get my balls blown off tomorrow."

For a moment there was silence, then Jobie Silver announced, "Okay, thank you all for coming, there's a pack for each of you on the table at the back of the room, containing copies of all the powerpoint slides, a CD-Rom and one of these rather nice posters..." He unfurled a glossy picture of a chimpanzee scratching its head, beneath a caption which read: '*You are a genius. Let the world know*.'

People were standing up to leave, when suddenly Jobie Silver remembered something. "Oh – there's also a course evaluation form which I'd be most grateful if you could fill in before you leave..."

Copies of the form were passed around. While the other delegates thoughtfully pondered their response to each question, Robert simply wrote the word 'BOLLOCKS' across all of the tick boxes. His contribution to the 'Feedback and Suggestions' section of the form read: '*Scrap bullshit courses like this and spend the money on ammunition, Minimis, 203 grenade launchers and decent radio kit'*. He signed the form 'Ben Dover'.

Brian Salter glanced at what Robert had written, and smiled wryly. "I can see you're not impressed."

"Too right. Don't these people have any idea what's going on a few miles away? My friends are being killed or maimed, while people like him are being paid a lot of money to talk bollocks. Does the Council know or care about the real world?"

"Oh they know perfectly well. But it suits them not to acknowledge it."

"Why not?"

"Because then they'd be obliged to do something about it. Far easier to stick your head in the sand and pretend everything's hunky dory." Salter extended a friendly hand. "It's been interesting talking to you, Corporal Taylor. I wish you the best of luck."

"Thanks."

They shook hands, then Robert turned and hurried from the room. On the way out, Jobie Silver handed him a course pack, which moments later was dumped into the bin in the hotel foyer.

He took a taxi back to his house in Rock Ferry, where he shaved, showered and changed into clean clothes, before driving to Susan's flat and arriving just as she returned from work. They made love with desperate passion, then lay happily in bed, holding hands and enjoying the peaceful, warm intimacy of the moment.

For a while there was silence, then he said, "I met your boss today."

"Brian?"

"Yep. Seemed like a decent bloke. Is he?"

"Yes. Very much so. He's a gentleman – one of the few senior people with real integrity. In fact, it was him who put my name down for that survey we did, so I suppose we've got him to thank for us being together. Did you tell him we're an item?"

"No, I didn't know whether I could trust him or not. But I reckon somehow he knew who I was."

"He's very astute, even if he does come across as a bit of a bumbling old fool. Gerald Radley hates him. In fact, I'm amazed he's managed to keep his job as long as he has."

"Does he actually oppose Radley?"

She pondered the question. "No, not really – at least, not blatantly." She lowered her voice to a melodramatic whisper. "But I wouldn't be surprised if he's involved in something..."

In fact, Brian Salter had not formulated any coherent subversive strategy, and was finding it extremely difficult to even ascertain the political allegiance of those colleagues who might be potential dissidents. He was well acquainted with a number of senior figures whose personalities were, he believed, inconsistent with Radley's regime and whom, he was sure, must be opposed to what was going on. But to broach the issue of insurrection was extremely risky, as the Senior Executive Committee had spies everywhere and seemed able to recruit the most unlikely candidates as informers. All Council buildings were now riddled with overt and covert surveillance systems, and several employees had already been arrested for treason. In such an environment, it would be suicidal to openly enquire as to someone's loyalty to Gerald Radley...

Brian Salter's lack of tangible action contrasted markedly with the efforts of his wife, whose seditious energies placed her firmly into the category identified by Radley as 'The Intellectual Threat.' Carol Salter had formed a secret 'reading society', which met once a week at the house of a solicitor who lived in Prenton. There were presently eight members, ostensibly gathering on a Wednesday evening to discuss George Orwell's *Nineteen Eighty-Four*, but in reality working on the production of a rebellious newsletter entitled *'Speaking Out'*. If caught in possession of the prohibited material, the conspirators would face severe punishment at the hands of George Lawton and his SCW thugs. In Gerald Radley's Wirral, everyone was entitled to freedom of speech, thought and personal expression - provided, of course, that what they said, thought or expressed was in complete accordance with Council policy and ideology...

When Gerald Radley arrived at the executive suite in the town hall one morning in late February, he found Duncan Silverlock waiting for him with a grave expression on his face and a piece of paper in his hand, which he held up to show the Council Leader.

"Have you seen this, Gerald?" he asked solemnly.

"No Duncan, what is it?"

"A subversive publication. Apparently, thousands of then have been distributed across Wirral. We're studying the CCTV footage to try to identify the perpetrators."

Radley took the copy of *'Speaking Out'* and read it slowly, scowling with outrage. The document consisted of a single sheet, but its small typeface enabled a large amount of text to be fitted into the limited space available. Amongst the issues discussed were the suppression of civil liberties, abuse of human rights, the legitimacy of the SCW, vote rigging, Council corruption including nepotism and financial embezzlement, the failure of the administration to pursue non-military routes to ending the war, and, most serious of all, the very legality of Radley's authority. The polemic ended by encouraging citizens to assert their rights and collective power through displays of public defiance and acts of civil disobedience, including non-payment of Wirral tax.

Radley was appalled. "How was this distributed? Through letterboxes?"

Silverlock shook his head. "No, they were stuck onto doors, walls, shop-fronts, bins, bus shelters and what-have-you, and small piles were left on street corners and other prominent places. It was all done last night during curfew."

"What was?" asked Terence McCarthy, striding into the room and flamboyantly removing his scarf and coat. Radley passed him the piece of paper, which he read with raised eyebrows. "Hmm. This is serious."

"Too bloody right. What do *you* suggest we do about it?"

"Well, find out who's doing it and shut down their operation, obviously. What do you think?"

"I think we need robust systems in place to make sure that this sort of thing doesn't happen again!" '*Robust systems*' were one of the Council Leader's favourite panaceas – his automatic response to any problem. Precisely what a 'robust system' actually involved was never explained.

McCarthy nodded hesitantly. "I think there's more to it than that, though, Gerald..."

Radley looked at him suspiciously. "Oh yes?"

"Yes. I know you think I'm trying to appease dissidents and defeatists, but I honestly believe you've got to acknowledge public opinion. People are fed up with the war and they're questioning our motives and integrity on other issues as well. I've received several letters from people complaining that friends or relatives have disappeared, and they're accusing the Council..."

Radley shrugged dismissively. "Just fob them off with the same old standard letter. Or better still, get one of the IT boffins to set up a complaints website which we can ignore. Brilliant idea, websites – they're cheap, have no staff costs and are excellent at keeping the plebs well away from us."

"I think it's going to take more than a standard letter or a website, Gerald. Some of these people are threatening legal action against us. We've got to recognise that we're losing public support – fast. We need to win back people's confidence before they start rioting in the streets."

Predictably, Radley's response to the situation was not to moderate his stance in any way, or adopt a more sensitive leadership style which acknowledged public opinion. Instead, he decided to create yet another Quasi-Autonomous Non-Council Organisation, or 'QANCO,' known as 'The Morale Bureau.' This had as its brief: *'To raise morale by assuaging public concerns and defeating defeatism, while simultaneously improving citizen's perceptions of the Council.'* The man appointed to manage this illustrious body was none other than Radley's brother-in-law.

Radley's brother-in-law was one of those people who earned an awful lot of money for doing something vague and nebulous, which nobody else quite understood. He drove an expensive car, wore expensive suits and lived in an expensive house full of expensive possessions, yet even his close friends were unable to explain what he actually *did* to fund his extravagant lifestyle. Radley decided that the War Effort would benefit from his esoteric talents, despite his exorbitant hourly rate.

One of the Morale Bureau's initial tasks was to produce what Radley described as "A glossy recruitment brochure with an upbeat theme," which might encourage more young men to join the Army, and to this end a Council photographer was sent out to the front line to take pictures. He arrived at Robert's trench one morning, accompanied by Lance-corporal Vahed from Seven Platoon.

"Good morning, Corporal Vah," Robert said with jovial surprise, when Vahed and the photographer appeared unexpectedly behind him. "To what do we owe this unexpected pleasure? Have you had enough of Seven Platoon, and want to join the elite?"

"No, Tayl, I'm just visiting. The Council's making some kind of booklet, and this guy wants a picture of me, looking out at Storeton from inside a trench."

"Oh, I see." Robert was confused. "But that still doesn't explain why you're here..."

Vahed grinned sheepishly. "Well, apparently, it's Council policy that one out of every three photos must have someone from an ethnic minority in it. So they've asked me!"

"But you're the only one in the whole company!"

"Yep, but they're paying me fifty quid, and it's a whole lot better than going out on patrol..."

The Morale Bureau was an ephemeral entity, which existed for little more than a month before it was shut down as a cost-saving measure. During that time, Radley's brother-in-law held numerous meetings, attended numerous lunches, made numerous phone calls and spent numerous hours at his computer. Virtually nothing of actual substance emerged from these activities, apart from the recruitment brochure, a few slogans, two posters, and an incomplete propaganda DVD with accompanying leaflet. But the generous severance pay settlement received by Radley's brother-in-law when his services were no longer required enabled him to pay-off his mortgage and continue living in the manner to which he had become accustomed. Nice work, if you can get it.

CHAPTER 38

Successes and Failures

I found the story itself tolerable, but the mock criticisms at the start of each chapter are frankly tiresome and irritating. In my opinion they detract from the plot, and a perceptive editor should have advised the author to leave them out. Sorry, Mr Roberts, but you really should find more skillful and subtle ways of expressing your arrogant opinions through the medium of literature.

Geraldine Bassenthwaite
Obsessive Cookery Magazine

Mr Roberts replies:
But I liked the idea of the mock criticisms! Oh well, maybe I can persuade the publishers to produce a 'director's cut.' Alternatively, I suppose, the reader could simply ignore them and get on with the main story...

While Gerald Radley and his cronies indulged in their executive games, the miserable routine of life on the front line continued unabated for Robert Taylor and his comrades. A brief spell of milder weather in early March was swiftly followed by a return to the cold, wet and windy conditions which had prevailed throughout the winter, and the woods remained a dismal quagmire with a steadily worsening hygiene status. During one visit to the lines, Colonel Hogan was so concerned by what he saw that he declared, "I know we're dug-in for static defence, but that doesn't mean we have to re-enact the bloody Somme!" At his insistence, the soldiers set about improving their living conditions by digging drainage channels, laying planks and pallets along the muddy paths of the track plan, installing field telephones in every trench, and constructing one chemical toilet per section. The ever-present threat of mortar or sniper fire made using these toilets a potentially hazardous operation, so Robert acquired a bucket with a lid - originally intended for soaking soiled baby clothes – which enabled him and Spencer to relieve themselves within the relative safety of their trench. A layer of strong disinfectant in the bottom of the bucket ensured that the smell remained tolerable for a couple of days, before the noxious slurry had to be emptied into the 'shit pit'. The system worked well, until Spencer knocked the bucket over one night and rendered the shelter bay of the trench uninhabitable by anyone with a functioning sense of smell.

There was a noticeable reduction in the activity of the enemy mortar in Storeton, leading to speculation that the French were running low on ammunition. As if to compensate, the Council's bureaucratic bombardment of the men in the trenches reached a new intensity. Every day, the officers and NCOs of C Company were burdened with letters and e-mails instructing them to implement some new administrative procedure, complete self-evaluation forms or provide data for statistical purposes. One such 'bureaucratic embuggerance' involved the weekly submission of 'body-count forecasts', and their subsequent evaluation. At the start of each week, Robert had to estimate how many enemy personnel his section would kill or incapacitate during the following seven days. At the end of the week, he was required to confirm the actual body-count figure and explain any discrepancy between it and the original forecast. If the difference was greater than the permitted 'tolerance limit', as it invariably was, he had to provide an 'action plan' explaining how he intended to improve his section's performance in the future. Continually failing to meet Council-imposed targets was demoralising, but Robert tried not to let it bother him too much, and was certainly never tempted to emulate the corporal in Seven Platoon who regularly took photos of his own men posing as French corpses in order to meet his body-count target.

While it was theoretically possible to invent a fictitious body-count to keep the Council happy, it was much more difficult to 'massage the figures' when it came to accurately predicting ammunition expenditure, as corporals were required to return empty cartridge cases as proof of the number of rounds fired by their section each week. This frequently caused problems, such as the occasion when Robert and his section were returning from a patrol early one morning, and were suddenly ordered to provide covering fire to support the withdrawal of an OP team which had been compromised. The section fired over a hundred rounds of ammunition per man, before coming under enemy fire and hurriedly withdrawing back to the woods under cover of smoke bombs from Monty's mortar, leaving their empty cartridge cases lying in the field. Unfortunately, the incident occurred the day *after* Robert had submitted his weekly ammunition estimate, which of course had not taken into account such a large and unexpected expenditure of rounds. As a result, his section was left in the potentially dangerous position of having very little ammunition for the remainder of the week, with no possibility of obtaining more because there were no empty cases to exchange for live rounds. The Council Liaison Officer, or 'Admin Gimp', was unsympathetic to Robert's plight, but fortunately the Company Sergeant-major came to his rescue. 'Taff' Jones miraculously conjured up a large metal box of ammunition from his stores, which he discretely handed over to a very grateful Robert Taylor with the comment, "Don't say I never give you anything, Corporal Taylor...Spoil you rotten, I do...But don't make a habit of it."

Unless disrupted by French activity, the daily routine began with reveille at around 5.30am, followed by washing, shaving, weapon cleaning and checking of kit and camouflage. Then the men would be summoned for breakfast in small groups, according to a carefully devised roster which ensured that no section of line was left unmanned.

Robert looked forward to the traditional army cooked breakfast of bacon, egg, sausage, beans, tomato and fried bread, although he always declined the black pudding. Several of his civilian friends who were fitness fanatics scoffed at the Army's predilection for stodgy fried food, and made superior comments like, "The best energy foods to start the day with are things like oats and dried apricots, or nuts and raisins..." What they failed to appreciate was that oats and dried apricots did little to raise the morale of tired, cold men in unpleasant circumstances, whereas, in Robert's experience at least, a full English breakfast steaming in his mess tin was reassuring proof that life was still worth living.

On this particular morning, when it was still dark, Robert unexpectedly found himself waiting with Farrell in the 'tactical feeding' queue. This was most unsatisfactory, as it meant that Two Section's stretch of front line was without an NCO.

"I told you to go first," Robert said.

"I thought *you* were going first," Farrell replied defensively.

Robert shrugged; arguing the point would achieve nothing. "Never mind. We'll get our scoff and get back to the position as quick as we can, before anyone notices. It'll be stand-to soon, anyway..."

Farrell's seemingly inexhaustible repertoire of movie quotes included an excellent impersonation of the Colonel Kilgore character from the film *Apocalypse Now*, and he entertained Robert with it as they crouched in the darkness with their mess tins at the ready, waiting to be fed. "I love the small of bacon in the morning. That smell – that fried fat smell...It smells like...*breakfast!* Some day this war's gonna end..."

They had just received their breakfast and filled their mugs with tea from the Norwegian urn, when Farrell's girlfriend Kirsty appeared from around the corner of the Traveller's Rest pub and hurried over to him, bearing a carrier bag of provisions. Visible only in silhouette, she waved flirtatiously in response to admiring wolf whistles from several soldiers who recognised her, then wrapped her arms around Farrell and kissed him passionately in a bizarre chemical exchange of lipstick and camouflage cream. He slid his hands up inside her duvet jacket, knowing that she would have deliberately left her bra off to please him. A few moments later she was gone, leaving a delighted Farrell with his bag of goodies, which included sweets, biscuits, batteries, razor blades, soap, a war novel and several 'top shelf' magazines.

Unbeknown to the soldiers, Gerald Radley had been watching proceedings with incredulity from the ground floor of the pub. He had expressed a desire "To see the men doing their normal duties, without changing anything because they know I'm watching," and had even borrowed a night-sight so as to be able to secretly observe the soldiers in darkness. This was the second time he had witnessed a rendezvous between Farrell and Kirsty. He was not impressed, and went straight to Alistair Blundell to demand an explanation.

"Oh, a few of the lads' wives or girlfriends - or even mums - come up and give them things when they get their meals," the major told him casually.

"I've gathered that. It happened the last time I was here, you may remember. On that occasion I assumed it was a one-off incident, but now I get the impression it's a regular event. Is it?"

"Fairly regular."

"It seems most unprofessional to me... Are you happy about it, Alistair?"

"I turn a blind eye, to be honest. Like the Colonel said last time, I don't really see any harm in it, provided it doesn't interfere with operational matters and there's no drugs or alcohol involved. Or cigarettes, now they've been banned by the health and safety people. But apart from that, I don't have a problem with it. It's good for morale, apart from anything else."

"Well, I think it's downright inappropriate! We're paying these men to fight a war, not grab a quick snog and a grope with their girlfriends whenever they can. Maybe that's why so little progress is being made here. It's got to stop – see to it, Major Blundell!"

Blundell sighed. "Yes, Council Leader Radley..."

Sometimes it seemed that the main priority of those in power was to snuff-out happiness wherever they found it, as part of some perverse grand design which would only be complete when everyone was thoroughly miserable.

Robert's confidence received a major dent in mid-March, when he was tasked with leading a mission to ambush French units operating in the vicinity of Storeton. There was a surprisingly dense network of hedgerows, tracks, ditches and streams to the west of the village, and it was through this natural labyrinth that enemy patrols were believed to be bringing ammunition and other supplies to Maurice's beleaguered force. The British had no specific intelligence relating to when or where these re-supply operations might take place, so Robert's ambush mission was a random gesture relying on pure luck. Every night, each of C Company's three platoons was required to set-up an ambush on a possible French supply route, in the hope that, against the odds, an enemy patrol might blunder into their trap. To date, only Seven Platoon had struck lucky, killing two Frenchmen near Thingwall, whose bergens were found to be full of small-arms ammunition.

"I can't overstate the importance of these operations," Blundell frequently told his section commanders before they set out into the night. "As you know, we're fighting a war of attrition here, grinding the French down, and at some point soon they're going to reach a critical situation where they simply run out of men or ammunition. These ambushes offer a chance to strike a decisive blow against the enemy and end his ability to continue waging war effectively from Storeton."

Robert was unhappy about this particular mission from the outset. Like an omen of things to come, the Battle Management System computer 'crashed' just as he was about to print the set of orders he had produced, forcing him to waste valuable time re-writing them by hand. As a consequence, he was left with insufficient time to properly deliver the orders and carry-out rehearsals and kit checks before setting out on the operation, which was in two phases. The first phase involved a daylight reconnaissance patrol to select a suitable ambush site; the second phase – the ambush itself – would take place after dark.

The computer problems had left Robert feeling flustered, frustrated and generally in the wrong frame of mind to lead a successful operation. To make matters worse, his section was supplemented by a fireteam from Nine Platoon, under the command of a surly Lance-corporal called Samson, whom Robert had never got on with. The four attached soldiers resented being shanghaied for what they regarded as an Eight Platoon task, and did their best to be querulous and uncooperative.

Late in the afternoon, the twelve-man patrol left British lines through the Dark Side of the Moon sentry position and proceeded cautiously in a wide arc to the north of Storeton. As they patrolled through the network of paths and hedges, Robert studied the surroundings carefully, trying to identify a suitable site for the ambush that night. His appraisal had to be conducted discretely, without stopping, in case the French were watching and realised what he was up to, but by the end of the patrol he believed he had found somewhere which suited his purpose: a small copse of trees, in a sloping field overlooking one of the tracks which the French might conceivably use.

By the time the patrol returned to British lines it was dark. Blundell wanted the ambush set by ten o'clock that evening, so preparations for phase two of the mission had to begin immediately. Robert delegated the task of model-building to Farrell, while he considered how best to deploy the different elements of the ambush. In the centre of the copse would go the six-man 'killer group', commanded by himself, which would deliver the majority of the firepower. Placed about thirty metres to either side of this would be the two-man 'cut-offs', commanded by Farrell on the left and Samson on the right. The role of the cut-offs was to provide early warning of approaching enemy, and prevent them escaping from the killing area once the ambush had been sprung. Finally, behind the killer group would go the two-man rear protection party, with a senior private in charge.

There was so much to prepare in such a short period of time that Robert had to miss the evening meal, although he snatched a few mouthfuls of cold boil-in-the-bag chicken pasta while writing his orders. The patrol set out on schedule at eight-thirty, but he still felt rushed and unprepared for the task ahead. Nevertheless, everything went smoothly and they reached the final rendezvous point in good time. Robert checked that he had radio contact with platoon HQ, and conducted a cautionary reconnaissance of the copse before placing his men in their positions, starting with the cut-offs. The soldiers of the killer group sat close together and checked that their weapons were set correctly: LSWs on fully automatic, and M16 rifles on single shot, so that they would not all run out of ammunition simultaneously. As the cut-offs were likely to be the first to spot approaching enemy, it was essential that they were able to pass information to the killer group without alerting their intended victims. This was to be achieved using coded bursts of radio static - three from Farrell and five from Samson – which would alert Robert to enemy troops approaching along the track from the left or right. As a back-up, two long pieces of comms cord with sticks tied to the ends were stretched from the cut-offs to the killer group, to be tugged repeatedly if the radios failed to work.

Robert peered at his dimly lit watch screen and was surprised to find that time had passed very quickly and it was now after ten o'clock. In his mind he hastily ticked-off items from a mental checklist: radio communications checked; HQ informed of location status; rear protection party in place, with Schermully rocket flares for illumination if required; cut-offs in position, with manually-operated trip flares and claymore mines; killer group arranged, with alternate rifles and LSWs; all soldiers aware of their role in the operation and briefed on the procedure to open fire, cease-fire, watch-and-shoot, send out searchers, and withdraw to the final rendezvous or emergency rendezvous. Satisfied that everything was in order, he was about to declare 'ambush set' – after which no-one was allowed to move – when suddenly there was a rustling in the undergrowth to his right and a shadowy figure appeared.

"Who's that?" he hissed angrily.

"Samson. My CWS isn't working – I think the batteries are dead. I can't see jack shit."

Robert sighed with exasperation. "Use the spares."

"There aren't any in the bag. Someone must've nicked them."

"Shit."

As an NCO, Samson should have made sure that his night-sight was working properly and had spare batteries before the patrol set out, but the ultimate responsibility lay with Robert, and due to the rushed nature of the preparations he had forgotten to check. He cursed under his breath and decided to take the batteries out of his own CWS sight and give them to Samson, as it was more important that the cut-offs had effective night vision than the killer group. Samson sloped off into the darkness, and shortly afterwards Robert declared "Ambush set."

The twelve men sat in the dark, damp copse for five hours, struggling desperately to stay awake, and fidgeting insanely as they fought to resist the urge to stand up and move their limbs to relieve the discomfort and boredom. It became steadily darker as the night progressed and clouds snuffed-out the moon, and Robert felt a growing sense of unease about how little he could actually see. In daylight, the path had been clearly visible from the copse, but now it was impossible to distinguish with the naked eye in the almost impenetrable blackness. He hoped that the cut-offs had better visibility, otherwise the entire operation was likely to be a complete waste of time.

At just after three o'clock in the morning, Robert heard the crackle of static in his headphones, although the sound did not seem to consist of clear, distinct bursts. Shivering with nervous excitement, he held his breath and waited for a repeat signal, or some confirmatory tugs on the comms cord. When none came, he decided that the headphone static must have been a spurious signal, most probably caused by Farrell or Samson leaning on their radio prestle switch by accident. Nevertheless, he peered anxiously into the night, looking for possible enemy troops, but seeing nothing. He exhaled slowly and began to relax. Then, suddenly, there came three clear bursts of static in his headphones, accompanied by unmistakable tugging on the comms cord leading from Farrell's cut-off position. But still Robert could see nothing...What really concerned him was that the initial burst of static might have been a deliberate signal from Samson, to warn him that enemy troops were approaching from the right. If that were so, Farrell's three bursts of static would mean that the enemy had passed through the ambush site from right to left, in which case it was now too late to open fire. If, however, the initial static had been spurious, it would mean that the enemy were moving from left to right and must currently be in the killing area directly ahead. Robert began to panic, trying to decide whether or not to give the order to open fire. His lack of night vision had put him in an impossible situation, rendering him effectively blind, and completely dependent upon the eyes of the cut-offs. If the killer group opened fire now, they might possibly succeed in wiping-out a French patrol; on the other hand, if he initiated the ambush too early or too late, the majority of enemy troops would be out of the main killing area and would probably survive to counter-attack, 'rolling-up' the ambush from its vulnerable flank. Which would, of course, be disastrous.

Swearing silently to himself, Robert waited, hoping to receive the five bursts of static from Samson which would confirm that the enemy was now between the two cut-offs. But no such signal came, and he began to suspect that the initial burst of garbled static had been genuine, and his mission had failed. He waited five minutes, before deciding to 'collapse' the ambush and lead his despondent patrol back towards Storeton Woods.

During the mission de-brief it emerged that the initial burst of static had indeed been spurious, although no-one owned up to it. Farrell had spotted a four-man patrol moving in the direction of Storeton, from left to right as expected, and had alerted Robert with three bursts of static. Samson, for some reason, had not seen the enemy, and had sent no signal as the French soldiers passed across his field of view.

"Did you fall asleep?" Robert asked suspiciously.

"No I fucking didn't!" snarled Samson defensively. "I couldn't see anything from that cut-off position. It was so bloody dark and there were bushes in the way - you should've put me nearer the bastard path, Corporal."

Everyone was extremely tired and disappointed, and apportioning blame was not going to rectify the situation. But it had been Robert's mission, and it was he who had to report to Major Blundell, with 'his tail between his legs', and explain that a valuable opportunity to strike a potentially decisive blow against the French had been lost, for the sake of two AA batteries.

To rub salt into Robert's wounded pride, Corporal Karl Brabander achieved a notable success only two days later, which placed him firmly at the top of Blundell's list of favourites.

Brabander was leading a four-man reconnaissance patrol at night along the bridleway known as 'The Roman Road', which was bordered on either side by barbed wire fences, incomplete hedges and stunted trees. Suddenly, the south-westerly wind carried to Brabander's ears a sound which he immediately recognised from countless training exercises in the Brecon Beacons: the unmistakable metallic *twang* of men climbing over a post-and-wire fence.

Brabander immediately deployed his men in a 'snap ambush' on either side of the path, using the hedges for concealment. From the darkness ahead materialised a ghostly French patrol, advancing slowly in staggered file from the direction of Storeton village. Brabander waited until the silhouette of the lead man was only about ten metres away before opening fire. The three other British soldiers followed suit, and the night erupted into sound and light as the surviving Frenchmen dived for cover and returned fire in blind panic. There were frantic shouts in French, and a smoke grenade fizzed and began spewing white vapour, through which bullets cracked in opposite directions.

Leaving his three comrades to exchange gunfire with the enemy in the narrow confines of the bridleway, Brabander squirmed through a gap in the hedge and crawled out into the furrowed field beyond. In a rash yet commendable display of heroics, he ran parallel to the Roman Road until he was level with the French soldiers on the other side of the hedge, then pulled the pin from a grenade and lobbed it onto the bridleway. After the grenade exploded, he fired repeated bursts through the hedge, hearing shouts and screams on the other side as the French broke contact and fell back towards Storeton in disarray. Two of their soldiers lay dead on the bridleway and a third man, seriously injured, crawled into an overgrown ditch and died several hours later. His body was overlooked by the French stretcher party which ventured out at daybreak under the protection of a white flag, and became one of several grisly discoveries awaiting dog walkers and ramblers in the months and years following the end of the war.

CHAPTER 39

The Dark Side of the Moon

A bored holidaymaker facing a long wait at an airport could, I suppose, do worse than take along this book to pass the time.

Dwight Schaltz
Paperback Review

Mr Roberts replies:
I shaltz take that as a compliment, Mr Schaltz!

The 'Dark Side of the Moon' sentry position was undoubtedly the least popular trench in the entire front line, yet it was arguably the most important. Concealed in a hedgerow on the edge of a huge field of ploughed earth, the remote outpost represented the farthest extremity of Eight Platoon's Tactical Area of Responsibility, and as such played a vital role in controlling the movement of all troops into and out of the British lines. Out of sight on the opposite side of the field lay an equivalent position belonging to Seven Platoon, known as 'The Black Hole of Calcutta'. The expanse of earth which lay between the two outposts was so wide that it constituted a weak point in the British defensive perimeter. Charlie Company had too few men to close the gap with troops on the ground, so the only alternative was to defend it with fire, and to this end both sentry positions were equipped with a general purpose machine-gun, a generous supply of flares and a radio with which to call-in mortar fire if necessary. Of greatest importance, of course, was that both trenches were manned by soldiers who were alert and competent.

Originally, The Dark Side of the Moon had come under Corporal Brabander's jurisdiction, and it had been Three Section's responsibility to man it, but after a while his soldiers began to complain that this was unfair. Why, they argued, did they always have to bear the stressful burden of manning the most dangerous trench in the entire perimeter, while other sections enjoyed a cushy time within the relative safety of the woods? In response to this complaint, Lieutenant Grudge instituted a new system, whereby every member of Eight Platoon had to perform a three-hour period of sentry duty in the dreaded outpost. One night, as Robert led his weary men back towards The Dark Side of the Moon after yet another uneventful patrol, he knew that the crucial job of commanding the notorious sentry position lay in the less than capable hands of Ben Spencer.

Robert radioed platoon HQ to inform them that he was about to re-enter the lines, but could not make contact with Spencer in the sentry post. This was worrying, as it could potentially result in him and his men being fired upon by their own side. Grudge advised him to stay where he was, while Brabander crawled out to the Dark Side of the Moon and alerted the sentries, who presumably had radio problems.

Robert's patrol lay impatiently in the field for several minutes, until Brabander's voice crackled over the net: "*Hello Two-Two Charlie, this is Two-Three Charlie, you can come in now, over.*"

"Two-Two Charlie, roger, out."

Robert's team negotiated their way through the coils of wire and the cunningly hidden trip-flares, but when they reached the sentry position they found Brabander in a furious mood. Next to him, shamefaced in the darkness and stripped of their rifles and equipment, stood Ben Spencer and his companion in the trench that night, young Private Mohr.

"Want to know why they didn't answer you over the net?" Brabander said, seething with rage. "They fell asleep. The most important position in the entire fucking line and they fell asleep on stag!"

The two disgraced soldiers were marched back to the woods to be severely reprimanded, first by their platoon commander, then by the CSM, and finally by Major Blundell himself. Suitably chastised, they were escorted under guard to the sangar at the entrance to the woods to await transfer to the military wing of Fort Perch Rock prison. Two weeks later, following court-martial, they were both dishonourably discharged from the Army as 'unfit for service', and spent the rest of the war making ammunition in the company of the borough's under-age mothers, which suited Spencer just fine.

The severity of Spencer's offence became all too apparent two days later, when slovenly Private Harding and inexperienced Private Cringle from One Section were sent to man the Dark Side of the Moon. Despite Lieutenant Grudge emphasising in no uncertain terms how important it was to remain awake and alert at all times, Harding was determined to be comfortable during his three-hour shift.

"Shove yer bivvi-bag in yer daysacks, Cringle boy," he told his impressionable companion, who assumed that Harding, being a veteran from pre-war days, must know what he was talking about. "Oh – and take some warm kit. I've got one of those little 'softie' sleeping bags to keep me nice and toasty. Look – fits in a daysack, so no-one can see it. You'll learn these tricks of the trade when you've been in a while..."

They made their way clumsily through Three Section's position and crawled along the umbilical-like hedgerow to reach the Dark Side of the Moon trench. The soldiers they were relieving regarded them resentfully when they arrived.

"Where the hell have you been?" asked Lance-corporal Dwyer angrily. "It's quarter past one!"

"We got a little delayed, Corporal..."

Dwyer briefed Harding on details such as of the arcs of fire, password, features on the range-card, friendly forces operating in the area that night, and the procedure for raising the alarm. Then he shouldered his daysacks and stood up to leave.

"Right, Harding, it's all yours. There're two patrols out at the moment – Brabander's and Kingsley's – so watch out for them coming back in. And remember what happened to those two dickheads the other night – stay switched-on!"

Within minutes of Dwyer's departure, Harding was sitting in his sleeping bag, smoking a cigarette and chuckling happily to himself. "Well, Cringle, this has got to be better than being in the woods with Tosser Taylor and General Grudge, 'asn't it? See what I told ya – there's ways of making yer stint on stag not so bad. Get yer warm kit on and get in yer bivvi-bag, and you can 'ave a coffee from me flask."

"But I was told we should never get into our doss bags on stag…" Cringle said uneasily.

"Bugger that for a game of soldiers," snorted Harding dismissively. "That's the sort of thing that the REMFs tell you - when they don't have to do stag themselves. Now get in yer bivvi-bag before you bastard freeze – we've got three hours to go..."

Cringle did as he was told. The two men made themselves warm and comfortable, and before long they were both asleep.

In order to ensure that the disgraceful incident involving Spencer and Mohr was not repeated, Lieutenant Grudge had decided that Platoon HQ would conduct a radio check with the Dark Side of the Moon every half-hour throughout the night, to confirm that the sentries were awake and vigilant. Unfortunately, a mere five minutes before this precautionary procedure was due to take place, a French patrol came visiting. Slipping unnoticed out from Storeton like predatory ghosts, the enemy soldiers crept silently along the hedgerow until they heard snoring coming from the British outpost…

When Grudge's radio check went unanswered, a quick reaction force led by Sergeant Murphy was sent out to investigate. They found Harding and Cringle still in their bivvi-bags, with multiple bayonet wounds and their throats cut. The GPMG, rifles and all items of value including the radio and BATCO wallet were gone.

Robert had never rated Harding as a soldier, but he had known him for a long time, and was saddened by the news of his death. Farrell, on the other hand, seemed to feel that the slovenly soldier had got what he deserved. He shrugged, and uttered a quote from *Zulu* in his best upper-class Lieutenant Bromhead voice: "I rather fancy he's nobody's son and heir now…"

"That's all very well," Robert replied soberly, "but the problem is, now we've got a section of six men, so the glass is definitely half empty. Any suggestions?"

"Put helmets on turnips and prop them up in the trenches!" Farrell joked. "Oh – Corporal T – what did Bromhead say when he found that Chard had taken his Japanese money?"

Robert thought for a moment. "Who said you could use my yen?"

"Bastard!"

In addition to his highly-publicised visits to the soldiers on the front line, Gerald Radley also toured his own Council departments periodically to "keep in touch with the staff". His powers of perception had by now deteriorated to such an extent that he genuinely believed that such visits raised morale, when in reality they achieved the opposite.

Today it was the turn of Brian Salter's Regeneration Department to be graced by the Council Leader's presence. Radley arrived slightly late as always, accompanied by Sean Simms and a pair of SCW 'heavies' whose job it was to keep the two young leopards, Nero and Caligula, under control. The magnificent animals strained at their leashes as they emerged from the lift, their muscles and sinews rippling under their beautifully spotted pelts. Staff at the entrance to the open plan office regarded the leopards with nervous admiration, and pretended to go about their usual business while watching the animals apprehensively from the corner of their eye.

The Council Leader greeted Salter with barely concealed indifference, and showed little interest in the department, until he reached Susan Fletcher's desk. She was busy producing computer-generated concept diagrams to illustrate how a greatly enlarged town hall could be integrated into the surrounding landscape, and looked up in surprise when Radley suddenly appeared and stood next to her.

"You look busy," he said, placing an unwelcome hand on her shoulder.

"I am," she replied, flinching as the two leopards lurched towards and were dragged back by their handlers. A stilted, perfunctory conversation followed for a few minutes, before Radley and Salter moved on.

"Isn't she great?" Radley said admiringly, when they were out of earshot. "She helps out in the War Office, as you know. I just can't believe she's single…"

Salter was about to reply that he was fairly certain that Susan was romantically involved with a soldier, but thought better of it. If Radley was unaware of the fact, it had to be because she had decided not to tell him. Trivial as it seemed, Salter felt a tingle of optimistic excitement at the thought of Susan deliberately withholding information from the most powerful man in Wirral. If she were being evasive or deceptive, then perhaps others were too, and from such seemingly insignificant origins a conspiracy might grow, if skilfully cultivated…

In early April, Alistair Blundell received an e-mail from Duncan Silverlock informing him that C Company's poor body-count scores made it a 'cause for concern', and the unit was consequently being issued with an official 'notice to improve'. As part of this process, a Milcheck inspector would be permanently stationed in the admin bunker to monitor performance and progress, until further notice. Silverlock stressed that the inspector's role was purely positive, and that the company should make him welcome and cooperate fully with his requests for data.

The soldiers resented the bureaucrat's prying presence, and his unannounced inquisitions made their jobs that much harder. Nevertheless, military operations continued apace and, one night, men from Seven Platoon successfully ambushed a French patrol which was escorting a quad-bike and trailer through the British perimeter to resupply Storeton. There was a fierce firefight, during which the vehicle and trailer caught fire, and moments later there was an explosion of such incredible force that every member of the French patrol was killed instantly, and several British soldiers were injured; evidently the trailer had been loaded with mortar bombs. A mile away in Storeton, Lieutenant Maurice heard the explosion and felt the shock-wave shake the floorboards of the farmhouse which he had fortified into his headquarters. He sighed with despair. His mortar team was down to its last twenty bombs, and without the desperately needed replacements, his ability to continue waging war was fast diminishing.

The following day, a fighting patrol from Nine Platoon captured two enemy soldiers who were setting rabbit snares along a hedgerow. The pair surrendered willingly, and seemed pleased to have been captured. During interrogation it became apparent that they were severely malnourished and their morale had sunk to breaking point, which was precisely the sort of information that Colonel Hogan had been waiting for. He decided that the time had finally come to comply with Gerald Radley's repeated requests, and bring the Storeton Campaign to a close.

CHAPTER 40

Dissent in the Ranks

I cannot understand why this author seems so vehemently opposed to public administrators. I work very hard at my job – harder, I suspect, than the majority of people in the private sector.

Henrietta Jamscone
Local authority middle manager

Mr Roberts replies:
I'm not suggesting that you don't work hard at what you do. I'm suggesting that not everything you do is entirely necessary. I'd like to see all jobs in Britain reclassified on the basis of this question: 'If you didn't turn up for work tomorrow, how long would it be before anyone noticed?' And I suspect that, according to that criterion, many of the humblest workers would emerge as those most crucial to society, while some of the highest paid pen-pushers would be exposed as largely superfluous.

Gerald Radley arrived in the executive suit carrying a gun case and wearing an expression of consummate delight. He waited for Maurine, his secretary, to make him a cup of coffee, before sitting down at the conference table with Duncan Silverlock and Terence McCarthy to discuss the day's business.

"You look very cheerful this morning, Gerald," observed McCarthy, intrigued.

"I am, Terence, I really am – for two reasons. Firstly, this arrived this morning..."

He opened the gun case and took out a brand new Purdey shotgun. "Look at that. Isn't she a beauty? Without doubt the finest guns in the world, and uniquely English. Here, Terence, I know you appreciate such things, even if Duncan doesn't..."

McCarthy put the weapon to his shoulder and looked along the gleaming barrel, admiring the beautiful bluing and fine engraving. "I thought they'd refused to sell to you," he remarked. "Weren't they worried that you might bring their distinguished name into disrepute or something?"

Radley looked perturbed. "I don't really care about their reasons, but yes, they did refuse to sell directly to me. I got my cousin in Cheshire to buy it on my behalf."

McCarthy made suitably appreciative noises before handing the gun back to Radley. "Are you really going to mutilate such a wonderful piece of craftsmanship by having the barrel and stock sawn off? There should be a law against that!"

"There was, but I rescinded it – just for me! And yes, I am going to have it cut shorter. Duncan, can I charge the cost of the modification work to the expense account, like we did for the gun itself? After all, it is essential for my work..."

"Oh absolutely, Gerald. If you're going to hide the purchase cost under the expenses umbrella you might as well hide the modification costs there as well, which presumably will be small by comparison."

"Anyway," said McCarthy, "What's the other reason for your ebullient mood this morning, Gerald? Has Lebovic sued for peace or something?"

"Oh no, it's far better than that. I just received a phone call from Colonel Hogan, to say that preparations are under way to surgically remove the Storeton excrescence in the very near future." He rubbed his hands with relish. "It's going to be the equivalent of a modern day Dien Bien Phu!" Radley had been studying military history, and now fancied himself as a qualified tactician. Indeed, so convinced was he of his own expertise in matters of military strategy and tactics that he was considering appointing himself as senior army commander, in place of Hogan. But first he wanted the Storeton issue resolved, as swiftly as possible.

"I really do think that this is a turning point," he declared confidently. "This will be our El Alamein. Once Storeton has been liberated, we can all relax a little and savour our achievements. Overall, I think we've made excellent progress. I'm especially pleased with the Army Administrative Initiative. It's put in place a really robust administrative system which focuses on individual standards and accountability, and I'm confident it'll start delivering improved performance very soon. What I'd like to do now is proceed with Phase Two of the process."

McCarthy looked startled. "There's more?"

"Oh yes. With the A.A.I. in place, the Army should qualify for the '*Investors in People*' award, and I'd also like to see it get the latest ISO accreditation. There's a Swiss-based firm in Ellesmere Port that deals with that sort of thing..."

Silverlock fumbled with his fingers and looked uncomfortable. "But Gerald, they charge a fortune...And our financial situation is something we need to discuss this morning as a matter of urgency..."

Radley waved his hand dismissively. "Oh, just sell some more land, raise parking fees again and siphon-off some more money from unnecessary traffic management schemes. They've always been good for raising some extra cash in the past."

McCarthy and Silverlock exchanged glances, then the chief executive said quietly, "I'm afraid it's not as simple as that, Gerald. You must appreciate the seriousness of the situation. I really do believe we're approaching crisis point."

"What do you mean?"

"The borough's on the verge of bancrupcy," stated Silverlock, with simple honesty.

"Then you've let me down, Duncan! Come on, there must be ways of obtaining the income we need to implement our latest policies and move Wirral forward. How about the financial reserves and the staff pension funds?"

"Already used and empty, I'm afraid."

"Well, there must be some public assets left which we can sell, like parks or libraries – schools, even…"

Silverlock shook his head sadly. "I can't think of any, Gerald. And in any case, people aren't exactly queuing up to buy land or property here, what with the war and everything."

"Then you must use your financial acumen to think of new ideas for revenue generation, like you've always done in the past. Come on, Duncan, can't you think of anything?"

"The environment is one possibility I've considered…"

Radley looked at him as if he were mad. "Environment-schmenvironment! You know I don't give a damn about the environment – unless I'm being interviewed, that is! How can limp-wristed green issues make us any money?"

"Well, I thought perhaps we could audit every household and then tax them according to how green they are. You know – if their boiler's too old or their loft insulation isn't thick enough, we could tax them at a higher rate, something like that. The audit could either be done by Council staff, or else I thought we could set up or own private company to do it, which might be a nice little earner for us in the future."

Radley nodded in approval. "I like it! There you are, you see – already we're solving the crisis. Anything else?"

"How about charging for services like bin collection?"

Radley shrugged. "Why not?"

"I'll tell you why not," interjected McCarthy with a frown of disapproval. "I know many people who regard waste collection as the only worthwhile service they receive from the Council. Make them pay extra for it and they're going to start wanting to know what they pay their Wirral tax for..."

Radley looked incredulous. "But surely it's obvious what they pay it for! They're paying for the administrative skills to *oversee* the services, rather than the actual services themselves. Surely even the thickest plebs can understand that!"

McCarthy shook his head solemnly. "Gerald, you can't go on like this – with this sort of attitude. When I said we're approaching crisis point, I wasn't just referring to the economy…"

"Oh yes?" Radley stared at him reproachfully. The Council Leader had aged a lot in recent months, and had developed a nervous tic under one eye, which gave him a sinister, almost psychotic appearance. "This isn't going to be another one of your namby-pamby 'We've got to do what the people want' speeches is it, Terence? – I've just about had enough of those, if you don't mind."

McCarthy sighed. "Okay then, Gerald, if you don't want my advice

I'll simply act as messenger. People are unhappy, and some are trying to take legal action against you. Yesterday I received a solicitor's letter on behalf of a group of women who are all wives, mothers or sisters of soldiers at the front – apparently they've formed some sort of pressure group. And they want to prosecute you personally for taking Wirral to war without the consent of the people…"

"The bloody people voted for me! How many times do I have to remind you of that?"

"They voted for partial autonomy, not war. People feel that you – we, the Council - haven't done enough to end the conflict through diplomatic channels."

Radley snorted dismissively. "Well, let them try taking me to court. They'll receive the same treatment as those two fools last month!" He was referring to a pair of brothers, who had tried – and failed – to prosecute him and George Lawton for the death of their father. Witnesses had seen the man – a known anti-Council activist – being dragged into an un-marked white van, which sped away towards SCW headquarters; three days later, a press release stated that he had resisted arrest and died in custody. The brothers had privately employed a local law firm to gather evidence against Radley and his regime, but at the last minute the case collapsed when the solicitors suddenly withdrew their services without explanation, leaving the brothers without legal representation. Unable to find replacement lawyers at any price, they were at the mercy of Radley's legal wrath, and were immediately found guilty of sedition and sentenced to ten years' hard labour.

"Okay, Gerald," McCarthy continued, "we may be able to temporarily stamp-out insurrection within our borders, but pressure from outside is growing as well. We've got the EU, UN, and Amnesty International and other human rights groups clawing at the gates, desperate to intervene, and in case you hadn't noticed there's a Royal Navy destroyer anchored in the Mersey directly opposite the town hall, keeping a watchful eye on us. Not only that, but the SCW guards along the southern border are reporting a build-up of British troops in Cheshire. Rumour has it that Westminster is so embarrassed by what's going on here that they're considering forcibly re-integrating us back into the UK, under central government rule."

At that moment, the meeting was interrupted by a phone call from George Lawton, head of the SCW, who wanted to speak to Radley as a matter of urgency. The Council Leader looked shocked as he listened to Lawton's report, and he put the phone down slowly and deliberately.

"What is it, Gerald?" asked Duncan Silverlock.

"Two SCW vans were attacked during the night, both at traffic lights. They were boxed-in by stolen cars and set alight with petrol. All the SCW personnel were either burned alive or beaten to death…" Radley's face turned puce with anger. "Bloody savages! I blame that subversive publication, that bloody leaflet thing – inciting people to break the law...Civil disobedience my arse – it's downright bloody murder!" He seized the Purdey shotgun in a gesture of symbolic defiance. "Right, no more Mr Niceguy – if people want to challenge me, they'll reap the whirlwind!"

"Gerald, please listen to me..." pleaded McCarthy. "Clamping down even harder won't work, it'll just antagonise people even more. You must consider doing the opposite – relax a bit, rescind a few laws, lower a few taxes, restore a few freedoms...Show your human side. Go out and meet the people like you used to, and listen to their grievances. They genuinely loved you for that. It might even be politic to be seen to enter into negotiations with Lebovic, even if they don't come to anything. You must try to be seen as a reasonable leader who's prepared to listen to public opinion. Otherwise I think we'll be facing a major uprising in the near future – even a full-scale revolution."

"I'm afraid I agree, Gerald," said Silverlock, a little sheepishly. "Our personal survival is at stake here. If a few token concessions will appease the masses and keep us in power, then surely it's got to be worth trying. Otherwise we could find some namby-pamby do-gooder reversing everything we've achieved."

Radley stared at the desk while he considered the advice from his two most senior colleagues, and the cheek muscle beneath his left eye began twitching uncontrollably. Eventually he looked up and nodded. "Alright, if that's what you both think, we'll try it for a while. But I have to say I'm not really convinced. I think that these social problems are due to low public morale caused by the failure of our armed forces to achieve even the most modest military victory. Once Storeton is back in our hands, I've no doubt that we'll see our popularity ratings soar to new heights..."

After McCarthy and Silverlock had gone, Radley retired to his personal quarters in the executive suite and sat for a while with his head in his hands. He did not agree with the chief executive's assessment of the situation, believing instead that the growing public disaffection was attributable not only to military procrastination but also to diminishing confidence in the Council itself, for which he blamed a number of poorly-performing individuals. Radley began compiling a mental list of key figures within the administration whom he regarded as unsatisfactory, for reasons varying from professional incompetence to lack of loyalty. He decided to wait until Storeton had been recaptured, then order a ruthless purge of all undesirable elements within his staff. "What we need here is a Night of the Long Knives," he muttered to himself, but as he was planning his pogrom he received a telephone call from his personal health consultant at Arrowe Park hospital, requesting that he submit himself for 'further tests' as a matter of urgency.

The following day, in accordance with McCarthy's advice, Gerald Radley undertook a 'walkabout' in Birkenhead Park to give the populace an opportunity to meet him in person and discuss issues which concerned them. However, as he strode along the paths amidst a phalanx of gorilla-faced SCW bodyguards, with the leopards Caligula and Nero straining at their leashes, he presented such an intimidating image that no-one dared even approach him, let alone air grievances. No-one, that was, until a very elderly man with a walking stick accosted him, and spoke in a voice which was almost scolding in its disapproval.

"I need to speak to you, sir," the wizened figure said.

Radley stopped, a little startled, while the leopards proceeded to sniff the old man's crotch. Pinned to the man's overcoat were several medals with faded ribbons, which revealed that he was a veteran of the Atlantic convoys in World War Two.

"Of course," the Council Leader said with a condescending smile. "How can I help you, sir?"

Without warning, the old man launched into a ferocious verbal attack on Gerald Radley, his Council, and his policies. He accused him of double standards, corruption, reneging on promises, and generally governing Wirral "In a way which would have made our old enemy Adolf proud."

Radley nodded with an expression of sincere understanding, while shuffling his feet impatiently and glancing around to see how many witnesses would have to be dealt with if he unleashed the leopards and set them upon the impudent geriatric. Eventually, he cut the man off in mid-sentence, declaring jovially, "Well thank you for your views – I've made a mental note of them and will see what I can do. Obviously you've got a few minor concerns but overall I'm glad to hear you're happy with what we've achieved. Good day!"

The entourage walked on. "What a delightful old codger!" Radley remarked to Simms when they were out of earshot. "It is so important that we respect the views of the elderly, and do our best to meet their needs in these difficult times." He turned to one of his SCW bodyguards. "Follow him home so we know where he lives. We really should arrange a nice fire for him, to keep him warm during this cold spell..."

Simon Beatty, the director of the Council's 'Adult Health and Social Care' department, was a man in mental turmoil, afflicted by an agonising conflict between his conscience on one side and concern for his personal welfare and that of his family on the other. There were many senior Council officials who lived in fear of losing their jobs or even their lives, but what made Beatty feel especially vulnerable was that he had been present during the original conversation at Caldy golf course, during which Gerald Radley had first mooted the idea of an artificial war as a catalyst for social change.

Shortly after the club house discussion, Beatty had found himself excluded from Radley's trusted circle of confidantes, and as a result had no way of knowing whether the war was a genuine conflict or an elaborate artifice created by the Council. Initially, it had seemed preposterous to even entertain the notion that the Council Leader might have fabricated the war as part of his grand 'strategic vision', but as the regime became increasingly Draconian, so Beatty's suspicions grew, until he was certain that conflict was artificial. He had always been a 'grey man' – someone who got on with his job without drawing attention to himself or 'rocking the boat' in any way, and as a result he had escaped persecution, unlike many of his colleagues. Beatty had never openly challenged or even criticised Gerald Radley, but he was a man of integrity, and found passive acquiescence increasingly difficult as the war grew more violent and costly and civil liberties were progressively eroded in Wirral. Eventually, his moral scruples got the better of him and he felt compelled to act.

Concerns for his family's safety ruled-out direct defiance, but he felt certain that his knowledge of the Caldy golf club conversation must be a powerful weapon against the hegemonic dictator that Radley had become. If the general public, or even the Army, learned that their leader had created the war for his own twisted ends, they would surely rise up against him.

The challenge facing Beatty was how to promulgate the taboo information without effectively signing his own death warrant in the process. Wirral's only newspaper and radio station were essentially Council-controlled propaganda machines, and in any case it would be virtually impossible to contact them, because he was unable to go anywhere without a SCW escort. Closed-circuit television cameras kept his house and garden under twenty-four hour surveillance, his telephone calls, text messages and e-mails were closely monitored, and his car was bugged and fitted with a satellite tracking device. He was not even permitted to post a letter or open his own mail – all items of correspondence were thoroughly checked by George Lawton's men before being allowed to proceed to their intended recipient. All of these measures were, ostensibly, for Beatty's own personal security, although his requests for a lower level of protection had been politely yet firmly declined. "You're a senior player, Simon," Radley had told him sternly, "and as such you qualify for the deluxe service. You need twenty-four hour protection – and so does your family. A SCW team will be permanently stationed at your house to keep an eye on your wife and children whenever you're away…" Beatty had little doubt that this last comment was a veiled threat - a reminder that, if he stepped out of line, his family would suffer.

After much careful consideration, he decided to write letters to three trustworthy friends, informing them of the golf club conversation and expressing his belief that the war was an artificial creation, deliberately engineered by Radley to justify extreme social policies. His three friends had, to his knowledge, no connections with the Council or the military, and as such should still hold passports granting them free movement into and out of Wirral. Beatty's letters would urge them to leave to peninsular and 'blow the whistle' to as many outside agencies as possible. Hopefully, news might then filter back into Wirral and ignite public fury which would precipitate regime change.

Beatty was fairly certain that the SCW had installed hidden cameras inside every room of his house, but thought of a way to thwart such surveillance. His four-year old daughter had a collapsible wendy-house which had been erected on the living room carpet, and one evening he crawled-in to play with her and hurriedly scribbled out his letters, hidden from view within the canvas structure. He did not sign the letters, but included a few intimate references in the text which would confirm to his friends that he was the author.

Later that evening, when it was dark and had started to rain, Beatty peered cautiously through his bedroom curtains at the SCW van parked in the driveway. Both occupants were sitting in the cab with the light on, reading magazines. He quickly donned a waterproof jacket with a hood, and wandered innocently out into the dripping garden, pretending to look for the family cat. To maintain the pretence, he called the cat's name repeatedly as he made his way along the edge of the lawn and discretely slipped through a gap in the hedge, into the garden of the house next door. Beatty quickly crossed his neighbour's lawn, climbed a high wall and jumped down onto the pavement of a deserted avenue. After checking to make sure no-one had seen him, he walked briskly to the pillar box at the end of the road and, with trembling fingers, posted the precious letters.

Suddenly a Special Council Worker appeared from around a hedge and shone a large torch at his face. "Mr Beatty – is that you? Everything alright, sir?"

Beatty panicked, and for a moment actually considered running away. "Er, I was just looking for our cat. It's run off..."

The SCW man had evidently seen Beatty at the pillar box, for he said sternly, "You know you're not allowed to post anything yourself, now, don't you, sir? I reckon we'll have to open this box up and have a look, now, won't we?"

Beatty stared at him imploringly in the darkness, aware that he was completely at the mercy of this man. "It was only a letter to a friend," he pleaded. "Can't you just look the other way this time? I'll get into trouble for breaking the rules – I could even lose my job..."

The SCW man thought for a moment. "Tell you what, sir. You give me two grand - cash, and I'll pour some petrol in there and we'll chuck in a match and blame it on vandals. No-one will ever know what you've posted. And I'm sure you'll never do it again, will you, sir?"

Beatty stared at him in momentary disbelief. Could it be that good old-fashioned corruption might be his salvation in this desperate situation? He hesitated. "Er – what guarantee have I got that you will actually set fire to it if I give you the money?"

"None at all," replied the man. "But you've got no real choice in the matter, have you, sir? I mean, if you're not interested in a deal, I'll contact the postal people now and ask them to open up the box..."

Beatty panicked. "I – I can't get two grand tonight. I doubt I'll be able to withdraw more than one from all of my accounts together."

"Okay, sir, a grand now and the other tomorrow." The SCW man chuckled. "I'm sure I can trust you, sir."

So Beatty climbed into the white van and they embarked upon a tour of various cash machines, from which he withdrew all of the money he could. Then, true to his word, the SCW man poured a small amount of petrol into the pillar box and set it alight.

Damp with rain and sweat, Simon Beatty returned dejectedly to his comfortable house, quietly closing the door behind him to avoid waking his sleeping wife and children. With trembling hands he poured himself a glass of red wine and collapsed into a chair, feeling crestfallen and foolish yet, at the same time, immensely relieved. It would be several days before his heart rate finally returned to normal – days during which he dreaded every phone call, e-mail and knock on the door. In his mind, he replayed the incident repeatedly and shuddered with dread as he thought about how close he had come to losing everything. He resolved never to attempt, or even to contemplate, such a foolhardy act of rebellion again, for the sake of his family's safety and his own well-being.

CHAPTER 41

Prior Planning and Preparation Prevent Piss-Poor Performance

This 'author' is simply an anarchic whinger. Throughout his pathetic story, he delights in ridiculing local authority revenue-raising schemes, yet even someone of his low intellect must appreciate that councils must pay for themselves somehow. In one chapter, he even has the effrontery to question the salaries paid to senior council executives. But, what he clearly fails to understand is that, if you want the best people running your local authority, you have to pay them competitive salaries which are on a par with those of similar jobs in the private sector.

Sigmund Fosberry-Snyde
Chief Executive, Wessex Council

Mr Roberts replies:
Firstly, councils exist to serve the local people, and no council official should ever forget that. However, with chief executives in some authorities receiving salaries equivalent to the combined council tax contributions from over one hundred and fifty households, it seems that perhaps the local people are in fact serving the council. Secondly, local authorities are not the private sector, they are not subject to the same hire-and-fire, profit-and-loss pressures, so there's no reason why they should enjoy the same pay scales at the tax payer's expense. And finally, how can our society claim to be truly democratic when the general population has no say in how many public administrators there are, what they do, or how much they are paid?

Robert Taylor's morale was slowly ebbing away. He had always regarded himself as a fairly stoic character, and had bragged to others in the past about his 'ability to endure discomfort', but as April slipped away with no end to the war in sight, his reserves of fortitude steadily deteriorated. What he had failed to appreciate before the war was the extent to which living in a perpetually traumatic environment, with the ever-present threat of being killed or injured, would inexorably erode his ability to perform effectively. During the day, when his duties kept him occupied and his thought processes were rational, he could usually suppress and control his fear. But at night, his wayward imagination roamed free and weakened his mental defences, treacherously leading him towards panic and hysteria. By now he had seen enough of the horrors of war to no longer feel guilty about shooting the Frenchman on Thurstaston Common, but no amount of conscious, rational, daytime thought could stop the nightmares which haunted him during sleep - in which the deceased soldier pursued him relentlessly, holding the remains of his brain and demanding an explanation as to why his skull had been so needlessly violated.

Robert was not alone in his psychological suffering. Few men in Charlie Company had slept well since Harding and Cringle had been butchered in the Dark Side of the Moon sentry position, and the terrified shrieks of dreaming - or nightmaring - soldiers could often be heard within trenches at night. What really troubled Robert was the cumulative impact which prolonged exposure to trauma might have upon his personality. As an erstwhile science teacher, he found himself visualising the phenomenon as a line graph, with 'Time in Trenches' along the horizontal x-axis, and 'Sanity' along the vertical y-axis. Plotted on such a graph, the line representing his mental condition would be a downward-sloping curve which became increasingly steep as time progressed. Spring was in the air, the weather was finally improving, and the first green dusting of leaf buds had appeared on many of the trees, yet Robert was fearful that, unless his situation improved dramatically in the very near future, he would end up as a permanently damaged nervous wreck by the time the war ended. Assuming he lived that long...

The transition from winter to spring was not the only change noticed by the men of C Company. In mid-April, the nature of Eight and Nine Platoon's tasks switched from predominantly 'aggressive' missions intended to dominate the ground, inflict casualties and prevent supplies reaching Storeton, to more 'passive' operations focusing upon detailed intelligence gathering. Each section was required to allocate two men to observation post duties, twenty-four hours a day, and record every detail of French activity, however insignificant. After repeated requests from Colonel Hogan, Radley eventually made funds available for the purchase of an expensive thermal-imaging night-sight, which was immediately put to good use throughout the hours of darkness to keep the enemy under continual surveillance. The standard piece of night-vision equipment issued to infantry units was the CWS image-intensifier, which worked by amplifying the available ambient light, but functioned poorly in total darkness or heavy rain. It was also defeated by traditional methods of camouflage and concealment, just like an ordinary human eye. Thermal-imaging equipment, by comparison, detected the infra-red radiation emitted by all objects, and opened up a completely new dimension on the nocturnal battlefield by enabling the user to see things which would have been invisible to the naked eye even in daylight. For example, a well-camouflaged soldier lying in the shadows of a hedgerow would be virtually impossible to spot during the day, or at night using a CWS sight, but he would be betrayed by his own body heat and stand-out as a conspicuous, glowing white shape when viewed through thermal-imaging equipment.

Robert's artistic talents resulted in Blundell appointing him Company Artist in Residence, and he began spending much of his time in observation posts, sketching Storeton and the surrounding landscape from different perspectives. His drawings were then photocopied and handed back to the men in the OPs, so that they could annotate them with details of any enemy activity which was observed. Within a week, this concerted surveillance effort provided Hogan and Blundell with sufficient information about enemy strengths and dispositions around the village to start planning their attack.

At the same time, Lieutenant Andrew Grudge was finally given permission to leave the platoon position and venture out into no-man's land on a series of reconnaissance missions. The purpose of these operations was to identify the most suitable approach route for a platoon-level deliberate attack on Storeton village. Grudge was thrilled to be chosen to perform the task, believing it implied that Eight Platoon would be spearheading the assault. He bragged to his NCOs that the honour of liberating the village had been bestowed upon the platoon because, "Quite simply, as everyone knows, we're the best in the regiment." However, he did have the decorum to acknowledge that the recent wounding of Lieutenant Evans by mortar fire might have contributed to the selection of Eight Platoon rather than Nine.

Colonel Hogan was adamant that the liberation of Storeton should be achieved swiftly, decisively and with the absolute minimum of British casualties. To ensure this, he concentrated on addressing the three main priorities which he considered crucial to the success of the operation. Firstly, he believed that the assaulting troops should have to do as little close-quarter fighting as possible, so insisted that the Council fund the purchase of large quantities of mortar bombs to allow a lengthy preliminary bombardment, which would hopefully destroy the majority of enemy positions before the foot soldiers arrived. Secondly, he appreciated that the men's morale would be raised if they knew that an effective system existed to get them off the battlefield quickly in the event of them being injured, and to this end he allocated considerable resources to the formation of casualty evacuation teams. And finally, Hogan recognised that his troops had been engaged in predominantly defensive operations since Christmas, and would need 'refresher training' to hone their offensive skills before going into battle.

Across the road from Nine Platoon's location in Mount Wood was a large field, surrounded on three sides by houses, and this became the training area for an 'offensive skills package' devised by Blundell and the RSM. Sappers created mounds, barbed wire obstacles, bunkers and trenches to enable the infantry to practice their section battle drills in a realistic environment. The Engineers also constructed some crude breeze-block houses in which to conduct FIBUA (Fighting In Built-Up Area) training. The beauty of the improvised training area was that it was so close to the woods that soldiers could swiftly return to their positions in the event of an emergency. Initially, men were taken from the trenches a section at a time, but after several days it became necessary for two or even three sections to train together, so gaps in the line had to be filled by engineers, transport troops or even cadets.

The training was as tough and realistic as possible, although it had to be conducted 'dry', without ammunition or pyrotechnics, in case the noise carried across to Storeton and alerted French suspicions. Robert and his comrades practiced section battle drills time and time again, advancing towards a trench or bunker, reacting to effective enemy fire, suppressing the position, and finally assaulting it with grenades before fighting-through and regrouping. They zig-zagged, crawled, shouted target indications, cut-through barbed wire, forced their way into buildings and bunkers and, most importantly, rehearsed working together as an effective team in the confusion of battle. It was physically and mentally exhausting work, and no sooner had the men refined their skills in daylight than they began repeating the whole process at night. The company's officers trained alongside their men for much of the time, but were also required to take part in 'Tactical Exercises Without Troops', or 'TEWTs'. These theoretical sessions focused upon the wider tactical issues relating to the impending attack on Storeton, and usually involved working through different scenarios using maps or models.

Robert's section was now back to full strength, following the arrival of two BCRs (Battle Casualty Replacements) fresh from basic training. The two new soldiers were very disparate personalities, and reinforced Robert's opinion that, in the Army, appearances could be deceptive and first impressions were best ignored. Slightly chubby Private Cunningham did not appear very soldier-like with his round-rimmed spectacles, but he proved to be a reliable and competent addition to the section, whereas square-jawed and athletic-looking Private Harold turned out to be lazy, arrogant and querulous.

After one particularly grueling simulated attack featuring no less than three 'depth' positions beyond the initial objective, Robert and Karl Brabander led their sections back to Storeton Woods for a well-deserved break. The weather was unusually warm and the men were dripping with sweat, their hearts still pounding from the exertion of running, crawling and shouting.

"Sod it, I'm taking this off," Brabander announced, removing his helmet and running his fingers through his greasy, sweat-soaked hair.

Several other soldiers followed suit, but Robert hesitated. "General Grudge will be most displeased if he sees you," he warned. Grudge was, of course, only a lieutenant, but it was a standing joke within the company that he regarded himself as being of considerably higher rank.

"Well, I'll tell him I'm giving two fingers to the Nanny State," Brabander replied defiantly. But, when they arrived at the line of folding tables at which packed lunches were being handed-out, the CQMS refused to serve them.

"No-one's getting any scoff until you've all got your helmets on - and properly done up", Colour-sergeant Morris told them sternly.

"Come on lads – get a grip. It's your own time you're wasting now. Corporal Brabander – you should know better."

Brabander grinned. "I'm giving two fingers to the Nanny State, Colour," he declared proudly.

"Well, here's two fingers back from me, you daft twat," replied the CQMS affectionately, making a reverse v-sign. "Now get your bin-lid on, before the Frogs put a bullet through your head."

Lunch that day consisted of a paper bag containing bland sandwiches and a packet of crisps, which the men collected without enthusiasm. Robert, Brabander and Farrell took their food a short distance into the wood and found a small, sunny glade in which to sit and eat. It was an idyllic spot, sheltered and warm, with a handy emergency bunker nearby for protection against sudden mortar attack. They were joined by Sergeant Murphy and, a short while later, by a barely recognisable Mark Conrad, who emerged from the undergrowth like a walking bush, wearing his heavily camouflaged ghillie suit. He nodded a silent greeting, carefully placed his rifle - which was festooned with strips of hessian and pieces of netting - on the ground, then sat down and began examining the contents of his packed lunch as if he were a forensic scientist.

"I recommend the cling-film," said Farrell wryly.

For a while they sat in virtual silence, chewing meditatively and drinking water or tea. This was the first time that the group of friends had been reunited in a relatively relaxed environment for many months, and they were able to enjoy each other's company without speaking. Then Farrell, who had been chewing thoughtfully on a grass stalk, produced a creased sheet of paper from his notebook and unfolded it with a gleeful twinkle in his eye.

"My mate in the Marines sent me a copy of *Murphy's Law of Combat*," he explained, perusing the sheet and chuckling to himself as he read each sentence. Farrell was a compulsive entertainer, and could not resist sharing the amusing quotes with his friends. "Here's a good one: '*If your attack's going well, it's an ambush*'...Or how about this: '*Friendly fire isn't*.' Too true. Or, '*Automatic weapons aren't*.' Whoever thought of these was spot-on. Oh – this is my favourite: '*A sucking chest wound is nature's way of telling you to slow down...*'"

At that moment, Robert felt a sudden surge of pressure in his bowels, which he sincerely hoped was a down-welling of gas rather than an attack of diarrhoea. Deciding that it was the former, he raised one buttock from the ground and broke wind noisily in the direction of his friends. In civilian life, flatulence was generally regarded as something to be ashamed of, but in the Army it was a talent to be flaunted. When it came to farts, the standard operating procedure was to ensure that each gaseous emission was expelled as loudly and grossly as possible, then judged on the offensiveness of its odour by all present – the fouler the better. Robert usually experienced a feeling of paternal pride towards his farts and revelled in their fruity bouquet, but on this particular occasion he was appalled by the demon he had unleashed from his bowels. It smelled like a municipal sewage treatment works the day after the entire population had dined on vindaloo curry, fried egg, cabbage and lager.

"Incoming!" exclaimed Brabander in mock alarm. "Gas gas gas!"

"Ease springs!" declared Murphy.

Farrell inhaled deeply through his nose and screwed up his face in revulsion. "That's disgusting! It's official – Taylor's got a sucking arse wound! And a severe case of gut rot. From now on we should call him 'Guffers' Taylor. Good old Guffers!"

Paul Murphy had been staring through the trees with a distant expression, but suddenly he sat upright and became serious. "Eh-up lads, looks like we've got a visitor. That's definitely Major Blundell, but who's he got with him?"

It was Duncan Silverlock, who had decided to visit the lines to show a token Council presence and feel self-important. Although escorted on his tour by Alistair Blundell, Silverlock took it upon himself to leave the major at the edge of the glade and walk over to speak to the soldiers alone.

"He's obviously someone important, although I don't recognise him," Robert remarked, as Silverlock came nearer. "Do you think we should stand up or something?"

"Naah," Murphy replied. "These people always want to see us acting naturally, so that's what we'll do."

"Fuck 'em," was Mark Conrad's contribution.

"Afternoon, guys," Silverlock said awkwardly, with unconvincing joviality. "Mind if I join you?" He sat down fastidiously in the long grass, looking hesitant and uncomfortable, as if unsure of how to speak to these men. Eventually he said, "So, how's it going?"

The soldiers exchanged glances, but no-one spoke. Then Farrell said, "Well, apart from the fact that the food and accommodation are shite, and people keep trying to kill us, everything's fine and dandy. How about you, whoever you are?"

Murphy grimaced. Robert and Karl Brabander grinned. Silverlock was stultified. Eventually he smiled idiotically and said, "Good, good... Oh – I should have introduced myself. I'm Duncan Silverlock, from the Senior Executive Committee. So, can we in the Council do anything to improve your situation?"

Sergeant Paul Murphy, as the senior NCO present, was about to enter into a constructive dialogue which might have brought the company some extra benefits, but unfortunately Mark Conrad answered first. "You can keep all your bureaucratic bullshit to yourself and let us get on with our job," he declared bitterly. "And you can tell me why that arse with a clipboard who struts self-importantly around our trenches telling us what to do gets paid shed loads more than we do. Oh – and you can explain why so much money was spent on those sodding computers when what we really need is more men, more ammunition and more fire support."

Silverlock flinched. He was unaccustomed to such aggressive insolence, and did not know how to deal with it. He realised that it had been a mistake to talk to these men on his own, without Blundell present to keep them in line. "I'm afraid I'm not responsible for salaries," he lied, "but I'll certainly look into it, and answer your query as soon as possible. As for the Battle Management System, it was intended to make your job easier. I know that a lot of the men are very happy with it."

"Well I've yet to meet one!" scoffed Robert.

Silverlock sneezed three times in quick succession and rose to his feet, brushing down his suit with sweating hands. He was most displeased. "Well, gentlemen, I shall waste no more of your time. I must say that I'm disappointed at the negativity I'm sensing here. Perhaps the Army might be making better progress at defeating the French if its soldiers adopted a more positive attitude..."

"Let's see how positive you are after five months doing what we've been doing," Conrad snorted contemptuously.

Silverlock was visibly riled. The Army, it seemed to him, was a hotbed of insolence and insurrection. He glared down at Conrad, trying to discern his facial features beneath all of the camouflage. "If you still want me to answer your query, you'll have to tell me your name."

"McCrackin," said Conrad obligingly. "First name's Phil."

"Well, Private McCrackin – "

"*Corporal* McCrackin," Conrad corrected.

"Whatever. You mentioned earlier about being allowed to get on with your job. Well, I think you should do just that, instead of sitting around complaining about how hard done by you are." Silverlock turned and stormed off towards Blundell, who was standing in the shade of the trees at the edge of the glade, talking to the CSM.

Conrad watched him go, his eyelids narrowed with loathing. "Someone ought to slot that boy," he declared quietly. "Give him the smoky hole..."

When Silverlock reached Blundell and the CSM he was fuming. "Alistair, those men were extremely disrespectful and their attitude was extremely negative, which does not reflect well on you, I'm afraid. There's one of them in particular who I must insist is made the subject of disciplinary action – a certain Corporal McCrackin."

The Company Sergeant-major, 'Taff' Jones, suppressed a grin. "Was his first name 'Phil' by any chance, sir?"

"That's right, Phil McCrackin..." Silverlock turned back towards the glade, intending to point out the offending soldier, but Phil McCrackin appeared to have vanished.

"Very good shot though, Phil," the CSM remarked casually. "Do you know, sir, that two weeks ago he killed a Frenchman at a range of over seven hundred metres? Shot him right through the centre of the chest, he did."

Silverlock suddenly began to feel very uneasy and very vulnerable. Behind his desk in the town hall, or on the streets of the borough amongst a phalanx of Special Council Workers, he was a man of power who commanded fear and respect. But here in these woods, which were the soldiers' domain, he realised that his authority counted for little. He glanced around nervously at the surrounding trees, wondering whether perhaps, even now, he was lined-up in the sniper's cross-hairs...Then, trembling with fear and anger, he hurried back to the town hall to report his findings to Gerald Radley.

The Council Leader was nowhere to be found when Silverlock arrived back at the executive suite, although Terence McCarthy was at his desk, checking his e-mails with an expression of languid boredom.

"Have you seen Gerald?" Silverlock asked.

"No, Duncan, I haven't." There was little friendliness in the chief executive's voice. Officially, McCarthy remained Radley's right-hand man, but in recent months his cynical and increasingly disillusioned attitude had created a widening rift between him and his former friend. Silverlock had sensed the souring of relations and turned the situation to his advantage. As McCarthy gradually slipped from favour, the erstwhile finance director moved in by a subtle process of diffusion to take his place at Radley's side, like an ever-faithful terrier. The chief executive was aware of this process, and although he did little to oppose it, he resented Silverlock's ambitions, and treated him with bland indifference.

Silverlock sat down at his desk, switched-on his computer and began sorting through his in-tray. Much of the correspondence related to the imminent increase in Value Added Tax to fifty percent, or to the plethora of new licences being introduced by the Council for the dual purposes of regulation and revenue-generation. He was in the process of scrutinising the prototype application forms and plastic licence cards when the door opened, and in waddled Radley's secretary, Maurine, encumbered by bags from her customary lunchtime shopping spree. Both Silverlock and McCarthy loathed Maurine, but they were always outwardly friendly towards her because she was arguably the second most powerful person in Wirral, after Radley himself. Maurine was effectively the Council Leader's bureaucratic bodyguard and censor, intercepting all items of correspondence and vetting all visitors before granting them access to the great man. Few things happened within the administration without Maurine's knowledge, and anyone who was not suitably obsequious towards her found all routes to Radley suddenly blocked - their appointments cancelled without explanation, their telephone calls perpetually unanswered and their letters condemned to an eternity at the bottom of the in-tray. She had her favourites within the Council – generally men who showered her with compliments and gifts – and Silverlock was certainly not one of them. He despised her so much that he was seriously considering having her killed, and often fantasised about shooting her through the back of the head with a pistol.

"Maurine dear," he called to her with false, fawning pleasantness. "My, what a lovely skirt! Is it new? You don't happen to know where Council Leader Radley is, do you?"

She shuffled over to his desk and nodded slyly, then placed her index finger against her nose and leant close to him to reveal her secret in a confidential whisper. "He's at the hospital again. They wanted to do more tests."

"Tests?"

She nodded solemnly. "Hmm, tests. He's been having heart flutters, you know."

Silverlock was taken aback. "Did you know about this, Terence?"

"I knew he'd been to the hospital a few times, but I didn't know why and I didn't ask."

"But his heart!"

"It doesn't surprise me, to be honest. He needs to relax, take a break, let things tick over for a while without dreaming-up any new schemes. Do you know, yesterday he came up with three ideas – to open up the wartime tunnels under Bidston Hill as his own personal bunker, to print counterfeit euros and introduce them into Normandy's economy, and to include gas attacks in the air raids...He kept going on about how adding a new, chemical threat would help bring people together and revitalise the War Effort! I mean, doesn't he appreciate that we're virtually bankrupt, the economy's on the verge of collapse and people are so disillusioned that we could have a revolution at any time? Has he completely lost the plot?"

Silverlock stroked his bald pate and looked personally hurt, as if McCarthy had been speaking about him. "He's a man with a vision!"

"He's a – " McCarthy began, but changed his mind. "He's exhausted. He needs to rest."

Later that week there was a further petrol bomb attack on an SCW van, and a number of demonstrations were staged outside the town hall by anti-Council activists. One group of people had gathered to protest against the imminent introduction of compulsory random conscription for men aged between eighteen and twenty-five. These conscripts were needed to satisfy the voracious appetite of the French Front for healthy human flesh, but they were to be paid a special 'emergency wage' which was substantially less than that received by existing soldiers. Another group, calling itself 'The War-Weary Women of Wirral' marched around the town hall waving banners and demanding that an end to the war be sought immediately by diplomatic means. Inside the building, Radley paced up and down in his office, listening to the chants outside and cursing what he referred to as a 'lack of moral fibre in modern society'. He then issued the order for George Lawton and his Special Council Workers to break-up the demonstrations using their usual brand of ruthless efficiency, employing batons, CS gas and water cannon.

As his unpopularity grew, Radley became increasingly concerned about the means of escape available to him should he need to leave Wirral in a hurry. In the event of revolution, he would probably not get far by road, so other options had to be considered. Boat seemed an attractive proposition, as the Mersey flowed within fifty metres of the town hall, but the river was so tidal that any craft moored at its edge would be beached high and dry for hours each day. What Radley really wanted was a helicopter on permanent standby, ready to pluck him to safety, but he knew that there was no way that the Council cabinet would authorise expenditure on such an extravagance. There were two possible solutions to this problem, both of which had received his serious consideration. One option was to ostensibly buy the helicopter for military use, which would involve persuading Colonel Hogan to argue, in writing, that the machine was essential for victory on the Wirral fronts at Thurstaston and Storeton. The other was to have the entire cabinet killed, with the exception of his most loyal and trusted confederates. Then he really would be free to do as he pleased...

Towards the end of April, Special Council Workers achieved a major breakthrough when they raided an industrial unit in Bromborough and caught four people in the act of producing the subversive publication *'Speaking Out'*. Radley was ecstatic, although his euphoria was tempered by disappointment that none of those arrested had any form of identification on them, and therefore could not be immediately 'named and shamed' by the media. Without hesitation, he authorised George Lawton to use any methods necessary to extract names from the prisoners, one of whom was Brian Salter's wife, Carol.

CHAPTER 42

A Grenade for a Rainy Day

While I applaud the use of imagery to create a particular mood, it can be overdone...It always seems to be raining in this dismal novel.

Persephone Woebegone
Intelligentsia magazine

Mr Roberts replies:
But it always seems to be raining in Britain these days...

The brief spell of sunny spring weather did not last long, and by late April dark clouds were once again mustering in the skies above Wirral. Sporadic showers dampened the woods and the soldiers' spirits, especially when the moisture brought forth swarms of midges which made life misery for susceptible individuals like Robert Taylor.

One evening, Robert was waiting in the tactical feeding queue on the road next to the sandstone boundary wall when he noticed Farrell's girlfriend, Kirsty, standing on the corner by the Traveller's Rest. She was peering at the line of soldiers in the fading light, trying to spot her lover, but Farrell was on the next feeding detail and would not be able to leave his trench for another half-hour. Robert was about to call-out to Kirsty to tell her, but then he noticed another woman standing hesitantly by the pub, and realised with a combination of excitement and alarm that it was Susan. He waved to her and she rushed across the road to him, clearly distressed.

"What is it?" he asked, knowing that she would never have come to find him here unless it was for something very important. "What's wrong?"

She glanced around furtively, and spoke in a virtual whisper. "The SCW have arrested Brian Salter's wife. Apparently she was one of the people producing that subversive leaflet..."

He felt a surge of relief, having expected bad news about something closer to home, but displayed a suitably concerned expression. "Oh..."

"Brian reckons they don't know who she is, otherwise they would have arrested him by now," Susan continued in a hurried whisper. "I said we'd try to help..."

Robert looked bewildered. "How?"

"Can you get a gun? Brian says if you can get him a gun he'll kill Radley. But he needs it quickly – his wife might talk at any time, and then he'll lose his chance."

Robert was taken aback. "Susan, I really can't think of anything I can do...I mean, I can't hand over my rifle – it's serial-numbered and everything. And anyway, anything I gave you would have my DNA on it..."

Like the rest of the population, Robert was unaware that the Council lacked the capability to perform DNA testing. Fabricated results were used in court cases to secure convictions and create the impression that the Council's forensic scientists were infallible, which in turn helped increase the fear and paranoia which kept the people cowed and subservient.

Suddenly, Robert remembered the French grenade buried on Thurstaston Common. "Hang on a minute. I might be able to get you something...But not before next week – not before my day off on Tuesday."

"That's too late! He needs it for Friday. Apparently there's going to be a cabinet meeting then, and that'll be his best chance of getting near to Radley. Can't you get anything by tomorrow?"

"I'm afraid I can't, my love." He noticed her despairing face and hurriedly added, "But I'll see what I can do."

After they parted, he hurried back down through the woods towards the trenches, and intercepted Brabander and Farrell, who were walking in the opposite direction to get their food.

"Hey, guys, have either of you two fine gentlemen got any leave in the next two days?"

Farrell shook his head, but Brabander nodded smugly. "Yes, thanks. Tomorrow, in fact."

"Would you consider doing a swap with me, as a massive personal favour? I really need a few hours off, and my day's not till Tuesday."

Brabander laughed. "No chance! I'd be more likely to donate both my testicles to you than swap my leave. We all know something big's about to kick off. We might not even be here on Tuesday!"

"I'll give you two hundred quid."

"Still no chance."

"Five hundred?"

"Sorry, Tayl, it's still no."

"How about five hundred just for covering for me for two hours?"

Brabander looked at him uncertainly. "Are you serious?" He had a large mortgage, a car loan, and a girlfriend at home who liked watching television shopping channels, armed with his credit card. Robert's offer was undeniably attractive.

"Completely serious. Five hundred in cash, all you have to do is sit in my trench for two hours and babysit my section."

"It's a deal. Five hundred quid! Jesus, Taylor – you must be absolutely desperate for a shag!"

Farrell chuckled mischievously, then piped-up like a cheeky schoolboy, "He could've had me for half that much!"

The next day, at noon, Robert signed-out of the guardroom sangar and ran to meet Susan, who was waiting in her car as close to the woods as the military exclusion zone would allow her to park. Without delay they drove straight to Thurstaston Common, where she dropped him off discretely on a stretch of rural road where there were unlikely to be CCTV cameras. He disappeared into the undergrowth while she drove back to the nearby village of Irby to wait for him in a car park. Twenty minutes later he was back in her passenger seat, the French grenade hidden in his rucksack.

Robert glanced at his watch. "I've still got an hour left…" he said hopefully.

"Then what are we waiting for?"

Back at her flat he showered and shaved, scrubbing his face and hands furiously to remove as much of the ingrained dirt and camouflage cream as possible. They made love and lay entwined in bed, staring resentfully at the clock as the seconds ticked away with relentless indifference to their plight.

"I don't want you to go," she said simply.

"I don't want to go."

For a few minutes they lay in silence, utterly miserable. Then Susan said, "Robert, I need to know how 'it' works so I can tell him."

"I'll write down some instructions. We'd better get up, I suppose…"

Wearing a pair of disposable gloves, Robert opened an item of 'junk mail' which he found on the doormat, and tore the bottom off the loan application letter within, to obtain an unmarked piece of paper which would not be contaminated with his or Susan's DNA. Then, taking care to disguise his handwriting, he quickly jotted down a step-by-step guide to using the grenade. He did not know how long the fuse on French grenades burned for, but assumed it would be similar to the British L2, at around five seconds. As he wrote down the final instruction, he became increasingly concerned.

"How are you going to get it to him? You're not intending to hand it over in person, are you?"

"I was…"

"But it's too dangerous!" He shook his head. "You can't – I don't want you to."

"Robert, I've got to. There's no time to do anything else. Don't worry, I'll be fine, no-one's ever searched me at work. I'll just hide it in some sanitary towels in my handbag…"

He stared at her in admiration. "You're amazing - and I love you!"

"I love you. Very much."

He slipped the grenade instructions into a small transparent freezer bag and handed them to her, then said, "I think something big's about to kick off, any time now. I reckon we're going to attack Storeton in the next few days."

"How do you know?"

"Well, we've been practising section attacks and offensive ops all week, and shed loads of ammo and stuff has been delivered. And I was asked to make a new model of the village – a large scale one."

She looked completely dismayed. "Can't you get out of it somehow?"

"I'm afraid not..." He sighed, and glanced at his watch once more. "It's two o'clock. Brabander's going to kill me..."

She drove him back to the woods via two bank cashpoint machines, from which he withdrew a total of five hundred pounds. By the time he arrived back at his trench it was almost two-thirty in the afternoon, and Brabander was looking distinctly unimpressed.

"What time do you call this, Tayl?"

"Sorry I'm late, Brab," Robert said apologetically. "Here's your five hundred quid."

Without a word, Brabander took the wad of notes and counted them suspiciously. Then he carefully peeled-off a single ten pound note from the top of the pile and put it in his pocket, before handing the rest of the money back to Robert. "Here you are, Tayl, yer shag's on me."

"But we agreed... I don't mind, honestly – take it Brab, please."

Karl Brabander shook his head solemnly and sighed. He, like Robert, could sense that something was afoot. "Tell you what, Tayl – if we're both still alive next week, the beers are most definitely on you."

That evening, a huge Foden flatbed truck rumbled quietly through the gates of the Teehey Lane allotments, and used its mechanical arm to unload crate after crate of bombs for Monty's mortar. Maurice and his men were going to receive an absolute pounding.

The bombardment commenced at seven o'clock, initially targeting the French positions at the northern edge of the village, guarding the bottom of Lever's Causeway. Colossal spurts of earth were blasted high into the air, and plumes of black smoke drifted skyward. At times, the explosions were occurring every three or four seconds, and many British soldiers, watching from the safety of their trenches, felt a certain sympathy towards the enemy troops who were enduring such a merciless onslaught.

Lieutenant Andrew Grudge grew steadily more excited as the evening wore on. From events and conversations which he had either participated in or overheard during the previous week, he was convinced that the operation to liberate Storeton was imminent, and that Eight Platoon would play a key role. After months of frustration, champing at the bit within the confines of the woods, Grudge felt sure that his moment of glory had finally arrived...

At eight o'clock, with a light drizzle falling and the thud of exploding mortar bombs still reverberating from Storeton, Grudge was summoned to the company command post for the customary evening briefing in which Blundell would outline the tasks and duties to be carried out that night. The lieutenant entered the CP in a state of great anticipation, hoping to receive a set of formal orders for an all-out assault on the village. But he was disappointed when the briefing followed the usual format, and related only to routine activities. In fact, Blundell announced that the company was to have a relatively relaxed night. Sentry and observation post duties would continue as normal, but the main priority was for the men to rest.

By the time Grudge left the command post it was almost dark, and the mortar bombardment had ceased temporarily to allow the weapon's barrel to cool. He was about to make his way along the comms cord to his position when he was accosted by the dour Milcheck inspector, who wanted to question Corporal Kingsley about some patrol reports, but could not find the right trench.

"Come with me," Grudge said, a little resentfully. "I'll take you down there."

They were in the process of following the muddy, trampled track-plan downhill towards the front-line trenches, when suddenly Grudge heard a distinctive sound above the patter of the rain, coming from the direction of Storeton. He decided to have a little fun at the Milcheck inspector's expense.

"Hang on a minute," the lieutenant said quietly. "Just wait right here – I'll be back in just a moment…"

Leaving the inspector nervously clutching the comms cord in the gloom, Grudge scurried off into the shadows and quickly took refuge in one of the unoccupied emergency bunkers which had been constructed at intervals along the track-plan for just such an eventuality. He threw himself down on the floor, as shouts of "Take cover!" erupted across the wood. The sound that he had heard had been the French mortar firing – a token five-round retaliatory salvo in pitiful response to Monty's sustained barrage. Grudge had expected the bombs to land a long way off, but they detonated in frightening proximity to his bunker, compressing his chest with the blast and sending foliage, soil and other debris showering down all around.

Caught in the open, the Milcheck inspector was fortunate to have been properly equipped with Kevlar helmet and body armour, and these protective items ensured that his head and torso escaped serious injury. Unfortunately, the two body parts were found some fifty metres apart.

"Sounds like poor skills and drills to me," remarked Farrell when he learned of the inspector's demise. "Perhaps if he'd practised a bit more of what he preached he'd still be alive, the stupid twat."

Monty's mortar continued stonking the French positions throughout the night, while in Storeton, Maurice's men braced themselves for an attack which did not come. By daybreak the survivors were shell-shocked, demoralised and exhausted, in stark contrast with the men of Eight and Nine Platoons across the valley, who emerged from their trenches feeling relatively refreshed, and tucked-in to extra-generous portions of full English breakfast. The British soldiers had been speculating about a possible offensive for days, and their suspicions were confirmed when the platoon sergeants began issuing ammunition at the rate of four hundred rounds per man, plus three smoke and three fragmentation grenades.

At midday on Friday, Gerald Radley was sitting in the executive suite with Duncan Silverlock and Terence McCarthy, when he received a call on his mobile phone from Colonel Hogan.

"Alan, good to hear from you, everything okay?"

"Yes, Council Leader, everything's in place here. Alistair and I have finalised the plan of attack and he's preparing his orders now, ready for offensive operations tonight. All we need now is the final thumbs-up from you."

"Consider my thumbs to be well and truly up, Colonel. Good luck to you and your men – hopefully by this time tomorrow it'll all be over."

"Let's hope so."

"I've got to attend a full cabinet meeting this afternoon, but I'll come along to the woods later to see the men…In fact, I'd like to watch the attack going in, if that's alright with you?"

"It's Alistair's operation really, Council Leader – perhaps you should check with him…"

"Oh he won't mind." Radley laughed. "And besides – I don't care if he does! Oh – Colonel, just one last thing…"

"Yes Council Leader?"

"Do you remember, a while ago, we discussed procuring a second helicopter, to support operations in Wirral?"

"I do…" Hogan replied cautiously.

"And do you still think it would be instrumental in achieving victory?"

"It would certainly be very useful, although to be honest I can think of better things to spend the money on…"

"I don't want to hear them! I'm intending to propose the purchase of a helicopter during this afternoon's cabinet meeting, and it would really lend weight to my argument if I could have your views on the matter, in writing. Could you just quickly jot down a statement to the effect that a Wirral-based helicopter would be a decisive asset in winning the war?"

"I suppose so…" Hogan replied, rather perturbed. He could not believe that, with only hours to go before the start of possibly the largest battle of the war to date, Radley intended to burden him with such a bizarre request.

"Splendid! So, if you could e-mail it across to me in, say, the next half-hour, it would be very much appreciated…"

CHAPTER 43

Bomb Plot

As the story progressed it became increasingly apparent that the author is an insecure individual with a great many chips on his shoulder. His book is simply a collection of twisted fantasies, in which stereotypes he dislikes get their just desserts. Council officials, health and safety inspectors, Rottweiler owners, four-by-four drivers, abusive drug addicts...all are subjected to ridicule, humiliation or a grisly end in this ghastly work. By the time I reached the chapter entitled 'Bomb Plot', I began to wish someone had put a bomb under the author before he started work on his unpleasant creation!

Birinda Kahnak
Opportunities magazine

Mr Roberts replies:
Charming, Birinda. I'll make sure you're suitably ridiculed in the sequel...

By two o'clock on Friday afternoon, Major Alistair Blundell had written his orders for a deliberate attack and summoned his platoon commanders to receive them. At the same time, the most significant figures in the Council, including the Senior Executive Committee, the departmental directors and the elected representatives, were convening in the town hall for what Radley intended as the last ever full cabinet meeting. The Council Leader had made sure that he arrived first, to stamp his authority upon proceedings and ensure that there was no pre-meeting seditious talk, or 'plotting,' as he called it. He took up a strategic position by the door as the various officials entered, greeting his friends and allies with jovial warmth and enthusiasm, while subjecting those he disliked or felt threatened by to a cold stare of contempt. Radley's hair had begun to look distinctly unkempt since he had stopped dyeing or even combing it, and this, together with the nervous tic under his left eye, gave him a manic, almost feral appearance.

Before being allowed to enter the conference room, each official was searched by a team of Special Council Workers, who frisked them roughly and wafted a hand-held metal detector over their bodies. This procedure was conducted with rigorous care on the first few individuals to arrive, but became noticeably less thorough as time went by and the trickle of delegates became a steady flow.

Gerald Radley looked at his watch and scanned the faces around the crowded conference table. Just as he had decided that everyone was present and the doors could be closed for the start of the meeting, a very flustered-looking Brian Salter hurried into the room, clutching a briefcase in one hand and a steaming mug of coffee in the other.

"Sorry I'm late, everyone," he panted, spilling coffee onto the carpet. "I was desperate for a coffee, but the kettle seemed to take ages to boil – you know what they say about a watched pot..."

There was a titter of laughter from some of those present, but Radley shook his head in contemptuous despair. Salter placed his dripping mug on a side desk and raised his arms obligingly while one SCW man frisked him and another searched his briefcase.

"Look at those sweat stains," someone muttered to their neighbour. "Jesus – the guy's dripping with it!"

After being given a cursory once-over with the metal detector, Brian Salter smiled affably and blundered over to the only vacant chair, which was next to Sylvia Fadden. The table was covered with folders and documents, so he carefully placed his briefcase and coffee on the floor.

Radley glared at him with an expression of exhausted patience. "Good afternoon, Brian, nice of you to make it...Now, I'd like to start the meeting, if that's alright with you?"

"Of course, of course, sorry if I've held things up..."

The meeting commenced with an introduction from Radley, in which he eulogized the Council and its post-autonomy achievements, but also warned that there was still much work to be done and there was no place for complacency, negativity or defeatism. He then sat down and listened while each of the departmental directors reported on the progress made by their teams toward meeting SEC-imposed targets, fulfilling their mission statements and generally contributing to the War Effort. While the finance director was speaking, Radley seized the opportunity to broach the subject of the desired helicopter purchase, and succeeded in obtaining approval for the necessary funds. Brian Salter seemed unusually nervous while delivering his summary, stammering severely and sweating profusely; several of his colleagues speculated that he was suffering from flu' or a similar illness.

When the last director had finished speaking, Radley nodded with satisfaction and rose to his feet. "Thank you, colleagues, that was splendid. You and your respective staffs are clearly working very hard for the borough and the War Effort, and I commend your dedication and professionalism."

He paused, taking a deep breath followed by a sip of water, before continuing. "As you all know, we are currently living through the greatest period of change and challenge in the borough's history, and if we are to prevail under such circumstances then we must all be proactive, resourceful and adaptable, to face the needs of the moment. We must all be prepared to suffer hardship and make sacrifices.

"Now, I know that many of you are concerned by what you perceive as disaffection amongst the population. I'm aware that the elected representatives amongst you are receiving complaints from your constituents that insufficient progress has been made towards ending the war by either military or diplomatic means. In some cases, this defeatism has become so extreme that certain individuals are even suggesting we sue for peace, at any price. But they should realise that such pessimistic and negative attitudes simply play into the hands of the enemy, and serve only to undermine our collective ability to win. We really must all adopt a unified stance on this. United we stand, divided we fall. Anyway, I'm convinced that public confidence will be restored very soon, when we finally achieve a decisive military victory. I've spoken to Colonel Hogan during the past hour and he assures me that Storeton will be back in our hands this weekend..."

In fact, even as Radley was speaking, warning orders were being issued to the soldiers of C Company to initiate preparations for a night attack, and Robert and his fellow corporals had been summoned to receive their formal orders. The company was in 'lock-down', with all communication with the outside world strictly forbidden and no-one allowed to leave the lines for any reason.

"Now," Radley continued, in an ominous tone of voice. "The impending victory at Storeton will undoubtedly raise morale throughout the borough and silence some of the Council's critics, but I believe further action is necessary to streamline our administration and make our systems work more efficiently, to achieve ultimate victory. Duncan, Terence and I have discussed this at length and we feel that radical and imaginative restructuring is required within the Council, to strip us down to fighting weight. The services of some of you will, I'm afraid, no longer be required, although I'm not going to read out a list of names now - the colleagues concerned will be notified in due course. I've also decided that it's no longer appropriate or justifiable to hold full cabinet meetings such as this one, so today is therefore an historic occasion, as it marks the last time we all gather here in this chamber."

"It sounds to me, Gerald," declared Sylvia Fadden with disgust, "that you've finally lost the plot and become the tin-pot dictator you've always aspired to be. What you're announcing here today is effectively the end of democracy on the Wirral."

Radlley smiled at her icily. "Thank you, Sylvia, and yes, yours is one of the posts which will be abolished." He chuckled, performed a theatrical double-take gesture, and stared at her questioningly. "Er, who are you? You remind me of someone who used to work for the Council. What are you doing here now?"

"Very funny, Gerald. You really have lost the plot. And you look terrible – hasn't anyone told you, or are your fawning lackeys all too scared to speak the truth nowadays?"

"You don't seem to realise, Sylvia, that as you no longer work for the Council, you no longer have the right to say anything at this meeting. So please shut up."

"I will not shut up! Don't patronise me like one of your pathetic 'yes' men!" She looked around the table with an expression of combined despair and contempt. "I can't believe you're all just sitting there, lapping-up everything he says like a bunch of brainwashed cretins! Can't you see what he's doing? Since when has Wirral been a dictatorship? We're all supposed to contribute to the decision-making process, but now he's effectively by-passed us all and made us either redundant or turned us into impotent puppets. And look at the state of the borough! The economy's on the edge of collapse, we've been living under totalitarian 'emergency powers' for months, people are dying every day in this ridiculous war, and no-one dares to say anything because of the prevailing culture of fear and intimidation! People have been disappearing, for heaven's sake! And we've all just sat back and let it happen because we're all too timid or corrupt or scared to voice any opposition. Maybe it doesn't matter if he *does* get rid of us all, we're so pathetically ineffectual..."

The muscle under Radley's eye twitched uncontrollably. "Thank you, Sylvia, very eloquent and impassioned and heartfelt, I'm sure." He gestured to the pair of SCW guards standing by the door. "Escort Ms Fadden from the building and make her comfortable at the Fort. Tell Mr Lawton that she's to be charged with sedition and extreme defeatism."

The two guards stepped towards Sylvia, and one of them unclipped some handcuffs from his belt. She stood up defiantly and looked at the SCW men with an expression of extreme disdain. "Don't you dare try to handcuff me, you Neanderthal oafs!" The men hesitated, and Sylvia looked around the table, subjecting each official to a piercing stare. Their response, she fancied, reflected their allegiance. Some stared defiantly back at her, some wilted and bowed their heads in shame, and a courageous few showed their support with a variety of facial expressions. Brian Salter held her gaze for a few moments and smiled strangely. The two Special Council Workers hovered either side of her, unsure of how to proceed.

"Well," she continued, taking advantage of the guard's hesitation, "all I can say is, if any of you have a conscience, then I sincerely hope you'll be able to live with it in future, because history will judge you on how you acted today..."

"Take her away!" Radley snapped impatiently. "And if she can't keep her big mouth shut, break her jaw."

The councillors and directors sat in stunned silence as Sylvia was escorted from the room, and Radley brought the meeting to a premature close with a final call for unity, proactive optimism and unswerving loyalty. As soon as he had finished speaking, the delegates aggregated into small groups, and a babble of conversation erupted within the conference chamber. No-one paid any attention to Brian Salter, as he reached down to get his mug of un-drunk coffee from the floor beneath his chair. He dipped his fingers into the lukewarm liquid and pulled-out the French grenade, protected within a sealed water-proof plastic bag. It seemed to take an age for his clumsy, trembling hands to prise the bag open, while keeping it hidden under the table. Eventually, he managed to pull out the grenade's pin, the splayed ends of which he had, on Robert Taylor's advice, squeezed together with pliers to make it easier to remove. Salter dropped the pin onto his coffee and slipped the grenade discretely into his jacket pocket, maintaining a firm grip on it to prevent the fly-off lever from detaching. Then he glanced around nervously until he spotted Radley in a corner of the room, talking to Terence McCarthy.

Tears welled up in Brian Salter's eyes as he released his grip on the grenade and felt the fly-off lever spring away inside his pocket. There was no going back now. He thought of his wife, imprisoned within the high security cells of the SCW headquarters by the docks, and strode purposefully towards the Council Leader.

"Gerald, can I just interrupt a moment?" he said, boldly stepping between Radley and McCarthy.

"Hang on a minute, Brian," declared the chief executive, grinning with amiable indignation, "I was in mid-sentence then!"

McCarthy was a large man, and he was able to grasp Salter's upper arms and physically move him gently yet firmly to one side. Unfortunately, this resulted in the chief executive being between Salter and his intended target when the grenade went off, and it was McCarthy who bore the brunt of the explosion and absorbed most of the shrapnel. Radley escaped with relatively minor injuries. Brian Salter sustained massive wounds but, amazingly, survived the blast. At Radley's insistence he was rushed to Arrowe Park hospital along with the other casualties, not for his own wellbeing but rather so that he could be nursed back to health and properly tortured. Mercifully, he died in the ambulance.

CHAPTER 44

Preparation for Battle

I was intrigued to read a local novel about an imaginary war in Wirral, yet simultaneously disappointed that no reference was made to the fascinating history of the area. For example, Mr Roberts fails to mention that Storeton was in fact the site of a major battle between Vikings and indigenous people during the first millennium. If only he had consulted the local history society – his book would have been greatly enriched.

Bob Forest
Local historian

Mr Roberts replies:
I agree with you, Mr Forest – we should all know something about the history of where we live...

In the immediate aftermath of the grenade explosion, there was pandemonium in the conference room. Although only Radley, McCarthy and Brian Salter had received significant injuries, many of those present had been hit by fragments of shrapnel, or sprayed with blood, and were in varying states of shock or hysteria. Duncan Silverlock almost fainted when he noticed a patch of blood on his shirt, but regained his composure when he realised that it was not his. Falteringly, he took control of the situation after Radley and McCarthy had been rushed off to hospital. His first response was to instruct the SCW guards to seal off the executive suite and prevent anyone from entering or leaving, apart from medical personnel. On Radley's orders, news of the assassination attempt was to be kept secret until at least the following morning, when hopefully its disclosure could be offset by the morale-raising announcement that Storeton was finally back in British hands.

Codenamed *Operation Excise*, the battle for Storeton had been planned by Hogan and Blundell as a deliberate attack at company level, to be executed in a number of distinct phases. The preliminary phase – which involved training, the gathering of intelligence, and the accumulation of stores – was already complete, and phase one – the prolonged bombardment of the French defences by mortar and machine gun fire – was well under way. Phase two - preparation for battle at all levels – would take place throughout Friday evening, to be followed by phase three, the covert movement of the various units to their 'lines of departure'. From these starting positions, the troops would be ready to commence phase four – the actual offensive. The first soldiers would start to advance at 3.00am, although these initial moves would in fact be purely diversionary, as part of a deception plan designed to confuse the enemy. Ten minutes later, the men of Eight Platoon would cross their line of departure to commence the operation's 'main effort' – a platoon attack against the relatively weak defences to the south of the village. This would follow the standard format of 'the approach', 'the assault' and 'the fight-through'. The platoon would secure a foothold in Storeton before launching into phase five - the advance through the village, which was expected to involve street fighting and house clearance operations. By this stage in the battle, it was hoped that any remaining French troops would either surrender or else attempt a withdrawal across the killing areas prepared by Seven Platoon to the west of the village, where they would be massacred. Finally, the inevitable 'mopping up' would be followed by an occupation and consolidation phase, in which the village would be secured against counter-attack, while booby-traps were disarmed and prisoners of war taken into captivity.

In Storeton Woods it was raining, and corporals Brabander, Taylor and Kingsley had received their orders from Lieutenant Grudge and were in the process of preparing their sections for the unenviable task ahead. From the moment Robert left Grudge's 'O' group, he felt as though an imaginary egg-timer had been turned over and the sand was trickling steadily away. He conducted a quick 'time appreciation' exercise, working back from H-hour to establish how long he had for each stage of the planning and preparation process. Of crucial importance was the 'No Move Before' time, which had been provisionally set for two o'clock in the morning, with troops on fifteen minutes 'notice to move'. Robert deducted the time needed for rehearsals, inspection and kit check, and preparing and delivering his orders, and came to the conclusion that he had about five hours at his disposal. How he used the time was largely down to him – all that really mattered was that, when his men were told to leave the wood, they were fully equipped and prepared for battle, knowing what they were to achieve, how they were to achieve it, and what fire support they could expect to receive.

Robert delegated the majority of administrative tasks to Farrell, who was given responsibility for building a detailed model of the objective, distributing ammunition and specialist equipment, and ensuring that each soldier performed the necessary personal preparations such as eating a proper meal, weapon cleaning, filling water bottles and checking personal camouflage. This left Robert free to consider how best to achieve his section's mission and prepare a full set of formal orders, which Colonel Hogan had decreed did not have to be computer-generated on this occasion. "I frankly don't care how they prepare them," the CO had told Blundell, "provided they follow the standard format from the tactical *aide memoire*, and achieve their purpose. The Council can slap our wrists afterwards if it wants to, but I'm not having my officers and NCOs fannying around with those bloody machines only to have the system crash at the last minute. Besides, I've never been convinced they're secure – if the French can somehow tap into our system, everything will go tits-up and pear-shaped, for sure..."

The primary mission for Robert's section that night was to capture one of a pair of enemy bunkers - codenamed "Scarlet' and "Pimpernel" - which defended the southern approaches to Storeton. Robert asked Grudge for permission to carry-out a visual reconnaissance of the objective area prior to writing his orders, which impressed the lieutenant.

"Good idea, Corporal Taylor," he said approvingly. "Time spent on reconnaissance is seldom wasted. But I'm sure we looked at that position last week..."

"We did, sir - I just want to have one last look at it before it gets dark, just to make sure nothing's changed. And to see what damage the mortar's done. I'm hoping there won't be a bunker there for me to attack..."

Grudge nodded. "Go on then. Oh – have you checked your e-mail recently?"

"No, sir. I can't say it was top of my list of priorities. Why?"

"The Council want us all to fill-in an online 'well-being' questionnaire. They want to know if we're happy in our workplace."

Robert laughed bitterly. "What's the point? No-one gives a damn about what we think. And if you tell the truth you get blacklisted as a whinger and a trouble-maker."

"Apparently this survey is completely anonymous. Every one of us will be given a number, and that number goes on the questionnaire instead of your name."

"And does the Council issue the numbers, sir?"

"Of course."

"Well, all I can say is, anonymous my arse! Anyway, with all due respect, sir, it's all bollocks and I'm not going to do it!"

"I don't blame you, Corporal. I'm not doing it, either. See you later."

Robert hurried across the road into Nine Platoon's position in neighbouring Mount Wood, where frantic preparations were evident all around. Lieutenant Evans remained incapacitated in hospital, leaving Sergeant Collins commanding the platoon for the night's operation. He emerged from the HQ tent just as Robert entered the platoon lines.

"Corporal Taylor!" he exclaimed. "What brings you here? Are you defecting to us?"

"I'm afraid not, Sergeant. I need to do a recce from one of your positions, to have a look at what I'm supposed to be attacking tonight."

"Of course. I don't envy you...I'm in charge the main diversionary attack, along Lever's Causeway."

"I know, and I know which job I'd rather have. Don't you just have to move along behind a Trojan until the Frogs start firing at you, then keep your heads down while we do the business in the actual village?"

"Something like that." Collins said with a grin, before his expression changed to one of concern. "I've got a really bad feeling about this one, Rob. I was supposed to be on leave today. The kids are so disappointed – and the missus! I'm sure it's some sort of bad omen or something."

Robert had always liked Pete Collins, and wanted to reassure him. "Don't worry about it, Sergeant – I'm sure you'll be fine. And if Monty's mortar keeps malleting them like it has been, there may not be much left for us to attack. Anyway, I'd better crack on. Good luck tonight."

"And you."

Robert made his way through the wood to some farm buildings located on the far side, overlooking the valley. Crouching low to the ground, he crossed the farmyard and entered what had once been a footpath but was now a shallow trench, bordered on either side by hawthorn hedges. He followed the trench through several changes in direction until he reached a concealed observation post, occupied by two men he vaguely knew. From there he could see out across the valley while remaining in good cover. A short distance away to his right lay a bunker, from which one of the tripod-mounted machine guns of the Sustained Fire (SF) Platoon was pouring tracer onto the very position he was due to attack that night, while from the north of the village came the muted crump of explosions, as Monty's mortar pounded the French defences at the bottom of Lever's Causeway. Although it was raining, several fires were visible in Storeton, and a pall of black smoke hung over the village. Feeling weak and nauseous with fear, Robert checked the time on his watch, took out his binoculars and notebook, and began studying the landscape over which he would have to lead his men in a few hour's time.

Not far away in the valley below lay the triangular conifer plantation where he and Susan had made love in the Land Rover the previous year. Despite its romantic associations, Robert had always regarded the wood as strangely sinister, and had nicknamed it 'The Forbidden Forest'. The term had been widely adopted throughout the company, not only because it struck a cord with the soldiers, but also because it would mean nothing to the French if they succeeded in intercepting British communications. During the attack that night, the forest would be where the assault troops would make their final preparations prior to moving to their start positions, and would also serve as the location of company HQ while the attack went in.

In order to avoid alerting the enemy, each section would make its way independently to the Forbidden Forest, so as to create the impression of routine patrols rather than a build-up to a major offensive. The plan was that Corporal Gorpe's section from Nine Platoon would move first, to mark the route and check that there were no enemy in the vicinity of the conifer plantation. Next would come Brabander's section, patrolling through Gorpe's position and along the hedge-lined road to

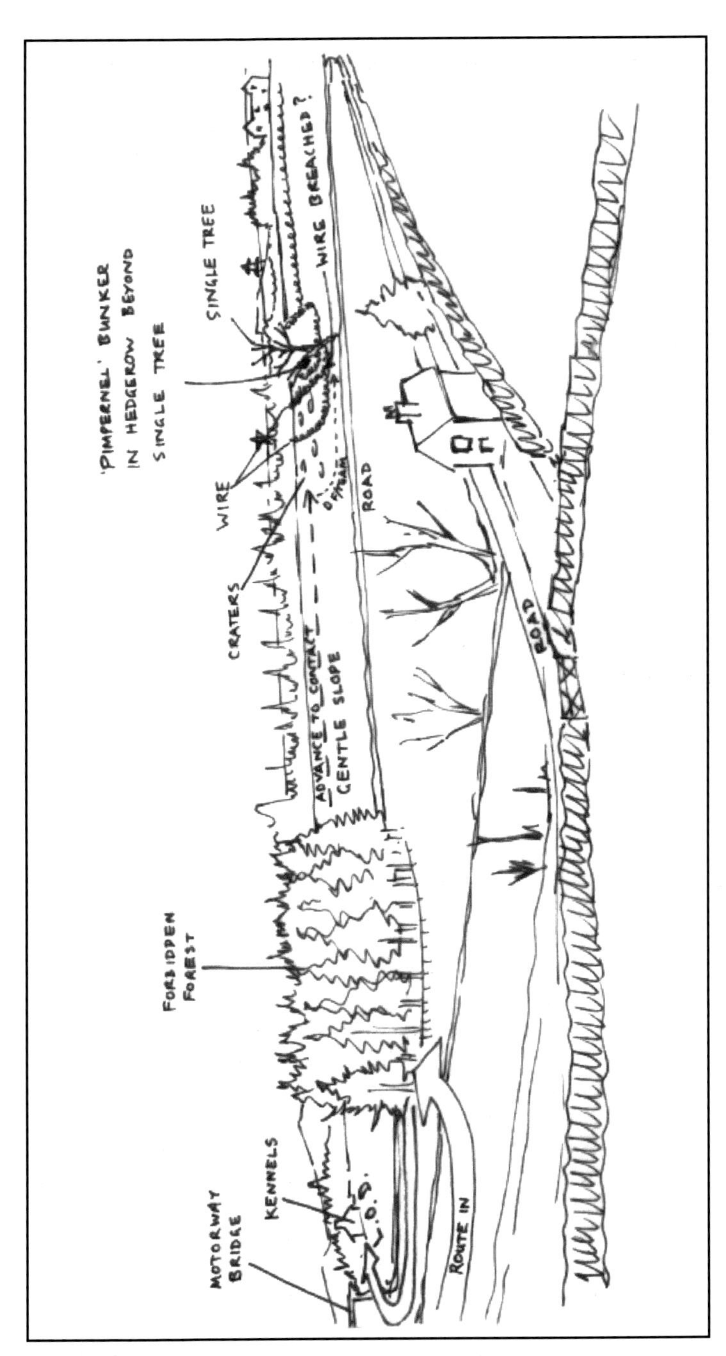

Robert Taylor's sketch of the southern approach to Storeton

secure the house and dog kennels by the motorway bridge. Brabander himself would then make his way back along the road and mark-out the line of departure using specially shrouded red, white and green torches fixed to flare pickets. While this was going on, Lieutenant Grudge would lead platoon HQ and assorted attached personnel into the wood, and shortly afterwards the lead assault sections under Robert and Corporal Kingsley would deploy along the roadside hedge which formed the line of departure. Finally, Blundell and Company HQ would move into the Forbidden Forest just before the attack was about to go in. Responsibility for the smooth and efficient deployment of all units that night would lie in the capable hands of the company Sergeant-major, Warrant Officer 'Taff' Jones.

From his concealed vantage point, Robert studied the ground between the line of departure and the enemy bunker which it was his mission to capture. The view was partly obstructed by the conifers of the Forbidden Forest, but he could see enough of the terrain to know that the approach would have to be made across a large expanse of grass, which was initially flat, then sloped gently up to the hedgerow in which the French bunker was located, close to the top of the hill. There was virtually no cover, apart from a few isolated bushes and a reed-filled pond, although the sloping landform might possibly provide a modicum of protected 'dead' ground for soldiers lying flat on their bellies. A post and wire fence which bisected the expanse of grass caused Robert some concern, as it could potentially hinder his progress at a crucial point in the advance. However, when he scrutinised it closely through his binoculars, he realised the French had unwittingly done him a favour by removing the barbed wire for use further up the slope.

Robert wiped the rain from his binocular lenses and examined the area around the bunker itself. It had been pounded by mortar fire since he had last seen it, and the ground was now pock-marked with muddy craters. The bombardment appeared to have destroyed the defensive wire in several places, but the actual bunker - which was well dug-in to the hedgerow - seemed to have escaped destruction. He sketched the scene in his notebook, taking particular care to make an accurate record of precisely where the wire had been breached and where it was definitely still intact, so that he could give Farrell as much information as possible; Lieutenant Grudge had decided that the actual assault on the two bunkers would be carried-out by each section's delta fireteam, led by the lance-corporals.

"Assaulting the bunkers is relatively straightforward – your 2ics are quite capable of handling that," the Lieutenant had told Robert and Kingsley. "I'm not saying they're expendable or anything, but I need my most experienced NCOs alive for when we enter the village and start the FIBUA phase. I can't afford to lose you right at the start."

In many respects, Robert was relieved to have been spared what was likely to be the most hazardous task of the entire operation, but he felt guilty that Farrell would have to do it instead.

When he had completed his annotated sketch of the objective area, Robert began formulating his plan of attack. According to Grudge's orders, the two bunkers defending the southern approaches to the village would be subjected to another mortar bombardment later that evening which might, hopefully, destroy them. However, it had to be assumed that the positions would survive, and require neutralizing in the traditional way - by infantrymen running and sweating and shouting and crawling and, finally, getting 'stuck-in' with rifles, grenades and bayonets. The advance up the slope was to be 'two-up', with Robert's section moving in extended line on the right and Kingsley's section on the left. Grudge and the platoon signaller and 'runner' would follow, separated from the lead sections by an arbitrary distance known as a 'tactical bound'. Behind them would come Brabander's section and Paul Murphy, the platoon sergeant.

In theory the attack was simple. Robert and Kingsley would lead their men towards the bunkers until they came under effective enemy fire. They would return fire until the enemy positions had been suppressed, then each 'delta' fireteam would conduct a flanking manoeuvre, approaching the bunkers from either side and destroying them with grenades. Of course, events were unlikely to proceed according to plan, so Robert tried to prepare in advance for possible eventualities, by asking himself a series of 'what if?' questions. What if his section suffered multiple casualties when the enemy first opened fire? What if the French directed accurate mortar fire onto them as they crossed the open ground? What if Farrell's assault failed? What if the French did not open fire at all – did it mean that the bunker was abandoned or destroyed, or was it a trap? There were so many possibilities that he began to feel overwhelmed and giddy with anxiety. He took a deep breath, put away his notebook and binoculars, and returned despondently to Eight Platoon's lines with the same sense of foreboding which was afflicting Pete Collins.

Back in his trench, Robert set about writing his orders. He set the time for his 'O' group at ten o'clock, but finished his preparations with about twenty minutes to spare, which gave him the opportunity to make a few last-minute changes to Farrell's model and rig-up a makeshift light-proof shelter around it using ponchos and bungee cords. At the same time, Monty's mortar began bombarding the two bunkers to the south of the village. Robert looked out through the trees and could see the flashes of the explosions far across the valley. He prayed that one of the bombs would land directly upon the 'Pimpernel' bunker, thereby sparing him and his men the unpleasantness of having to attack it. Then Farrell rounded-up the men, who emerged in solemn procession out of the rain-drenched darkness to lie on their bellies in the mud beneath the ponchos and stare at the model, which Robert illuminated dimly with a red-filtered torch. He waited until everyone was present, and glanced from one anxious, camouflaged face to the next. Then he swallowed hard to try to clear the lump in his throat, glanced down at his notebook, and sighed.

"Right, gents, this is it – the moment we've all been waiting for. For the benefit of Mister Shite, there will be a show tonight..." He was shaking almost uncontrollably. "Orders for a deliberate attack..."

When Robert had finished delivering his orders, he supervised rehearsals in a muddy clearing behind the trenches. The men of Two Section practised patrolling down to the Forming Up Point, deploying along the Line of Departure, advancing to contact, reacting to effective enemy fire, winning the firefight and assaulting the bunker. Finally, they rehearsed regrouping on the objective and responding to mortar bombardment or fire from depth positions. Shortly before midnight, Robert conducted a thorough kit inspection and then decided that any further preparation might be counter-productive.

"We'll call it a day for now," he told Farrell wearily. "There's no point in kicking the arse out of it – the lads'll start switching off, if they haven't already. I reckon they'll benefit more from an hour's rest. No Move Before time is zero-two-hundred hours. We'll get up at one-thirty for a final run-through and kit check, ready to hand-over the positions to the cadets. Make sure everyone packs away all their personal kit – hopefully we won't be coming back here again."

"Sure thing, boss."

"Oh – Farrell...?"

"Yeah?"

"Sorry about dumping the shitty job on you."

"What do you mean?"

"Attacking the bunker. Believe me, it's not my decision."

"Never mind. How else am I going to win my V.C.?"

Robert returned to his trench and wriggled into his sleeping bag, but could not relax, which was not surprising. He was far too worried about the night's mission and about Susan, with whom he had had no contact since giving her the French grenade almost two days ago. It was far too risky to try contacting her by mobile phone, as all calls made by soldiers were being monitored for security reasons until Operation Excise was over. He knew that Brian Salter's only chance of using the grenade against Radley had been during the cabinet meeting that afternoon, but as there had been no mention of any assassination attempt on the radio news bulletins, it had to be assumed that the desperate plan had failed. Suddenly, Robert became gripped with dread and panic as his mind concocted various worst case scenarios, including one in which Susan had been caught with the grenade and was now being tortured so horrifically that she was shouting his name repeatedly to betray him as the provider of the weapon. He abandoned the idea of sleep, even though he was exhausted, and occupied his mind by reading through his orders several times and checking that he had loaded tracer rounds into the top of his rifle magazines. At midnight, he changed the frequency on his radio and memorised the new password for the day, then decided that only one thing could raise his morale in such a dismal situation, and made himself a final mug of tea.

It was still drizzling with rain at a quarter to two in the morning, when the soldiers emerged from their trenches like condemned men on the day of execution, carrying their heavy bergens which were packed with all of their personal kit. They handed-over the positions to a force of nervous and excited cadets, who arrived with their manually-operated 'Ensign' rifles. The cadet's role that night was to occupy the trenches and fire tracer in the direction of Storeton when the attack began, in order to convince the French that the woods remained occupied, and hopefully deter a counter-offensive. Robert paused in the entrance to his trench and stared back into the dank, gloomy space. He had hated living there, but over the course of five months the squalid hole had become his home, and had faithfully sheltered him from weather, bullets and shrapnel. Now that the time had come to finally abandon its protection, he felt a sentimental attachment towards it and, like a baby about to emerge from the womb, was reluctant to leave. He really was very scared.

Robert carried out a final kit-check and inspection of his men and then, satisfied that preparations were as complete as they were ever going to be, led them up through the woods and onto the road. Corporals Brabander and Gorpe were already there with their sections, as were some assault pioneers and various soldiers from Company HQ. Corporal Kingsley arrived shortly afterwards with One Section. The bergens were loaded onto a four-tonne truck, while the Company Sergeant-major, 'Taff' Jones, lined the assault sections up along the wall in the correct order of march. Colour-sergeant Morris, the CQMS, provided the men with tea and soup as they waited in the rain, listening apprehensively to the distant *thump* of exploding mortar bombs and watching the minutes and seconds tick away on their watches.

Although fear was Robert's overwhelming emotion at that time, he also experienced a sense of excitement and pride at being a key player in such a momentous event. He felt a tingle of exhilaration at seeing so many people working together as a single entity with a common purpose, and was impressed by the professionalism of everyone he encountered. Each man knew what part he had to play in events that night, and even the cooks, clerks, storemen and drivers were fully prepared for battle and had an air of grim determination about them. Lance-corporal 'Duffer' Dudley brought packets of biscuits over to Robert's section and was virtually unrecognisable in full fighting order, with a heavily camouflaged face, bandoliers of ammunition draped around his neck, and a collapsible stretcher resting across one shoulder. His job that night was to supply the combat troops with ammunition, and assist in evacuating them to the Company Aid Post if they became casualties.

A tall figure, unidentifiable in the darkness, approached Robert's section and asked, "Who have we got here, then – Two or Three section?"

Robert recognized the voice as belonging to the CO, Colonel Hogan. "Two section, sir,"

"Ah – Corporal Taylor. You're taking out the right hand bunker aren't you?"

"For my sins yes, sir..."

"Good. Well, you don't need me to tell you how important your task is to the success of the whole operation. What I will say though is don't be afraid to use ammunition. When it comes to winning the firefight, let loose with everything you've got – absolutely mallet that position so no-one will dare even look out, let alone fire back at you. Be reassured that you will be get continuous ammo re-supply throughout the attack, so use maximum firepower and remember to call in fire support if you need to. By this time tomorrow I want Charlie Company occupying Storeton, without having sustained a single casualty, okay?"

"Sounds good to me, sir."

"Good luck"

"Thank you, sir."

Hogan moved on to talk to Corporal Kingsley and One section, while at the far end of the line, the Company Sergeant-major and Corporal Gorpe's section were setting off to occupy the Forbidden Forest. In his headphones, Robert could hear their radio checks crackling over the company net.

For a while, Robert and his men sat waiting by the wall, checking and re-checking their equipment and feeling increasingly despondent. Robert thought about Susan, and his family and friends, and wished that he could be with them all now, in a warm, dry room, wearing clean casual clothes, laughing and joking without any threat of death or injury or having to inflict death or injury upon others. All he wanted at that moment was to be in a civilised environment with people who cared about him. He hated waiting by the wall, as it gave him time to dwell upon unhealthy issues such as how he might be killed or injured, or whether he might fail to perform as required and, in doing so, put his men at risk. Jobie Silver and his *Challenging Negative Thinking* course had evidently failed, he thought wryly.

Eventually, Lieutenant Grudge emerged from the darkness to issue the order for Robert and Kingsley to proceed to the Forbidden Forest. The lieutenant was accompanied by several silhouetted figures, including the platoon 'runner' and the indispensable radio operator. There was also a diminutive man, whom Robert could not identify until he heard him speak. It was Lieutenant Monty, who was accompanying platoon HQ in his role as Mortar Fire Controller, or MFC. His job that night was to advance with the combat troops and direct accurate mortar fire onto enemy positions as and when required. Monty was clutching his SA80 rifle with gung-ho zeal, eager to use it against a human target during the operation.

Robert and Kingsley led their sections south along the road, heading away from Storeton. They followed the roadside hedgerow downhill until they came to a luminous green glow-stick, which the pathfinders had placed at a gateway in the hedge. There, they veered to the right into a field, and used the contours of the ground to conceal them from view as they descended towards the Forbidden Forest in the floor of the valley. In the distance, they could see the flashes of mortar bombs exploding in the vicinity of Storeton, although initially no sound could be heard; the muted *thud* of each detonation arrived several seconds later.

In the darkness of the forest there was more waiting to be done by Robert and his men, while the CSM guided Kingsley's section into position along the line of departure. Robert experienced a moment of panic when he suddenly thought that he might have forgotten to put fresh batteries in his night-sight, but then remembered that he had done so only an hour before. After what seemed like an age but was actually only a few minutes, 'Taff' Jones returned to collect Robert's section. The soldiers followed the CSM out of the conifer plantation, across the edge of a field, through a gateway and onto the road, which was out of sight of the French positions thanks to a high hawthorn hedge. Mortar bombs were still exploding about five hundred metres away at the top of the slope, sending fragments of shrapnel and debris pattering down onto the tarmac. 'Taff' Jones reached a gateway in the hedge and stopped.

"Right, Corporal Taylor, put your section along the hedge, from here back down the way we've just come – towards the conifer forest. Get your boys down in the ditch and await further orders, alright?"

"Right, sir."

Crouching low to the ground, Robert scurried back along the road and placed each of his men in the correct position, making sure that they knew in which direction the enemy positions lay, and instructing them to get down into the ditch at the base of the hedge.

"Bollocks to that, Corporal!" declared Private Harold indignantly. "It's full of bloody water!" Robert marvelled at how some soldiers would prefer to play Russian roulette with bullets and shrapnel rather than get their legs wet.

"Get down in it, you big girl's blouse!" he said, pushing Harold into the ditch, before moving on along the line.

When Robert reached Farrell, he checked that his second-in-command knew what was expected of him during the attack, and then asked teasingly, "What did Bromhead say when he found that Chard had taken his famous architect?"

Farrell thought for a moment. "Hmm. Don't tell me..."

"I'll leave it with you. Better go."

Robert scuttled back to his position near the centre of the extended line of soldiers, and slid down into the ditch. He was dismayed to find that it was rather deeper than he had expected - the cold water reached up to his thighs and made him shiver even more. By listening to the radio traffic over the company net he was able to get an impression of how the build-up to H-Hour was progressing, as various callsigns reported their status. He wiped the rain off his watch face and illuminated the faint screen. It was 02.40am: twenty minutes to go.

Peering through the hedge, Robert could see the flashes of mortar bombs exploding at the top of the slope with earth-shaking power, along with streams of tracer which were pouring onto the enemy positions from at least two SF guns firing from Mount Wood. It was an impressive spectacle, even though he knew that this was low-tech, low-budget warfare...High-tech, no-expense-spared total war, with its massed armour, artillery and air power, would be altogether more terrifying. Watching the display of firepower pounding the French positions, Robert came to the conclusion that this was no place for a man to be - no matter how much Kevlar you wrapped him in.

At 02.50am, Grudge arrived and moved into position to the rear of the hedge, behind Robert's section. Moments later, on Lieutenant Monty's order, smoke bombs were combined with the high-explosive ordnance being fired by the mortar in the Teehey Lane allotments. The quantity and urgency of radio traffic increased noticeably, as events swiftly began to gather momentum, like a steamroller released at the top of a hill. H-hour had finally arrived.

In the distance, several Schermully rocket flares lit up the night sky above Seven Platoon's TAOR, accompanied by the crackle of gunfire and the thud of explosions. This was the first of the diversionary attacks, and it was followed shortly afterwards by the distant sound of vehicle engines, as the two Trojans rumbled into life and clattered forward, with their attendant infantry sheltering behind them. One machine, accompanied by Sergeant Collins and a mixed force of sappers and men from Nine Platoon, began advancing slowly along Lever's Causeway towards Storeton. At the same time, the other Trojan, supported by a single section from Nine Platoon, lumbered down Rest Hill Road, bulldozing aside the burned-out wrecks of the two cars which had been ambushed by the British during Maurice's initial break-out back in November and had remained there ever since. As the Trojans advanced as noisily and ostentatiously as possible, the cadets in the woods opened fire with tracer rounds in the general direction of Storeton, to demonstrate that the line remained manned.

And to the south of the village, the men of Eight Platoon crouched grimly in the rain, and waited.

Lieutenant Maurice looked out from his command post inside the fortified three-storey farmhouse in the middle of the village, and knew that, finally, the day of reckoning had arrived. The British were about to launch an all-out assault which his beleaguered defenders could not hope to repulse. From the radio reports coming in from positions all around his defensive perimeter, it was clear that the British were approaching from several different directions. Maurice evaluated each piece of information as he received it, and decided that the main attack was almost certainly the one advancing along Lever's Causeway. He had no reserves with which to reinforce the positions in that area, but sent his platoon sergeant there with a rucksack of extra ammunition. Then he ordered his mortar, which was dug-in in a walled garden nearby, to fire all of its remaining rounds at the British forces on Lever's Causeway - more as a symbolic gesture of defiance than a serious attempt to halt the advance. All other troops were to remain in their allocated positions around the village perimeter until further notice, covering their arcs and firing at anything that moved.

In fact, having endured two days of sustained mortar and machine-gun bombardment, as well as five months' hardship under siege, during which they had subsisted on meat and bland flour cakes, many of the French defenders were by now so exhausted and demoralised that they had already laid down their weapons and were in the process of preparing white flags. They knew, as Maurice knew, that the outcome of the battle was a foregone conclusion - in which case there was no point in fighting to the bitter end. All that most of them wanted was to return home, alive and intact.

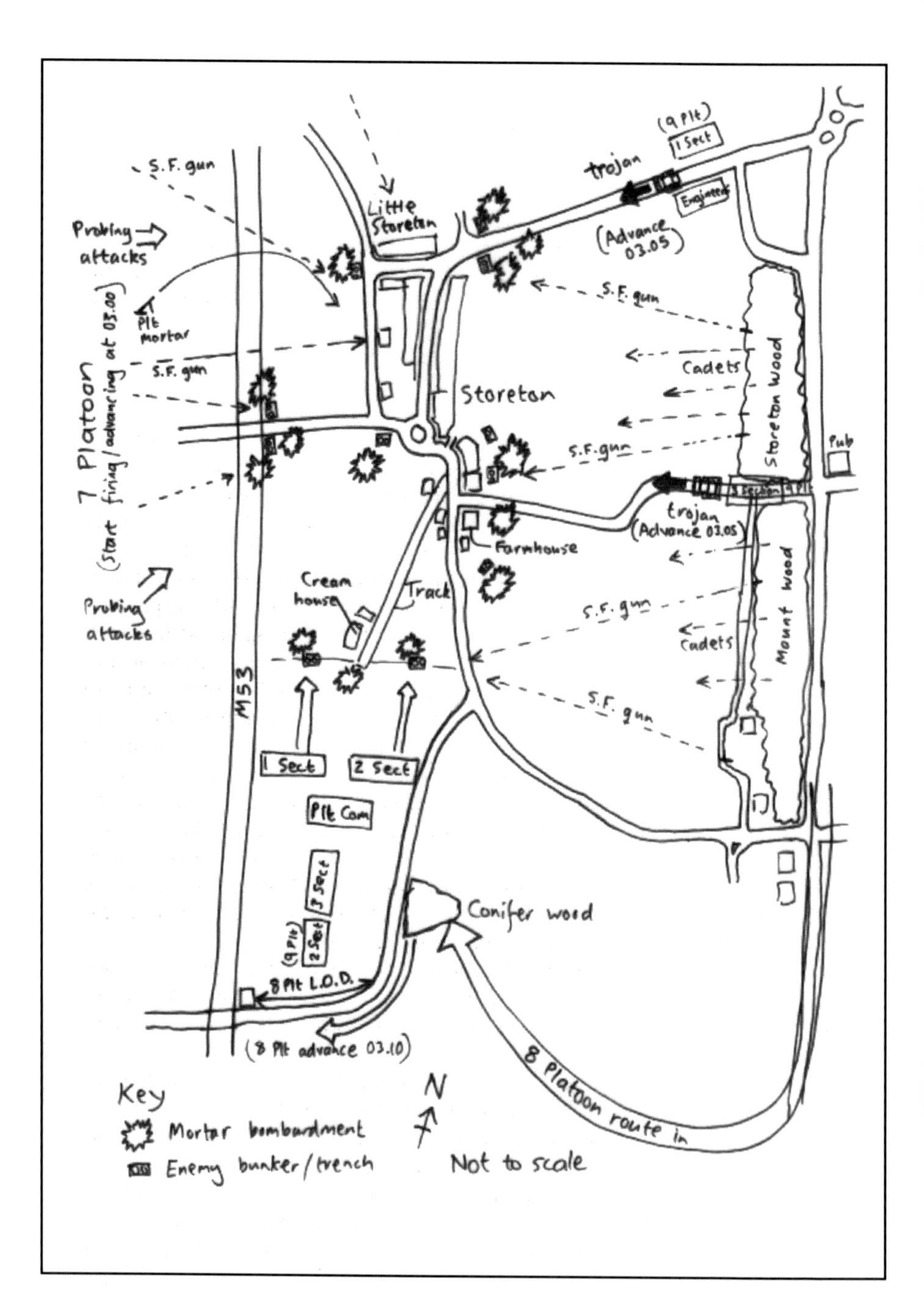

Major Blundell's sketch plan for the attack on Storeton

CHAPTER 45

The Battle for Storeton

A passable fictitious account of a small-scale infantry engagement.
Major Farah-Fawcett
2RWR Newsletter

Mr Roberts replies:
That's good enough for me, sir!

At just after three o'clock in the morning, with Eight Platoon in position and ready to advance, Sergeant-major 'Taff' Jones walked along the line of soldiers and issued the order to fix bayonets. Robert's hands were shaking so badly that, in an involuntary tremor of nervous clumsiness, he dropped his bayonet into the ditch, and had to grope around frantically in the black water to retrieve it. Lieutenant Grudge's voice crackled in his radio earpiece, instructing him and Kingsley to move their sections forward into the 'final attack position' in the field beyond the hedge. The soldiers had practised this manoeuvre during their rehearsals and it was executed quickly and efficiently, with the men at the far end of the line 'peeling off' and passing through the gateway in single file until they ended up in the same formation as before, but on the other side of the hedge. A long, gentle grassy slope was now all that separated them from the French positions at the top of the hill, which were shrouded in smoke. There were more flashes and deafening concussions as the final high-explosive bombs detonated, then Lieutenant Monty ordered his mortar team to make adjustments so that the rounds landed a considerable distance behind the bunkers, to avoid the risk of 'friendly fire' casualties.

Suddenly, a frantic voice crackled over the company radio net. "*Hello Zero this is Three-One Charlie, we have been DF'd and there are men down here. I say again, we have men down including Sunray, over...*"

Robert's heart sank. Three-One Charlie was one of the callsigns advancing down Lever's Causeway, and the word 'Sunray' referred to the unit commander, which meant that kind Sergeant Collins had been killed or wounded. It later emerged that Collins and his men had been blasted by shrapnel from French mortar bombs landing just behind the Trojan. A shard of steel had severed the sergeant's spine, just below his body armour, leaving him paralysed from the waist downwards and confined to a wheelchair for the rest of his life. War was indiscriminate in its random cruelty.

Lying in the soggy grass of the field, Robert used his night-sight to scan the view ahead but could distinguish little due to the darkness, the rain and the smoke. In a way this was reassuring, as the enemy would be similarly impaired when trying to spot the advancing British troops. His heart was pounding in his rib cage, and his breathing was rapid and shallow. Now that the mortar bombardment of the bunkers had ceased, it could only be a matter of minutes before the order to advance was given. He took advantage of the momentary lull in proceedings to empty his bladder into the grass upon which he was lying.

Suddenly Farrell called-out from the darkness over to Robert's right. "I've got to know, Corporal T!"

Robert grinned and put him out of his misery. "Who said you could use my *wren!*"

"Quiet in the ranks!" snarled the CSM from behind the hedge. "Come on boys – maintain battlefield discipline!"

Finally, just as the waiting was becoming unbearable, Lieutenant Grudge's voice came over the radio: "*Two-two Charlie and Two-three Charlie, this is Two-zero, prepare to move, over...*"

Robert acknowledged the message and relayed it to his men. He checked that his webbing pouches were secure, his helmet properly fastened and his rifle magazine was firmly in place, then waited for the order to advance. He did not have to wait long.

"*Two-two Charlie and Two-three Charlie, this is Two-zero. Move now. I say again, move now.*"

"Two section – move now," Robert called out to the men either side of him. He rose stiffly to his feet and, with great trepidation, began to walk across the grass towards the smoke-shrouded bunkers, which were still under fire from the Mount Wood machine guns; a steady stream of tracer continued to arc gracefully through the night sky before disappearing into the mass of smoke. Robert's greatest fear was being caught in the open by mortar fire, so he was eager to cross the field as quickly as possible. In the darkness it was impossible to discern anyone apart from the two men immediately to his left and right, and he prayed that the section was advancing in some sort of workable formation. They made good progress, passing between the wire-less posts of the fence which Robert had spotted during his visual reconnaissance the previous afternoon, and pressing on up the slope.

Suddenly, a tracer bullet whined through the air, very close by. It was, in fact, a ricochet from one of the British SF guns, but young Private Craven mistook it for effective enemy fire and loosed-off a couple of rounds in the general direction of the bunkers, before throwing himself to the ground. His actions precipitated a domino effect within the section, as other soldiers panicked and opened fire as well.

Confused and startled, Robert dropped down onto the wet grass and peered through his night-sight at the drifting curtains of smoke, trying to ascertain what was happening. "Can anyone see the enemy?" he shouted.

As if in response, there was a burst of automatic fire from the top of the slope, and bullets cracked overhead. Robert squirmed down into the grass in terror, trying to make himself as small a target as possible, but he retained sufficient composure to spot the enemy muzzle flashes. "Rapid fire!" he screamed. "Watch my tracer!"

He fired five shots in quick succession at the place where he had seen the muzzle flashes, sending tracer rounds streaking into the smoke. The rest of his section followed suit, the riflemen firing single shots with their M16s and the LSW gunners unleashing longer bursts. Tracer poured onto the enemy position, with some rounds ricocheting off into the sky while others bounced around on the ground like glowing embers. Over the radio net came the excited voice of Lieutenant Grudge, demanding to know what was going on.

"Contact, wait out," Robert replied quickly, as he tried to judge the distance to the enemy position. It was impossible to make an accurate estimate, but he guessed that the bunkers lay about two hundred metres away, which was further than he would have liked.

The enemy position had fallen silent, so he brought his section's fire under control and used the radio to tell Farrell to move his 'Delta' fireteam ten metres further forward. As soon as Farrell's men had advanced and had resumed laying-down suppressive fire on the bunker, Robert and his 'Charlie' fireteam dashed forward, zig-zagging as they ran, and threw themselves down onto the grass. They began firing at the bunker again, and the whole process was repeated. This alternating 'fire and movement' was exhausting for troops laden with ammunition and equipment, but it enabled them to cover ground without sustaining casualties, until the first coils of defensive barbed wire emerged from the smoke and Robert realised that his frontal attack could proceed no further. He contacted Grudge by radio to request that the SF guns switch their fire away from the bunker, then got in touch with Farrell: "Hello Two-two Delta, this is Two-two Charlie. Prepare to go right flanking, over."

"*Two-two Delta, roger that, over.*"

"*Two-two Charlie, move now, over.*"

"*Two-two Delta, moving now, out.*"

Delta fireteam peeled-off and sprinted away into the darkness off to Robert's right. Farrell led them down the side of the hill into dead ground, then followed the contours of the slope until he reached a hawthorn hedge. This hedge, the lance-corporal knew, ran all the way back up the slope to the top of the hill, and somewhere along its length lay the concealed bunker which was his target. He put Smythe in the lead, and the four of them began crawling cautiously up towards the enemy position.

By now the smoke was starting to dissipate, enabling Robert and the three other men of Charlie fireteam to put down fairly accurate suppressive fire onto what they assumed to be the bunker, located in the hedge to the left of an isolated ash tree. No enemy fire came back at them, effective or otherwise. Grudge continued to harass Robert over the radio, so he quickly provided a brief situation report to keep the lieutenant happy while Farrell's assault went in. In the darkness somewhere over to the left, shots could be heard as Corporal Kingsley's section advanced on the 'Scarlet' bunker, near to the M53 motorway.

Meanwhile, Farrell's fireteam had made good progress and was passing beneath the silhouetted branches of the distinctive ash tree, which meant that the bunker was not far away. The lance-corporal dropped-off Privates Cunningham and Craven at a point from which they could provide extra covering fire if necessary, then he and Smythe crawled onwards, staying close to the hedgerow for concealment. A bomb crater enabled them to slip undetected through a breach in the outermost coils of barbed wire, but then Smythe unwittingly set off a trip-flare hidden at the edge of the field. Behind him, Farrell threw himself to the ground, expecting to be on the receiving end of a murderous hail of bullets at any moment. In the flickering orange glare he could see the enemy position, protruding from the hedge about thirty metres away. "Go for the bunker, Smythe!" he shouted. "I'll cover you!"

Farrell began firing at the dark slits of the bunker while Smythe dashed forward, unaware that the trip-flare wire had also been attached to a delayed-action pipe bomb. Suddenly there was an explosion, and both men collapsed onto the grass. Concussed by the blast and peppered with shrapnel, Farrell rolled back down the slope, clutching his face.

Robert Taylor heard the explosion but could not see what was happening at the bunker. His initial attempts at contacting Farrell by radio were unsuccessful, but then there was a long burst of static and his second-in-command's voice came through the headset.

"*We're down, we're both down – there was an IED in the hedge, over...*"

Robert hesitated. He was desperate to help Farrell, but knew that his priority must be to neutralise the bunker. "Two-two Charlie, what is the situation with the bunker? Is it neutralised, over?"

"*No – negative, the bunker is not neutralised...over.*"

Painfully aware that his attack was in danger of losing its momentum or petering out altogether, Robert contacted Grudge. "Hello Two-zero, this is Two-two Charlie, be advised we have men down here and the position has not been neutralised, over."

"*Two-zero, how many men down? Can you provide zap numbers, over?*"

Robert cursed under his breath. Grudge had a fixation with zap numbers, which were reference codes for identifying individual soldiers without using their names, but in the heat of the moment Robert could not even remember his own number, let alone those of his men. So he simply replied, "It's Farrell and Smythe, over."

"*Two-zero, you will have to take that position before casevac can proceed. I say again, you must take that position immediately, before we can casevac your wounded...Out."*

Robert tried to stay calm, but was on the verge of panic. His mind raced frantically as he tried to assess the different options open to him. He considered firing an anti-tank missile at the bunker, but the poor visibility would create a high probability of missing, and might endanger Farrell and Smythe. In any case, there was no escaping the fact that the only way of confirming that the position was neutralised was to physically occupy it. So he decided to leave his two LSW gunners firing at the bunker from their present position while he and Stevenson moved around the right flank to finish what Farrell had started. Before he could move, however, Farrell's voice crackled over the radio again.

"*Hello Two-two Charlie, this is Two-two Delta, you need to switch fire, coz I'm about to assault the bunker, over.*"

In amazement, Robert complied with the request, and the two LSW gunners aimed off to the left but continued firing. Then, from out of the darkness behind, Lieutenant Grudge crawled up alongside without warning, and peered at the bunker through his night-sight.

"What's the situation, Corporal T?"

"I think Farrell's about to assault the bunker, sir."

In a display of great courage and determination, Farrell had crawled through the grass and mud towards the enemy position, which remained silent. Blood was trickling down his face, and his right arm was numb and only partially responsive, but somehow he reached the bunker and collapsed against the earth wall next to one of the firing slits. For a few moments he lay there, his chest heaving. Then he pulled a grenade from his webbing pouch and attempted to remove the pin. But his numb right hand lacked the strength and coordination to achieve the task, so he tried using his teeth, which was similarly unsuccessful – the ring almost ripped out his incisors without showing any sign of budging. After several attempts, he finally managed to pull the pin free by hooking the ring over the bayonet on the end of his rifle and giving the grenade a violent tug with his good hand. As soon as the pin was out, he posted the grenade into the bunker, shouted "Grenade!" and closed his eyes.

There was a loud explosion which shook the ground, and smoke poured from the bunker's firing slits. Farrell dropped a second grenade inside and, after it had detonated, poked his rifle muzzle into the bunker and sprayed the interior with bursts of automatic fire. The noise roused Private Smythe from unconsciousness and he started moaning, while overhead a Schermully flare *popped* and bathed the scene in flickering light. Farrell's rifle ran out of ammunition and he slumped down against the bunker, fumbling for his radio prestle switch. "Er, Hello Two-two Charlie, Two-two Delta here...Position clear, I think. Two grenades inside, can't do any more...it's all yours...Out."

Grudge slapped Robert on the back. "Superb effort! Now get in there, Corporal Taylor, and give 'em the good news!"

In the crazily lurching light of the spiraling parachute flare, Robert left his two LSW gunners with Grudge and, accompanied by Private Stevenson, followed the right-flanking route used earlier by Delta fireteam. He collected Private's Craven and Cunningham, who had been lying in the grass where Farrell had left them, and the four of them advanced up the slope in alternating pairs until they reached the bunker. Smythe was clearly in a bad way, but Robert could not risk tending to him until the bunker was confirmed as neutralized. He scurried over to Farrell and dropped down beside him.

"Well done, mate. We'll soon get you sorted, but we need to get inside first. Is there a way in?"

"I don't know. I didn't get that far..."

Robert left his men covering the bunker's firing slits while he tried, without success, to find a way inside. Grudge was pestering him over the radio again, but he was determined not to be pressured into acting rashly; once, on exercise, he had carried out an almost flawless attack against a bunker similar to this one, only to be 'killed' when he carelessly stood up and exposed himself to an enemy depth position which suddenly opened fire from a hundred metres away. If he made such a mistake now there would be no second chance, no miraculous return to the land of the living at the end of the scenario. He had only one life, and was determined to keep it. Personal survival was his overriding priority now – he had not endured months of misery to get killed just as the end was in sight.

Grudge fired up another rocket flare while Robert crawled cautiously around the bunker, looking for an entrance. Mortar rounds were exploding in the centre of the village and, not far away across the field on the other side of the hedge, the cream-coloured house which was Brabander's objective that night was being pummelled by machine gun fire from Mount Wood. Over the radio came Corporal Kingsley's voice, joyfully announcing that the 'Scarlet' bunker had received a direct hit from a mortar bomb and been captured without a fight. Tormented by Farrell's groans and Smythe's screams, Robert felt envious and resentful.

Suddenly Private Craven, who had moved further along the hedge to cover the approach from Storeton, called out, "Corporal – over here!"

Robert crawled over to where Craven crouched in a bomb crater. The mortar bomb had severed the hedge and, in the process, unearthed a low, narrow tunnel leading to the bunker.

"Craven – I need you to get in there and make sure the position's clear, okay?"

Unsurprisingly, young Private Craven, who had only recently joined the section, was less than enthusiastic about the proposal. "I'm not going in there, Corporal, no way."

Robert hesitated for a moment, wondering whether to threaten the soldier with court-martial for disobeying a direct order. But it was obvious that Craven was scared, just as they were all scared, and shouting at him would serve no purpose. Time was of the essence here and decisive action was required if the attack was not to falter.

"Okay, I'll do it," Robert declared wearily. "You keep watch here. Make sure you cover that opening there, in case anyone comes down the tunnel from the other side, okay?"

Craven nodded. "Okay, Corporal."

Robert crouched down and fired several bursts into the tunnel. Then he shrugged-off his daysacks and webbing, tucked a spare magazine into his combat smock, and squirmed into the cramped aperture with his rifle held out in front of him. The tunnel had a bare earth floor, but strips of wood had been used to prevent the walls and roof from collapsing. It was only slightly wider and higher than the dimensions of a man lying down, forcing Robert to squirm and wriggle like a worm, using his elbows, knees and toecaps to push himself along.

Ahead, he could just make out a patch of slightly lighter darkness, which suggested that he was nearing the actual bunker. He fired another precautionary burst, which deafened him in the confines of the passageway, and moments later his bayonet embedded itself in something firm yet slightly yielding. Suddenly, the impetuous bravado which he had displayed to Craven disappeared, replaced by a claustrophobic panic, as he realised that something was blocking the tunnel ahead. This was a personal nightmare of his – to be trapped in a dark, confined space, unable to go forward or back. He closed his eyes with a whimper and was on the verge of succumbing to despair, when some innate survival instinct took over and galvanized him into action. Summoning all of his strength, he rammed his rifle forward, and the object yielded a little, enabling him to force his head and arms into the bunker. He clawed desperately with his hands to push aside whatever it was that was preventing access. It felt initially like a large, warm, slippery sandbag, but then he realised with horror that it was in fact a corpse. His face contorted in revulsion as he frantically rolled onto his back, grasped the wooden lintel above the tunnel opening and, using a combination of arm and leg power, forced himself up over the body and into the chamber beyond. Panting and trembling almost uncontrollably, he retrieved his rifle and used the torch taped beneath the barrel to check that he and the bearded Frenchman – who was undoubtedly very dead – were the bunker's only occupants. Almost delirious with relief, he contacted Grudge by radio to tell him that the position was clear. Then he shouted "Two section! Re-org! Reorg!" out of the firing slits, and crawled as fast as he could from the smoky, tomb-like chamber, back into the wonderful damp freshness of the open air.

When the rest of his section arrived, Robert detailed two men to tend to Farrell and Smythe, and deployed the remainder in defensive positions around the bunker. He nominated Private Stevenson to take over from Farrell as section second-in-command, and tasked him with finding out how much ammunition each man possessed, so that it could be re-distributed if necessary.

Another Schermully flare ignited overhead and illuminated a motley group of soldiers, who were toiling up the slope towards the captured position. They were led by Lieutenant Grudge, who immediately crawled onto the grass roof of the bunker to try to see the platoon's next objective – the isolated cream-coloured house, which stood at the end of a track leading right into Storeton. Accompanying the officer and his radio operator were the platoon 'runner', who was laden with bandoliers of ammunition, Lieutenant Monty and a stretcher party under the command of Sergeant-major Morris, the CQMS. In the darkness, Robert watched the silhouettes of Morris and 'Duffer' Dudley as they tended to Farrell, who was entering a state of shock as the anaesthetising effect of natural adrenalin and endorphins wore off.

"Don't worry, Farrell son, we'll have you out of here in no time," the CQMS said reassuringly, placing the absorbent pad of a field dressing against the side of Farrell's face, before rolling him onto a stretcher. "Just hang in there, everything's going to be fine...Right, Dudley, one two three – lift!" They heaved Farrell up off the ground and disappeared into the night, running back down the slope towards one of the ambulances waiting under the motorway bridge. Moments later, Smythe had been evacuated too.

Brabander's section arrived, accompanied by a party of assault pioneers armed with SA80s. They hurried past Robert and moved further up along the hedge, ready to attack the cream-coloured house. Robert could not help chuckling to himself as he watched them go by. The assault pioneers were mostly short, stocky men with glasses – Conrad always referred to them as 'The Munchkins' – and several of them were carrying ladders and grappling hooks... To the emotionally drained Robert Taylor, they seemed a bizarre and comical sight – reminiscent of 'The Keystone Cops' – and he laughed out loud with nervous relief, smug in the knowledge that he had achieved his objective and survived, for the time being at least. Now it was Brabander's turn.

Grudge disappeared with the house-clearing party, leaving Robert leaning wearily against the bunker, listening to the radio traffic over the company net. From the various exchanges of dialogue, he ascertained that the RSM, who had taken over from the injured Pete Collins on Lever's Causeway, had led a small force right up to the edge of the village and captured two trenches, from which white flags were flying. Other reports indicated that French resistance was crumbling, and enemy troops were fleeing westwards, across the motorway and into the killing areas prepared by Seven Platoon.

Suddenly the SF guns stopped firing at the cream-coloured house, and a cacophony of small-arms fire erupted nearby as Brabander's assault went in. There was a lot of strident shouting and some more shooting, followed by an enormous *bang!* as the assault pioneers used an explosive 'mousehole' charge to blast through one of the walls and create an entry point into the house. Robert peered over the bunker to try to see what was going on, but the building was hidden from view behind a screen of tall conifers which were silhouetted against the night sky. Several muted explosions – presumably grenades detonating within the house – were followed by bursts of automatic fire and frantic shouting, as Brabander's entry team stormed the first room. Meanwhile, Gorpe's section arrived on the scene from the Forbidden Forest to act as reserves, and Sergeant Murphy laboured up the slope carrying a bergen full of ammunition and grenades, which he passed to the runner for distribution to the sections. Moments later, Murphy was hurrying back down the slope, dragging behind him two stumbling French prisoners with sandbags over their heads.

Gorpe's section was called forward, and crouched behind the hedge at the top of the slope, awaiting orders. It was still raining, but the sky had begun to lighten slightly as dawn approached. Robert slid off the roof of the bunker into a safer position behind the earth walls. Now that the excitement of his section's attack was over, he was feeling cold and immensely tired, and was drifting gradually into a state of blissful semi-consciousness. Suddenly, Brabander's voice crackled over the radio, jolting him back to reality with the welcome news that the house had been captured without British casualties. Operation Excise was proceeding as planned: Eight Platoon now had a foothold in Storeton, from which they could launch the next phase of the attack and liberate the entire village.

Another group of unidentifiable soldiers made its way up the slope from the Forbidden Forest and approached Robert's location, until challenged by one of his men.

"Halt! Advance one and be recognized! Sierra Lima!"

"Uniform Golf," replied a familiar voice, which Robert could not quite identify. "Who've we got here then? I'm hoping it's Corporal Taylor and Two Section."

Robert was intrigued. "It is. Who's that?"

"The O.C."

"Oh, hello, sir."

"So you managed to take your first objective, Corporal T – well done."

"Lance-corporal Farrell deserves the credit, sir. He did all the hard work. I just turned up at the end when it was all over."

"Well, well done anyway. Now, I've just heard that Three Section have taken the cream-coloured house. I need you to get your men ready to press on into the village, as soon as I've spoken to Lieutenant Grudge. We need to maintain the momentum of our attack. Be ready to move in, shall we say, minutes four, okay Corporal?"

"Right, sir," Robert replied sullenly, feeling resentful at being re-tasked so swiftly.

"Keep up the good work, Corporal T." Blundell said, then he and his entourage hurried on up the slope towards the cream-coloured house.

Robert called after them: "Oh – sir! How's the whole thing going? The big picture, I mean?"

"Very well, from the reports we're receiving," Blundell called back, as he vanished into the darkness. "All indications are that they're routed!"

In the war office in the town hall, Susan Fletcher listened with great anxiety to the radio traffic and casualty reports coming from the battlefield. Her main job that night was to make sure that the positions of the model soldiers representing the various units were continually updated on a large model of Storeton and its environs. Coloured flags and labels were used to record where casualties had been sustained or inflicted, and she had a list of soldier's names and zap numbers with which to initiate the sensitive process of informing next of kin. There had been nine British casualties during the operation so far. Her relief that none of them had been Robert was accompanied by a sense of guilt, arising from the realisation that, while they were unknown to her, the injured or dead men were *somebody's* lover, or son, or father, or brother, or friend.

In the centre of the room, Duncan Silverlock paced up and down, rubbing his hands impatiently and muttering comments such as, "Come on, get it over with!" or, "Why on earth is it taking them so bloody long?" He was desperate to bring glad tidings to his beloved Council Leader.

CHAPTER 46

A Despicable Act

A delicious blend of cynicism, horror, black humour and good old-fashioned far-fetched fantasy. I loved it! If you only read one book this year, make it this one.

Katie Burrows
Female Fitness magazine

Mr Roberts replies:
Cheers - the cheque's in the post!

At dawn, Lieutenant Grudge sent Corporal Gorpe's section forward along the track which led from the cream-coloured house right into the centre of Storeton. Robert and his remaining men were ordered to advance in extended line through the fields and gardens to the right of the track, while Kingsley's section moved up on the left side. Progress was slow and cautious, as it was vital that the advance did not bypass any hidden Frenchmen, who might suddenly emerge to shoot the liberators in the back.

Halfway along the track, Gorpe's men came across a badly injured enemy soldier lying on the tarmac, who had evidently been caught in the open when Monty's mortar had switched fire away from the bunkers. The British troops disarmed and searched him, then administered basic battlefield first aid, called for a medic, and pressed on until they reached some cottages. Each dwelling had to be cleared room by room, which was a time-consuming and nerve-wracking process.

By now there was sufficient daylight to see unaided, so Robert removed the night-sight from his M16 and put it away in one of his daysacks. A few minutes later, his section discovered a trip wire stretched across a gateway, connected to something nasty hidden in a hedge. They made no attempt to disarm the device, but carefully tied strips of white mine tape around the wire to make it more conspicuous, before leaving it for the assault pioneers and moving on.

The rain had finally stopped, leaving the morning cool and overcast and the landscape damp and dreary. Sporadic gunshots could be heard in the distance from Seven Platoon's area, but Storeton itself was eerily quiet, and the advancing British troops began to relax a little. All indications were that the enemy had abandoned their positions during the night and attempted a withdrawal across the killing areas to the west of the village, where they had been slaughtered by mortar and machine gun fire. The RSM, entering Storeton from Lever's Causeway, reported a similar absence of enemy troops in the northern part of the village.

Shortly after dawn, Corporal Gorpe's section reached a junction where the track leading from the cream-coloured house joined the main metalled road passing through the centre of the village. There they halted, while the scout in the lead crouched down next to a stone wall and cautiously scanned the view ahead for signs of enemy activity. Suddenly, there was a single loud *crack!* and he collapsed. Behind him, the rest of the section immediately took cover, but Gorpe bravely dashed forward, grabbed the scout's ankle, and dragged him back into the shelter of the wall. Gorpe fumbled frantically for the scout's field dressing, but blood was gushing from a bullet wound to his throat, and he was almost certainly beyond help. As Gorpe reported the situation to Lieutenant Grudge by radio, all of the British soldiers in the vicinity sighed with despair: evidently the fighting was not over yet.

Sensing that his corporals were flagging, Grudge hurried along the track and took charge of the situation. The shot which had killed the scout had been fired at an angle which suggested that it had come from the large three-storey farmhouse on the other side of the road. Under the cover of smoke grenades, Grudge deployed Gorpe's men in an arc focusing upon the farmhouse, with instructions to watch and shoot, and dispatched Robert's and Kingsley's sections to completely encircle the building. Then the lieutenant forced his way into one of the cottages at the end of the track and crept into the front room, from where he was able to peer through the net curtains at the farmhouse across the road. After studying it closely for a while, he shivered with dismay: the building showed obvious signs of having been fortified into a strongpoint, which was bad news for his platoon.

Grudge knew that a fortified building could be an infantry soldier's worst nightmare - a veritable haunted house of horrors, filled with every conceivable means of killing or maiming which the ingeniously cruel human brain could devise for inflicting misery upon fellow men. Inside the building, the walls and ceilings would be shored up with timber props to prevent collapse, ensuring that the house could withstand all but a direct hit from mortar or artillery fire. Within each room, sandbags and soil-filled furniture would be used to create sangars from which the defenders could fire with virtual impunity. All doors would be barricaded shut, and the glass in the windows replaced with chicken-wire screens and strips of Hessian, to prevent grenades being thrown in while simultaneously allowing the defenders to fire out. Attacking soldiers who succeeded in gaining entry through a window would find themselves confronted by a mass of razor wire and booby-traps. The house would have to be cleared a room at a time, enabling the defenders to slip away to safety using secret escape holes knocked through walls and hidden inside cupboards or under beds. The attacking force would be denied movement between floors by sheets of greased corrugated iron, or planks with six-inch nails driven through them, which would be fixed over the stairs and complemented by grenade booby-traps suspended at face height. With sufficient time, the entire building could be turned into a terrifying labyrinth of death, into which assaulting soldiers entered at their peril. It was even possible for a ruthless enemy to escape un-noticed along sewers or tunnels, and then blow-up the building with the attackers trapped inside. Grudge was aware that a single, well-constructed and resolutely defended fortified house could turn an entire platoon into casualties before it finally succumbed. He had no intention of sending his men into this one.

Alistair Blundell arrived on the scene, and he and Grudge discussed how to proceed. The major was being repeatedly pestered by Colonel Hogan for situation reports, while Hogan himself was being harassed by Duncan Silverlock in the War Office, who wanted to know how long it would be before he could inform Gerald Radley that the entire village was back in British hands.

By mid-morning, it had become apparent that the fortified farmhouse was the only remaining pocket of French resistance in Storeton. The British had completely surrounded the building with a ring of troops, reinforced by the RSM's small force and a Trojan, which had advanced south from Lever's Causeway and linked-up with Eight Platoon. Both Blundell and Grudge were extremely reluctant to assault the house so, to save time and lives, the major contacted the War Office and asked Silverlock to send an interpreter, who, it was hoped, might be able to persuade the French to surrender. Silverlock agreed, but announced that he was on his way, "To assess the situation and maybe hurry things along." He met Colonel Hogan at the top of Lever's Causeway at midday and, accompanied by the interpreter and a phalanx of bodyguards, they drove in convoy through the smouldering, rubble-strewn village to where Grudge and Blundell were waiting.

"So, what's the situation, Alistair?" Silverlock asked brusquely. "Why is this taking so long?"

Blundell had never been particularly fond of Duncan Silverlock, and today he liked him even less than usual. "Well, Duncan, we're fairly sure we've taken the entire village except for that farmhouse across the road. We reckon it's been fortified into a strongpoint, and whoever's in command here is probably holed-up inside...anyone else would probably have surrendered by now."

Silverlock was unimpressed. "Well, we need to resolve this unsatisfactory situation right away, don't we, gentlemen?"

The interpreter was put to work immediately with her megaphone, reading out a message written by Hogan which acknowledged the heroic stand made by the occupants of the house, but urged them to surrender. Repeated readings of the message failed to elicit a response from the French, and Silverlock tutted impatiently.

"Listen," he told the three officers curtly, "we haven't got time to waste here. Council Leader Radley is lying wounded in a hospital bed, and the one thing that'll help him pull through will be the news that the French have been completely defeated here in Storeton. So let's stop being so bloody chivalrous and deliver these bastards an ultimatum."

He turned to the interpreter. "Tell them that unless they surrender and come out with their hands up in the next five minutes, we'll destroy the house and everyone in it, okay?"

The interpreter dutifully did as she was told and the ultimatum, in French, echoed through the village. Silverlock checked his watch, and the countdown began.

"Destroying the house may be easier said than done, Duncan," Blundell pointed out. "It's a good solid building and it's probably been reinforced, remember."

"Honestly, I thought you soldiers were supposed to be experts at destroying things," Silverlock snorted dismissively. "Surely it's simple – we just burn them out. You've got petrol, presumably?"

His proposal was frankly repellent to the officers, but they could not oppose his wishes without being guilty of disobeying orders from a higher authority. So, after five minutes had elapsed without any response from the French in the farmhouse, some jerry cans of petrol were brought up by Land Rover and stacked on the platform at the rear of the Trojan. Smoke grenades were thrown at the building, then the order 'Rapid fire!" was given and every British soldier in the encircling cordon began shooting at the doors and windows of the house to 'keep the enemy's heads down'. Under cover of the smokescreen and suppressive fire, the Trojan clattered across the road, smashed through the garden wall and rammed its bulldozer blade into the side of the house just below a window, knocking out bricks and dislodging the chicken-wire anti-grenade screen. Two assault pioneers, who had been sheltering behind the machine, ran forward and heaved jerry cans of fuel - from which the caps had been unfastened – though the window and into the room beyond. One man draped a petrol-soaked bed sheet over the window sill to make a crude fuse, while the other poured fuel over the front lawn. Then they both ducked back behind the protective bulk of the Trojan, which reversed across the road and retreated into cover behind one of the cottages. Lieutenant Grudge gave the command, "Stop! Watch and shoot, watch and shoot!" and the suppressive fire petered out. Silence descended over the village once again. The British watched the house intently, but there were still no signs of life.

"The whole place must stink of fuel," Colonel Hogan remarked. He turned to the interpreter with the megaphone. "Give them another chance to surrender..."

A second message was directed at the house, warning those inside that, unless they came out immediately, the entire building would be set alight. Moments later, an improvised white flag was waved from an upstairs window, and a dejected-sounding voice shouted:

"We come out now. Don't shoot, please."

There was a commotion inside one of the ground floor rooms, presumably as barricades were cleared aside and booby-traps disarmed to allow the occupants to exit. An unarmed Frenchman climbed out of the window onto the petrol-soaked grass. He turned to help lift a casualty on a stretcher out through the window, then assisted the exit of another soldier, whose face was covered with bloodstained bandages. The final man to emerge was a lance-corporal with one arm in a sling. All four soldiers were bearded, sullen, haggard and filthy.

"Over here!" shouted Sergeant Murphy, gesturing urgently with his rifle, and the Frenchmen walked wearily across the road and into captivity. The lance-corporal with the injured arm was clutching a piece of paper, which he handed to Murphy. On it was written:

I do not surrender. Damn you English! Burn me you bastards - like the children!

Lieutenant Philippe Maurice

Duncan Silverlock leant over, read the note and shrugged callously. "Well, if that's what the man wants, let's give him what he asks for!"

A Molotov cocktail was duly prepared using a glass bottle found in one of the cottages, but no soldier would volunteer to throw it, and their officers refused to order any of them to do so. Exasperated by the Army's lack of cooperation, Silverlock turned to one of his own bodyguards. "You'll have to do it, Littler. There's a thousand pound bonus in it for you."

So the SCW bodyguard lit the petrol bomb's cloth fuse, ran out from behind cover and hurled the burning bottle at the farmhouse. It smashed against a wall and burst into flames, setting the garden alight and swiftly igniting the fuel inside the downstairs room. The flames spread quickly, and very soon the entire house was ablaze, consumed by a truly horrific inferno which roared and screamed and hissed and crackled, pouring billowing clouds of black smoke into the sombre grey sky.

The fatigued British troops watched the building burn in respectful silence, mourning the death of a man who had won their respect and admiration during the past months, even though they knew nothing about him. Suddenly their victory in Storeton seemed hollow and of dubious morality, and any soldier who witnessed Duncan Silverlock strutting up and down with self-satisfied smugness while filming the blaze with his mobile phone could not help but suspect that the real enemy was not the French, but rather the dishonourable, immoral and self-serving autocrats of their own loathsome Council.

CHAPTER 47

And Then There Were Two

A rogue councillor leading his community into an unnecessary war, funded by increased parking charges and the sale of school playing fields...Of course, beneath it all lies Tony Blair's war in Iraq. As an allegory it lacks subtlety, but I found it fairly entertaining nonetheless.

Percival Pilchard
Borehamwood Gazette

Mr Roberts replies:
For your information, Mr Pilchard, the idea for my story originated during a conversation between the real Mark Conrad and myself, which took place a year before Mr Blair even came to power.

Gerald Radley was so delighted by the news of Storeton's liberation that he immediately contacted Paul Ryder in Public Relations and instructed him to arrange a press conference that very afternoon.

"This is precisely the sort of positive news the public have been waiting for," he declared proudly, as if he had led the assault himself. "So let's tell them about it straight away and watch our popularity ratings soar. Even our most negative, defeatist critics can't scoff at this. At last – a real victory!"

Radley's doctors forbade him from leaving the hospital, so the press conference would by necessity have to be a small-scale affair, held in the intimate surroundings of his room. Only three representatives from the media would be present: a journalist from the *Herald;* a radio reporter from Wirral FM; and a cameraman from the PR Department, who would record the interview for broadcast via the Council website. When the necessary arrangements had been made, Radley demanded to be wheeled into the room next door, where Terence McCarthy lay in bed, attached to numerous monitors and drips.

"Terence, how the devil are you?"

McCarthy looked at him with reproach. "Well, Gerald, I'm waiting to hear whether I'll get to keep one or both of my kidneys, but apart from that I'm bloody awful." The grenade had evidently not blasted away the chief executive's cynicism.

"Well, I've got some great news to help cheer you up: Duncan's just informed me that we've booted the Frogs out of Storeton!"

"Great. I'd rather have my kidneys to be honest, Gerald."

"Don't worry – we'll sort you out, old chum. I'm sure you'll soon be on the mend, but if there's a problem we'll just find some peasant who's a suitable donor and whisk their kidneys out for you in a jiffy. The privileges of power!"

McCarthy was in no mood for joviality or facetious remarks of any kind. The medical team at Arrowe Park was still in the process of assessing his injuries, but the prognosis was not looking good, and he blamed Radley for his condition.

The Council Leader sensed his former friend's hostility and tried adopting a more compassionate tone. "Where's Helen?" he asked. Helen was McCarthy's devoted wife of twenty-six years, who had been at his bedside throughout the night.

"She's popped back home to check on Sarah and pick up a few things for me."

"And how is Sarah these days? She must be seventeen by now, am I right?"

"Eighteen. She's fine."

"And what about your son? You don't seem to mention him much these days..."

"He's surviving, as far as I know. He's moved out of the area – work commitments, you know how it is these days..."

Radley sighed. "I'll leave you to it, then. Remember, I'm just next door if you need me. Oh, Terence – I'm holding a press conference this afternoon in my room, and I'd like you to be involved. After all, you saved my life, and I want the proles to know about what's happened to you, and how these bloody barbaric activists will stop at nothing to create instability. Will you say a few words for me?"

McCarthy tilted his face towards the ceiling and closed his eyes with a weary sigh. "I'll think about it, Gerald. Right now I just want to be left alone..."

Meanwhile, three kilometers away in Storeton, a jubilant Duncan Silverlock had insisted on being taken on an escorted tour of the liberated village. Accompanied by Major Blundell and some soldiers from Eight Platoon, he made his way through the houses and gardens, displaying an almost perverse fascination with the damage and debris of war.

In one garden, the group came across the abandoned French mortar, protected within a deep pit which had been dug right down to the subsoil. Discarded bomb packaging littered the site, but not a single live round was evident, suggesting that the crew had run out of ammunition before destroying the weapon with a phosphorous grenade down the barrel. Further on, in a beautiful garden in the northern part of the village, the group made the poignant discovery of a small cemetery comprising seven neat graves in a row, each marked with an improvised cross, upon which the name, rank and number of the deceased had been painstakingly carved by hand. The garage of the house next door was found to contain a portable two-stroke petrol generator, which explained how the French had managed to keep the batteries for their radios and other equipment charged throughout the siege.

"I think it might be best if we don't go right to the end of the lane," Blundell advised as they neared the edge of the village, close to the fields across which the enemy had fled during the night. "We can't be sure that the area's secure...Shall we call it a day, Duncan?"

"Oh no!" Silverlock declared indignantly. "I want to see everything! Show me where we finished them off last night – I insist!"

So they walked solemnly to the low sandstone wall which marked the western extent of the village, and stared out across the muddy, bomb-cratered field, upon which lay a few scattered corpses.

"Aha," declared Silverlock with satisfaction. "The killing fields..."

Mark Conrad had spent the duration of the battle lying hidden in a hedgerow to the north-west of Storeton, with orders to keep watch on a stream culvert under the motorway which represented a possible escape route for enemy troops trying to withdraw back to Thurstaston. The hours of darkness had been uneventful, but shortly after first light a single French soldier had emerged furtively from the culvert and crept along the hedgerow towards his position. Conrad had killed him with a single bullet through the chest, and his body lay in the grass about a hundred metres away.

Conrad remained concealed in the hedgerow until the afternoon, when he received a radio message recalling him back to Storeton. He waited a few minutes, scanning the surrounding landscape through his binoculars until he was satisfied that it was safe to move. Then, emerging from cover, he crept cautiously down to where the French soldier lay at the edge of the meadow. After confirming that the man was definitely dead, Conrad relieved him of his rifle, bayonet, magazines and grenades. He wrapped the items in a heavy-duty polythene bag and sealed it with electrical tape, before stuffing it into his bergen and setting off towards Storeton via a cross-country route. In a patch of dense scrubland near the motorway, he used his entrenching tool to dig a deep hole, in which he buried the bag containing the French rifle and equipment.

Using copses and hedgerows for concealment, Conrad approached to within three hundred metres of Storeton, then stopped. He knew that, the closer he got to the village, the greater was the risk of being mistakenly shot by his own comrades, so he decided to notify them of his approach. But, just as he was about to send his radio message, something caught his eye: a group of figures, standing by the wall at the edge of the village, looking out across the fields. Intrigued, Conrad viewed them through his telescopic sight. Major Blundell he recognised instantly, together with a couple of soldiers from Brabander's section, but two mysterious civilians wearing helmets and body armour defied initial identification. When he studied them more closely he felt sure that he knew the bespectacled man from somewhere, although he could not place him out of context. Then a cold shiver of malicious excitement passed through him, as he realised that he was looking at none other than Duncan Silverlock, the senior Council executive to whom he had taken a dislike the previous month. Revenge really would be very sweet…

Conrad unfolded his rifle's bipod, and adopted a comfortable position from which he could fire out across the field while remaining concealed within the hedge. Usually, he would have aimed for the 'central body mass' of any human target, but there was a possibility that someone of Silverlock's importance might be wearing ceramic plate body armour capable of stopping a rifle bullet, so he raised his point of aim before squeezing the trigger.

The Deputy Council Leader's head jerked backwards and he dropped to the ground like a marionette with its strings cut, shot through the face from a range of three hundred metres. A second later the sound of the gunshot arrived. Blundell and the rest of Silverlock's entourage dived for cover, while Conrad slipped away unnoticed, almost invisible in his heavily camouflaged ghillie suit. He skirted around to the north of the village and entered Storeton along the Roman Road, listening with amusement to the agitated radio traffic over the company net which was warning all callsigns to be extra vigilant, as an enemy sniper had appeared and seemed able to pick-off targets at will.

Colonel Hogan immediately telephoned Gerald Radley at Arrowe Park hospital and informed him of Silverlock's death. Upon receiving the news, the Council Leader turned cold and was unable to speak.

"We've got all available units out there looking for this sniper," the colonel told him, "and I can assure you, Council leader, that he won't get away…"

Radley's heart monitor displayed a sudden increase in beats per minute, as it occurred to him that the French sniper who had killed Duncan Silverlock was less than two miles from his own hospital bed, and might make a desperate bid to assassinate him. Then he thought about the situation some more, and decided that there probably was no French sniper...In which case, he was in fact facing a far more serious and sinister threat: the Army itself. Suddenly, Radley believed that he had experienced a moment of mental clarity, in which the mists of deceit had momentarily lifted to expose the bare bones of an unfolding *coup d'etat*. Hogan undoubtedly lay at the heart of the plot, of that he was convinced. It must have been Hogan who had supplied Brian Salter with the grenade and taught him how to use it, and now the power-hungry colonel had lured poor Duncan to Storeton and had him murdered. Isolated in his hospital bed with only a token bodyguard to protect him, the Council Leader began to feel very vulnerable. His mind worked frantically, trying to second-guess his adversary and regain the upper hand before it was too late. He decided to call the colonel's bluff.

"Alan, are you still there?"

"Yes, Council Leader."

"Er, listen, I need you out of there - now. Let Alistair deal with the sniper. We're approaching crisis point, to be honest. Duncan's dead, Terence is badly injured and I'm not exactly fighting fit myself. I really can't afford to lose you as well. I need you over here to give me a thorough debrief on the whole operation and advise me how to proceed now. Oh – and there's a press conference at three and I'd like you to be there, to represent your men, who've done such a splendid job. Can you do that for me, Alan?"

Radley had expected Hogan to find some excuse for declining the request, but to his surprise the colonel replied, "I'm on my way, Council Leader."

"Excellent. I'll see you shortly."

Radley ended the call and immediately dialed the direct-line number for George Lawton, leader of the SCW.

While Radley was making devious arrangements in a last-ditch attempt to cling to power, Terence McCarthy lay in the adjacent room, reflecting bitterly on events of the previous two years. The door opened and his wife Helen entered. Like a hopeless ghost, she walked slowly and silently over to her husband's bedside and burst into tears.

"It's alright, Helen," he told her gently. "It'll be alright..."

"No it won't," she sobbed, holding up an official-looking letter. "This came this morning. Darren's been killed in Normandy..."

Saying nothing, Terence McCarthy held out his bandaged hand to comfort her. She placed her head against his damaged chest and he tenderly stroked her hair, while staring at the wall which separated him from Gerald Radley with an expression of consummate hatred.

Leaving Alistair Blundell in charge in Storeton, Colonel Hogan headed for Arrowe Park in a Land Rover driven by Lance-corporal Dudley. Driving towards Prenton, they found the road ahead blocked by a SCW checkpoint and were forced to stop. The black-clad paramilitary in command of the roadblock sauntered over to the Land Rover, brandishing his Heckler and Koch sub-machine gun, and peered inside. At the same time, a white van pulled up behind the army vehicle and nudged up against its rear bumper.

"Colonel Hogan?" asked the SCW commander brusquely.

"That's right. I'm on my way to see Council Leader Radley."

More armed SCW personnel climbed out of the van and surrounded the Land Rover. Suddenly, Hogan began to feel uneasy. He glanced around nervously, looking for possible escape options but finding none. Once, as a young officer serving in Ulster in the late nineteen eighties, Hogan had found himself in a similar situation when he had inadvertently driven into a vehicle checkpoint manned by the IRA. On that occasion, he had followed the correct drills and, by a miracle, had escaped unscathed. However, this SCW roadblock was rather more substantial. Noting the telegraph pole barrier and spiked caltrops blocking the road ahead, and the white van parked directly behind to make reversing impossible, Alan Hogan knew that any attempt to fight his way out would be foolhardy to the point of being suicidal.

"Colonel Hogan," the Special Council Worker said, "I'm sorry, but my orders are to place you under arrest for treason and escort you to The Fort to await trial and sentencing. Should you refuse to cooperate then I must inform you that I'm authorised to use whatever force is necessary to secure your arrest. So, out you come, there's a good chap..."

In Storeton, Robert Taylor was having a sense of humour failure. After the farmhouse had been razed to the ground, his section had been detailed to search nearby buildings for enemy and then take up defensive positions allocated by Lieutenant Grudge. Although the possibility of the French mounting a serious counter-attack was virtually non-existent, the lieutenant insisted that it was "better to be safe than sorry."

Robert had just deployed his men when a four-tonne truck arrived, carrying the platoon's bergens, and a short while later, the CSM gave permission for one soldier per pair to rest while the other remained vigilant. Throughout the village, foam mats were unrolled, sleeping bags unpacked and hexamine stoves lit to boil water for tea. To everyone's surprise and delight, the CQMS appeared in a Land Rover bearing burgers and chips for every man, purchased by one of the cooks, who had been sent on a morale-boosting mission to a fast food restaurant in Bromborough. The weary troops were just starting to relax and savour their victory, when suddenly the whole company was stood-to in response to the shooting of Duncan Silverlock, and a message came through over the company radio net instructing all callsigns to prepare for immediate counter-sniper operations.

Robert sighed with despair and swore copiously. He turned to Stevenson, who was carefully placing boil-in-the bag meals into a mess tin of water, and declared in the voice of a sulky child, "I don't want to play this game any more. I want to go home..."

He felt as though his reserves of energy and stoicism were finally exhausted and he could no longer motivate himself to perform as required. According to his own definition, he was no longer a 'good soldier,' able to endure endless hardship with alacrity and determination. He was tired of being filthy, wet, cold, hungry and scared...most of all he was tired of being tired. The novelty of living in a glorified hole in the ground, getting three or four hours of interrupted sleep every night, defecating in a bucket, drinking tea made with powdered 'non-dairy whitener', and generally leading a nocturnal existence which alternated between boredom and terror, had long ago worn off. All he wanted was to go home to a clean and civilized environment.

Blundell summoned Grudge, the section commanders and Mark Conrad to a house in the middle of the village for a hurried briefing. The basic plan was that two sections would be sent out to hunt the sniper, while the remaining troops covered them from positions along the western edge of the village. Every copse, ditch and hedgerow would have to be systematically searched, forcing the sniper to either open fire or break cover - either of which would hopefully betray his position and give the British the upper hand in the deadly game of cat and mouse.

"Corporal Taylor," Blundell said, "I want you to advance along Storeton Road towards Barnston, checking the hedgerows and field boundaries until you rendezvous with Seven Platoon's roadblock, okay?"

Robert nodded sullenly. "Yes, sir."

"Corporal Brabander, I need you to patrol down the track which leads under the motorway to Landican – the one with the shot-up Council van on it. Check the hedges and the small copse by the track, then conduct a sweep of Cow Hey Covert in extended line, in case he's gone to ground in there. Got that?"

Brabander looked uncomfortable. "I don't want to go into Cow Hey Covert, sir."

"Why not?"

"I don't like the bodies, sir."

"What do you mean, Corporal?"

"There's some sort of mass grave in there, with a JCB and bodies. It gives me and the boys the creeps – I'm sure it's haunted."

For a moment Blundell simply stared at Brabander in stunned silence. Then he asked, "Is it a French grave?"

"I don't think so. It looks like civvies in there to me."

"I see..." The major looked shocked. "Corporal Conrad, will you go in there? After all, they say the most effective weapon against a sniper is another sniper..."

Conrad nodded reluctantly. "I will, sir, but what bothers me is being slotted by our own boys by mistake. They're going to be looking for a sniper to shoot, aren't they?"

"I can understand your concern, Corporal, but we'll make sure all callsigns are kept informed of your whereabouts and no-one fires without checking with me first. Mind you, with your stalking skills, I doubt whether any of our lads will see you anyway. So, has anyone got any questions?" There was silence. "Does everyone know what they've got to do?" The men nodded grimly. "Right, crack on – the quicker we get this over with, the quicker we can all get our heads down."

CHAPTER 48

McCarthy Blows the Whistle

More pearls of wisdom than an oyster-bed university.

Mary Mungomidge
Cleverclogs fanzine

Mr Roberts replies:
What a delightful description! Fancy dinner?

At just before three o'clock that afternoon, the triumvirate of media representatives was escorted up to Radley's hospital room for the press conference. Paul Ryder from the PR Department directed proceedings, issuing scripts to the reporters and making it clear to them that certain issues were taboo and were not, under any circumstances, to be discussed during the interview.

"If anyone decides to start asking unauthorised questions I'll pull the plug on the whole thing immediately," he warned. "But try to make it seem spontaneous – we don't want the public to know you're reading from a script, okay? And remember, the emphasis should be on celebrating the victory at Storeton and demonising the subversives who have attacked Council Leader Radley..."

The radio reporter and her technician prepared their equipment whilst listening intently through their headphones to the three o'clock news bulletin, waiting for the newsreader in the Birkenhead studio to pass over to them so that they could start broadcasting from the Council Leader's bedside. The bulletin's headlines broke the news of both the liberation of Storeton and the assassination attempt, before leading in to the exclusive live interview with Gerald Radley. The technician gave the thumbs up to indicate that they were 'on air,' and the reporter introduced the Council Leader, who immediately launched into one of his customary 'People of Wirral' speeches. He announced to the masses that there had been both good and bad news during the preceding twenty-four hours.

"I'll start with the good news. It gives me great pleasure to inform you all that a major offensive by our forces has finally driven the French out of Storeton, and ensured that they will never return. No longer do they have two fronts on our soil. The operation was a resounding success and inflicted heavy casualties on the enemy, and this will surely diminish their ability to continue waging war here in Wirral. I am convinced that this is the beginning of the end of this conflict, and I ask you all to remain supportive, loyal and unflinching in your determination to win. But it will not be easy – hard times still lie ahead, and certain defeatist or downright treasonous elements within our own society seem intent on exploiting the situation, to undermine the Council's authority and promote pacifist views, which only serve to play into the hands of the French. Let me assure you all that these subversive elements within our own population are every bit as ruthless and dangerous as the enemy."

He paused, to look earnestly into the lens of the digital video camera, which was recording his speech for broadcast via the Council website.

"Which brings me to the bad news. A mere twenty-four hours ago, during a routine Council meeting, a callous and cowardly attempt was made to kill me using an explosive device. As you can see, I survived, but a number of other people were injured, including two colleagues who are close personal friends of mine - Terence McCarthy and Brian Salter. Mr Salter has since died of his injuries and Mr McCarthy – our very own chief executive – was severely injured. People must not allow themselves to be fooled by the treacherous subversives within our society. Be under no illusion – these are not idealistic intellectuals trying to provoke political debate. They are unscrupulous, violent terrorists and murderers, who will stop at nothing to get their way, and they must be dealt with robustly. Arrests have already been made, and all of those responsible for this outrage will be brought to justice.

"Finally, I should like to end on a more positive note. We should not allow what happened in the town hall yesterday to overshadow the momentous victory achieved by our armed forces. We should also remember that victory at Storeton came at a price, and our thoughts and prayers should be with those who were killed or injured, and with their families. They are an inspiration to us all – they did not falter or shy away from noble sacrifice, and neither should we. If we follow their example we will ultimately triumph."

For a few moments there was silence, then Paul Ryder nodded at the female radio reporter and she obligingly asked her pre-arranged question: "Council Leader Radley, with both yourself and Mr McCarthy in hospital, people will inevitably be concerned about whether leadership within the borough remains strong and effective. Are you able to assuage such concerns?"

"Oh, most definitely, of course. I should like to reassure the public that it's definitely business as usual as far as I'm concerned, and the fact that Mr McCarthy and myself remain in total control should demonstrate to everyone that the Council has a very resilient and determined leadership. I always ask for fortitude from the people of Wirral, and they have a right to expect the same from me..."

While the interview was in progress, Paul Ryder slipped next door, to forewarn the injured chief executive that he was about to have visitors. "Don't worry, Terence," Ryder said reassuringly. "The reporters will only be here for a few minutes at most. Gerald just wants people to know what's happened to you. You're a popular figure – seeing you like this will help turn people against the subversives."

"But I've got nothing to say!" McCarthy protested.

"You'll be fine, trust me..."

Ryder hurried back to the adjacent room, where Radley was in the process of bringing the interview to a close with his usual stirring clichés about everyone working together and making sacrifices to achieve the common goal of 'ultimate victory'. When the Council Leader had finished speaking, Ryder gave him the thumbs up, and ushered the media representatives into McCarthy's room next door. Once again, the radio reporter asked the first question.

"Mr McCarthy, presumably this attempt on the Council Leader's life during a high-security Council meeting has come as quite a shock to you, is that right?"

"No. It doesn't surprise me in the least, to be honest."

This was not the response which the reporter had expected, and she floundered for a moment, before glancing at the script and selecting another question.

"And what are your feelings towards this person – the person who tried to kill you?"

"I respect him, and I feel very sorry for him and for his family. He was a good man - and a brave man, who should be thanked for doing what the rest of us should have done a long time ago."

An alarmed Paul Ryder stepped towards the reporter and technician to try to stop the broadcast, but they turned their backs on him and squeezed into the narrow space between the bed and the wall, preventing him from reaching their equipment. McCarthy knew that he only had a few seconds at most, so he spoke with sudden urgency. "People need to know that this war is completely artificial - Gerald Radley arranged it with Claude Lebovic, so he could feel important. The SCW fired the shots at the Tranmere match, the air raids are actually a SCW mortar firing on our own people, and the SCW kidnap and murder anyone that Radley doesn't like. I urge the people to rise up against him, and I beg the Army to help, because he's a tin-pot dictator who's lost the plot...Oh, hello, Gerald."

Radley was standing in the doorway in his pyjamas, brandishing his sawn-off shotgun in one hand and supporting himself against Sean Simms with the other. For a few seconds he stared silently at McCarthy with an expression of pure malice. McCarthy met his gaze defiantly.

"Go on then, you bastard."

Radley blasted him in the chest with both barrels, then turned and limped from the room, leaving the media people shocked and deafened. In the corridor outside, startled medical staff rushed to the scene. Simms waved his pistol threateningly and shouted at them to move back. He turned to Radley's two SCW bodyguards and said, "We need to go - give the Council Leader a hand!"

The two men seized Radley under each arm and followed Simms through the ward towards the stairs. Doctors, nurses, visitors and patients leapt aside as the group descended to the ground floor and charged along the corridors like a rugby wedge, until they reached a fire exit at the rear of the building. Radley's Hummer was parked in a delivery bay nearby. When the group reached the vehicle, the two young leopards, Nero and Caligula, sprang up and began leaping around in their cage, hissing and spitting with agitation.

"Better get rid of those flags," Radley said, pointing at the official pennants which were fixed above each headlight to ensure that the vehicle received privileged status wherever it went. The two SCW men helped Radley into the back of the armoured Hummer and sat either side of him, their sub-machine guns at the ready. Sean Simms snapped off the two pennants, then slid into the driver's seat and started the engine. "Where to, boss?"

Radley's mind was racing as he tried to decide between his two main options – returning to the town hall or fleeing for the border. After a few moments he declared, "The town hall."

They left the hospital by bumping over a grass verge to bypass cars waiting at a red traffic light, then drove at speed along the dual carriageway towards the M53 motorway. As they passed the Woodchurch estate, Radley peered through the tinted windows and saw people emerging from their houses and gathering in angry groups, which began moving purposefully in the direction of Birkenhead. The Council Leader shuddered, recognising in the congregating crowds the beginnings of a vengeful, rampaging mob which might prevent him from reaching the town hall. The only person who could offer any real protection against such a threat was George Lawton, so Radley contacted him immediately on his mobile phone.

"George, Gerald here."

"Gerald, how are you?"

"I could be better, but never mind – George, where are you now?"

"At headquarters."

"Did you hear the radio broadcast?"

"I did...Jesus!"

"Exactly. Listen, I'm heading back towards the town hall now, George, but there are people taking to the streets everywhere, and if we're not careful we're going to find ourselves being lynched. I need you to call-in all of your SCW boys and get them together to protect the town hall and disperse the crowds, okay?"

"I'll do my best, Gerald. Bloody hell!"

"What is it?"

"I'm looking out of the window, and there's a lot of people – hundreds I'd say – heading this way from the direction of the college. Looks like a full-blown uprising to me. Can we open fire on them?"

"Whatever it takes to restore order, George, whatever it takes. Listen, I'll go the long way round - along the M53, and come to you past the docks and the *Onyx*. That way I might avoid some of the crowds. Just try to get as many Special Council Workers together as you can, okay?"

"Will do. What about the Army? Have you called Alistair for help?"

"No. I really don't know where we stand with the Army at the moment. I suppose it all depends on whether any of them heard the radio broadcast...Anyway, I'd rather not involve them if I can help it - hopefully we can sort things out ourselves. Make sure you leave your phone on – I'll speak to you later."

"Right you are, Gerald."

"Oh – George?"

"Yes?"

"Get some of your boys on standby in vans ready to come and get me if things get tricky. There's a lot of traffic around, and it's not going to be easy getting through to you."

"Will do."

As soon as he had finished speaking to the Council Leader, George Lawton hurried to the communications room to tell the radio operator to contact all SCW personnel, both on and off duty, and order them to make their way immediately to the headquarters building at Four Bridges. A few loyal teams and individuals obeyed the instruction, but the majority of Special Council Workers did not. From their roadblocks, white vans or unmarked cars they could see the angry crowds gathering, and knew that attempting to quell such a massive uprising would be as hopeless as trying to hold back the tide. Many SCW personnel leapt into their vehicles and raced south for the border with Cheshire. Some went into hiding. Others changed into civilian clothes and mingled with the crowds, which was a potentially risky strategy, as the incensed masses were not inclined to be merciful to those who had subjugated them so brutally for so long.

All across Wirral, scores were being settled, as off-duty SCW men were dragged from their houses and beaten to death in the streets, or left hanging from lamp-posts. White vans were rammed by brave citizens in cars, or attacked with bricks and petrol bombs. The SCW fought back, of course, and the peninsular echoed with the staccato crackle of gunfire, as civilians caught up in the struggle paid a heavy price for their rebellious defiance.

Hidden in the woods on Bidston Hill, the SCW mortar team sat in their white panel van and listened gloomily as George Lawton spoke to them directly over the radio.

"Get yourselves back here now!" he growled. "I need you to give fire support to cover HQ and the town hall. I repeat, get back here now. Do you hear me? Answer me, you numpty bastards!"

The mortar team leader switched off the radio and stared at the others in the cab. "Basically, boys, it's over. Who wants to go and help him and Radley, and kill lots more people - and probably get killed ourselves?"

There was silence. Then someone said, "Let's get the fuck out of here..." This proposal was greeted with a murmur of agreement from everyone present. The men quickly changed out of their black uniforms and into civilian tracksuits and trainers. A few of them decided to keep their sub-machine guns, while others stripped the weapons and threw the parts into the undergrowth. Then they doused the panel van with petrol, set it alight, and ran like hell before the mortar ammunition went off.

In Storeton, Blundell and Grudge were directing the anti-sniper operation from an upstairs room in a house at the edge of the village, when suddenly the major's mobile phone began to vibrate. He expected the caller to be either Gerald Radley or Colonel Hogan, and was surprised to find that it was in fact Major Hubbard, who commanded B Company at Thurstaston.

"Alistair, have you been listening to the radio – Wirral FM, I mean, over?"

Blundell laughed. "No Edward, believe it or not, directing a company attack has rather taken up most of my time during the past twenty-four hours, over!"

"Well, apparently, Council Leader Radley has killed Mr McCarthy, the chief executive. It seems that he shot him at Arrowe Park hospital, because McCarthy told everyone on live radio that the war has been arranged deliberately, with the cooperation of the French. Sounds incredible, I know, but apparently Radley's disappeared and people are taking to the streets in open revolt. One of my corporals got a phone call from his wife to say that his brother's been shot by the SCW while marching on the town hall. I can't get comms with the CO, so I thought I'd contact you for advice. What shall we do, over?"

Blundell's heart started beating very rapidly. "Er, my advice is to do nothing for the time being, until we get more information. Keep your attention focused on the French, but have an officer and a few men ready to speak to any civilians which come your way. Make it clear to them that the Army will not get involved in any civil unrest. Our job is to fight the French. Whatever happens, don't use force against civilians… Remember, technically we're still TA, and it's never been the TA's role to suppress civil disorder. I'll try to get through to the Colonel, and get back to you when I've spoken to him, okay, over?"

"Thanks Alistair. Out."

Blundell turned to Grudge, who had overheard the entire conversation and was looking at him with an expression of keen expectation. "There's some sort of civil unrest or uprising going on," he explained. "I need to speak to the CO."

The major tried dialing Hogan's number several times, but only succeeded in getting through to his voicemail service. Then Blundell remembered that Radley had summoned the colonel several hours previously, and realised that he had not been seen nor heard from since. With a shiver of foreboding, he took a deep breath and dialed Radley's number. To his surprise, the Council Leader answered almost immediately, although he sounded stressed and distracted.

"Alistair! What is it?"

"Gerald, I'm getting reports of riots and people on the streets, and I can't make contact with Colonel Hogan. Is he with you?"

Radley hesitated. "Er, no, Alistair, he's not. He never reached me. It's possible he got hijacked by this rabble I'm going through now."

"What do you want me to do? What do you want the Army to do, Gerald?"

Radley could scarcely believe his luck. Could it be that, despite the souring of relations in recent months, the Army might actually be prepared to come to his rescue?

"Alistair, I need you to come and help restore order at the town hall. I'm on my way there now, but there's rioters everywhere – we've had a couple of close shaves already and we've still got quite a way to go."

"Where are you?"

"Just coming up to Poulton roundabout."

"Right, Gerald. It'll take a while to get to you, so leave your phone on and keep letting me know where you are, okay?"

"Okay, Alistair. And thanks – I won't forget this, you know."

Radley rang-off, leaving Blundell to assimilate the flood of information which had swept upon him during the past few minutes. It occurred to him that, suddenly, he had become a key player in events of great gravity, a pivotal figure upon whom circumstance had unexpectedly bestowed the power to decide the fate of Gerald Radley and indeed Wirral itself. Alistair Blundell thought back to the historic conversation at Caldy Golf Club, and frantically reviewed his personal conduct since then, trying to decide whether he was guilty of questionable deeds and complicity in atrocities, or whether he could legitimately claim to have been an honourable soldier who had simply followed orders in the course of his duty. Eventually he made up his mind, and delivered his verdict to Grudge.

"Andrew, I need you to take Eight Platoon and go and get Council Leader Radley. Basically he's to be arrested, but don't tell him that. It's a tricky situation – he needs to be saved from lynching, but must not be allowed to escape, if you know what I mean. If you find yourself confronted by crowds of angry civilians, try to negotiate your way through them but do not use force unless they actually attack you, in which case it's self-defence only. The important thing is to make sure they know you're on their side, not the Council's."

"What about the sniper, sir?"

"He'll have to wait. Seven Platoon and Corporal Conrad can deal with him."

"And what about you, sir? Isn't the Council Leader more likely to listen to you than me?"

"Possibly, but I don't think it would be a good idea for me to be involved. Remember, technically I'm still a Council official, and I have links with the Council Leader…I don't want people to misinterpret my intentions. Oh – once you've got Mr Radley, go to the Fort and SCW headquarters and try to find Colonel Hogan, okay?"

Grudge nodded. "Okay, sir. And what about the Special Council Workers?"

Blundell thought for a moment, then smiled. "Show them no mercy."

Lieutenant Andrew Grudge quickly recalled his patrols by radio, and while they were withdrawing back to Storeton he mustered a motley convoy of vehicles on Lever's Causeway. A Trojan formed the vanguard of the column, providing protection for the soft-skinned Land Rovers and four-tonne trucks which would carry the men of Eight Platoon, plus Corporal Gorpe's section from Nine Platoon. The company ambulance joined the rear of the formation.

One by one, the weary sections arrived at the vehicles. The soldiers, who were unaware of the latest turn of events, looked sullen and confused and generally unimpressed at being re-tasked yet again.

"Where are we going, sir?" asked young Private Howell, in almost child-like bewilderment.

"To the town hall," Grudge replied, as though it were obvious.

Machine guns were positioned to fire over the cabs of the trucks and Land Rovers, and extra ammunition was loaded aboard, together with the platoon's remaining LAW94 anti-tank missiles.

"Good luck, sir," called the Company Sergeant-major, as vehicle engines rumbled into life and Grudge climbed aboard his Land Rover.

The lieutenant grinned at him with an expression of smug satisfaction, bordering upon delight. "Thank you, Sergeant-major. Who'd've thought it? Eight Platoon, Main Effort again - second time in twenty-four hours!"

George Lawton had hoped to have sufficient personnel at his disposal to secure the entire area between the SCW headquarters at Four Bridges in the south and the town hall in the north. However, scarcely a tenth of the potential force of four hundred Special Council Workers had reported for duty, and the number of angry citizens on the streets was growing exponentially every few minutes, swelling rapidly from tens to hundreds to thousands. According to the SCW anti-aircraft gunners situated on the roof of the town hall, the building was besieged by an enraged mob which was demanding that Radley be handed over immediately for trial and sentencing. Knowing that the Council Leader was elsewhere, Lawton decided to abandon the town hall as a lost cause, and concentrate his efforts and manpower on defending his own headquarters in the converted pump-house by the docks. He advised Radley to make his way directly to the blackened tower at Four Bridges, where he could be protected until the Army intervened and restored order.

From the top of the pump-house's sinister-looking gothic turret, the SCW anti-aircraft gun team were keeping the crowds at bay with bursts of withering fire from their general-purpose machine-gun, although they could only effectively cover a semi-circular arc in the direction of Birkenhead. The opposite direction – towards Wallasey and the town hall – was being covered by a small force of Special Council Workers, who were firing their sub-machine guns from behind a barricade of white vans at the end of the line of bridges which gave the area its name. Initially, the paramilitaries had aimed above the people's heads, but as the rioters became more aggressive and audacious, Lawton ordered his men to shoot to kill, "To show them we mean business." The enraged crowds fell back in disarray, leaving several of their number lying dead or injured in pools of blood on the road.

In the War Office at the town hall, Susan Fletcher and her colleagues listened apprehensively to the chants from the mob outside, and wondered how they would be treated when the protesters finally forced their way in, as they inevitably would.

"We're better off staying here, I think," she advised the others. "I mean, now there's no senior Council staff here, we can say we're supporting the Army in Storeton. I really think we should emphasise our army connections. It's the Council and SCW that people hate, not the Army..."

On the roof above, the two-man SCW anti-aircraft gun crew stared bleakly over the top of their sandbag emplacement at the chanting masses below. So far the gunners had not fired a shot, although they *had* cocked the GPMG and aimed it down at the crowds; both men knew that, by opening fire, they would be signing their own death warrants.

"Come on, our Dean," one said to the other. "It's time we made a move..."

They hurried inside the building and took refuge in a toilet, where they disassembled the machine-gun and hid some of the smaller parts in the bowl and cistern to prevent the weapon being used by anyone else. Then they changed into boiler suits and walked casually out into the corridor, hoping to pass themselves off as innocent repairmen.

Downstairs in the entrance hall, the Army guards in their ceremonial uniforms were standing behind the locked doors, engaged in a nervous dialogue with the protesters outside.

"Just let us in, mate," a man in the crowd shouted through the glass. "It's not you we're after, it's that bastard Radley."

"We'll smash our way in anyway," threatened another man, brandishing a sledgehammer. "So you might as well just open up..."

The lance-corporal in the entrance hall thought for a moment. Then he unlocked the door and stepped aside, as the masses flooded in like a rampaging torrent. Relieving the two soldiers of their Lee-Enfield rifles but leaving them unharmed, the protesters swept towards the lift and stairs and swarmed through the building in search of the

Council Leader. It was not long before some of them arrived at the War Office control centre and burst through the door, wielding kitchen knives, pieces of wood and metal bars. Susan Fletcher and her colleagues regarded them fearfully, but remained seated at their desks with a certain dignity.

"What do you do here?" demanded a middle-aged man, who seemed to be the leader of this particular group.

"We're part of the Army," Susan replied. "We deal with all of the military planning and communications. We've just spent the night handling all radio traffic relating to the fighting at Storeton." She gestured towards the large model of the village and its environs, hoping it might convince the man that she was telling the truth.

"Have you seen that bastard Radley?"

"Not since Thursday."

"Know where he is?"

"No. The last I heard he was in Arrowe Park hospital."

This answer seemed to satisfy the rioters, although for a while they prowled around the room, looking under desks and behind partitions in search of the Council Leader or other high-ranking officials. Finding no-one, they headed for the exit.

"What shall we do?" Susan called after them.

The middle-aged man paused on his way out and said, "Just stay in here and wait, and you won't get hurt."

Unable to find Gerald Radley, the crowds vented their pent-up anger on substitute villains, including the two disguised SCW gunners who were identified, dragged out into the street, and summarily executed with a single .303 bullet to the head.

Meanwhile, Gerald Radley was discovering that even reaching SCW headquarters was going to be easier said than done. He had hoped to arrive at the docks to find massed ranks of SCW personnel restoring order with brutal efficiency. Instead, there were large numbers of unruly citizens confronting a few scattered white vans, with pockets of paramilitaries whose plight appeared to be every bit as desperate as his own.

Suddenly, a Ford Mondeo appeared from nowhere and rammed Radley's Hummer, shunting it against the kerb. Simms fought to retain control of the vehicle, bumping onto the pavement and braking sharply before colliding with a lamp-post. The Hummer suffered little damage, and reversed back towards the stationary Mondeo, so that one of the Special Council Workers sitting next to Radley on the back seat could lower his window and spray the car with bullets. Protesters milling around nearby threw themselves to the ground in terror and looked around frantically for the source of the gunfire. Seeing the shiny black Hummer, with its tinted windows and remnants of chrome pennant stalks on each wing, several astute citizens realised that the vehicle must belong to the Council Leader, and they began attacking it with stones and other missiles. Simms slammed his foot down on the accelerator to get them out of danger. A brick hit the rear window and the two already distressed leopards went berserk. Ahead, several cars were blocking the dock road and Simms had to drive into them at speed to force a passage through.

"At this rate we're not even going to make it to George," Radley commented, gesturing towards the blackened tower of the SCW headquarters at the far end of the dock, which looked so near yet so far away. "The *Onyx* is just up ahead. We'll go there and wait for Alistair to come and get us..."

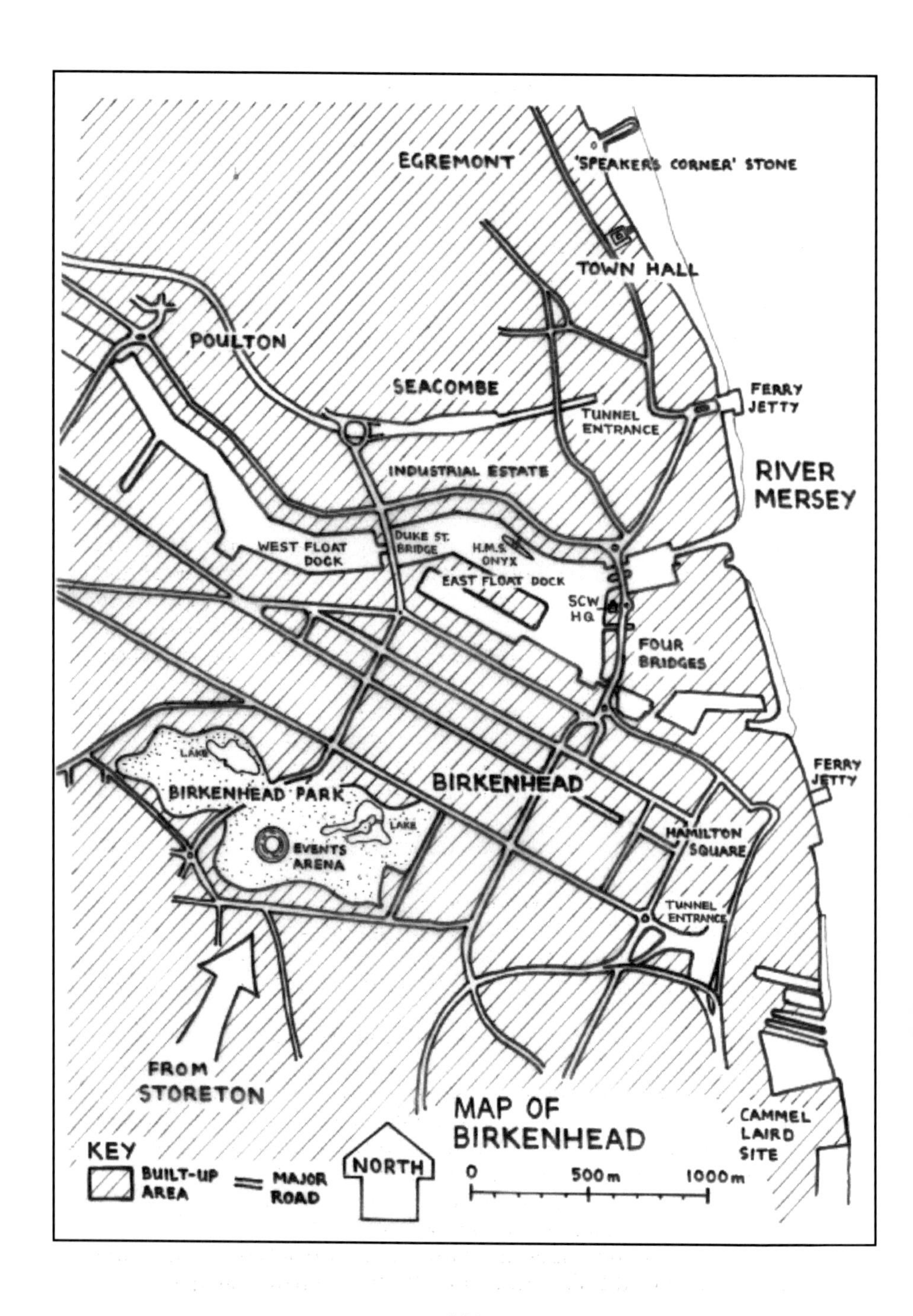
EGREMONT
'SPEAKER'S CORNER' STONE
TOWN HALL
POULTON
SEACOMBE
FERRY JETTY
TUNNEL ENTRANCE
INDUSTRIAL ESTATE
RIVER MERSEY
WEST FLOAT DOCK
DUKE ST. BRIDGE
H.M.S. ONYX
EAST FLOAT DOCK
SCW HQ
FOUR BRIDGES
LAKE
FERRY JETTY
BIRKENHEAD PARK
BIRKENHEAD
LAKE
HAMILTON SQUARE
EVENTS ARENA
TUNNEL ENTRANCE
FROM STORETON
MAP OF BIRKENHEAD
CAMMEL LAIRD SITE
KEY
BUILT-UP AREA
MAJOR ROAD
NORTH
0
500m
1000m

CHAPTER 49

Radley in the Dock

A great book. It expresses the anger felt by many of us towards the anal, bureaucrat-dominated culture of superfluous targets, excessive regulation and internecine competition which has made modern Britain such a miserable place. I found the final chapter particularly satisfying - in which the self-serving, autocratic leader gets his come-uppance in a way which I personally would like to see our pompous, pontificating politicians get theirs.

Damien Slaughter
Intellectual Anarchist (college publication)

Mr Roberts replies:
Hear hear!

With the smoke-spewing Trojan clattering along in the lead, the convoy carrying Eight Platoon rumbled along Lever's Causeway and turned left towards Prenton. On the main road they came across the abandoned SCW roadblock, where Colonel Hogan had been apprehended earlier in the day. The Trojan bulldozed the obstacles aside and the column pressed on. There were a considerable number of people on the streets, many wearing illegal balaclavas or hooded tops to conceal their identity, but in the absence of the SCW or any other obvious enemy their revolutionary fervour had begun to wane and they appeared aimless and frustrated. Many of them regarded the military convoy with suspicion, unsure as to whether the soldiers were friend or foe. Lieutenant Grudge did his best to clarify the situation, with the help of a megaphone.

"Move aside please. We are on your side. We are going to arrest Council Leader Radley. Move out of the way, please."

At the cross-roads by the Halfway House pub the cavalcade encountered a large, agitated crowd of people surrounding a white SCW van. The Special Council Workers who crouched around the vehicle had succeeded in keeping the encroaching mob at bay by firing over their heads, but some of the more brazen rioters were edging ever nearer and it would not be long before the paramilitaries would be forced to choose between inflicting casualties or becoming them. When the Trojan arrived at the scene, the SCW squad leader hoped that the Army might be his salvation, until Grudge's megaphone-amplified voice disabused him of that optimistic notion: "Lay down your weapons and surrender, or you will be killed."

With a euphoric cheer, the crowd parted obligingly to give the soldiers a clear field of fire. Two Land Rovers, each mounting a GPMG on the cab roof, swung-out to either side of the Trojan, and for a few moments there was a tense stand-off between the two sides. Then the SCW squad leader suddenly opened fire in the direction of the troops, and urged his driver to "Go go go!" The soldiers returned fire, riddling the van with bullets, and those Special Council Workers who escaped death or injury surrendered immediately. Grudge ordered the prisoners to be taken into the pub and made to lie down on the floor, guarded – and protected – by a single soldier. Surrounded by a euphoric throng of cheering locals who were delighted to find the Army on their side, the convoy advanced again in the direction of Birkenhead Park, beyond which lay the docks and the town hall.

On the dockside overlooking the submarine *Onyx*, Gerald Radley paced up and down anxiously, muttering frustrated comments like, "Where's the rest of my Special Council Workers?" or "What's taking the bloody Army so long?" Gripping his sawn-off Purdey tightly, he walked around the perimeter of the dockside compound, peering through the spiked metal railings in the hope of spotting his rescuers. A small force of Special Council Workers was firing out through the palisades at an increasing number of people who were hurling ineffective bottles, stones and petrol bombs from the industrial estate across the road. Initially, the civilian uprising had largely involved a disorganised rabble which lacked cohesion or coordination, but as time went by, emergent leaders in different areas began communicating with each other by mobile phone, and word spread that Radley was cornered down at the docks. Vengeful citizens converged on the site from the surrounding area, their numbers swelling steadily until it became clearly apparent to the beleaguered Council Leader that he could not possibly hope to escape by road. He contacted George Lawton at SCW headquarters, a mere few hundred metres away across the dock, but the situation there was equally dire.

"Sorry, Gerald," Lawton told him, shouting over the sound of gunfire. "I've got a massive crowd of people here and it's getting bloody hard to keep them back. Where's the sodding Army?"

"I'll find out," Radley replied, quickly dialling Blundell's number. "Alistair, it's me. I thought you were coming to get me..."

"We are, Gerald. A platoon's on its way now."

"Well, if they don't hurry up it might be too late. Where the hell are they?"

"Going through Birkenhead Park. Where are you, Gerald?"

"I'm at the *Onyx*. The way things are going here, I'll probably be inside with the hatches shut and the drawbridge up by the time your men arrive."

"Okay Gerald, hold tight there, help's on its way."

Blundell rang-off, and immediately contacted Lieutenant Grudge.

"Hello Two-Zero this is Zero, message, over."

"Two-Zero, send, over."

"He's at the *Onyx*. I say again, don't bother with the town hall, he's at the *Onyx*, over."

"Two-Zero, roger your last, out."

As the soldiers of Eight Platoon approached the docks through the streets of Birkenhead, the top of the pump-house clock tower came into view above the rooftops, and they could see and hear the SCW machine gun firing from between the blackened crenellations. The convoy drew nearer and encountered a chaotic crowd of citizens armed with knives, rocks, sticks and petrol bombs. One man was even wielding a Samurai sword. Some people were running in seemingly random directions, but most were sheltering behind walls and any other solid structures which provided protection from the machine-gun fire. Several walking-wounded were limping away from the scene, while the more seriously injured were carried away on makeshift stretchers, screaming and leaking enormous quantities of blood.

The convoy drew to a halt beside a large warehouse close to the docks, and Lieutenant Grudge went forward on foot to assess the situation and reassure people that the Army was on their side. He crawled across a disused level crossing to where he could peer cautiously around the edge of a derelict footbridge, and was appalled by what he saw. Immediately to his front lay a roundabout, and beyond it stretched a series of bridges which carried the road across the eastern end of the dock. Situated to the left of the road, between two of the bridges, was the SCW headquarters. The entire area was littered with civilian corpses, and among the dead crawled wounded citizens who were unable to run or walk to safety. Two white vans were blocking the road on the far side of the roundabout, and from behind the vehicles, black-clad paramilitaries fired indiscriminately at the crowd, forcing people back from the headquarters building so that the machine-gun at the top of the tower could slaughter them more effectively. To further worsen the plight of the courageous citizens, the anti-aircraft machine-gun on the top of the Mersey tunnel ventilation tower half a mile away suddenly opened up, and anyone in the vicinity of the roundabout found themselves caught in a lethal crossfire. Grudge stared at the carnage, and became very angry. Gentlemanly negotiation and honourable surrender were, he decided, no longer appropriate. It was time for revenge.

Returning to the platoon convoy, the lieutenant sent Corporal Gorpe and his section down to the far end of the dock to cross the Duke Street Bridge and approach the *Onyx* from the opposite direction, thereby cutting-off a potential escape route for the Council Leader. Grudge intended to lead the rest of the platoon across the four bridges to reach the submarine, trapping Radley in a pincer movement, but knew that this would only be possible when all resistance from the SCW Headquarters building – and in particular its machine-gun –

had ceased. To achieve this, he sent one of his lance-corporals in a GPMG-equipped Land Rover through the side streets to a position near the Twelve Quays college building, from where it could fire at the top of the clock tower at long range. Additional fire support was provided by the platoon 51mm light mortar, which began dropping smoke bombs around the old pump-house building. Meanwhile, Grudge hurriedly prepared a set of quick battle orders and briefed his section commanders, before unleashing them upon the Special Council Workers.

The Trojan led the attack, clattering across the level crossing and opening fire on the SCW vans on the far side of the roundabout. Robert's section provided additional covering fire as a Land Rover carrying Corporal Kingsley and three of his men raced out from behind the Trojan and sped across the roundabout in a brave attempt to reach the car park on the far side. Unfortunately, the smoke screen was not fully developed, and Kingsley and his driver were hit by a hail of bullets from the clock tower machine gun. The soldiers in the rear of the vehicle jumped clear as it collided with some sturdy railings and came to an abrupt halt, throwing Kingsley and his driver into the dashboard. More bullets raked the stricken Land Rover as the survivors crawled for cover and hid behind a low wall. Meanwhile, Brabander's section advanced by alternate fireteams along the side of the Tower Quays office building, trading shots with Special Council Workers as they moved steadily nearer to the clock tower.

Smoke bombs continued to burst around the SCW headquarters, tracer streaked in different directions, and the whole situation became very confused. Grudge sent the Trojan forward to dominate the ground in the vicinity of the roundabout and provide covering fire for a right-flanking manoeuvre by Robert's section. Through the deafening cacophony of gunfire could be heard the characteristic shouts and commands of an infantry battle: "Put some fire down!" "Changing mag!" "Delta fire team prepare to move, Charlie fire team - rapid fire!" "Delta move now! – go go go go GO!"

Robert and his section sprinted through the smoke and reached the safety of the car park on the other side of the roundabout. They took cover behind the low wall which already sheltered the two surviving soldiers from Kingsley's Land Rover, and Robert crawled toward the vehicle to see if either occupant was still alive. Both men were slumped against the dashboard and were covered in blood, but as he crawled nearer, a tracer cracked through the air nearby and reminded him of his priorities; the injured and dead would have to wait until the battle was won. Recruiting Kingsley's men into his own section, Robert pressed on through the smokescreen.

Not far ahead, the group came across an injured Special Council Worker, lying in a flower bed with one of his knees shot away. "Don't shoot!" he screamed at the approaching soldiers through clenched teeth. "Jesus Christ - help me!"

"Throw away the weapon!" Robert shouted, gesturing at the man's MP5 submachine-gun.

The Special Council Worker threw the gun obligingly towards the soldiers. He was obviously in great pain. Robert and Private Cunningham crawled over to him and aimed their rifles at his face. He stared at them with a combination of fear and outrage. "Aren't you going to help me?"

Robert was surprised by how little compassion he felt towards the wounded SCW man. "Why should we?" he asked, callously.

"Look at my fucking leg!" the man sobbed. "I didn't want any of this! I'm a groundsman, for Christ's sake – a fucking groundsman!"

The remark struck Robert like a slap in the face, as he realised how Gerald Radley had ensnared so many ordinary people, and succeeded in seducing or coercing them into becoming participants in his warped scheme. The SCW man was not a real paramilitary, just as Robert was not a real soldier...They were both pawns in a bizarre game, dreamt up by a deranged tyrant who had to be brought to justice without further delay, so that everyone could get back to their normal lives and restore sanity to Wirral.

Ironically, Gerald Radley had unwittingly put his Special Council Workers at a severe disadvantage in the battle, by arming them with sub-machine guns which were incapable of penetrating a soldier's helmet or body armour at normal combat ranges. Furthermore, many SCW personnel had not even fired their weapons, let alone zeroed them, whereas the men of Eight Platoon were battle-hardened and combat-proficient after months of fighting the French at Storeton. It was not long before the surviving Special Council Workers were falling back across the bridges in disarray, heading for the *Onyx*.

From a window of the old pump-house building, George Lawton watched with disgust as his routed paramilitaries fled past in panic. So incensed was he by their lack of resoluteness that he leaned out and shouted, "Stand and fight, yer bastards!" When this failed to have the desired effect, he fired a contemptuous burst from his MP5 in their general direction. A few diehard SCW personnel remained in the headquarters building, nervously aiming their weapons out of the windows, and Lawton addressed them sternly. "Don't any of you think about running away, like those pussies," he warned, "or I'll shoot you myself." He cocked his head to one side like an intrigued dog and listened for a moment: the GPMG at the top of the clock tower had ceased firing. Lawton scowled ferociously. "Now why have *they* stopped, the stupid bastards?"

In fact, the two men operating the machine-gun had found themselves in an increasingly untenable situation, as the soldiers below advanced steadily nearer and took up positions from which they could shoot accurately at the top of the tower. There was now such a heavy volume of fire hitting the blackened masonry that it would have been suicidal to attempt so much as a quick glance over the parapet, and there was certainly no possibility of continuing to use the GPMG effectively. The smoking weapon lay on the turret floor amongst hundreds of spent cartridge cases, while its crew cowered behind the pointed Gothic crenellations, waiting for an opportunity to surrender.

Lieutenant Grudge peered cautiously from behind the armoured cab of the Trojan and was satisfied with how the operation was proceeding. Eight Platoon had won the firefight, and was now in an ideal position to assault the SCW headquarters and press on across the bridges to claim the prize of the *Onyx* and its infamous occupant. However, the lieutenant was wary of advancing impetuously and exposing his men to unnecessary risk, so he ordered the platoon mortar man to drop some high explosive bombs onto the SCW headquarters "to soften it up a little." A few minutes later, when flames could be seen inside the building and black smoke rose skyward from the roof, Grudge used his megaphone to tell his men to hold their fire, and urged the remaining Special Council Workers to surrender.

The firing from the old pump-house petered out, and for a few moments there was virtual silence. Then the barrel of the GPMG appeared above the crenellations at the top of the tower, pointing vertically upwards with a piece of white rag tied to its muzzle. With a sigh of relief, Grudge ordered the SCW gunners to lay down their weapon and stand up in full view, with their arms raised.

Delighted to have been given the opportunity to surrender, the two gunners obligingly placed the GPMG on the roof, rose to their feet and held their hands high in the air. Through the dissipating smoke they could see numerous soldiers aiming various weapons up at them from the ground below, but neither man noticed George Lawton as he emerged silently onto the turret roof behind them. Like an enraged bull, Lawton charged towards the gunners, his palms outstretched. The soldiers below watched in fascinated horror as the two men fell screaming from the tower and landed on the concrete with a *thud!*

Snarling with anger, Lawton seized the GPMG and stood up above the parapet, just as the men of Eight Platoon fired simultaneously and abruptly ended his career.

From the metal gangway connecting *Onyx* to the dockside, Gerald Radley watched soldiers and military vehicles advancing over the Four Bridges, past the burning clock tower of the SCW headquarters, and realised that it was all over. He now knew for certain that Alistair Blundell had betrayed him, and the Army was coming to arrest rather than rescue him. George Lawton had been unable to halt the military advance across the Four Bridges, and at the other end of the dock, two army Land Rovers had crossed the Duke Street Bridge and approached to within a few hundred metres of the submarine before halting, as if awaiting orders. From the industrial estate across the road, a large crowd of rioters continued to hurl missiles and verbal abuse, despite being fired upon by Special Council Workers manning the perimeter fence. Radley knew that he was trapped.

The demoralised SCW personnel who had been routed at the Four Bridges began to arrive in white vans or on foot, and reported to Radley with expressions of bewildered expectation, as if believing him capable of rectifying the situation with a wave of his hand. But instead, the weary, deflated-looking Council Leader simply pointed them in the direction of the submarine, while he stared vacantly at the approaching military force. Eventually he turned to Sean Simms and said, "Go and get 'The Lads' – and bring some food for them. We'd better get below deck."

Radley went aboard *Onyx* while Simms hurried back to the Hummer to fetch the two leopards, Nero and Caligula. They lurched and strained at their leashes in agitation as he led them across the gangway and onto the deck of the old submarine.

Several months earlier, as Radley's paranoia steadily worsened, he had insisted that the gangway be lengthened to incorporate a drawbridge section, which could be raised to completely isolate *Onyx* from the shore. Now, as the Army's noose squeezed tighter and the advancing Trojan was only a couple of hundred metres away, the Council Leader told his two bodyguards to start winding the winches to raise the drawbridge. Several Special Council Workers who were still defending the compound's perimeter fence turned in alarm to see the steel gantry rising slowly into the air, and made a frantic dash for it. They just managed to leap across the widening gap and scramble aboard the submarine before the drawbridge reached its vertical position.

Bullets began striking the nearby warehouse buildings and several landed in the water around *Onyx*, sending up fountains of spray. Radley scurried across the black deck to the forward access hatch and paused for a moment, taking one last lingering look at Wirral before descending into the torpedo room, closely followed by Sean Simms, the leopards, and his two SCW bodyguards.

The Council Leader had just climbed through the circular hatchway leading into the forward accommodation area when, back in the torpedo chamber, Caligula and Nero suddenly and unexpectedly turned on Sean Simms and began to tear him apart in an attack of terrifying ferocity. Radley's bodyguards dived through the hatchway in terror, and pulled with all of their strength to close the massively thick and heavy steel door. It slammed shut with a resounding metallic *clang*, silencing Simms's screams on the other side.

Shaken and ashen-faced, Radley made his way unsteadily along the narrow corridor to his quarters in the former captain's cabin. With trembling hands he closed the door, poured himself a stiff drink and sat down on the bed to take stock of the situation. He thought back over the past two years, trying to identify what had caused his noble scheme to come to such an unsatisfactory conclusion. There were, he decided, many culprits, including the disloyal Army, treacherous colleagues within the Council...and the people of Wirral themselves, who had proved unworthy of the *greatness* he had tried to bestow upon them. To a certain extent he also blamed himself for his current predicament...He had been too *trusting* and too *lenient*, graciously allowing society to entertain too many personal liberties and social freedoms, which had enabled defeatism and dissent to spread like a terminal disease through the borough. He resolved to learn from his mistakes and do better next time.

Outside, the fighting was over. Feeling abandoned and resentful after the raising of the gangway drawbridge, the Special Council Workers who had been left stranded on the dockside quickly surrendered. The Trojan rammed its way through the padlocked gates and soldiers rushed in to disarm the SCW prisoners. As they did so, a crowd of civilians surged out from the industrial estate and swarmed across the road, seething with vengeful fury. Fearing that he might lose control of the situation if the crowd overwhelmed the compound, Grudge ordered the Trojan to push the twisted gates closed with its bulldozer blade. Then he left Corporal Gorpe and some troops to try to placate the angry citizens, while he and the other NCOs proceeded cautiously towards the submarine. They reached the edge of the dock and stared across at the *Onyx*, which lay in the water about thirty metres away like some malevolent black beast - a floating metal casket of pure evil. All of the hatches were closed, and there was no sign of activity anywhere on or around the vessel.

Grudge positioned his men in a line along the dockside, with orders to fire at anyone who emerged from the submarine, unless they were clearly trying to surrender. He then gathered together Sergeant Murphy and corporals Brabander and Taylor, and together they crouched on the cobbles with sweat trickling down their grimy faces and their chests heaving from the exertion of combat. Robert had a terrible headache and could feel blood pounding under high pressure in his temples. Desperate for a drink and a rest, he turned to Grudge and asked, "What now, sir?"

The lieutenant stared at the silent submarine and thought for a moment. "Well, we've got him trapped, so I suppose we just keep him here until Major Blundell arrives. He can decide what to do with Council Leader Radley."

Robert scowled and rubbed his throbbing forehead. He thought about the casualties of Gerald Radley's ridiculous war – of Farrell and Kingsley and Pete Collins, and his good friend Mark Conrad, who had never been the same since returning from France. He thought about his own personal psychological suffering – the nightmares and paranoia, the wildly fluctuating moods and the sudden panic attacks – together with the physical toll on his body in the form of dark, sunken eyes and prematurely greying hair. And the more he thought about it, the more the bloodlust rose within him, and the more he wanted vengeance. "I say we sink the bastard," he declared angrily. "Come on sir – think about all the good lads he's wasted or left in bits. He doesn't deserve any mercy."

"I agree with Taylor," said Karl Brabander with quiet malice.

Paul Murphy nodded. "Me too…" It was less than half an hour since the sergeant had led a team of soldiers into the burning SCW headquarters to free the prisoners held in the sound-proofed cells. Having seen the torture chambers with his own eyes, and learned of the unspeakable deeds committed within them, Murphy was not inclined to show clemency towards the occupants of the submarine.

Grudge remained unconvinced. "Look, he's not a threat to anyone now, is he? It's not our job to decide what happens to him – that's for a court of law to decide, not us!"

"Oh yeah, sir!" Robert snorted bitterly. "You know what'll happen: he'll end up in some nice cushy detention centre or under house arrest or something, while people he probably plays golf with decide his fate. These people look after their own, you know that! And before you know it, he'll be living abroad under a false name with an obscenely generous pension, paid for by the rest of us. Come on sir, let's strike while the iron's hot – we won't get another chance! It'll be a crime of passion if we do it now!"

"I still think we should wait for Major Blundell," Grudge said firmly.

"Do you mean Major Blundell who used to be one of Radley's best buddies in the Council? Come on, sir – that bastard in the sub has killed a lot of people. They deserve justice…"

Clearly troubled by the dilemma facing him, Grudge stared at *Onyx* for a long time. Finally, he nodded slowly and delivered his verdict. "All right, let's do it. Sergeant Murphy – get the 94s, if you will."

While the men of Eight Platoon kept the submarine's hatches covered with a variety of weapons, Murphy gathered together the five remaining LAW 94 anti-tank missiles. With appropriate solemnity, the weapons were prepared for firing and the back-blast area checked for safety.

"We're quite close to the warehouse here, sir," Murphy remarked. "I suggest we fire them at an angle, you know," he made a cross with his arms to represent the missile trajectories if the firer opposite the stern of the sub aimed at the bow, and vice versa.

Grudge nodded. "Good idea. That'll also help the warheads to arm properly. Can anyone remember the minimum range – is it twenty or forty metres?"

"It's twenty," said Brabander, flipping up the hologram sight on one of the throw-away rocket launchers. "So we should be fine…"

The lieutenant decided that Sergeant Murphy and corporals Brabander and Taylor would each fire a missile at the *Onyx* – one at the bow, one at the stern and one amidships, directly beneath the conning tower. "Aim at the waterline," he told them. "We need to start getting some water in…"

The three NCOs practiced with their tracer spotting rounds until they found the correct aiming point for the main armour-piercing warheads. Grudge lay down and pushed his fingers into his ears. "Missile detail!" he shouted. "Target to your front, in your own time, carry on!"

There were three loud bangs in quick succession, followed immediately by three unspectacular explosions along the side of the *Onyx*. Black smoke began pouring from the vessel and flames could be seen licking up from the missile entry holes, but the submarine showed no sign of sinking.

"Give it another one," Grudge instructed Sergeant Murphy. "Aim higher up this time, below the conning tower."

A fourth missile was fired, and more smoke and flame belched out from the puncture. It was as if the soldiers were trying to cull a great whale which refused to die. Then, very slowly, the conning tower began to tilt towards the soldiers, and *Onyx* keeled over and capsized, creaking and groaning and hissing steam from the fires raging within her. Frantic banging could be heard from inside the upturned hull, but still the vessel remained afloat.

"Must be air trapped inside," Grudge declared. "We need to hole her again to release the pressure. She should sink then."

"Go on, sir," urged Robert Taylor. "You deliver the *coup de grace*."

The lieutenant accepted the honour, and a fifth missile was fired into the condemned submarine. *Onyx* seemed to shudder, and released a hiss of trapped air rather like a resigned sigh, as if finally accepting her fate. Then she started to sink slowly into the turbulent water, which foamed and frothed around her as she descended into the dock. It seemed a fitting end to Gerald Radley and his tyrannical ambitions. Several soldiers cheered as the submarine disappeared from view, sending huge bubbles rolling up from the depths and making the surface appear to boil for many minutes afterwards.

Robert Taylor watched the *Onyx* sink beneath the waves with a sense of overwhelming relief. He closed his eyes, put his head in his hands, and let out a long, weary sigh. Perhaps now, at last, he could go home to Susan and get some sleep.

Epilogue

Standing on the cliff-top at Thurstaston, Sylvia Fadden and Alan Hogan watched as lines of heavily-laden French troops filed across the beach below and waded into the muddy water of the Dee, to board small boats which would ferry them to the support vessel *Dauphin*, moored out in the estuary.

Following Radley's death, Sylvia had been put in charge of a caretaker administration, tasked with securing an immediate end to the war. This had been achieved through the use of leaflets and repatriated prisoners to inform French forces that the conflict had been artificially engineered by Radley and Lebovic. Shortly afterwards, the French leader had been overthrown in a military coup and executed in public on a specially constructed guillotine. An armistice was immediately signed between the two sides, while formal arrangements for a permanent cessation of hostilities were finalised.

Sylvia shook her head. "What a disgraceful state of affairs..."

Hogan nodded. "And such a terrible waste - of lives, and effort, and money."

"You're right, Colonel. And what a ridiculous idea in the first place! What was he thinking? And why did so many people go along with it? I mean, why go to war with the French, when our real enemy is just over there - across the river?" Her eyes narrowed, and she gazed maliciously across the Dee estuary at the distant landscape of Flintshire. "Personally, I've never had anything against the French. My problem's always been with the bloody Welsh..."